KT-571-229

PETERSBURG

ANDREI BELY

PETERSBURG

Translated from the Russian
by John Elsworth

PUSHKIN PRESS
LONDON

English translation © John Elsworth 2009

First published in Russian as
Petersburg in 1916

This edition first published in 2009 by
Pushkin Press
12 Chester Terrace
London N1 4ND

British Library Cataloguing in Publication Data:
A catalogue record for this book is available
from the British Library

ISBN 978 1 901285 96 3

All rights reserved. No part of this publication may be
reproduced, stored in a retrieval system or transmitted in
any form or by any means, electronic, mechanical,
photocopying, recording or otherwise,
without prior permission in writing from
Pushkin Press

Cover: *Demonstration on 17 October 1905* Ilya Yefimovich Repin
Courtesy of the State Russian Museum St Petersburg

Frontispiece: *Andrei Bely 1905* Leon Bakst
Courtesy of the State Russian Museum St Petersburg

Map from *Baedeker's Russia* 1914

Set in 10 on 12 Monotype Baskerville
by Alma Books Ltd
and printed in the United Kingdom
by TJ International

PETERSBURG

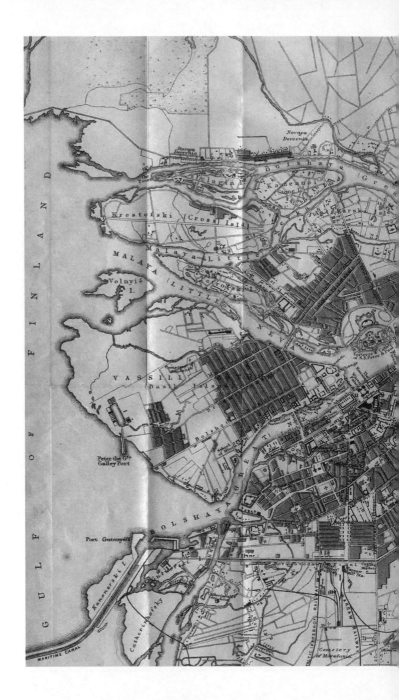

HANDBOOK MAP
OF
ST. PETERSBURG.

Scale of English Miles

Reference.

1. Palace of the G. Duke Michael
2. Michael Theatre
3. Palace of the late Grᵈ Duchess Helen
4. Preobrajensky Church
5. British Embassy
6. Roman Catholic Ch.
7. Palace of the Grᵈ Duke Nicholas
8. Post & Telegraph Offices
9. English Church
10. Minist. of Foreign Affairs
11. Minist. of Marine
12. Circus
13. Marie Theatre
14. State Bank
15. Foundling Hospital
16. Bazaar
17. Imperial Public Library
18. Town Hall

PROLOGUE

Y OUR EXCELLENCIES, *your Highnesses, Lords and Ladies, Citizens!*

What is this Russian Empire of ours?

The Russian Empire is in the first place a geographical unit, which is to say: part of a certain planet. And the Russian Empire comprises: first of all— Greater Rus, Lesser Rus, White Rus and Red Rus; secondly—the Georgian, Polish, Kazan and Astrakhan kingdoms; thirdly, it comprises ... But—etcetera, etcetera, etcetera.

This Russian empire of ours consists of a multitude of cities: metropolitan cities, provincial capitals, regional capitals, cities of no administrative importance; and furthermore—of the Ancient Capital and of the Mother of Russian Cities.

The Ancient Capital is Moscow; and the Mother of Russian Cities is Kiev.

Petersburg, or Saint Petersburg, or Peter (which is the same thing) belongs properly to the Russian Empire. And Tsargrad, Konstantinograd (or, as people say, Constantinople), belongs by right of inheritance. We will not expatiate further about that.

Let us expatiate further about Petersburg: there exists—Petersburg, or Saint Petersburg, or Peter (which is the same thing). On the basis of these same judgements Nevskii Prospect is a Petersburg Prospect.

Nevskii Prospect possesses an astonishing quality: it consists of space for the circulation of the public; it is delimited by numbered houses; the numbering proceeds in the order of the houses—and the quest for the required house is greatly facilitated. Nevskii Prospect is, like any other Prospect, a public Prospect; that is to say: a Prospect for the circulation of the public (not of the air, for instance); the houses that form its lateral limits are—ahem ... quite so: ... for

11

the public. In the evenings Nevskii Prospect is illuminated by electricity. In the daytime Nevskii Prospect requires no illumination.

Nevskii Prospect forms a straight line (between ourselves), because it is a European Prospect; and every European Prospect is not merely a Prospect, but (as I have already said) a European Prospect, because … well … yes …

And that is why Nevskii Propsect forms a straight line.

Nevskii Prospect is a Prospect of no little importance in this—not Russian— metropolitan—city. Other Russian cities consist of a pile of mean little wooden houses.

And Petersburg is strikingly different from them all.

If, however, you persist in asserting the quite ridiculous legend to the effect that there exists a population of a million-and-a-half in Moscow—then it will be necessary to concede that Moscow must be the capital, for it is only in capital cities that we find a population of a million-and-a-half; in provincial capitals there is not, never was and never will be a population of a million-and-a-half. And in accordance with that ridiculous legend it transpires that the capital is not Petersburg.

But if Petersburg is not the capital, then Petersburg does not exist. It merely seems to exist.

However that may be, Petersburg not only seems, but truly manifests itself— on maps: in the form of two concentric circles with a black point in the middle; and from this mathematical point, which possesses no dimensions, it energetically proclaims that it exists: from there, from that said point, swarms of printed books issue in a torrent; from this invisible point with great momentum issue circulars.

CHAPTER ONE

In which is told of a certain worthy person, his cerebral play and ephemerality of being.

Once there was a dreadful time.
The memory of it is not stale.
It is of this, my friends, that I
Will now commence for you my tale—
A sad one will my story be.
                    A Pushkin

Apollon Apollonovich Ableukhov

APOLLON APOLLONOVICH ABLEUKHOV was of exceedingly venerable stock: he had Adam for his ancestor. And that is not the main thing: incomparably more important here is the fact that a high-born ancestor of his was Shem, that is to say, the very progenitor of the Semitic, Hessitic and red-skinned peoples.

Here we shall make a transition to ancestors of less distant times.

These ancestors (so it appears) had their dwelling in the Kirgiz-Kaisak Horde, from where, in the reign of Empress Anna Ioannovna, Mirza Ab-Lai, the senator's great-great-grandfather, valiantly entered the service of Russia, receiving at his baptism the Christian name Andrei and the sobriquet Ukhov. Thus the Armorial of the Russian Empire discourses upon this descendant scion of the Mongol race. For the sake of brevity Ablai-Ukhov was later turned into simply Ableukhov.

This great-great-grandfather, it is said, proved to be the source of the line.

A grey, gold-braided servant was dusting the writing desk with a feather duster; a cook's cap peeped in at the open door.

"The master's up, you know … "

"He's rubbing himself with eau de cologne, soon be down for coffee … "

"The postman this morning said there was a letter for the master—from Spain: with a Spanish stamp on."

"Let me tell you something: you shouldn't be sticking your nose into letters so much … "

"I suppose Anna Petrovna … "

"You suppose, do you … "

"I was just saying … What's it to do with me … "

The cook's head suddenly vanished. Apollon Apollonovich Ableukhov strode through into the study.

A pencil lying on the desk seized Apollon Apollonovich's attention. Apollon Apollonovich conceived the intention of giving the pencil's point acuteness of form. Swiftly he walked up to the desk and grasped … a paperweight, which he twisted around in deep thought for a long time, before realizing that in his hands was a paperweight, and not a pencil.

His absent-mindedness arose from the fact that at that moment he had been struck by a profound idea; and at once, at this inopportune time, it extended into a far-reaching train of thought (Apollon Apollonovich was hurrying to the Establishment). His *Diary*, which was to appear in the periodical press in the year of his death, became longer by a page.

Apollon Apollonovich quickly wrote down his extended train of thought: once it was written down, he thought: "It's time to go to the office." And he passed through into the dining room to take his coffee.

Before doing so he set about interrogating his old valet with a certain unpleasant persistence:

"Is Nikolai Apollonovich up yet?"

"No, indeed, sir: he hasn't got up yet … "

Apollon Apollonovich rubbed the bridge of his nose in displeasure:

"Hmm … tell me: when does—tell me—Nikolai Apollonovich, as it were … "

" He gets up quite late, sir … "

"Well, how late?"

And at once, without waiting for a reply, he strode through for his coffee, with a glance at his watch.

It was precisely half-past-nine.

At ten o'clock he, an old man, would leave for the Establishment. Nikolai Apollonovich, a young man, would rise from his bed—a couple of hours later. Every morning the senator inquired about the hour of his waking. And every morning he frowned.

Nikolai Apollonovich was the senator's son.

In short, he was the head of a certain Establishment

Apollon Apollonovich Ableukhov had distinguished himself by acts of valour; more than one star had fallen on to his gold-embroidered breast; the stars of Stanislav and Anna: even the White Eagle.

The ribbon he wore was a blue ribbon.

And recently from a red lacquered box the rays of bejewelled insignia had come to gleam on this receptacle of patriotic feelings, that is to say, the insignia of the Order of Alexander Nevskii.

What then was the social station of this person who has arisen from non-existence?

I think that is a somewhat unseemly question: the whole of Russia knew Ableukhov from the exquisite prolixity of the speeches he uttered; these speeches glittered without exploding and soundlessly spread poisons over the opposing party, as a result of which that party's proposal was rejected in the appropriate place. Since Ableukhov had been installed in that responsible post the ninth department had been inactive. Apollon Apollonovich had conducted relentless hostilities with that department by means of papers and, where necessary, of speeches, facilitating the import into Russia of American reaping-machines (the ninth department was not in favour of their import). The senator's speeches flew round all the regions and provinces, some of which in spatial terms yield nothing to Germany.

Apollon Apollonovich was the head of an Establishment: you know ... that one ... what's it called?

In short, he was head of an Establishment with which you are certainly familiar.

If one were to compare the emaciated, utterly unimpressive figure of my venerable statesman with the immeasurable immensity of the mechanisms he directed, one might well surrender to a long bout of naïve wonderment; but then—absolutely everyone did wonder at the explosion of mental forces that issued from this cranium in defiance of the whole of Russia, in defiance of the majority of departments, with the exception of one: but it was nearly two years now since the head of that department had by the will of fate fallen silent beneath his tombstone.

My senator had just reached the age of sixty-eight; and his face was redolent in its pallor both of a grey paperweight (in solemn moments)—and of papier-mâché (in leisure hours); the senator's stony eyes, surrounded by a green-black cavity, seemed in moments of fatigue to be yet bluer and more huge.

On our own account we will add: Apollon Apollonovich was not in the least discomposed by the contemplation of his own ears, completely green, magnified to immensity, on the bloody background of a burning Russia. That was how he had recently been depicted: on the title page of a humorous little gutter-rag, one of those *yid* magazines, whose blood-red covers in those days were multiplying with astounding speed on the city Prospects that teemed with folk.

North-East

In the oak-panelled dining room the wheezing of a clock could be heard; with a bow and a hiss a little grey cuckoo cuckooed; at that signal from the antique cuckoo Apollon Apollonovich took his seat before his porcelain cup and broke off warm crusts of white bread. And at his coffee Apollon Apollonovich recalled his past years; and at his coffee he would—even, even—make jokes:

"Who, Semyonych, do people defer to most?"

"I presume, Apollon Apollonovich, that people defer most of all to an Actual Privy Councillor."

Apollon Apollonovich smiled with his lips only.

"You presume wrongly: people defer most of all to a chimney-sweep … "

The valet already knew how the joke ended: but out of deference he kept quiet about it.

"Why, if I may be so bold as to ask, sir, does a chimney-sweep enjoy such honour?"

"People stand aside, Semyonych, for an Actual Privy Councillor … "

"I presume so, your Excellency … "

"But a chimney-sweep … Even an Actual Privy Councillor will stand aside for him, because: the chimney-sweep will dirty him."

"So that's how it is, sir," the valet interposed deferentially …

"That's it: only there is one profession people defer to even more … "

And he immediately added:

"A lavatory attendant … "

"Ugh! … "

"A chimney-sweep will stand aside for him, not only an Actual Privy Councillor … "

And—a sip of coffee. But let us note: Apollon Apollonovich was himself an Actual Privy Councillor.

"There was another thing, Apollon Apollonovich, sir: Anna Petrovna used to say to me … "

But at the words "Anna Petrovna" the grey-haired valet stopped short.

"The grey coat, sir?"

"The grey coat … "

"The grey gloves, too, sir, I presume?"

"No, I'll have the suede gloves … "

"If you would be so good as to wait a moment, your Excellency; the gloves are in the chiffonier: shelf B—North-East."

Only once had Apollon Apollonovich entered into the trivia of life: one day he had conducted a review of his inventory; his inventory had been sequentially catalogued and a nomenclature established for all the shelves, large and small; shelves had appeared by letter: A, B, C; and the four sides of the shelves had assumed the designation of the four points of the compass.

When he put his spectacles away, Apollon Apollonovich would note in his register in fine, minute handwriting: spectacles, shelf B and NE, that is to say, North-East: a copy of the register was also received by the valet, who memorised the compass-bearings of the appurtenances of the inestimable toilet; sometimes during insomnia he would recite these compass-bearings unerringly by heart.

In the lacquered house the storms of life took their course quietly; nevertheless the storms of life here took their course calamitously: they did not thunder with events; they did not shine a cleansing light into the inhabitants' hearts with arrows of lightning; but from a hoarse throat they wrung the air in a torrent of poisonous fluids; and in the consciousness of the inhabitants cerebral games swirled round, like dense gases in hermetically sealed jars.

Grocer, grow, sir

A cold long-legged bronze sculpture rose up from the table: the lamp-shade did not gleam with its delicate decoration of a purple-pink hue: the nineteenth century had lost the secret of that colour; the glass had darkened with time; the delicate decoration had darkened with time too.

On all sides the gold pier glasses between the windows swallowed the drawing room into the green-hued surfaces of their mirrors; there one was crowned by the wing of a golden-cheeked cupid; and over there the laurels and roses of a golden wreath were pierced by the heavy flames of torches. On all sides there glittered mother-of-pearl encrusted tables between the pier glasses.

Apollon Apollonovich quickly threw open the door, resting his hand on the cut-glass doorknob; his footsteps resounded on the gleaming blocks of the parquet floor; on all sides clustered a profusion of porcelain knick-knacks; they had brought these knick-knacks back from Venice, Anna Petrovna and he, thirty years ago. Memories of a misty lagoon, a gondola and an aria, sobbing in the distance, flashed inopportunely through the senator's head ...

He immediately turned his gaze to the piano.

From its polished, yellow lid the leaves of bronze incrustations gleamed forth; and again (importunate memory!) Apollon Apollonovich remembered: a white Petersburg night; through the windows the wide river running; and the moon standing there; and a Chopin roulade pealing out: he remembered—it was Chopin that Anna Petrovna used to play, not Schumann.

The leaves of incrustations gleamed forth—mother-of-pearl and bronze—on little boxes, and little shelves protruding from the walls. Apollon Apollonovich settled himself in an Empire armchair, on the pale-blue satin seat of which little wreaths were entwined, and from a Chinese tray he grasped with his hand a sheaf of unopened letters: his bald head bent towards the envelopes. While waiting for the servant with his invariable "The horses are ready", he immersed himself here, before leaving for his office, in reading the morning's mail.

He did just the same today.

And the envelopes were torn open: envelope after envelope; an ordinary one, bought at the post office—the stamp stuck on crooked, indecipherable handwriting.

"Hmm ... Yes, yes, yes: very well ... "

And the envelope was carefully secreted.

"Hmm ... A petition ... "

"One petition after another ... "

The envelopes were torn open carelessly; that one—in due course, later: some time ...

An envelope made of heavyweight grey paper—sealed, with a coat of arms, without a stamp and with an imprint on the sealing wax.

"Hmm ... Count W ... What is this? ... Asking me to receive him in the Establishment ... On a personal matter ... "

"Hmm ... Aha! ... "

Count W, the head of the ninth department, was an opponent of the senator's and an enemy of farmstead husbandry.

Then ... A miniature, pale pink envelope; the senator's hand faltered; he recognised this handwriting—it was Anna Petrovna's; he examined the Spanish stamp, but did not open the envelope:

"Hmm ... money ... "

"The money's been sent, hasn't it?"

"The money will be sent!! ... "

"Hmm ... make a note ... "

Apollon Apollonovich, thinking he had taken hold of a pencil, pulled out of his waistcoat an ivory nail brush and made to jot down with it "Return to sender", when ...

"? ... "

"They're ready, sir ... "

Apollon Apollonovich raised his bald head and walked out of the room.

On the walls hung pictures, shimmering with the lustre of oils: only with difficulty was it possible to make out through the lustre French women reminiscent of Greek women, in the close-fitting tunics of the distant time of the Directoire and with towering coiffures.

Above the piano hung a reduced copy of David's picture *The Distribution of the Eagle Standards*. The picture depicted the great Emperor in a wreath and a robe of purple and ermine; the Emperor Napoleon was stretching out his hand to a plumed gathering of marshals; his other hand was clutching a metal staff; on the top of the staff was perched a heavy eagle.

The drawing room's magnificence was cold on account of the total absence of rugs: the parquet gleamed; if the sun lit it up for a moment, you would screw up your eyes willy-nilly. The drawing room's hospitality was cold.

But senator Ableukhov made a principle of it.

Its imprint was felt: in the owner, in the statues, in the servants, even in the dark stripy bulldog that lived somewhere near the kitchen; in this house everyone felt ill at ease, yielding to the parquet, the pictures and the statues, smiling in embarrassment and swallowing their words: bowing obsequiously, rushing to meet one another—on this echoing parquet; cracking their cold fingers in an access of fruitless obsequiousness.

Since Anna Petrovna's departure: the drawing room was silent, the piano lid was lowered: roulades pealed out no more.

Yes—concerning Anna Petrovna, or (to put it more simply) concerning the letter from Spain: hardly had Apollon Apollonovich gone striding past, when two boisterous servant-boys began to chatter briskly.

"He didn't read the letter … "

"Well he wouldn't, would he … "

"Will he send it back?"

"Looks like it … "

"What a heart of stone, may the Lord forgive me … "

"You'd better be more mindful of the proper way to talk, I can tell you."

As Apollon Apollonovich went down into the entrance-hall, his grey-haired valet, also on the way down to the entrance-hall, glanced from below at the venerable ears and clutched in his hand his snuffbox, a present from the minister.

Apollon Apollonovich stopped on the staircase, trying to find a word:

"Hmm … Listen … "

"Your Excellency?"

Apollon Apollonovich searched for a suitable word:

"What in general—yes—does he … does he … do with himself … "

"? … "

"Nikolai Apollonovich."

"Nothing in particular, Apollon Apollonovich, he's well … "

"Anything else?"

"The same as ever: he chooses to lock himself in and read books."

"Books, then?"

"Then he walks around his rooms, sir … "

"Walks—yes, yes … And? … And? How?"

"He walks … In his dressing gown!"

"Reading, walking … I see … What else?"

"Yesterday he was expecting a visit from … "

"A visit from whom?"

"From a costumier … "

"What costumier might that be?"

"Just a costumier, sir … "

"Hm-hm … Whatever for?"

"I presume he's going to a ball … "

"Aha—I see: going to a ball … "

Apollon Apollonovich rubbed the bridge of his nose: his face lit up with a smile and suddenly became an old man's:

"Are you from the country?"

"Yes, indeed, sir!"

"Then—you know—you must have been a grocer."

"?"

"What did you grow in the country?"

"Grow, sir?"

"There you are, you see … "

Taking his top hat, Apollon Apollonovich passed through the open door.

The carriage flew off into the mist

Fine rain sprinkled the streets and Prospects, the pavements and the roofs; it spattered down in cold rivulets from the tin drainpipes.

The fine rain sprinkled the passers-by: it bestowed influenza upon them; along with the fine dust of the rain colds and influenza crept under the upturned collars: of schoolboy, student, civil servant, officer, nondescript; and the nondescript (the man-in-the-street, so to speak) looked around in anguish; and gazed at the Prospect with his worn grey face; he circulated in the infinity of the Prospects, overcame infinity, without complaint—in an infinite flow of others like himself—amidst the rush, the roar, the tremor, the horse-cabs, listening to the tuneful voice of the motor cars' roulades in the distance and the swelling rumble of the red and yellow trams (a rumble which later died away again), in the incessant clamour of the lusty newspaper vendors.

From one infinity he ran into another; then he stumbled upon the Embankment; this was where everything came to an end: the tuneful voice of the motor cars' roulades, the red and yellow trams and every kind of nondescript; this was the edge of the world and the end of infinity.

But over there, over there: depth, a turbid greenish bilge; far, far away, further than it seemed was right, the islands had sunk down in fear and were lying low; the earth was lying low; and the buildings were lying low; it seemed—the waters would sink down, and upon them at that moment would come surging: depth, a turbid greenish bilge; and above this greenish bilge thundered and shuddered, running away over there in the mist, the black, black Nikolaevskii Bridge.

On this louring Petersburg morning the heavy doors of a magnificent yellow house were thrown open: the yellow house's windows looked out on to the Neva. A clean-shaven servant with gold braid on his lapels rushed out of the entrance-hall to make signs to the coachman. Dappled grey horses lurched towards the entrance; they pulled up to it a carriage on which were traced the arms of an ancient noble family: a unicorn piercing a knight.

A sprightly constable who was passing the entrance porch lost his wits and stood to attention when Apollon Apollonovich in his grey coat and his tall black top hat, with his stony face redolent of a paperweight, ran quickly out of the entrance and more quickly still mounted the footboard of his carriage, pulling on a black suede glove as he did so.

Apollon Apollonovich Ableukhov cast a momentary, puzzled glance at the constable, at the carriage, at the coachman, at the big black bridge, and at the expanse of the Neva, where the misty, many-chimneyed distances were so faintly outlined, and from where Vasilevskii Island cast a fearful glance.

The grey servant hastily slammed the carriage door. The carriage flew off into the mist full-tilt; and the constable who had chanced by, shaken by all he had seen, gazed for a long, long time over his shoulder into the grimy mist—where the carriage had flown off full-tilt; and he sighed, and went his way; soon this constable's shoulder, too, was hidden in the mist, just as all shoulders, all backs, all grey faces and all wet, black umbrellas were hidden in the mist The venerable servant also had a look in that direction, he looked to the right, and to the left, and at the bridge and the expanse of the Neva, where the misty, many-chimneyed distances were so faintly outlined, and from where Vasilevskii Island cast a fearful glance.

Here, at the very beginning, I have to interrupt the thread of my narration, in order to introduce the reader to the location of a certain drama. In advance I must correct an inaccuracy that has crept in; it is not the fault of the author, but of the author's pen: at this time trams were not yet running through the city: the year was nineteen hundred and five.

Squares, parallelepipeds, cubes

"Gee-up, Gee-up … "

That was the coachman's fitful call.

And the carriage spattered mud in all directions.

Over there, where there was nothing but a misty dampness hanging, first there appeared as a faint intimation, then there descended from the sky to the earth—grimy, grey-black St Isaac's; another intimation took on a clear outline: the equestrian statue of Emperor Nikolai; the metallic Emperor was in the uniform of the Life-Guards; at his foot a grenadier of the Nikolaevskii regiment emerged from the mist with his furry cap and disappeared back into it.

The carriage, however, flew on to the Nevskii Prospect.

Apollon Apollonovich rocked on the satin cushions of his seat; he was separated from the grime of the street by four perpendicular walls; thus was he detached from the crowds of people flowing by, from the red covers of the magazines, offered for sale at a crossing and becoming disconsolately drenched.

System and symmetry soothed the senator's nerves, which were upset both by the unevenness of his domestic life and by the impotent rotation of our wheel of state.

His tastes were marked by a harmonious simplicity.

Most of all he loved the rectilinear Prospect; this Prospect reminded him of the flux of time between two points in life; and of another thing too: all other cities consist of a cluster of wooden houses, and Petersburg is astonishingly different from all of them.

The wet, slippery Prospect: the cubes of houses there were joined together into a systematic, five-storey row: this row differed from the line of life in one respect only: this row had neither end nor beginning; what was the middle of life's journey for this bearer of bejewelled insignia had for so many high officials turned out to be the end of their life's path.

Inspiration took possession of the senator's soul every time his lacquered cube cut through the Nevskii like an arrow: there, outside the window, the numbering of the houses could be seen; and circulation took place; there in the distance, far, far away, on bright days a golden spire gleamed blindingly, and clouds, and crimson rays of sunset; there on cloudy days—there was nothing, nobody.

Over there were the Lines: the Neva, the islands. Surely in those distant days when out of the mossy marshes high roofs and masts and spires rose up, piercing the dank, greenish mist with their points—

—the Flying Dutchman on his shadowy sails came winging to Petersburg from far away in the leaden expanses of the Baltic and German seas, to raise here as an illusion his misty lands and give the name of islands to a wave of scudding clouds; for two hundred years the Dutchman lit the hellish lights of drinking-dens, and the Christian people thronged and thronged into the hellish drinking-dens, spreading putrid pestilence ...

The dark shadows receded. But the hellish drinking dens were left. Long years the Christian people caroused here with the ghost: a bastard race arose from the islands—neither men nor shadows—settling on the border between two alien worlds.

Apollon Apollonovich did not like the islands: the population there were factory folk, vulgar; a thousands-strong swarm of people strolls along the streets of a morning to the many-chimneyed factories; and now he knew too that revolvers were in circulation there; and other things too. Apollon Apollonovich reflected: the inhabitants of the islands were reckoned among the population of the Russian Empire; the general census had been introduced for them too; they too had numbered houses, police stations, official Establishments; an inhabitant of the islands might be a solicitor, a writer, a worker, a police officer; he regards himself as a Petersburger, but as a resident of chaos, he threatens the capital of the Empire in a scudding cloud ...

Apollon Apollonovich did not wish to continue this thought: the restless islands should be crushed, crushed! Chained to the earth with the iron of a huge bridge and pinned on all sides with the arrows of the Prospects ...

And now, gazing dreamily into the limitless mists, the statesman suddenly expanded in all directions from the black cube of the carriage and began to hover above it; he wanted the carriage to fly onwards, the Prospects to come flying to meet them— Prospect after Prospect, he wanted the whole spherical surface of the planet to be embraced, as though by the coils of a snake, by the grey-black cubes of houses; he wanted the whole earth, compressed by Prospects, in its linear cosmic course to intersect with the immeasurable in accordance with a rectilinear law; he wanted a network of parallel Prospects, intersected by a network of Prospects, to spread out into the abysses of interstellar space in planes of squares and cubes: a square to each man-in-the-street, he wanted ... he wanted ...

After the line, of everything symmetrical the figure that soothed him most was the square.

He would give himself over for long periods to the unreflecting contemplation of: pyramids, triangles, parallelepipeds, cubes, trapezoids. Disquiet took hold of him only at the contemplation of a truncated cone.

Zigzag lines he could not bear.

Here, in his carriage, Apollon Apollonovich for long periods delighted without reflection in the quadrilateral walls, sitting in the centre of a perfect black cube, upholstered in satin: Apollon Apollonovich was born for solitary confinement; it was only his love for the plane geometry of state that had clothed him in the many facets of responsible office.

The wet, slippery Prospect was intersected by a wet Prospect at a ninety-degree angle; at the point of the lines' intersection stood a policeman ...

And houses of exactly the same kind towered up there, and grey streams of people of exactly the same kind passed by there, and exactly the same kind of yellow-green mist was hanging there. Faces ran by in deep concentration; the pavements whispered and clicked their heels; they were scraped by galoshes; the nose of a man-in-the-street floated solemnly by. Noses flowed by in their multitudes: aquiline noses, noses like ducks' or like cockerels', greenish ones, white ones; and a lack of nose flowed by here too. People on their own flowed by here, couples, groups of three or four; bowler hat after bowler hat; bowlers, feathers, caps; caps, caps, feathers; tricorn, top hat, cap; scarf, umbrella, feather.

But parallel to this receding Prospect was another receding Prospect with just the same series of boxes, the same numbering, the same clouds; and with the same civil servant.

There is an infinity in the infinity of receding Prospects with the infinity of intersecting shadows receding into infinity. The whole of Petersburg is the infinity of the Prospect raised to the power of n.

But beyond Petersburg—there is nothing.

The inhabitants of the islands astound you

The inhabitants of the islands astound you with some thievish tricks they have; their faces are greener and paler than those of any other earth-born creature; an islander—a man of uncertain status, with a little moustache, perhaps—can squeeze through a keyhole; and before you know it he's touched you for a contribution to the arming of the factory workers; he starts chattering, and whispering, and chuckling: and you give him some money; and then you won't any longer be able to sleep at night; your room will start chattering, and whispering, and chuckling: that's him, an inhabitant of the islands—a stranger with a little black moustache, fugitive, invisible, he's not there at all; he's away in the provinces; and just you watch—the distant backwoods, out there in the spaces, will start chattering and chuckling; out there in the distant backwoods—Russia itself will start chattering and roaring.

It was the last day of September.

On Vasilevskii Island, in the depths of the Seventeenth Line a huge grey house peered out of the mist; from the yard a dark, grimy staircase led into the house: there were doors and doors; one of them opened.

A stranger with a little black moustache appeared on the threshold.

Then, closing the door, the stranger began to descend; he was coming down from the height of five storeys, stepping carefully on the stairs; in his hand swung a package, not a small one exactly, but not a very big one either, wrapped in a dirty napkin with a red fringe of faded pheasants.

My stranger treated the package with exquisite caution.

The staircase was, of course, the back staircase, and was littered with cucumber skins and a much-trodden cabbage leaf. The stranger with the little black moustache slipped upon it.

Then with one hand he grabbed hold of the banister, while the other (with the package) described in dismay a nervous zigzag in the air; but the describing of the zigzag related properly to his elbow: my stranger evidently wished to protect the package from a vexing mishap—from a violent fall on to the stone step, for the movement of his elbow revealed a truly deft acrobatic feat: some instinct prompted this delicate dexterity.

Then when he met the caretaker, who was ascending the stairs with a load of aspen wood over his shoulder and blocking the way, the stranger with the little black moustache began with redoubled intensity to display once again a delicate concern for the welfare of his package, which was in danger of getting caught against a log; the objects contained in the package must have been objects of especial fragility.

Otherwise my stranger's behaviour would not have been comprehensible.

When the significant stranger descended cautiously to the outer door, a black cat at his feet snorted, and crossed his path with its tail in the air, dropping at the stranger's feet a chicken's entrails; my stranger's face twisted convulsively; his head, though, was thrown back nervously, revealing his delicate neck.

Such movements were characteristic of young ladies in olden times, when young ladies of those days began to feel thirsty: a way of confirming by an extraordinary gesture the interesting pallor of their faces, which was imparted by the drinking of vinegar and the sucking of lemons.

And just such gestures sometimes mark our young contemporaries, exhausted by insomnia. The stranger suffered from such insomnia: the smell of tobacco that impregnated his residence indicated as much; the bluish shade of the tender skin of his face bore witness to the same— skin so tender that had my stranger not been the owner of a moustache, you might well have taken him for a young lady in disguise.

Here the stranger is—in the yard, a quadrangle asphalted all over and confined on all sides by a five-storeyed colossus with many windows. In the middle of the yard damp lengths of aspen wood were piled; and from here a piece of the Seventeenth Line could be seen too, whistled at by the wind.

Lines!

Only in you does there remain a memory of the Petersburg of Peter.

It was Peter who once upon a time drew parallel lines across the marshes; those lines grew a casing of granite or stone, or perhaps a wooden fence. Not a trace is left in Petersburg of Peter's regular lines; Peter's lines turned into the lines of a later epoch: into the rounded line of Catherine's time, or the Alexandrine structure of white stone colonnades.

Only here, among the colossi, are any of Peter's little houses left; there's a log house over there; and there is a green one; there a blue one, single-storeyed, with a bright red sign saying '*Eating-house*'. It was exactly houses like that that used to be scattered here in ancient times. Various smells still strike the nose directly here: there's a smell of sea salt, herring, hawsers, leather jackets, pipes, and tarpaulin by the shore.

Lines!

How they have changed: how these severe days have changed them!

The stranger recalled to mind: in the window of that gleaming little house over there on a summer evening in June an old woman was sucking her teeth; from August the window was closed; in September a brocaded coffin was brought.

He thought how life was becoming more expensive and that working people would soon have nothing to eat; that from the bridge over there Petersburg was plunging the arrows of its Prospects into the islands along with a horde of stone giants; that horde of giants would soon bury in their attics and cellars, shamelessly and flagrantly, all the poor of the islands.

My stranger from the island had long since come to hate Petersburg: over there Petersburg rose up in a wave of clouds; and buildings hovered there; and someone malicious and dark, whose breath clamped firmly in the ice of granite and of stone the once green and rippling islands, seemed to hover above the buildings; someone dark, ominous and cold stared with stony gaze from the howling chaos over there, and beat his bat-like wings, hovering dementedly; he lashed out at the poor of the islands with an authoritative utterance, standing out—with skull and ears—against the mist; that was how someone had recently been depicted on the cover of a magazine.

The stranger clenched his fist in his pocket as he thought all this; he remembered a circular and remembered that the leaves were falling: my stranger knew it all by heart. These fallen leaves—for how many they would be the last leaves: my stranger became a bluish shadow.

For our own part we will say: O, Russian people, Russian people! Do not let the crowds of slippery shadows come over from the islands! Beware of the islanders! They have the right to settle freely in the Empire: for that purpose black and grey bridges have been thrown across the waters of Lethe to the islands. They ought to be dismantled …

Too late …

The police had no thought of dismantling the Nikolaveskii bridge; dark shadows thronged across the bridge; one of the shadows in the throng that crossed the bridge was the shadow of the stranger. In his hand swung a package, not a small one exactly, but not a very big one either.

Catching sight of him, they opened wide, they shone, they flashed

In the greenish light of the Petersburg morning, in a protective 'or so it seems', a quite ordinary phenomenon was also circulating before senator Ableukhov: an atmospheric phenomenon—a stream of people; people here became dumb; the streams of them, scurrying like waves breaking on the shore, thundered and roared; the ordinary ear did not register at all that this surge of people was a surge of thunder.

Welded together into one by an optical illusion, the stream broke down into the segments of the stream: segment after segment flowed by; every segment could be surmised to distance itself from every other, like one planetary system from another; the relation of neighbour to neighbour was much like the relation of a pencil of rays from the firmament to the retina, which carries to the brain centre along the telegraph of the nerves a vague, astral, flickering message.

The aged senator communicated with the crowd that flowed before him by means of wires (telegraph and telephone wires); and the flood of shadows was presented to his consciousness as a message that flowed peacefully beyond the compass of the world. Apollon Apollonovich thought: about the stars, about the incoherence of the thunderous stream flowing past; and, rocking on his black cushion, he tried to calculate the power of the light received from Saturn.

All at once …

—his face wrinkled and was convulsed by a tic; his stony eyes, ringed with blue, rolled upwards in a spasm; his hands, clothed in black suede, flew up to the level of his chest, as though he were defending himself with his arms. His body was thrown back, and his top hat, striking the side of the carriage, fell on to his knees from his bared head …

The involuntary nature of the senator's demeanour was not subject to an ordinary interpretation; the senator's code of conduct did not anticipate anything of that nature …

As he contemplated the flowing silhouettes—bowlers, feathers, caps, caps, caps, feathers—Apollon Apollonovich likened them to points in the firmament; but one of those points, breaking loose from its orbit, rushed with dizzying speed straight at him, taking on the form of a huge, crimson sphere, that is to say, I mean:—

—as he contemplated the flowing silhouettes (caps, caps, feathers), among those caps, feathers and bowlers Apollon Apollonovich caught sight, at the corner, of a pair of wild eyes: the eyes expressed one impermissible quality: the eyes recognised the senator; and, recognising him, went wild; maybe the eyes had been waiting for him at the corner; and, catching sight of him, they opened wide, they shone, they flashed.

This crazed glance was a glance cast with full awareness and it belonged to a man of uncertain status with a little black moustache, wearing a coat with its collar raised; as he later immersed himself in the details of the occurrence Apollon Apollonovich intuited, rather than remembered, another thing: the man of uncertain status was holding in his right hand a package wrapped in a wet napkin.

The matter was so simple: squeezed in by the stream of horse-cabs, the carriage had stopped at a crossroads (a policeman there had raised his white baton); the stream of men of uncertain status walking past, squeezed by the flood of cabs up against the stream of those flying at right angles to it, crossing the Nevskii—this stream now simply pressed itself up against the senator's carriage, destroying the illusion that he, Apollon Apollonovich, as he flew along the Nevskii, was flying at a distance of billions of versts from that human myriapod which was trampling the selfsame Prospect: disconcerted, Apollon Apollonovich moved right up to the windows of the carriage, and saw that he was separated from the crowd by no more than a thin wall and a four-inch space; then he caught sight of the man of uncertain status; and began to examine him calmly; there was something about that unimposing figure that was worthy to be noticed; and no doubt a physiognomist, chancing to meet that figure in the street, would have stopped in astonishment: and afterwards would have recalled at odd moments that face he'd seen; the peculiarity of its expression lay simply in the difficulty of attributing that face to any of the existing categories—nothing else ...

This observation would have flashed through the senator's head, if his observation had lasted another second; but it did not last. The stranger raised his eyes and—through the mirror-like glass of the carriage, at a four-inch distance from himself, he saw not a face, but ... a skull in a top hat and a huge pale-green ear.

In the same quarter of a second the senator saw in the stranger's eyes—that same unbounded chaos, out of which the misty, many-chimneyed distance and Vasilevskii Island had immemorially surveyed the senator's house.

That was when the stranger's eyes had opened wide, and shone, and flashed; and that was when, through the window, separated by a four-inch space and the wall of the carriage, arms had been thrown up swiftly to cover eyes.

The carriage flew on: and with it Apollon Apollonovich flew on into those damp expanses; over there—on bright days there rose in beauty—a golden spire, clouds and a crimson sunset; over there today—billows of grimy mists.

There, in the billows of grimy smoke, as he leant back against the carriage wall, his eyes saw nothing else: billows of grimy smoke; his heart began to beat faster; it expanded, expanded, expanded; in his chest the sensation was born of a growing, crimson sphere, on the point of exploding and bursting into pieces.

Apollon Apollonovich Ableukhov suffered from dilation of the heart.

All of this lasted a moment.

Apollon Apollonovich, mechanically replacing his top hat and holding his black suede-clad hand to his galloping heart, once again gave himself over to his beloved contemplation of cubes, in order to come to terms, calmly and rationally, with what had happened.

Apollon Apollonovich glanced once more out of the carriage: what he saw now obliterated what had been before: the wet, slippery Prospect; wet, slippery flagstones, gleaming feverishly this September day.

The horses stopped. A policeman saluted. Through the glass of the entrance, under the bearded caryatid that supported the stones of the balcony, Apollon Apollonovich saw the same sight as ever: a ponderous bronze mace was gleaming there; the doorman's dark tricorn had fallen across his octogenarian shoulder. The octogenarian doorman tended to fall asleep over *The Stock Exchange Gazette*. In just the same way he had fallen asleep yesterday and the day before. In just the same way he had slept through those fatal five years ... And in just the same way he would sleep through the five years to come.

Five years had passed since Apollon Apollonovich had rolled up to the Establishment as its unquestioned Head: five years and a bit had passed since that time! And there had been events: China had been through turmoil and Port Arthur had fallen. But the sight of those years was unchanging: an octogenarian shoulder, gold braid, beard.

The door was thrown open: the bronze mace rattled. From the carriage door Apollon Apollonovich cast his stony gaze across to the wide-open entrance. And the entrance closed.

Apollon Apollonovich stood and breathed.

"Your Excellency ... Sit down, sir ... Why, look how out of breath you are ... "

"You keep running around like a little boy ... "

"Sit still for a bit, your Excellency: get your breath back … "

"That's the way, sir, that's it … "

"Some water, perhaps?"

But the distinguished statesman's face brightened all over, became childlike, senile; and was covered in wrinkles:

"Can you tell me: who is the husband of a Duchess?"

"A Duchess, sir? … Which duchess, if I may ask?"

"No, just a Duchess?"

"?"

"The husband of a Duchess is a Dutchman."

"Tee-hee-hee, sir … "

But his recalcitrant heart defied his mind, and fluttered and beat; and because of that everything around was: the same—but not the same …

Two poorly dressed girl-students …

Amidst the crowds flowing slowly by the stranger flowed by too; or rather he flowed away in complete confusion from the crossroads where he had been squeezed by the stream of people up against the black carriage, out of which a skull, an ear and a top hat had stared at him.

That ear and that skull!

Recalling them, the stranger took to flight.

Couple after couple flowed by: groups of three and four flowed by: from every group a conversation rose into the sky in a column of vapour which entwined and merged with the vaporous column running alongside; intersecting the columns of conversations, my stranger caught fragments of them; out of those fragments phrases and sentences were composed.

This was how the Nevskii gossip was woven.

"D'you know?" swept past from somewhere on the right and was smothered in the oncoming clatter.

Then something else surfaced:

"They're going to … "

"What?"

"Throw … "

There was a whispering behind him.

The stranger with the little black moustache turned round and saw: a bowler hat, a cane, an overcoat; ears, moustache and nose …

"Who at?"

"Who, who"—a whisper was exchanged in the distance; then a dark couple said:

"Abl … "

And so saying, the couple walked past

"Ableukhov?"

"At Ableukhov?!"

But away over there the couple continued …

"A tabula rasa … you just try!"

And the couple hiccuped.

But the stranger stood there, shaken by all he had heard:

"They're going to? … "

"Throw? … "

"At Abl … "

"Why no: they're not … "

Whispering all round:

"High time … "

Then again from behind:

"A proper … "

And as one disappeared at the crossroads, another attacked from the next:

"Time … a proper … "

The stranger heard "provo … " instead of "proper"; and completed it himself:

"Provo-cation?!"

Provocation was abroad on the Nevskii. Provocation changed the meaning of all the words that were heard: an innocent "proper" it endowed with "provo-cation"; and turned "a tabula rasa" into the devil only knows what:

"At Abl … "

And the stranger thought:

"At Ableukhov."

He had just added the preposition 'at' on his own account; the addition of the letters 'a' and 't' had turned an innocent fragment of words into a fragment of terrible import; and the main thing was: it was the stranger who had added the preposition.

So the provocation must be sitting inside him; while he was running away from it: running away—from himself. He was his own shadow.

O, Russian people, Russian people!

Do not let the crowds of fitful shadows come over from the island: surreptitiously those shadows penetrate into your physical habitation; from there they penetrate into the nooks and crannies of your soul: you become the shadows of the swirling, billowing mists: since time immemorial those mists have come flying in from beyond the world's edge: from the leaden expanses of the Baltic with its seething waves; and from time immemorial the thunderous apertures of cannon have stared out into the mist.

At twelve o'clock, in accordance with tradition, a dull cannon shot solemnly rent the air of Saint Petersburg, capital of the Russian Empire: all the mists dispersed and all the shadows scattered.

Only my shadow—the fugitive young man—was not effaced and did not dissolve at the cannon shot, but continued without let or hindrance to pursue his course to the Neva. Suddenly my stranger's keen ear caught behind his back an excited whisper:

"The Fugitive! … "

"Look—the Fugitive!"

"What daring! … "

And when, thus exposed, he turned his islander's face, he saw, staring at him intently, the eyes of two poorly dressed girl-students …

You hold your tongue! …

"Yutter … "

The thunderous shout of a man sitting at a table: a man of immense proportions; he was stuffing a piece of yellow smoked salmon into his mouth, and, choking on it, shouting out incomprehensible things. He was probably shouting:

"You ought to … "

But what was heard was:

"Yutter … "

And a group of gaunt men in jackets started squealing:

"Aaah—ha-ha-ha—aha! … "

The Petersburg street in autumn penetrates your whole organism: it turns the marrow of your bones to ice and tickles your freezing spine; but as soon as you escape from it into a warm room, the Petersburg street flows in your veins like a fever. The stranger now experienced the quality of this street as he entered a grimy vestibule, densely crammed with black, blue, grey and yellow overcoats, swanky hats, lop-eared hats, dock-tailed hats, and galoshes of every description. A warm dampness enveloped him; in the air hung a milky steam: steam that smelled of pancakes.

When he had received a token for his coat which scorched his palm, the man of uncertain status with the moustache finally went into the room …

"A-a-a … "

At first he was deafened by voices.

"Crayfish … a-a-a … ha-ha-ha … "

"You see, you see, you see … "

"Don't tell me … "

"Mmm   mmm … "

"And some vodka … "

"You don't say … Oh, really … What did you expect … "

All this was hurled into his face; but from behind him, from the Nevskii, he was still being chased by:

"Proper … provo … "

"What's proper?"

"Station—cassation—vocation … "

"Bl … "

"And some vodka … "

The restaurant consisted of a small, grimy room; the floor was polished with mastic; the walls were decorated by the hand of a house painter to depict the remnants of the Swedish fleet, from the heights of which Peter was pointing to the distant expanses; and the distant expanses came flying in from there in the blue of white-crested waves; but in the stranger's head it was a carriage flying, surrounded by billows of …

"Proper … "

"Going to throw … "

"At Abl … "

"Prov … "

O, idle thoughts! …

On the wall an ornate green spinach plant leapt to the eye, describing in its zigzags the *plaisirs* of nature at Peterhof, with wide expanses, clouds and a sugary Easter-cake in the form of a stylised pavilion.

"Some syrup in that?"

The bloated landlord addressed our stranger from behind the counter.

"No, no syrup for me."

But he was thinking: why that terrified gaze from inside the carriage window: the eyes had opened wide, become transfixed, and then closed; the dead, shaven head had rocked back and disappeared; from the hand—the black suede hand—not even the wicked scourge of a circular had struck his back; the black suede hand dangled powerlessly; not so much a hand, more a drooping flipper …

He looked round: on the counter the vodka-snacks were languishing, various wilting leaves were mouldering under glass covers along with a pile of three-day-old overdone rissoles.

"Another glass … "

Over in the distance an idly perspiring man was sitting, with a huge coachman's beard, in a short blue coat and blacked boots over grey trousers the colour of soldiers' uniforms. The idly perspiring man was throwing back glass after glass; the idly perspiring man called the tousled waiter:

"What would you like? ... "

"Some sort of ... "

"Some melon, sir?"

"Like hell: tastes like soap and sugar, your melon ... "

"A banana, then, sir?"

"That's an indecent sort of fruit ... "

"Grapes from Astrakhan?"

Thrice my stranger swallowed the acerbic, colourlessly gleaming poison, whose effect is reminiscent of the street's effect: its vengeful fires lick at the alimentary canal and the stomach, while the consciousness, splitting off from the body, like the lever of a machine begins to revolve around the whole organism, in extraordinary clarity ... for a single moment.

And the stranger's consciousness became lucid for a moment: he remembered: the unemployed were starving there; the unemployed had begged him; and he had promised them; and had accepted from them—yes? Where was the package? Here it was, just here—beside him ... He had accepted from them the package.

Truly: that meeting on the Nevskii had put his memory put of joint.

"Some watermelon, sir?"

"To hell with your watermelon: just a crunch in your teeth; but in your mouth—nothing at all ... "

"Have some vodka, then ... "

But suddenly the bearded man burst out:

"I'll tell you what I want: some crayfish ... "

The stranger with the little black moustache settled down at a table to wait for the person who ...

"Would you care for a glass?"

The idly perspiring man with the beard winked merrily.

"No thank you ... "

"Why not? ... "

"I've had a drink … "

"Well, you could have another: in my company … "

My stranger reflected a moment: he gave the bearded man a suspicious glance, took hold of the wet package, took hold of a torn sheet of newspaper (for customers to read); and, as though inadvertently, covered the package with it.

"From Tula, are you?"

The stranger broke off his thought with displeasure and said quite rudely—and in a falsetto:

"Not from Tula at all … "

"Where are you from, then? … "

"What's it to you?"

"Just asking … "

"Well, I'm from Moscow … "

And with a shrug of his shoulders he turned angrily away.

And he thought: no, it was not him thinking—the thoughts thought themselves, spreading out and revealing a picture: tarpaulins, ropes, herring; and sacks filled with something: a limitless mass of sacks; among the sacks a workman dressed in black leather was hoisting a sack on to his back with a blue-tinged hand; he stood out against the mist, against the rushing expanses of water; and the sack fell with a dull sound: from his back into a barge loaded with beams; sack after sack; and the workman (a workman he knew) stood over the sacks and pulled out a pipe along with a flap of clothing that danced absurdly in the wind.

"In business?"

(Lord Almighty!)

"No: nothing in particular … "

And he said to himself:

"A snooper … "

"I see: as for me, I'm in the coaching business … "

"My brother-in-law works as a coachman for Konstantin Konstantinovich … "

"So what?"

"So nothing: doesn't matter—we're all friends here … "

Obviously a snooper: if only the person would come soon.

The man with the beard meanwhile fell into hapless rumination over the plate of uneaten crayfish, making the sign of the cross over his mouth as he yawned:

"O, Lord, O, Lord! … "

What were his thoughts about? The Vasilevskii people? Sacks and the workman? Yes—of course: life was getting dearer, workers had nothing to eat.

Why? Because: Petersburg was piercing the islands with its black bridge: with its bridge and the arrows of the Prospects—in order to crush the poor under heaps of stone coffins; he hated Petersburg; above the accursed regiments of buildings that rose from the other bank out of a billow of clouds—someone small soared up out of the chaos and hovered there like a black dot: everything screamed from there and wept:

"Crush the islands! … "

Only now did he realise what had happened on the Nevskii Prospect, whose green ear had stared at him from a four-inch distance—through the glass of the carriage; the little death-spawn trembling there was that selfsame bat who, soaring up—in agony, cold and ominous—threatened and screamed …

All at once—

… But we'll tell about "all-at-once" later.

The desk stood there

Apollon Apollonovich focused his mind on the current day's business; in the flash of an eye there rose before him in complete clarity: yesterday's reports; with complete clarity he visualised the papers laid out on his desk, their order and the notes he had made on those papers, the shape of the letters in those notes, the pencil with which he had nonchalantly jotted in the margins: a blue *'approved for action'* with a flamboyant cross on the *t*, or a red *'check and report back'* with a squiggly tail on the *k*.

In the brief moment between the departmental staircase and the doors of his office Apollon Apollonovich shifted the centre of his consciousness by an act of will; all cerebral play retreated to the edge of his field of vision, like those pale patterns on the white background of the wallpaper: the neat pile of papers, lying parallel, shifted into the centre of that field, like the portrait that had just come to occupy that centre.

And the portrait? That is to say:

He is no more—and Russia he has left …

Who was this? The senator? Apollon Apollonovich Ableukhov? Why no: Viacheslav Konstantinovich … And what of him, Apollon Apollonovich?

And now, methinks, my turn has come,
And my beloved Delvig calls me …

My turn—your turn: turn and turn about—

New clouds have gathered now above the earth,
And in their tempest …

Idle cerebral play!

The pile of papers leapt up to the surface: Apollon Apollonovich, focusing his mind on the current day's business, turned to his assistant:

"Would you please, German Germanovich, be so kind as to prepare that file for me—that one, what's it called … "

"The file on deacon Zrakov with appended material evidence in the form of a tuft of beard?"

"No, not that one … "

"On landowner Puzov, number? … "

"No: the file on the potholes in Ukhtomsk … "

He was on the point of opening the door into his office when he remembered (he had all but forgotten): yes, yes—the eyes: they had opened wide, shown astonishment, gone wild—the eyes of the man of uncertain status … And why, why that zigzag with his hand? …

Most unpleasant. And he felt he had seen the man of uncertain status—somewhere, some time: maybe nowhere, never …

Apollon Apollonovich opened the door to his office.

The desk stood there in its proper place with the pile of official papers: in the corner the open fire crackled with logs; as he prepared to immerse himself in his work, Apollon Apollonovich warmed his frozen hands at the fire, while his cerebral play, limiting the senator's field of vision, continued to erect its misty planes.

He had seen the man of uncertain status

Nikolai Apollonovich …

Then Apollon Apollonovich …

"Surely not: good heavens."

"? … "

"What devilry is this?"

Apollon Apollonovich stopped at the door, because—what else would he do?

His innocent cerebral play once again moved forward of its own accord into his brain, that is to say into the pile of papers and petitions: Apollon Apollonovich would have regarded this cerebral play rather as the wallpaper of the room in whose confines projects came to fruition; Apollon Apollonovich's attitude to the arbitrariness of thought combinations was like his attitude to a plane; this plane, however, sometimes moved apart and admitted something unexpected into the centre of mental life (as it did now, for instance).

Apollon Apollonovich remembered: he had once seen the man of uncertain status.

He had once seen the man of uncertain status—can you imagine—in his own house.

He recalled: once he had been going down the stairs on the way to the outer door; on the stairs Nikolai Apollonovich, leaning over the banisters, had been cheerfully talking to someone: the statesman did not consider he had the right to inquire about Nikolai Apollonovich's acquaintances; a sense of tact naturally prevented him then from asking directly:

"Tell me, Kolenka, who was that who came to see you, old boy?"

Nikolai Apollonovich would have lowered his eyes:

"No one in particular, Papa: people call on me … "

And the conversation would have ended.

That was why Apollon Apollonovich took no interest at all in the identity of the man of uncertain status who had been looking up from the entrance-hall in his dark overcoat; the stranger had the same little black moustache and the same astonishing eyes (you might have met exactly such eyes at night in the Moscow chapel to the Martyr Panteleimon, which is beside the Nikolskii Gate: the chapel is famed for curing those who are possessed; you might also have seen such eyes on the portrait attached to the biography of a great man; or indeed: in a neurological clinic or even a psychiatric one).

Then, too, the eyes had opened wide, glinted, flashed; so: it had happened once, and might quite well happen again.

"About all this—just so, just so … "

"We'll have to … "

"Make detailed inquiries … "

The statesman made his detailed inquiries not directly, but by a roundabout route.

Apollon Apollonovich looked through the office door: desks upon desks! Piles of files! Heads bent over files! The scratch of pens! The rustle of papers as they were turned over! What powerful, seething paper production!

Apollon Apollonovich calmed down and immersed himself in work.

Strange qualities

The cerebral play of the bearer of bejewelled insignia was distinguished by strange, very strange, exceedingly strange qualities: his cranium became the womb of mental images, which were forthwith embodied in this spectral world.

Taking into account this strange, very strange, exceedingly strange circumstance, it would have been better for Apollon Apollonovich not to project from himself a single idle thought, but instead to go on carrying the idle thoughts in his own head: for every idle thought obstinately developed into a spatio-temporal image, continuing its now uncontrollable activities—outside the senator's head.

Apollon Apollonovich was in a certain sense like Zeus: from his head there emerged gods, goddesses and genii. We have already seen: one such genius (the stranger with the little black moustache), arising as an image, continued as a *being* there and then in the yellowish expanses of the Neva, claiming it was from them he had emerged: and not the senator's head; this stranger turned out to have idle thoughts of his own; and his idle thoughts possessed all the same qualities.

They escaped and acquired solidity.

And one such escaping thought of the stranger's was the thought that he, the stranger, existed in fact; this thought ran back from the Nevskii into the senator's brain and there established the idea that the very existence of the stranger in that head was an illusory existence.

And so the circle was closed.

Apollon Apollonovich was in a certain sense like Zeus: hardly had Athene the Stranger been born from his head, armed with the package, than another, exactly identical Pallas-Athene emerged as well.

This Pallas was the senator's house.

The stone colossus had escaped from his brain; and now the house opens its hospitable door—to us.

A servant was climbing the stairs; he suffered from breathlessness, but he's not the point now; the point is the staircase: a beautiful staircase! It had steps on it: as soft as the convolutions of the brain. But the author won't have time to describe to the reader this said staircase, which ministers have on many occasions climbed (he'll describe it later), because—the servant is already in the grand hall …

And again—the grand hall: beautiful! Windows and walls: the walls are a little cold … But the servant was in the drawing room (we have seen the drawing room).

We have cast a glance round the beautiful residence, taking our lead from the general feature with which the senator was wont to endow all objects.

45

For example:—

> —on those rare occasions when Apollon Apollonovich found himself in the bosom of nature he saw there just what the rest of us see; that is to say: he saw the blossoming bosom of nature; but for us this bosom immediately divides into different features: violets, buttercups, dandelions and carnations; but the senator restored these individual features to unity. We, of course, would have said:
>
> "There's a buttercup!"
>
> "There's a forget-me-not … "
>
> Apollon Apollonovich said simply and concisely:
>
> "Flowers … "
>
> "A flower … "

Let it be said between ourselves: for some reason Apollon Apollonovich regarded all flowers as bluebells …

He would have described with laconic brevity his own house too, consisting for him of walls (that formed squares and cubes), of windows cut through them, parquet floors, chairs, tables; the rest is mere detail …

The servant went into the corridor …

And it will do no harm for us to recall: the things that flashed by (pictures, piano, mirrors, mother-of-pearl, veneered tables)—in short, whatever flashed by could not possess any spatial form: it was all just an irritation of the cerebral membrane, unless it was a chronic malfunction … of the cerebellum, perhaps.

The illusion of a room was built up; and then it flew apart, leaving no trace, erecting its own misty surfaces beyond the bounds of consciousness; and when the servant slammed the heavy drawing room doors behind him, when his boots clattered down the echoing corridor, it was only a hammering in the temples: Apollon Apollonovich suffered from haemorrhoidal rushes of blood.

Beyond the door that had been slammed there was no drawing room: there were … cerebral expanses: convolutions, grey and white matter, pineal gland; and the heavy walls, consisting of sparkling spray (conditioned by the rushes of blood)—the bare walls were only a painful, leaden sensation: in the occipital, frontal, temporal and sincipital bones belonging to the venerable skull.

The house—this stone colossus—was not a house; the stone colossus was the Senator's Head: Apollon Apollonovich sat at his desk, at his files, distressed by a migraine, feeling that his head was six times larger than it should have been, and twelve times heavier.

Strange, very strange, exceedingly strange qualities!

Our role

The streets of Petersburg possess a most indubitable quality: they turn passers-by into shadows; shadows, however, the streets of Petersburg turn into people.

We saw that in the instance of the mysterious stranger.

Arising as a thought in the senator's head, he for some reason became associated with the senator's own house as well; it was there that he came to the surface of memory; most of all, however, he established himself on the Prospect, following immediately behind the senator in our humble tale.

From the crossroads to the little restaurant on Millionnaia Street we have described the stranger's route; we have described, further, how he sat in the restaurant up to the much-vaunted expression "all at once" with which everything broke off; suddenly something happened to the stranger there; an unpleasant sensation came over him.

Let us now examine his soul; but before that let's examine the restaurant; we have good grounds for that; for if we, the author, record in pedantic detail the path of the first person we meet, then the reader will believe us: this action of ours will be vindicated in the future. All that we have done in initiating this natural investigation is to anticipate senator Ableukhov's wish that an agent of the security department should follow unremittingly in the footsteps of the stranger; the glorious senator would have grasped hold of the telephone himself, in order by its means to communicate his thought to the appropriate place; fortunately for himself he did not know the stranger's place of residence (but we do know his residence). We are coming to meet the senator; and while the thoughtless agent is sitting idly in his station, we will be the agent ourselves.

But surely, surely …

Haven't we put our foot in it? Come on, what sort of an agent are we in fact? There *is* an agent. And he isn't asleep, honest to God, he isn't. Our role turns out to be an idle role.

When the stranger disappeared into the doors of the restaurant and we were seized by a desire to follow him there, we turned round and saw two silhouettes slowly cutting through the mist; one of the two silhouettes was quite tall and fat, clearly distinguished by his build; but we could not make out the silhouette's face (silhouettes don't have faces); still we were able to discern: a new, open, silk umbrella, blindingly gleaming galoshes and a half-sealskin hat with ear-flaps.

The moth-eaten figure of a squat little gent comprised the principal content of the second silhouette; the silhouette's face was reasonably visible: but this face too we failed to see, because we were taken aback by the immense proportions of its wart: thus the facial substance was obscured from us by the importunate accidence (as it behoves it to act in this world of shadows).

Pretending that we were looking at the clouds, we let the dark couple past; in front of the restaurant door the dark couple stopped and said a few words in human language.

"Hm?"

"Here … "

"That's what I thought: steps have been taken; that was in case you didn't point him out to me at the bridge."

"What steps have you taken? … "

"I've put a man there in the restaurant."

"Oh, there's no point in taking steps! I've told you time and time again … "

"I'm sorry, I did it out of zeal … "

"You ought to have consulted me first … Your steps are all very well … "

"You say yourself … "

"Yes, but your splendid steps … "

"Hm … "

"What? … Your splendid steps will get everything mixed up … "

The couple went on five paces and stopped; and again they said a few words in human language.

"Hm! ... I'll have to ... Hm! ... Wish you success now ... "

"Oh, what doubt can there be about that: the business is set up like clockwork; if I wasn't standing behind this whole matter, you can take my word for it as a friend, it would be done and dusted."

"Hm?"

"What are you saying?"

"This wretched cold."

"I'm talking about the business ... "

"Hm ... "

"Souls are tuned like musical instruments: and they're creating a concert—what did you say? The conductor just has to wave his baton from behind the scenes. Senator Ableukhov has to send out a circular, and the Fugitive will have to ... "

"Wretched cold ... "

"Nikolai Apollonovich will have to ... In a word: it's a triple concerto, with Russia as the stalls. D'you understand me? D'you understand? Why don't you say anything?"

"Listen: you ought to take a salary ... "

"No, you'll never understand me!"

"I do, I do: hm-hm-hm—I really haven't got enough hand-kerchiefs."

"What's the matter?"

"It's this cold! ... And the beast—hm-hm-hm—won't get away?"

"Go on, how could he ... "

"You really ought to take a salary ... "

"Salary! I don't work for a salary: I'm an artist, don't you understand, an artist!"

"In a manner of speaking ... "

"What's that?"

"Nothing: I'm treating myself with a tallow candle."

The moth-eaten figure took out a snotty handkerchief and made snorting noises with its nose.

"I'm talking about the business! Tell them, anyway, that Nikolai Apollonovich made a promise ... "

"A tallow candle is a marvellous cure for a cold ... "

"Tell them everything you've heard from me: the business is set up ... "

"Rub your nostril with it in the evening, and in the morning—right as rain … "

"The business is set up, I tell you again, like clock … "

"Your nose is clear, you can breathe freely!"

"Like clockwork! … "

"Eh?"

"Clockwork, damn it."

"My ear's bunged up: can't hear."

"Clo-ck-work … "

"Atchoo! … "

The handkerchief made another sortie round the wart: the two shadows slowly drifted away into the sodden murk. Soon the shadow of the fat man in the half-sealskin hat with ear flaps reappeared out of the mist, glanced absent-mindedly at the spire of the Peter and Paul cathedral.

And went into the restaurant.

And the face, moreover, had a glossy shine

Reader!

You are familiar with "all-at-once". Why ever do you hide your head under your wing like an ostrich at the approach of a fatal and ineluctable "all-at-once"? If some stranger started talking to you about "all-at-once", you would probably say:

"Excuse me, sir: you must be an out-and-out decadent."

And no doubt you will find me guilty of decadence too.

There you are before me now, just like an ostrich; but there's no point in hiding—you understand me perfectly well; and you understand the ineluctable "all-at-once" too.

So listen …

Your "all-at-once" creeps up behind your back, though sometimes it precedes your entry into a room; in the first case you are terribly disconcerted: an unpleasant feeling develops in your back, as though a host of invisible forces had come thronging into your back, as through an open door; you turn round and ask the lady of the house:

"Madam, would you mind if I closed the door; I have a particular nervous sensation: I cannot bear to sit with my back to an open door."

You laugh, she laughs.

Sometimes as you enter a drawing room you are met by a general murmur:

"We were just talking about you … "

And you reply:

"Heart speaking to heart, no doubt."

Everyone laughs. You laugh as well: as though this wasn't a case of "all-at-once".

Sometimes it happens that someone else's "all-at-once" peeps at you from over the shoulder of the person you're talking to, trying to snuggle up to your own "all-at-once". Something passes between the two of you which makes your eyes start fluttering, while the person you're talking to becomes very distant. For the rest of your lives there will be something he never forgives you.

Your "all-at-once" feeds on your cerebral play; it loves to gobble up everything vile in your thoughts, like a dog; as it becomes bloated, you melt like a candle; if your thoughts are vile and a tremor comes over you, then "all-at-once", sated with vileness of all varieties, like a well-fed but invisible dog, starts to precede you everywhere, creating in the detached observer the impression that you are veiled from view by a black cloud, invisible to the eye: that is your hairy "all-at-once", the faithful demon of your house (I knew one unfortunate person whose *black cloud* was all but visible to the eye: he was a writer …).

We left the stranger in the restaurant. All at once the stranger turned round abruptly; he felt as though some horrid slime had slipped under his collar and was trickling down his spine. But when he turned round there was no one behind him: the door into the restaurant was gaping open gloomily; and from there, from the door, the *invisible* thronged in.

Then he realised: the person he was waiting for was climbing the stairs, of course; and was about to enter; but was not entering yet; there was no one in the doorway.

But when my stranger turned away from the door, through the door there came at once the unpleasant fat man; and, going up to the stranger, he made the floorboards squeak; the yellowish, clean-shaven face, slightly tilted to one side, swam smoothly in its own second chin; and the face, moreover, had a glossy shine.

At this my stranger turned round and shuddered: the *person* gave him a friendly wave with his half-sealskin hat with ear-flaps:

"Aleksandr Ivanovich … "

"Lippanchenko!"

"None other … "

"Lippanchenko, you've kept me waiting."

The collar at the person's neck was tied with a cravat—red satin, garish, pinned with a large imitation diamond; the person was clad in a striped, dark-yellow suit; and gleaming polish glinted on his yellow shoes.

Taking a seat at the stranger's table, the person called out with satisfaction:

"A pot of coffee … And—listen—some cognac: I've got my own bottle there—with my name on."

And around them could be heard:

"You drank with me, didn't you?"

"I did … "

"And you ate? … "

"I did … "

"Well what a swine you are, if you don't mind my saying so … "

"Careful," cried my stranger: the unpleasant fat man, whom the stranger called Lippanchenko, had been about to put his dark-yellow elbow on the sheet of newspaper: the sheet of newspaper was covering the package.

"What is it?" then, as he removed the sheet of newspaper, Lippanchenko caught sight of the package: and Lippanchenko's lips quivered.

"Is that … it?"

"Yes, that is it."

Lippanchenko's lips went on quivering: Lippanchenko's lips resembled pieces of sliced smoked salmon—not the yellow-red sort, but greasy and yellow (you have probably eaten salmon like that with pancakes at the home of an impecunious family).

"Aleksandr Ivanovich, I have to say, how careless you are." Lippanchenko stretched his coarse fingers towards the package; and imitation gemstones glittered on the rings on his swollen fingers, with their chewed nails (there were also dark traces on his fingernails of a brown dye, which corresponded to the colour of his hair; the attentive observer might reach the conclusion: the person dyed his hair).

"Why, just one more movement (if I'd just put my elbow on it), and there could have been … a catastrophe … "

And with especial solicitude the person transferred the package to a chair.

"Yes, indeed, we'd both have been … off the wall … " the stranger joked unpleasantly. "We'd both have been … "

Evidently he was enjoying the discomfiture of this person whom (we can add on our own account) he hated.

"Not for myself, of course … "

"Of course not, you're not … for yourself, but for … " the stranger concurred.

And around them could be heard:

"Don't you call me names … "

"I'm not calling you names."

"Yes, you are: you've got it in for me because you paid … Well so what, if you paid; you paid that time, now I'm paying … "

"Let me give you a kiss, my friend, for that act of yours … "

"Don't be cross about the swine: I'm just eating and eating … "

"Yes, you just eat: that's the way … "

"Now then, Aleksandr Ivanovich, that package, old chap"— Lippanchenko gave him a sideways glance—"you take it straight round to Nikolai Apollonovich."

"Ableukhov?"

"Yes, to him—for safe keeping."

"But surely: for safe keeping the package can stay at my place … "

"It's awkward: you might get caught; there it will be safe and sound. Say what you will, senator Ableukhov's house … By the way, have you heard the venerable dodderer's latest authoritative utterance? … "

Thereupon the fat man bent over and started whispering something into my stranger's ear:

"Sh-sh-sh … "

"At Ableukhov?"

"Sh-sh … "

"To Ableukhov? … "

"Sh-sh-sh … "

"With Ableukhov? … "

"Yes, not with the senator, but with the senator's son: when you go to his house, would you be so kind, along with the package give him this note: here it is … "

Lippanchenko's low-browed head hove right alongside the stranger's face; his little eyes, hidden in their sockets, bored inquisitively into him; his lip quivered slightly and sucked the air. The stranger with the little black moustache listened intently to the fat man's whispering, trying attentively to make out the import of the whisper, which was drowned by the voices in the restaurant; the voices in the restaurant obscured Lippanchenko's whisper; something barely rustled from his hideous lips (like the rustle of many hundred ants' articulated legs, when their nest is disturbed) and it seemed that that whisper had a fearful import, as though this were a whisper about whole worlds and planetary systems; but you only had to listen hard to the whisper and the fearful import of the whisper turned out to be a perfectly mundane import:

"You hand him the note … "

"How's this, does Nikolai Apollonovich have special relations then?"

The person narrowed his eyes and clicked his tongue.

"I thought all contact with him was through me … "

"But it isn't, you see … "

Around them could be heard:

"Eat, my friend, eat … "

"Chop me a piece of that beef-brawn."

"Truth is in food … "

"What is truth?"

"Truth's what suits your tooth … "

"I know that … "

"Well, if you know it, then fine: pass your plate and get eating … "

Lippanchenko's dark-yellow suit reminded the stranger of the dark-yellow colour of the wallpaper in his abode on Vasilevskii Island—a colour with which his insomnia was linked on white spring nights, and the gloomy nights of September; it must have been that cruel insomnia that all of a sudden evoked in his memory a certain fateful face with narrow, Mongoloid eyes; that face had many a time gazed at him from a patch of his yellow wallpaper. When he examined this spot by day, the stranger could discern only a patch of damp with a woodlouse crawling across it. In order to distract himself from the recollection of the hallucination that tormented him, my stranger lit a cigarette and to his own surprise became loquacious:

"Listen to the noise … "

"Yes, they're pretty noisy."

"The sound of the noise is 'ee-ee-ee', but I keep hearing 'ugh' … "

Lippanchenko was preoccupied, lost in thoughts of his own.

"There's something dull and blubbery in the sound 'ugh' … Or am I wrong?"

"No, no, not at all," Lippanchenko grunted without listening, and for a moment tore himself away from his own thought-processes …

"All words with that '-u-' sound are hideously trivial: it's not like that with 'ee-ee'; 'ee-ee' is the blue firmament, thought, crystal; the sound 'ee-ee' creates for me the impression of the hooked beak of an eagle; but words with '-u-' are trivial; take 'slug', for instance; just listen to it: 'slu-u-u-g', something foul and slippery … Or again 'slu-u-dge': something sticky; 'lump'—something shapeless; 'rump'—the debauched bits … "

My stranger broke off his speech: Lippanchenko was sitting in front of him like a shapeless *lump*; the *fug* from his cigarette was making *smuts* in the atmosphere: Lippanchenko was sitting in a cloud; my stranger looked at him and thought, "Ugh, muck—Tartar hordes … " In front of him was sitting one great '*ugh*'.

With a hiccup someone at the next table cried out:

"You *ugh*-er! … "

"Excuse me, Lippanchenko: are you a Mongol?"

"Why such a strange question? … "

"No reason, I just thought … "

"All Russians have Mongol blood in their veins … "

A fat paunch slumped down at the next table; and the paunch was greeted at the table by a roar of:

"Anofriev the knacker! … "

"Our respects!"

"Greetings to the knacker of the city slaughterhouse … Have a seat … "

"Waiter! … "

"Well, how are things with you? … "

"Waiter: put on *The Negro's Dream* … "

And the tubes of the machine bellowed to the health of the knacker like a bull under the knacker's knife.

What costumier might that be?

Nikolai Apollonovich's apartments consisted of the following rooms: bedroom, study, sitting room.

The bedroom: the bedroom was occupied by an immense bed; it was covered by a red satin bedspread—with lace pillowcases on the luxuriously fluffed-up pillows.

The study walls were lined with oak shelves, tightly packed with books, in front of which a silk curtain slipped easily on bronze rings; an attentive hand could either conceal the contents of the shelves entirely from the gaze, or, alternatively, could reveal rows of black leather-bound spines, studded with inscriptions saying: '*Kant*'.

The study furniture was upholstered in dark green; and a bust was resplendent there … also of Kant, of course.

For two years now Nikolai Apollonovich had taken to rising no earlier than midday. Two-and-a-half years previously he had woken up earlier: he would wake at nine o'clock, and would appear at half-past nine in his uniform, buttoned to the top, for the family's morning coffee.

Two-and-a-half years ago Nikolai Apollonovich did not stride round the house in a Bukhara robe; no skullcap adorned his oriental sitting room; two-and-a-half years ago Anna Petrovna, Nikolai Apollonovich's mother and Apollon Apollonovich's spouse, had finally abandoned the family hearth, inspired by an Italian singer; since that elopement with the singer Nikolai Apollonovich had appeared on the parquet floors of the frigid family hearth in a Bukhara robe: the daily meetings of father and son over morning coffee had somehow ceased of their own accord. Nikolai Apollonovich had his coffee brought to him in bed.

And Apollon Apollonovich was pleased to take his coffee significantly earlier than his son.

Meetings between father and son took place only at dinner; and even then: of short duration; meanwhile the robe began to appear on Nikolai Apollonovich in the morning; he acquired Tartar slippers, trimmed with fur; on his head there appeared a skullcap.

And the brilliant young man turned into an oriental man.

Nikolai Apollonovich had just received a letter; a letter in unfamiliar handwriting: some wretched doggerel with hints of revolution and love and with the striking signature: '*An ardent soul*'. Desiring for precision's sake to acquaint himself with the contents of the doggerel, Nikolai Apollonovich started rushing helplessly around the room in quest of his spectacles, riffling through books, pens, pencils and sundry knick-knacks, and muttering to himself:

"A-ah … Where are my glasses? … "

"Damn it … "

"Lost them?"

"Well I never."

"Ah? … "

Nikolai Apollonovich, just like Apollon Apollonovich, talked to himself.

His movements were abrupt, like those of his Excellency his father; just like Apollon Apollonovich he was distinguished by his unimpressive stature and the restless gaze of his incessantly smiling face; when he immersed himself in the serious contemplation of something, however, that gaze gradually turned to stone: the lines on his completely white countenance, which resembled the face on an icon, stood out drily, sharply, coldly, with a striking aristocratic nobility of a specific kind: it was his forehead that most noticeably displayed the nobility of his face—it was chiselled, with swollen veins: the rapid pulsation of those veins left on his forehead the distinct mark of premature sclerosis.

The bluish colour of his veins coincided with the blue around his huge, seemingly made-up eyes, of a dark-cornflower shade (only in moments of emotion did his eyes become black from the dilation of the pupils).

Nikolai Apollonovich stood before us in a Tartar skullcap; but if he were to take it off—then a head of flaxen white hair would appear and soften this cold, almost severe exterior with its imprint of obstinacy; it would be hard to find hair of this shade in a grown man; this shade, rare in an adult, can often be found in peasant children—especially in Belorussia.

Throwing the letter down casually, Nikolai Apollonovich sat down at his open book; what he had been reading the day before arose distinctly before him (a treatise of some sort). He remembered the chapter and the page: he called to mind the lightly traced zigzag made by his rounded fingernail; the sinuous trains of thought and his own notes—in pencil in the margins; his face now came to life, while remaining both stern and precise: it was animated by thought.

Here, in his room, Nikolai Apollonovich truly grew into an autonomous, self-existent centre—into a series of logical premises flowing out from that centre, which determined thought, the soul and this table right here: here he comprised the sole centre of the universe, both conceivable and inconceivable, flowing cyclically through all the aeons of time.

This centre—performed logical processes.

But today Nikolai Apollonovich had barely managed to push aside all the everyday trivia and the morass of incoherence called the world and life, he had barely managed to find his way back to himself, when incoherence burst back into his world; and in this incoherence his self-awareness became shamefully bemired: just like a fly, trotting at liberty round the rim of a plate on its six little paws, that suddenly gets its paw and its wing inescapably stuck in a viscous mass of honey.

Nikolai Apollonovich tore himself away from his book: there was a knock at his door:

"Well? … "

"What is it?"

From the door came a muffled and deferential voice.

"There, sir … "

"Someone's asking for you, sir … "

When he was deeply immersed in thought, Nikolai Apollonovich used to lock the door of his study: then it began to seem to him that both he and the study, and the objects in that study, were instantly transforming from objects of the real world into mental symbols of purely logical constructions; the space of the study merged with his desensitized body into a general chaos of being, which he called the *universe*; and Nikolai Apollonovich's consciousness, separating from his body, was directly linked to the electric lamp on the writing desk, which was called "the sun of consciousness". Behind locked doors and thinking through his system, which was being raised step by step to unity, he felt that his body was spilt out into the 'universe', that is to say, the study; the head of this body was then transposed into the rotund glass head of the electric lamp under its flirtatious shade.

And thus transposed, Nikolai Apollonovich became a truly creative being.

That was why he liked locking himself in: a voice, a rustle, or the footstep of another person, transforming the *universe* into a study, and the *consciousness* into a lamp, shattered the fastidious structure of Nikolai Apollonovich's thought.

So it was now.

"What is it?"

"I can't hear … "

But from the distant expanses the servant's voice responded:

"There's a man come."

Then Nikolai Apollonovich's face all at once took on a satisfied expression:

"Ah, that will be from the costumier: the costumier has brought me my costume … "

What costumier might that be?

Gathering up the folds of his robe, Nikolai Apollonovich strode off towards the front door; on the landing he leant over the banister and called:

"Is that you? … "

"The costumier?"

"From the costumier?"

"Has the costumier sent me my costume?"

And once more we will repeat on our own account: what costumier might that be?

In Nikolai Apollonovich's room there appeared a cardboard box, Nikolai Apollonovich locked the door; he anxiously cut the string; and raised the lid; further, he pulled out of the box: first a small mask with a black lace beard, and after the mask Nikolai Apollonovich pulled out a splendid bright red domino, that rustled as he unfolded it.

Soon he stood before the mirror—all satin and red, with a tiny mask poised over his face; the black lace of the beard, twisted aside, fell on to his shoulders, forming to right and left of him a pair of outlandish, fantastic wings; and from the black lace of those wings, from the semi-darkness of the room, there gazed at him in the mirror, tormentingly strange—that very thing: his own face; you might have said that it was not Nikolai Apollonovich gazing at himself from the mirror, but an unknown, pale and languishing—demon of space.

After this masquerade Nikolai Apollonovich, with an extremely satisfied expression on his face, tidied back into the box first the red domino and then the little black mask.

A sodden autumn

A sodden autumn winged its way over Petersburg; and the September day flickered cheerlessly.

Ragged clouds scudded by in billows of green; they condensed into a yellowish vapour that settled ominously on the roofs. The billows of green kept rising endlessly above the distant, limitless expanses of the Neva; the dark depths of the water beat against their barriers with scales of steel; from the Petersburg Side a spire shot up into the greenish billows.

Dark strips of soot rose high from steamers' funnels, described an arc of mourning, and collapsed tail first into the Neva.

The river seethed, and cried out in despair through steamers' sirens, shattering its watery steel scales on stone abutments; it licked the granite; in the onslaught of its biting winds it tore off caps from working men and officers, it snatched umbrellas, raincoats. And everywhere the air was heavy with a pale grey putrescence; and from afar, into the Neva, into that pale grey putrescence, the sodden statue of the Horseman went on hurling from its rock its heavy, green-stained bronze.

And on this louring background of dangling soot-tails above the damp stones of the embankment parapet, staring into the murky, germ-infested water of the river, the silhouette of Nikolai Apollonovich was moulded distinctly in his grey Nikolaevan cloak and his student's cap, worn askew. Slowly Nikolai Apollonovich moved towards the grey, dark bridge, not smiling, and presenting a somewhat comical figure: wrapped in his overcoat, he seemed hunched and somehow armless with the flap of his coat dancing absurdly in the wind.

By the big black bridge he stopped.

An unpleasant smile flashed across his face for a moment and faded again; memories of unrequited love seized him, rushing over him with the onslaught of the biting wind; Nikolai Apollonovich remembered a misty night; on that night he had leant over the parapet; he had turned round and seen that there was no one there; he had raised his leg; and had lifted it, with its smooth rubber galosh, over the parapet, yes … and stayed like that: with his leg raised; it would seem that further consequences ought to have ensued; but … Nikolai Apollonovich went on standing there with his leg raised. A few moments later Nikolai Apollonovich lowered his leg.

And it was then that he had conceived an ill-considered plan: to give a terrible promise to a certain reckless party.

Recalling now that unsuccessful act of his, Nikolai Apollonovich smiled in a most unpleasant way, presenting a somewhat comical figure: wrapped in his overcoat, he seemed hunched and somehow armless with the long flap of his coat dancing in the wind; and presenting such a figure, he turned off on to the Nevskii; it was beginning to turn dark; here and there a light gleamed in a shop window.

"How handsome," was heard constantly around Nikolai Apollonovich.

"An ancient mask … "

"The Belvedere Apollo."

"Handsome man … "

Most probably it was the ladies coming the other way who said such things about him.

"The pallor of his face … "

"That marble profile … "

"Like a god … "

Most probably the ladies coming the other way said such things to each other.

But if Nikolai Apollonovich had made to engage them in conversation, they would have said under their breath:

"What a freak … "

At the point where two melancholy lions in a doorway mockingly place paw on grey granite paw—there, at that spot, Nikolai Apollonovich stopped in surprise, seeing in front of him the back of a passing officer; tripping over the flaps of his coat, he made to catch the officer up:

"Sergei Sergeevich?"

The officer (a tall fair-haired man with a pointed beard) turned and watched apprehensively and with a shade of irritation through the blue lenses of his spectacles as, tripping over the flaps of his overcoat, the figure of a student struggled clumsily towards him from the familiar spot where in a doorway two melancholy lions with smooth granite manes mockingly place paw on paw. It seemed that for a moment a certain thought crossed the officer's face; from the expression of his trembling lip one might have thought that the officer was flustered: as though he was wondering whether to recognise the other or not.

"Ah … good day … Where are you going?"

"I'm on my way to Panteleimonovskaia," Nikolai Apollonovich lied, in order to walk with the officer along the Moika.

"We can go together, then … "

"Where are you going?" Nikolai Apollonovich lied a second time, in order to take a walk with the officer along the Moika.

"I'm going home."

"We're going the same way, then."

Between the windows of a yellow official building rows of stone lions' muzzles hung over the two of them; each muzzle hung above a coat of arms, entwined in a garland of stone.

As though in an effort to avoid touching on some difficult past, they both began to talk anxiously, interrupting each other: about the weather, about the way the disturbances of recent weeks had affected Nikolai Apollonovich's philosophical work, about the shenanigans the officer had uncovered in the provisioning commission (the officer was in charge of provisions somewhere out there).

Between the windows of a yellow official building a row of stone muzzles hung over the two of them; each hung above a coat of arms entwined in a garland.

And so they talked all the way.

And here they were at the Moika: the same bright, three-storeyed building with five columns from the time of Alexander; and the same frieze of ornamental stucco above the first floor: one circle after another; and in each circle a Roman helmet on crossed swords. Now they were past the building; after the building was a house; and there were its windows … The officer stopped by the house and for some reason suddenly reddened; and after reddening he said:

"Goodbye, then … You're going on? … "

Nikolai Apollonovich's heart began to thump more violently; he was on the point of asking something; but—no: he didn't ask; now he stood on his own in front of the door that had been slammed shut; memories of unrequited love, or rather—of sensual infatuation— these memories enveloped him; and the bluish veins on his temples began to beat more strongly; he was now considering his revenge: an outrage against the feelings of the person who had insulted him, and who lived behind this entrance; he had been considering his revenge for about a month now; and—for the time being not a word about it!

The same bright building with five columns and a frieze of ornamental stucco; one circle after another; and in each circle a Roman helmet on crossed swords.

In the evening the Prospect is flooded by a pall of fire. The spheres of electric light in the middle hang evenly on high. At the sides the shifting gleam of signboards plays; here, here and here a flash of ruby lights; over there—a flash of emeralds. One moment—and the ruby lights are over there; and the emeralds are here, here and here.

In the evening the Nevskii is flooded by a pall of fire. And the walls of many buildings burn with gemstone light: words composed of diamonds sparkle brilliantly: '*Coffee House*', '*Farce*', '*Tate Diamonds*', '*Omega Watches*'. A shop window, in daytime greenish, now resplendent, opens wide its fiery maw on to the Nevskii; everywhere are tens, hundreds of hellish fiery maws; these maws disgorge their bright white light tormentingly on to the pavement; they spew out a turbid fluid in fiery rust And the Prospect is chewed to shreds by fire. A white gleam falls on bowler hats, on top hats, plumes; the white gleam surges further, to the middle of the Prospect, shoving the evening darkness off the pavement: and above the Nevskii the evening fluid evaporates as it glistens, to form a dull yellow and blood-red murk mixed from blood and dirt. Thus from the Finnish marshes the city will show you the place of its demented settlement with a red, red spot: and that spot is to be seen in silence from afar against the sombre night. As you wander the length of our far-flung land, you will see from afar a spot of red blood, that stands out against the sombre night; and in consternation you will say: "Is that not the location of the fires of Gehenna?" And having said it—you will trudge off into the distance: you will try to circumvent Gehenna.

But if, you madman, you were to venture out to meet Gehenna, that bright-red gleam that so horrified you from afar would slowly dissolve into a whitish, not entirely wholesome brilliance, and would encircle you with houses and their many lighted windows—and nothing else: and in the end it would dissolve into a multitude of lights.

And there would be no Gehenna.

Nikolai Apollonovich did not see the Nevskii, in his eyes was nothing but that one same house: windows, shadows behind the windows; behind the windows merry voices perhaps: that of the yellow cuirassier, Baron Ommau-Ommergau; of the blue cuirassier, Count Aven, and her—*her* voice … And Sergei Sergeevich, the officer, was sitting there and maybe slipping in among the merry pleasantries:

"I was just walking along with Nikolai Apollonovich Ableukhov … "

Apollon Apollonovich remembered

Yes, Apollon Apllonovich remembered: he had recently heard a certain innocuous joke about himself.

Officials were saying:

"Our old bat (Apollon Apollonovich's nickname in the Establishment) doesn't behave at all according to Gogol's types of officials when he shakes hands with petitioners; when he shakes petitioners' hands he doesn't use the full scale of handshakes from utter contempt, via disdain, to complete non-contempt: from collegiate registrar to state counsellor ... "

"He only strikes a single note: contempt ... "

Thereupon some intervened in his defence:

"Gentlemen, please stop it: that's because of his piles ... "

And everyone agreed.

The door was flung open: and Apollon Apollonovich came in. The joke broke off in fear (just as a nimble little mouse shoots abruptly into its hole as soon as you enter the room). But Apollon Apollonovich did not take offence at jokes; and anyway there was an element of truth in it: he did suffer from haemorrhoids.

Apollon Apollonovich went to the window; two children's heads in the windows of the house opposite saw facing them behind the glass of the house across the road the facial blur of an unknown old man.

And the little heads in the windows disappeared.

Here, in his office in the exalted Establishment, Apollon Appollonovich truly grew into a certain centre: into a series of state Establishments, offices and green tables (only more modestly appointed). Here he was a point that radiated forces, the point of intersection of forces, and the impulse for many manifold manipulations. Here Apollon Apollonovich was a force in the Newtonian sense; and a force in the Newtonian sense, as you are probably not aware, is an occult force.

Here he was the final instance—of denunciations, petitions and telegrams.

This instance in the organism of state he attributed not to himself: but to that centre contained in himself—his consciousness.

Here his consciousness separated from his valiant personality, seeping all round between the walls, taking on an improbable brightness, concentrating with such great force in a single point (between his eyes and forehead), that it seemed an invisible, tiny white light-source, flashing between his eyes and forehead, was casting all around it sheaves of snake-like lightning flashes; these lightning-thoughts spread out like snakes from his bald head; and if a clairvoyant were to stand at that moment before the face of the venerable statesman, he would without doubt see before him the head of the Gorgon Medusa.

And Apollon Apollonovich would envelop him in Medusan terror.

Here his consciousness separated off from his valiant personality: his personality, though, with its vortex of multifarious emotions (this collateral consequence of the existence of the soul) was taken by the senator to be the cranium, seen as an empty case, vacated at this very moment.

In the Establishment Apollon Apollonovich spent hours reviewing the production of papers: from the effulgent centre (between his eyes and forehead) flew all the circulars to the heads of subordinate Establishments. And just as he, from this armchair here, cut through his own life with his consciousness, so too his circulars, from this same place, cut at right angles through the haphazard life of the man-in-the-street.

Apollon Apollonovich was wont to compare this life with the sexual, the vegetative or any other kind of urge (for example, with the urge for fast travel along the Petersburg Prospects).

When he left these walls, permeated as they were with cold, Apollon Apollonovich suddenly became a man-in-the-street.

It was only from here that he towered up and hovered madly over Russia, evoking in his enemies the fateful comparison (with a bat). All these enemies of his—down to the last—were men-in-the-street; once outside these walls he was just such an enemy to himself.

Today Apollon Apollonovich was particularly precise: his bald head did not nod a single time during a report; Apollon Apollonovich was afraid of revealing weakness: in the performance of his official responsibilities! ... Rising to logical clarity was especially difficult for him today: heaven alone knows why, Apollon Apollonovich had come to the conclusion that his own son, Nikolai Apollonovich—was an out-and-out scoundrel.

The window allowed a view of the lower part of the balcony. Approaching the window it was possible to see the caryatid at the entrance: a bearded man of stone.

Like Apollon Apollonovich the bearded man of stone rose above the noise of the street and above the seasons of the year: the year 1812 had freed him from his scaffolding. The crowds of 1825 had raged beneath him; a crowd was passing now, too—in 1905. For five years now Apollon Apollonovich had seen from here every day the smile sculpted in stone; the tooth of time was gnawing at it. In those five years events had flown by: Anna Petrovna was in Spain; Viacheslav Konstantinovich was no more; the yellow heel had impertinently mounted the lofty ridges of Port Arthur; China had been through turmoil and Port Arthur had fallen.

As he made ready to go out and meet the crowds of petitioners, Apollon Apollonovich had a smile on his face; his smile arose, however, from anxiety: what might be waiting for him outside those doors.

Apollon Apollonovich spent his life between two desks: his desk in the study and his desk in the Establishment. The third place the senator favoured was his carriage.

And here: he was anxious.

And the door opened; the secretary, a young man with a minor decoration dangling in a somewhat liberal fashion from his starched collar, rushed up to the lofty personage, flicking respectfully the over-starched edge of his snow-white cuff. And in answer to his timid question Apollon Apollonovich roared out:

"No, no! ... Do as I said ... And you know," said Apollon Apollonovich, then stopped and corrected himself.

He had meant to use the polite form, but the familiar form had come out by mistake.

His absent-mindedness was legendary; on one occasion Apollon Apollonovich had appeared at an important reception—can you imagine?—without a tie; stopped by a palace servant, he suffered extreme embarrassment, from which he was rescued by the servant, who offered to lend him his own.

Cold fingers

Apollon Apollonovich in his grey overcoat and tall black top hat, with his stony face redolent of a paperweight, stepped swiftly out of his carriage and ran up the steps of the entrance, removing a black suede glove on the way.

He quickly went into the entrance-hall. The top hat was passed with care to the servant. With equal care his overcoat, his briefcase and his scarf were surrendered likewise.

Apollon Apollonovich stood in front of the servant in thought; suddenly Apollon Apollonovich addressed a question to him:

"Would you be so kind as to tell me: does a young man come here very often—yes: a young man?"

"A young man, sir?"

An awkward silence ensued: Apollon Apollonovich was unable to formulate his thought in any other way. But the servant, of course, had no way of guessing what young man the master was asking about.

"Young people do come, your Excellency, not often … "

"Well … what about young people with moustaches?"

"With moustaches, sir?"

"Black ones … "

"With black ones, sir?"

"Well yes, and—in overcoats … "

"They all come in overcoats, sir … "

"Yes, but with the collar turned up … "

Suddenly something dawned upon the doorman.

"Ah, you mean the one who … "

"Well yes, that one … "

"One like that did come once, sir … came to see the young master: only that was quite a while ago; that's how it is, sir … they come to inquire … "

"How's that?"

"That's how it is, sir!"

"With a moustache?"

"Exactly so, sir!"

"A black one?"

"With a black moustache … "

"And with his coat collar turned up?"

"The very same, sir ... "

Apollon Apollonovich stood for a moment as though rooted to the spot and suddenly: Apollon Apollonovich walked on past.

The staircase was covered with a grey velvet carpet; the staircase was framed, of course, by heavy walls; the grey velvet carpet covered those walls. On the walls an ornamental arrangement of ancient weapons gleamed; beneath a verdigris encrusted shield there shone a Lithuanian helmet with its spike; the cruciform hilt of a knight's sword glittered; here swords were rusting; there—halberds ponderously sloped; chain-mail armour gave the walls a muted brilliance; a blunderbuss and a pike were leant against the wall.

The top of the staircase led to the landing; here from a lustreless plinth of white alabaster a white Niobe raised on high her alabaster eyes.

Apollon Apollonovich threw open the door in front of him deliberately, resting his bony hand upon the cut-glass doorknob: across the cold hall, that stretched a disproportionate distance, the tread of his heavy steps rang out coldly.

So it is always

Over the empty streets of Petersburg barely-lit amorphous forms were flying by; scraps of cloud were overtaking one another.

A patch of phosphorescence floated—nebulous and deathly—across the sky; the sky was shot through with a misty, phosphorescent brilliance; and it made the roofs and chimneys glisten. The green waters of the Moika flowed past there; on one side of it the same three storeyed building still rose up with its five white columns; at the top were cornices. There, on the bright background of the bright building, a cuirassier of Her Majesty was passing slowly by; he had a gleaming golden helmet.

And a silver dove raised its wings above that helmet.

Nikolai Apollonovich, shaven and scented, was making his way along the Moika wrapped in furs; his head was sunk into his coat, and his eyes held a strange light; in his soul—nameless tremors were rising; something terrible and sweet was singing there: as though within him Aeolus' storm-filled wineskin had flown apart and the sons of unearthly impulses were cruelly driving him away with whistling whips to strange and incomprehensible lands.

He was thinking: can this *too* be love? He recalled: one misty night, rushing impetuously from that doorway over there, he had set off at a run towards that cast-iron Petersburg bridge, and there, on the bridge ...

He shuddered.

A sheaf of light flew past: a black carriage from the royal court: it bore its bright-red, as though bloodshot, lamps past the bright window cavities of that self-same house; on the black current of the Moika the lamps played and glittered; the ghostly outline of a servant's tricorn hat and the outline of a flapping overcoat flew by with the light from one mist into another.

Nikolai Apollonovich stood for some time in thought in front of the house: his heart was pounding in his chest; he stood and stood—and suddenly disappeared into the familiar doorway.

In the old days he used to come here every evening; now he had not crossed the threshold for two months and more; and now he crossed it like a thief. In the old days a girl in a white apron used to open the door to him in welcome; she would say:

"Good evening, sir," with a sly smile.

And now? No one would come out to meet him; and if he rang, the same girl would blink her eyes at him in fear and would not say, "Good evening, sir"; no, he wasn't going to ring.

What was he here for?

The outer door opened wide in front of him; and the sound of its closing struck him in the back; the darkness enveloped him; as though everything behind him had dropped away (that is probably how it is in the first moment after death, as the temple of the body collapses away from the soul into the abyss of corruption); but Nikolai Apollonovich gave no thought now to death—death was far away; in the darkness he evidently thought of his own gestures, because his behaviour in the darkness took on a fantastic tinge; he settled down on the cold step by an inner door, sinking his face into the fur and listening to the beating of his heart; a black void began behind his back; and a black void was in front.

And so Nikolai Apollonovich sat in the darkness.

And while he sat there the Neva still opened out between Alexander Square and Millionnaia; the stone arch of the Winter Canal displayed its lachrymose expanse; the Neva thrust itself from there in an onslaught of moist wind; the fleeting surfaces of its waters glinted from there soundlessly, their pale gleam reflected furiously in the mists. The smooth walls of the four-storeyed palace wing, criss-crossed with lines, glistened with malice in the moonlight.

No one, nothing.

As ever the canal disgorged its choleric water into the Neva: the same bridge still bent over it; as ever a nightly female shadow ran out on to the bridge, to—cast herself into the river? … Liza's shadow? No, not Liza's, but simply—some Petersburg woman's; the woman ran this way, but did not throw herself into the river: crossing the Winter Canal, she ran hurriedly away from a yellow house on the Gagarin Embankment, beneath which she would stand every evening, gazing for a long time at the windows.

The quiet plashing was left behind her: in front a square spread out; endless statues, green-tinged, bronze, appeared from all sides above the dark-red walls; Hercules and Poseidon surveyed the expanses by night as well; across the Neva a dark mass rose up—in the outlines of islands and houses; and cast its amber eyes sadly into the mist; and it seemed it was weeping; a row of lights along the bank dropped tears into the Neva; its surface was seared by their seething flashes.

Up above—vague outlines spread their ragged grieving arms across the sky; swarm on swarm they climbed above the waves of the Neva, racing to the zenith; and when they touched the zenith, then a phosphorescent blur, rushing to attack, thrust itself upon them from the sky. Only in one place, untouched by chaos—where by day a heavy stone bridge was cast across—huge nests of gemstones glinted strangely in the mist.

The woman's shadow, her face buried in her muff, ran along the Moika to that same doorway which she came running out of every evening and where now Nikolai Apollonovich was sitting on a cold step by the door; the street door opened before her; the street door slammed shut behind her; the darkness enveloped her; as though everything had fallen away behind her; the lady in black was thinking there in the hallway of simple, mundane things; how she would give orders for the samovar to be prepared; she had already stretched her hand out to the bell—and then she saw: a kind of outline—it seemed a mask stood up from the step in front of her.

And when the door to the apartment opened and a sheaf of light from the door momentarily lit the darkness of the hallway, her terrified chambermaid's exclamation confirmed everything for her, because first there appeared in the open door an apron and starched cap; and then the apron and cap started back from the door. In the bright flash of light a picture of indescribable strangeness was revealed, and the black outline of the lady rushed into the open door.

Behind her back there rose from the darkness a rustling, dark-crimson clown in a trembling, bearded mask.

From the darkness it could be seen how the fur of a Nikolaevan cloak fell slowly, soundlessly from shoulders rustling with velvet, and two red arms stretched out in anguish to the door. But then, of course, the door closed, cutting off the sheaf of light and casting the entrance stairway back into utter emptiness and darkness: just as we, as we cross death's threshold, cast our body back into the darkened abyss that had just shone with light.

A second later Nikolai Apollonovich slipped out on to the street; a piece of red silk was flapping beneath the skirts of his cloak; his nose buried in the Nikolaevan cloak, Nikolai Apollonovich hastened away in the direction of the bridge.

Petersburg, Petersburg!

Sediment of mist, you have pursued me too with idle cerebral play: you are a cruel-hearted tormenter; you are a restless ghost; for years you used to assail me; I would run along your terrible Prospects and my impetus would carry me up on to that cast-iron bridge which starts from the edge of the world and leads to the limitless distance; beyond the Neva, in the green distance of the other world—the ghosts of islands and houses rose, seducing me with the vain hope that that land was real and not—a howling endlessness that drives the pale smoke of clouds out on to the Petersburg streets.

Restless shadows trudge from the islands; thus a swarm of visions repeats itself, reflected in the Prospects, chasing along the Prospects that are reflected in each other like a mirror in another mirror, where a moment of time itself expands into immeasurable aeons: and as you wander from one doorway to another you live through ages.

O, great bridge, gleaming in electric splendour!

I remember a fateful moment; I, too, one September night leaned over your parapet: another moment—and my body would have tumbled into the mists.

O, green waters, teeming with bacilli!

Another moment, and you would have turned me too into one of your shadows. A restless shadow, maintaining the appearance of a man-in-the-street, would have flickered ambiguously in the draughts of the damp canal; a passer-by might have seen over his shoulder: a bowler hat, a stick, a coat, ears, a nose and a moustache …

He would have passed on … to the cast-iron bridge.

On the cast-iron bridge he would have turned round; and would have seen nothing: above the damp parapet, above the green water teeming with bacilli, in the gusts of the Neva gale—only a bowler hat, a stick, ears, a nose and a moustache—would have fluttered by.

You will never forget him!

In this chapter we have seen Senator Ableukhov; we have also seen the senator's idle thoughts in the form of the senator's house, and in the form of the senator's son, who carries in his head idle thoughts of his own; and lastly, we have seen another idle shadow—that of the stranger.

This shadow arose by chance in Senator Ableukhov's consciousness, receiving there its ephemeral existence; but Apollon Apollonovich's consciousness is a shadow consciousness, because he too is possessed of ephemeral existence, being the product of the author's imagination: needless, idle cerebral play.

The author, having once displayed these pictures of illusions, ought quickly to remove them and break off the thread of the narration with this very sentence; but … the author will not behave like this: he has sufficient right not to do so.

Cerebral play is only a mask; beneath this mask proceeds the invasion of the brain by forces unknown to us: and what if Apollon Apollonovich is woven from our brain—he will still be able to terrify with another startling existence that attacks at night. Apollon Apollonovich is endowed with the attributes of this existence; and with the attributes of this existence all his cerebral play is endowed too.

Once his brain has erupted in the mysterious stranger, that stranger exists—exists in fact: he will not vanish from the Petersburg Prospects, as long as the senator exists with thoughts of this kind, because thought, too, exists.

So let our stranger be a real stranger! And let my stranger's two shadows be real shadows!

Those dark shadows will keep following on the stranger's heels, just as the stranger follows straight after the senator; and the senescent senator, dear reader, will come chasing after you too in his black carriage: and from now on you will never forget him!

CHAPTER TWO

In which is told of a certain meeting, fraught with consequences.

> *And I, though in their books and chat*
> *My confreres like to mock at me,*
> *Of middle class I'm known to be,*
> *And in that sense a democrat.*
> A Pushkin

The Chronicle of Events

O<small>UR VENERABLE CITIZENS</small> do not read the newspaper section *The Chronicle of Events*; in October 1905 *The Chronicle of Events* was not read at all; our venerable citizens probably used to read the leaders in *The Comrade*, unless they were subscribers to the very latest fulminating papers; these latter carried a chronicle of other events.

Nevertheless all other genuinely Russian men-in-the-street threw themselves upon *The Chronicle of Events* without a care in the world; I, too, threw myself upon *The Chronicle*; and since I read this *Chronicle* I am very well informed. Well, who, in all honesty, read all the communications about burglaries, witches or spirits in the aforementioned year of 1905? Everyone read the leaders, of course. Most likely nobody will recall the communication set forth here.

It is a true story ... Here are some newspaper cuttings of that time (the author will remain silent): along with reports of burglaries, rape, the theft of diamonds and the disappearance from a provincial town of a certain writer (Daryalskii, I think) together with diamonds to a substantial sum, we have a series of interesting news items—pure fantasy, perhaps, from which the head of any reader of Conan Doyle will start to spin. In short—here are the cuttings.

Chronicle of Events

1st October. *From the account of N N, a young lady attending the Higher Nursing Courses, we print the story of a certain exceedingly enigmatic occurrence. Late in the evening of 1st October the young lady was passing by the Chernyshev Bridge. There by the bridge she noticed a very strange sight: right over the canal by the parapet of the bridge in the middle of the night a red, satin domino was dancing; on the red domino's face was a black lace mask.*

2nd October. *From the account of M M, a schoolteacher, we inform our venerable readers of an enigmatic occurrence near one of the suburban schools. The teacher, M M, was giving her morning lesson in the O O community school; the windows of the school looked out on to the street; suddenly outside the window a column of dust began to whirl with ferocious force, and the teacher M M along with the high-spirited children naturally rushed to the windows of O O community school; what was the consternation of the class and its teacher when a red domino in the middle of the whirling dust ran up to the windows of O O community school and pressed its black lace mask to the window? In O O community school lessons were stopped ...*

3rd October. *At a spiritualist séance held in the apartment of the much-respected Baroness R R the foregathered spiritualists formed a spiritualist chain: but hardly had they formed the chain, when among the chain was discovered a domino, who during the dance touched the tip of titular councillor C's nose with the folds of his cloak. A doctor at the G hospital discovered on titular councillor C's nose a serious burn: the tip of his nose, it is rumoured, will be covered in purple spots. In short, the red domino is everywhere.*

Finally:

4th October. *The entire population to a man of the suburb of Y ran away at the appearance of the domino: a series of protests is being arranged; the U Cossack squadron has been sent to the suburb of Y.*

Domino, domino—what's it all about? Who is the girl-student N N, who is the class-teacher M M, Baroness R R and so on? In 1905 you, dear reader, were of course not in the habit of reading *The Chronicle of Events*. So you can blame yourself, and not the author: but *The Chronicle of Events*, you may be sure, has found its way into the library.

What is a newspaper reporter? In the first place, he is a representative of the periodical press; and as a representative of the press (the sixth continent of the world) he receives five copecks per line, or seven, or ten, sometimes fifteen or twenty, as he conveys in his lines everything that has happened and much that has not. If you were to put together the newspaper lines of any representative of the press, then the single line compiled from all the lines would encircle the entire globe with what has happened and what has not.

Such are the venerable qualities of the majority of contributors to extreme right-wing, right-wing, centre, moderate liberal, and finally revolutionary newspapers, together with the calculation of their quantity and quality—and with these venerable qualities the key to the truth of the year 1905 can be revealed quite simply—the truth of *The Chronicle of Events* under the rubric *The Red Domino*. Here's what it's about: a certain venerable contributor to an undoubtedly venerable newspaper, who received five copecks, suddenly decided to make use of a fact which had been narrated in a certain house; the hostess of this house was a lady. So it turns out that it isn't a matter of the venerable newspaper contributor who was paid by the line; it's a matter of the lady …

Who is the lady?

Let's start with her.

A lady: ahem! And a pretty one … What is a lady?

The attributes of a lady have not been revealed by any chiromancer; the chiromancer stands forlorn before the enigma entitled 'lady': that being the case, how is the psychologist to approach this enigma, or—gracious me!—how is the writer to do so? The enigma becomes yet profounder if the lady is a young one, and if it is said of her that she is pretty.

So here we go: there was a lady; and out of boredom she attended courses for young ladies; and also from boredom she sometimes took the place of a teacher in the O O community school, unless she had been at a spiritualist circle in the evening on a day on which there were no balls; it hardly needs saying that the girl-student N N, and M M the class-teacher, and R R (the spiritualist baroness) were simply a lady: and a pretty one. It was at her house that the venerable newspaper contributor would spend the evenings.

One day this lady told him with a laugh that she had just

encountered some kind of red domino in the unlit doorway. That was how the pretty lady's innocent confession reached the columns of the newspapers under the rubric *Chronicle of Events*. And once it had found its way into *The Chronicle of Events* it unravelled into a series of occurrences that had never occurred, but which were a threat to public order.

What had happened? Without fire there is even no fabricated smoke. What then was the fire that had caused the smoke in this venerable newspaper, about which the whole of Russia had read, but about which you, to your shame, had probably not?

Sofia Petrovna Likhutina

That lady ... But that lady was Sofia Petrovna; we shall have to devote a lot of words to her straight away.

Sofia Petrovna Likhutina was distinguished, you might say, by an excess of vegetation: and she was extraordinarily supple: if she loosened her black hair, this black hair would cover her entire frame and fall as far as her calves; and Sofia Petrovna Likhutina, if the truth be told, simply did not know what to do with this hair of hers, so black that I dare say there was no object blacker; whether from the excess of her hair, or from its blackness—only, only: on Sofia Petrovna's upper lip a slight fluff was to be seen, which threatened her with a real moustache in later years. Sofia Petrovna Likhutina was possessed of an extraordinary facial complexion; this complexion was—simply the colour of pearls, distinguished by the whiteness of apple blossom, or sometimes—by a tender pink; if something caused her a sudden agitation, then Sofia Petrovna would all at once become completely crimson.

Sofia Petrovna Likhutina's eyes were much bigger than her irises: if I were not afraid of falling into a prosaic tone, I would call Sofia Petrovna's irises not just eyes, but—saucer eyes of a dark, blue—dark-blue colour (let us call them orbs). These orbs would sometimes flash and sometimes fade, would sometimes seem dull, colourless, sunk in their collapsing orbits, an ominous bluish shade: and squinting. Her bright-red lips were lips too large, but ... her teeth (oh, her little teeth!): teeth of pearl! And add to that—her childlike laugh … This laugh lent a certain charm to her flared lips; and her supple frame lent a certain charm; but again it was supple to excess; all the movements of this frame and of her somewhat nervous back were either impulsive, or languid—clumsy to the point of ugliness.

Sofia Petrovna dressed in a black woollen dress that fastened at the back and clung to her magnificent figure: if I say *magnificent figure* that means that my vocabulary is exhausted, that the banal expression "*magnificent figure*" signifies for Sofia Petrovna—no escaping it—a threat: of premature plumpness by the time she was thirty. But Sofia Petrovna Likhutina was twenty-three.

Ah, Sofia Petrovna!

Sofia Petrovna Likhutina lived in a small apartment that looked out on to the Moika; from the walls tumbled cascades of the brightest, most irrepressible flowers: here—fiery red, there—sky-blue. On the walls hung Japanese fans, laces, pendants, ribbons, and on the lamps: velvet lampshades flapped their velvet and paper wings, like butterflies from tropical lands; and it seemed that a swarm of these butterflies, suddenly descending from the walls, would sprinkle all round Sofia Petrovna Likhutina the celestial blue of their wings (officers of her acquaintance used to call her the Angel Peri, probably merging the two notions of 'Peri' and 'Angel' into one: the Angel Peri).

Sofia Petrovna Likhutina had draped the walls with Japanese landscapes, depicting views of Mount Fujiyama—every one; in the landscapes that hung there there was no perspective; but in the rooms, too, crammed as they were with armchairs, sofas, pouffes, fans and living Japanese chrysanthemums, there was no perspective either: the only perspective was the velvet alcove, from which Sofia Petrovna would skip out, or the whispering fern, dangling from the door, from which she might skip out too, while Fujiyama formed a bright-coloured background for her magnificent hair; it must be said: when Sofia Petrovna Likhutina wafted by of a morning from door to alcove, she was a genuine Japanese lady. But there was no perspective.

The rooms were small rooms: each was occupied by a single huge object: in the tiny bedroom the bed was the huge object; the bath—in the tiny bathroom; in the drawing room—the blue-tinged alcove; the table and sideboard—in the dining room; that object in the servants' quarters was the chambermaid; and in her husband's room that object was, of course, her husband.

How could there be any perspective?

All six tiny rooms were heated by steam, for which reason you were suffocated in the little flat by a damp, greenhouse heat; the panes of the windows sweated; Sofia Petrovna's visitor sweated; the chambermaid and the husband sweated endlessly; and Sofia Petrovna herself was covered in perspiration like a Japanese chrysanthemum in warm dew.

So where would any perspective come from in such a hothouse?

Nor was there any perspective.

Sofia Petrovna's visitors

A visitor to Sofia Petrovna, the Angel Peri's, greenhouse (incidentally, such a visitor was obliged to present the Angel with chrysanthemums), always praised the Japanese landscapes to her, adding as he did so his own reflections on painting in general; and the Angel Peri, furrowing her thin black brows, would blurt out momentously: "That landscape is from the pen of Hadusai ... " The Angel resolutely confused all proper names, as well as all foreign words. The visitor who was an artist took offence at this; and thereafter did not address to the Angel his homilies on painting in general: nevertheless this Angel bought up landscapes with the last of her pin-money and spent hours in solitude admiring them.

Sofia Petrovna did nothing to occupy her visitor: if it was a young man-of-the-world, devoted to amusements, she thought it necessary to shriek out laughing on account of his every humorous word, or indeed his every not entirely humorous word, or even his entirely serious ones; she laughed at everything, turning crimson with mirth, and perspiration covered her tiny nose; the young man-of-the-world then for some reason also turned crimson; and perspiration covered his nose too: the young man-of-the-world was struck by her youthful, but by no means genteel shrieks of laughter; thus struck, he thought of her as belonging to the demi-monde; in the meantime a tankard would appear on the table with the words *Charity Collection* written on it and Sofia Petrovna Likhutina, the Angel Peri, would exclaim with

a shriek of laughter: "That's another *whiffy* you've told—pay up."
(Sofia Petrovna had recently established a charity collection for the
benefit of the unemployed in punishment for every fashionable *whiffy*:
for some reason she called every deliberately uttered frivolity a *whiffy*,
because it had a whiff of naughtiness about it.) And Baron Ommau-
Ommergau, the yellow cuirassier of Her Majesty, and Count Aven,
the blue cuirassier, and the hussar of the Life-Guards Shporyshev,
and Vergefden, the official seconded for special duties to the chancery
of Ableukhov (all young men-of-the-world) told *whiffy* upon *whiffy*,
dropping one twenty-copeck piece after another into the tin tankard.

Why was she visited by so many officers? Goodness, she danced at
balls; and while not being a lady of the demi-monde, she was a pretty
lady; and lastly, she was an officer's wife.

If on the other hand Sofia Petrovna's visitor turned out to be either
himself a musician, or a music critic, or simply a music lover, then
Sofia Petrovna would explain to him that her idols were Duncán
and Nikísch; she would explain, in rapturous expressions more
gesticulatory than verbal, that she intended to study meloplastics
herself, in order to perform the dance of the flight of the Valkyries
in no less a place than Bayreuth itself; the musician, music critic
or simply music lover, shaken by the inaccurate pronunciation of
the two proper names (he himself pronounced them Dúncan and
Níkisch, not Duncán and Nikísch), came to the conclusion that Sofia
Petrovna Likhutina was quite simply an empty-headed flibbertigibbet;
and he became more playful; in the meantime the extremely pretty
chambermaid would bring a gramophone into the little room: and
out of a red tube the tin throat of the gramophone would spew
forth on to the visitor the flight of the Valkyries. The fact that Sofia
Petrovna Likhutina did not miss a single fashionable opera the guest
would forget: he would turn crimson and become excessively free in
his manners. Sofia Petrovna would show such a guest the door; and
so musicians who played in good society were rare in the greenhouse;
other representatives of good society in the persons of Count Aven,
Baron Ommau-Ommergau, Shporyshev and Vergefden did not
allow themselves improper behaviour in relation to a lady who was,
when all is said and done, an officer's wife, and bore the name of
the ancient noble line of the Likhutins: so Count Aven, and Baron
Ommau-Ommergau, and Shporyshev and Vergefden continued to

visit. At one time a student, Nikolenka Ableukhov, had also often moved in their circles. And then he had suddenly disappeared.

Sofia Petrovna's visitors fell of their own accord into two categories: the category of guests from good society and of guests so-to-speak. These guests so-to-speak were not guests at all: they were all desired visitors ... for her soul's solace; these visitors did not strive for admittance to the greenhouse; not in the least! The Angel almost dragged them to her house by force; and, having dragged them there by force, she immediately returned their visit: in their presence the Angel Peri sat with pursed lips: she did not shriek with laughter, was not moody, did not flirt at all, but showed extreme timidity and speechlessness, while the guests so-to-speak argued furiously with one another. And all that was to be heard was: "revolution—evolution". And again: "revolution—evolution". That was the one thing these guests so-to-speak argued about constantly; this was not the golden youth, nor even the silver youth: this was the bronze, pauper youth, who bought their education with their own hard-earned pennies; in short, they were students at the higher education institutions, and showed off with an abundance of foreign words: "social revolution". And again: "social evolution". The Angel Peri invariably got those words confused.

The officer: Sergei Sergeich Likhutin

Among the student youth that frequented the Likhutins' house was one noble soul, who attended courses for young ladies and enjoyed the circle's respect: Varvara Evgrafovna (here Varvara Evgrafovna was occasionally able to meet Nicolas Ableukhov himself).

Under the influence of this noble person the Angel Peri once graced with her presence—can you imagine—a political meeting! Under the influence of this noble person the Angel Peri had placed on the table the tin tankard with the nebulous inscription: *Charity Collection*. It goes without saying that this tankard was designed for the guests; all persons belonging to the guests so-to-speak had once and for all been released by Sofia Petrovna from liability; but Count Aven, and Baron Ommau-Ommergau, and Shporyshev and Vergefden were all liable to taxation. Under the influence of that same noble person the Angel Peri had begun to drop in of a morning to the O O community school and without the slightest sense to din into the children the *Manifesto* of Karl Marx. The point is that at that time she used to receive daily visits from the student Nikolenka Ableukhov, whom she could safely introduce both to Varvara Evgrafovna (who was in love with Nikolenka), and to the yellow cuirassier of Her Majesty. Ableukhov, as the son of Ableukhov, was, of course, received everywhere.

However, since the time when Nikolenka had suddenly stopped visiting the Angel, this Angel had flitted off, unbeknown to the guests so-to-speak, to the spiritualists, to Baroness (what's her name?), who was about to enter a nunnery. Since that time a magnificently-bound book *Man and his Bodies*, by some Madame Henri Besançon, sat in splendour on her table (Sofia Petrovna had got things confused again: not Henri Besançon—Annie Besant).

Sofia Petrovna took pains to keep her new infatuation a secret both from Baron Ommau-Ommergau and from Varvara Evgrafovna; notwithstanding her infectious laughter and her diminutive forehead, the Angel Peri's secrecy reached improbable proportions: for example, Varvara Evgrafovna never once met Count Aven, nor even Baron Ommau-Ommergau. Just once she chanced to see in the entrance-hall the plumed fur hat of a Life-Guard. But nothing was ever said thereafter about this Life-Guard's hat.

What was hidden under all his, Lord alone knows.

Sofia Petrovna Likhutina had one further visitor; the officer: Sergei Sergeevich Likhutin; to tell the truth, he was her husband; he was in charge of provisions somewhere out there; he left the house early in the morning; and appeared at home no earlier than midnight; he greeted equally meekly both the guests and the guests so-to-speak, with equal meekness he told a whiffy for decency's sake, dropping a twenty-copeck coin into the tankard (if Count Aven or Baron Ommau-Ommergau was present), or he modestly nodded at the words "revolution—evolution", drank a cup of tea and went to his room; among themselves the young men-of-the-world called him the *conscript*, and the students—the *martinet* (in 1905 Sergei Sergeich had the misfortune to defend the Nikolaevskii Bridge from the workers with his half-company). In truth, Sergei Sergeich would have preferred to refrain both from whiffies and from the words "revolution—evolution". In truth, he wouldn't have minded going to a nice spiritualist séance at the Baroness'; but he did not use his status as her husband to insist on this modest wish, since he was by no means a despot in his relations with Sofia Petrovna: he loved Sofia Petrovna with all his soul; more than that: two-and-a-half years before he had married her against the wishes of his parents, immensely wealthy landowners from Simbirsk; and since that time he had been cursed by his father and deprived of his inheritance; since that time he had astonished everyone by modestly entering the Gr...skii regiment.

There was another visitor: the sly Ukrainian Lippanchenko; this one was extremely sensual and called Sofia Petrovna not an Angel, but ... a sweetie; under his breath the sly Ukrainian called her simply: poppet, popsy, popsicle (there are some fine words for you!) But Lippanchenko stayed within the bounds of decency; and so he was admitted to the house.

Sofia Petrovna's eminently good-natured husband, Sergei Segeevich Likhutin, second lieutenant of the Gr...skii Regiment of his Majesty the King of Siam, adopted an attitude of humility towards his better half's revolutionary circle of acquaintances; towards the representatives of the men-of-the-world his attitude was simply one of emphatic equanimity; but the sly Ukrainian he merely tolerated: this sly Ukrainian, by the way, did not look like a Ukrainian at all: he looked more like a mixture of Semite and Mongol; he was both tall and fat; the yellowish face of this gentleman floated unpleasantly in his own chin, which was pushed up by his starched collar; and Lippanchenko wore a yellow and red velvet tie, pinned with an imitation diamond, and boasted a striped dark-yellow suit and shoes of the same colour; but for all that Lippanchenko unashamedly dyed his hair brown. Of himself Lippanchenko said that he exported Russian pigs abroad and planned to make a swine of a fortune out of it.

Be all that as it may, Lippanchenko was the one person that Second Lieutenant Likhutin disliked: dark rumours circulated about Lippanchenko. But why ask after Second Lieutenant Likhutin's likes: Second Lieutenant Likhutin, it goes without saying, loved everyone: but if there was one person he had at one time particularly loved, then that was Nikolai Apollonovich Ableukhov; they had known each other, after all, since earliest youth: Nikolai Apollonovich had, in the first place, been best man at Likhutin's wedding, and secondly, had been a daily visitor at the apartment on the Moika for nigh on a year-and-a-half. But then he had disappeared without trace.

It was not, of course, Sergei Sergeevich's fault that the senator's son had disappeared, but that of the senator's son or indeed of the Angel Peri herself.

Ah, Sofia Petrovna, Sofia Petrovna! In a word: a lady … And what can you ask of a lady!

The handsome, elegant best man

On the very first day of her 'lady-hood', as it were, during the performance of the sacrament of marriage, when Nikolai Apollonovich held the ceremonial crown over her husband, Sergei Sergeevich, Sofia Petrovna had been painfully struck by the handsome, elegant best man, the colour of his huge, unearthly, dark-blue eyes, the whiteness of his marble face and the godlike quality of his flaxen hair: those eyes were not gazing then, as they often did later, from behind the dull lenses of a pince-nez, and his face was cradled by the gold collar of a smart new uniform (not every student has a collar like that). Well, and … Nikolai Apollonovich became a regular visitor at the Likhutins' at first once every two weeks; then once a week; two, three, four times a week; and in the end, every day. Soon Sofia Petrovna noticed beneath the mask of those everyday visits that Nikolai Apollonovich's face, godlike, severe, had turned into a mask: grimaces, an aimless rubbing of his sometimes sweaty hands, finally the unpleasant frog-like expression of his smile, arising from the way the most diverse mannerisms played across his face, obscured that face from her forever. And as soon as Sofia Petrovna noticed that, she realised to her horror that she had been in love with *that* face, *that* one, but not *this*. The Angel Peri wished to be an exemplary wife: and the terrible thought that, while faithful, she had already become infatuated with someone other than her husband—this thought completely shattered her. But things went further: from beneath the mask, the grimaces, the frog-like lips, she tried unconsciously to summon back her irretrievably lost infatuation: she tormented Ableukhov, showered him with insults; but, in secret from herself, she dogged his tracks, discovered his tastes and strivings, unconsciously followed them, trying all the while to recapture in them the genuine, godlike countenance; and so she began to act a part: first meloplastics appeared on the scene, then the cuirassier Baron Ommau-Ommergau, and finally Varvara Evgrafovna appeared with the tin tankard for collecting whiffies.

In short, Sofia Petrovna became confused: hating, she loved; loving, she hated.

From that time her real husband, Sergei Sergeich Likhutin, turned into nothing more than a visitor to the little apartment on the Moika: he began to take charge of provisions somewhere out there; left the house early in the morning; appeared around midnight: told a whiffy for decency's sake, dropping a twenty-copeck piece into the tankard, or nodded modestly at the words "revolution—evolution", drank a cup of tea and went to his room to sleep: he had to be up as early as possible in the morning and go off out there somewhere to take charge of provisions. It was only because he did not wish to inhibit his wife's freedom that he had begun to take charge of provisions somewhere out there.

But Sofia Petrovna could not bear freedom: she had after all such a tiny, tiny forehead; along with her tiny forehead there were volcanoes of unplumbed passion secreted within her: because she was a lady; arousing chaos in ladies is wrong: in this chaos there are hidden in a lady all manner of cruelties, crimes, falls, all manner of frenzied rage, and also all manner of heroism unheard of on earth; in every lady a criminal is hidden: but once the crime is committed, nothing will be left in the heart of a true lady but holiness.

Soon we shall prove to the reader beyond doubt the division that also exists in Nikolai Apollonovich's soul, into two independent quantities: a godlike ice—and simply a frog-like slime; a duality like that is a property of any lady: duality is in essence not a masculine, but a feminine property: the figure two is the symbol of the lady; the symbol of the male is unity. That is the only way to achieve a trinity, without which is any hearth and home conceivable?

We remarked Sofia Petrovna's duality above: her highly-strung movements—and her clumsy listlessness; the insufficiency of her forehead and the excess of her hair; Fujiyama, Wagner, the faithfulness of a female heart—and "Henri Besançon", the gramophone, Baron Ommergau and even Lippanchenko. If Sergei Sergeich Likhutin or

Nikolai Apollonovich had been real unities and not dualities, there would have been a trinity; and Sofia Petrovna would have found the harmony of life in a union with a man; the gramophone, meloplastics, Henri Besançon, Lippanchenko, even Ommau-Ommergau would all have gone to the devil.

But there was no unified Ableukhov: there was number one, god-like, and number two, the little frog. That is why it all happened.

What was it that happened?

Nikolai Apollonovich the little frog became infatuated with Sofia Petrovna's profound heart, raised above all vanity: not with her tiny forehead—with her hair; but Nikolai Apollonovich's divinity, despising love, took cynical delight in meloplastics; the two disputed inside him: whom to love: the flibbertigibbet or the angel? Sofia Petrovna the angel, as naturally befits an angel, fell in love only with the god: but the flibbertigibbet became confused: she was at first indignant at the unpleasant smile, then she came to love precisely that indignation of hers; coming to love her hatred, she came to love the nasty smile, but with a strange (everyone would say, perverse) kind of love: in all of this there was something unnaturally poignant, unwontedly sweet, fatal.

Could it be that in Sofia Petrovna a criminal had awakened? Ah, Sofia Petrovna, Sofia Petrovna! In a word: a lady, a lady ...

And what can you ask of a lady!

The red clown

To tell the truth, in recent months Sofia Petrovna had behaved towards the object of her affections in an extremely provocative way: in front of the gramophone speaker spewing out *The Death of Siegfried* she practised body movements (and what movements!), raising her rustling silk skirt almost to her knees; moreover: her foot touched Ableukhov under the table more than once or twice. It is not surprising that this latter made to embrace the angel on more than one occasion; but then the angel slipped away, dousing her admirer in a wave of cold: and then she started all over again. But when once, in her zeal to defend Greek art, she proposed setting up a circle for the practice of chaste nakedness, Nikolai Apollonovich lost control: all the pent-up passion of many days rushed to his head (in the struggle Nikolai Apollonovich threw her down on to the sofa) ... But Sofia Petrovna bit most painfully the lips that were seeking her lips, and when Nikolai Apollonovich became crazed with pain, a slap resounded loudly through the Japanese room.

"Ugh ... You freak, you frog ... Ugh—you red clown."

Nikolai Apollonovich answered calmly and coldly:

"If I'm a red clown, then you are a Japanese doll ... "

With extreme dignity he straightened to his full height at the door; at that moment his face assumed precisely that distant expression she had once caught, and remembering which she had imperceptibly come to love him; and when Nikolai Apollonovich had left, she collapsed to the floor, scratching and biting the carpet in her grief; suddenly she jumped up and stretched out her arms to the door:

"Come to me, come back—my god!"

But in reply to her the street door banged: Nikolai Apollonovich was running towards the great Petersburg bridge. Further on we shall see him take a certain fatal decision at the bridge (in the performance of a certain act to destroy life itself). The expression "Red Clown" had hurt him to the quick.

Sofia Petrovna Likhutina did not see him again: in furious protest at his preoccupation with *revolution—evolution* the Angel Peri involuntarily recoiled from the student group, and attached herself to Baroness R R and her spiritualist séances. Varvara Evgrafovna also began to visit more rarely. On the other hand, Count Aven, and Baron Ommau-Ommergau, and Shporyshev, and Vergefden, even ... Lippanchenko—began to appear more frequently; Lippanchenko most of all. With Count Aven, Baron Ommau-Ommergau, with Shporyshev and with Vergefden, even ... with Lippanchenko she shrieked with laughter tirelessly; suddenly she would break off laughing and ask petulantly:

"Of course I'm a doll, aren't I?"

And they responded with whiffies, pouring silver into the tin tankard with the inscription *Charity Collection*. And Lippanchenko told her in reply: "You're a sweetie, a poppet, a popsy." And brought her a present of a yellow-faced doll.

When she told all this to her husband, her husband, Sergei Sergeich Likhutin, second lieutenant of the Gr...skii Regiment of His Majesty the King of Siam, made no reply, but went away as though to bed: he was in charge of provisions somewhere out there; but when he entered his room, he sat down to write a meek and mild letter to Nikolai Apollonovich: in this letter he took the liberty of informing Ableukhov that he, Sergei Sergeevich, second lieutenant of the Gr...skii Regiment, most respectfully requested the following: having as a matter of principle no wish to interfere in the relations between Nikolai Apollonovich and his dearly beloved wife, he nevertheless requested him emphatically (the word emphatically was underlined three times) to relinquish their house forever, since his dearly beloved wife's nerves were overwrought. Sergei Sergeich kept his act a secret; his behaviour did not change one iota: just as before he left in the early morning; returned towards midnight; told a whiffy for decency's sake, if he saw Baron Ommau-Ommergau, frowned slightly if he saw Lippanchenko, nodded most benevolently at the words *evolution—revolution,* drank a cup of tea and quietly made himself scarce: he was in charge of provisions somewhere out there.

Sergei Sergeich was tall, wore a blonde beard, and possessed a nose, a mouth, hair, ears and wonderfully sparkling eyes: but unfortunately he wore dark-blue spectacles, and nobody knew either the colour of his eyes, nor those eyes' wonderful expression.

A cad, a cad, a cad

In those bitter days of early October Sofia Petrovna was in a state of unusual agitation; on her own in the greenhouse she would suddenly start furrowing her little brow, and colouring: she would turn crimson; she would go up to the window to wipe the misted panes with her delicate cambric handkerchief; the glass would begin to squeal, revealing a view of the canal and a passing gentleman in a top hat—nothing else; as though disappointed in her premonition, the Angel Peri began to pick at the dampened handkerchief and crumple it with her little teeth, and then she ran to put on her coat of black plush and her hat of the same (Sofia Petrovna dressed most modestly), in order to mooch fretfully, her fur muff pressed to her nose, from the Moika to the Embankment; on one occasion she even went into Cinizelli's circus and saw there a wonder of nature:

a bearded woman; most often, though, she ran to the kitchen and whispered with the young chambermaid Mavrushka, an exceedingly pretty girl in an apron and butterfly cap. And her eyes squinted: her eyes always squinted like that in moments of agitation.

One day, in the presence of Lippanchenko, she snatched the pin from her hat with a shriek of laughter and pushed it into her little finger:

"Look: it doesn't hurt; and there's no blood: I'm made of wax … a doll."

But Lippanchenko understood nothing: he laughed out loud and said:

"You're not a doll: you're a sweetie."

And the Angel Peri became angry and sent him packing. Seizing his hat with the earflaps from the table, Lippanchenko departed.

Then she rushed about the greenhouse, furrowed her brow, coloured, wiped the glass; a view emerged of the canal and a carriage flying past: nothing else.

What else might there be?

Here's what it's all about: a few days earlier Sofia Petrovna Likhutina was on her way home from Baroness R R's. At the Baroness' that evening there had been knockings; lustreless sparks had travelled across the walls; and once the table had even jumped: nothing more; but Sofia Petrovna's nerves were strained to breaking point (she wandered round the streets after the séance), and the entrance to her flat was not lit (in cheap flats they don't light the entrances): and inside the black doorway Sofia Petrovna saw with such clarity, blacker than the darkness, a shape like a black mask staring at her; something gleamed a dull red under the mask, and Sofia Petrovna tugged with all her might at the bell. And when the door was thrown open and a beam of bright light from the hall fell on to the staircase, Mavrushka screamed and threw up her hands: Sofia Petrovna did not see anything, because she flew full tilt through into the apartment. Mavrushka did see: behind the mistress' back a red velvet domino stretched forward its black mask, surrounded from below by a dense fan of lace, black too, of course, so that this black lace fell on to Sofia Petrovna's shoulders (a good thing she didn't turn her head); the red domino stretched out to Mavrushka its blood-red sleeve, from which a visiting card protruded; and when the door slammed shut in front of the hand, then Sofia Petrovna too saw by the door a visiting card (it must have slipped through the aperture); and what was inscribed on that visiting card? A skull and crossbones in place of a crown of the nobility and in a fashionable typeface the words: 'I shall expect you at the masquerade—such-and-such a place, such-and-such a date'; and then the signature: '*The Red Clown*'.

Sofia Petrovna spent the whole evening in terrible agitation. Who might dress up in a red domino? Of course it was him, Nikolai Apollonovich: hadn't she once called him by just that name? ... So the red clown had come. In that case what do you call an act like that towards a defenceless woman? Isn't it the act of a cad?

A cad, a cad, a cad.

If only her husband would come back soon, the officer: he would teach that bounder a lesson. Sofia Petrovna reddened, squinted, chewed her handkerchief and became covered in perspiration. If only somebody would come: even Aven, even Baron Ommau-Ommergau, or Shporyshev, or even ... Lippanchenko.

But nobody appeared.

But what if it wasn't him? And Sofia Petrovna felt a distinct sense of annoyance: she was reluctant to part with the idea that the clown was him; in these thoughts along with anger was mixed that same sweet, familiar, fatal feeling; evidently she wanted him to prove himself an out-and-out cad.

No—it wasn't him: he wasn't a cad, he wasn't a delinquent! ... Well, what if it was the red clown himself? Who the red clown might be, she could not give herself a coherent answer: all the same ... And her heart sank: it wasn't him.

She told Mavrushka at once to keep quiet: but she did go to the masquerade; and without telling her meek husband: it was the first time she had been to a masquerade.

The point was that Sergei Sergeich Likhutin had most strictly forbidden her to go to masquerades. He was odd: he set great store by his epaulettes, his sword, his honour as an officer (perhaps he *was* a martinet?).

His meekness was all very well ... up to the point where his honour as an officer came into play. He only needed to say: "I give you my word as an officer—this shall happen, that shall not." And he would not budge: there was an inflexibility, even a cruelty about him.

When he raised his spectacles on to his forehead and became curt, unpleasant, wooden, as though he was made of white cypress wood, and banged his cypress-wood fist on the table—then the Angel Peri flew out of her husband's room in fear: she screwed up her nose, the tears trickled, and in high dudgeon the bedroom door was locked.

Among Sofia Petrovna's visitors, one of the guests so-to-speak, who argued about revolution—evolution, there was one venerable newspaper contributor: Neintelpfain; dark, wrinkled, with a downward-hooked nose and a goatee beard hooked in the opposite direction. Sofia Petrovna had frightful respect for him: and he was the one she confided in; it was he who took her to the masquerade, where miscellaneous clowns and Harlequins, Italian, Spanish and oriental women flashed the unfriendly lights of their eyes from under their black velvet masks; on the arm of Neintelpfain, the venerable newspaper contributor, Sofia Petrovna modestly paraded through the rooms in her black domino. And a red velvet domino kept rushing around the rooms, looking for someone, his black mask protruding in front of him, under which fluttered a dense fan of lace, also black, of course.

It was then that Sofia Petrovna told the faithful Neintelpfain about the enigmatic occurrence, hiding all the threads, of course; little Neintelpfain, the venerable newspaper contributor, earned five copecks per line: and from then on there was no stopping it, every single day—a note in the *Chronicle of Events*; red domino here, red domino there!

People discussed the domino, became excited about it, argued; some saw revolutionary terror in it; others simply kept quiet and shrugged their shoulders. Telephones rang in the security department.

Even in the little greenhouse there was talk about the strange appearance of the domino on the streets of Petersburg; Count Aven, and Baron Ommau-Ommergau, and the hussar of the Life-Guards Shporyshev, and Vergefden uttered whiffies in this connection, and an endless rain of twenty-copeck pieces showered into the tin tankard; only the sly Ukrainian Lippanchenko laughed in a somewhat crooked way. And Sofia Petrovna, beside herself, turned crimson, paled, became covered in perspiration and bit her handkerchief. Neintelpfain had shown himself to be simply a swine, but Neintelpfain did not show himself here: from day to day he zealously spun out line after line for the newspaper; and the newspaper's nonsense stretched and stretched, covering the world with the most utter balderdash.

An utterly smoke-ridden face

Nikolai Apollonovich Ableukhov stood by the landing balustrade in his multicoloured gown, casting in all directions an iridescent gleam that formed a complete contrast to the pillar and the alabaster plinth, where the white Niobe raised her alabaster eyes on high.

Leaning over the balustrade, Nikolai Apollonovich called down in the direction of the entrance-hall, but his call was answered first by silence, then, with excessive distinctness, by an unexpected, reluctant falsetto:

"Nikolai Apollonovich, you must have taken me for someone else … "

"I'm—me … "

Down below stood the stranger with the little black moustache and the coat with the upturned collar.

From the balustrade Nikolai Apollonovich bared his teeth in an unpleasant smile:

"It's you, Aleksandr Ivanovich? … what a pleasant surprise!"

And then he added hypocritically:

"I didn't recognise you without my glasses … "

Overcoming the unpleasant impression made by the stranger's presence in the lacquered house, Nikolai Apollonovich went on nodding over the balustrade:

"I have to admit, I'm only just up: that's why I'm in my dressing gown," (as though with this casual mention Nikolai Apollonovich wished to let the visitor understand that he had chosen an inopportune time for his visit; on our own account we will add: recently Nikolai Apollonovich had been absent every night).

The stranger with the little black moustache presented with his person an extremely pitiful sight on the background of the ornamental ancient weaponry; all the same the stranger put on a show of bravery, continuing to reassure Nikolai Apollonovich fervently—either making fun of him, or acting like a perfect simpleton:

"It doesn't matter in the slightest, Nikolai Apollonovich, that you're only just up … An absolute trifle, I assure you: you aren't a young lady, and I'm not a young lady either … Why, I only got up quite recently myself … "

Nothing to be done. Suppressing in his heart the unpleasant impression (it was caused by the stranger's appearance—here, in the lacquered house, where the servants might be thoroughly dumbfounded, and where, after all, the stranger might be encountered by Papa)—suppressing in his heart the unpleasant impression, Nikolai Apollonovich conceived the intention of proceeding downstairs, in order to introduce his scrupulous guest into the lacquered house in a manner befitting the dignity of the Ableukhovs; but to his consternation his fur-lined slipper slipped off his foot; and his bare foot started flapping about from the folds of his dressing gown; Nikolai Apollonovich tripped on the steps; and to make matters worse he misled the stranger: on the assumption that Nikolai Apollonovich was about to rush down to meet him in an outburst of his customary courtesy (Nikolai Apollonovich had already demonstrated in this sense all the impetuosity of his gestures), the stranger with the little black moustache had rushed in his turn towards Nikolai Apollonovich and left his grimy trace on the grey velvet steps; and now the stranger stopped in confusion halfway between the entrance-hall and the top of the stairs; and thereupon he noticed that he was leaving stains on the carpet; my stranger smiled in embarrassment.

"Please take your coat off."

The discreet reminder that one cannot by any manner of means gain admittance to the master's rooms in an outdoor coat belonged to the servant, into whose hands the stranger discarded his wet overcoat with a desperate show of independence; now he stood in a grey checked suit, slightly moth-eaten. Seeing that the servant intended to stretch out his hand for the damp package, my stranger coloured; and colouring, he became doubly embarrassed:

"No, no … "

"If I may, sir … "

"No, I'll take *this* with me … "

The stranger with the little black moustache trod the slippery glistening parquet in his worn-through shoes with the same despairing obstinacy; he cast momentary glances of astonishment at the splendid perspective of rooms. Nikolai Apollonovich, gathering the folds of his gown, preceded the stranger with especial gentleness. But they both found their wordless peregrination through those gleaming perspectives wearisome; they maintained a melancholy silence; Nikolai Apollonovich was relieved to present to the stranger with the little black moustache his iridescent back instead of his face; no doubt that was why the smile absconded from his hitherto unnaturally smiling lips. Let us note directly on our own account: Nikolai Apollonovich was in a funk; round and round in his head was flashing: "Probably some kind of charitable collection—a worker who's been injured; at most—for weapons ... " And in his heart came a forlorn moan: "No, no—it's not that, but the other thing?"

In front of the oaken door to his study Nikolai Apollonovich suddenly turned round sharply to the stranger; across the faces of both a smile slipped momentarily; each suddenly looked the other in the eye with an expectant expression.

"Please go in, then ... Aleksandr Ivanovich ... "

"Don't trouble yourself ... "

"Do go ahead ... "

"No, no ... "

Nikolai Apollonovich's sitting room constituted a total contrast with the severity of his study: it was as multicoloured as ... as a Bukhara dressing gown; it was as though Nikolai Apollonovich's gown continued into all the appurtenances of the room: into the low divan, for example; it bore more resemblance to an oriental couch, upholstered in variegated colours; the Bukhara gown continued into the stool in dark-brown shades; it was encrusted with delicate strips of ivory and mother-of-pearl; the gown continued further into the Negro shield made from the thick leather of a long-fallen rhinoceros, and into the rusted Sudanese spear with its massive haft; for some reason it had been hung there on the wall; and finally, the gown continued into the multicoloured leopard skin, cast at their feet with its gaping jaws; on the stool stood a dark-blue hookah-set and a three-legged golden incense-burner in the form of a sphere pierced all over with holes and a crescent moon on the top; but most surprising of all was a bright-coloured cage, in which green budgerigars would now and then start fluttering their wings.

Nikolai Apollonovich drew up the multicoloured stool for his guest: the stranger with the little black moustache lowered himself on to the edge of the stool and pulled out of his pocket a cheap cigarette case.

"Do you mind?"

"Not at all."

"Don't you smoke yourself?"

"No, I'm not in the habit … "

And, immediately embarrassed, Nikolai Apollonovich added:

"However, when others smoke, I … "

"You open the window?"

"Goodness, no! … "

"You switch on the fan?"

"Oh, not at all … quite the contrary—I meant to say that smoking gives me … " Nikolai Apollonovich hastened to say, but his guest, not listening to him, continued to interrupt:

"You leave the room?"

"Absolutely not: I was going to say that I like the smell of tobacco smoke, and especially of cigars."

"You shouldn't, Nikolai Apollonovich, you really shouldn't: after people have been smoking … "

"Yes? … "

"You ought to … "

"Really?"

"Ventilate the room quickly."

"Oh, I don't think so!"

"Open the window and switch on the fan."

"On the contrary, on the contrary … "

"Don't defend tobacco, Nikolai Apollonovich: I'm telling you this from experience … Smoke penetrates the grey matter of the brain … The hemispheres of the brain become contaminated: a general inertia spreads through the organism … "

The stranger with the little black moustache winked meaningfully and in a familiar way; the stranger also saw that his host had some doubts about the permeability of the grey matter of the brain, but that being in the habit of acting the gracious host was not going to argue with his guest: then the stranger with the little black moustache began in chagrin to pluck out his black whiskers:

"Just look at my face."

Unable to find his glasses, Nikolai Apollonovich brought his blinking eyelids right up to the stranger's face.

"Do you see that face?"

"Yes, a face … "

"A pale face … "

"Yes, it's a bit on the pale side," and all manner of politeness formulae with all their nuances played across Ableukhov's cheeks.

"A completely green, smoke-ridden face," the stranger interrupted him, "the face of a smoker. I'll get your whole room full of smoke, Nikolai Apollonovich."

Nikolai Apollonovich had long since begun to feel an uneasy heaviness, as though the atmosphere of the room were impregnated not with smoke, but lead; Nikolai Apollonovich could feel the hemispheres of his brain becoming contaminated and a general inertia spreading through his organism, but he was not now thinking about the properties of tobacco smoke, but was thinking about how he might extract himself with dignity from a ticklish situation, how he would behave—he thought—in the risky event that the stranger were to …

This leaden heaviness bore no relation at all to the cheap cigarette that exuded upwards its wispy stream of blue, but was related rather to the host's depressed state of mind. Nikolai Apollonovich was expecting his restless visitor to break off any second his chatter, which had been set in motion, evidently, for a single purpose—to torment him with anticipation—yes: he would break off his chatter and remind Nikolai Apollonovich of how he, Nikolai Apollonovich, had once upon a time, through the mediation of this weird stranger, given—how exactly to put it …

In short, he had once upon a time given what was for him a terrible undertaking, which not just honour now forced him to fulfil; Nikolai Apollonovich had given the terrible undertaking out of nothing but despair; a personal disaster had made him do it; gradually thereafter the disaster had been effaced. You might think that the terrible promise would be cancelled of its own accord: but the terrible promise remained in force: it remained if only because it had never been withdrawn: to tell the truth, Nikolai Apollonovich had thoroughly forgotten about it; but it, the promise, went on living in the collective consciousness of a certain incautious circle, just at the time when the feeling of the bitterness of being, brought on by the disaster, was effaced; Nikolai Apollonovich himself would doubtless have regarded his promise as belonging to the humorous category.

The appearance of the man of uncertain status with the little black moustache, for the first time since the passage of these two months, filled Nikolai Apollonovich's heart with well-founded fear. Nikolai Apollonovich remembered with absolute precision that exceedingly sad event. Nikolai Apollonovich remembered with absolute precision all the minute details of the circumstances in which he had made his promise and found those details lethal for himself.

Why ever … —not so much had he made the terrible promise, but had he made the terrible promise to a reckless party?

The answer to this question was simple in the extreme: Nikolai Apollonovich, in his study of the principles of social phenomena, condemned the world to fire and the sword.

And now he paled, turned grey and finally became quite green; his face even took on suddenly a dark-blue shade; probably this last hue depended simply on the atmosphere of the room, which was permeated through and through with tobacco smoke.

The stranger stood up, stretched, squinted tenderly at the package and suddenly broke out in a childlike smile.

"You see, Nikolai Apollonovich (Nikolai Apollonovich shuddered in fear) … it's not really tobacco I came to see you about, I mean, not to talk about tobacco … what I said about tobacco is really by the way … "

"I see."

"Tobacco's all very well: but I'm not really talking about tobacco, but about business … "

"I'm glad to hear it … "

"And not really business, even: the whole point is a favour—and this is a favour you can do for me … "

"Very well, I'll be happy … "

Nikolai Apollonovich turned a deeper blue: he sat there plucking at a button in the divan; and failing to pull out the button, he took to plucking out the horsehair from the divan.

"I feel very awkward, but remembering … "

Nikolai Apollonovich shuddered: the stranger's high-pitched, strident falsetto cut the air: this falsetto was preceded by a second of silence; but that second had seemed to him like an hour, like an hour at that time. And now, hearing that strident falsetto pronounce "remembering", Nikolai Apollonovich all but cried out aloud:

"My offer? ... "

But he at once regained control; and he merely observed:

"I see, I'm at your service," and in so doing thought how his politeness had destroyed him ...

"Remembering your sympathy, I came ... "

"Anything I can do," Nikolai Apollonovich cried out and in so doing thought that he was an idiot of the first water ...

"A small favour, oh, a very small favour ... " (Nikolai Apollonovich strained to hear):

"I'm sorry ... could you pass me the ashtray? ... "

Quarrels on the street became more frequent

Those were strange, misty days: across the north of Russia venomous October was passing with its freezing tread; and across the south it draped dank mists. Venomous October fanned the forest's golden whisper, and the forest's golden whisper submissively lay down upon the ground—and the rustling purple of the aspens submissively lay down upon the ground, to wind and chase at the feet of a passing pedestrian, and to murmur as it wove from leaves a red-and-yellow web of words. That sweet chirruping of blue tits that in September bathes in waves of foliage had long since ceased to bathe in foliage: and the blue tit herself was now hopping forlornly in the black network of boughs, which all autumn long, like the mumble of a toothless dotard, sends its whistle from the forests, leafless groves, the gardens and the parks.

Those were strange, misty days; an icy hurricane was making its approach in tattered clouds, leaden and blue; but everyone believed in spring: the newspapers wrote about spring, officials of the fourth class discussed spring; a minister who was popular at the time pointed to spring; and the effusions of a Petersburg girl-student carried the scent of nothing less than violets in early May.

Ploughmen had long since ceased to scratch the mouldering earth; the ploughmen had put aside their harrows and ploughs; the ploughmen gathered in their huts in wretched clusters for the communal discussion of what the papers said; they argued and wrangled, only to throw themselves in concert on the landowner's colonnaded house reflected in the waters of the Volga, Kama or even of the Dnieper; all the long nights there shone over Russia the blood-red glow of village fires, that resolved themselves by day into black columns of smoke. But then through the thinning leaves of a thicket you might catch sight of a concealed detachment of dishevelled Cossacks, the muzzles of their rifles trained in the direction of the blaring alarm; the Cossack detachment then rushed out at a gallop on their ragged mounts: blue men with beards, whooping and brandishing their whips, would then career across the autumn meadow hither and thither for a very long time.

That is how it was in the villages.

But it was like that in the towns too. In workshops, printing-houses, barbers' shops, in dairies and in taverns a loquacious nondescript kept turning up; pulling down over his forehead his rough black hat, evidently brought back from the fields of blood-soaked Manchuria; and sticking into his side-pocket a revolver brought from somewhere, the loquacious nondescript kept shoving into the hands of all and sundry a badly printed leaflet.

Everyone was expecting something, fearing, hoping; at the slightest noise they spilled out quickly on to the street, gathering in a crowd and then dispersing; in Arkhangelsk the Lapps, Karelians and Finns behaved like this; in Nizhne-Kolymsk—the Tungus; on the Dnieper—the Jews and the Ukrainians. In Petersburg, in Moscow—everyone behaved like that: they behaved like that in elementary, secondary and higher educational institutions: they expected, they feared, they hoped; at the slightest rustle they quickly spilled out on to the street; they gathered in a crowd and dispersed again.

Quarrels on the street became more frequent: with caretakers and night-watchmen; quarrels became more frequent on the street with down-at-heel constables; the caretaker, the policeman, and most of all the local constable found themselves the butt of brazen jibes from worker, schoolboy, craftsman—Ivan Ivanovich Ivanov and his wife Ivanikha—even from the shopkeeper—merchant of the first guild

Puzanov, from whom in better and recently past days the constable had received backhanders in the form of a piece of sturgeon, or smoked salmon, or unpressed caviar; but now instead of salmon, sturgeon or caviar the merchant of the first guild, the staid Puzanov, had suddenly turned against the constable along with the rest of the riff-raff; he was a well-known person, who had often been to the governor's house, because, say what you will—the fishing-trade and then a steamship-line on the Volga: so the constable piped down a bit from an event like that. A grey little man himself, in his grey overcoat, he walked by like an unnoticed shadow, holding his sword deferentially by his side and keeping his eyes down: and behind his back came verbal comments, rebukes, laughter and even obscene abuse; and all the station superintendent could say was: "If you can't gain the trust of the population, you'll have to retire." So he set about gaining their trust: he too rebelled against the arbitrary actions of the government, or else he entered into a special agreement with the occupants of the transit prison.

In just the same way in those days the constable somewhere in Kem dragged out his existence: and he dragged out his existence in the same way in Petersburg, Moscow, Orenburg, Tashkent, Solvychegodsk, in short, in those cities (provincial capitals, regional capitals, cities of no administrative importance) which comprise part of the Russian Empire.

Petersburg is surrounded by a ring of many-chimneyed factories.

A swarm of many thousand humans wanders towards them of a morning; the suburbs seethe; and swarm with people. At that time all the factories were in terrible turmoil, and the workers' representatives in the crowds, every man-jack of them, turned into loquacious nondescripts; among them revolvers were in circulation; and other things too. The usual swarms were growing excessively in those days and merging with one another into one immense blackness with many heads and many voices; and then the factory inspector would reach for the telephone: and as soon as he reached for it, then you could be sure: a hail of stones would come flying from the crowd and through the window panes.

This turmoil, surrounding Petersburg in a ring, was somehow penetrating into the city's very centre; first it seized the islands, then it sprang across the Liteinyi and the Nikolaevskii Bridges; and from there surged on to the Nevskii Prospect: and although the circulation of the human myriapod on the Nevskii Prospect was the same as ever, yet the composition of the myriapod was changing strikingly; an observer's experienced gaze had long since been able to detect the appearance of a rough black hat, pulled down, brought back from the fields of blood-soaked Manchuria: as the loquacious nondescript began to stride along the Nevskii Prospect, so the proportion of top hats passing was suddenly reduced; the loquacious nondescript here revealed his intrinsic quality: he jostled with his shoulders, stuffing his freezing fingers into his sleeves; there also appeared on the Nevskii the restive cries of anti-governmental urchins, rushing for all they were worth from the station to the Admiralty brandishing cheap magazines, coloured red.

There were no changes in anything else: just once—the Nevskii was flooded by crowds accompanied by clergy: they were carrying aloft the coffin of a professor, making for the station: in front there swept a sea of green; red velvet ribbons fluttered.

Those were strange, misty days: venomous October was passing with its freezing tread; frozen dust blew around the city in drab-brown vortices; and the golden whisper of foliage lay down submissively on the paths of the Summer Garden, and the rustling purple lay down submissively at people's feet, to wind and chase at the feet of a passing pedestrian, and to murmur as it wove from leaves a red-and-yellow web of words; that sweet chirruping of blue tits that all August had bathed in waves of foliage had long since ceased to bathe in foliage: and the Summer Garden blue tit herself was now hopping forlornly in the black network of boughs, along the bronze railing and across the roof of Peter's house.

Such were the days. As for the nights—did you go out on those nights, did you find your way to the distant wastelands in the suburbs, to hear the insistent, angry note of "*u*"? *Uuuu-uuuu-uuuu*: that was how it sounded in those spaces; that sound—was it a sound? If it was a sound, then it was certainly the sound of some other world; this sound reached an unusual strength and clarity: "*uuuu-uuuu-uuu*" rang out quietly in the suburban fields of Moscow, Petersburg, Saratov: but the factory siren did not sound, there was no wind; and the dog held its peace.

Did you too hear this October song of 1905? That song was not heard before; and it will not be heard again: ever.

My beloved Delvig calls me

As he climbed the red-carpeted staircase of the Establishment, his hand resting on the cold marble of the banister, Apollon Apollonovich Ableukhov caught the toe of his shoe on the material, and—tripped; he could not but slow his pace; and consequently: it was entirely natural that his eyes (quite without prior intention) were held by the huge portrait of a minister, whose sad and sympathetic gaze was directed straight in front.

A shiver ran up Apollon Apollonovich's spine: there was not much heating in the Establishment. This white room seemed to Apollon Apollonovich an open plain.

He was afraid of spaces.

He was more afraid of them than of zigzags, broken lines or sectors; rural landscape simply terrified him: beyond the snows, beyond the ice, out there beyond the forest's jagged line the blizzard raised the blast and counterblast of clashing air currents; there, by a stupid chance, he had all but frozen to death.

That had happened fifty years ago.

At that hour of his solitary freezing it was as though someone's cold fingers, ruthlessly inserted into his breast, had callously caressed his heart: the icy hand had led him on; following the icy hand he had climbed the steps of his career, keeping always before his eyes that fatal, unbelievable expanse; over there, from there—the icy hand had beckoned; and the measureless was hurtling by: the Russian Empire.

Apollon Apollonovich Ableukhov settled down for many years behind urban walls, hating with all his soul the forlorn provincial spaces, the smoke rising from villages and the jackdaws sitting on scarecrows; only once did he venture to cross those spaces in an express train, making for Tokyo on a vital mission.

Apollon Apollonovich told no one about his sojourn in Tokyo.

Yes—concerning the minister's portrait … He used to say to the minister:

"Russia is an icy plain where for hundreds of years wolves have roamed … "

The minister would glance at him with a velvet gaze that soothed the soul, smoothing his dapper grey moustache with his white hand;

he was silent, and sighed. The minister accepted the number of departments under his direction as an agonising, sacrificial cross on which he was crucified; when he retired he was planning to …

But he died.

Now he rested in his coffin; Apollon Apollonovich Ableukhov was now completely alone; behind him—the centuries ran off into infinity; in front of him—the icy hand revealed: infinity.

Infinity came flying towards him.

Russia, Russia! It was you he saw, you!

It is you who have set up the howl of winds, of blizzards, of snow and rain and ice—a howl of living, incantatory voices in their millions! At that moment it seemed to the senator that a voice was calling him from a solitary burial mound in these expanses; no solitary cross was teetering there; no lamp was blinking at the swirling snow; only the hungry wolves, gathering in packs, howled their plaintive accompaniment to the winds.

The fear of spaces had undoubtedly developed in the senator with the years.

The illness had become acute: since that tragic death; the image of his departed friend surely visited him at night, to keep glancing at him in the long nights with that velvet gaze, smoothing his dapper grey moustache with his white hand, because the image of his departed friend was now permanently linked in his consciousness with a passage of verse:

He is no more—and Russia he has left,
Upraised by him …

That passage arose in Apollon Apollonovich's consciousness when he, Apollon Apollonovich, crossed the hall.

After the passage just quoted another passage of verse arose:

And now, methinks, my turn has come,
And my beloved Delvig calls me,
The comrade of my merry youth,
The comrade of my youth downhearted,
The comrade of my vernal songs,
My feasts and uncorrupted notions,

The genius who fore'er has fled
To join the beckoning shades that greet him.

The even tenor of the verse was angrily interrupted:

New clouds have gathered now above the earth,
And in their tempest …

As he recalled these passages Apollon Apollonovich became especially distant; and he dashed out to offer his fingers to petitioners with an especial deliberateness.

Meanwhile the conversation was continued

Meanwhile Nikolai Apollonovich's conversation with the stranger was continued.

"I have been charged," the stranger said, taking the ashtray from Nikolai Apollonovich, "yes: I have been charged with handing you this little package for safe keeping."

"Is that all!" Nikolai Apollonovich exclaimed, not yet daring to believe that the disconcerting arrival of the stranger had no bearing whatsoever on that terrible offer, but merely had to do with this utterly innocuous little package; and in an access of absent-minded joy he was on the point of covering the package with kisses; and his face twitched all over, revealing a tempestuous life; he stood up abruptly and moved towards the package; but then for some reason the stranger also stood up, and for some reason suddenly thrust himself between the package and Nikolai Apollonovich; and when the senator's son's hand stretched out towards the infamous package, the stranger's hand unceremoniously seized with its fingers the fingers of Nikolai Apollonovich:

"Be careful, for goodness' sake … "

Nikolai Apollonovich, drunk with joy, muttered an incoherent apology and again absent-mindedly stretched out his hand towards the object; and once again the stranger prevented him from grasping the object, stretching out his own hand in entreaty:

"No, seriously, Nikolai Apollonovich, I beg you to be more cautious, more cautious … "

"Ah … yes … yes … " Nikolai Apollonovich did not hear clearly this time either: but hardly had he taken hold of the package by the corner of the towel, when the stranger shouted in his ear this time in a quite infuriated voice …

"Nikolai Apollonovich, I repeat to you for the third time: be more cautious … "

This time Nikolai Apollonovich did show surprise …

"Literature, I suppose? … "

"Well, no … "

At that moment a distinct metallic sound rang out: something clicked; in the silence the high-pitched squeak of a trapped mouse was heard; at the same moment the soft stool was overturned and the stranger's steps pattered off into the corner:

"Nikolai Apollonovich, Nikolai Apollonovich," his frightened voice rang out. "Nikolai Apollonovich—it's a mouse, a mouse … Tell your servant quickly … to, to … clear it up: for me it's … it's more than I can bear … "

Nikolai Apollonovich put the package down, astonished at the stranger's distress:

"Are you afraid of mice? … "

"Please hurry, take it away … "

Darting out of his room and pressing the bell-push, Nikolai Apollonovich presented, it must be admitted, a most absurd spectacle; the most absurd thing of all was the fact that in his hand he was holding … a timorously trembling mouse; the mouse was running round, granted, in a wire trap, but Nikolai Apollonovich had absent-mindedly bent his remarkable face right down to the trap and was now scrutinising his grey prisoner with the greatest attention, passing his long manicured fingernail of a yellowish colour back and forth across the metal wire.

"A mouse," he raised his eyes to the servant; and the servant deferentially repeated after him:

"A mouse, sir … That's what it is, sir … "

"Just look at it: running around like that … "

"Running around, sir … "

"It's afraid, you can tell … "

106

"Bound to be, sir … "

The stranger now glanced out of the door of the drawing room, took one frightened look and withdrew again:

"No—it's more than I can bear … "

"Is the gentleman afraid, sir? … It's no matter: a mouse is one of God's creatures … Bound to be, sir … It's one too … "

For several minutes both servant and master were occupied in the contemplation of the prisoner; finally the venerable servant took the trap into his own hands.

"A mouse … " Nikolai Apollonovich repeated in a contented voice and returned with a smile to his waiting guest. Nikolai Apollonovich was particularly gentle in his attitude to mice.

Nikolai Apollonovich finally took the package into his study: he was struck in passing merely by the heavy weight of the package; but he did not stop to reflect on this; as he went through into the study he tripped on the bright Arabian carpet, catching his foot on a soft fold; then something in the package rattled with a metallic sound, at which the stranger with the little black moustache jumped up; behind Nikolai Apollonovich's back the stranger's arm described that same zigzag which had recently aroused such fear in the senator.

But nothing happened: the stranger merely saw that in the neighbouring room a red domino and a black satin mask were spread out in splendour on a massive armchair; the stranger stared in surprise at this black mask (it had astonished him, it must be said), while Nikolai Apollonovich unlocked his desk and, having cleared a sufficient space, carefully stowed the package there; the stranger with the little black moustache, still scrutinising the domino, meanwhile began an animated elaboration of a thought of his which had had a long gestation.

"You know … Loneliness is killing me. I have completely forgotten how to hold a conversation these last months. Haven't you noticed, Nikolai Apollonovich, how I get my words mixed up?"

Nikiolai Apollonovich, presenting his Bukhara-clad back to his guest, merely muttered absent-mindedly:

"Well, you know, that happens to everyone."

In the meantime Nikolai Apollonovich was carefully concealing the package behind a desktop portrait depicting a brunette; as he covered the package with the brunette, Nikolai Apollonovich paused for thought, without removing his eyes from the portrait; and a frog-like expression momentarily passed across his colourless lips.

But at his back the stranger's words went on resounding.

"I get mixed up in every sentence. I want to say one word, and instead I say something completely different: I keep going round and about … Or I suddenly forget what some perfectly ordinary object is called; and when I remember I start doubting whether that's still right. I repeat: lamp, lamp, lamp; and then I suddenly get the feeling that there's no such word as 'lamp'. And often there's no one to ask; and even if there were, you'd feel ashamed asking just anyone—you know, they'd think you were mad."

"Oh, I don't know … "

About the package, by the way: if Nikolai Apollonovich had paid a little more attention to his guest's words about being careful with the package, then he might well have realised that what he took to be the most innocuous of packages was not so innocuous, but, I repeat, he was preoccupied with the portrait; so preoccupied that the thread of the stranger's words got lost in his head. And now that he caught the words he hardly understood them. At his back the strained falsetto went drumming on:

"It's hard, Nikolai Apollonovich, to live shut out as I do, in a Torricellian vacuum … "

"Torricellian?" Nikolai Apollonovich uttered in surprise without turning round, not sure he had heard properly.

"Exactly so—Torricellian, and this, you understand, is in the name of the community; community, society—and what society, I ask you, do I see? The society of a certain person you don't know, the society of the caretaker at my house, Matvei Morzhov, and the society of grey woodlice: brrr … there's a plague of woodlice in my attic … Eh? How do you like that, Nikolai Apollonovich?"

"Yes, I see … "

"Common cause! Why, for me it's long since turned into a personal cause which doesn't allow me to meet other people: that common cause has struck me off the list of the living."

The stranger with the little black moustache had apparently quite by chance hit upon his favourite topic: and, having hit quite by chance upon his favourite topic, the stranger with the little black moustache forgot the purpose of his visit, probably forgot his damp package, even forgot the quantity of cigarettes he was consuming, which were increasing the foul smell: like all people who are by nature garrulous but forcibly compelled to be silent, he sometimes felt an inexpressible need to communicate the sum of his thoughts to someone or other: to a friend, an enemy, a caretaker, a constable, a child, or even … to a hairdresser's dummy in a shop window. At night the stranger sometimes talked to himself. In the environment of the magnificent, brightly coloured sitting room this need suddenly awoke irresistibly, like a drinking bout after a month's abstinence from vodka.

"I'm not joking: it's no joking matter; I've been living for over two years in this joke, you know; it's all right for you to joke—you're included in society of every kind; but society for me is the society of woodlice and bedbugs. I'm—me. Can you hear me?"

"Of course I can hear you."

Now Nikolai Apollonovich was really listening.

"I am me: but they tell me that I'm not me, but some kind of 'us'. But I ask you—why should that be? And now my memory's failing: that's a bad sign, a bad sign, indicating the onset of mental illness," the stranger with the little black moustache started striding from one corner to the other—"you know, loneliness is killing me. And sometimes you even get angry: common cause, social equality, but … "

At this point the stranger interrupted his speech, because Nikolai Apollonovich, having closed his desk, had turned to face the stranger and, noticing that this latter was already striding about his study, dropping ash on the desk, on the red satin domino—noticing all this, Nikolai Apollonovich for some incomprehensible reason blushed deeply and rushed to remove the domino; it was only by this that he facilitated a change of the focus of attention in the stranger's brain:

"What a beautiful domino, Nikolai Apollonovich."

Nikolai Apollonovich rushed over to the domino as though he meant to conceal it with his bright-coloured gown, but he was too late: the stranger felt the bright rustling silk with his hand:

"Wonderful silk … Must be expensive: I suppose you go to masquerades, Nikolai Apollonovich … "

But Nikolai Apollonovich blushed even more:

"Yes, now and then … "

He almost snatched the domino and went to hide it away in the cupboard, as though found guilty of a crime; like a thief caught in the act, he busily tidied the domino away; like a thief caught in the act, he ran back for the mask; once everything was put away, he calmed down, breathing heavily and casting suspicious glances at the stranger; but the stranger had in fact already forgotten the domino and now returned to his pet topic, still continuing to stride about scattering ash.

"Ha, ha, ha!" the stranger prattled on, quickly lighting another cigarette on the move. "Does it surprise you that I can still go on being active in a notorious movement that is liberating for some and extremely restricting for others, well, for your papa, for instance? It surprises me myself; it's all rubbish that up to the last minute I have been acting according to a strictly elaborated programme: that's just—listen: I act according to my own discretion; but what can you expect, my discretion just draws a new track every time in their activity; to tell the truth, it's not me who is in the party, the party is in me … Does that surprise you?"

"Yes, I must confess: that does surprise me; and I have to confess that I would never agree to act together with you." Nikolai Apollonovich was beginning to listen more attentively to the stranger's speeches, which were becoming more and more rounded, more and more resonant.

"But you did take my little package from me: so that means we are acting in concert."

"Well, that can't possibly count; what sort of action is that … "

"Of course, of course," the stranger interrupted him, "I was just joking." And he fell silent for a while, cast a gentle glance at Nikolai Apollonovich and said perfectly frankly this time:

"You know, I've been wanting to see you for a long time: to have a heart-to-heart talk; I see so few people. I wanted to tell you about myself. You see, I'm a fugitive not only for the opponents of the movement, but also for its less than committed supporters. The quintessence of revolution, as it were, but what's strange is this: you know all about the principles of social phenomena, you immerse yourself in diagrams and statistics, you probably know Marx perfectly; but me—I haven't read anything; don't get me wrong: I'm well read, very, only not in those things, not in statistics."

"What in, then? … No, just a moment: I have some cognac in the cupboard—would you like some?"

"I wouldn't mind … "

Nikolai Apollonovich rummaged in a little cupboard: soon there appeared in front of the guest a cut-glass decanter and two cut-glass glasses.

During conversations with guests Nikolai Apollonovich was in the habit of treating his guests to cognac.

As he poured his guest the cognac with the greatest absent-mindedness (like all the Ableukhovs, he was absent-minded), Nikolai Apollonovich kept thinking that a most convenient occasion had now presented itself for withdrawing completely the offer he had made *then*; but when he wanted to express his thought in words, he became embarrassed: out of cowardice he did not wish to display cowardice in front of the stranger; and besides: in his joy he did not wish to burden himself with a most ticklish conversation, when it was possible to withdraw the undertaking in writing.

"I'm reading Conan Doyle just now, for relaxation," the stranger twittered on, "Don't be angry—that's a joke, of course. However, maybe it isn't a joke: if I'm honest, my reading will be just as preposterous to you: I'm reading the history of gnosticism, Gregory of Nissa, Sirianin, the Apocalypse. That's my prerogative, you know; say what you like— I am a colonel in the movement, transferred from active service to headquarters (for services rendered). Yes, yes, yes: I'm a colonel. For long service, of course; but you, Nikolai Apollonovich, with your principles and your intelligence, you're an NCO: you're an NCO in the first place because you're a theoretician; and our generals aren't very well up on theory; you have to admit they aren't very well up on it; they are just like bishops, only bishops who have risen from being monks; and a young student from the theological academy who has studied Harnack but has missed the school of experience, and hasn't been through the sternest training—for a bishop he's just an irritating appendage to the church; and you, too, with all your theories, are an appendage; an irritating one, for sure."

"In your words I can hear a trace of populism."

"So what? It's the populists who have the strength, not the Marxists. But forgive me, I am digressing … what was I talking about? Yes, about length of service and reading. Well, then: the originality of my mental fare comes from exactly the same eccentricity; I'm just as much a braggart of the revolution as any bragging old soldier with a St George's cross: an old braggart, an old campaigner, gets everything forgiven."

The stranger fell to thinking, poured a glass: he drank it—and poured another.

"And why ever shouldn't I be able to find something of my own, something personal, independent of others: as it is I seem to live privately—in four yellow walls; my fame grows, society repeats my party nickname, but the circle of people with whom I have human relations is, honestly, zero; people first learned about me at that wonderful time when I got stuck in minus forty-five ... "

"You were exiled, weren't you?"

"Yes, to the Yakutsk province."

An awkward silence ensued. The stranger with the little black moustache looked out of the window at the expanse of the Neva; a putrid pale-grey mass was hanging there: the edge of the earth was there and the end of all infinities; there, through the greyness and the putrid mass venomous October was already whispering something, beating against the windows with tears and wind; and the tears of rain on the panes chased each other, to twist into streams and trace the hieroglyphs of words; in the chimneys the sweet chirruping of the wind could be heard, and a network of black chimneys, from far, far away, sent its smoke up into the sky. And the smoke tumbled in tails over the dark-coloured waters. The stranger with the little black moustache touched his lips to his glass and looked at the yellow liquid: his hands were shaking.

Nikolai Apollonovich, now listening intently, said with a certain ... almost anger:

"But I trust that for the time being, Alexandr Ivanovich, you're not saying a word to the crowds about your dreams? ... "

"Of course, I shall keep quiet for now."

"That means you're lying; forgive me, but the words aren't what matters: you really are lying, once and for all."

The stranger gave a look of astonishment and continued rather irrelevantly:

"For the time being I'm just reading and thinking: and it is all exclusively for myself: that is why I am reading Gregory of Nissa."

A silence ensued. Downing another glass, the stranger peeped out of his cloud of smoke victoriously; it goes without saying that he was smoking all the time. It was Nikolai Apollonovich who broke the silence.

"Well, and after you returned from the Yakutsk province?"

"I managed to escape from the Yakutsk province; I was brought out in a cabbage barrel; and now I am what I am: an underground agent; only don't you imagine that I operate in the name of social utopias or in the name of your railway-line thinking: your categories remind me of rails, and your life—of a carriage flying along the rails: at that time I was a desperate Nietzschean. We are all Nietzscheans: you, too, you know, the engineer of your railway line, the creator of your scheme—are a Nietzschean; only you will never admit to it. Well, then: for us Nietzscheans the masses, disposed to rebellion and aroused by their social instincts (as you would put it), turn into an operational mechanism (that's an engineering expression of yours, too), where people (even people like you) are the keyboard, on which the fingers of the pianist (please note, that expression is mine) fly freely, overcoming difficulties for difficulty's sake; and while some milksop in the stalls sits beside the concert platform revelling in the divine sounds of Beethoven, for the pianist and for Beethoven too—the point isn't the sounds, but a particular seventh chord. You do know what a seventh chord is, don't you? And we are all like that."

"Athletes of revolution, you mean."

"Why not? Isn't an athlete an artist? I am an athlete out of pure love of the art: and therefore I am an artist. It would be good to sculpt from the unformed clay of society an extraordinary bust for all eternity."

"But come on, come on—you are slipping into a contradiction: a seventh chord, a formula, that is, a term—and a bust, that is to say, something living? Technique—and creative inspiration? I understand technique perfectly."

Again an awkward silence ensued: in irritation Nikolai Appollonovich plucked horse-hairs out of his brightly woven couch; he saw no sense in getting involved in a theoretical argument; he was in the habit of arguing correctly, not jumping from one topic to another.

"Everything in the world is built on contrasts: and my usefulness for society brought me to the cheerless icy expanses; while they still remembered me here, they no doubt completely forgot that there I was alone, in emptiness: and as I went off into that emptiness, rising above the foot-soldiers, even above the NCOs (the stranger grinned without malice and plucked at his moustache)—gradually all party prejudices dropped away from me, all categories, as you would say: since Yakutsk, do you know, I have only known one category. Do you know what category that is?"

"Tell me."

"The category of ice … "

"How do you mean?"

Whether from his thoughts or from the alcohol he had drunk, only Alexandr Ivanovich's face really did take on a strange expression; it changed markedly in colour, and even in its dimensions (there are such faces that can be transformed in an instant); he now looked as though it was the cognac that had finally drunk him.

"The category of ice—that is the ice of the Yakutsk province; I carry it in my heart, you know: that is what separates me off from everyone; I carry the ice with me; yes, yes, yes: the ice separates me; it separates me, in the first place, as an illegal, living under a false passport; and secondly, it was in that ice that a special sensation first developed in me: that even when I was among people, I was cast out into infinity … "

The stranger with the little black moustache had imperceptibly crept up to the window; there, beyond the window panes, a platoon of grenadiers was passing in the greenish mist: fine, strapping lads were passing by, all in grey overcoats. Swinging their left arms, they passed by: row after row passed by, their bayonets gleaming black in the mist.

Nikolai Apollonovich had a strange sensation of cold: an unpleasant feeling returned to him: his promise to the party had not been taken back; listening to the stranger now, Nikolai Apollonovich lost his nerve: Nikolai Apollonovich, just like Apollon Apollonovich, disliked spaces; he was even more alarmed by icy spaces, such as now wafted over him so distinctly from Alexandr Ivanovich's words.

Over there, by the window, Alexandr Ivanovich was smiling …

"I have no need of the articles of revolution: it's you, the theoreticians, the propagandists, the philosophers, who need the articles."

At that moment, as he looked out of the window, he abruptly broke off his speech; jumping away from the windowsill, he began to stare out into the misty slush; the point was that out of that misty slush a carriage had rolled up; Alexandr Ivanovich also saw the carriage door open wide, and Apollon Apollonovich Abezlukhov in his grey overcoat and his tall black top hat, with his stony face, redolent of a paperweight, quickly jump out of the carriage, casting a momentary and fearful glance at the mirror-like reflections in the window panes; quickly he rushed up to the entrance, unbuttoning as he went a black kidskin glove. Alexandr Ivanovich, now frightened by something in his turn, suddenly raised his hand to his eyes, as though he was trying to hide from an importunate thought. A suppressed whisper burst from his chest.

"It's him … "

"What did you say?"

Now Nikolai Apollonovich also came up to the window.

"Nothing in particular: your papa has just driven up in his carriage."

The walls were snow, not walls!

Apollon Apollonovich did not like his spacious apartment; the furniture in it gleamed so irksomely, so eternally: and when it was covered, the furniture under its white covers presented itself to the gaze as snow-clad hills; the senator's footfalls made a sharp and hollow echo on the parquet.

The senator's footfalls made a sharp and hollow echo in the hall, which had more the character of a corridor of the broadest proportions. From the ceiling with its flourish of white garlands, from the circle of stucco fruit a chandelier with beads of rock crystal hung down, enveloped in a sheath of lace; the chandelier seemed transparent, rocking evenly and trembling with a crystal tear.

And the parquet with its little square blocks gleamed like a mirror.

The walls were snow, not walls; everywhere tall chairs were set against those walls; golden fluting sprouted everywhere from their tall white legs; between the chairs, upholstered in beige plush, everywhere white alabaster plinths arose; and from each of those white plinths an alabaster Archimedes sprang. Not Archimedes—various exemplars of Archimedes, for their collective name is—ancient Greek sage. Severe, icy glass glittered coldly from the walls; but someone's solicitous hand had hung circular frames along the walls; under the glass pale-hued paintings were revealed; these pale-hued paintings imitated the frescoes of Pompeii.

Apollon Apollonovich glanced in passing at the Pompeian frescoes and remembered whose solicitous hand had hung them along the walls; the solicitous hand belonged to Anna Petrovna: Apollon Apollonovich pursed his lips in distaste and passed through into his study; in his study Apollon Apollonovich was in the habit of locking himself in; the expanses of the enfilade of rooms aroused in him an unaccountable sadness; it was as though from there someone eternally familiar and strange was forever about to rush upon him; Apollon Apllonovich would most gladly have moved from his immense apartments into apartments more modest; his subordinates, after all, lived in more modest accommodation; but he, Apollon Apollonovich, had to forego forever such captivating congestion: his lofty post required that of him; and so Apollon Apollonovich was compelled to languish idly in his cold apartment on the Embankment; he often recalled his former fellow-occupant of these brilliant rooms: Anna Petrovna. It was two years now since Anna Petrovna had left him for an Italian singer.

A certain person

At the senator's appearance the stranger became nervous; his hitherto smooth talk broke off: it was probably the effect of the alcohol; generally speaking, Alexandr Ivanovich's health gave grounds for serious anxiety; his conversations with himself and others aroused in him a sinful state of mind, and reflected agonisingly upon his spinal cord; a kind of gloomy disgust arose in him towards a conversation that excited him: then he would transfer that disgust on to himself; apparently these innocent conversations weakened him terribly, but the most unpleasant thing was the fact that the more he talked, the more he developed the desire to go on talking: to the point of hoarseness, a feeling of constriction in the throat; he was no longer able to stop, and wore himself out more and more: sometimes he went on talking until he experienced real attacks of persecution mania: arising in his words, they continued in his dreams: on occasions his extraordinarily ominous dreams became more frequent: dream followed dream; sometimes three nightmares in one night; in these dreams he was surrounded by terrible faces (most often, for some reason, Tartars, Japanese or oriental persons in general); these faces always bore the same foul imprint; they kept winking at him with their foul eyes; but the most astonishing thing of all was that at such times there invariably came to his mind the most meaningless of words, apparently cabbalistic, but actually the devil only knows what: *enfranshish*; with the help of this word he battled in his dreams with surrounding throngs of spirits. Moreover: one fateful face would appear even in a waking state on a patch of dark-yellow wallpaper in his lodgings; in the end all manner of drivel would sometimes begin to haunt him: and it haunted him in the broad light of day, if in Petersburg in autumn the daylight is broad at all, and not a greenish-yellow hue with flashes of dark saffron; and then Alexandr Ivanovich experienced exactly what the senator himself had experienced the day before, when he met his, Alexandr Ivanovich's, gaze. All these fateful phenomena began in him with attacks of mortal anguish, most probably occasioned by sitting too long in one place: and then Alexandr Ivanovich would start running out into the yellow-green mist (despite the danger of being detected); as he ran round the Petersburg streets he dropped into taverns. And so alcohol also appeared on the scene. As he drank a shameful feeling arose at once, too: towards the leg, no, sorry, towards the stocking on the leg of an artless girl-student, without any relation to the girl herself; seemingly quite innocent jokes would start, sniggers, grins. And it would all finish in an absurd nightmare with *enfranshish*.

Alexandr Ivanovich remembered all this and a shudder went down his back: as though all this had arisen in his soul once more with the senator's arrival at the house; it was an extraneous thought that would give him no peace; now and then he went inadvertently up to the door and listened to the barely perceptible sound of distant steps; it was probably the senator striding to and fro in his study.

In order to interrupt his thoughts, Alexandr Ivanovich began again to pour out those thoughts in opaque orations.

"Here you are, Nikolai Apollonovich, listening to my chatter: but it's the same here: in all my conversations, in my assertion of my own identity, for example, here again there's an admixture of illness. I am talking to you, arguing with you—but it's not you I'm arguing with, but myself, only myself. The person I'm talking to has no meaning for me whatever: I can talk to the walls, the hoardings in the street, total idiots. I don't listen to other people's ideas: I mean, I hear only what concerns me or mine. I am struggling, Nikolai Apollonovich: I am assailed by loneliness: I sit for hours, for days, for weeks in my attic, smoking. Then it begins to seem to me that everything is something else. Do you know that condition?"

"I can't quite imagine it. I've heard that it's due to the heart. At the sight of empty space, for instance, when there's nothing all round … I can understand that better."

"Well, I can't: it's like this, you're sitting there by yourself and you say, why am I—me: and it seems I'm not me … And you know, there's a coffee table standing there in front of me. And the devil alone knows what it is: the table isn't a table. And you say to yourself: the devil only knows what life has done to me. And I so want me to be me … But there's this 'us' … Altogether I despise all words with that 'u' sound, there's something Tartar in them, or Mongol, anyway, eastern. Just listen: '*u*'. No cultured language knows that sound: it's got something obtuse in it, cynical, slippery."

Then the stranger with the little black moustache remembered the face of a certain person that irritated him; and it reminded him of the sound '*u*'.

Nikolai Apollonovich deliberately, it seemed, engaged Alexandr Ivanovich in conversation.

"You keep talking about greatness of personality: but tell me, isn't there any control over you; are you not tied in any way yourself?"

"Do you mean, Nikolai Apollonovich, a *certain person?*"

"I don't mean anyone at all: I just … "

"Yes—you're right: *a certain person* appeared shortly after my escape from the ice: appeared in Helsingfors."

"This person, who is it—someone with authority in your party?"

"The highest: the whole course of events revolves around him; maybe the most important events of all: do you know this *person?*"

"No, I don't."

"I do, though."

"There you are, then: you said just now that you're not in the party at all, but the party is in you; but it turns out that you must be in this *certain person*."

"Ah, but he sees his centre in me."

"What about the burdens?"

The stranger shuddered.

"Yes, yes, yes: a thousand times yes; the *certain person* imposes the heaviest burdens upon me; my burdens imprison me all the time in that same coldness: the cold of the Yakutsk province."

"So that means," Nikolai Apollonovich quipped "the physical plains of a not-so-distant province have after all turned into the metaphysical plains of your soul."

"Yes, my soul is like outer space; and from there, from outer space, I look down upon everything."

"Listen, do you have ... "

"Outer space," Alexandr Ivanovich interrupted him "sometimes weighs so heavily upon me, desperately heavily. Do you know what I call outer space?"

And without waiting for an answer, Alexandr Ivanovich added:

"It's my lodgings on Vasilevskii Island that I call outer space: four perpendicular walls with dark-yellow wallpaper on them; when I settle down between those walls, nobody comes to see me: the caretaker of the house, Matvei Morzhov, might come; and then the *person* finds his way into those precincts."

"How did you come to be there?"

"Why—the *person* ... "

"The person again?"

"It's all him: here he has turned out to be the guardian, so to speak, of my damp threshold; if he so decides in the interests of security I might sit there for weeks on end without emerging; my appearance on the streets always represents a danger, you know."

"So it's from there that you cast your shadow over the life of Russia—the shadow of the Fugitive?"

"Yes, from four yellow walls."

"But listen: where is your freedom, where does it come from," Nikolai Apollonovich was making fun of him, as though in revenge for his recent words, "your freedom, such as it is, comes from twelve cigarettes smoked one after another. Listen, the *person* has trapped you. How much do you pay for your accommodation?"

"Twelve roubles, no, I mean—twelve-and-a-half."

"And that's where you give yourself over to the contemplation of outer space?"

"That's right: and that's where everything is something else, objects are not objects: this is where I came to the conviction that the window is not a window; the window—is a opening to infinity."

"And I suppose this is where you came to the idea that the upper echelons of the movement know things that aren't accessible to the lower ones, because the upper echelons," he continued his mockery, "what are the upper echelons?"

But Alexandr Ivanovich answered calmly:

"The upper echelons of the movement—are the limitless emptiness of outer space."

"So what is everything else for?"

Alexandr Ivanovich became more animated.

"It's all in the name of illness … "

"How do you mean, illness?"

"The very same illness that torments me so: I don't know the strange name of that illness yet, but I know its symptoms perfectly: an unaccountable longing, hallucinations, fears, vodka, smoking; from the vodka—a frequent, nagging pain in the head; and finally, a particular feeling in the spine: it torments you in the morning. Do you imagine I'm the only one who's ill? Nothing of the sort: you, too, Nikolai Apollonovich—you—are ill, too. Nearly everyone is ill. No, don't, please; I know, I know in advance what you will say, and all the same: ha-ha-ha!—nearly all the party's ideological workers—are ill with the same illness; it's just that its features are more clearly marked in me. You know—even in the old days when I met a party comrade, I always liked, you know, to study him; you'd have a meeting lasting several hours, business, smoke, conversations all on such noble, lofty topics, and my comrade would get really worked up, and then, you know, this same comrade would invite you to a restaurant."

"What follows from that?"

"Well, it goes without saying, vodka; and so on; one glass after another; and I'd be watching; if after a glass of vodka there appeared on the face of man I was talking to a certain kind of smile (what kind, Nikolai Apollonovich, I can't tell you), then I would already know: my ideological interlocutor was not to be relied on; his words couldn't be believed, and nor could his actions: this man was suffering from weakness of will, neurasthenia; and there was nothing, you can be sure, to guarantee he wouldn't have softening of the brain: a man like that is not only capable of failing to fulfil a promise at a difficult moment (Nikolai Apollonovich shuddered); he's quite capable of simply stealing, betraying, or raping a little girl. And his presence in the party is provocation, provocation, a terrible provocation. And that was when I came to understand the full meaning of, you know, all those little wrinkles by the lips, those weaknesses, giggles, grimaces; and wherever I turn to look, everywhere, everywhere I'm met by an unvarying mental derangement, one general, secret, evasively contrived provocation, one of those little giggles in the midst of the common cause—what kind, I dare say I can't tell you exactly, Nikolai Apollonovich. But I know how to detect it unfailingly, and I have detected it in you."

"And do you not have it?"

"I have it too: I have long since ceased to trust in any common cause."

"So that means you are a provocateur. Don't be offended: I'm talking about purely ideological provocation."

"I am. Yes, yes, yes. I am a provocateur. But all my provocation is in the name of a single great idea, that secretly draws us away somewhere; and again, not an idea, but—something in the air."

"What something is that?"

"If we're to talk about what's in the air, I can't define it with words: I can call it a universal hankering for death; and I revel in it, with delight, with bliss, with horror."

"And I suppose it was when you started to revel in this sense of death in the air that that little wrinkle appeared on your face."

"That's when."

"And when you started smoking, and drinking."

"Yes, yes, yes: and a particular kind of erotic feeling appeared too: you know, I wasn't in love with any of the women: I was in love—how shall I put it: with specific parts of a woman's body, with articles of her toilet, stockings, for instance. And men started falling in love with me."

"And was it just then that *a certain person* appeared?"

"How I hate him. You know, of course—I expect you know it not by your own willing, but by the will of the fate that has been raising me up—the fate of the Fugitive—my personality, the personality of Alexandr Ivanovich, has turned into an appendage of my own shadow. Everyone knows the shadow of the Fugitive; but me, Alexandr Ivanovich Dudkin, nobody knows at all, and nobody wants to know. But it wasn't the Fugitive who starved or froze or had any experiences in general, it was Dudkin. Alexandr Ivanovich Dudkin, for example, was marked by a great sensitivity; the Fugitive, however, was cold and cruel. Alexandr Ivanovich Dudkin was naturally distinguished by a clearly expressed sociability and wasn't the least disinclined to live for his own perfect pleasure. But the Fugitive had to be ascetically silent. In short, the fugitive shadow of Dudkin even now continues its victorious onward march: in the minds of the young, of course; but I myself, under the influence of *that certain person*, have become—just look and tell me what I look like."

"Yes, you know … "

And again they both fell silent.

"And in the end, Nikolai Apollonovich, another strange nervous ailment waylaid me: and under the influence of this ailment I came to some unexpected conclusions: I fully realised, Nikolai Apollonovich, that emerging from the cold of my *outer space* I had begun to burn with a concealed hatred not of the government at all, but of *a certain person*; why, this person, by turning me, Dudkin, into the shadow of Dudkin, had driven me out of the world of three dimensions, and spread-eagled me, so to speak, on the wall of my attic (my favourite position during insomnia, you know, is to stand against the wall and spread-eagle myself, stretching out my arms on either side). And in that spread-eagled position by the wall (I stand like that for hours on end, Nikolai Apollonovich) I came one day to my second conclusion; that conclusion was somehow strangely connected—somehow strangely connected with a phenomenon that was quite comprehensible, if you take into account my developing illness."

Alexandr Ivanovich thought it appropriate to remain silent about that phenomenon.

The phenomenon consisted in a strange hallucination: on the

yellow-brown wallpaper of his lodgings there appeared from time to time a ghostly face; the features of that face composed themselves on occasions into a Semite; most often, though, Mongol lineaments were what stood out: the whole face was swathed in an unpleasant, saffron-yellow glow. This Semite, or Mongol, stared at Alexandr Ivanovich with a hate-filled gaze. Then Alexandr Ivanovich would light a cigarette; and the Semite or Mongol would move his yellow lips through the bluish haze of cigarette smoke, and in Alexandr Ivanovich a single word would seem to echo over and over again:

"Helsingfors, Helsingfors."

Alexandr Ivanovich had been in Helsingfors after his escape from places not so distant: he had no particular connections with Helsingfors: he had simply met *a certain person* there.

So why Helsingfors specifically?

Alexandr Ivanovich went on drinking the cognac. The alcohol affected him gradually and evenly; when he drank spirits (he could not afford wine) there always followed a uniform effect: the wavelike lines of his thought turned into zigzags; the zigzags intersected with each other; if he were to go on drinking, the lines of thought would dissolve into a series of fragmentary arabesques, which for him who thought them were the fruit of genius; but only for him were they the fruit of genius, and only at that one moment; he only had to sober up slightly, and the quality of genius disappeared; and his inspired thoughts seemed nothing but a farrago, for at those moments his thought undoubtedly anticipated both his tongue and his brain, beginning to revolve with furious rapidity.

Alexandr Ivanovich's agitation communicated itself to Ableukhov: the bluish wisps of tobacco smoke and the twelve squashed cigarette butts definitely irritated him; it was as though someone invisible, a third person, had suddenly come to stand between them, raised out of this smoke and this pile of ash; this third, once arisen, now dominated everything.

"Wait a moment: perhaps I'll go out with you; my head is splitting: and after all, outside in the open we can continue our conversation without problems. Wait. I'll just go and change."

"That's an excellent idea."

A sharp knock, sounding at the door, interrupted their conversation; before Nikolai Apollonovich could formulate the intention of inquiring who had knocked, the absent-minded and half-drunk Alexandr Ivanovich quickly threw the door open; from the door's opening a bare skull with ears of magnified proportions thrust itself, almost threw itself, upon the stranger; the skull and Alexandr Ivanovich's head came within an inch of clashing foreheads; Alexandr Ivanovich leapt back in consternation and glanced at Nikolai Apollonovich, and in that glance saw only … a hairdresser's dummy: the pale, waxen figure of a handsome man with an unpleasant, timid smile on lips that extended all the way to his ears.

He glanced again at the door, and in the open doorway stood Apollon Apollonovich with … an immense watermelon under his arm …

"I see, I see … "

"I seem to have disturbed you … "

"I was bringing you, Kolenka, this watermelon, you know—here … "

It was a tradition of the house that in the autumn Apollon Appollonovich on the way home sometimes bought an Astrakhan watermelon, for which both he and Nikolai Apollonovich—both had a liking.

For a moment all three were silent; each of them in that moment felt an utterly unconcealed, purely animal fear.

"This is my university colleague, Papa … Alexandr Ivanovich Dudkin … "

"I see … Glad to meet you."

Apollon Apollonovich proffered two fingers: *those eyes* held no horror; was that really the face that had looked at him in the street: Apollon Apollonovich saw in front of him only a timid man, evidently oppressed by need.

Alexandr Ivanovich seized the senator's fingers fervidly; that *fateful* aspect disappeared: Alexandr Ivanovich saw before him only a pathetic old man.

Nikolai Apollonovich looked at both of them with the same unpleasant smile; but he too calmed down; it was just an apprehensive young man shaking hands with a weary skeleton.

But the hearts of all three were beating fast; but the eyes of all three were avoiding each other. Nikolai Apollonovich ran off to change; he now had only one thought on his mind: how *she* had been wandering under the window yesterday: so she was pining; but there was something in store for her today—what was it? ...

His thought broke off: from his cupboard Nikolai Apollonovich pulled out his domino and put it on over his frock coat; he fastened the red satin flaps with pins; on top of everything he threw on his cape.

Apollon Apollonovich had in the meantime entered into conversation with the stranger; the disorder in his son's room, the cigarettes, the cognac—all this left an unpleasant and bitter sediment in his soul; he was reassured only by Alexandr Ivanovich's replies: his replies were incoherent. Alexandr Ivanovich blushed and answered out of turn. All he saw before him was good-natured wrinkles; from those good-natured wrinkles eyes peeped out: the eyes of a hunted animal: and a rumbling, broken voice was shouting something out; Alexandr Ivanovich listened carefully only to the last words; and caught nothing but a series of abrupt exclamations ...

"You know ... even as a schoolboy Kolenka knew all the birds ... He used to read Kaigorodov ... "

"He was eager for knowledge ... "

"But now it's different: he's dropped everything ... "

"And doesn't go to university any more ... "

Thus the old man of sixty-eight shouted his abrupt opinions at Alexandr Ivanovich; and something akin to sympathy stirred in the Fugitive's heart ...

Nikolai Apollonovich now entered the room.

"Where are you going?"

"I've got some business, Papa ... "

"You're going with ... as it were ... with Alexandr ... Alexandr ... "

"With Alexandr Ivanovich ... "

"I see ... with Alexandr Ivanovich, then ... "

To himself Apollon Apollonovich was thinking: "Well, maybe it's for the best: as for the *eyes*, maybe I imagined it ... " And furthermore Apollon Apollonovich thought that poverty was no crime. Only why had they been drinking cognac (Apollon Apollonovich had an antipathy to alcohol).

"Yes: we have some business ... "

Apollon Apollonovich started searching for something appropriate to say:

"Perhaps … you would have dinner … And Alexandr Ivanovich would stay for dinner with us … "

Apollon Apollonovich looked at the clock:

"But anyway … I don't want to cramp your style … "

"Goodbye, Papa … "

"My respects to you … "

When they opened the door and set off along the echoing corridor, the small figure of Apollon Apollonovich appeared behind them—there in the half-darkness of the corridor.

And while they walked along in the half-darkness of the corridor, Apollon Apollonovich stood there; craning his neck after the two of them, he gazed with curiosity.

All the same, all the same … the eyes had looked at him yesterday: there was hatred in them, and fear; those were the eyes: they belonged to *him, the man of uncertain status.* And the zigzag was—most unpleasant, or had it not happened—never happened at all?

"Alexandr Ivanovich Dudkin … University student."

Apollon Apollonovich strode after them.

In the magnificent entrance-hall Nikolai Apollonovich stopped in front of the old servant, trying to catch his escaping thought.

"Yee-ee-s … "

"Certainly, sir!"

"A-ah … the mouse!"

Nikolai Apollonovich went on helplessly rubbing his forehead, trying to remember what he was supposed to express with the help of the verbal symbol 'mouse': this often happened to him, especially after reading extremely serious treatises that consisted exclusively of a concatenation of the most unimaginable words: every object, even more than that—every name of an object seemed after reading such treatises unthinkable, and vice versa: everything thinkable turned out to be utterly divorced from things, from objects. And on this account Nikolai Apollonovich once more uttered with an offended mien.

"Mouse … "

"Exactly so, sir!"

"Where is it? Listen, what have you done with the mouse?"

"The one just now, sir? I let it out on to the Embankment … "

"Did you really?"

"Indeed I did, sir: like I always do."

Nikolai Apollonovich was distinguished by an unusual tenderness towards these little creatures.

Reassured about the mouse's fate, Nikolai Apollonovich and Alexandr Ivanovich set out on their way.

The two of them set out, however, because they both had the impression that from the landing of the staircase someone was looking at them intently and sadly.

He sallied forth all right

A gloomy building rose up on a gloomy street. It was just turning dark; the lamps began to glimmer, lighting up the entrance; the fourth floors were still red from the sunset.

And it was there, from all ends of Petersburg, that nondescripts were making their way; their complement was of two kinds; their complement was recruited, in the first place, from the class of worker—nondescript, tousle-headed—in a hat brought back from the fields of blood-soaked Manchuria; and secondly, their complement was recruited from the class of protester in general: this protester strode in profusion on his long legs; he was pale and weakly; sometimes he had phytin to drink, sometimes he had cream; today he strode along with a huge knobbly stick; if you were to put my protester on one pan of the scales, and put his knobbly stick on the other pan, then the implement would no doubt outweigh the protester: it was not entirely clear who was following whom; whether the cudgel was springing along in front of the protester, or he was striding along behind the cudgel; but most probably it was the cudgel that had come galloping here by itself from the Nevskii, from Pushkinskaia, the Vyborg Side, even from Izamailovskaia Rota; the protester was dragged along behind it; and he got out of breath, he could hardly keep up; and the sprightly urchin who was rushing by at the hour when the newspaper's evening supplement came out—this sprightly urchin would have knocked the protester over, if my protester had not been a protester from the working-class, but just an ordinary protester.

It was not by chance that this ordinary protester had latterly started strolling around: around Petersburg, Saratov, Tsarevokokshaisk, Kineshma; it wasn't every day he strolled around like that … He might just go out of an evening for a stroll: the sunset quiet and peaceful; and a young lady laughing so peacefully in the street; and my nondescript protester would have a peaceful little laugh with the young lady—without a cudgel at all: he'd swap a joke, have a smoke; and with the most benign expression chat with the caretaker, with the most benign expression chat with the constable, Brykachev.

"Bet you're fed up with standing here, Brykachev, aren't you?"

"Of course, guv'nor: this job isn't an easy one."

"Just be patient: it will change soon."

"I hope to God it will: not much good in it like this; you can't keep the free spirit down, as you well know."

"You're right there … "

He's all right, the nondescript; and the constable, Brykachev, is all right too: and they both laugh; and a five-copeck piece slips into Brykachev's fist.

The next day he might go out for a stroll again in the evening—and what's this? The sunset quiet and peaceful; just the same contentment in nature; and the theatres and the circuses—all working; and the city water supply in perfectly good condition too; and—but no: everything's different.

Crossing the public garden, the street, the square, or shifting sadly from one foot to the other in front of the monument to a great man, the good-natured nondescript of yesterday now strides out with his huge cudgel; threateningly, silently, solemnly, emphatically, you might say, the nondescript puts his best foot forward in galoshes and rolled-down gaiters; threateningly, silently, solemnly the nondescript strikes the pavement with his cudgel; not a word for Brykachev the constable; and Brykachev has no word for him either, he simply mutters into space, but with determination:

"Move along, gentlemen, move along, don't stand still."

And look: somewhere Podbrizhnii the superintendent is circulating.

My protester's eye darts around: this way and that; to see if other protesters like himself have gathered in a group in front of the monument to the great man. Have they gathered on the square in front of the transit prison? But the monument to the great man is surrounded by police; and on the square—there is no one.

So he walks around a bit, my nondescript, he walks around and sighs with sympathy; and goes back to his home; and his mama gives him tea with cream to drink … Then you can be sure: that day something was printed in the papers: something—some measure— for the prevention, so to speak: of something or other; when some measure is published—the nondescript begins to wander round.

The next day there is no such measure: and no nondescript to be seen on the streets: and my nondescript is happy, and Brykachev the constable is happy; and Podbrizhnii the superintendent is happy. The monument to the great man is not surrounded by police.

Did my protesting nondescript sally forth on that October day? He sallied forth all right! There were shaggy Manchurian hats sallying forth on to the street; and the nondescripts and the hats dissolved in the crowd; but the crowd wandered hither and thither with no purpose; the nondescripts and the Manchurian hats, however, walked in one direction—to the gloomy building whose upper storeys still shone crimson; and by that crimson building, gloomy from the sunset, the crowd consisted exclusively of nondescripts and hats; there was a young lady from an educational institution mixed up with them as well.

They pushed and shoved into the doorways—how they pushed, how they shoved! What do you expect? The working man has no time to concern himself with propriety: and there was a bad smell; but the crush began at the corner.

At the corner, right beside the pavement, a small detachment of police were stamping their feet (it was cold) in good-natured embarrassment; the local constable—was even more embarrassed; a grey little man himself, in a grey overcoat, he shouted intermittently like an unnoticed shadow, holding his sword deferentially by his side and keeping his eyes down; and behind his back came verbal comments, rebukes, laughter and even: obscene abuse—from the craftsman Ivan Ivanovich Ivanov, from his wife, Ivanikha, from the staid merchant of the first guild, Puzanov (the fishing-trade and a steamship-line on the Volga), who was walking by there and had rebelled along with the others. The little grey constable called out more and more timidly:

"Move along there, gentlemen, move along!"

But the more his lustre faded, the more insistently the furry-legged horses there behind the fence snorted: from behind the pointed panels every now and then a shaggy head rose up; and if you were to stand up and look over the fence, you would see men just lately rushed here from the steppes with whips in their fists and the muzzles of rifles over their shoulders, who for some reason were growing angrier by the minute; impatiently, angrily, silently those ragamuffins danced up and down in their saddles; and the shaggy little horses—danced up and down as well.

It was a detachment of Cossacks from Orenburg.

Inside the gloomy building was a saffron-yellow murk; the only lighting was by candles; nothing could be seen but bodies, bodies, bodies: bent over, half-straightened, bent over slightly, not bent at all: and surrounding those bodies, sitting or standing, were others in every space that could be sat or stood in; they filled an ascending amphitheatre of seats; the lectern could not be seen, nor could the voice be heard that was declaiming from the lectern:

"*Uuu-uuu-uuu.*" There was a buzzing in the space around and through that "uuu" there resounded now and then:

"Revolution … Evolution … Proletariat … Strike … " And then again: "Strike … " And again: "Strike … "

"Strike … " a voice would fire off; the buzzing would increase: between two loudly uttered *strikes* you might just catch a fleeting "Social democracy." And then it would melt back into the deep, bass, universal *uuu-uuuu* …

Evidently the issue was that there, and there, and there as well the strike was under way; that there, and there, and there as well the strike was being prepared, and so a strike must happen—here and here: must happen in this very place; and not a yard be yielded!

Flight

Alexandr Ivanovich was walking home along the empty Prospects beside the Neva; the light of a carriage from the royal court flew past him; a view of the Neva opened up under the arch of the Winter Canal; there, on the humpbacked bridge, he noticed the same shadow that appeared there every night.

Alexandr Ivanovich was walking home to his squalid lodgings, to sit in solitude among brown stains and observe the life of woodlice in the damp crevices of the walls. His morning sortie after the night was more like a flight from the crawling woodlice; Alexandr Ivanovich's repeated observations had long since brought him to the thought that the peace of his night was directly dependent on the peace of the day he had passed: recently it was only what he experienced on the streets, in restaurants or tea-houses that he brought home with him.

What was he bringing back today?

His experiences dragged along behind him like a receding tail made up of forces not visible to the eye; Alexandr Ivanovich experienced these experiences in reverse order, as his consciousness ran away into that tail (behind his back, that is): at moments like this it always seemed to him that his back had split open and that out of his back, as though from a door, the body of a giant was about to hurl itself into an abyss: that giant's body was his experience of the past twenty-four hours; his experiences began to billow out in his tail.

Alexandr Ivanovich reflected: as soon as he returned home the events of today would come bursting through the door; he would try to crush them in the attic door, tearing the tail from his body: but the tail would still burst in.

Alexandr Ivanovich left the bridge with its glittering diamonds behind him.

Further on, beyond the bridge, against the background of the nocturnal St Isaac's that same rock rose before him out of the green murk: stretching out his heavy, verdigris-encrusted hand the same enigmatic Horseman raised above the Neva his wreath of bronze laurels; above a grenadier, asleep beneath his shaggy hat, the steed thrust out its two front hooves in consternation; and below, beneath those hooves, the dozing old grenadier's shaggy hat rocked slowly. A metal badge, falling from the hat, struck against his bayonet.

A fitful half-shadow covered the Horseman's face; and in its ambiguous expression his metallic face seemed doubled; the palm of his hand sliced the turquoise air.

Since that fraught time when the metal Horseman came hastening

131

to the banks of the Neva, since that time, fraught with days, when he thrust his steed on to the grey Finnish granite—Russia has been split in twain; the very fates of the fatherland have been split in twain as well; suffering and weeping, until the final hour—Russia has been split in twain.

You, Russia, are like the steed! Your two front hooves are raised over the dark, the emptiness; and your two rear hooves are firmly set in the granite earth.

Do you, too, wish to split yourself from the stone that holds you, as so many of your demented sons have done—do you, too, wish to split yourself from the stone that holds you and hang in the air without a bridle, to come crashing down anon into the waters of chaos? Or perhaps you wish to hurl yourself through the air, ripping apart the mists, to vanish in the clouds along with your sons? Or is it, Russia, that, rising on to your hind legs, you have sunk into thought for many years to come over the ominous fate that cast you here—amidst this gloomy north, where the sunset lasts for hours, where time itself tosses between frosty night and the luminescence of day? Or, taking fright at the leap, will you lower your hooves and, snorting, carry the great Horseman off into the depths of those endless expanses of plains, those illusory lands?

Let it not be! …

Once it has risen on to its hind legs and measures the air with its eyes, the metal steed will not lower its hooves: the leap over history— shall be; there will be a great disturbance; the earth shall fly apart; the mountains themselves shall collapse from the great quake; and the native plains shall be covered with hills from that quake. On the hills will stand Nizhnii, Vladimir and Uglich.

But Petersburg will sink.

All the nations of the earth will rush in those days from their places; there will be a great battle—a battle such as the world has never seen: yellow hordes of Asiatics, moving from the places they have settled, will turn the fields of Europe crimson with oceans of blood; there will be—Tsushima! There will be—a new Kalka! …

Field of Kulikovo, I await you!

On that day the last Sun will shine forth over my native land. If, Sun, you do not rise, then, O, Sun, the shores of Europe will sink under the heavy Mongol heel, and above those shores foam will froth; the creatures of the earth will sink again to the bottom of the oceans—into primeval, long-forgotten chaos …

Rise, O, Sun!

A gash of turquoise raced across the sky; and coming to meet it a patch of burning phosphorus flew through the clouds, turning all of a sudden into a complete, brightly shining moon; for a moment everything flashed with light: the waters, the chimneys, the granite blocks, the silvery drainpipes, two goddesses over an arch, the roof of a four-storeyed building; the dome of St Isaac's looked translucent; the Horseman's brow and his wreath of bronze laurels flashed with light; the lights of the islands dimmed; and an enigmatic vessel in the middle of the Neva turned out to be a simple fishing boat; from the captain's bridge a point of light shone out more brilliantly; maybe it was a spark from the pipe of a blue-nosed boatswain in a Dutch hat, with ear-flaps, or—the bright torch of a sailor on watch. The light half-shadow fell away from the Bronze Horseman, like a thin layer of soot; and the shaggy grenadier, along with the Horseman, was outlined a deeper black against the slabs.

For a moment the fates of men were illuminated distinctly for Alexandr Ivanovich: it was possible to see what would happen, and it was possible to know what would never come to pass: everything became so clear; it seemed that fate was clarified; but he was afraid to glance at his fate; he stood face to face with fate shaken, disturbed, in anguish.

And—the moon was swallowed by a cloud …

Again the ragged arms of clouds rushed madly on; the misty wisps of witches' braids rushed on; and a burning patch of phosphorus flickered ambiguously among them …

And then a deafening, inhuman roar was heard: gleaming unbearably with its massive headlights an automobile rushed past, puffing petrol fumes, under the archway towards the river. Alexandr Ivanovich made out ugly yellow, Mongol faces cutting across the square; from the shock he fell over; his wet hat fell off in front of him. Behind his back there then arose a mumbling, that sounded like a lamentation.

"Lord Jesus Christ! Have mercy on us and save us!"

Alexandr Ivanovich turned round and realised that the old Nikolaevskii grenadier had started whispering beside him.

"Good Lord, what was that?"

"An automobile: important Japanese visitors … "

There was no trace of the automobile left.

The ghostly outline of a footman's tricorn hat and the folds of an overcoat protruding in the wind were borne from mist to mist by the two lamps of a carriage.

Styopka

Not far from Petersburg the highway winds along from Kolpino: there is no gloomier place than this! Approaching Petersburg in the morning, you wake up and out you look: outside the carriage windows all is dead; not a single soul, not a single village; as though the human race had died out and the earth itself was a corpse.

Here on the surface, which consists of a confusion of frozen bushes, a black, black cloud leans down to the earth from afar; the horizon there is leaden; gloomy lands crawl away beneath the sky …

Many-chimneyed, smoke-infested Kolpino!

And from Kolpino to Petersburg the highroad winds along: winds in a grey ribbon; bordered by crushed stone and a line of telegraph wires. A workman was making his way there with a bundle on a stick; he had been working at the powder factory and had been sacked for something; and was on his way by shanks' pony to Petersburg; yellow reeds bristled around him; and the roadside stones lay numb; the barriers were raised and lowered, the striped milestones passed in turn, the telegraph wires hummed without beginning or end. The workman was the son of an impoverished shopkeeper; his name was Styopka; he had only been working at a factory outside town for a month or so; and he had left it: now Petersburg lay hunched before him.

Many-storeyed blocks lay hunched behind the factories; the factories themselves lay hunched behind the chimneys—one there, another here, and there—another still; in the sky there was not a single cloud, but the horizon seen from there seemed smeared with soot, the population of a million-and-a-half breathed its lungs full of soot.

Here, there, and there again: toxic ash was smeared about; and chimneys bristled on the ash; here a chimney rose up high; another squatted somewhat—there; further off—a row of chimneys so slender that in the end they came to look like hairs; in the distance those hairs could be counted in their tens; above the soot-grimed opening of one nearby chimney the protruding arrow of a lightning conductor threatened the sky with a pinprick.

My Styopka saw all this; and to all of this my Styopka paid no attention at all; he sat for a while on a pile of crushed stone, with his boots off; he bound his feet again, chewed a morsel of bread. And he was off again: plodding on to that poisoned place, the patch of soot: to Petersburg itself.

It was the evening of that day when the door of the caretaker's lodge was opened: the door squealed; and the pulley-block clattered: in the middle of the room the caretaker, Matvei Morzhov, was immersed in reading the newspaper—*The Stock Exchange Gazette*, of course; the plump caretaker's wife, meanwhile (she had earache), had piled on to the table a heap of fluffy pillows and was engaged in the extermination of bedbugs with the aid of Russian turpentine; and a harsh and acrid smell pervaded the room.

At that moment the door of the caretaker's lodge opened with a squeal and the pulley-block clattered; on the threshold stood Styopka apprehensively (the Vasilevskii Island caretaker, Matvei Morzhov, was the only person in the whole of Petersburg from the same village: so of course Styopka had come to him).

Towards evening a bottle of vodka appeared on the table; salted cucumbers appeared, and Bessmertnyi the cobbler appeared with his guitar. Styopka said no to the vodka: it was Morzhov the caretaker and Bessmertnyi the cobbler who drank it.

"Now then … My neighbour here's got things to tell us," Morzhov grinned.

"It's all because they haven't got the right ideas," Bessmertnyi the cobbler shrugged his shoulders; he touched his finger to the string; bam, bam—it went.

"And how's the Tselebeyevo priest?"

"The same old story: drinking."

"And the schoolmarm?"

"The schoolmarm's all right: they say she's going to get married to Frol the hunchback."

"Now then … my neighbour's got things to tell," Matvei Morzhov turned sentimental; and, taking a cucumber in two fingers, he bit into it.

"It's all because they haven't got the right ideas," Bessmertnyi the cobbler shrugged his shoulders: touched his finger to the string; bam, bam—it went. And Styopka went on telling all about the same old thing: how some mysterious folks had turned up in the village and what had happened to those mysterious folks concerning everything else, how they'd announced in the village that an infant would be born, and that meant: liberation: universal liberation; and then they said it was going to come about soon; about the fact that he too, Styopka, used to go himself to these mysterious people's prayers, he didn't say a word; and then he told about the gentry fellow who'd turned up, and all the rest of it taken all together; what the gentleman was like about everything else: he'd run away to the village from his aristocratic bride; and so on; he went off to the mysterious people himself, but still he didn't get to grips with their mysteries (even though he was a gent); they'd written in the papers, he heard, that he had disappeared—in regards to everything else; and what's more, he'd robbed a merchant's wife; and it all turned out together: the birth of the infant, liberation, and all the rest—it was all going to happen soon. Morzhov the caretaker was exceedingly surprised at all this buffoonery, but Bessmertnyi the cobbler wasn't surprised: he was at the vodka.

"It's all because they haven't got the right ideas—that's the reason for the thefts, and the gent, and the granddaughter, and universal liberation; that's where the mysterious people come from; they've got no ideas: why, nobody has."

He touched his finger to the string, and—*bam, bam*!

Styopka didn't utter a sound at this: he kept quiet about how he'd had notes from those people even at the Kolpino factory; and all the rest: how and what. Most of all he kept quiet about how he'd struck up an acquaintance at the Kolpino factory with a *circle*, who had meetings just outside Petersburg; and so on. How some of the gentry themselves, if those people could be believed, had been attending those meetings since last year—quite extreme they were: and—all together … Styopka didn't say a word to Bessmertnyi about all this; but he sang a song:

Wimble-wamble—wimble-wed—
Juicy grains of barley:
Cockerel with his comb so red
Pecking while we parley.
Wimble-wamble—wimble-word—
Pretty little Jenny,
Don't you touch the cockerel-bird,
And I'll give you a penny.

At this song Bessmertnyi the cobbler merely shrugged his shoulders; but with all five fingers he thundered out on the guitar: "Wimble-wamble, wimble-wamble: pam-pam-pam-pam."

And he sang:

Oh, never again shall I see you,
I know I shall see you no more:
In my pocket I've kept a wee capsule
In case such a day was in store.

I'll take out that tiny wee capsule
And pour all it holds down my throat:
I'll collapse on the ground, and perhaps you'll
Understand that life's not worth a groat.

And with all five fingers on the guitar: wimble-wamble, wimble-wamble: pam-pam-pam ... But Styopka wasn't going to be outdone: he surprised them.

Over all temptation and all grief
An angel stood with golden trump—
Light, Oh, Light,
Light Immortal!
Immortal, shed thy light upon us—
Before you, we are nought but children:
Thou—art
In heaven.

137

The young gentleman who lived in the attic apartment and had dropped into the caretaker's lodge listened attentively to this: he asked Styopka a lot of questions about the mysterious people: how they announce the end of the world; and when this was to come about; but most of all he asked about that gentleman who'd appeared, Daryalskii—and the why's and wherefore's. He was a skinny gentleman to look at: clearly wasn't well; and from time to time the gentleman downed a glass, so that Styopka had some words of remonstrance for him:

"You're a sickly gentleman; and from tobacco and from vodka you'll soon be kaput: I used to drink myself, sinner that I am: but now I've taken the oath. It's from tobacco and vodka that it all started; and I know who's making us drink: the Japanese!"

"How do you know?"

"About vodka? First it was Count Lev Nikolaevich Tolstoi—have you had a read of his book *The First Distiller?*—who said that; and then those same people near Petersburg say so."

"And how do you know about the Japanese?"

"About the Japanese, that's common knowledge: everybody knows about the Japanese ... And if you remember, there was that hurricane that passed over Moscow, they said—it was, like, the souls of those who'd been killed; back from the other world, like, and swooping over Moscow, because they'd died without absolution. And that means there'll be an uprising in Moscow."

"And what will happen to Petersburg?"

"What d'you think? The Chinese are building some kind of temple!"

The gentleman took Styopka with him to his attic: it was a nasty room the gentleman had; and he was terrified there on his own: so he took Styopka with him; they spent the night there.

He took Styopka with him, sat him down in front of him, took a dog-eared letter out of his wretched trunk; and read the letter to Styopka:

"Your political convictions are as clear as daylight to me: the same old devilry, the same possession by the force of terror; you don't believe me, but I already know: I know what you will shortly learn, what many will shortly learn ... I have been snatched from the unclean claws.

"The great time is approaching: ten years are left until the beginning of the end: remember this, write it down and pass it on to future generations; the most

important of all years is the year 1954. This will concern Russia, because in Russia is the cradle of the Church of Philadelphia; Our Lord Jesus Christ himself blessed this church. I now see why Solovyov spoke of the cult of Sophia. That was in connection—do you remember?—with what the sectarian woman from Nizhnii Novgorod ..."

"And so on ... and so on ... "

Styopka made snuffling noises, and the gentleman went on reading the letter: he was a long time reading it.

"So that's it—right. And what gentleman wrote that?"

"He's abroad, he's a political exile."

"Oh, I see."

"What's going to happen, Styopka?"

"What I've heard is that first of all there'll be killings, and then general discontent; afterwards there'll be all kinds of diseases—plague, famine, and then, the cleverest people say, all kinds of disturbances: the Chinese will rise up against themselves: there will be turmoil among the Mohammedans, but nothing will come of that."

"Well, and after that?"

"Well, everything else will come together at the end of 1912; only then in 1913 . But what! There is a certain prophecy, master: let us take heed, they say ... the sword will be raised against us ... and the crown will go to the Japanese: and then again—the birth of a new child. And they say that the Emperor of Prussia ... Anyway. Here's a prophecy for you: we must build Noah's Ark!"

"How do we build it?"

"It's all right, master, we'll see: you whisper it to me, I'll whisper it to you."

"But what are we whispering about?"

"It's all about the same thing: the second coming of Christ."

"That's enough; that's all nonsense ... "

"Even so, come, Lord Jesus!"

CHAPTER THREE

In which it is described how Nikolai Apollonovich Ableukhov comes a cropper in his enterprise.

> *Though he's an ordinary fellow,*
> *Not some sub-standard Don Juan,*
> *Nor yet a demon, nor a gypsy,*
> *But just a metropolitan man,*
> *The like of whom we meet in thousands,*
> *Not by his beauty nor his brains*
> *Distinguished from us other swains.*
> A Pushkin

A ceremony

IN A CERTAIN IMPORTANT PLACE a spectacle occurred, important in the extreme; the spectacle occurred, that is to say, it took place.

On the occasion of this event there appeared in the aforementioned place extraordinary people in embroidered uniforms and with extraordinarily serious faces; they turned up in the right place, as it were.

This was a day of extraordinary things. It was, of course, clear. From the very earliest hours the sun had been sparkling in the sky: and everything began to sparkle that could sparkle: the Petersburg rooftops, the Petersburg spires, the Petersburg domes.

Somewhere firing was heard.

If you had found time to cast a glance at that important place you would have seen only lacquer, only lustre; the gleam on the mirror-like windows; well, of course, the gleam through the mirror-like windows, too; on the columns—gleam; on the parquet—gleam; at the entrance—gleam too; in a word, lacquer, lustre and gleam!

And that is why from an early hour at the most varied points in the capital of the Russian Empire all ranks, from the third class up to and including the first, silver-haired sages with perfumed side-whiskers and pates gleaming like lacquer energetically donned their starch, as though it were some knightly armour; and thus clad in white, they took from little cupboards their red-lacquered boxes reminiscent of ladies' jewellery cases; an aged yellow fingernail pressed the spring, and as a result a red lacquer lid sprang open with an agreeable elasticity, elegantly revealing its dazzling star on a bed of soft velvet; at the same time an equally grey-haired valet would bring in a coat hanger on which were to be seen firstly: a pair of dazzlingly white trousers; secondly: a lustrous black uniform with a gilded breast; a bald pate blazing like lacquer bent over to those white trousers, and a little grey-haired old man, without wheezing, clothed himself, on top of the pair of white, white trousers, in a uniform of bright-black lustre with a gilded breast, on to which the silver of his hair tumbled aromatically; he then wound round himself diagonally a bright-red satin ribbon, if he was a knight of the order of St Anna; if, however, he was a knight of a higher order, then his sparkling breast would be adorned by a ribbon of blue. After this festive ceremony the corresponding star took its place on the golden breast, the sword was attached, the three-cornered hat with its plumes was taken out of a specially shaped cardboard box, and the grey-haired decorated knight—himself all gleam and tremor—set off in his lacquered black carriage to the place where everything was gleam and tremor; to the extraordinarily important place where stood an array of extraordinarily important people with extraordinarily solemn faces. This brilliant array, dressed in ranks by the rod of the master of ceremonies, comprised the central axis of our wheel of state.

This was a day of extraordinary things; and it was bound, of course, to shine; and shine it did, obviously.

Right from the early morning all darkness disappeared, and there was light whiter than electricity, the light of day; and in that light everything began to sparkle that could sparkle: the Petersburg rooftops, the Petersburg spires, the Petersburg domes.

At noon a cannon shot rang out.

On that extraordinarily bright morning, from the dazzling white sheets that suddenly soared up from the bed in the dazzling bedroom, out leapt a figure—a small figure, all in white; somehow the figure resembled a circus-rider. This brisk figure began, in accordance with time-hallowed tradition, to strengthen its body with Swedish gymnastics—arms apart, arms together—and then squatting down on its haunches up to twelve (or more) times. After this wholesome exercise the figure sprayed its bare skull and its hands with eau de cologne (triple strength, from the Petersburg chemical laboratory).

Further, after performing ablutions on skull, hands, chin, ears and neck with fresh tap water, after replenishing his organism with coffee brought by way of exception to his room, Apollon Apollonovich Ableukhov, like all the other ageing dignitaries, confidently fastened himself this day in starch, drawing through the opening of his breastplate of a shirt front two astonishing ears and a bald pate gleaming like lacquer. After this, going through to his dressing room, Apollon Apollonovich took from a cupboard (as did all the other ageing dignitaries) his red-lacquered boxes, where lay, beneath the lid on a bed of soft velvet, all the rare and precious medals. For him, as for others (smaller than others), a lustrous uniform with a breast of gold was brought in; white trousers of heavy cloth were brought in, a pair of white gloves, a specially shaped cardboard box, the black scabbard of a sword, over which a silver fringe dangled from the hilt; under the pressure of a yellow fingernail all ten red-lacquered lids flew open, and from those lids were extracted: a White Eagle, the corresponding star and a blue ribbon; finally an item of bejewelled insignia was extracted; all of this took its place on the embroidered bosom. Apollon Apollonovich stood before the mirror, gold and white (all gleam and tremor!), with his left hand holding his sword to his hip, and with his right—holding to his chest the plumed three-cornered hat and the pair of white gloves. In this tremulous state Apollon Apollonovich hastened the length of the corridor.

But in the drawing room the senator for some reason held back in perplexity; he was evidently struck by the extraordinary pallor of his son's face and his dishevelled appearance.

On this day Nikolai Apollonovich had risen earlier than he was wont; indeed, Nikolai Apollonovich had not slept at all that night: late in the evening a cab had come hurtling up to the entrance of the yellow house; Nikolai Apollonovich had jumped from the cab in consternation and begun to ring at the door for all he was worth; and when the grey, gold-braided doorman had opened the door to him, then Nikolai Apollonovich, without taking off his overcoat, stumbling over its flaps, had run up the stairs, and then—run through a series of empty rooms; and his door had clicked shut behind him. Soon some shadows started walking by the yellow house. Nikolai Apollonovich kept striding around in his room; at two o'clock in the morning footsteps could still be heard in Nikolai Apollonovich's room, they could be heard at half-past-two, at three, at four.

Unwashed and heavy-eyed, Nikolai Apollonovich sat sullenly by the fireplace in his bright-coloured gown. Apollon Apollonovich, all radiance and tremor, stopped involuntarily, his brilliance reflected in the parquet and the mirrors; he stood on the background of a pier glass, surrounded by a family of plump-cheeked cupids, who had thrust their flaming torches into golden wreaths; and Apollon Apollonovich's hand drummed something on the incrustation of the side-table. Nikolai Apollonovich, suddenly coming to his senses, jumped up, turned round and unintentionally screwed up his eyes: he was blinded by the little gold and white old man.

The little gold and white old man was his papa; but at that moment Nikolai Apollonovich experienced no surge of familial feelings at all; he experienced something quite the contrary, perhaps that which he had experienced in his study; in his study Nikolai Apollonovich had been committing acts of terrorism on himself—number one upon number two: the socialist upon the aristocrat; the corpse upon the lover; in his study Nikolai Apollonovich had been cursing his mortal nature and, inasmuch as he was the image and likeness of his father, he cursed his father. It was clear that his godlike side was bound to hate his father; but perhaps his mortal nature loved his father all the same? Nikolai Apollonovich would hardly admit that to himself. Love? … I do not know whether that word is appropriate here. It was as though Nikolai Apollonovich knew his father sensually, knew him down to the tiniest inflections, to the imperceptible quivering of the most inexpressible feelings; and beyond that: sensually he was his father's absolute equal; he was most of all astonished by the fact that psychically he could not tell where he finished and where in him the spirit of the senator began, the bearer of those sparkling bejewelled insignia that glistened on the gleaming leaves of his embroidered breast. In a flash he not so much imagined, as rather experienced himself in that magnificent uniform; what would he feel at the sight of an unshaven lout like himself in a multicoloured Bukhara dressing gown; it would seem to him a breach of etiquette. Nikolai Apollonovich understood that he would feel disgust, and that in his own way his father would be right to feel disgust, and that his parent was feeling such disgust precisely here and now. He also understood that it was a mixture of anger and shame that made him jump up so quickly in front of the little gold and white old man:

"Good morning, Papa!"

But the senator, continuing sensually in his son, feeling instinctively, perhaps, something not entirely alien to him (like the voice of doubts he had fostered once—in his days as a professor), imagined in his turn himself in deliberate déshabillé, contemplating his upstart careerist of a son, all in gold and white—in front of his parent's déshabillé—began to blink his eyes fearfully with a naiveté exaggerated beyond all reason, and answered merrily and with especial familiarity:

"My respects to you!"

Probably the bearer of bejewelled insignia had no knowledge of his own conclusion, as he continued in the psyche of his son. In both of them logic was conclusively developed to the detriment of the psyche. Their psyche appeared to them as chaos, from which nothing but surprises could be born; but when the two of them came into contact psychically, they resembled two dark vent holes into an utter abyss, turned to face each other; and from one abyss to the other blew a most unpleasant draught; both of them felt that draught as they stood in front of each other; and the thoughts of both mingled, so that the son could no doubt have continued his father's thought.

They both lowered their heads.

This unaccountable intimacy was least of all like love; Nikolai Apollonovich's consciousness, at all events, knew no such love. Nikolai Apollonovich felt this unaccountable intimacy as a shameful physiological act; at that moment he might have adopted the same attitude to the discharge of familial duties as he would to the natural discharges of the organism: such discharges are not a matter of love, merely of disgust.

A helpless frog-like expression appeared on his face.

"Are you taking part in the parade today?"

Fingers grasped fingers; and fingers withdrew. Apollon Apollonovich evidently wanted to express something, most likely to give a verbal explanation of the reasons for his appearance in this uniform; and he also wanted to ask a question about the reason for his son's unnatural pallor, or at the very least to inquire why his son had appeared at such an unaccustomed hour. But his words somehow became stuck in his throat, and Apollon Apollonovich only had an attack of coughing. At that moment the servant appeared and announced that the carriage was ready. Apollon Apollonovich, gladdened by something, gave the servant a grateful nod and began to bustle about.

"I see, I see: very good!"

Apollon Apollonovich, all gleam and tremor, flew past his son; soon his footsteps ceased to sound.

Nikolai Apollonovich gazed after his parent: a smile reappeared on his face; abyss turned away from abyss; the draught ceased to blow.

Nikolai Apollonovich Ableukhov recalled Apollon Apollonovich Ableukhov's last authoritative circular, which comprised a total contradiction of Nikolai Apollonovich's own plans; and Nikolai Apollonovich came to the decisive conclusion that his father, Apollon Apollonovich, was nothing more than an out-and-out scoundrel ...

Soon the little old man was climbing a tremulous staircase, which was carpeted completely in bright-red material: on this bright-red material his short legs began to bend and with unnatural rapidity to construct angles, which quickly calmed Apollon Apollonovich's spirit too; he loved symmetry in everything.

Soon many other little old men, just like himself, came up to him: side-whiskers, beards, bald patches, moustaches, chins, golden-breasted and bestrewn with medals, directing the movement of our wheel of state; and over by the staircase balustrade stood a golden-breasted group, discussing in a thunderous bass the fateful passage of that wheel over the potholes, until the master of ceremonies, passing with his rod, invited them to form up in a line.

As soon as the extraordinary inspection and graciously uttered words were done, the little old men once again swarmed together— in the great hall, in the anteroom, by the columns of the balustrade. For some reason one sparkling swarm stood out, from the centre of which was heard the sound of tireless, but restrained voices; a deep bass emerged from the centre of the group, like a velvet bumblebee of immense dimensions; he was shorter than all the others, and when he was surrounded by golden-breasted old men, he could not be seen at all. And when Count W, the size of a folklore *bogatyr*, with a blue ribbon across his shoulder, passing his hand across his grey locks, went up to the cluster of old men with a certain nonchalance and screwed his eyes up, he saw that this humming centre was Apollon Apollonovich. At once Apollon Apollonovich broke off his speech, and without marked cordiality, but with cordiality all the same, extended his hand to that fateful hand that had just signed the terms of a most important treaty: the treaty had been signed—in America. Count W bent down gently to the bare skull that came up only to his shoulders, and a hissing witticism slipped nimbly into the ear of pale-green tints; the witticism, however, evoked no smile: nor did the golden-breasted little old men around them smile; and the cluster dissolved of its own accord. Apollon Apollonovich went down the stairs in the company of this dignitary of folkloric appearance; in front of Apollon Apollonovich Count W walked bent double; above them descended sparkling old men, below them—the hook-nosed ambassador of a distant country, a little red-lipped old man, oriental; between them Apollon Apollonovich—small, gold and white, erect as a pole—descended on the fiery background of the carpet that covered the staircase.

At that hour on the Field of Mars a great parade was taking place; a square of the imperial guard was standing there.

From afar, through the crowd, beyond the bristling steel of the bayonets of Preobrazhenskii, Semyonovskii and Izmailovskii grenadiers, rows of cavalry on white horses could be seen; it seemed that one unbroken, golden mirror, reflecting all the rays, had set off slowly from one point to another; bright regimental banners fluttered in the air; silver wind bands wept and called melodically from the distance: a line of squadrons could be seen there—of cuirassiers and cavalry-guards; then a single squadron could be seen—of cuirassiers and cavalry-guards; then the gallop could be seen of horsemen from the line of squadrons—cuirassiers and cavalry-guards—fair-haired, huge and clad in armour, in smooth, tight-fitting, white kidskin breeches, in sparkling golden breastplates, in glittering helmets, surmounted by a silver dove or by a double-headed eagle; the horsemen from the line of squadrons pranced; the lines of the squadron pranced. And, surmounted by a metal dove, Baron Ommergau with his pale whiskers danced on his steed in front of them; and surmounted by an identical dove Count Aven pranced arrogantly—cuirassiers, cavalry-guards! And from the dust, like a blood-red cloud, their plumes lowered, the hussars galloped past on their grey mounts; their pelisses showing scarlet, their fur capes showing white in the wind behind them; the earth hummed, and sabres clanged as they were raised: and above the roar, above the dust, there suddenly rushed a stream of bright silver. The red hussar-cloud flew past to the side, and the parade ground was emptied. And again, out there in the expanses, there arose now azure horsemen, rendering to the distances and to the sun the silver of their armour: that must have been a division of gendarmerie of the guard: from afar it trumpeted a complaint at the crowd; but it was hidden from view by brown dust; a drum rattled; the infantry went past.

To the meeting

After the dank slush of early October the Petersburg rooftops, the Petersburg spires and, last but not least, the Petersburg domes bathed blindingly one day in the frosty October sun.

The Angel Peri was on her own that day; her husband was not there: he was taking charge of provisions—out there somewhere; the uncombed angel flitted around in her pink kimono between vases of chrysanthemums and Mount Fujiyama; the folds of the kimono flapped like satin wings, and the owner of the kimono, the aforesaid angel, still hypnotised by a single idea, nibbled now at her handkerchief, now at the end of her black plait. Nikolai Apollonovich remained, of course, a cad to end all cads, but the newspaper contributor Neintelpfain—he too!—was a scoundrel. The angel's feelings were utterly in tatters.

In order to bring her tattered feelings into some semblance of order, the Angel Peri curled up on her quilted *causeuse* and opened her book: Henri Besançon *Man and His Bodies*. The angel had opened this book many times before, but … and but: the book had slipped from her hands, the Angel Peri's eyes had swiftly closed, and in her tiny nose vigorous life had awakened: it snuffled and snorted.

No, today she was not going to fall asleep: Baroness R R had already inquired about the book once; and learning that the book had been read, she had slyly asked: "So what do you say of it, *ma chère*?" But "*ma chère*" had nothing to say; and Baroness R R shook a finger at her: it wasn't without reason, after all, that the inscription in the book began with the words: "My Devachanic friend", and the inscription ended with the signature: "Baroness R R—frail shell, but with a Buddhist spark".

But—come on, come on: what is this "Devachanic friend", "shell", "Buddhist spark"? That is what Henri Besançon would explain. And this time Sofia Petrovna would really immerse herself in Henri Besançon; but no sooner had she popped her nose into Henri Besançon, sensing distinctly in the pages the smell of the Baroness herself (the Baroness used opopanax), when the bell rang and in like a whirlwind flew Varvara Evgrafovna from the Women's Courses: the Angel Peri did not have time to conceal the treasured book properly; and the angel was caught *in flagrante*.

"What's this?—" Varvara Evgrafovna cried out sternly, placed her pince-nez on her nose and bent over the book …

"What's this you've got? Who gave it you?"

"Baroness R R … "

"Well, of course … What is it?"

"Henri Besançon … "

"You mean Annie Besant … *Man and His Bodies*? … What drivel is this? … Have you read Karl Marx's *Manifesto*?"

Blue eyes blinked in anxiety, while crimson lips pouted in offence.

The bourgeoisie, sensing its demise, has seized upon mysticism; let's leave the heavens to the sparrows and from the realm of necessity create the realm of freedom.

And over her pince-nez Varvara Evgrafovna cast her incontestable gaze victoriously at the angel: and the Angel Peri blinked her eyes even more helplessly; this angel had equal respect for Varvara Evgrafovna and Baroness R R. And now she was being asked to choose between them. But Varvara Evgrafovna fortunately did not create a scene; crossing her legs, she polished her pince-nez.

"This is what I've come about … You're going to be at the Tsukatovs' ball, aren't you?"

"I am," the angel answered guiltily.

"This is the point: according to rumours that have reached me, our common acquaintance Ableukhov is also going to be at the ball."

The angel flushed.

"Well, then: you just hand him this letter." Varvara Evgrafovna slipped a letter into the angel's hands.

"Just hand it him; that's all there is to it: will you?"

"I'll … I'll do it … "

"That's it then, but I've no time to be kicking my heels here: I'm on my way to a meeting … "

"Varvara Evgrafovna, my dear, take me with you."

"Aren't you afraid? There may be violence … "

"No, do take me, do take me—please … "

"All right: if you like, let's go. Only you're going to dress and everything, put on your make-up … You really must be quick … "

"Oh, at once: I'll only be a second! … "

"Oh, my goodness, hurry, hurry … Mavrushka, my corset! … The black woollen dress—that one: and the shoes—you know, those that … No, not those: the high-heeled ones." And skirts rustled as they fell: the pink kimono flew across the table on to the bed … Mavrushka got mixed up: Mavrushka knocked a chair over …

"No, not like that, tighter: still tighter … You've got stumps instead of hands … Where are the laces—eh, eh? How many times do I have to tell you?" And the whalebone of the corset creaked; and trembling hands were quite unable to fix on her head the black night of her plaits …

Sofia Petrovna Likhutina, with a bone hairpin in her teeth, squinted: she squinted at the letter; on the letter there was a clear inscription: "*to Nikolai Apollonovich Ableukhov.*"

The fact that she would meet "him" tomorrow at the Tsukatovs' ball, would talk to him, hand him the letter—was both frightening and painful: there was something fateful in it—no, better not to think, not to think!

A rebellious black strand of hair tumbled from the back of her head.

Yes, the letter. On the letter it said quite distinctly: "*to Nikolai Apollonovich Ableukhov.*" There was one strange thing about it, though: that handwriting was Lippanchenko's handwriting ... What nonsense!

Now in her black woollen dress that fastened at the back she skipped out of the bedroom:

"Well, let's go, let's go ... By the way, that letter ... Who's it from? ... "

"?"

"All right, never mind, never mind: I'm ready."

Why was she in such a hurry to go to the meeting? In order to make inquiries on the way, to ask questions, to find things out?

What could she ask?

At the entrance they ran into the Ukrainian Lippanchenko:

"Well I never: where are you off to?"

In irritation Sofia Petrovna waved both plush-clad hand and muff:

"I'm going to a meeting, a meeting."

But the cunning Ukrainian persisted:

"Fine: I'll go with you."

Varvara Evgrafovna flushed and stood still: she stared at the Ukrainian.

"I think I know you: don't you rent a room ... from Manponshi?"

At that the shameless cunning Ukrainian became extremely embarrassed: he started huffing and puffing suddenly, he took a step backwards, raised his hat, and left them alone.

"Tell me, who is that unpleasant type?"

"Lippanchenko."

"That's not true at all: he's not Lippanchenko, he's a Greek from Odessa: Mavrokordato; he visits the room through the wall from me; I advise you not to receive him."

But Sofia Petrovna was not listening. Mavrokordato, Lippanchenko— what did it matter ... Now the letter, the letter ...

Noble, elegant and pale

They walked along the Moika.

To their left the last gold and the last crimson fluttered in the leaves of the garden; on coming closer, a blue tit could be seen; a rustling thread stretched submissively from the garden on to the stones, to wind and chase between the feet of a passing pedestrian, and to murmur as it wove from leaves a red-and-yellow web of words.

"*Uuuu-uuu-uuu* ... " resounded in the expanses.

"Can you hear?"

"What is it?"

"*Uuu-uuu.*"

"I can't hear anything ... "

But that sound was resounding quietly in the cities, the forests and the fields, in the suburban expanses of Moscow, Petersburg, Saratov. Did you hear that October song of 1905? That song was not heard before; it will not be heard again ...

"It must be a factory siren: there's a strike somewhere in the factories."

But the factory siren did not sound, there was no wind; and the dog held its peace.

Beneath their feet on the right was the blue of the Moika canal, while behind them above the water the reddish line of the Embankment stonework rose up to be crowned with the lace of a cast-iron lattice: the same bright three-storeyed building from the time of Alexander stood supported by five stone columns; and between the columns the entrance glowered; above the first floor ran the same old strip of ornamental stucco: circle after circle— plaster circles everywhere.

Between the canal and the building an overcoat flew past in a privately-owned carriage, hiding the freezing tip of its arrogant nose in a beaver collar; a bright-yellow cap-band bobbed up and down, and the soft pink top of the coachman's hat swayed slightly. Drawing level with Likhutina, the bright-yellow cap-band of Her Majesty's cuirassier soared high above a bald patch: it was Baron Ommau-Ommergau.

In front, where the canal made a bend, there rose the red walls of a church, running away into a tall tower and a green spire; and further to the left, over the jutting stone of a house, the blinding dome of St Isaac's rose severely into the glassy turquoise.

And here was the Embankment: depth, a greenish blue. Far, far away—further than it seemed was right—the islands had sunk down, and were lying low: and the buildings were lying low; the depth, the greenish blue, would surge upon them, wash them all away. And above that greenish blue an unrelenting sunset cast its brilliant crimson blows in all directions: and the Troitskii Bridge turned crimson; and the palace turned crimson too.

Suddenly amidst this depth and greenish blue, on the crimson background of the sunset, a distinct profile emerged: a grey Nikolaevan cloak beat its wings in the wind; and a waxen face was thrown back nonchalantly, lips apart; in the bluish expanses of the Neva the eyes were searching for something they could not find, and swept past her modest little hat; they did not see that hat: they did not see anything—neither her nor Varvara Evgrafovna: they only saw the depth, the greenish blue; they rose and fell again—fell over there, beyond the river, where the shores lay low and the buildings on the islands shone crimson. In front of him ran snuffling a dark, stripy bulldog, carrying its little silver whip in its teeth.

As he drew level he recollected himself, screwed his eyes up slightly, touched his hand to his cap; he said nothing—and went away towards the place where there was nothing but the crimson gleam of buildings.

Sofia Petrovna, with eyes asquint, her face buried in her muff (she was redder than a peony), shook her head helplessly in the direction—not of him, but of the bulldog. But Varvara Evgrafovna simply stared, snorted, fastened her eyes on him.

"Ableukhov?"

"Yes … I think so."

And, hearing the affirmative answer (she was short-sighted herself), Varvara Evgrafovna started whispering excitedly under her breath:

Noble, elegant and pale,
Locks of hair like flax;
Rich in thought and poor in feeling,
N A A—who's that?

Here he was:

An agitator of renown,
Though aristocrat by birth,
But still a hundred times more worth
Than his unworthy clan.

Here he was, who would transform this rotten order, and to whom she (soon, soon) was going to propose common-law marriage once he had fulfilled his designated mission, after which a general, universal explosion would follow: at that point she choked (Varvara Evgrafovna was in the habit of swallowing her saliva too loudly).

"What is it?"

"Nothing: I just thought of a progressive idea."

But Sofia Petrovna was not listening any more: to her own surprise she had turned round and now she saw that away over there, beside the jutting wall of the palace that was struck by the Neva's last crimson rays, Nikolai Apollonovich was standing strangely turned towards her, his back arched and his face buried in his collar, so that his student's cap was slipping from his head,: it seemed to her that he was smiling in a most unpleasant way and that at all events he presented a pretty ridiculous figure: wrapped in his overcoat, he seemed both hunched and somehow armless, with the flaps of his coat dancing absurdly in the wind; and when she had seen all this, she swiftly turned her head back again.

For a long time yet he stood there, hunched, smiling in a most unpleasant way, and at all events presenting a pretty ridiculous figure, armless and with the flaps of his coat dancing absurdly in the wind, against the slanting beam of the crimson sunset. But in any case he was not looking at her: how could he with his myopia make out such little figures as they moved away; he laughed to himself and gazed far, far away, further than it seemed was right—where the island buildings sank down, where they were barely outlined in the crimson haze.

But she—she felt like crying: she wanted her husband, Sergei Sergeich Likhutin, to go up to that cad and suddenly punch him in the face with his cypress-wood fist, and utter in this connection his honest word as an officer.

The relentless sunset was casting blow after blow from the very horizon; higher up came a measureless expanse of pink ripples; higher still the clouds, so lately white (now pink), like iridescent dimples in mother-of-pearl, were softly vanishing in the general turquoise; this general turquoise flowed evenly among the fragments of pink mother-of-pearl: soon those fragments, drowning in the heights, as though disappearing into the ocean's depths—would extinguish in the turquoise their oh, so tender glow: blue darkness, the blue-green depths, would surge over everything—houses, granite, water.

And the sunset would be no more.

Comte—Comte—Comte

The servant served the soup. In front of the senator's plate he placed in anticipation the pepper-pot from the cruet.

Apollon Apollonovich appeared in the doorway in his grey jacket; he took his place with equal alacrity; and the servant took the lid from the steaming soup tureen.

The door on the left opened, through the left-hand door Nikolai Apollonovich swiftly dashed in, wearing his student's uniform with all the buttons done up; his uniform had an immensely high collar (from the time of Emperor Alexander the First).

They raised their eyes to each other; and they both felt awkward (they always felt awkward).

Apollon Apollonovich allowed his gaze to wander from object to object; Nikolai Apollonovich experienced his daily confusion: he had two totally unneeded arms hanging from his shoulders on either side of his torso; in an access of fruitless obsequiousness he ran up to his parent and started to rub his slender fingers together (one finger against another).

The daily spectacle awaited the senator: his unnaturally polite son overcame the distance from door to dining table unnaturally quickly, in a few bounds. Apollon Apollonovich hastily stood up (anyone would say, jumped up) to meet his son.

Nikolai Apollonovich tripped over the leg of the table.

Apollon Apollonovich extended to Nikolai Apollonovich his puffy lips; to these puffy lips Nikolai Apollonovich pressed two lips; the lips came into contact with each other; and a usually sweaty hand shook two fingers.

"Good evening, papa!"

155

"My respects to you … "

Apollon Apollonovich sat down. Apollon Apollonovich took hold of the pepper pot. As a rule Apollon Apollonovich put too much pepper in his soup.

"From the university? … "

"No, I went for a walk … "

And a frog-like expression crossed the grinning mouth of the deferential son, whose face we have had an opportunity to examine in isolation from the various grimaces, smiles or gestures of courtesy which constituted the curse of Nikolai Apollonovich's life, if only because of the Greek mask not a trace remained; these smiles, grimaces, or simply gestures of courtesy streamed in an unceasing torrent before the fluttering gaze of his absent-minded papa; and the hand that raised the spoon to his lips was clearly shaking, spilling the soup.

"Have you come from the Establishment, papa?"

"No, I was at the minister's … "

We saw above how Apollon Apollonovich, sitting in his study, reached the conviction that his son was a thorough villain: thus the sixty-eight-year-old papa performed every day on his own flesh and his own blood a certain, albeit notional, but nonetheless terrorist act.

But those were abstract, study-bound conclusions, which were not brought out into the corridor or, far from it, into the dining room.

"Would you like some pepper, Kolenka?"

"I'd like some salt, Papa … "

Apollon Apollonovich, as he looked at his son, that is to say, as he fluttered round the squirming young philosopher with his restless eyes, in accordance with the tradition of this hour was wont to surrender to a rush of, as it were, paternity, avoiding the study in his thoughts.

"I like pepper: it's tastier with pepper … "

Nikolai Apollonovich, lowering his eyes to his plate, drove from his memory the insistent associations: the sunset on the Neva and the inexpressibility of the pink ripples, the tender glow of mother-of-pearl, the blue-green depths; and on the background of that tenderest mother-of-pearl …

"I see! ... "

"I see! ... "

"Very good ... "

Apollon Apollonovich occupied his son (or rather—himself) in conversation.

A heavy silence hung over the table.

Apollon Apollonovich was not troubled in the least by this silence as they took their soup (old people are not troubled by silence, but nervous young people—certainly are) ... Nikolai Apollonovich suffered genuine torment over his plate of cold soup in the quest for a topic of conversation.

And to his own surprise he burst out:

"I've ... just ... "

"What exactly?"

"No ... Nothing in particular ... Doesn't matter ... "

A heavy silence hung over the table.

And again to his own surprise Nikolai Apollonovich burst out (he was so on edge!):

"I've ... just ... "

Only just what? He had still not thought up a continuation to the words that had slipped out; and there was no thought to add to "I've ... just ... " And Nikolai Apollonovich faltered ...

"What can I think up," he wondered, "to add to 'I've just'." And he couldn't think of anything.

Apollon Apollonovich, meanwhile, disturbed by this second senseless verbal debacle on his son's part, suddenly raised his eyes questioningly, sternly, capriciously, indignant at his 'mumbling'.

"Come now, what are you saying?"

But in his son's head senseless words were spinning wildly.

"Perception ... "

"Apperception ... "

"Pepper's not pepper, but a term: terminology ... "

"-ology, logic ... "

And suddenly out came:

"Cohen's Logic ... "

Relieved that he had found a way out to some words, Nikolai Apollonovich blurted out with a smile:

"I've ... just ... read in Cohen's *Theorie der Erfahrung* ... "

And came to a halt again.

"So, what book is that, Kolenka?"

Apollon Apollonovich involuntarily observed, in addressing his son, the traditions of childhood; and in his intercourse with this thorough villain he called the thorough villain "Kolenka, sonny, old chap" and even—"darling ... "

"Cohen, a most important representative of European Kantianism."

"Did you say—Comteianism?"

"Kantianism, papa ... "

"Kan-ti-an-ism?"

"Yes, exactly ... "

"But surely Kant was refuted by Comte? It's Comte you're talking about?"

"No, not Comte, papa, I'm talking about Kant! ... "

"But Kant isn't scientific ... "

"It's Comte who isn't scientific ... "

"I don't know, I don't know, old chap: in our days people didn't think like that ... "

Apollon Apollonovich, tired and not in the best of spirits, slowly rubbed his eyes with his cold fists, absent-mindedly repeating:

"Comte ... "

"Comte ... "

"Comte ... "

Lustre, lacquer, gleam and red flashes of some kind began to jump about in his eyes (Apollon Apollonovich always saw before his eyes two different kinds, so to speak, of space: our space and another space, made up of a whirling network of lines, which became golden at night).

Apollon Apollonovich reckoned that his brain was once again suffering from very severe rushes of blood, occasioned by his very severe haemorrhoidal condition of the past week; his cranium slumped against the dark back of his chair, into its dark depths; his dark-blue eyes took on a fixed, interrogative gaze:

"Comte … Yes, Kant … "

He thought for a moment and turned his eyes on to his son:

"So what book was that, Kolenka?"

It was through an instinctive cunning that Nikolai Apollonovich had initiated a conversation about Cohen; a conversation about Cohen was the most neutral conversation; through this conversation other conversations were avoided; and a certain explanation was postponed (from day to day—from month to month). And moreover: the habit of instructive conversations had been retained in Nikolai Apollonovich's soul since childhood: ever since his childhood Apollon Apollonovich had encouraged his son in such conversations: when he came home from school Nikolai Apollonovich used to explain to his papa with apparent enthusiasm the details of the *cohort, testudo* and *turris*; he explained all the other details of the Gallic War too; then Apollon Apollonovich listened with pleasure to his son, indulgently encouraging his school interests. In later times Apollon Apollonovich even used to put his hand on Kolenka's shoulder.

"You ought to read Mill's *Logic*, Kolenka: it's a very useful book, you know … Two volumes … I read it from cover to cover once upon a time … "

And Nikolai Apollonovich, who had only just devoured Sigwart's *Logic*, nevertheless turned up at tea in the dining room with a vast volume in his hand. Apollon Apollonovich gently asked, for no apparent reason:

"What's that you're reading, Kolenka?"

"Mill's *Logic*, papa."

"I see, I see … Very good!"

And now, utterly divided, they came back unwittingly to old memories: their dinner often ended with an instructive conversation …

Apollon Apollonovich had once been professor of the philosophy of law: at that time he had read many things right through. All of that—had passed without trace: Apollon Apollonovich found the elegant pirouettes of filial logic inconsequentially burdensome. Apollon Apollonovich was not able to raise objections to his son.

However, he thought: "You have to be fair to Kolenka: his mental apparatus is precisely tuned."

At the same time Nikolai Apollonovich had the pleasant sensation that his parent was an extraordinarily attentive listener.

And a semblance of friendship usually arose between them by the dessert: they were sometimes sorry to break off their dinner-time conversation, as thought they were each afraid of the other; as though each of them, alone, were sternly signing a death-warrant for the other.

They both rose: they began to stroll along the enfilade of rooms together; white busts of Archimedes rose into the shadows: one here, one there, and there another; the enfilade of rooms led into blackness; from the distance, from the drawing room, came red-tinged flashes of a colour-ferment; from the distance came a crackle of firelight.

Just like this they had once wandered along the empty enfilade—a little boy and … a still fond father; the fond father still patted the fair-haired little boy on the shoulder; then the fond father would take the little boy up to the window and raise his finger towards the stars:

"The stars are a long way away, Kolenka: a ray of light from the nearest star takes two years and more to reach the earth … That's how it is, old chap!" And once the fond father even wrote a little verse for his son:

> *Silly laddie, simple chap,*
> *Little Nicky's dancing:*
> *On his head a dunce's cap,*
> *On a horse he's prancing.*

And when the outlines of the side-tables emerged from the shadows, a ray from the Embankment lights shot through the windowpanes: the tables began to gleam with their incrustations. Was it really true that the father had come to the conclusion that the blood of his blood—was the blood of a scoundrel? Or that the son had made a mockery of his advancing years?

> *Silly laddie, simple chap,*
> *Little Nicky's dancing:*

On his head a dunce's cap,
On a horse he's prancing.

Had that really happened—perhaps it had not happened ... anywhere, ever?

Now they both sat on the satin drawing room couch, drawing out without purpose meaningless words: they stared each other in the eye expectantly, and the red flame of the fireplace breathed warmth on the wallpaper; clean-shaven, grey and old,

Apollon Apollonovich was outlined against the flickering flame with his ears and his jacket: it was with just such a face that he had been depicted on the cover of a gutter-rag on the background of a burning Russia. Stretching out his lifeless hand and not looking his son in the eye, Apollon Apollonovich asked in a downcast voice:

"Do you often have visits, old chap, from that ... mmm ... that ... "

"Who do you mean, Papa?"

"That, what's his name ... young man ... "

"Young man?"

"Yes—with the little black moustache."

Nikolai Apollonovich curled his lip and wrung his suddenly sweaty hands ...

"The one you found in my study just recently?"

"Yes—that one ... "

"Alexandr Ivanovich Dudkin! ... No ... Of course not ... "

And as soon as he had said, "of course not", Nikolai Apollonovich thought:

"Now why did I say 'Of course not'?"

And after a moment's reflection, he added:

"Now and then, he drops in."

"If you ... if you don't mind my asking, I ... suppose ... "

"What, papa?"

"I suppose he comes to see you on ... university business?"

"However ... if my question is, so to speak, out of place ... "

"Why should it be? ... "

"It's not important ... he seems a pleasant young man: not well off, you can tell ... "

"A student, is he? ... "

"A student."

"At the university?"

"Yes, the university ... "

"Not the technical institute? ... "

"No, papa ... "

Apollon Apollonovich knew his son was lying; Apollon Apollonovich looked at the clock; Apollon Apollonovich stood up indecisively. Nikolai Apollonovich was painfully aware of his hands; in his embarrassment Apollon Apollonovich's eyes began to wander:

"Yes ... There are many special branches of knowledge: every specialism is deep—you're right. Do you know, Kolenka, I'm tired."

Apollon Apollonovich made as if to ask a question of his son, who was rubbing his hands together ... He stood for a moment, gave a look, and ... did not ask, but lowered his gaze: Nikolai Apollonovich had a momentary feeling of shame.

Apollon Apollonovich mechanically extended to his son his puffy lips: and his hand shook ... two fingers.

"Good night, Papa!"

"My respects to you!"

Somewhere to one side was heard the scratching and rustling of a mouse, and then its sudden squeal.

Soon the door of the senator's study opened: candle in hand Apollon Apollonovich hurried along to the room that is comparable with no other, to immerse himself ... in the newspaper.

Nikolai Apollonovich went up to the window.

A patch of phosphorescence mistily and madly rushed across the sky; the distances of the Neva were shrouded in a phosphorescent gleam so that the level planes of water glinted green in their soundless flight, giving off now here, now there a spark of gold; a little red light would flash out here and there on the water, twinkle for a moment, and withdraw into the pervasive phosphorescent murk. Beyond the Neva the huge buildings of the islands rose darkly and thrust into the mist their wanly shining eyes—endlessly, soundlessly, tormentingly: and it seemed they were weeping. Up above—dim outlines stretched out madly their ragged arms; swarm after swarm, they rose over the waves of the Neva; and the patch of phosphorescence hurled itself at them from the sky. Only in one place, untouched by chaos, where by day the Troitskii Bridge arches across, huge nests of diamonds pierced the shroud of mist above the glistening swarm of ringed and shining snakes; coiling and uncoiling, the snakes slid away in a sparkling string; then they rose to the surface from their dive in starry streams.

Nikolai Apollonovich lost himself in contemplation of those streams.

The Embankment was empty. Occasionally the black shadow of a policeman went by, standing out black in the bright mist and then again merging with it; the buildings across the Neva also stood out black and disappeared in the mist; the spire of the Peter and Paul Cathedral stood out black and was lost in the mist.

For a long time the shadow of a woman had been standing out black in the mist: poised by the parapet, it did not disappear into the mist, but gazed straight at the windows of the yellow house. Nikolai Apollonovich grinned a most unpleasant grin: putting his pince-nez to his nose, he scrutinised the shadow; Nikolai Apollonovich stared wide-eyed, with a sensual cruelty, at this shadow; joy distorted his features.

No, no: it wasn't her; but she too, like that shadow, was wandering around the yellow house: he had seen her; everything was in turmoil in his soul. No doubt she did love him; but a fatal, terrible vengeance was in store for her.

The chance black shadow had already merged with the mist.

In the depths of the dark corridor a metal latch clicked, in the depths of the dark corridor a light glimmered: Apollon Apollonovich, candle in hand, was returning from the place that is comparable with no other: his mouse-grey dressing gown, his grey, shaven cheeks and the immense contours of his utterly lifeless ears were clearly visible from afar, etched in the dancing lights, disappearing from the circle of light into utter darkness; from utter darkness Apollon Apollonovich passed on to the doors of his study, only to drop into utter darkness once more; and from the open door the place of his passing gaped gloomily.

Nikolai Apollonovich thought: "It's time."

Nikolai Apollonovich knew that today's meeting would last till night, that *she* was on her way to the meeting (the guarantee of that was the company of Varvara Evgrafovna: Varvara Evgrafovna took everyone to meetings). Nikolai Apollonovich reflected that two hours and more had passed since he had met them on the way to the gloomy building; and now he thought: "It's time … "

The meeting

In the spacious hallway of the gloomy building there was a desperate crush.

The crush carried the Angel Peri, rocking her backwards and forwards between people's chests and backs, as she desperately tried to make her way through to Varvara Evgrafovna: but Varvara Evgrafovna, taking no notice, was over there, pushing and struggling, thrusting her way: and suddenly vanished in the crush; together with her the chance of asking about the letter also vanished. But what of the letter! The crimson spots of sunset still glinted in her eyes: and— away over there: strangely turned towards her beside the jutting palace wall that was struck by the Neva's last brilliant crimson rays, his back arched and his face buried in his collar, Nikolai Apollonovich was standing with a most unpleasant smile. At all events he presented a pretty ridiculous figure: he seemed both hunched and somehow armless with the flaps of his coat dancing absurdly in the wind; she felt like bursting into tears from the bitter insult, as though he had struck her painfully with the silver whip, that same silver whip that the dark, stripy bulldog had carried past, snorting, in its teeth; she wanted her husband, Sergei Sergeich Likhutin, to go up to that cad and suddenly punch him in the face with his cypress-wood fist, and in this connection utter his word as an officer; in her eyes the little Neva clouds still glittered, like little dents in broken mother-of-pearl, amongst which the universal turquoise smoothly flowed.

But in the crowd that tender glow was extinguished, and from all sides surged chests, backs and faces, black darkness—into the misty-yellow murk.

And all the time there was a press of nondescripts, of shaggy hats, young ladies: body pressed against body; a nose was crushed against a back; a chest was obstructed by a pretty schoolgirl's head, while a second-former squealed among the feet; under pressure from behind an immoderately extended nose disappeared in one place into someone's coiffure and was pierced by a hatpin, while in another the sharp angle of an elbow threatened to smash someone's chest; taking coats off was beyond the strength of anyone; the air was full of steamy vapour, lit by candles (as it later turned out, the electricity supply had suddenly broken down—the electricity station had evidently started misbehaving: soon its misbehaviour would be of long duration.)

Everyone pressed, everyone struggled: Sofia Petrovna, of course, got herself stuck at the bottom of the staircase for a long time, while Varvara Evgrafovna, of course, had struggled out and was now thrusting and pushing and struggling right up near the top; alongside her an extremely respectable Jewish gentleman in a lambskin hat and spectacles and with a broad grey streak in his hair had also struggled out: turning back, he tugged in utter horror at the tails of his own coat; and could not pull them free; and, failing to pull them free, he started to shout:

"A fine publikum! It's not a publikum, it's a pig-sty, real R-r-russian! ... "

"What'ya doing here, then, what d'you want in our R-r-russia?" came a cry from somewhere below.

This was a Jewish socialist who was a member of the *Bund* having it out with another Jew who was not a member of the *Bund*, but still a socialist.

In the hall body sat on body, body pressed against body; bodies rocked; they became excited and shouted to each other that there, and there, and there as well the strike was under way, that there, and there, and there as well the strike was being prepared, that they were going to strike—here, here and here: they were going to strike right on this spot; and—not to yield a yard!

First an intelligent party worker had his say about this, after him a student repeated the same thing; after the student came a young lady from the Women's Courses; after her—a politically aware proletarian, but when a politically unaware proletarian, a representative of the lumpen-proletariat, tried to repeat the same, then such a deep voice thundered out across the room, as though issuing from a barrel, that everyone shuddered:

"Com-rades! ... I'm a ... you might say, a poor man—a proletarian, com-rades! ... "

Thunderous applause.

"So, then, com-rades! So that means, all this arbitrary stuff by the government is ... I mean to say ... I'm a poor man—and I say: strike, com-rades!"

Thunderous applause (He's right! He's right! Deny him the floor! It's disgusting, ladies and gentlemen! He's drunk!)

"No, I'm not drunk, com-rades! ... I mean, the bourgeoisie have got it coming to them ... you just work and work, and ... Nothing else for it, grab'em by the legs and into the water with'em; that's it ... strike!"

(A blow on the table with his fist: thunderous applause.)

But the chairman denied the worker the floor.

The one who spoke best was a venerable contributor to a certain venerable newspaper, Neintelpfain: as soon as he had spoken, he disappeared. A young lad tried from the fourth step of the platform to declare a boycott against someone: but he was laughed out; what was the point of such trivial things when they were striking there, and there, and there as well, when they were striking right here—and not yielding a yard? And the young lad, almost in tears, came down again from the fourth step of the platform; and then a sixty-five-year-old lady from the *zemstvo* organisation mounted those steps and said to the assembled gathering:

Sow what is good, what is wholesome, eternal,
Sow, and the thanks of the people of Russia
Will come from their hearts.

But the sowers laughed. Then suddenly someone proposed destroying everybody and everything: that was a mystical anarchist. Sofia Petrovna did not hear the anarchist, she was squeezing her way out again, but it was strange: Varvara Evgrafovna had explained to her time and time again that at such meetings the wholesome, the good was always sown, which deserved heartfelt thanks on her part. But it wasn't like that, it wasn't! They had all just laughed desperately at the sixty-five-year-old *zemstvo* lady, who had said just the same to them (about sowing); and then why was it that the seed had produced no shoots in her heart? Just some miserable nettles had pushed their way through; and her head was splitting; whether because she had seen *him* just before, or because she had such a tiny forehead, or because on all sides she met the stares of fanatical faces, who were striking there and there, and had now come to strike right here, to gaze at her from the misty yellow murk and bare their teeth in mockery. And out of that chaos an anger awoke in her that she did not herself understand; she was, after all, a lady, and chaos must not be awoken in ladies; all manner of cruelty is concealed in that chaos, all manner of crime and depravity; then there is a criminal lurking in every lady; something criminal had long been lurking in her as it was.

She was now approaching a corner together with a puny officer who was walking beside her, who in there had aroused smiles and patronising whispers, and who had suddenly taken offence at the boycott declared by the young lad, and had quickly left in high dudgeon—she was approaching a corner, when from the gates of the next house a detachment of Cossacks hurtled out in front of her at full tilt on their unkempt horses; blue, bearded men in shaggy *papakhas* and with rifles at the ready, downright ragamuffins, they pranced by in their saddles, silent, overbearing, impatient—towards that building. A workman who saw all this from the corner ran up to the officer, stretched out his hand to him and began talking breathlessly:

"Officer, excuse me, officer!"

"I'm sorry, I haven't any change … "

"That's not what I'm after: what's going to happen there now? … What's going to happen? … There are defenceless young women there—girl students … "

The officer became embarrassed and reddened, for some reason he saluted:

"I don't know, really … It's nothing to do with me … I'm only just back from Manchuria myself; look—here's my St George medal … "

But something really was happening there.

Tatam: tam, tam

It was late.

Sofia Petrovna was making her way home unobtrusively, hiding her nose in her downy muff; the Troitskii Bridge behind her reached out endlessly towards the islands, ran off into those silent places; and shadows drifted across the bridge; on the big cast-iron bridge, above the damp, damp parapet, over the greenish waters teeming with bacilli she was followed in the gusts of the Neva gale—by bowler hat, cane, overcoat, ears, moustache and nose.

Suddenly her eyes came to rest, opened wide, began to blink and squint: beneath the damp, damp parapet sat a dark, splay-legged, tiger-striped beast, snorting and slavering as it chewed on a little silver whip; the dark stripy beast had its snub-nosed snout turned away from her; and when she cast a glance in the direction of that averted snout, she saw: that selfsame waxen face, with lips apart over the damp parapet, above the greenish waters teeming with bacilli, stretched forward from its overcoat; with lips apart, he seemed to be engrossed in a single baneful thought, which had been echoing in her too these recent days, for in these recent days she had kept hearing with such torment the words of a simple song:

Your eyes upon the purple of the sunset,
You stood upon the bank of the Neva …

And here he was: standing on the bank of the Neva, staring somehow dully into the green, or no—with his gaze soaring away to where the banks were lying low, where the buildings on the islands squatted submissively and from where over the white walls of the fortress the tormentingly sharp, merciless, cold spire of the Peter and Paul cathedral stretched hopelessly and coldly up into the sky.

She reached out towards him with her whole self—what were words and what were thoughts! But he—again he did not notice her;

with lips apart and glassy eyes wide open, he seemed nothing but an armless freak; and again in place of arms the flaps of his coat flew up into the gusts above the damp parapet of the bridge.

But when she moved away, Nikolai Apollonovich slowly turned towards her and hurried off with mincing gait, tripping and catching his feet in the long tails of his coat; at the corner of the bridge a cab was waiting for him: and the cab flew off; and when the cab overtook Sofia Petrovna Likhutina, then Nikolai Apollonovich, leaning forwards and clasping in his hands the bulldog's collar, turned with drooping shoulders towards the little dark figure that had so forlornly pressed its nose into its muff; he looked, he smiled; but the cab flew by.

All at once the first snow began to fall; and it glittered as it danced like living diamonds in the streetlamp's pool of light; the pool of light now barely lit the side of the palace, the little canal and the wooden bridge: the Winter Canal ran off into the depths; it was empty: a solitary cabby was whistling on the corner, waiting for someone; on the cab a grey Nikolaevan cape lay negligently.

Sofia Petrovna Likhutina stood on the hump of the little bridge and gazed dreamily—into the depths, into the mistily splashing canal; Sofia Petrovna Likhutina had stopped at this point before; once she had stopped here with him; and she had sighed over Liza, arguing seriously about the horrors of *The Queen of Spades*—about the divine, entrancing, marvellous harmonies of a certain opera, and then she had sung under her breath, conducting with her finger:

"Tatam: tam, tam! ... Tatatam: tam, tam! ... "

And now she was standing here again; her lips opened, and a little finger was raised:

"Tatam: tam, tam! ... Tatatam: tam, tam!"

But she heard the sound of running feet, she looked—and did not even scream: suddenly from around the side wall of the palace a red domino emerged with an air of perplexity, it bustled here and there, as though in search of something, and, seeing the shadow of a woman on the hump of the bridge, rushed towards her; in its impulsive rush it stumbled over the cobblestones, sticking out in front its mask with the narrow slits for the eyes; beneath the mask a gust of the icy Neva gale played with the thick fan of lace—black, too, of course; and while the mask was running in her direction towards the bridge, Sofia Petrovna Likhutina had no time even to work out that the red domino was a piece of buffoonery, that some tasteless jester (and we know which) had simply decided to have a joke at her expense, that under the velvet mask and the black lace beard was simply concealed a human face; now it was fixing her with a sharp stare through the oval slits. Sofia Petrovna thought (after all she had such a small forehead) that a chasm had opened in this world, and from there, from that chasm, on no account from this world, some imp of Satan had hurled himself upon her: who this imp might be, she probably would not have been able to say.

But when the black lace beard flew stumbling up on to the bridge, then in a gust from the Neva the clownish velvet flaps flew up with a rustle and landed in a red flash beyond the railings—in the dark-hued night; the all-too-familiar light-green trouser straps were revealed, and the terrible clown turned into a clown who was simply pathetic; at that moment his galosh slipped on a convex cobblestone: the pathetic clown crashed on to the stone from his full height; and over him there now resounded—not laughter even—but simply an unrestrained guffaw.

"You little frog, you freak—you red clown! … "

A swift female foot angrily rewarded the clown with a barrage of kicks.

Some bearded men now started running along the canal; and a police whistle was heard in the distance; the clown jumped up; the clown rushed off to the cab, and from afar something red could be seen struggling impotently inside it, trying in flight to put a Nikolaevan cape on over its shoulders. Sofia Petrovna burst into tears and ran away from this accursed place.

Soon, chasing the cab, the snub-nosed bulldog ran barking from the Winter Canal: its short legs flashed through the air, and behind them, behind those short legs, on rubber tyres, chasing, wobbling from side to side, there hurried two agents of the security department.

Shadows

Shadow said to shadow:

"My good fellow, you missed one circumstance of considerable importance, which I found out about with the help of my own resources."

170

"What circumstance?"

"You haven't uttered a sound about the red domino."

"So you know already?"

"I not only know: I followed him all the way to his flat."

"So, who is the red domino?"

"Nikolai Apollonovich."

"Hm! Yes, yes: but the incident isn't ripe yet."

"Don't try to wriggle out: you simply lost sight of him."

"?!?"

"Yes you did: you lost sight of him … And then you go telling me off for forging money, you told me off about that fifty-copeck piece—remember? And I didn't say anything about your false hair."

"It isn't false—it's just dyed … "

"Same thing."

"How's your cold?"

"Thank you, it's better."

"I didn't lose sight of him."

"Your proof?"

"What do you need that for: I can easily provide it."

"Your proof?!"

"You can believe me anyway."

"Your proof!!!"

But in reply only sardonic laughter rang out.

"Proof? You want proof? The proof is *The Petersburg Chronicle of Events.* Have you read *The Chronicle* for the last few days?"

"I must confess, I haven't."

"But it's your obligation to know what Petersburg is talking about. If you had glanced into *The Chronicle* you would understand that the news about the domino preceded his appearance at the Winter Canal."

"Hm-hm."

"There, you see, you see, you see: and you go on about it. You can ask me who wrote all that in *The Chronicle.*"

"Well, who did?"

"Neintelpfain, my contributor."

171

"I must confess, that's a trick I didn't expect."

"And yet you attack me, you heap reproaches on me: but I've told you a hundred times that I work for ideological reasons, that the business is set up like clockwork. You're still in blissful ignorance, and my Neintelpfain is already creating a sensation."

"Hm-hm-hm: talk louder—I can't hear."

"I hope you will order your agents to leave Nikolai Apollonovich completely in peace, otherwise: otherwise—I can't guarantee further success."

"I must admit, I have already told the newspapers about this latest incident."

"Lord above, you have to be an absolute … "

"What?"

"An absolute id … idealist: you've done it again, you've poked your nose into matters that are within my competence … God grant at least that his father doesn't find out!"

A mad dog had howled

We left Sofia Petrovna Likhutina in a difficult situation; we left her on the Petersburg pavement on that cold night when police whistles could be heard somewhere in the distance, and dark silhouettes had started running all around. Then she too ran off, offended, in the opposite direction; into her soft muff, offended, she shed tears; she could see no way of coming to terms with this terrible occurrence, the shame of which would last forever. Better if Nikolai Apollonovich had insulted her some other way, if he had struck her, if he had even thrown himself off the bridge in his red domino—then she would have remembered him all the rest of her life with a shudder of horror, remembered him till she died. Sofia Petrovna Lihutina did not regard the Canal as a prosaic place, where you could allow yourself the kind of behaviour he had just allowed himself; it was not for nothing that she had sighed so often at the sounds of *The Queen of Spades*: there was something similar to Liza in this situation of hers (where the similarity lay she could not have said precisely); and it went without saying that she dreamt of seeing Nikolai Apollonovich here in the role of Hermann. But Hermann? ... Hermann had behaved like a pickpocket: in the first place, he had stuck out his mask at her from the side of the palace with laughable cowardice; secondly, after waving his domino in front of her with laughable haste, he had measured his length on the bridge; and then from the folds of his velvet the trouser straps had prosaically appeared (at that moment these straps had finally driven her out of her wits); and to complete the outrages so uncharacteristic of Hermann, this Hermann had run away from a mere Petersburg policeman; he hadn't stood his ground and torn the mask from his face in a heroic, tragic gesture; he hadn't said, in a dull, faint voice, in the presence of all, the audacious words: "I love you"; and after that Hermann had not shot himself. No, the shameful behaviour of Hermann had extinguished in her forever the dawning light of all these tragic days! No, the shameful behaviour of Hermann had turned the very thought of the domino into a piece of pretentious buffoonery; and the main thing was that this shameful behaviour had disgraced her; after all, what kind of Liza could she be if there was no Hermann! Revenge on him, then, revenge!

Sofia Petrovna Likhutina flew into the apartment like a tempest. In the lighted entrance-hall hung an officer's greatcoat and cap: so her husband was home now, and without taking off her coat, Sofia Petrovna Likhutina flew into her husband's room; throwing open the door with a prosaically vulgar gesture—in she flew: with her boa flapping, with her soft muff, and with her face inflamed and unattractively swollen: in she flew—and stopped.

Sergei Sergeevich Likhutin was evidently preparing to go to bed; his grey tunic was hanging modestly on a hanger, and he himself in his blindingly white shirt, criss-crossed by braces, presented a faint silhouette, snapped in two, it seemed—as he knelt; in front of him the icon glimmered and the lamp crackled. In the blue lamp's half-light Sergei Sergeevich's face was outlined in matt, with his pointed beard and his raised hand at his brow both of exactly the same colour; his hand, his face, his beard, and his white chest all seemed to be carved from some strong, aromatic wood; Sergei Sergeevich's lips moved slightly; and Sergei Sergeevich nodded his head slightly at the blue flame, and his blue-tinged fingers, pressed to his forehead, moved slightly, clasped together—to make the sign of the cross.

Sergei Sergeevich Likhutin first placed his blue-tinged fingers on his chest and both shoulders, he bowed, and only then did he somewhat reluctantly turn round. Sergei Sergeevich Likhutin showed no shock or embarrassment; as he rose from his knees, he began carefully to brush off the flecks of dust that had attached themselves to his knees. After these leisurely actions he asked unconcernedly:

"What's the matter, Soniushka?"

Sofia Petrovna was irritated and even offended by her husband's calm unconcern, just as she was offended by that little blue flame in the corner. She collapsed abruptly on to a chair and, covering her face with her muff, burst into sobs that filled the room.

Then the whole of Sergei Sergeevich's face became kinder, gentler; his fine lips drooped and a horizontal line furrowed his brow, bringing a sympathetic expression to his face. But Sergei Sergeevich had no clear conception of how he ought to act in this ticklish instance—whether to let those feminine tears flow, only to put up with a scene later and be reproached for coldness, or on the contrary: to kneel down cautiously in front of Sofia Petrovna, deferentially move her head away from the muff with his gentle hand, and with that hand wipe away her tears, put his arms round her like a brother and cover her face with kisses; but Sergei Sergeevich was afraid of seeing a grimace of contempt and boredom; and Sergei Sergeevich chose a middle path: he simply patted Sofia Petrovna on her trembling shoulder:

"Come on, now, Sonia … That's enough … That's enough, little one! My child, my child!"

"Leave me alone, leave me alone! … "

"What is it? What's the matter? Tell me! … Let's discuss it calmly."

"No, leave me alone, leave me alone! … Calmly … leave me alone! It's clea-ear … you've got … cold, fish's blood … "

Offended, Sergei Sergeevich moved away from his wife, stood for a while in indecision, and then dropped into the adjacent armchair.

"Aaah … to leave your wife like that! … Just take charge of provisions out there somewhere! … to go away! … and not know anything! … "

"You're wrong, Sonechka, if you think I don't know anything at all … You see … "

"Oh, leave me, please! … "

"You see how it is, old girl: since the time when ... when I moved out of our room into this one ... In short, I have my pride: and I don't want to infringe on your freedom, you understand ... Moreover, I can't restrict you: I understand you; I know perfectly well that it isn't easy for you, old thing ... I do have hopes, Soniushka: that maybe one day again ... All right, I won't, I won't! But you must understand me too: my distance, my unconcern, if you like, doesn't come, as it were, from coldness ... All right, I won't, I won't ... "

"Perhaps you'd like to see Nikolai Apollonovich Ableukhov? Something's happened between you, hasn't it? Tell me all about it: tell me without hiding anything; we'll discuss your situation together."

"Don't you dare speak to me about him! ... He's a scoundrel, a scoundrel! ... Any other husband would have shot him long ago ... Your wife is pursued, is mocked ... And what do you do? ... No, leave me alone."

And incoherently, disconsolately, dropping her head on to her breast, Sofia Petrovna told the whole story.

Sergei Sergeevich Likhutin was a simple man. And simple people are more astonished by the inexplicable absurdity of an action than by an act of baseness, than by a murder, or a bloody display of bestiality. A man is capable of understanding human betrayal, crime, even human shame; after all, to understand means almost to find a justification; but how can you explain to yourself the action of a man-of-the-world, an apparently perfectly honest man, if this worldly and perfectly honest man suddenly gets an utterly absurd fantasy into his head: to get down on all fours in the doorway of a high-society drawing room waving the tails of his frock coat? That would be, I have to say, an act of total infamy! There can be no justification for the incomprehensibility, the purposelessness of such infamy, just as there can be no justification for blasphemy or profanity or any purposeless mockery! No, it would be better for such a perfectly honest man to get away with embezzling state funds, so long as he never gets down on all fours, because after such an action everything is sullied.

Sergei Sergeevich Likhutin pictured to himself vividly, distinctly, angrily the clownish appearance of the velvet domino in the unlit doorway, and … Sergei Sergeevich began to redden, he turned a bright carrot colour: the blood rushed to his face. Why, he had played with Nikolai Apollonovich as a child: later Sergei Sergeevich had been impressed by Nikolai Apollonovich's philosophical capabilities; Sergei Sergeevich had nobly allowed Nikolai Apollonovich, as a man-of-the-world, an honest man, to come between himself and his wife and … Sergei Sergeevich Likhutin pictured to himself vividly, distinctly, angrily the clownish grimaces of the red domino in the unlit doorway. He stood up and began to pace around the tiny room, clenching his fingers to a fist and raising his clenched fingers furiously at every sharp turn; when Sergei Sergeevich lost his temper (he had only ever lost his temper two or three times—no more), this gesture always made its appearance; Sofia Petrovna sensed this gesture perfectly; she was a little afraid of it; she was always a little afraid— not of the gesture, but of the silence that expressed the gesture.

"What's that you're? … "

"Never mind … it's nothing … "

And Sergei Sergeevich Likhutin went on striding around the tiny room with his fingers clenched to a fist.

Red domino! … It was foul, foul, foul! And there it had stood, behind the entrance door—how about that!?

Second Lieutenant Likhutin was astonished in the extreme by the behaviour of Nikolai Apollonovich. He was now experiencing a mixture of disgust and horror; in a word, he was experiencing that feeling of disgust which usually seizes us at the sight of complete idiots discharging their excretions just like that, where they squat, or at the sight of a black, hairy-legged insect—a spider, perhaps … His bewilderment, his sense of insult, his fear turned simply into fury. To take no notice of his insistent letter, to insult his honour as an officer with his clownish antics, to insult his beloved wife with his spiderish posturing!! … And Sergei Sergeevich Likhutin swore to himself on his honour as an officer—that he would crush that spider, cost what it may; and having made that decision he went on pacing up and down, red as a lobster, clenching his fingers into a fist and tightening his muscular arm on the turns; now he involuntarily struck Sofia Petrovna too with fear: red too, with her puffy lips half-open and her cheeks still streaked with glistening tears, she watched her husband attentively from where she sat in the armchair.

"What's that you're? … "

But Sergei Sergeevich now replied in a harsh voice: his voice resounded now with threat, severity and repressed fury—all at the same time.

"Never mind … it's nothing."

To tell the truth, Sergei Sergeevich at that moment was feeling something like disgust towards his beloved wife too; as though she also shared the clownish disgrace of the red mask that had performed its tomfoolery there by the entrance door.

"Go to your own room: get some sleep … leave all this to me."

And Sofia Petrovna Likhutina, who had long since stopped crying, stood up uncomplainingly and went quietly to her own room.

Left on his own, Sergei Sergeevich Likhutin went on pacing and clearing his throat; it came out like a dry cough, very unpleasant, distinct, a constant *khe-khe, khe-khe*. Sometimes his wooden fist, as though carved from strong, aromatic wood, was raised over the coffee-table; and it seemed that the table was about to fly into smithereens with a deafening crash.

But his fist unclenched again.

Finally Sergei Sergeevich began to undress quickly; he undressed, he covered himself with a flannelette blanket, and—the blanket flew off again; Sergei Sergeevich lowered his feet to the floor, stared with unseeing eyes at a particular point and even to his own surprise whispered out loud:

"Aaah! How do you like that? I'll shoot him like a dog … "

Then through the wall a high-pitched, injured voice rang out, tearful and loud:

"What's that you're? … "

"Never mind … it's nothing … "

Sergei Sergeevich dived under his blanket again and pulled it over his head, to sigh, and whisper, and implore, and threaten—somebody, for something …

Sofia Petrovna did not call Mavrusha. Quickly she threw off her fur coat, her hat, her dress; and out of the cascade of things that she contrived to cast around herself in those two or three minutes, she threw herself, all in white, on to the bed; and now she sat there with her feet tucked up and her angry face, framed with black hair, resting in her hands with parted lips, above which a moustache was clearly evident, and all around her was a cascade of things; that is how it always was. All Mavrusha ever did was to tidy up after her mistress; Sofia Petrovna had only to remember an article of her toilet and the article was not to hand; then blouses, handkerchiefs, dresses, hair-clips, hatpins—everything flew about in all directions, higgledy-piggledy; from Sofia Petrovna's hands a multicoloured waterfall of miscellaneous objects began to flow. This evening Sofia Petrovna did not call Mavrusha; so the cascade of things took place.

Sofia Petrovna listened despite herself to the tireless pacing of Sergei Sergeevich behind the partition; she also listened to the nightly sounds of the piano above her head: there someone was playing over and over the tune of an old mazurka, to the sounds of which her mother had danced with her, laughing, when she was still only an infant of two. And to the sounds of this mazurka, so ancient and so innocent of knowledge, Sofia Petrovna's anger began to subside, to be replaced by weariness, complete apathy and a spot of irritation towards her husband, in whom she herself, Sofia Petrovna, had aroused, as she thought, jealousy of *him*. But as soon as jealousy, as she thought, awoke in Sergei Sergeevich, her husband, then her husband, Sergei Sergeevich, became distinctly inimical to her; she had a feeling of awkwardness, as though some stranger's hand had reached out for her secret box of letters, locked away there, in the drawer. On the contrary: just as Nikolai Apollonovich's smile had first aroused her disgust, and she had then extracted for herself from that disgust a sweet mixture of delight and horror towards that same smile, so too in the shamefulness of Nikolai Apollonovich's behaviour there on the bridge there now revealed itself to her a sweet source of revenge: she regretted that when he had fallen in front of her in his pathetic clownish garb she had not set about kicking and trampling him; she suddenly wanted to torment and torture him, but her husband, Sergei Sergeevich, she did not want to torture; neither to torture, nor to kiss. And it suddenly became clear to Sofia Petrovna that her husband had nothing to do with this fateful occurrence between them; that occurrence ought to have remained a secret between her and *him*; and now she had told it all to her husband herself. Any involvement on her husband's part not only with her, but also with *him*, Nikolai Apollonovich, became above all offensive to her: Sergei Sergeevich was bound to draw thoroughly false conclusions from this incident; above all, he of course would not be able to understand anything at all in this: not the fateful, eerie-sweet sensation, nor the dressing-up itself; and against her will Sofia Petrovna listened intently to the ancient sounds of the mazurka and to the restless, rebarbative footfalls behind the partition; from the excess of her loosened black plaits she fearfully extended her pearly face with its dark-blue, lustreless gaze, clumsily pressing her face to her faintly trembling knees.

At that moment her gaze fell upon the toilet mirror: under the toilet mirror Sofia Petrovna noticed the letter that she was supposed to hand *him* at the ball (she had quite forgotten about the letter). In the first moment Sofia Petrovna decided to send the letter back with a messenger, to send it back to Varvara Evgrafovna. How dare they foist some letters or other on her! And she would have sent it back, if only her husband had not just become involved in everything (if only he'd go to bed!). But now under the influence of her protest against all interference in *their* personal matters she looked at the issue simply, too simply: of course, she had every right to tear open the envelope and read whatever secrets were there (how dare he have secrets at all!). A moment— and Sofia Petrovna was by the table; but hardly had she touched this letter that was not hers, when there through the wall a ferocious whispering started up; the bed creaked.

"What's that you're? ... "

From the other side of the wall she was answered:

"Never mind ... it's nothing."

The bed squealed plaintively; everything fell silent. With trembling hand Sofia Petrovna tore open the envelope ... and as she read, her little swollen eyes became larger and larger; their dullness cleared, replaced by a blinding brilliance, the pallor of her face took on first the shade of pale pink apple-blossom, then that of bright pink roses; and by the time she had finished reading her face was simply crimson.

Now Nikolai Apollonovich was entirely in her hands; her whole being trembled with terror on his account and on account of the possibility of dealing him a fearful, irreparable blow in return for her two months of suffering; and he would receive that blow from these very hands. He had wanted to frighten her with his clownish masquerade; but he had not been able even to see this clownish masquerade through properly, and, caught unawares, he had committed a series of outrages; let him now efface himself in her, let him be Hermann! Yes, yes, yes: she would deal him the evil blow herself simply by handing over this letter of terrible import. One moment: she was overcome by a feeling of dizziness at the course to which she was committing herself; but it was too late to hold back, to step aside from that course: had she not herself sought to summon the blood-red domino? And if he had then called forth before her the image of the terrible domino, then let all the rest come about too: let the bloody domino tread a bloody path!

The door creaked: Sofia Petrovna barely managed to screw up the opened letter in her hand, when her husband, Sergei Sergeevich Likhutin, already stood on the threshold of the bedroom; he was all in white: white shirt and white underpants. The appearance of this completely irrelevant person in such an indecent state of dress drove her to fury:

"You might at least get dressed … "

Sergei Sergeevich Likhutin quickly left the room, covered in confusion, but nevertheless he appeared again a minute later; this time he was, at least, wearing a dressing gown; Sofia Petrovna had had time to hide the letter. Sergei Sergeevich addressed her simply, with an unpleasant, dry firmness that was not customary for him:

"Sophie … Make me one promise: I really beg you not to go to the Tsukatovs' tomorrow evening … "

Silence.

"I hope you will promise me that; your own good sense will prompt you: don't make me explain."

Silence.

"I would like you to acknowledge yourself that it's impossible to go to the ball after what has just happened."

Silence.

"At all events, I have given my word as an officer on your behalf that you will not be at the ball."

Silence.

"And if you don't agree then I would simply have to forbid you."

"I shall go to the ball … "

"No, you won't!!"

Sofia Petrovna was astonished at the threat in the wooden voice with which Sergei Sergeevich uttered this sentence.

"Yes, I will."

A burdensome silence ensued, during which all that could be heard was a kind of gurgling in Sergei Sergeevich's chest, which made him grasp at his throat nervously and toss his head a couple of times, as though he was trying to ward off the inevitability of some terrible event; suppressing with an immense effort the explosion rising inside him, Sergei Sergeevich Likhutin sat down quietly, straight as a rod; in an unnaturally quiet voice he began to speak:

"Look: it wasn't me who pressed you for the details. You yourself called me in as a witness to what had just happened."

Sergei Sergeevich was unable to utter the words "red domino": the thought of all the recent events forced him instinctively to experience a kind of vicious abyss, into which his wife had begun to slip down a steep incline; what was vicious about it, apart from the unheard-of absurdity of the whole event, Sergei Sergeevich was not in a position to know: but he sensed what had happened, and that this was not just an everyday love affair, not a betrayal or merely a fall. No, no, no: over all this hung the smell of satanic excesses which could poison the soul for ever, like prussic acid; he had caught so clearly the slightly sweet smell of bitter almonds when, on entering his wife's room, he had suffered a powerful attack of breathlessness; and he knew, knew for certain: if his wife, Sofia Petrovna, should be found at the Tsukatovs' tomorrow, and should she meet there the repulsive domino—everything would be destroyed: his wife's honour, his own honour as an officer.

"Don't you see? After what you have told me, don't you understand that you must not meet; that it's a horrible, filthy business; that, finally, I have given my word that you will not be there. Take pity, Sophie, on yourself, on me, and even … on him, because otherwise … I … don't know … I can't guarantee … "

But Sofia Petrovna was becoming more and more outraged at the impertinent interference of this completely irrelevant officer, an officer who, moreover, had the effrontery to appear in her bedroom with his interference in most indecent dress; picking up some dress or other from the floor (she had suddenly noticed that she was *déshabillée*) and covering herself with it, she moved away into a dark corner; and from there, from her shadowy corner, she suddenly shook her head emphatically:

"Maybe I wouldn't have gone, but now, after all your interference, I shall, I shall, I shall!"

"No: that shall not be!!!"

What was that? It seemed to her that a deafening shot rang out in the room; at the same time an inhuman scream rang out: a thin, hoarse falsetto shouted something incomprehensible; the man of cypress wood leapt up and an armchair fell with a crash, while the blow of a fist smashed the cheap little table in two; then a door slammed; and everything fell silent.

The sounds of the mazurka up above broke off; over her head feet began to stamp; voices started buzzing; finally the neighbour above, outraged by the noise, began to bang on the floor with a broom; evidently someone up above was trying to express an enlightened protest.

Sofia Petrovna Likhutina shivered and broke into injured sobs from her dark corner: it was the first time in her life that she had encountered such fury, because what had stood before her just now was not even a man … not even a beast. Here in front of her just now a mad dog had howled.

The senator's second space

Apollon Apollonovich's bedroom was small and simple: four walls, perpendicular to one another, and a single window aperture with a white lace curtain; the sheets, the towels and the pillowcases on the puffed-up pillows were distinguished by the same whiteness; before the senator went to bed, his valet sprinkled the sheet with a scented spray.

Apollon Apollonovich acknowledged only triple strength eau de cologne from the Petersburg chemical laboratory.

Further: the valet placed a small glass of lemon water on the bedside table and hastened to make his departure. Apollon Apollonovich undressed by himself.

In a most fastidious way he discarded his dressing gown; in a most fastidious way he folded it, laying it skilfully upon the chair; in a most fastidious way he discarded his jacket and his minute trousers, and was left in tight-fitting knitted underpants and vest; left thus in his underwear, before he settled for the night Apollon Apollonovich strengthened his body with gymnastics.

He spread out his arms and legs; then he stretched them and twisted his torso, squatting on his haunches up to twelve times and more, and then, finally, moved on to an even more beneficial exercise: turning over on to his back, Apollon Apollonovich began to work with his legs in order to strengthen the muscles of his stomach.

Apollon Apollonovich had especially frequent recourse to these most beneficial exercises on days when he was suffering from haemorrhoids.

Following these most beneficial exercises Apollon Apollonovich pulled the blanket over himself, in order to surrender himself to peaceful repose and set off on a journey, for sleep (we make this comment ourselves)—is a journey.

All of this Apollon Apollonovich performed today. Pulling the blanket over his head (with the exception of the tip of his nose), he hung from his bed over a timeless void.

But at this point we shall be interrupted and asked: "What do you mean: void? What about the walls, and the floor? And ... so on? ... "

We shall reply.

Apollon Apollonovich always saw *two* spaces: one was material (the walls of the rooms and the sides of his carriage), the other was—not spiritual exactly (it was also material) ... How shall we put it: above senator Ableukhov's head senator Ableukhov's eyes saw strange currents: flashes, gleams, nebulous blurs, dancing in all the colours of the rainbow and emerging from swirling cores, obscured in the half-light the limits of material spaces; and so within one space there seethed another, and this latter, screening everything else, ran off in its turn into infinities of volatile, palpitating perspectives, consisting ... well, of something like Christmas tree tinsel, of stars, sparks, lights.

Sometimes Apollon Apollonovich would close his eyes before going to sleep and then open them again; and what would he see? Lights, nebulous blurs, threads and stars, as though a bright froth of immense gurgling blacknesses suddenly (for no more than a quarter-of-a-second) formed itself into a distinct picture: of a cross, a polyhedron, a swan, a light-filled pyamid. And everything would fly apart.

Apollon Apollonovich had a strange secret of his own: a world of figures, contours, tremors, weird physical sensations—in short: a *universe* of oddities. This *universe* always arose on the brink of sleep; and it arose in such a way that, at the moment he dropped off to sleep, Apollon Apollonovich would remember all the incoherences of the past, the rustling sounds, the crystallographic figures, the golden, chrysanthemum-shaped stars that coursed through the darkness on their legs of light-rays (sometimes one of these stars would shower the senator's head with boiling water: a tingling in his scalp): in short, before he fell asleep he remembered everything he had seen the previous day, only to lose it all from memory the following morning.

Sometimes (not always), just before the final moment of daytime consciousness, Apollon Apollonovich would notice, as he dropped to sleep, that all the threads, all the stars, as they formed a gurgling vortex, whirled together to create a corridor running off into infinity and (the strangest thing of all) he felt that that corridor—began in his head, that is to say that it, the corridor, was an endless continuation of his head itself, whose crown had suddenly burst open—a continuation into infinity; thus it was that the old senator received on the edge of sleep the most extraordinary impression that he was looking not with his eyes, but with the centre of his head itself, in other words that he, Apollon Apollonovich, was not Apollon Apollonovich, but *something* that had settled in his brain and was now gazing out from there, from his brain; when the crown of his head opened this something could freely and easily run the length of the corridor to the place *where everything is cast into the abyss* that revealed itself there at the end of the corridor.

This was the senator's *second space*—the land of the senator's nightly travels; and that's quite enough about it ...

With the blanket pulled over his head, he was already hanging from his bed over the timeless void, the lacquered floor had already dropped away from the legs of the bed and the bed was standing, so to speak, on the unfathomable—when a strange, distant clattering sound reached the senator's ears, like the clatter of swiftly beating hooves.

"Tra-ta-ta ... Tra-ta-ta ... "

And the clatter of hooves came nearer.

A strange, very strange, exceedingly strange circumstance: the senator poked his ear out from under the red blanket in the direction of the moon: and—yes: very probably it was someone making a knocking sound in the mirrored gallery.

Apollon Apollonovich poked his head out.

The golden gurgling vortex suddenly flew apart in all directions above the senator's head; the chrysanthemum-shaped many-legged star moved towards the crown of his head, disappearing abruptly from the field of vision of the senator's eyes; and, as always, the blocks of the parquet floor came flying back out of the abyss to the legs of the iron bed; Apollon Apollonovich, small and white, looking like a plucked chicken, suddenly rested his two yellow heels on the bedside rug.

The clatter continued: Apollon Apollonovich jumped up and ran out into the corridor.

The rooms were lit by the moon.

In nothing but his undervest and with a lighted candle in his hand Apollon Apollonovich journeyed through the rooms. The bulldog, happening to be there, laboured after its distressed master, twitching its docked tail condescendingly, clinking its collar and snuffling with its stunted nose.

His hairy chest, like a flat, wood-panelled lid, heaved with a heavy wheezing, and his ear of pale-green hue heeded to the clattering sound. The senator's gaze chanced to fall on the pier glass: how strangely the pier glass reflected the senator: his arms, legs, hips and chest suddenly turned out to be strapped in dark-blue velvet: the velvet cast from it in all directions a metallic gleam: Apollon Apollonovich was clad in dark-blue armour; Apollon Apollonovich turned out to be a tiny knight and from his hands protruded not a candle, but a kind of luminous emanation, that glittered like a sabre-blade.

Apollon Apollonovich felt a surge of courage and rushed into the gallery; the clatter reverberated there:

"Tra-ta-ta ... Tra-ta-ta ... "

And he snapped at the clattering sound:

"On the basis of which article of the *Code of Laws*?"

As he uttered this exclamation he noticed that the complacent bulldog was snuffling away beside him sleepily and placidly. But—what impertinence—from the gallery came an answering exclamation:

"On the basis of the extraordinary regulation!"

Outraged by this impertinent response, the little blue knight brandished the luminous emanation clasped in his hand and rushed into the gallery.

But the luminous emanation dissolved in his fist: it flowed between his fingers like air and dropped at his feet as a little ray of light. But the clattering—Apollon Apollonovich now detected—was the clicking of the tongue of some wretched Mongol: there a fat Mongol with a face Apollon Apollonovich had seen during his stay in Tokyo (Apollon Apollonovich had once been sent to Tokyo)—there a fat Mongol had appropriated the face of Nikolai Apollonovich—I say *appropriated*, because that was not Nikolai Apollonovich, but simply a Mongol, previously seen in Tokyo; nevertheless his face was Nikolai Apollonovich's face. Apollon Apollonovich had no desire to understand this, he rubbed his astonished eyes with his fists (but once again he could not feel his hands, just as he could not feel his face: it was just two intangible points rubbing against one another—the space of his hands in contact with the space of his face). But the Mongol (Nikolai Apollonovich) was approaching with an ulterior motive.

Then the senator cried out a second time:

"On the basis of what regulation?"

"And what paragraph?"

And the space replied:

"There are no paragraphs or regulations any more!"

And Apollon Apollonovich, lost without trace, robbed of sensation, suddenly bereft of the very awareness of his body, transformed into nothing but vision and hearing, imagined that he had raised up the space of his pupils (with the sense of touch he could not say for certain that his eyes were raised up, for the awareness of his body had been discarded)—and, raising up his eyes in the direction of where the crown of his head should be, he saw that there was no crown of his head, since at the point where the brain is compressed by strong, heavy bones, where there is neither gaze nor vision—at that point Apollon Apollonovich inside Apollon Apollonovich caught sight of a round aperture pierced through into the dark-azure distance (in the place of the crown); this aperture—a blue circle—was surrounded by a wheel of flying sparks, glints, gleams; at the fatal moment when by Apollon Apollonovich's calculations the Mongol (merely impressed on the consciousness, but no longer visible) was already stealing up to his powerless body (the blue circle in that body was the exit from the body)—at that same time something began, with a roar and a whistle, like the sound of the wind in the chimney, to drag Apollon Apollonovich's consciousness out of the glittering vortex (through the blue aperture in his crown) into the starry realm beyond.

Thereupon an outrage occurred (at that moment Apollon Apollonovich's consciousness noted that such an event had happened before: where and when—he could not remember)—thereupon an outrage occurred: the wind whistled Apollon Apollonovich's consciousness out of Apollon Appollonovich.

Apollon Apollonovich flew out through the round aperture into the blue, into the darkness, as a gold-plumed star; and, once he had flown up high enough above his head (which seemed to him to be the planet Earth), the gold-plumed star, like a rocket, flew apart soundlessly into sparks.

For a moment there was nothing: there was the darkness before time; and in the darkness consciousness moved not some other consciousness, such as a universal consciousness, but a perfectly simple one: Apollon Apollonovich's.

This consciousness now turned back, issuing from itself only two sensations: the sensations lowered themselves like hands; and this is what the sensations felt: they felt a kind of form (resembling the form of a bathtub), filled to the brim with a sticky, stinking filth; the sensations splashed in the bathtub like hands; that with which the bathtub was filled Apollon Apollonovich could only compare with the dung-water in which the hideous hippopotamus wallowed (he had seen this several times in the zoos of enlightened Europe). A moment—and the sensations grew together with the vessel, which was filled, as we would say, to the brim with *ordure*; Apollon Apollonovich's consciousness struggled to escape into space, but the sensations were dragging something weighty along behind that consciousness.

The eyes of the consciousness opened and the consciousness saw that in which it resided: it saw the little yellow old man resembling a plucked chicken; the old man was sitting on the bed; with his yellow heels he was resting on the bedside rug.

A moment: the consciousness turned out to be that selfsame little yellow old man, for that little yellow old man was listening from the bed to a strange distant clattering sound, like the clatter of swiftly beating hooves:

"Tra-ta-ta … Tra-ta-ta … "

Apollon Apollonovich realised that all his journeying along the corridor and through the gallery and, finally, through his own head—was a dream.

And no sooner did he think that, than he awoke: it was a double dream.

Apollon Apollonovich was not sitting on the bed, but Apollon Apollonovich was lying with the blanket pulled over his head (except for the tip of his nose): the clattering in the gallery turned out to be the sound of a slamming door.

No doubt that was Nikolai Apollonovich coming home: Nikolai Apollonovich came home late at night.

"I see … "

"I see … "

"Very good … "

Only there was something wrong with his back: a fear of touching his spine … He wasn't developing *tabes dorsalis*, surely?

CHAPTER FOUR

In which the thread of the narrative snaps.

God grant I may not lose my mind …
A Pushkin

The Summer Garden

PROSAICALLY, SOLITARILY the paths of the Summer Garden ran this way and that; now and then a sombre pedestrian, as he cut across these spaces, would hasten his step, only to lose himself conclusively in an emptiness without escape; the Field of Mars is not to be surmounted in five minutes.

The Summer Garden wore a frown.

The summer statues were concealed by wooden boards; the grey boards suggested coffins standing on their ends; and coffins lined the paths; in these coffins delicate nymphs and satyrs found sanctuary, that the tooth of time might not nibble them with snow, rain and frost, for time whets its iron tooth on all things; and its iron tooth will gnaw away equally body and soul, and the very stones themselves.

Since times long gone this garden has grown empty, grown grey, grown smaller; the grotto has fallen in, the fountains have ceased to plash, the summer gallery has collapsed and the waterfall has dried up; the garden has grown smaller and squatted down behind its railings, those same railings that foreign guests from English lands would gather to admire, in wigs and green kaftans; and they would smoke their soot-stained pipes.

Peter himself planted this garden, watering with his own watering can the rare trees, melliferous tansies, varieties of mint; from Solikamsk the Tsar had cedars sent here, from Danzig barberry, and apple trees from Sweden; fountains he built, and the fragmented, reflective spray, like a delicate spider's web, was shot through long thereafter with the red camisole of persons imperial, their coiled ringlets, with black negro faces and the farthingales of ladies; here a grey-haired cavalier, leaning on the faceted glass knob of his black and gold cane, would lead his lady to a pool; and in the green, frothing waters, rising with a snort from the very bottom, the black snout of a walrus would emerge; the lady gasped, the grey-haired cavalier smiled jokingly and held out his cane to the black monster.

In those days the Summer Garden extended further, taking away space from the Field of Mars for avenues lined with yews and meadow-sweet, so dear to the Tsar's heart (the Garden, too, has evidently been gnawed by the ruthless tooth of time); huge seashells from the seas of the Indies raised their pink-hued trumpets from the porous stones of the severe grotto; and the imperial person, doffing his feathered hat, would put his lips in curiosity to the opening of the pink-hued trumpet: and the noise of chaos would be heard from there; other persons at this time would be drinking fruit cordials in front of this mysterious grotto.

In later times, too, beneath the graceful figure of Rastrelli's statue that stretched out its fingers into the gathering evening, the laughter, whispering and sighs of the Empress' ladies-in-waiting would be heard, and their big, rounded pearls would glisten. That would be in spring, at Whitsuntide; the atmosphere of evening thickened; suddenly it was disturbed by a powerful organ voice, flooding in from beneath a clump of sweetly slumbering elms: and suddenly light spread out from there—green light, amusing; and there, among green lights, bright red musicians, dressed as huntsmen, raised their horns, and filled with melody the air around, disturbing the zephyr and cruelly stirring the soul, already deeply wounded: the languorous plaint of these upraised horns—have you not heard it?

All that used to be, but now it is no more; now the paths of the Summer Garden run so sullenly; a black, ferocious flock circled above the roof of Peter's house; its raucous noise and the heavy flapping of its ragged wings were beyond endurance; all at once the ferocious flock descended on the branches.

Nikolai Apollonovich, clean-shaven and scented, was making

his way along a frosty path, wrapped in his overcoat: his head was buried in the fur, and his eyes gleamed in a strange way; that morning he had just decided to immerse himself in work, when a messenger had brought him a note; unfamiliar handwriting invited him to a rendezvous in the Summer Garden. And it was signed "*S*". Who might this mysterious "*S*" be? Why, obviously, "*S*" was Sofia (evidently she had changed her handwriting). Nikolai Apollonovich, clean-shaven and scented, was making his way along a frosty path.

Nikolai Apollonovich seemed agitated; in recent days he had lost both appetite and sleep; for a week now fine dust had been falling unimpeded on to the page of his commentary on Kant; but in his soul was an uncharted flow of feeling; he had felt this vague, rapturous flow in himself in previous times ... granted, only dimly, distantly. But since the moment he had called forth nameless tremors in the Angel Peri by his behaviour, nameless tremors had been aroused in him too: as though he had summoned from their mysterious depths some inchoately surging forces, as though in him himself the wine-skin of Aeolus had been ruptured, and the scions of otherworldly gales had pulled him through the air on whistling whips to unfamiliar lands. Surely this condition could not betoken merely the return of sensual longings? Might this be—love? But he did not acknowledge love.

He was already glancing round in agitation, looking for the familiar silhouette on the paths, in the black fur-coat with the black fur muff; but there was no one there; a little way off a frumpish woman was sprawled on a bench. Suddenly that frump stood up from the bench, dithered on the spot for a moment and stepped out towards him.

"Don't you ... recognise me?"

"Ah, how do you do!"

"You don't seem to recognise me even now. I'm—Solovyova, you know."

"Of course, by all means, you're Varvara Evgrafovna!"

"Well, let's sit down here, on this bench ... "

Nikolai Apollonovich lowered himself down beside her in torment: why, his rendezvous had been arranged in precisely this avenue; what an unfortunate circumstance! Nikolai Apollonovich began to wonder how best to get rid of this frump as quickly as possible; still seeking the familiar silhouette, he looked to right and left; but the familiar silhouette was still nowhere to be seen.

The dry path started tossing yellow-brown, worm-eaten leaves at their feet; a dark network of criss-crossed branches stretched out drably, standing straight against the steely horizon; sometimes the dark network began to hum; sometimes the dark network began to rock.

"Did you receive my note?"

"What note?"

"Why, the note signed '*S*'."

"What, was it you who wrote that?"

"Well, of course … "

"But why the '*S*'?"

"How do you mean? My surname is—Solovyova … "

Everything collapsed, how could he! … The nameless tremors suddenly sank to the bottom.

"What can I do for you?"

"I … I wanted, I thought, did you receive a little poem over the signature '*An ardent soul*'?"

"No, I didn't."

"How is that possible? Are the police intercepting my correspondence? Oh, how annoying! Without that poetic fragment, I must admit, it's very difficult to explain it all to you. I wanted to ask you a few things about the meaning of life … "

"You must excuse me, Varvara Evgrafovna, I really don't have time."

"How is that? How is that?"

"Goodbye! Please forgive me—we'll arrange a more convenient time for this conversation. Won't we?"

Varvara Evgrafovna pulled hesitantly at the fur trim of his overcoat; he stood up with determination; she stood up after him; but he with even more determination stretched out his scented fingers to her, touching her red hand with the tip of his rounded fingernails. She had no time at that moment to dream up anything to detain him; while he ran away from her in total vexation, wrapped arrogantly and angrily in his Nikolaevan cape, his face immersed in its fur. Leaves began to move sluggishly, encircling the flaps of his coat in dry, yellow rings; but the circles narrowed, began to twist in ever more restless swirls; a golden swirl, whispering something, danced with ever greater vigour. The vortex of leaves twisted swiftly, darted here and there and, no longer swirling, ran off somehow sideways; a ribbed, red leaf moved slightly, flew forwards and lay flat. A dark network of criss-crossed branches stretched out drably, standing straight against the steely horizon; he passed into this network; and when he passed into the network, a ferocious flock of crows shot upwards and started circling above the roof of Peter's House; the dark network began to rock; the dark network began to hum; and timorously melancholy sounds began to blend together; they merged into a single sound—the sound of an organ voice. The atmosphere of evening thickened; once more the soul sensed that there was no present; that this dense evening atmosphere would be tremulously lit by a bright-green cascade from those distant trees; and there the bright-red huntsmen, fiery-red all over, their horns outstretched, would once again elicit from the zephyrs melodic waves of organ music.

Madame Farnois

It was pretty late today when the Angel Peri deigned to open her innocent eyes from her pillows; but her eyelids were too heavy; and in her little head a dull, vague pain was definitely developing: the Angel Peri deigned to remain a long time in a state of drowsiness; beneath her curls all manner of incoherence, anxiety and half-grasped intimations swarmed around: her first complete thought was a thought about the evening: what was going to happen! But when she attempted to develop this thought the weight of her eyelids completely overcame her, and the incoherence, anxiety and half-grasped intimations returned; and out of this confusion there rose again exclusively: Pompadour, Pompadour, Pompadour—what was this Pompadour? But brightly that word was lit up in her soul: a costume in the style of Madame Pompadour—light blue, with flowers, Valenciennes lace, silver slippers, pompons! She had had such a long argument with her dressmaker the other day about a costume in the style of Madame Pompadour; Madame Farnois simply would not give way to her on the matter of blonde lace; she kept saying: "What do you want the blonde lace for?" But how could you manage without blonde lace?

In Madame Farnois's opinion blonde lace had to look like this and be used on such-and-such occasions; and in Sofia Petrovna's opinion blonde lace didn't have to look like that at all. At first Madame Farnois had said to her, "My taste, your taste—that's not how we get the Pompadour style!" But Sofia Petrovna was not willing to give way, and Madame Farnois was so offended that she suggested she should take the material back. Take it to Maison Tricotons: "They won't start contradicting you there, Madame … " But take it to Maison Tricotons:—what an idea! And they dropped the blonde lace, just as they dropped various other contentious issues as regards the style of Madame Pompadour: for example, a light chapeau Bergère for her hands, but there was no way she could do without a pannier skirt.

And so they came to terms.

As she immersed herself in thoughts about Madame Farnois, Pompadour and the Maison Tricotons, the Angel Peri had a tormenting feeling that something was wrong, that something had happened after which Madame Farnois and Maison Tricotons must surely dissolve into thin air; but, taking advantage of her state of semi-sleep, she consciously avoided catching the elusive impression left by the real events of the previous day; in the end she did remember—no more than two words: *domino* and *letter*; and she jumped out of bed and wrung her hands in objectless anxiety; there was a third word too, with which she had gone to sleep the day before.

But the Angel Peri could not remember the third word; it might, after all, be any of those totally unprepossessing sounds: husband, officer, second lieutenant.

The Angel Peri made a firm decision not to think about the first two words until the evening; as for the third, unprepossessing word—it was not worthy of attention. But it was precisely this unprepossessing word that she came up against; for she had barely fluttered out of her stuffy bedroom into the drawing room and taken wing in total innocence into her husband's room, assuming that her husband, the officer, Second Lieutenant Likhutin, had, as usual, left to take charge of provisions—when, all of a sudden, to her immense surprise, this Second Lieutenant's room turned out to be locked against her: Second Lieutenant Likhutin, in defiance of all his habits, in defiance of constricted space, convenience, common sense and honour—had evidently settled in there.

It was only then that she remembered yesterday's ugly scene; and with pouting lips she slammed the bedroom door shut (if he had locked himself in, then she would do so too). But, having locked herself in, she caught sight of the shattered coffee table.

"Madam, shall I bring your coffee in?"

"No, I don't want any … "

"Sir, shall I bring your coffee in?"

"No, I don't want any."

"Sir, the coffee's gone cold."

Silence.

"Madam, there's someone to see you!"

"From Madame Farnois?"

"No, from the laundress!"

Silence.

There are sixty minutes in an hour; and a minute consists entirely of seconds; the seconds trickled by, forming into minutes; massive minutes came in throngs; hours dragged by.

Silence.

In the middle of the day the yellow cuirassier of Her Majesty Baron Ommau-Ommergau called with a two-pound box of chocolates from Kraft's. The two-pound box of chocolates was not refused; but he was.

Around two o'clock in the afternoon the blue cuirassier of His Majesty Count Aven called with a box of chocolates from Balle's; the chocolates were received, but he was not.

A hussar of the Life-Guards in a tall fur hat was also refused; the hussar shook his plume and stood there with a veritable bush of chrysanthemums of a bright lemon colour; he called in after Aven shortly after four o'clock.

Vergefden came flying in too with a box at the Mariinskii Theatre. Only Lippanchenko didn't come flying in: Lippanchenko did not call.

Finally, late in the evening, just before ten, a girl from Madame Farnois appeared with a huge cardboard box; she was received at once; but when she was admitted and a giggling arose in the entrance-hall on this account, the bedroom door clicked, and a tear-stained face emerged from there inquiringly; a hurried, angry shout was heard:

"Bring it in quickly."

But then the lock clicked in the study too; from the study there emerged an unkempt head: it took one glance and retreated. That was surely not the Second Lieutenant?

Petersburg vanished into the night

Who does not remember the evening before a memorable night? Who does not remember that day's sad flight to rest?

Above the Neva a huge crimson sun floated behind the factory chimneys: the buildings of Petersburg were veiled by the thinnest of hazes and seemed to have started melting, turning into flimsy, smoky-amethyst lace; from the windowpanes a fiery gold glint penetrated everywhere; and from the tall spires came a gleam of rubies. All the usual solid objects—corbels and coping-stones—withdrew into a blazing incandescence: the entrances with their caryatids, and the cornices of brick-built balconies.

The rust-red palace turned a fierce incarnadine; this old palace was built by Rastrelli; in those days this old palace rose with mild blue walls amid a white host of pillars; the late Empress Elizaveta Petrovna used to open her windows on to the distances of the Neva and gaze from there in delight. In the reign of Emperor Alexander Pavlovich this old palace was repainted a pale-yellow shade; in the reign of Alexander Nikolaevich it was repainted a second time: since then it became rust-red, turning sanguine in the sunset.

On this memorable evening everything was ablaze, the palace too; everything else, that was not included in the blaze, gradually gathered dusk; the string of lines and walls gradually gathered dusk while over there, on the fading lilac sky, in pearly cloud-wisps, sparkling light-spots kindled languidly; the flimsiest of flames gradually kindled too.

You might say it was the glow of the past.

A small, plump lady dressed all in black, who had released her cab over by the bridge, had been walking up and down beneath the windows of the yellow house for a long time; her hand was trembling strangely; and in that trembling hand there trembled slightly a tiny *réticule* which was not in the Petersburg fashion. The plump lady was of advancing years and looked as though she suffered from shortness of breath; her plump fingers grasped now and then at her chin, which protruded impressively from her collar and was sprinkled here and there with grey whiskers. Taking up a position across from the yellow house, she made with trembling fingers to open her *réticule*: the *réticule* resisted; at last the *réticule* opened, and, with a haste uncharacteristic of her years, the lady took from it a patterned lace handkerchief, turned towards the Neva and burst into tears. Then her face was lit by the sunset, and whiskers became clearly visible above her lips; setting her hand upon the stone, she gazed with childlike and quite unseeing eyes into the misty many-chimneyed distance and the watery depths.

Finally, the lady hurried anxiously to the entrance of the yellow house and rang the bell.

The door opened; a little old man with braid on his lapels stuck his bald head out of the opening into the sunset; he screwed up his watery eyes against the unbearable gleam from across the Neva.

"Yes, madam?"

The lady of advancing years became agitated: her features were lit up either by emotion or by carefully concealed timidity.

"Dmitrich? ... Don't you recognise me?"

Then the servant's bald pate trembled and fell on to the tiny *réticule* (on to the lady's hand):

"My dear lady, mistress! ... Anna Petrovna!"

"Yes, here I am, Semyonych ... "

"Fancy that, madam ... Where have you come from?"

Emotion—unless it was carefully concealed timidity—could again be heard in her pleasant contralto.

"From Spain ... I wanted to see how you're getting on without me."

"Our dear mistress ... Please come in! ... "

Anna Petrovna went up the stairs: the staircase was still swathed in the same velvet carpet. On the walls the same ornamental weaponry still gleamed: under the mistress' attentive scrutiny once upon a time the bronze Lithuanian helmet had been hung here, and there—the thoroughly rusted sword from the Knights Templar; and they gleamed just the same today: from here—the bronze Lithuanian helmet; from there—the cross-shaped hilts of thoroughly rusted swords.

"Only there's no one here, ma'am: neither the young master nor Apollon Apollonovich."

Above the banister the same white alabaster plinth still stood, as before, and, just as before, the same white Niobe raised her alabaster eyes on high; this *before* enveloped her again (but three years had passed, and so much had been experienced in those years). Anna Petrovna recalled the dark gaze of her Italian cavalier, and felt again within her that carefully concealed timidity.

"Would you care for some chocolate, some coffee? Shall I have the samovar brought in?"

With a slight gesture Anna Petrovna waved away the past (everything here was just the same as before).

"How have you managed without me all these years?"

"We haven't, madam … Only I may make so bold as to say, madam, that without you—there's no order … But everything else is unaffected: same as before … Apollon Apollonovich, the master— have you heard?"

"I've heard … "

"Yes, ma'am, all the decorations … The favour of the Tsar … What would you expect: the master's a very important man!"

"The master—has he aged?"

"The master's being appointed to a post: a responsible one:—the master is a minister in all but name: that's the sort of man he is … "

All of a sudden it seemed to Anna Petrovna that the servant had given her a slightly reproachful glance; but that was an illusion: he had merely screwed up his eyes at the unbearable gleam from across the Neva, as he opened the door into the grand hall.

"And what about Kolenka?"

"Kolenka, ma'am, Nikolai Apollonovich, that is, is such a clever fellow, if I may say so! He's making such progress in his studies; doing well in everything he's supposed to … He's become so handsome … "

"Has he really? He always took after his father … "

Saying this, she dropped her gaze—and fingered her *réticule*.

As before, long-legged chairs stood against the walls; between the chairs, with their pale upholstery, there rose on all sides cold white pillars; and from each of these white pillars a stern sage in cold alabaster gazed at her reproachfully. And from the walls the antique, greenish glass, under which she had had her decisive conversation with Apollon Apollonovich, glinted at her with plain hostility: while over there—pale-hued paintings—were the Pompeian frescoes; the senator had brought her these frescoes when she was still his fiancée: thirty years had passed since then.

Anna Petrovna was seized by the drawing room's same old hospitality: seized by the lacquer and lustre; she felt a constriction in her breast, just as before; her throat tightened with an age-old disaffection; maybe Apollon Apollonovich would forgive her; but she would not forgive him: in the lacquered house the storms of life had taken their course quietly, but all the same the storms of life had taken their course here calamitously.

So a tide of dark thoughts drove her to hostile shores; she leant absent-mindedly against the window—and saw pink clouds wafting over the waves of the Neva; lumpy clouds were disgorged from the smokestacks of passing steamers, as they cast a glittering ruby strip from their bows on to the shore: after a lick at the stone pier, that strip was cast back again and merged with another coming to meet it, sweeping all the rubies into a single serpentine string of tinsel. Higher up—the flimsiest of flames became edged with ash on the clouds; ash was scattered generously: all the sky's light-shafts were choked with ash; then everything conspired to turn into a weightless monotone; and for a moment it appeared that the dim vista of lines, spires and walls with the faintly drifting darkness of shadows falling on to the stone walls' mass—it appeared that this dim vista might be the most delicate lace.

"What will you do, mistress, will you stay with us?"

"Me? ... At a hotel."

In this melting greyness a multitude of points suddenly stood out faintly, staring in astonishment: specks of light, flecks of light; these specks of light, these flecks of light swelled with strength, to spring out of the darkness as russet spots, while up above them waterfalls cascaded: dark-blue, violet, black.

Petersburg vanished into the night.

Tip-tap went their slippers

The doorbell kept ringing.

Out of the entrance-hall into the ballroom came angelic creatures in pale-blue, white or pink dresses, silvery, sparkling; they wafted by with gauze, and silks, and fans, spreading all round a balmy scent of violets, lilies and tuberose; their marble-white shoulders, lightly dusted with powder, in an hour or two would be heated and flushed, covered in perspiration; but now, before the dancing, their delicate little faces, their shoulders and their slender bare arms seemed even paler and more slender than on ordinary days; all the more meaningfully, then, these creatures' charm lit up with a kind of restrained sparkle in their pupils, as the creatures, veritable angels, formed rustling, colourful swarms of billowing muslin; their white fans, fluttering apart and folding together, created a light breeze; tip-tap went their slippers.

The doorbell kept ringing.

Briskly out of the entrance-hall into the ballroom came firm-chested genii in tautly fastened tailcoats, uniforms and pelisses—law students, hussars, gymnasium students and just ordinary people—with moustaches and without—beardless—all of them: all around they spread a kind of dependable joy and restraint. Without a hint of importunity they infiltrated the circle of brilliant gauze and seemed to the young ladies more pliant than wax; and look—now here, now there—a light, feathery fan began to beat against the breast of a moustachioed genius, like the wing of a butterfly that had settled trustingly upon that breast, and a firm-chested hussar began circumspectly to trade his vacuous innuendo with the young lady; it is with just the same circumspection that we bend our face to a delicate moth that has chanced to settle on our finger. And on the red background of the hussar's gold-threaded apparel, as though against the magnificent rising of an unheard-of sun, a slightly pink-hued profile stood out simply and distinctly; the surging whirlwind of the waltz would shortly change the pink-hued profile of this innocent angel into the profile of a fiery demon.

It was not, in truth, a ball that the Tsukatovs were giving: it was nothing more than a children's party, in which the adults too had expressed a wish to take part; true, a rumour was going around that there would be masks coming to the party too; their impending appearance perplexed, it must be admitted, Liubov Alekseevna; say what you would, it wasn't Christmas; but evidently such were the traditions of her beloved husband that he was ready to break all the rules of the calendar for the sake of dancing and children's fun; her beloved husband, the possessor of two sets of silver side-whiskers, was to this day known as Koko. In this cavorting mansion, it hardly need be said, he was Nikolai Petrovich, head of the household and father of two pretty girls of eighteen and fifteen.

These sweet fair-haired creatures were in gauze dresses and silver slippers. Since shortly after eight they had been waving their feathery fans at their father, at the housekeeper, at the chambermaid, even ... at the venerable member of the *zemstvo*, a mammoth of a man (and a relative of Koko's), who was staying in the house. At last a long-awaited timid ring at the bell was heard; the door of the ballroom, lit to full whiteness, was flung open, and the pianist, tightly buttoned into his tailcoat, like some long-legged black bird, rubbing his hands, all but tripped over a passing waiter (invited into this gleaming house on the occasion of the ball); in the waiter's hands a sheet of cardboard tinkled and trembled, studded with forfeits for the cotillion: medals, ribbons, bells. The modest pianist spread out rows of sheet music, raised and lowered the piano lid, solicitously blew on the keys and for no apparent purpose pressed the pedal with his gleaming shoe, bringing to mind a meticulous engine driver testing the locomotive's boilers prior to the departure of the train. Satisfied with the working order of the instrument, the modest pianist gathered up the folds of his tailcoat, lowered himself on to the low stool, leant backwards with his whole frame, dropped his fingers on to the keys, froze for a moment—and a thunderous chord rattled the walls: as though a summoning whistle had blown for the distant journey.

And amongst these delights, entirely in his element, no stranger, Nikolai Petrovich Tsukatov circulated lithely, spreading out the silvery lace of his side-whiskers with his fingers, gleamed with his bald pate and his clean-shaven chin, rushed from one couple to another, cracking an innocent joke with an adolescent in blue, firmly prodding with two fingers a firm-chested man with a moustache, and muttering into the ear of a man of more mature years: "It's all right, let them have their fun: people tell me that I danced my life away; but, you know, that innocent pastime saved me in those days from the sins of youth: from wine, women and cards." And amongst these delights, not at all in his element, quite a stranger, the member of the *zemstvo* lumbered clumsily about with nothing to do, nibbling at the yellow felt of his beard and treading on the trains of ladies' dresses; he ambled about on his own among the couples and then went away to his room.

Dancing to the end

Today, as usual, visitors to the drawing room occasionally made their way through the ballroom—they passed through condescendingly along the walls; impudent fans might brush their chests, beaded skirts might lash them, the warm breeze from the whirling couples might blow across their faces; but they passed through soundlessly.

A plump man with an unpleasantly pockmarked face was the first to cross the ballroom; the lapels of his frock coat stuck out inordinately because he had tightened that frock coat to excess around his ample stomach: this was the editor of a conservative newspaper, descended from a family of liberal clergy. In the drawing room he kissed the puffy hand of Liubov Alekseevna, a lady of forty-five with a flabby face that sagged with its double chin on to her corset-supported bosom. If one looked from the ballroom through two intermediate rooms he could be seen in the distance standing in the drawing room. There in the distance burned the azure sphere of an electric ceiling-lamp; there in the trembling azure light the editor of the conservative newspaper stood ponderously on his elephantine legs, expatiating nebulously in the floating wisps of blue tobacco smoke.

And no sooner had Liubov Alekseevna asked him some innocent question, than the rotund editor turned that question too into a question of great significance:

"Don't you believe it—no, madam! They only think like that because they are all idiots. I undertake to prove it precisely."

"But my husband, Koko, you know … "

"That's nothing but trickery by the Jews and the masons, my good lady: organisation, centralisation … "

"But there are some very nice, well-mannered people among them and besides—they're people of our society," the hostess put in apprehensively.

"Yes, but our society doesn't know where the power of the conspiracy lies."

"What is your opinion?"

"The power of the conspiracy is in—Charleston."

"Why ever in Charleston?"

"Because that is where the head of the entire conspiracy lives."

"Who is that head?"

"The antipope … " the editor roared.

" What do you mean exactly—the antipope?"

"Oh, you evidently haven't read anything."

"Oh, but this is all so interesting: do tell me, please."

And Liubov Alekseevna sighed and gasped as she invited the pockmarked editor to make himself comfortable in a soft armchair; and as he did so, he said:

"Yes, that's how it is, gentlemen!"

From the drawing room they could see, through the two intermediate rooms, the palpitating gleams and tremors coming through the open door of the ballroom. Thunderous sounds were heard.

"*Rrreculez!* … "

"*Balancez vos dames!* … "

And again.

"*Rrreculez* … "

Nikolai Petrovich Tsukatov had danced his life away; now Nikolai Petrovich was dancing this life to its end; dancing it lightly, inoffensively, not vulgarly; not a single cloud darkened his soul; his soul was pure and innocent, just like that sunburnt pate or that smoothly shaven chin protruding between his side-whiskers, as though it were the moon peeping out between clouds.

Everything had danced out as he wished.

He had started dancing as a small boy: he danced better than anyone; and as an accomplished dancer he had been invited to people's houses; by the end of his gymnasium days he had

203

danced himself many an acquaintance; from this immense circle of acquaintances by the time he graduated from the Law Faculty a circle of influential patrons had danced out of its own accord; and Nikolai Petrovich Tsukatov set about dancing attendance on the civil service. By that time he had danced away his estate; having danced it away, he took, with simple-hearted frivolity, to attending balls; and from such balls he brought home with remarkable ease his life's companion Liubov Alekseevna; quite by chance this companion turned out to have an enormous dowry; and from that day on Nikolai Petrovich danced at home; children were danced into existence; the children's upbringing came out dancing, all was danced with lightness, simplicity and joy.

Now he was dancing to the end of himself.

The ball

What is a drawing room during a merry waltz? It is nothing but an appendage to the ballroom and a refuge for mothers. But the astute Liubov Alekseevna, taking advantage of her husband's good nature (he did not have a single enemy), and of her own immense dowry, taking advantage, furthermore, of the fact that their house was profoundly indifferent to everything, except dancing, of course, and was therefore a neutral location for meetings—taking advantage of all these things, the astute Liubov Alekseevna, leaving her husband to conduct the dancing, conceived the desire to conduct encounters between the most diverse persons; here a member of the *zemstvo* might meet a member of the civil service; a publicist might meet the director of a department; a demagogue a Judaeophobe. Among those who visited this house, and even lunched here, was Apollon Appollonovich.

And while Nikolai Petrovich wove the *contredanse* into unforeseeable figures, it happened that in the indifferently hospitable drawing room many a conjunction was woven and unwoven.

Dancing went on here too, but of a particular kind.

Today, as usual, visitors to the drawing room occasionally made their way through the ballroom; and the second so to make his way was a man of truly antediluvian appearance, with a sweet and horrendously absent-minded face, and with a fold of his frock coat caught up on his fluff-covered back in such a way that an artless black half-belt protruded indecently between its flaps; this was a professor of statistics; a ragged yellow beard hung from his chin, and on to his shoulders tumbled matted locks that had never seen a comb. His swollen blood-red lip, detached, to all appearance, from his mouth, was particularly striking.

The point was that in view of developing events something in the nature of an accommodation was being prepared on the part of a group that supported, so to speak, not sweeping, but at all events decidedly humane reforms—men with truly patriotic hearts—not a fundamental accommodation, but a provisional one, brought about for the time being by the roar of this avalanche of meetings that had descended on everyone. The supporters of, so to speak, gradual, but at all events decidedly humane reforms, shaken by the thunder of this terrifying avalanche, had suddenly started drawing closer to the supporters of the status quo, but had not taken the crucial step to meet them; the liberal professor was the first who ventured in the name of the common good to cross this, so to speak, fateful threshold. It should not be forgotten that he was respected by the whole of society and that the most recent protest declaration had borne his signature; and at the most recent banquet his glass had been raised in welcome to the spring.

But as he entered the ballroom with its dazzling illumination, the professor lost his nerve: the gleams and tremors evidently blinded him; his swollen lip became detached from his mouth in surprise; he scanned the jubilant ballroom in the most good-natured manner, he marched up and down on the spot, he dithered, he took his unfolded handkerchief from his pocket, to wipe from his moustache the dripping moisture he had brought in from the street, and he blinked at the couples who had momentarily fallen silent between two figures of the quadrille.

And then he passed through into the drawing room, into the tremulous light of the azure electric ceiling-lamp.

The editor's voice detained him on the threshold:

"Do you understand now, madam, the connection between the war with Japan, the Jews, the threat of a Mongol invasion and this conspiracy? These Jewish tricks and the Boxer Rebellion in China are most closely and obviously connected with each other."

"I understand, now I understand!"

That was Liubov Alekseevna's cry. But the professor stood still in fear: he remained, come what may, a liberal to the marrow of his bones and a supporter of, so to speak, decidedly humane reforms: this was the first time he had entered this house, expecting to meet Apollon Apollonovich; but he was evidently not there: there was only the editor of the conservative newspaper, that same editor who had just lately slung, to put it humanely, a lump of the most disgusting mud at the collector of statistical data's twenty-five year record of enlightened activity. And the professor suddenly began to huff and puff, he began to blink angrily at the editor, began to snort ambiguously into his ragged beard, and to gather with his bright-red lip the moisture dripping from his moustache.

But the hostess' double chin turned first to the professor, then—it turned to the editor of the conservative newspaper and, indicating each to the other with her lorgnette, she introduced them to one another, which at first took them both aback, but then they proffered each other their cold fingers, puffy-sweaty ones to puffy-dry ones, liberal-humane ones—to ones not humane at all.

The professor became even more embarrassed; he bent over, snorted ambiguously, dropped into an armchair, got stuck and started wriggling there restlessly. Mr Editor, however, as though nothing were the matter, continued his interrupted conversation with their hostess. Ableukhov could have helped him out, but … Ableukhov wasn't there.

Could this really all be demanded of the professor by this astute conjunction, by the recently signed protest declaration and the glass raised at the banquet in welcome to the spring?

And the fat man went on:

"Do you understand, madam, this Jewish-Masonic activity?"

"I do, I do now."

The professor, grunting liberally and sucking his lips, could take no more; turning to the hostess, he observed:

"Allow me, madam, to add a modest word—the word of science: the information communicated here has an absolutely obvious source of origin."

But the fat man suddenly interrupted him.

While over there, over there …

Over there with one hand the pianist suddenly broke off his musical dance with an elegantly thunderous bass chord, while in the twinkling of an eye he turned the page of his music with his other hand in one flamboyant movement, and with his hand suspended in the air, the fingers spread expressively between the keyboard and the music, he turned his body towards the master of the house in a gesture of expectancy, the enamel of his blindingly white teeth gleaming.

And then in response to the pianist's gesture Nikolai Petrovich Tsukatov swiftly thrust his smoothly shaven chin out of his luxuriant side-whiskers, sketching with his smoothly shaven chin a gesture of approval and encouragement to the pianist; and then, head bowed, as though he were head-butting empty space, he rushed hastily in front of the couples on to the gleaming parquet, twisting the end of his greying whiskers between two fingers. And behind him an angelic creature flew with no will of her own, her heliotrope shawl waving in the air. Nikolai Petrovich Tsukatov, taking inspiration from his own flight of choreographic fancy, flew like lightning at the pianist and roared like a lion at the whole room:

"*Pas-de-quatre, s'il vous plaît!*"

And the angelic creature flew along behind him with no will of her own.

Meanwhile scampering servants appeared industriously in the corridor. For some reason tables, stools and chairs were brought out from somewhere and then brought in again; a mountain of fresh sandwiches was carried through into the dining room on a porcelain dish. The tinkle of forks was heard. A pile of delicate plates was carried through.

Couple after couple thronged into the brightly-lit corridor. Jokes and laughter rained down in a universal cackle, and chairs were pulled out in a universal rumble.

A cigarette haze arose in the corridor, in the smoking-room; a cigarette haze arose in the entrance-hall. A cadet, pulling his glove from his fingers and stuffing his hand into his pocket, was fanning his cheeks with a discoloured glove; two girls with their arms round each other were sharing some treasured secrets, possibly of very recent origin; the brunette told the blonde, and the blonde snorted and bit her delicate handkerchief.

Standing in the corridor, it was possible to glimpse the corner of the dining room, crowded with guests; sandwiches were carried in there too, bowls laden with fruit, and bottles of wine, and bottles of a sour fizzy drink that bubbles in your nose.

Now only the pianist was left in the over-illuminated ballroom, gathering up his music; having scrupulously wiped his overheated fingers, carefully cleaned the piano keyboard with a soft cloth, and tidied his music into a pile, this modest pianist, in whose presence the servants did not hesitate to open all the ventilation windows in the ballroom, set off hesitantly through the lacquered corridor, for all the world like a long-legged black bird. He too was eagerly looking forward to tea and sandwiches.

In the doorway to the drawing room a lady of forty-five floated out of the semi-darkness, her fleshy chin sagging on to her corset-supported bosom. And she gazed through her lorgnette.

And behind her there floated through into the ballroom an immensely portly man with an unpleasantly pockmarked face, with a paunch of venerable proportions tightly constrained by a fold of his frock coat.

Somewhere further off the professor of statistics was pottering about; till now he had been as though on tenterhooks; but now he had come across the *zemstvo* member, languishing on his own by the passageway, had suddenly recognised him, smiled in greeting, and even pinched between two fingers, in his anxiety, a button of his frock coat, as though he were grasping at a life jacket thrown to save him; and out rang the words:

"According to the statistical data … The annual per capita consumption of salt by the average Dutchman … "

And out there rang again:

"The annual consumption of salt by the average Spaniard … "

"According to statistical data … "

As though someone were weeping

They were expecting masks. And still the masks hadn't come. Clearly it was nothing but a rumour. They expected the masks all the same.

And then the tinkle of the bell was heard: it rang out timidly; it was as though someone uninvited were drawing attention to himself and begging admittance out of the damp, malevolent mist and the slush of the street; but no one answered. And then the bell jangled again, more loudly.

As though someone were weeping.

At that moment a ten-year-old girl rushed breathlessly out of the two intermediate rooms and saw the ballroom, so recently full, glittering in its emptiness. There, by the entrance to the vestibule, a door banged questioningly, and its cut-glass doorknob, gleaming as though with diamonds, wobbled slightly; and when the empty space between walls and door had defined itself sufficiently, out of that emptiness a black mask cautiously emerged as far as its nose, and two gleaming sparks shone through the eye-slits.

Then the ten-year-old child saw between the wall and the door a black mask and two unfriendly sparks from the eye-slits directed straight at her; then the whole mask emerged and a black beard made of curly lace revealed itself; after the beard there gradually appeared in the doorway, with a rustle, something velvet, and the ten-year-old first raised her fingers fearfully to her eyes and then smiled in joy, clapped her hands and with a cry: "The masks have come, they've come!", set off at a run into the depths of the enfilade, to the place where, out of the suspended wisps of blue tobacco smoke, the nebulous professor could be distinguished on his elephantine legs.

A bright, blood-red domino, treading jerkily, dragged its velvet across the lacquered panels of the parquet; it left faint traces on the parquet panels in the floating crimson flicker of its own reflections; it was as though a fitful pool of blood, spreading crimson across the ballroom, ran from panel to panel of the parquet; weighty feet came tramping to meet it, from afar huge boots came squeaking towards the domino.

The *zemstvo* member, now more acclimatised to the ballroom, stood still in perplexity, grasping a tuft of his beard in one hand; meanwhile the lonely domino seemed to be begging him mutely not to drive it from this house back into the Petersburg slush, begging him not to drive it from this house back into the dense, malevolent mist. The *zemstvo* member evidently had it in mind to make a joke, because he cleared his throat; but when he attempted to express his joke verbally, the joke assumed a somewhat incoherent form:

"Mm ... Yes, yes ... "

The domino walked towards him with its body thrust out imploringly, walked towards him with its rustling red arm thrust out, and from its head, which drooped from its hunched shoulders, transparent lace swirled upwards slightly.

"Tell me, are you a mask?"

Silence.

"Mm … Yes, yes … "

The mask was begging; it flung itself forwards with its body thrust right out—in emptiness, across lacquer and gleams, over a pool of its own reflections; it scurried in solitude about the ballroom.

"What a business … "

And again it flung itself forwards, and again red reflections slithered forwards too.

Now the *zemstvo* member, puffing and panting, began to retreat.

Suddenly he waved an arm in exasperation; and he turned round; he began hurriedly, Lord alone knows why—to go back where he had come from, where the azure electric lamp shone, where in the azure electric light stood the professor of statistics with his frock coat sticking up, expatiating nebulously in the wisps of tobacco smoke; but the *zemstvo* member was all but knocked off his feet by a swarm of careering damsels: their ribbons fluttered, their cotillion trinkets fluttered in the air and their knees rustled.

This twittering swarm had run out to have a look at the mask that had wandered in; but the twittering swarm stopped at the door, and its merry exclamations suddenly turned into a sibilant whisper; in the end that whisper fell silent; the silence weighed heavily. All of a sudden behind the backs of the young ladies a bold cadet declaimed:

Who are you, sombre visitor,
Fateful domino?
See—the cloak of crimson
Wraps him head to toe.

Against the lacquer and the lights, over the ripples of its own reflections, the domino made a pathetic sideways dash, and the wind from the open ventilator whistled in an icy stream on the bright velvet; poor domino: as though it had been caught out in some misdemeanour—it remained bent over in a jutting silhouette; with its rustling red arm thrust out, as though it were mutely imploring them all not to drive it from this house back into the Petersburg slush, imploring them not to drive it back from this house into the damp, malevolent mist.

The cadet broke off.

"Tell us, domino, aren't you the one who runs around the Petersburg Prospects?"

"Gentlemen, have you read today's *Petersburg Chronicle*?"

"What's in it?"

"Why, the red domino again … "

"Gentlemen, that's rubbish."

The solitary domino stayed silent.

Suddenly one of the young ladies at the front with her head bowed, the one who had frowned so sternly at the uninvited guest—whispered something with feeling to her friend:

"Rubbish … "

"No, no: it gives you the jitters … "

"I suppose our dear domino has lost his tongue: call yourself a domino … "

"Really, we shouldn't have anything to do with him … "

"Domino, indeed! … "

The solitary domino stayed silent.

"Wouldn't you like some tea and sandwiches?"

"Wouldn't you like some of this?"

With that exclamation, the cadet swung his arm and let fly with a rustling stream of serpentin over the heads of the young ladies. For a moment a ribbon of paper unwound in the air in an arc; and when the end of it struck the mask with a dry clatter, the arc of paper, winding together again, lost its force and fell to the floor; the domino made no answer to this amusing trick, but simply thrust out its arms, imploring them not to drive it from this house on to the Petersburg streets, imploring them not to drive it from this house into the dense, malevolent mist.

"Come on, let's go away from here … "

And the swarm of damsels ran off.

Only the one who had been standing closest of all to the domino hesitated for a moment; she measured the domino with a sympathetic gaze; sighing for some reason, she turned and went away; and she turned round again, and again said to herself:

"All the same … It … It isn't right."

A small withered figure

It was still him, of course: Nikolai Apollonovich. He had come today to say—to say what?

He had forgotten his own self; forgotten his thoughts; and forgotten his hopes; he was intoxicated by his own predestined role: the godlike, passionless creature had flown away; naked passion remained, and passion turned to poison. A feverish poison penetrated his brain, poured unseen from his eyes in a cloud of flame, entwining him in clinging blood-red velvet: as though he now looked at everything with a charred face out of flames that seared his body, and that charred countenance turned into a black mask, and the flames that seared his body—into red silk. He had now truly become a clown, an ugly red clown (as she had once called him). Now this clown was pouring scorn—perfidiously, vengefully, incisively—on someone's truth—his own, or hers?—and once again the question: was it love, or hate?

It was as though all these recent days he had been casting spells on her, stretching his cold arms from the windows of the yellow house, stretching his cold arms from the granite into the mist of the Neva. He wanted to embrace in love the mental image he had evoked, he wanted to smother in vengeance the faintly wafting silhouette; it was for this that all these days cold arms had stretched from one space to another, and that was why all these days from such a space unearthly confessions had been whispered in her ears, sibilant invocations and hoarse passions; and that was why inchoate whistles had echoed in her ears, and the crimson of the leaves had chased between her feet a rustling web of words.

And that was why he had now come to that house: but she, unfaithful, was not there; in the corner he fell to thinking. He saw the venerable and astonished *zemstvo* member as though in a haze; somewhere far off, in the labyrinth of mirrors, it seemed, the figures of the laughing girls floated past as fitful blurs; and when, emerging from this labyrinth, from the cold greenish surface, the distant echoes of questions and the paper ribbon of the serpentin had struck him, his surprise was like surprise in a dream: he was surprised to see how a reflection, with no existence of its own, emerged before him into the bright world; but just as he regarded them as unstable, fleeting dream reflections, so these reflections themselves evidently took him for an emanation from the other world; and as an emanation from the other world, he drove them all away.

Now distant echoes reached him again, and he turned round slowly: dimly, indistinctly—somewhere over there, over there—a small withered figure quickly crossed the room, without hair, without moustache, without eyebrows. Nikolai Apollonovich had difficulty making out the details of this figure that had rushed into the room— from the effort of looking through the eye-slits he felt a stinging in his eyes (besides, he suffered from short-sightedness), all that could be made out clearly was the outline of a pair of greenish ears— somewhere over there, over there. There was something familiar in all of this, something live and close, and Nikolai Apollonovich impulsively, in forgetfulness, leapt towards the figure to see it from close to; but the figure started back, seemed even to grasp at its heart, ran off a little way and looked at him from there. And what was Nikolai Apollonovich's astonishment: standing right in front of him was a face belonging to his family; it seemed to him to be covered all over with wrinkles that had worn away the cheeks, the forehead, chin and nose; from a distance that face could be taken for the face of a eunuch, a young one rather than an old one; from close to, though, it was a feeble, frail old man, marked by barely noticeable side-whiskers: in a word—right under his nose Nikolai Apollonovich saw his father. Apollon Apollonovich, fingering the links of his watch-chain, stared with ill-concealed terror at the velvet domino that had so suddenly rushed up to him. Something like a conjecture flashed across those blue eyes; Nikolai Apollonovich felt an unpleasant shiver, there was something eerie about gazing shamelessly from under a mask at those dispassionate eyes, before which at normal times he would lower his eyes in unaccountable diffidence; there was something eerie about reading in those eyes now fear and a kind of helpless, frail senescence; and the conjecture that flashed across so quickly, was read as a good guess: Nikolai Apollonovich thought he had been recognised. But that was not the case: Apollon Apollonovich merely thought that some tactless joker was terrorising him, a man of the imperial entourage, with the symbolic colour of his bright cape.

All the same he began to feel his own pulse. More than once of late Nikolai Apollonovich had noticed this secret gesture of the senator's fingers (evidently the senator's heart was weary of working).

Seeing this gesture now, he felt something akin to compassion; and involuntarily he thrust out his rustling red arms towards his father; as though he were imploring his father not to run away from him, choking in a heart attack, as though he were imploring his father to forgive him for all his past trespasses. But Apollon Apollonovich went on feeling his pulse with trembling fingers and in his heart attack ran off—somewhere over there, over there …

Suddenly the bell rang: the entire room was filled with masks; a string of black Capuchins burst in; the black Capuchins quickly formed a chain around their red comrade, and began dancing some kind of dance around him; their velvet tails fluttered apart and folded together; the tips of their hoods flew upwards and fell down again hilariously; on the chest of each was embroidered a skull and crossbones; and the skull danced.

The red domino, fighting free of them, then ran out of the ballroom; the black flock of Capuchins chased after him guffawing; they flew like that along the broad corridor and into the dining room; all those sitting at the tables tapped their plates in greeting.

"Capuchins, masks, clowns."

Flocks of pearly-pink and heliotrope damsels jumped up from their seats, hussars, law students, university students jumped up from their seats. Nikolai Petrovich Tsukatov jumped up in his place with a glass of Rhine wine, roaring out his thunderous "*vivat*" in honour of this weird company.

Then someone commented:

"Gentlemen, this is too much … "

But he was dragged away to dance.

In the ballroom the pianist arched his spine, as his bristling quiff of hair danced above his fingers that ran up and down pouring out roulades; the treble pranced away while the bass dragged its feet.

And glancing with an innocent smile at a black Capuchin that had swung its velvet cape with a particularly brash gesture, an angelic creature in a violet skirt suddenly bent under the opening of its hood (the mask was staring her in the face); and this creature grasped in her hand the hump of a stripy clown, whose one (blue) leg soared up into the air, while the other (red) one bent down to the parquet; but the creature was not afraid: it gathered up the hem of its skirt, and a silver slipper emerged from under it.

And off they went—one, two, three …

And after them came Spanish ladies, monks and devils; harlequins, pelisses, fans, bare backs, silver scalloped stoles; above them all, swaying, danced a long-legged palm-tree.

Only over there, on his own, leaning against the windowsill between the lowered green blinds, Apollon Apollonovich gasped for breath in an attack of the heart disease whose extent was not known to a single person.

Pompadour

The Angel Peri stood in front of the dull oval mirror, leaning slightly backwards: everything ran away down there and at the bottom became blurred: the ceiling, the walls, the floor; and she herself ran down there into the depths, into the greenish murk; and there, there—emerging from a foam of lace and muslin and a fountain of various articles was a beautiful woman with luxuriously bouffant hair and a beauty spot on her cheek: Madame Pompadour!

Her hair, wound into curls and barely fastened by a ribbon, was as white as snow, and the powder-puff was frozen over the powder-compact in such slender fingers; her tightly girt, pale-azure waist was bent ever so slightly to the left with a black mask in her hand; from the tight, décolleté bodice, like living pearls, her bosom swelled, moving with her breath, and from the tight sleeves, rustling with velvet, Valenciennes lace frothed out in delicate folds; and everywhere, everywhere around the décolletage, beneath the décolletage—was the froth of lace; beneath the bodice the pannier skirt, as though rising in the breath of languid zephyrs, swayed, played with its flounces, and glittered with a garland of silver grasses in the form of delicate scallops; below were exactly similar slippers; and on each slipper a silver pompon shone. But it was strange: in this costume she seemed suddenly older and less pretty; instead of her little pink lips, indecently red lips, overly heavy lips, splayed out, spoiling her face; and when her eyes squinted, then in Madame Pompadour something of the witch appeared for a moment: at that moment she hid the letter in her décolletage.

At that moment too Mavrusha came running into the room, carrying a cane of light wood with a golden knob, festooned with ribbons: but when Madame Pompadour stretched out her hand to take the cane, she found her hand holding a note from her husband; it said: "If you go out this evening, you will never again return to my house. Sergei Sergeevich Likhutin."

That note, of course, was a matter for Sofia Petrovna Likhutina, and not for her, Madame Pompadour, and Madame Pompadour smiled at the note in contempt; she stared into the mirror—into its depths, into the greenish murk: far, far away down there something seemed to ruffle the surface; suddenly out of those depths and greenish murk there seemed to emerge into the crimson light of the dark-red lampshade a waxen face; and she turned round.

Behind her back stood motionless her husband, the officer; but again she laughed out loud in contempt, and lifting her pannier skirt slightly by the scallops, she glided smoothly away from him in a series of curtsies; the hushed currents of the zephyr bore her away from him, and her crinoline rustled, swaying like a bell, in the zephyr's sweet gusts; and when she found herself at the door, she turned to face him, and with a hand on which a velvet mask was wound, she thumbed her nose at the officer with a sly smile; through the door a peal of laughter resounded and an innocent exclamation:

"Mavrusha, my fur coat!"

Then Sergei Sergeevich Likhutin, second lieutenant of His Majesty's Gr…skii regiment, pale as death but perfectly calm, sprang with an ironic smile after the graceful mask and then, clicking his spurs, stood to attention ever so deferentially with the fur coat in his hands; with yet greater deference he threw the coat over her shoulders, opened the door wide and considerately pointed her with his hand out there—into the tenebrous darkness; and when she passed through into that darkness, rustling, her head held high before such a humble servant, then the humble servant made her another low bow, clicking his spurs. The tenebrous darkness rushed in upon her—rushed in from all sides: it flooded her rustling outlines; something went on rustling, down there on the steps of the staircase. The outside door slammed; then Sergei Sergeevich Likhutin began with the same exaggeratedly abrupt gestures to walk round everywhere switching off the lights.

The hand of fate

The pianist broke off his musical dance with an elegantly thunderous bass chord, while with the other hand he turned over the page of his music in one flamboyant movement; but at that moment Nikolai Petrovich Tsukatov suddenly thrust his smoothly-shaven chin out of his luxuriant side-whiskers, rushing swiftly with bowed head in front of the couples on to the glittering parquet, pulling behind him at great speed a creature with no will of her own.

"*Pas-de-quatre, s'il vous plaît!* ... "

"Come with me," some Madame Pompadour attached herself to Nikolai Apollonovich, and Nikolai Apollonovich, not recognising Madame Pompadour, reluctantly gave her his arm; jerking her mask upwards with a particularly cruel gesture, Madame Pompadour glanced with a barely perceptible grin at her red cavalier, and stretched out her arm to lay it, as though with no will of her own, upon the arm of the domino; with the other hand, in close-fitting kid-skin and with her fan dangling from it, Madame Pompadour hitched up her hem of floating azure haze, and from it with a rustle a silvery slipper peeped.

And off they went.

One-two-three—and a movement of her foot as she bent from the waist:

"Have you recognised me?"

"No."

"Are you still looking for someone?"

One-two-three—and another bend from the waist, and again a slipper peeped out.

"I have a letter for you."

After the first couple—the domino and the marquise—harlequins set off, Spanish ladies, pearly-pale damsels, law students, hussars and will-less, muslin creatures; fans, bare shoulders, silvery backs and shawls.

Suddenly the red domino's hand embraced the slender, azure waist, while his other hand, grasping his partner's, felt a letter in it; at the same moment the dark-green, black gloved hands of all the couples, and the red hands of the hussars embraced all the slender waists of the heliotrope, *gris-de-perle*, rustling ladies, to whirl again and again in the turns of the waltz.

217

Shooting out in front of them all, the grey-haired master of the house roared at the couples:

"*A vos places.*"

And along behind him flew an adolescent with no will of her own.

Apollon Apollonovich

Apollon Apollonovich recovered from his attack; Apollon Apollonovich gazed into the depths of the enfilade of rooms; hidden in dark curtains, he stood there unnoticed by anyone; he tried to move away from the curtains in such a way that his appearance in the drawing room should not betray his unstatesmanlike behaviour. Apollon Apollonovich hid from everyone these attacks of his heart disease; but it would have been even more unpleasant for him to admit that today's attack was occasioned by the red domino's appearance before him: the red colour was, of course, an emblem of the chaos that was destroying Russia; but he had no wish to admit that the domino's ridiculous attempt to frighten him had any political implications.

Apollon Apollonovich was, moreover, ashamed of his fear.

As he recovered from the attack he kept glancing into the ballroom. Everything that he saw there struck his gaze with its strident mass of colour; the images flashing by had something repugnant about them, striking him personally: he saw a monster with a double-headed eagle for its head; over there somewhere, over there—the small withered figure of a knight with a gleaming sword blade quickly crossed the room, for all the world like some luminous emanation; he was so indistinct, so faintly drawn, as he ran by, with no hair, no moustache, marked only by the contours of green ears and a glittering item of bejewelled insignia dangling on his chest; and when a creature with a single horn emerged from the masks and Capuchins to throw itself upon the little knight, with its horn it broke the knight's luminous emanation; something clattered in the distance and fell on to the floor in the likeness of a moonbeam; it was strange that this picture awoke in Apollon Apollonovich's consciousness a recent event that had happened to him but had been forgotten, and he felt his spine: for a moment Apollon Apollonovich thought he might have *tabes dorsalis*. He turned away from the motley ballroom in disgust; and went through into the drawing room.

On his appearance here everyone rose from their seats; Liubov Alekseevna flowed amicably towards him; and the professor of statistics, who had risen from his seat, muttered:

"We had occasion to meet once: extremely glad to see you; there is a matter, Apollon Apollonovich, I would like to discuss with you."

To which Apollon Apollonovich, after kissing his hostess' hand, replied a little drily:

"But I have reception times in my office in the Establishment, you know."

With this reply he was cutting off the possibility of a certain liberal party making a rapprochement with the government. The conjunction fell apart; and it was left to the professor simply to depart with dignity from this gleaming house, and henceforth to sign without inhibition all expressions of protest, and raise his glass without inhibition at all liberal banquets.

As he made ready to leave he went up to the hostess, upon whom the editor was still practising his eloquence.

"You believe that the destruction of Russia is being planned in the hope of social equality. How should that be so? They simply want to sacrifice us to the devil."

"How do you mean?" asked the hostess in surprise.

"It's very simple, madam: you are only surprised because you haven't read anything on this topic … "

"But come now, come!" the professor again interposed, "you are relying on the inventions of Taxille … "

"Taxille?" the hostess interrupted, suddenly took out a little notebook and started writing:

"Taxille, you say? … "

"We are to be sacrificed to Satan because the higher echelons of the Jewish-Masonic conspiracy are followers of a particular cult, Palladism … This cult … "

"Palladism?" the hostess interrupted, and again started noting something in her little book.

"Pa-lla- … How was that?"

"Palladism."

From somewhere the housekeeper's anxious sigh was heard, and then a tray was carried in with a cut-glass decanter, filled to the brim with a cooling beverage, and placed in the room between the drawing room and the ballroom. Standing in the drawing room it was possible to see first one, then another light-spangled girl with face flushed and translucent blonde plaits dishevelled, tear loose from the melodic tide of sounds beating at the walls, and from the swell of lace-and-muslin couples swaying in the waltz, and run, laughing, into the adjacent room in her white silk slippers, her high heels tapping, to pour hastily from the decanter some of the sour, ruby-red liquid: thick ice-cold cordial. And drink it greedily.

And the hostess blurted out distractedly to the editor:

"Tell me, though … "

Putting her minute lorgnette to her eyes, she saw a law student, his tight-waisted uniform rustling with silk, dart out of the ballroom and up to the flushed girl in the next room who was drinking cordial, and, rolling his 'r's in his throat with an unnaturally deep bass voice, snatch the glass of ruby-red cordial from the girl in jest and bashfully take a cold sip. And, interrupting the editor's fierce utterances, Liubov Alekseevna stood up with a rustle and glided through into the half-dark room to observe sternly:

"What are you doing in here? Dance, dance."

And then the happy couple returned to the ballroom that seethed with light; the law student put his snow-white glove round the girl's wasp waist; the girl—leant her weight on that snow-white glove; and suddenly the two of them began to swoop and sway entrancingly, tripping along on brisk, brisk toes, cleaving through the flying dresses, shawls and fans that wound sparkling patterns around them; in the end they themselves turned into luminescent spray. Over there the pianist, elaborately arching his spine, bent with a surreptitious air over his fingers as they flew across the keys, to pour out somewhat strident treble sounds: they raced away after one another; then the pianist, leaning back in languor, his piano stool squealing, ran his fingers down to the deepest bass …

"Taxille spun an utter cock-and-bull story about the masons," the acerbic voice of the professor rang out, "unfortunately many people believed it; but later Taxille quite decisively renounced the story; he publicly confessed that his sensational declaration to the Pope was nothing but a straightforward mockery of the backwardness and ill-will of the Vatican. But for that Taxille was cursed in a papal encyclical … "

At this point a new person entered—a rather fidgety, rather taciturn gent with a huge wart beside his nose—and he suddenly started nodding in approval, started smiling at the senator, rubbing the fingers of one hand against those of the other; and with an ambiguous humility he drew the senator away into a corner:

"You see … Apollon Apollonovich … The director of N N Department suggested … how should I put it … Well … asking you a certain rather ticklish question."

After that it was hard to make anything out: all that could be heard was the gent whispering something into a pale ear with an ambiguous humility, and Apollon Apollonovich turning on him with a kind of pathetic fear.

"Tell me straight … my son?"

"Well, exactly, exactly: that precisely is the ticklish question."

"My son has dealings with? … "

After that nothing at all could be made out; all that was heard was: "It's trivial … "

"This is all really quite trivial … "

"Though it is a pity, of course, that this unseemly joke has acquired such an unseemly character that the press … "

"And you know: we have ordered the Petersburg police, I have to admit, to keep an eye on your son … "

"Merely for his own good, of course … "

And again a whisper trembled in the air. And the senator asked:

"The domino, you say?"

"Yes—that very one."

With these words the fidgety gent pointed in the direction of the next room, where somewhere over there with jerky steps the anxious domino was dragging his velvet across the lacquered panels of the parquet.

Uproar

After handing over the letter, Sofia Petrovna Likhutina slipped away from her cavalier and collapsed in prostration on to a soft stool; her arms and legs refused to function.

What had she done?

She had seen the red domino rush past her from the ballroom into the corner of the empty communicating room; there, unnoticed, the red domino had torn open the envelope; the note had crackled in those brightly rustling hands. Struggling better to see the fine, minute handwriting of the note, the red domino had unwittingly raised the mask on to his forehead, which made the black lace of the beard, with its two luxurious folds, frame the pale face like two wings of a black silk cap; from those trembling wings that face had protruded, waxen, motionless, with lips apart, and the hand had shaken, and the note had shaken in the hand; and a cold sweat had appeared on the forehead.

The red domino could not now see Madame Pompadour as she observed him from her corner; he was completely immersed in reading; making anxious movements, he opened the flaps of his long garment, revealing his ordinary suit—a dark-green frock coat; Nikolai Apollonovich pulled out his golden pince-nez and, putting it to his eyes, bent his face over the note.

Nikolai Apollonovich straightened abruptly; he gazed in her direction with a fixed stare; but he did not see her: his lips must have been whispering quite incoherent things—and Sofia Petrovna was on the point of rushing over to him from her corner, because she could no longer bear those dilated eyes fixed upon her. Then people came into the room; the red domino nervously concealed the note in his fingers as they slipped into the folds of the cape; but the red domino forgot to lower the mask. And so he stood with the mask raised on to his forehead, with his mouth half-open and an unseeing gaze.

Even more wildly than before the little girl came rushing in after the waltz to cool down; she almost knocked the *zemstvo* member off his feet, who for some reason was standing dreamily by himself at the entrance, stopped in front of the pier glass, adjusted the loose ribbon on her hair, retied her white silk slipper, putting her foot up on to a chair; she set up a suspicious whispering there in the corner with her friend, a little girl like herself, as they listened to the stream of sounds, the discordant rustle and shuffle of feet, the hoarse cries from the drawing room, the laughter, the calls of the master of ceremonies, as they listened to the faint tinkle of the cavaliers' spurs.

Suddenly she noticed the domino with his raised mask; and, seeing him, she cried out:

"So that's who you are! Good evening, Nikolai Apollonovich, good evening: who would have recognised you?"

Sofia Petrovna Likhutina saw Nikolai Apollonovich give the girl a smile full of suffering, then start away strangely and set off at a run into the ballroom.

Two rows of dancers stood there, floating into vision in a delicately blinding play of pearly-pink, *gris-de-perle*, heliotrope, blue and white velvets and silks: on the silks and velvets lay shawls and scarves, veils, fans and beads, on the shoulders lay heavy lace in silvery scallops; at the slightest movement a scaly back shot sparks; now everywhere flushed arms were seen, fingers that played unthinkingly with the blades of fans, unbecoming stains on the white velvet and the swaying décolletages, cheeks now wholly crimson, all in a haze of hairstyles troubled by the dance.

Two rows of dancing couples stood there, floating into vision with the black, green and bright-red cloth of hussars' uniforms, gold collars that chafed the chin, false chests and shoulders of the uniforms, snow-white openings revealing waistcoats that creaked at every effort, gleaming tailcoats the colour of a raven's wing.

Nikolai Apollonovich flew headlong past the masks and cavaliers, treading jerkily on trembling legs; and the blood-red satin dragged behind him on the lacquered parquet panels, barely registering on the parquet panels in a fleeting, crimson swell of its own reflections; like a fitful red lightning flash that crimson swell licked the parquet in front of the monstrous fleeing figure.

The red domino's flight with its mask raised on to its forehead, revealing the protruding face of Nikolai Apollonovich, created total uproar; the merry couples rushed away; one young lady had an attack of hysterics; in terror two masks suddenly disclosed their astonished faces; and when the hussar of the Life-Guards Shporyshev, recognising the fleeing Ableukhov, grabbed him by the sleeve with the words: "Nikolai Apollonovich, Nikolai Apollonovich, for goodness' sake tell us what's the matter," then Nikolai Apollonovich, like a hunted animal, grinned pitifully with a demented face, in an attempt to laugh, but no smile transpired; snatching his sleeve away, Nikolai Apollonovich disappeared through the door.

An indescribable confusion ran through the ballroom; the young ladies and their cavaliers busily told each other their impressions;

all were in distress; the masks, which had just now been gliding by mysteriously, all those little blue knights, harlequins, Spanish ladies lost their fascination; from under the mask of the two-headed monster that ran up to Shporyshev an anxious and familiar voice was heard:

"For goodness' sake, explain what all this means?"

And Shporyshev, hussar of the Life-Guards, recognised Vergefden's voice.

The commotion in the ballroom was instinctively communicated through the two connecting rooms to the drawing room: and there, there—where the azure sphere of the electric lamp shone, where in that trembling azure light the drawing room guests stood somewhat ponderously, expatiating nebulously among the suspended wisps of blue tobacco smoke—these guests gazed in anxiety—there, into the ballroom. Among this whole group the gaunt figure of the senator stood out, the pale face, as though of papier-mâché, with firmly compressed lips, two small sideburns, and the outline of the greenish ears: that was exactly how he had been depicted on the title page of a gutter magazine.

In the ballroom a plague of conjectures, perplexities and rumours was on the loose concerning the strange, very strange, exceedingly strange behaviour of the senator's son; it was said there, in the first place, that this behaviour was occasioned by a certain drama; in the second place a rumour was circulated to the effect that Nikolai Apollonovich, who had so mysteriously visited the Tsukatovs' house, was that very red domino that had created such a sensation in the press. There were discussions about what all this might mean. It was said that the senator knew nothing about it; from the distance, from the ballroom, nods were directed into the drawing room, where the figure of the senator now stood and where his gaunt face stood out so indistinctly among the suspended wisps of blue tobacco smoke.

But what if? …

We left Sofia Petrovna Likhutina—alone, at the ball; now we shall return to her.

Sofia Petrovna Likhutina stood still in the middle of the ballroom.

Her terrible vengeance now dawned upon her for the first time: the crumpled envelope had passed into his hands, Sofia Petrovna

Likhutina hardly understood what she had done; Sofia Petrovna had not understood what she had read in the crumpled envelope the day before. But now the import of the terrible note dawned on her with clarity: the letter was inviting Nikolai Apollonovich to throw a bomb with a clockwork mechanism, which, apparently, was already lying in his desk; to judge by the implication, he was expected to throw this bomb at *the senator* (everyone called Apollon Apollonovich *the senator*).

Sofia Petrovna stood distractedly amongst the masks, bending slightly from her pale-azure waist, wondering what all this might mean. It was, of course, someone's wicked, base joke; but she had so wanted to give him a scare with this joke: he was, after all, a … base coward. But what if … what if what the letter said was true? And what if … Nikolai Apollonovich did keep in his desk things of such terrible import? And if this became known? And now he would be caught? … Sofia Petrovna stood distractedly amongst the masks with her pale-azure waist, fiddling with her locks, all silver-white with powder and curled magnificently.

And then she began to twist and turn uneasily amongst the masks; and then the Valenciennes lace she wore began to flutter; and her pannier skirt, below her corsage, as though rising in the breath of languid zephyrs, swayed with its frills and glittered with its garland of silver grasses in the form of delicate scallops. Around her voices, merging in a single murmur, unchangingly, unceasingly, importunately droned their fateful refrain. A little group of grey-browed matrons, their satin skirts rustling, were preparing to depart from *such* a merry ball; this one, her neck stretched forward, summoned her daughter, a *paysanne*, from the swarm of clowns; while that one fussed around with her tiny lorgnette at her eyes. Over them all hung the alarming atmosphere of scandal. The pianist stopped rending the air with sounds; of his own accord he placed his elbow on the piano lid; he waited for an invitation to re-start the dancing; but no invitation came.

The cadets, the schoolchildren, the law students—all dived in among the waves of clowns, and, diving, disappeared; they weren't there any more; from all sides could be heard—grumbles, rustles, whispers.

"No, did you see, did you see? Do you understand it?"

"You don't need to tell me, it's terrible … "

"I always said so, I always said so, *ma chère:* he's produced a good-for-nothing. And *tante* Lise always said so; and Mimi said so; Nicolas said so."

"Poor Anna Petrovna: I can understand her! … "

"Yes, I understand her too: we all understand."

"Here he is himself, here he is … "

"His ears are really awful … "

"They say he's going to be a minister … "

"He'll ruin the country … "

"Someone ought to tell him … "

"Just look: the *bat* is looking at us; it's as though he senses that we're talking about him … And the way the Tsukatovs are fawning on him—you feel ashamed to watch … "

"They won't dare to tell him why we're leaving … They say Madame Tsukatov comes from a clergy family."

Suddenly the whistle of the ancient serpent resounded from the agitated little group of grey-browed matrons:

"Look! He's gone: more like a chicken than a chancellor."

But what if … if Nikolai Apollonovich was really keeping a bomb in his desk? Why, it might be discovered; why, he might jolt the desk (he's absent-minded). Maybe in the evenings he sits at this desk working with an open book. Sofia Petrovna vividly imagined the sclerotic Ableukhov forehead with its blue veins leaning over the desk (there was a bomb in the desk). A bomb is something round which you must not touch. And Sofia Petrovna Likhutina shuddered. For a moment she vividly pictured Nikolai Apollonovich rubbing his hands over the tea tray; on the table—the red horn of the gramophone was regaling their ears with passionate Italian arias; oh, why did they have to quarrel? And what was the sense of this ridiculous delivery of the letter, the domino and all the rest …

An extremely fat man attached himself to Sofia Petrovna (a Spaniard from Granada); she moved aside, the fat man moved aside too (the Spaniard from Granada); for a moment he was pressed against her by the crowd, and she had the impression his hands were rubbing up and down her skirt.

"You aren't a lady: you're a sweetie-pie."

"Lippanchenko!" And she hit him with her fan.

"Lippanchenko, explain to me … "

But Lippanchenko interrupted her:

"You're in a better position to know, madam: don't play at being naïve."

And Lippanchenko, clinging to her skirt, pressed firmly against her; she struggled to tear away from him; but the crowd squeezed them even closer together; what was he up to, this Lippanchenko? Oh, he was really obscene.

"Lippanchenko, you mustn't do that."

He gave a greasy laugh:

"I saw you there handing over … "

"Not a word about that."

He gave a greasy laugh:

"Very well, very well! Now come out with me into this wonderful night … "

"Lippanchenko! You are a cad … "

She tore free of Lippanchenko.

The Spaniard from Granada clicked along behind her with some castanets, performing some passionate Spanish dance steps.

But what if—the letter was not a joke: what if … if his fate was sealed. No, no, no! Such terrible things as that don't happen in the world; there aren't such beasts as would force a demented son to raise his hand against his father. It was all a joke on the part of his comrades. How silly of her— to be so frightened by nothing more than his friends' joke. But what about him, though? He had been frightened by his friends' joke, too; but he was just a coward: look how he had run away from her (there at the Winter Canal) at the sound of a police whistle; she didn't regard the Winter Canal as some prosaic kind of place that you could run away from at a police whistle …

He hadn't behaved like Hermann: he had slipped and fallen over, showing his trouser straps under the silk. And now: he hadn't laughed at the naïve joke by his revolutionary friends, and he hadn't recognised her as the transmitter of the letter: he had run off across the ballroom with his mask in his hands, letting his face become the laughing stock of all the ladies and their cavaliers. No, let Sergei Sergeich Likhutin teach that cad and coward a lesson! Let Sergei Sergeich Lihutin challenge him to a duel …

The Second Lieutenant! ... Sergei Sergeich Likhutin! ... Second Lieutenant Likhutin had been behaving in a most reprehensible manner since the previous evening: he had been muttering things into his moustache and clenching his fist; he had had the audacity to come into her bedroom to talk things through in nothing but his underwear; and then he had had the audacity to march around on the other side of the partition until morning.

She vaguely recalled the crazed shouts of yesterday, the bloodshot eyes and the fist crashing down on the table: had Sergei Sergeich lost his mind? She had begun to suspect him a long time ago: his silence these three months had been suspicious; his disappearances to work had been suspicious. Oh, how lonely she was, poor thing! She so needed his firm support now; she wanted her husband, second lieutenant Likhutin to put his arms around her like a child and carry her away ...

Instead of that the Spaniard from Granada darted up to her again and whispered in her ear:

"Aren't you coming, then? ... "

Where was Sergei Sergeich now, why wasn't he here beside her; she was a little afraid to go back to the apartment on the Moika as she used to as though nothing had happened, with her mutinous husband feverishly lying in wait there like an animal in its lair.

And she stamped her foot;

"I'll show him!"

And again:

"I'll teach him a lesson!"

And the Spaniard from Granada slipped away from her in confusion.

Sofia Petrovna Likhutina shuddered as she recalled the grimace with which Sergei Sergeich had handed her her cloak and pointed to the door. The way he stood there behind her back! The way she had laughed in contempt then, and, raising her pannier skirt slightly by the scallops, had glided away from him so smoothly, curtseying (why hadn't she curtseyed when she handed Nikolai Apollonovich the letter—she was so good at curtseys)! The way she had spoken to him in the doorway, and thumbed her nose at the officer with a sly smile! Only she was a little afraid to go home.

228

And in irritation she stamped her foot again:

"I'll show him!"

And again:

"I'll teach him a lesson!"

But she was still afraid to go home.

She was even more afraid to stay here; almost everyone had already left: the young people and the masks had left; the good-natured host, with a depressed, distracted expression on his face, was going up to one person and another, to tell a funny story; in the end he cast a forlorn glance around the emptying room, cast a forlorn glance at the crowd of clowns and harlequins, and by his expression frankly recommended that the gleaming room should be relieved of any further merriment.

But the harlequins had gathered into a motley bunch and were behaving in a most improper way. Some impudent person emerged from their throng, started dancing and began to sing:

Departed now the Famusovs,
Departed Ableukhov …
The streets, the Prospects, harbour ways
Are full of fearsome rumours!…
And you extolled the senator,
Though treachery's your trademark …
But there's no legislation now,
No rules and regulations!
A patriotic cur, he wore
Distinctive decorations;
But acts of terrorism now
Occur on all occasions.

Nikolai Petrovich Tsukatov realised in the twinkling of an eye that the respectability of his merry house was being disrupted by this poisonous doggerel. Nikolai Petrovich Tsukatov turned a deep red, glanced at the daring harlequin in a most good-natured fashion, turned on his heel and walked away from the door.

The white domino

It really was time to go. Almost all the guests had already left: Sofia Petrovna Likhutina wandered on her own around the unpeopled rooms; only the Spaniard from Granada clicked away at his loud castanets in reply to her distress. There, in the empty enfilade, she chanced to catch sight of a solitary white domino; the white domino seemed to arise quite suddenly, and—then:

—someone tall and sad, whom she felt she had seen many, many times before, seen recently, even today—someone tall and sad, all swathed in white satin, came towards her through the vacant rooms; from the slits in the mask the bright light of his eyes was gazing at her; it seemed to her that light was streaming sadly from his brow, from his immobile fingers …

Sofia Petrovna called trustingly to the dear wearer of the white domino:

"Sergei Sergeevich! … Hey, Sergei Sergeevich! … "

There was no doubt: it was Sergei Sergeich Likhutin: he had thought better of yesterday's scene; he had come to take her home.

Sofia Petrovna called again to the dear wearer of the white domino—tall and sad:

"It is you, isn't it? Surely it's you?"

But the tall and sad one slowly shook his head, put his finger to his lips and bade her be silent.

Trustingly she held out her hand to the white domino: how the satin gleamed, how cool the satin was! And her azure sleeve rustled as it touched that white arm and hung upon it impotently (the wearer of the white domino turned out to have an arm of wood); for a moment the radiant mask bent over her head, revealing under the white lace a tuft of beard like a sheaf of ripe corn.

She had never seen Sergei Sergeevich in such a gleaming aspect: and she whispered:

"Have you forgiven me?"

Her answer was a sigh from under the mask.

"Shall we be friends again?"

But the tall and sad one slowly shook his head.

"Why don't you say anything?"

But the tall and sad one slowly put his finger to his lips.

"Is it … you, Sergei Sergeevich?"

But the tall and sad one slowly shook his head.

They were passing through into the entrance-hall: they were surrounded by the inexpressible, the inexpressible stood all around. Sofia Petrovna Likhutina took off her black mask and her face drowned in the caressing fur, while the tall and sad one, putting on his coat, did not remove his mask. Sofia Petrovna gazed at the tall and sad one with astonishment: she was surprised that he had not been handed an officer's greatcoat; instead of that he had donned a ragged overcoat, from the sleeves of which his long hands protruded, reminding her of lilies. Her whole being rushed to meet him among the astonished servants watching the scene; they were surrounded by the inexpressible; the inexpressible stood all around.

But the tall and sad one slowly shook his head on the lighted threshold and bade her be silent.

Since evening the sky had turned into undifferentiated, dirty slime; with the onset of night that undifferentiated, dirty slime had descended on to the earth; fog had descended on to the earth; everything had now descended on to the earth and become for the time being a black darkness, through which the rusty spots of street lights penetrated horribly. Sofia Petrovna Likhutina saw that above one such rusty spot a caryatid by the entrance, arching out, had fallen and was hanging there; she saw that a section of the neighbouring house protruded in one such spot with semi-circular windows and little sculptures carved in wood. The tall outline of her unknown companion towered up in front of her. And she whispered to him imploringly:

"I need a cab."

The tall outline of her unknown companion with the flaxen beard pulled down a rust-red cap above his mask, and waved an arm into the fog:

"Cabby!"

Now Sofia Petrovna Likhutina understood everything: the sad outline had a beautiful and gentle voice …

> —a voice that she had heard many, many times before, heard so recently, today: yes, today in her dream; and she had forgotten, just as she had altogether forgotten her dream of the night before …

He had a beautiful and gentle voice, but … —there was no doubt:

he did not have the voice of Sergei Sergeevich. But she had hoped, she had wished this beautiful and gentle, but unfamiliar man (she wished)—to be her husband. But her husband had not come, he had not led her out of hell: it was a stranger who had led her out of hell.

Who could it be?

The unfamiliar outline raised its voice more than once: its voice grew stronger and stronger, and it seemed that beneath the mask someone was growing stronger too, someone immense beyond measure. The silence could only worry the voice; behind some stranger's gate a dog gave an answering bark. The street ran off into the distance.

"Tell me, who are you?"

"You all deny me: but I keep watch over you all. You deny me, and then you call me … "

Then Sofia Petrovna Likhutina grasped for a moment what it was that stood before her: tears constricted her throat; she wanted to fall at these slender feet and wind her arms around the stranger's slender knees, but at that moment a carriage trundled up prosaically and a hunched, sleepy cabby entered the bright light of the streetlamp. The wondrous outline helped her into the cab, but when she held out her trembling hands to him in entreaty from the cab, the outline slowly put his finger to his lips and bade her be silent.

But the cab had already set off: if only she had stopped, and, oh, if only she had turned back—back to that bright spot, where a moment before the tall and sad one had been standing and where he was no more, because nothing but the yellow eye of the streetlamp now glimmered on the paving-stones.

She forgot what had happened

Sofia Petrovna Likhutina forgot what had happened. Her future collapsed into black night. The irreparable was creeping up; the irreparable embraced her; and house, apartment, husband—disappeared. She did not know where the cab was taking her. A segment of the recent past broke away into that grey-black night: the masquerade, the harlequins; and even (can you imagine!)—even the tall and sad one. She did not know where the cab was bringing her from.

After that segment of the recent past the whole of the past day broke away: her quarrel with her husband and her quarrel with Madame Farnois about the 'Maison Tricotons'. No sooner did she move on in quest of some support for her consciousness, no sooner did she try to evoke the impressions of the previous day—than the previous day broke away again, like a piece of a huge road, paved with granite; it broke away and crashed down to some utterly dark depths. And somewhere a blow rang out, smashing stone to smithereens.

There flashed before her the love of this unhappy summer; and the unhappy summer's love, like everything, broke away from her memory; and again a blow rang out, smashing stone to smithereens. Her conversations in the spring with Nicolas Ableukhov flashed by and dropped away; her years of marriage, her wedding flashed by and dropped away: a void was tearing them away and swallowing them, piece by piece. And metallic blows were carried in the air, smashing stone. The whole of her life flashed by, the whole of her life dropped away, as though her life had never happened and she herself—was just a soul as yet unborn. A void began immediately behind her back (because everything had fallen away there, crashing down into the depths); the void stretched into aeons, and in those aeons nothing could be heard but blow upon blow: pieces of her lives falling away and tumbling into the depths. It was as though a metallic steed, clanging loudly against the stone, was trampling behind her back everything that had dropped away; as though there behind her back, clanging loudly against the stone, a metallic horseman had set off to chase her.

And when she turned round, a vision presented itself to her: the outline of the Mighty Horseman ... There—two equine nostrils pierced the fog, flaming in an incandescent pillar.

Death, crowned in bronze, was chasing her.

Then Sofia Petrovna came to her senses: a military messenger overtook the cab, holding a torch out into the fog. His heavy bronze helmet gleamed for a moment; behind him, with a rumble and a flash, a fire engine flew off into the fog as well.

"What's going on there, a fire?" Sofia Petrovna addressed the cabby.

"Seems to be a fire: they say the islands are burning ... "

The cabby announced this to her from the fog: the cab was standing at the entrance to her house on the Moika.

233

Sofia Petrovna remembered everything: everything floated up before her alarmingly prosaically; as though there had not been that hell, those cavorting masks or the Horseman. The masks now seemed to her just unknown jesters, probably some of her acquaintances who visited their house too; and the tall and sad one—he, no doubt, was one of the comrades (a thank-you to him for taking her to the cab). Only Sofia Petrovna bit her plump lip now in vexation: how could she make such a mistake and confuse that acquaintance with her husband? And whisper in his ear confessions about some utterly nonsensical guilt? Why, now that unknown acquaintance (thank-you to him for taking her to the cab) would go and tell everyone some absolute rubbish about her being afraid of her husband. And that gossip would get all round the city … Oh, bother that Sergei Sergeich Likhutin: you'll pay me for this quite needless shame, just you look out!

She indignantly kicked open the street-door; the street-door indignantly slammed to behind her bowed head. The darkness enveloped her, for a moment she was seized by the inexpressible (that is no doubt how it must be in the first moment after death); but death was not on Sofia Petrovna's mind in the least: on the contrary, her mind was occupied with very simple things. She was thinking about how she was about to tell Mavrusha to light the samovar; while the samovar was warming, she was going to scold and nag her husband (she could nag for more than four hours on end without falling silent); and when Mavrusha brought the samovar in she and her husband would be reconciled.

Now Sofia Petrovna rang at the door. The loud bell informed the nocturnal apartment of her return. She was about to hear Mavrusha's hurried footsteps in the entrance-hall. No hurried footsteps were heard. Sofia Petrovna took offence and rang again.

Evidently Mavrusha was asleep: the minute she left the house, that silly girl dropped on to the bed … But her husband was a fine one, too: of course he had been anxiously waiting for her for hours; and of course he had heard the bell, and of course he realised that the servant was asleep. And he didn't lift a finger! What do you think of that! Offended, is he?

In that case he could go without both tea and reconciliation.

Sofia Petrovna began to ring continuously at the door: peal after peal, her ringing resounded ... Nobody, nothing! She put her ear right to the keyhole of the door; and when she put her ear to the keyhole of the door, then on the other side of that keyhole, at a distance of an inch from her ear, she heard quite distinctly: irregular heavy breathing and a match being struck. Lord Jesus Christ Almighty, who could be breathing heavily in there? And Sofia Petrovna stepped back from the door in astonishment, her head still bent forward.

Mavrusha? No, it wasn't Mavrusha ... Sergei Sergeich Likhutin? Yes, him. Why was he standing there in silence, not opening the door, with his head pressed to the keyhole and breathing heavily?

With a premonition of something untoward Sofia Petrovna started hammering desperately at the prickly felt of the door. With a premonition of something untoward Sofia Petrovna cried out:

"Open up!"

But on the other side of the door whoever it was went on standing in silence and breathing heavily, in fear and terribly irregularly.

"Sergei Sergeich! Come on, that's enough ... "

Silence.

"Is that you? What's the matter with you?"

A patter of feet—away from the door.

"Whatever is going on? Oh, Lord, I'm afraid, I'm afraid ... Open up, please, darling!"

Something howled loudly on the other side of the door and ran at full tilt into the further rooms, scrabbled around at first, then moved the chairs; she thought she heard the lamp in the drawing room clinking; the rumbling sound of a table being moved was heard in the distance. For a minute everything fell silent.

And then a horrendous crash rang out, as though the ceiling had fallen and the ceiling-plaster had come scattering down; in that crash Sofia Petrovna was struck by just one sound: the muffled sound of a heavy human body falling from somewhere high.

Alarm

Apollon Apollonovich Ableuhkov, speaking trivially, could not stand leaving his house; for him the only sensible reason for leaving the house was leaving it to go to the Establishment or to make a report to the minister. That was what the director of the Ministry of Justice had once remarked to him in jest.

Apollon Apollonovich Ableukhov, speaking frankly, could not stand direct conversations that entailed looking another person in the eye: conversation with the aid of a telephone line obviated that inconvenience. From Apollon Apollonovich's desk telephone lines ran to all departments. Apollon Apollonovich listened with pleasure to the ringing of the telephone.

Just once some joker, in reply to Apollon Apollonovich's question about which department he was from, struck the mouthpiece of the telephone as hard as he could with the palm of his hand, so that Apollon Apollonovich had the impression that someone had slapped him in the face.

Every verbal exchange, in Apollon Apollonovich's view, had a clear purpose, straight as a line. Everything else he attributed to the category of tea-drinking and the smoking of cigarette stubs: Apollon Apollonovich relentlessly called every cigarette a cigarette stub; and he considered that Russian people were worthless tea-drinkers, drunkards and consumers of nicotine (he had frequently proposed raising the taxes on these latter products); for that reason the Russian man, in Apollon Apollonovich's opinion, was betrayed by the age of forty-five by an unseemly paunch and a blood-red nose; Apollon Apollonovich charged like a bull at anything red (at a nose, among other things).

Apollon Apollonovich himself was the possessor of a deathly grey little nose and a slender waist—you would say it was the waist of a sixteen-year-old girl—and was proud of it.

Nevertheless Apollon Apollonovich had a peculiarly adroit way of explaining to himself why people pay each other visits: at-homes were for most people a place for collective tea-drinking and smoking of fag-ends, unless the visitor was planning to find himself a niche in the idle department and therefore trying to ingratiate himself in the house he was visiting, or he was trying to find his son a niche in that department, or trying to marry his son to the daughter of one of the officials in that department: there was one such idle department. Apollon Apollonovich conducted a ceaseless struggle with that department.

Apollon Apollonovich had gone to the Tsukatovs with a single purpose: to strike a blow at that department. That department had started a flirtation with an undoubtedly moderate party, which was suspicious not on account of its rejection of order, but on account of its desire to make small changes in that order. Apollon Apollonovich despised compromises, he despised the representatives of that party, and, above all, the department. He wished to show the representative of the department, as well as the representative of the party, what his immediate behaviour would be like in relation to the department in the lofty post that had recently been offered to him.

That is why Apollon Apollonovich considered himself unpleasantly obliged to sit out the evening at the Tsukatovs', with the most distasteful object of contemplation right under his nose: the convulsions of the dancing feet and the blood-red, offensively rustling folds of the harlequins' costumes; he had seen these red rags before: yes, on the square in front of the Kazan Cathedral; there such red rags were designated banners.

These red rags now, at a simple party and in the presence of the head of that Establishment, struck him as an unseemly, unworthy, and straightforwardly shameful joke; and the convulsions of the dancing feet recalled to his mind a certain unfortunate measure (unavoidable, however) for the prevention of state crimes.

Apollon Apollonovich gave his hospitable hosts an inimical, side-long glance and became ungracious.

The dances of the red clowns turned for him into other, sanguinary dances; these dances started, as, indeed, they all did, on the street; these dances continued, as they all did, beneath the crossbar of two notorious uprights. Apollon Apollonovich thought: if these apparently innocent dances are allowed here, then, for certain, these dances will continue on the street; and these dances will end, of course—there, up there.

Apollon Apollonovich had, however, danced himself in his youth: the polka-mazurka—for sure, and possibly the lancers.

One circumstance deepened the miserable mood of this person of lofty rank: he found one ridiculous domino exceptionally unpleasant; it caused him a particularly severe attack of angina pectoris (whether it was indeed an attack of angina, Apollon Apollonovich doubted; and it's strange: absolutely everyone whose lot it has been to turn, however little, the wheels of such impressive mechanisms as the

Establishment, for example, knows what angina is). This was what happened: the ridiculous domino, the buffoon, had met him in a most impudent way when he appeared in the ballroom; as he entered the room the ridiculous domino (buffoon) had run up to him making grimaces.

Apollon Apollonovich tried in vain to remember where he had seen those grimaces: and could not remember.

With unconcealed boredom and barely surmounted disgust Apollon Apollonovich sat as straight as a rod with a tiny china cup in his diminutive hands; his spindly legs with their sinewy calves rested perpendicularly on the bright Bukhara carpet, comprising the lower parts which formed a ninety-degree right-angle to the upper parts at the kneecaps; perpendicularly to his chest his thin arms extended to the china cup. Apollon Apollonovich, a person of the first class, seemed to be the figure of an Egyptian, depicted on the carpet—angular, broad-shouldered, contemptuous of all laws of anatomy (Apollon Apollonovich, after all, did not have muscles: Apollon Apollonovich consisted of bones, sinews and veins).

And it was with just the same habitual self-imposed angularity that Apollon Apollonovich, the Egyptian, expounded a most judicious system of prohibitions to the professor of statistical data who had turned up at this evening—the leader of a recently formed party, a party of *moderate* state treason, but *treason nonetheless*; and it was with just the same habitual self-imposed gaunt angularity that he pedantically expounded to the editor of a conservative newspaper from a clerical family of liberal leanings a system of the most judicious advice.

Apollon Apollonovich, a person of the first class, wanted nothing to do with either of them: both had fat, so to speak, stomachs (from self-indulgence in respect of tea); both, incidentally, had red noses (from the excessive consumption of alcoholic beverages). To cap it all one of them came from a clerical family, and towards the families of the clergy Apollon Apollonovich Ableukhov had an understandable and, moreover, hereditary weakness: he could not stand them. When in the line of duty Apollon Apollonovich talked to village priests, urban priests or consistorial priests, or to the sons or grandsons of priests, he was distinctly aware of a bad smell from their feet; village priests, urban priests ... even consistorial priests along with their sons and grandsons all had such long, black, unwashed necks and yellow fingernails.

Suddenly Apollon Apollonovich became quite flustered, standing there between the two paunchy frock coats belonging to the priest's son and the moderate traitor, as though his olfactory sense had distinctly detected a bad smell of feet; but the distinguished statesman's agitation did not derive at all from the irritation of his olfactory organs; this agitation derived from a sudden assault on his sensitive ear-drums: at that moment the pianist had once again dropped his fingers on to the piano, and Apollon Apollonovich's auditory equipment perceived all euphonious accords and all melodic modulations through networks of harmonious dissonances as the purposeless scratching of fingernails, at least ten of them, across glass.

Apollon Apollonovich turned round with his whole body; there, over there, he caught sight of the convulsions of grotesque legs belonging to a company of state criminals: beg pardon: young people dancing; among these diabolical dances his attention was caught by that same domino, his blood-red satin swirling in the dance.

Apollon Apollonovich tried in vain to remember where he had seen all those gestures. And he could not remember.

And when the saccharine little gent with the moth-eaten look sidled respectfully up to him, Apollon Apollonovich became exceedingly animated, and sketched with his arm a triangle of greeting in space.

The point is that the moth-eaten gent, despised by everyone, was, as it were, an essential figure: it goes without saying—a figure belonging to a transitional period, whose existence Apollon Apollonovich in principle rejected, whose existence within the bounds of legality was, of course, deplorable, but ... what were you to do?—essential, convenient and ... in any case, once the figure existed, there was nothing for it but to come to terms with it. Taking into account the tricky situation in which he found himself, the moth-eaten gent had the positive quality that, although he knew his own value, he didn't get above himself; he didn't preen himself in vacuous, ostentatious words, like that professor; he didn't thump the table with his fist in a most unseemly manner, like that editor. The saccharine little gent just got on with quietly serving a variety of departments, while an employee of one department. Apollon Apollonovich valued him despite himself, for he never tried to be on an equal footing with civil servants or just people in society—in short, the moth-eaten little gent was an undisguised lackey. So what? With lackeys Apollon

Apollonovich was exquisitely courteous: no lackey who had served in the Ableukhov household had ever had grounds for complaint.

And with accentuated courtesy Apollon Apollonovich immersed himself in a circumstantial conversation with that figure.

What he elicited from this conversation struck him like a thunderclap: the blood-red, nasty domino, the buffoon he had just had thoughts about, according to the gent who had sat down beside him, turned out to be ... No, no (Apollon Apollonovich pulled a face, as though he had seen someone cutting a lemon and the knife tarnishing in the acid juice)—no, no: the domino, it transpired, was his own son! ...

But was he truly his own son? His own son might, after all, be nothing but Anna Petrovna's son as a result of the fortuitous, so to speak, predominance in his veins of his mother's blood; and in his mother's blood—in Anna Petrovna's blood—there had turned out, according to the most scrupulously conducted inquiries, to be ... clergy blood (these inquiries Apollon Apollonovich had initiated after his wife's elopement)! This clergy blood had most probably contaminated the unblemished Ableukhov line, bestowing upon the distinguished statesman simply a *nasty* son. Only a *nasty son*—a real *mongrel*—could do things like that (in the Ableukhov line ever since the time of Ab-Lai, the Kirghiz-Kaisak's, migration into Europe—since the time of Anna Ioannovna—there had been nothing of the sort).

Apollon Apollonovich was struck most forcefully by the fact that the nasty domino cavorting about there (Nikolai Apollonovich) had, as the little gent reported, a nasty past, and that the Jewish press had been writing about those nasty exploits; now Apollon Apollonovich regretted most emphatically that he had not found time these recent days to cast an eye over *The Chronicle of Events*; in the place that is comparable with no other he had only had time to acquaint himself with the headlines belonging to the pens of moderate state criminals (the headlines of immoderate criminals Apollon Apollonovich did not read at all).

Apollon Apollonovich changed the position of his body: he quickly stood up and made to run through into the next room in quest of the domino, but from there, from that room, a clean-shaven schoolboy came rushing towards him, in a tightly-buttoned frock coat; absent-mindedly Apollon Apollonovich very nearly shook his hand; the clean-shaven schoolboy turned out on closer inspection to be senator Ableukhov: in his momentum Apollon Apollonovich had almost hurtled into the mirror, having mistaken the disposition of the rooms.

Apollon Apollonovich changed the position of his body, turning his back to the mirror; and there, over there: in the anteroom between the drawing room and the ballroom, Apollon Apollonovich once again caught sight of the vile domino (mongrel), immersed in reading a note (a vile one, probably—most likely of pornographic import). And Apollon Apollonovich did not have sufficient courage to expose his son.

Several times Apollon Apollonovich changed the position of the combination of sinews, skin and bones called his body, and seemed to be a little Egyptian. He rubbed his hands with immoderate nervousness, and many times approached the cardtables, suddenly revealing an extraordinary politeness and an extraordinary curiosity about the most disparate things: Apollon Apollonovich asked the statistician inopportunely about the potholed roads of the Ukhtomsk district of the Ploshchegorsk Province; and the member of the Ploshchegorsk *zemstvo* he asked about the consumption of pepper on the island of Newfoundland. The professor of statistics, touched by the attention of the distinguished statesman, but completely ignorant about the pothole question in the Ploshchegorsk Province, promised to send this person of the first class a sound guidebook to the geographical peculiarities of the whole planet Earth. The *zemstvo* member, who was quite uninformed about the question of pepper, hypocritically observed that pepper was consumed by the Newfoundlanders in enormous quantities, which was a permanent feature of all countries with constitutions.

Before long a whispering, a rustling and a surreptitious giggling, of indeterminate provenance, reached Apollon Apollonovich's ears; Apollon Apollonovich noticed clearly that the convulsions of the dancing feet had suddenly stopped: for a single moment his agitated spirit calmed down. But then his head began working again with terrifying clarity; the fateful premonition of all these restlessly flowing hours was confirmed: his son, Nikolai Apollonovich, was the most terrible scoundrel, because only the most terrible scoundrel could behave in such a manner: for days on end to wear a red domino, for days on end to attach a mask, for days on end to disturb the Jewish press.

Apollon Apollonovich realised with decisive clarity that while there in the ballroom officers, girls, ladies and final-year students about to leave school had been dancing together, his son, Nikolai Apollonovich, had danced himself to … But Apollon Apollonovich could not bring distinct lucidity to his thought about what it was exactly that Nikolai Apollonovich had danced himself to; Nikolai Apollonovich was still his son, and not just no one in particular … —a person of the male gender that Anna Petrovna had brought into the world from the devil only knows where; Nikolai Apollonovich did, after all, have the ears of all the Ableukhovs—ears of improbable size, and moreover protruding.

This thought about ears slightly softened Apollon Apollonovich's anger: Apollon Apollonovich postponed his intention of banishing his son from the house without initiating the most precise inquiry into the reasons that had led his son to wear the domino. But in any event Apollon Apollonovich would lose the post, he would have to decline the post; he could not accept the post without removing the shameful stains of his son's behaviour (say what you will—an Ableukhov) that sullied the honour of the house.

With this disconsolate thought and with twisted lips (as though he had sucked a pale-yellow lemon) Apollon Apollonovich proffered a finger to everyone and rushed impetuously out of the drawing room in the company of his hosts. And when, flying through the ballroom, he looked round in utter horror at the walls, finding the expanse of the lighted ballroom too huge, he saw distinctly: a little cluster of grey-browed matrons was whispering away maliciously.

Only one word found its way to Apollon Apollonovich's ears: "Chicken."

Apollon Apollonovich detested the sight of the plucked and headless chickens sold in shops.

Be that as it may, Apollon Apollonovich ran headlong across the ballroom. In his complete naivety he did not know that in the whispering room there was no longer a single soul for whom it remained a secret who the red domino was that had so recently been dancing here: nor did anyone say a word to Apollon Apollonovich about the fact that his son, Nikolai Apollonovich, had a quarter of an hour before taken to undignified flight through this same ballroom where he was now fleeing with such evident haste himself.

The letter

Nikolai Apollonovich, dumbstruck by the letter, had raced past the merry *contredanse* a quarter-of-an-hour before the senator. How he had made his exit from the house he had no recollection. He came to his senses in a state of utter prostration in front of the Tsukatovs' entrance; he went on standing there in a clinging dark dream, in the clinging dark dampness, mechanically counting the number of carriages standing there, mechanically following the movements of someone tall and sad who was supervising public order: this was the district constable.

Suddenly the tall and sad one strode past Nikolai Apollonovich's nose: Nikolai Apollonovich was suddenly singed by his dark-blue gaze; the district constable, angered by the student in his greatcoat, shook his flaxen beard: he took one look and passed by.

Quite naturally Nikolai Apollonovich moved off too in a clinging dark dream, in the clinging dark dampness, through which the rusty blur of a streetlamp glimmered obstinately: into that blurred light from the mist above, over the streetlamp's point, the caryatid at the entrance tumbled lifelessly, and in that blur of light a piece of the neighbouring house protruded; it was a black, single-storey house, with semi-circular windows and little sculptures carved in wood.

But no sooner had Nikolai Apollonovich moved off, than he noticed without concern that his legs were completely missing: there were some flaccid appendages floundering senselessly in a puddle; he tried in vain to gain control of those appendages: the flaccid appendages would not obey him; to look at they had all the outward appearance of legs, but he could not feel his legs (he had no legs). Nikolai Apollonovich sank down involuntarily on the step of the little black house; he sat there for a minute or so, with his overcoat wrapped round him.

This was natural in his position (all his behaviour was entirely natural); equally naturally he opened his overcoat, revealing a red patch of his domino; equally naturally he rummaged in his pockets and pulled out the crumpled envelope, and read over and over again the contents of the note, trying to find in it some trace of a simple joke or a trace of mockery. But he could not discover any trace of either ...

"Remembering your offer made in the summer, we hasten to inform you, comrade, that your turn has now come; you are now charged with immediate preparations for carrying out the action against ... " Nikolai Apollonovich could not read further, because there stood his father's name—it went on: "The necessary material in the form of a bomb with a clockwork mechanism has been conveyed to you in advance in a package. Hurry: there is no time to lose; it is desirable that the entire undertaking should be completed within the next few days." ... There followed a slogan: Nikolai Apollonovich was equally familiar both with the slogan and with the handwriting. It was written by the Incognito: he had several times received notes from that same Incognito.

There could not be any doubt.

Nikolai Apollonovich's arms and legs dangled loosely; Nikolai Apollonovich's lower lip fell away from his upper lip.

From the fateful moment when some lady had handed him the crumpled envelope, Nikolai Apollonovich had been trying somehow to seize hold of simple contingencies, of extraneous and totally idle thoughts, which were like a flock of ferocious crows, frightened by a shot, that take off from a bare-branched tree and start to circle—hither and thither, hither and thither, until another shot rings out; in his head totally idle thoughts circled just like that, for example: about the number of books that could be accommodated on a shelf in his bookcase, about the patterns with which the frilly petticoat of a person he had once loved were embroidered, as that person tripped flirtatiously out of the room with a slight hitch of her skirt (that this person was Sofia Petrovna Likhutina, he somehow failed to remember).

All the time Nikolai Apollonovich tried not to think, tried not to understand: thinking, understanding—what *understanding* could there be of *that*; *that—just arrived, overwhelmed you, and roared;* if you thought about it—you'd go straight and throw yourself through a hole in the ice ... What could you think? There was nothing to think here ... because *that* ... *that* ... What was that?

No, here no one was capable of thought.

In the first moment after reading the note something bellowed pitifully in his soul: bellowed as pitifully as a meek bull under the knacker's knife; in the first moment he looked round to see his father; and his father seemed to him quite ordinary, quite ordinary: he seemed small and old—he seemed like a plucked chicken; he felt sick with horror; in his soul something bellowed pitifully again: submissively and pitifully.

And then he had rushed out.

And now Nikolai Apollonovich kept trying to seize hold of appearances: there was the caryatid at the entrance; a caryatid like any other ... And—no, no! It was not like any other caryatid—he had never seen anything of the sort: hanging there above the flame. And there was the little house: a little black house like any other.

No, no, no!

The house was not straightforward, just as nothing here was straightforward: everything in him was dislodged, disrupted; he was dislodged from himself; and from somewhere (no idea where), where he had never been, he was watching!

And his legs here—legs like any others ... No, no! They weren't legs—but utterly unfamiliar flaccid appendages dangling idly.

But Nikolai Apollonovich's attempt to seize hold of extraneous thoughts and trifles broke off at once when the entrance to that tall house where he had just been running amok began to open noisily and out of it tumbled group after group; carriages started off in the mist, the lights of their lamps started off at their sides. With an effort Nikolai Apollonovich started up from the step of the little black house, and turned into an empty alleyway.

The alleyway was empty, like everything else: like the expanses up there above; empty as the soul of man is empty. For a minute Nikolai Apollonovich tried to remember about transcendental matters, about the fact that the events of this ephemeral world do not infringe at all upon the immortality of its centre, and that even the thinking brain is only a phenomenon of the consciousness; that inasmuch as he, Nikolai Apollonovich, acted in this world, he was not he; and he was—a frail integument; his true contemplative spirit was still as capable as ever of illuminating his path: of illuminating his path even with *that*; of illuminating even ... *that* ... But all around him *that* rose up: rose up in the shape of fences; and at his feet he noticed: an archway and a puddle.

And there was no illumination.

Nikolai Apollonovich's consciousness vainly strove to give illumination; it illuminated nothing; the terrible darkness that had been, remained. Glancing round in fear, he managed somehow to crawl as far as the streetlamp's blur; beneath this blur a stream of water trickled across the pavement, and a piece of orange-peel floated past. Nikolai Apollonovich again turned his attention to the note. Flocks of thoughts flew up from the centre of consciousness like flocks of ferocious birds frightened by a storm, but there was no centre of consciousness: there was a gloomy chasm yawning there, before which Nikolai Apollonovich stood bewildered as though before a gloomy well-shaft. Where and when had he stood like this? Nikolai Apollonovich struggled to recall; and could not recall. And he turned again to the note: flocks of thoughts, like birds, plummeted headlong into that empty chasm; and now some feeble little thoughtlets began to stir down there.

"Remembering your offer made in the summer," Nikolai Apollonovich re-read and tried to find something to object to. He could find no objection.

"Remembering your offer made in the summer ... " He had indeed made an offer, but he had forgotten about it: he had once remembered it, but then it had been submerged by the events of the recent past, submerged by the domino; Nikolai Apollonovich cast an astonished glance over the recent past and found it simply uninteresting; there was some lady with a pretty face there; but anyway, just a lady—like any other! ...

Flocks of thoughts flew up from the centre of consciousness a second time; but there was no centre of consciousness; before his eyes was an archway, while in his soul was an empty hole; above that empty hole Nikolai Apollonovich became lost in thought. Where and when had he stood like this? Nikolai Apollonovich strained to remember; and—remembered: he had stood like this in the gusts of the Neva gale, leaning over the parapet of the bridge and gazing into the water infested with bacilli (why, it was that night that everything had started: the terrible offer, the domino, and now ...) There: Nikolai Apollonovich stood bent so low, still reading the note of terrible import (all this had happened before: had happened multitudes of times).

"We hasten to inform you that your turn has now come," Nikolai Apollonovich read. And he turned round: footsteps were ringing out behind him; some restless shadow loomed up ambiguously in the draughts of the alleyway. Behind his back Nikolai Apollonovich caught sight of: a bowler hat, a cane, an overcoat, a beard and a nose.

Nikolai Apollonovich went towards the passer-by, staring at him expectantly; and he saw a bowler hat, a cane, an overcoat, a beard and a nose; all that walked by and did not pay the least attention (only steps to be heard and his heart beating to breaking point); Nikolai Apollonovich turned round to look at *all that* and gazed behind him into the grimy mist—where the bowler hat, cane and ears had just rushed by; for a long time he went on standing with his back arched (and all that had happened before, too), his mouth open in a most unpleasant manner and at all events presenting a pretty ridiculous figure, armless (he was in his Nikolaevan cape), with the flaps of his greatcoat dancing absurdly in the wind ... How could he make out anything except the edge of the fence, short-sighted as he was?

He returned to his reading.

"The necessary material in the form of a bomb with a clockwork mechanism has been conveyed to you in advance in a package ... " Nikolai Apollonovich found an objection to this sentence: no, it hadn't been conveyed, it hadn't been conveyed! And having found an objection, he felt something akin to hope that it was all a joke ... A bomb? ... He didn't have a bomb?! ... But, but—no!! ...

In a package?!

Then everything came back to him: the conversation, the package, the suspicious visitor, the September day, and all the rest. Nikolai Apollonovich recalled distinctly taking the package and putting it away in his desk (the package was wet).

Only then was Nikolai Apollonovich able to appreciate for the first time the full horror of his situation. How could that be? And for the first time he was seized by a fear beyond expression: he felt a sharp thumping in his heart: the side of the archway in front of him began to revolve; no sooner did the darkness touch him than the darkness enveloped him; his 'self' was nothing but a black receptacle, unless it was a cramped box room buried in absolute darkness; and there in the darkness, in the place of his heart, a spark ignited ... with frantic speed the spark turned into a crimson ball: the ball expanded, expanded, expanded; and the ball burst: and everything burst ... Nikolai Apollonovich came to his senses: the restless shadow was once again nearby: bowler hat, cane and ears; and a moth-eaten gent with a wart beside his nose (would you believe it: he felt he had only just seen that gent; that he had seen him at the ball; that the gent had been standing in the drawing room next to that other one, the old one, rubbing his hands)—the moth-eaten gent with the wart beside his nose had stopped two paces away from him in front of the old fence—for a call of nature; but as he stood in front of the old fence he turned his face towards Ableukhov, made a clicking sound with his lips and grinned slightly:

"Been at the ball, I suppose?"

"Yes, at the ball ... "

Nikolai Apollonovich was caught unawares; but what did it matter: being at a ball wasn't yet a crime.

"I can tell ... "

"Really? How can you tell?"

"There's something showing under your coat, what do you call it: a bit of a domino."

"Well, yes, a domino ... "

"It was seen yesterday, too ... "

"What do you mean, yesterday?"

"By the Winter Canal ... "

"My good sir, you are taking liberties ... "

"Come off it: you are the domino."

"What domino do you mean?"

"You know which one."

"I don't understand you: and in any case it's very odd to come up like that to a person you don't know ... "

"You aren't a person I don't know: you're Nikolai Apollonovich Ableukhov: and moreover, you're the Red Domino that's being written about in the papers ... "

Nikolai Apollonovich was as white as a sheet:

"Listen," he held out a hand to the saccharine gent, "listen ... "

But the gent kept at him:

"And I know your papa, too, Apollon Apollonovich: I've just had the honour of chatting with him."

"Oh, believe me," Nikolai Apollonovich became flustered, "this is all some horrid rumour … "

But having completed his call of nature, the gent slowly moved away from the fence, buttoned his coat, stuck his hand unceremoniously into his pocket and winked meaningfully:

"Where are you going?"

"To Vasilevskii Island," Nikolai Apollonovich snapped.

"I'm going to Vasilevskii Island, too: we can go together."

"I meant, I'm going to the Embankment … "

"You clearly don't know yourself where you're supposed to be going," the moth-eaten gent grinned, "and since that's the case—let's pop into a restaurant."

One alleyway led into another: the alleyways led out into the street. Perfectly ordinary men-in-the-street were running along the street in the form of little black, restless shadows.

A companion

Apollon Apollonovich Ableukhov, in his grey overcoat and tall black top hat, with a face resembling grey chamois leather, tinged with green, darted with a touch of fear through the open entrance door and ran with staccato steps down the steps of the portico, to find himself suddenly on the drenched and slippery porch, which was shrouded in dampness.

Someone called out his name and at that respectful cry the black outline of a carriage moved from the reddening murk into the streetlamp's pool of light, displaying its coat of arms: a unicorn, piercing a knight; no sooner had Apollon Apollonovich Ableukhov, bending his leg at an angle, in order to rest it upon the step of the carriage, formed an Egyptian silhouette in the moist mist, no sooner had he made ready to jump into the carriage and fly away together with it into that moist mist, than the house door was thrown open behind him; the moth-eaten gent, who had just revealed to Apollon Apollonovich a veracious, though lamentable truth, appeared in the street; pulling his bowler down over his nose, he trotted off to the left.

Apollon Apollonovich then lowered the leg he had raised at an angle, touched the brim of his top hat with the tip of his glove and gave a curt command to the dumbstruck driver: to go back home without him. Then Apollon Apollonovich performed an incredible act; the history of his life had known no such act for fully fifteen years: Apollon Apollonovich himself, blinking in bewilderment and pressing his hand to his heart in order to moderate his breathlessness, ran after the disappearing back of the gent as it slipped away in the mist; bear in mind an essential fact: the lower extremities of the distinguished statesman were minute in the extreme; if you bear this essential fact in mind, you will understand, of course, that as he ran Apollon Apollonovich assisted himself by waving his arm.

I am communicating this valuable behavioural feature of the lately deceased person of the first class exclusively for the attention of the many collectors of material for his future biography, about which I believe the newspapers have been writing so recently.

I resume.

Apollon Apollonovich Ableukhov performed two most unlikely digressions from the code of his balanced life; in the first place, he did not avail himself of the services of his carriage (taking into account his agoraphobia, this can be called a veritable feat of courage); secondly: in the most literal, and not transferred meaning, he sped in the dark night along the quite unpopulated street. And when the wind blew off his tall top hat, when Apollon Apollonovich Ableukhov squatted down over a puddle to extract his top hat, then in a cracked voice he shouted after the disappearing back:

"Mmm ... Listen! ... "

But the back did not listen (actually, not the back—the ears running along above the back).

"Stop ... Pavel Pavlovich!"

The dimly visible back stopped, turned its head and, recognising the senator, ran towards him (it was not the back that ran towards him, but its owner—the gentleman with the wart). The gentleman with the wart, seeing the senator squatting in front of a puddle, was astonished in the extreme and began trying to fish the floating top hat out of the puddle.

"Your Excellency! ... Apollon Apollonovich! What a strange meeting! ... Here you are, be so kind as to take it," (with these words the moth-eaten gent handed the distinguished statesman his towering top hat, having given it a preliminary wipe with his coat sleeve).

"Your Excellency, where's your carriage? ... "

But Apollon Apollonovich, putting on his top hat, interrupted his effusions.

"The night air is good for me ... "

They both set off in the same direction: as they walked the gent tried to keep in step with the senator, which was truly impossible (Apollon Apollonovich's tiny paces could have been distinguished in the lens of a microscope).

Apollon Apollonovich raised his eyes to his companion: he blinked and said—said with evident embarrassment:

"I ... you know," (this time too Apollon Apollonovich used the wrong form of the verb) ...

"Yes?"—the gent answered guardedly.

"You know ... I would like to have your precise address, Pavel Pavlovich ... "

"Pavel Iakovlevich! ... " his companion timidly corrected him.

"I'm sorry, Pavel Iakovlevich: I'm afraid I have a bad memory for names, you know ... "

"Not at all, sir, never mind: it really doesn't matter."

The moth-eaten gent thought slyly: it's all to do with his son ... He so wants to know ... but he's ashamed to ask ...

"So there, Pavel Iakovlevich: please give me your address."

Apollon Apollonovich Ableukhov unbuttoned his coat and took out his notebook, bound in the leather of a fallen rhinoceros; they stood together under a streetlamp.

"My address," the gent suddenly became flustered, "is an impermanent one: most often I'm to be found on Vasilevskii Island. Here you are: Eighteenth Line, house number 17. Care of Bessmertnyi the cobbler. I rent two rooms from him. For Voronkov the police clerk."

"Very well, very well, very well, I shall come to see you shortly ... "

Suddenly Apollon Apollonovich raised the arches of his eyebrows: his features depicted astonishment:

"But why," he began. "Why … "

"Why is my name Voronkov, when I am really Morkovin?"

"Yes, exactly … "

"Well, you see, Apollon Apollonovich, that's because I live there with a false passport."

Disgust could be read upon Apollon Apollonovich's face (in principle, after all, he denied the existence of such figures).

"My real apartment is on the Nevskii … "

Apollon Apollonovich thought: "It can't be helped: the existence of such figures at a transitional time and within the bounds of strict legality is an unfortunate necessity; but a necessity nevertheless."

"As you see, your Excellency, I am currently engaged entirely in detective work: we live in extremely important times."

"Yes, you are right," Apollon Apollonovich concurred.

"A crime of great state significance is being planned … Careful: there's a puddle here … This crime … "

"I see … "

"Will very soon be successfully exposed … Here's a dry patch, sir: allow me to take your arm."

Apollon Apollonovich was crossing an immense square: his fear of such open spaces reawakened in him; and involuntarily he pressed against the gent.

"I see, I see: that's very good … "

Apollon Apollonovich tried to keep his spirits up in this immense space, but was still losing his nerve; suddenly Mr Morkovin's icy hand made contact with him, took him by the arm, steered him past the puddles: and he kept following the icy hand; and the spaces flew to meet him. All the same Apollon Apollonovich became downcast: the thought of the fate that threatened Russia overcame for a moment all his personal fears: his fear for his son and his fear of crossing such a huge square; Apollon Apollonovich cast a glance full of respect at the selfless guardian of the existing order: Mr Morkovin had after all brought him to the pavement.

"A terrorist act is being prepared?"

"Exactly so, sir … "

"And its victim? … "

"Is to be a certain highly-placed dignitary … "

Shivers ran up Apollon Apollonovich's spine: Apollon Apollonovich had recently received a threatening letter; the letter had informed him that in the event of his accepting the highly responsible post a bomb would be thrown at him; Apollon Apollonovich despised all anonymous letters; and he tore the letter up; the post, however, he accepted.

"I beg your pardon, if it isn't a secret: who is it they're targeting now?"

Here something truly strange took place; all the objects around them suddenly seemed to sink down, to be visibly infused with dampness and to be closer than was right; Mr Morkovin himself seemed to sink down too and appeared closer than was right: he appeared ancient and somehow familiar; a faint smile passed across his lips as, lowering his head towards the senator, he uttered in a whisper:

"Who, you ask? Why you, your Excellency, it's you!"

Apollon Apollonovich saw: there, a caryatid at an entrance; a caryatid like any other. But—no, no! It was not like any other caryatid—he had never seen anything of the sort in his life: hanging there in the mist. There was the side of a house; a house-side like any other, just a house-side, a stone one. But—no, no: it wasn't straightforward, just as nothing here was straightforward: everything in him was dislodged, disrupted; he was dislodged from himself and was now muttering senselessly into the midnight murk:

"How can that be? … Come now, come now … "

Apollon Apollonovich was completely unable to imagine for real that this tightly gloved hand, twisting the button of another man's coat, that these very legs and this tired, utterly tired (believe me!) heart might, as a result of the expansion of gases inside some bomb or other, in the twinkling of an eye suddenly turn into … into …

"I don't understand … "

"Nothing to understand, Apollon Apollonovich, it's all very simple … "

Apollon Apollonovich found it hard to believe that *that* could be quite so simple: first he snorted defiantly into his side-whiskers (—the side-whiskers too!), he pouted his lips (there wouldn't be any lips then), and then he drooped, dropped his head right down and gazed unthinkingly at the dirty trickle of water burbling across the pavement. Everything around was burbling in patches of moisture, spluttering, whispering: it was the old crone of autumn's whisper carried in the air.

Apollon Apollonovich stood under the streetlamp, rocking backwards and forwards with his ash-grey countenance, his eyes wide in astonishment, the pupils hidden, the whites rolling (a carriage clattered by, but it seemed to be the clatter of something terrible, momentous: like blows of metal, shattering a life).

Mr Morkovin evidently began to feel exceedingly sorry for this aged silhouette that seemed to sink into the grime in front of him. He added:

"Don't be afraid, your Excellency, the strictest measures have been taken; we shall not allow it: there is no immediate danger today or tomorrow ... In a week's time you will be fully informed ... Just bear with us a while ... "

As he observed the blur of his pathetically trembling face, resembling a corpse, lit by the pale gleam of the streetlamp's flame, Mr Morkovin thought involuntarily: "How he's aged: why, he's nothing but a wreck ... " But with a barely perceptible creaking sound Apollon Apollonovich turned to that gent his beardless countenance and suddenly smiled sadly, whereupon huge wrinkled bags formed under his eyes.

A moment later, however, Apollon Apollonovich recovered completely, became younger, whiter: he shook Morkovin's hand firmly and set off, straight as a rod, into the grimy autumnal murk, his profile resembling the mummy of Pharaoh Ramses the Second.

The night was black and blue and indigo, as it merged into the reddish blurs of streetlamps, like spots from some fiery rash. The archways, walls and fences, the yards and entrances towered up—and from them came all manner of burbling and all manner of sighing; the many uncoordinated sighs in the windy gales that rushed along the side streets combined together, somewhere over there, beyond the houses, fences, walls and archways, into coordinated sighs; and the liquid burbles of the streams, somewhere over there, beyond the houses, fences, walls and archways all came together into a single liquid burble: all the burbles turned to sighs; and all the sighs began to burble.

Oh! How damp it was, how dank, how the night turned blue and indigo, as it merged into the sickly, bright-red rash of streetlamps, how Apollon Apollonovich came running from that indigo blue into the streetlamps' pools of light and ran off back again from those red pools into the indigo.

Out of his mind

We left Sergei Sergeevich Likhutin at that fateful moment in his life when, pale as death, completely calm, with an ironic smile on his tightly compressed lips, he had rushed headlong into the entrance-hall (that is to say, simply into the vestibule) after his disobedient wife and then, clicking his spurs, had stood so deferentially in front of the door with her fur coat in his hands; and when Sofia Petrovna had swished defiantly past the angry Second Lieutenant's nose, Sergei Sergeevich Likhutin, as we saw, had started, with the same excessively abrupt gestures, going round switching out all the lights.

Why did he reveal his extraordinary state of mind in this strange act? Well, what connection can there be between all this *beastliness* and the lights? There is just as little sense and connection here as there is sense and connection between the tall, ungainly and sad figure of the Second Lieutenant in his dark-green uniform, his excessively abrupt gestures and the defiant, flaxen beard on his youthful face that might have been carved from aromatic cypress-wood. There was no connection at all; maybe just—the mirrors: in the light they reflected—a tall ungainly man with a suddenly youthful face: the tall ungainly reflection with the suddenly youthful face, coming up close to the surface of the mirror, seized itself by its slender white neck—oh dear, oh dear! So there wasn't any connection between the light and the gestures.

"Click-click-click,"—all the same the switches clicked, immersing in darkness the tall ungainly man with excessively abrupt gestures. Maybe it wasn't Second Lieutenant Likhutin?

No, put yourself in his terrible position: to be reflected in the mirrors in such a beastly way, just because some domino had inflicted an insult upon his honourable house, because, in accordance with his word as an officer, he was now obliged to stop his wife from crossing the threshold. No, put yourself in his terrible position: it really was Second Lieutenant Likhutin—none other.

"Click-click-click,"—the switch clicked in the next room. He clicked the same way in the third. This sound disturbed Mavrusha too; and when she came shuffling through from the kitchen she was totally enveloped in utter darkness.

And she grumbled:

"Whatever's going on here?"

But out of the darkness came a dry, slightly restrained cough:

"Go away … "

"What do you mean, master … "

From the corner someone hissed at her in an indignant, peremptory whisper:

"Go away … "

"How do you mean, sir: I've got to tidy up after the mistress … "

"Go away from our rooms altogether."

"And then, you know, the beds isn't made yet … "

"Get out, get out, get out! … "

And no sooner had she gone out into the kitchen than the master came into the kitchen after her:

"Clear out of the house altogether … "

"How can I, master … "

"Clear out, clear out at once … "

"Where am I going to go?"

"Wherever you like: I don't want any trace of you here … "

"Master! … "

"Until tomorrow … "

"But master!! … "

"Get out, get out, get out … "

He shoved her coat into her hands, and her—out of the door: Mavrushka burst into tears: she was terrified—not half she wasn't: obviously the master wasn't quite right: should have gone to the porter and then the police station, but—silly girl—she went to her friend's.

Oh dear, Mavrushka …

How terrible is the fate of an ordinary, perfectly normal man: his life is resolved by a vocabulary of readily understood words, and by the practice of exceedingly clear actions; those actions carry him into the boundless distance, like a little boat rigged with words and gestures that are entirely expressible; if, however, that boat should chance to founder on an underwater reef of quotidian incomprehension, then, foundering, the boat is shattered, and in a trice the simple-hearted sailor drowns ... Gentlemen, at the slightest jolt in their lives ordinary people are robbed of their understanding; no, madmen do not know such risks of damage to their brains: their brains must surely be woven from the lightest ethereal substance. For the simple brain everything that these brains penetrate is quite impenetrable: the simple brain has nothing left but to be shattered; and shattered it is.

Since the previous evening Sergei Sergeich Likhutin had felt in his head a most acute cerebral pain, as though he had banged his head at speed against a wall of iron; and while he stood before that wall he had seen that the wall was not a wall, that it was permeable and that there, beyond the wall, there was some light he could not see and some laws of the absurd, just as there, outside the walls of the apartment, there was light and carriage traffic ... Then Sergei Sergeich Likhhutin bellowed deeply and gave a shake of his head, feeling the most acute cerebral effort, such as he had not known before. Reflected lights crept across the wall: no doubt that was a boat chugging by along the Moika, leaving bright stripes upon the water.

Sergei Sergeich Likhutin bellowed again and again: again and again he shook his head: his thoughts were conclusively confused, as was everything. He began his cogitation by analysing the actions of his unfaithful wife, but at the end he caught himself in senseless drivel: perhaps it was only to him that a solid plane was impenetrable, and rooms reflected in the mirror were genuinely rooms; and in those genuine rooms lived the family of some recently arrived officer; he would have to cover the mirrors: it was awkward to be examining with inquisitive glances the behaviour of a married officer with his young wife; you might come up against all kinds of drivel there; and Sergei Sergeich Likhutin started catching himself out in such drivel; and he found that he was himself engaged in drivel, getting

257

distracted from the essential, the absolutely essential thought (it was a good thing that Sergei Sergeich Likhutin had switched the electricity off; the mirrors would have been a terrible distraction to him, and at this moment he needed all his strength of will to discover in himself some train of thought).

So that was why, after his wife's departure, Second Lieutenant Likhutin had started going round switching the lights off everywhere.

What was he to do now? Since the previous evening *it—had begun, had come creeping up, and hissing:* what was that *it*—why had it started? Apart from the fact of Nikolai Apollonovich Ableukhov's disguise there was absolutely nothing here to seize hold of. The Second Lieutenant's head was the head of an ordinary man: that head refused to serve in this delicate matter, and the blood rushed to his head: it would be a good thing to put a wet towel on his temples; and Sergei Sergeich Likhutin put a wet towel on his temples: put it on and tore it off again. In any event, something had certainly happened; and in any event he, Likhutin, had become involved: and, becoming involved, he had become linked with it; here—*it* was: knocking, playing, beating, tugging at the veins in his temples.

The most simple-hearted of men, he had shattered against the wall: but through into the depths beyond the looking glass he could not penetrate: all he had done was to say out loud, in his wife's hearing, that he had given his word of honour as an officer that he would not voluntarily allow his wife back in if she went to the ball without him.

What was he to do? What was he to do?

Sergei Sergeich Likhutin became deeply agitated and struck another match: rusty-red lights flickered around him; the rusty-red lights lit up the face of a madman; it was now anxiously concentrated on the clock: two hours had passed since Sofia Petrovna had left; two hours, that is one hundred and twenty minutes; having calculated the number of minutes that had elapsed, Sergei Sergeich took to calculating the seconds:

"Sixty times a hundred and twenty? Twice six is twelve; carry one ... "

Sergei Sergeich Likhutin grasped his head:

"Carry one; keep one in mind; yes—the mind: the mind shattered against the mirror ... Ought to take the mirrors out! Twelve, keep one in mind—yes: one piece of glass ... No, one second lived ... "

His thoughts were confused: Sergei Sergeich strode up and down in complete darkness: *tu-tu-tu*—went Sergei Sergeich's footfalls; and Sergei Sergeich went on calculating:

"Two sixes are twelve; carry one: one six is six: plus one: an abstract unit—not a piece of glass. And two zeros: total—seven thousand two hundred seconds."

And having triumphed over this most complex piece of mental work, Sergei Sergeich rather inappropriately revealed his enthusiasm. Suddenly he remembered: his face darkened.

"Seven thousand two hundred seconds since she ran away: two hundred thousand seconds—no, it's all over!"

After the expiry of seven thousand seconds, the two hundred and first second inaugurated in time the beginning of the fulfilment of his word of honour as an officer: he had lived these seven thousand two hundred seconds like seven thousand years; little more than that, after all, had passed from the creation of the world till now. And it appeared to Sergei Sergeich that he had been imprisoned in this darkness since the creation of the world with the most acute mental illness: the illness of spontaneous thought, the autonomy of the brain regardless of the tormented personality. And Sergei Sergeich Likhutin, in the corner, became feverishly busy; he became quite quiet for a moment; began to cross himself; hurriedly pulled a rope (the likeness of a snake) out of a drawer, unwound it, and made a noose with it: the noose would not tighten. And in despair Sergei Sergeich ran into the study; the rope dragged along behind him.

What was Sergei Sergeich Likhutin doing? Keeping his word as an officer? No, goodness me—no. He simply took some soap out of a soapbox for some reason, squatted on his haunches and soaped the rope over a basin placed on the floor. And as soon as he had soaped the rope, all his actions assumed a quite fantastic tenor; you might say: never in his life had he done anything so original.

Judge for yourselves!

For some reason he climbed on to the table (as a precaution he removed the tablecloth first); and he lifted a bentwood chair from the floor on to the table; clambering on to the chair, he carefully disconnected the lamp; he carefully lowered it between his feet; in place of the lamp Sergei Sergeich Likhutin firmly attached to the hook the rope, slippery with soap; he crossed himself and froze; and he slowly raised the noose over his head with his hands, looking like a man who has decided to put a snake round his neck.

But Sergei Sergeich was struck by a brilliant thought: he really must shave his stubbly neck; and, apart from that, he must calculate the number of thirds and fourths: that meant multiplying seven thousand two hundred by sixty—twice.

With this brilliant thought Sergei Sergeich Likhutin marched through into the little study; there by the light of a candle-end he started shaving his stubbly neck (Sergei Sergeich had excessively tender skin and as he shaved, the tender skin on his neck became covered in spots). When he had shaved his neck and chin Sergei Sergeich accidentally caught his moustache with the razor: now he must shave himself entirely clean, because—what other choice was there? When they broke the door down and came in they would see him there with half a moustache, and moreover ... in such a position; no, there was no way he could start this undertaking without shaving himself clean first.

And Sergei Sergeich shaved himself clean: and clean-shaven he looked an utter idiot.

Well, now there was no reason to delay: it was all over—his face was shaved entirely clean. But at precisely that moment the bell rang in the hall; in vexation Sergei Sergeich threw down the razor, getting his fingers all covered in bits of whisker, glanced regretfully at the clock (how many hours had flown by?)—what was he to do, what was he to do? For a minute Sergei Sergeich thought of postponing his undertaking: he hadn't known that he would be caught in the act: he was reminded that there was no time to lose by the bell ringing a second time; and he leapt up on to the table to take the noose off the hook; but the rope slipped in his soapy fingers and would not obey him; Sergei Sergeich climbed down as quickly as possible and started creeping into the hall; and as he was creeping into the hall, he noticed that the blue-black darkness in the rooms, that all night long had been drowning him in ink, was slowly starting to dissolve; the inky darkness slowly became infused with grey and turned into a grey darkness: and in the greying darkness objects began to be outlined;

the chair standing on the table, the lamp lying there; and over all of this—the damp noose.

In the hall Sergei Sergeich put his ear to the door; he froze; but evidently his agitation had generated such a degree of forgetfulness in Sergei Sergeich that it was impossible for him to undertake any action at all: Sergei Sergeich Likhutin did not notice at all how heavily he was breathing; and when he heard through the door his wife's anxious calls, he shouted out at the top of his voice from fear; and having shouted out, he saw that everything was lost, and rushed off to put into execution his original plan; he swiftly jumped up on to the table and stretched out his freshly shaven neck; and on to his freshly shaven neck, covered in spots, he quickly began to tighten the noose, for some reason sticking two fingers between the noose and his neck as a precaution.

After this he for some reason shouted:

"In the name of the Tsar!"

He pushed the table away with his foot; and the table rolled away from Sergei Sergeich on its copper casters (that was the noise that Sofia Petrovna heard—outside the door).

What next?

A moment ...

—Sergei Sergeich Likhutin twitched his legs in the darkness; at the same time he distinctly saw the reflected gleam of the streetlamp on the air-vent of the stove; he also distinctly heard a knocking and scratching at the outer door; something crushed his two fingers forcefully against his chin, so that he could no longer pull them out; then he felt that he was choking; and above him a crash was heard (no doubt the veins bursting in his head), plaster flew all around him; and Sergei Sergeich Likhutin tumbled down (straight into death); and at once Sergei Sergeich Likhutin rose again from this death, having received a lusty kick in the next world; then he realised that he had come to; and when he came to, he realised that he had risen only to a sitting position—on a solid flat surface: he was sitting on the floor in his own room, with a pain in his spine and the fingers he had unwittingly stuck through now crushed between the rope and his throat: Sergei Sergeich Likhutin started tearing at the rope on his throat; and the noose expanded.

It was then that he realised that he had nearly hanged himself: he had just failed to hang himself—only just. And he breathed a sigh of relief.

All at once the inky darkness became infused with grey; and became a grey darkness: greyish—at first; then greying bit by bit; Sergei Sergeich Likhutin saw distinctly that he was sitting senselessly surrounded by walls, and that those walls were turning grey with Japanese landscapes as they imperceptibly merged with the surrounding night; the ceiling, so distinctly tinged at night by the rusty tracery of the streetlamp, began to lose its tracery; the streetlamp's tracery had long since started fading, turning into drab spots that gazed astonished at the greyish morning.

But let us return to the unfortunate Second Lieutenant.

We must say a few words about Sergei Sergeich by way of justification: the sigh of relief was expelled by Sergei Sergeich quite instinctively, just as the gestures of people drowning themselves, just before they sink in the cold, green depths, are instinctive. Sergei Sergeich Likhutin (you're not to smile!) had intended in all seriousness to settle his accounts with the world, and he would without the slightest doubt have realised this intention, were it not for the rotten ceiling (for that you can blame the builder); so that the sigh of relief can be attributed not to the personality of Sergei Sergeich, but to his fleshly, animal and impersonal integument. Be that as it may, however, the said integument was squatting on the floor and listening to everything (thousands of rustlings); while Sergei Sergeich's spirit revealed from the depths of the integument the most total composure.

In the flash of an eye all his thoughts were clarified; in the flash of an eye a dilemma presented itself to his consciousness: what was he to do now, what was he to do? His revolvers were hidden away somewhere; it would take too long to find them ... The razor? Do it with a razor—ugh! Everything inside him turned upside down: making another attempt with the razor after what had just happened with the first ... No: much the most natural thing was to stretch out here on the floor and leave all the rest to fate; yes, but in that natural event Sofia Petrovna (there was no doubt she had heard the crash) would immediately rush to the porter (if she hadn't already done so); they would phone the police, a crowd would gather; their pressure would break open the outer door, and they would come crashing in here; and, once crashed in, they would see him, Second Lieutenant Likhutin, with an unwontedly shaven face (Sergei Sergeich did not suspect what a complete idiot he looked without his moustache) and with a rope around his neck squatting among scraps of broken plaster.

No, no, no! The Second Lieutenant would never let things come to that: the honour of his uniform was dearer to him than his word to his wife. There was only one thing left: to open the door shamefacedly, make peace as quickly as possible with his wife, Sofia Petrovna, and give a plausible explanation of the chaos and the ceiling-plaster.

He hastily thrust the rope under the sofa and ran in utter abjection to the entrance door, through which there was no longer anything to be heard.

With the same involuntary heavy breathing as before he opened the outer door and stood hesitantly on the threshold; he was seized by a burning sense of shame (he had failed to hang himself!); and the storm that had been raging in his soul fell calm; as though by crashing down from the hook he had put an end to everything that had been raging just before: an end to his anger with his wife, an end to his anger over Nikolai Apollonovich's disgraceful behaviour. Why, now he had himself performed an act of unheard-of, incomparable disgracefulness: he'd planned to hang himself—and instead he had torn the hook out of the ceiling.

A moment ...

—No one ran into the room: but there was someone standing there (he could see); in the end Sofia Petrovna Likhutina came flying in; she flew in and burst out sobbing:

"What's all this? What's all this? Why is it dark?"

Sergei Sergeich lowered his head in embarrassment.

"What was all the noise and kerfuffle about?"

Embarrassed, Sergei Sergeich pressed her cold fingers in the dark.

"Why are your hands covered in soap? ... Sergei Sergeich, darling, what does this mean?"

"You see, Soniushka ... "

But she interrupted him:

"Why are you so hoarse? ... "

"You see, Soniushka ... I ... stood in front of the open window (careless of me, of course) ... And well, I lost my voice ... But that isn't the point ... "

He stopped short.

"No, don't, don't," Sergei Sergeich Likhutin almost shouted, pulling away his wife's hand as she tried to switch on the light, "don't come in here, not now—come into this room."

And he pulled her by force into the little study.

In the study things were already clearly outlined; and for a moment it seemed that the grey pattern created by the geometry of the chairs and the walls with the surfaces of shadows barely lying on them and the endless quantity of shaving paraphernalia scattered higgledy-piggledy all round—was nothing but ethereal lace, or gossamer; and through this finest gossamer the dawn sky percolated timidly and gently. Sergei Sergeich's face was indistinct; but when Sofia Petrovna looked at it close to, she saw before her ... No, it's indescribable: she saw before her the completely blue face of an unknown idiot; and this face was guiltily lowered.

"What have you done? Have you shaved yourself? Why, you're nothing but a fool! ... "

"You see, Soniushka," his frightened whisper rasped in her ear, "there's something I need to ... "

But she was not listening to her husband and rushed with instinctive anxiety to look at the rooms. She was followed from the study by a surge of tearful, hoarsely rasping cries:

"You'll find a mess in there ... "

"You see, my love, I was mending the ceiling ... "

"The ceiling had a crack in it ... "

"I had to ... "

But Sofia Petrovna Likhutina was not listening at all: she was standing terrified in front of a pile of scraps of plaster that had fallen on to the carpet, amongst which the hook, where it had fallen on the floor, stood out in black; the table with the overturned chair upon it had been shunted aside; from under the soft sofa, on which Sofia Petrovna had so recently been reading *Henri Besançon*—from under the soft sofa a grey noose protruded. Sofia Petrovna Likhutina trembled, turned deathly pale and hunched her shoulders.

Outside the windows was a spatter of the lightest flames, and everything was suddenly bathed in light, when a pink ripple of clouds moved into the flames like a network of mother-of-pearl; and in the gaps in that network something now shone a faint blue: such a tender blue; all was filled with a tremulous timidity; all was filled with an astonished question: "How can that be? How can that be? Am I not shining?" Over there on windows and spires the tremor became more and more visible; on the tall spires the ruby gleam stood out loftily. The lightest of voices now suddenly passed across her soul: and for her everything was bathed in light, when a pale-pink, palely patterned slanting ray from the rising sun fell through the window on to the grey noose. Her heart filled with an unexpected tremor and an astonished question: "How can that be? How can that be? Why did I forget?"

Then Sofia Petrovna bent down to the ground and stretched out her hand to the rope, on which such delicate pink lace flimmered; Sofia Petrovna kissed the rope and quietly began to weep: someone's image from a distant but regained childhood (an image not utterly forgotten—where had she seen it: somewhere recently, today, perhaps?): this image rose to stand over her, stood at her back. And when she turned round she saw: at her back her husband was standing, Sergei Sergeevich Likhutin, long-limbed, sad and shaven: he raised his meek blue eyes to her:

"Please forgive me, Soniushka!"

She for some reason fell at his feet, embracing them and weeping: "My poor love: my darling! … "

What they whispered between themselves God only knows: all that remained between them; his gaunt hand could be seen raised over her towards the dawn:

"God will forgive … God will forgive … "

The shaven head laughed so happily: who could help laughing, when such delicate flames were laughing in the sky?

A ragged, pink-hued cloud stretched along the Moika: this was a cloud from the funnel of a passing steamer; from the steamer's prow a strip of green glistened with cold, striking the bank with a flash of amber, reflecting—here and there—a spark of gold, reflecting—here and there—a diamond; as it sprang back from the bank this strip shattered against another strip that came to meet it, making them both glisten in swarms of coiling snakes. The boat sailed into this swarm; and all the snakes were cut into diamond strings; the strings at once wound into one another to make a silver thread, in order then to bobble on the water surface like stars. But the momentary movement of the water settled down; the waters became smooth and the stars upon them ceased to shine. Now just gleaming watery-green surfaces rode between stone banks. Soaring into the sky like a green-black sculpture, a green building with white columns rose strangely from the bank like a living piece of the Renaissance.

Man-in-the-street

Over a great distance, this way and that, alleyways and side streets were scattered, simply streets, Prospects; here a house's high-topped gable-end stood out, brick-built, made entirely out of gravity, while there a wall gaped from the darkness with a portico on which two stone Egyptians bore aloft on their hands the stone protrusion of a balcony. Past the high-topped house, past the brick gable-end, past all the million-ton colossi—from darkness into darkness—Apollon Apollonovich walked and walked in the Petersburg mist, overcoming all the gravity: in front of him appeared the outline of a grey, decrepit fence.

Then somewhere at one side a low door was thrown open swiftly and left open; white steam billowed out, foul language was heard, the pitiful twanging of a balalaika and a voice. Apollon Apollonovich listened despite himself to the voice as he scrutinized the lifeless archways, the lamp rattling in the wind and the outside toilet.

The voice sang:

With our spirit, Lord, to Thee
In our thoughts we're heaven-bent,
With our hearts we gratefully
Thank Thee for our nourishment.

Thus sang the voice.

The door slammed shut. In the man-in-the-street Apollon Apollonovich had always suspected something mean flying by outside the glazed apertures of his carriage (Apollon Apollonovich, after all, calculated the distance between the nearest wall and the door of his carriage as many millions of versts). And now all the spaces before him had been displaced: the life of the man-in-the-street had suddenly surrounded him with archways and walls, while the man-in-the-street himself had come to face him as a voice.

And that voice sang:

With our spirit, Lord, to Thee
In our thoughts we're heaven-bent,
With our hearts we gratefully
Thank Thee for our nourishment.

Was that what the man-in-the-street was like? Apollon Apollonovich conceived an interest in the man-in-the-street, and there was a moment when he was ready to knock on the first door, in order to find him; but then he remembered that the man-in-the-street was preparing to do him to death in a most humiliating way: his top hat slipped to one side, and his enfeebled shoulders hung limply over his chest:—

—yes, yes, yes: they had blown him to pieces: not him, Apollon Apollonovich, but the other, his best friend, the friend that fate sends only once; for a moment Apollon Apollonovich recalled the white moustache, the greenish depths of the eyes fixed upon him as they both leant over the map of the Empire, their so youthful old age afire with dreams (that was exactly one day before) ... But they had blown to pieces even his best friend, the leader among leaders ... They say it only lasts a second; and then—just nothing ... What is that? Every statesman is a hero, but—brr-brr ...

—Apollon Apollonovich adjusted his top hat and straightened his shoulders, as he passed into the putrid mist, into the putrid life of the man-in-the-street, into this network of walls, archways, fences, all full of slush, subsiding pitifully, limply, in short—into that ubiquitous, worthless, rotten, empty universal latrine. And now it seemed to him that even that blind wall hated him, even that rotting fence; Apollon Apollonovich knew from experience that *they* hated him (day and night he walked enveloped in the mist of their malice). But who were *they*? A negligible little bunch, noisome like them all? Apollon Apollonovich's cerebral play erected misty planes before his gaze; but all the planes blew up: the gigantic map of Russia rose up before him, who was so small: could it be that these were his enemies: his enemies were the gigantic totality of all the peoples living in these spaces: a hundred million. No, more ...

"From the cold Finnish cliffs to flaming Colchis" ...

What was that? They hated him? ... No, Russia lay stretched out. And him? ... They were going to ... going to ... No: brr-brr ... Idle cerebral play. Better to quote Pushkin:

'Tis time, my friend, 'tis time; for peace my heart now aches;
Days hasten after days, and each, departing, takes
Away with it a part of being; you and I
Had thought to live together: lo, we die.

Who was he planning to spend his life with? With his son? His son was an appalling scoundrel. With the man-in-the-street? The man-in-the-street was going to ... Apollon Apollonovich recalled that once upon a time he had planned to spend his life with Anna Petrovna, to settle in his country house in Finland at the end of his civil service career, but, well, there you are: Anna Petrovna had left—yes, left! ...

"She left, you know: it can't be helped ... "

Apollon Apollonovich realised that he had no companion in life (up to that moment he had somehow not found time to recall the fact) and that death in office would in fact be an adornment to the life he had lived. He began to have a childish feeling of both sadness and calm—he felt so calm, comfortable somehow. All he could hear around him was the patter of a trickling puddle, like someone's prayer—about one and the same thing: about that which was not, but which might have been.

The grey-black murk, which all night long had stifled him, began slowly to dissolve. The grey-black murk slowly became infused with grey and turned into grey murk: at first just greyish, later greying slightly more; the walls of houses, lit at night by streetlamps, started to merge palely with the dissipating night. And it seemed that the rusty lamps, that had just now been casting rusty pools of light around them, had begun suddenly to fade; and gradually they faded out. The feverishly burning torches disappeared from the walls. At last the streetlamps became nothing but dull points gazing in surprise into the greyish mist; and for a moment it seemed that the grey vista of lines, spires and walls with surfaces of shadow barely lying on them, with an infinity of window apertures—was not a stone colossus, but a structure of ethereal lace that stood there, made out of the most delicately worked patterns, and that through those patterns the dawn sky percolated timidly.

Suddenly a poorly dressed adolescent girl came rushing towards Apollon Apollonovich; the girl was about fifteen, with her hair in a headscarf; and behind her in the dawn mist came the silhouette of a man: bowler hat, cane, overcoat, ears, moustache and nose; the silhouette had evidently been pestering the girl with indecent propositions; Apollon Apollonovich considered himself a knight; to his own surprise he doffed his top hat:

"Madam, may I make so bold as to offer you my arm as far as your home; at this late hour it is not without danger for young persons of your sex to appear on the street."

The poorly dressed girl saw distinctly that a strange black figure had respectfully raised his top hat to her; a shaven, deathlike head emerged for a moment from the collar and retreated back again.

They walked in profound silence; everything seemed nearer than was right: wet and old, retreating into the ages; Apollon Apollonovich had seen all this before from a distance. But now—here it was: archways, houses, walls and this adolescent girl, pressed to his arm by fear, for whom he, Apollon Apollonovich, was not a villain, not a senator: just ordinary—a kind old stranger.

They walked as far as a little green house with lopsided gates under a rotting arch; on the doorstep the senator raised his top hat, bidding the girl farewell; and when the door slammed behind her, his aged mouth twisted plaintively; his lifeless lips munched utter emptiness; at that moment something like the singing of a violin rang out in the distance: the singing of the Petersburg cockerel bearing tidings of none knew what and rousing none knew whom.

Somewhere to one side there was a spattering of the lightest flames, and everything was suddenly bathed in light, as a pink ripple of clouds moved into the flames like a network of mother-of-pearl; and in the gaps in that network a scrap of blue shone out. The vista of lines and walls took on weight and form; to one side heavy things protruded—ledges, shelves; porticoes protruded, caryatids and the cornices of brick-built balconies; but on the windows, on the spires a tremor could be noticed more and more; and from the windows, from the spires a ruby brilliance broke forth.

This lightest lace turned out to be the morning Petersburg: Petersburg took on colour lightly and fantastically, there were sandy-coloured houses standing there five storeys high; there were dark-blue houses, grey ones; the rust-red palace gleamed with dawn.

CHAPTER FIVE

In which is told of the gent with the wart on his nose and the sardine-tin of terrible import.

> *The rays of dawn illume the morning,*
> *And day's new brilliance grows apace,*
> *While I, perchance, beneath the awning*
> *Of veilèd death shall find my place.*
>
> A Pushkin

The gent

NIKOLAI APOLLONOVICH stayed silent all the way.

Nikolai Apollonovich turned round and stared straight into the face of the gent running along behind him:

"I beg your pardon: with whom do I ... "

The Petersburg slush squelched in melting rivulets; over there a carriage flew by, its lights melting into the mist ...

"With whom do I have the honour? ..., "

All the way he could hear the irritating splash of the galoshes pursuing him and sensed, running up and down his back, the inflamed little eyes of the bowler hat that had attached itself to him back in the alley, beside the archway.

"Pavel Iakovlevich Morkovin ... "

And then Nikolai Apollonovich turned right round and stared straight into the gent's face; the face told him nothing: bowler hat, cane, overcoat, beard and nose.

After that he fell into forgetfulness, turning away to the wall, where all the way the shadow bowler hat was running, set slightly at an angle; the sight of this bowler hat aroused a feeling of disgust in

271

him; the Petersburg damp crept under the skin; the Petersburg slush squelched in melting rivulets; the black ice and the drizzle soaked his overcoat.

The bowler hat on the wall stretched its shadow out, then drew it in again; once more a distinct voice rang out behind Ableukhov's back:

"I'm willing to bet that this tone of indifference you're putting on is nothing but an affectation … "

All this had happened before.

"Listen," Nikolai Apollonovich tried to say to the bowler hat, "I must admit, I'm most surprised; I must admit … "

Over there the first sphere of light blazed up; there—a second: there—a third; and the line of electric spheres delineated the Nevskii Prospect, where the walls of stone buildings are shrouded in a fiery pall all the round Petersburg night and where glaring restaurants show off to the tumult of the night their vivid blood-red signs, beneath which plumed ladies flutter to and fro, hiding in their boas the carmine of their painted lips—amidst top hats and bowlers, high-collared shirts and overcoats—into the dully gleaming murk that from the wretched Finnish marshes over far-flung Russia reveals the gaping, incandescent jaws of Gehenna.

Nikolai Apollonovich kept a constant watch as the shadowy black bowler, the immemorial dark shadow, progressed along the walls; Nikolai Apollonovich knew: the circumstances of his meeting with the mysterious Pavel Iakovlevich did not permit him to break the meeting off right there—by the fence—maintaining his own dignity unblemished: he had to elicit from him, with the greatest caution, what this Pavel Iakovlevich truly knew about him, what had truly passed between him and his father; and that was why he delayed his leave-taking.

Now the Neva opened out: the stone arch over the Winter Canal revealed a lachrymose expanse, from where rushed gusts of sodden wind; across the Neva there rose the outlines of islands and houses; their amber eyes pierced the mist with melancholy; and it seemed they were weeping.

"But in fact you're not averse to hobnobbing with me, as they call it, either, are you?" the same moth-eaten voice kept at him from behind.

Here was the square; the same grey rock still reared up on the square; the same steed flourished its hoof; but strange to say: a shadow obscured the Bronze Horseman. And it seemed the Bronze Horseman was not there; there far away on the Neva lay a fishing schooner; and on the schooner a light was glinting.

"It's really time I went home … "

"No, be my guest: what's home to you now!"

And they passed across the bridge.

There were two men walking in front of them: a sailor of forty-five or so, dressed in black leather; he had a hat with ear-flaps, he had blue-tinged cheeks and a bright red beard with flecks of grey; his companion, a downright giant in immense boots, with a dark-green felt hat, strode along—black eyebrows, black hair, with a small nose and a small moustache. Both of them were redolent of something; and both of them went through the open door of a restaurant under a gleaming signboard.

Beneath the letters of the gleaming signboard Pavel Iakovlevich Morkovin grabbed Ableukhov by the flap of his cape with an incomprehensible effrontery:

"This way, Nikolai Apollonovich, into the restaurant: here we are — just the thing, this way, sir! … "

"Now look here … "

But Pavel Iakovlevich, keeping hold of the flap of the cape, at this point began to yawn: he twisted and turned, bent over and stretched, presenting his open oral cavity to Nikolai Apollonovich like some kind of cannibal who was about to swallow Ableukhov: swallow him for sure.

This attack of yawning was communicated to Ableukhov; the latter's lips contorted:

"*Aaa—a: aaaa* … "

Ableukhov tried to break away:

"No, it's really time for me to go."

But the mysterious gentleman, having regained the gift of speech, interrupted him unceremoniously:

"Hey, get on with you—I know all that: bored, are you?"

And without giving him time to reply, interrupted again:

"Yes, I'm bored too: and on top of that you might add that I've got a cold: all these last few days I've been treating it with a tallow candle … "

Nikolai Apollonovich wanted to make some interjection, but his mouth split open in a yawn:

"*Aaa: aaa—aaa!* … "

"There you are—look how bored you are!"

"I'm just sleepy ... "

"Well, you may be, but all the same (put yourself in my position): it's a unique opportunity, most unique ... "

There was nothing for it: Nikolai Apollonovich gave a slight shrug of his shoulders and with barely perceptible disgust opened the door of the restaurant ... Coat-hangers draped in blackness: with bowler hats, canes, overcoats.

"A unique opportunity, most unique," Morkovin snapped his fingers, "I'll tell you that straight: a young man of such exceptional talents as yourself? ... And let him go? ... Leave him in peace?! ... "

Dense white steam smelling somewhat of pancakes, mixed with the damp from the street; the cloakroom token dropped into his palm with an icy burn.

"Hee-hee-hee," Pavel Iakovlevich let himself go, rubbing his hands, as he took off his coat, "the young philosopher is curious to find out about me: isn't that so?"

Now, inside the room, the Petersburg street began to give off an acrid, feverish heat, like dozens of red-pawed ants crawling all over the body:

"Why, everyone knows me ... Alexandr Ivanovich, your papa, Butishchenko, Shishiganov, Peppóvich ... "

After these words Nikolai Apollonovich began to feel the liveliest curiosity for three reasons; in the first place: the stranger—for the umpteenth time!—had emphasised his acquaintance with his father (that certainly meant something); secondly: the stranger had slipped in a word about Alexandr Ivanovich and had mentioned this name along with that of his father; finally, the stranger had mentioned a series of names (Butishchenko, Shishiganov, Peppóvich) which sounded so strangely familiar ...

"She's interesting," Pavel Iakovlevich drew Ableukhov's attention to a bright-lipped prostitute in a light-orange dress and with a Turkish cigarette in her teeth ...

"What sort of women d'you like? ... We could ... "

"?"

"All right, I won't, I won't: I can see you're the innocent type ... Anyway this isn't the time ... We have things to ... "

All around there reverberated:

"Who's that then?"

"Who? … Ivan! … "

"Ivan Ivanych! … "

"Ivan Ivanych Ivanov … "

"Just what I was saying: Ivan-Ivanch? … A? … Ivan-Ivanch? … What'ya up to, Ivan Ivanch? Oh dear, oh dear! … "

"As for Ivan Ivanych … "

"That's all lies."

"No, it's not lies … You just ask Ivan Ivanych: there he is, in the billiard-room … Hey, hey!"

"Ivan! … "

"Ivan Ivanych!"

"Ivan Ivanych Ivanov … "

"Ivan Ivanych, what a swine you are!"

Somewhere a shindig broke out; a machine suddenly roared out, like a dozen howling horns that hurled ear-splitting sounds into the fug; beside the machine a merchant, Ivan Ivanych Ivanov, waving a green bottle, took up a dancing position with a lady in a torn blouse; the dirt on her grimy cheeks could be seen gleaming; from under her red hair, from under the raspberry-coloured feathers that had slipped on to her forehead, pressing a handkerchief to her lips so as not to burp out loud, the goggle-eyed lady laughed; as she laughed her bosom bounced; Ivan Ivanych Ivanov neighed with laughter; the drunken audience caterwauled all round.

Nikolai Apollonovich looked round in astonishment: how could he have got into such a ghastly place in such ghastly company at a time when? …

"Ha-ha-ha-ha-ha-ha," the same drunken bunch roared out again, when Ivan Ivanych Ivanov seized his lady by the hair and pinned her to the ground, pulling out a huge raspberry-coloured feather; the lady was crying, expecting to be beaten; but they managed to pull the merchant off her in time. Viciously, tormentingly, in that wild machine, with a bellow and a clash of tambourines, terrible antiquity, like a volcanic explosion of subterranean paroxysms hurtling upon us from the depths, grew ever louder, swelled and wailed out into the restaurant from golden trumpets: *"Be soothed now, you feelings of passion …* "

"And sleep now, you heart without hope … "

"Ha-ha-ha-ha-ha-ha! … "

A glass of vodka

There were the rooms of the ancient, hellish drinking-den; there were its walls; these walls had been decorated by a painter's hand: the foam of Finnish breakers, from where—from afar, piercing the dank and greenish mist, on great shadowy sails a ship's tarred rigging once again came flying towards Petersburg.

"You have to admit ... Hey, two glasses of vodka!—admit it ... " Pavel Iakovlevich Morkovin shouted—white as white: flabby—all swollen and bloated; his white face, tinged with yellow, still seemed thin, although it was swollen and bloated: here a bag under his eyes; here a bump like a nipple; here a white wart ...

"I'll wager that for you I represent a conundrum which your mental apparatus is at this moment trying in vain to resolve ... "

Away over there was a table: at the table a forty-five-year-old sailor, dressed in black leather (and apparently a Dutchman), was leaning his blue-shaded face over his glass.

"Some syrup in that? ... "

The Dutchman's blood-red lips—for the umpteenth time—sucked in the flaming kümmel.

"With syrup, then?"

And beside the Dutchman a cumbersome colossus, hewn, it seemed, from stone, lowered himself ponderously at the table.

"With syrup."

Black-browed, black-haired—the colossus laughed ambiguously in the direction of Nikolai Apollonovich.

"Well, young man?" the stranger's shrill tenor piped up at this moment by his ear.

"What is it?"

"What do you have to say about my behaviour in the street?"

And it seemed that if that colossus were to strike the table with its fist—a crash of sundered planks, a peal of broken glass would echo through the restaurant.

"What to say about your behaviour in the street? Oh, why are you talking about the street? I really don't know."

Then the colossus took a pipe from the heavy folds of his kaftan, stuck it between his powerful lips, and the heavy smoke of the stinking tobacco wafted across the table.

"Another?"
"Another."

The pungent poison gleamed in front of him; in an attempt to calm himself he selected some withered leaves to put on his plate; there he stood with the full glass in his hand, while Pavel Iakovlevich anxiously fussed about, trying to catch on his trembling fork a slippery saffron milk-cap; having impaled the slippery mushroom, Pavel Iakovlevich turned round (there were scraps clinging to his moustache).

"Don't you agree, it was all rather strange there?"

He had stood like this before (for all this had happened before) … But the glasses clinked loudly; glasses had clinked like this … —where had they clinked?

"Where?"

Nikolai Apollonovich strained to remember. Unfortunately Nikolai Apollonovich was unable to recall.

"Why, *there*, by the fence … No, landlord, we don't want sardines: they float in yellow slime."

Pavel Iakovlevich made an explanatory gesture to Ableukhov.

"The way I caught you there: you were standing by a puddle reading a note: well, I thought, this is a unique opportunity, most unique … "

There were tables standing all round; at the tables a hybrid race was carousing; and this race kept on crowding in: neither men nor shadows—with astounding thievish tricks; they were all inhabitants of the islands, and the inhabitants of the islands are a hybrid race, a strange one: neither men nor shadows. Pavel Iakovlevich Morkovin was also from the island: smiling, chuckling, with astounding thievish tricks.

"Do you know, Pavel Iakovlevich, I have to say I'm expecting an explanation from you … "

"Of my behaviour?"

"Yes!"

"I'll explain it … "

Again the pungent poison gleamed: he was becoming drunk—everything was revolving; the drinking-den glimmered more ghostly; the Dutchman seemed more blue, the colossus—more colossal; its shadow fractured on the walls and seemed to be crowned with some kind of wreath.

Pavel Iakovlevich's face had a more and more glossy shine—he was swelling up, becoming bloated: here a bag under his eyes; here a bump like a nipple; here a white wart; this puffy face aroused in his memory the tip of a tallow candle, oozing pig-fat.

"A third one, then?"

"Yes, let's … "

"So what do you say about our conversation by the archway?"

"About the domino?"

"Well, yes, goes without saying! … "

"I'll say what I said before … "

"You can be perfectly frank with me."

Nikolai Apollonovich wanted to turn away in disgust from Mr Morkovin's malodorous lips, but he restrained himself; and when he received a smacking kiss on the lips, he instinctively cast his tortured gaze up to the ceiling, brushing a wisp of hair from his lofty brow with his hand, at the same time as his lips spread unnaturally in a smile and began to tremble, twitching with tension (the paws of laboratory frogs twitch unnaturally like that when they come into contact with the ends of electric wires).

"There: that's better; and don't get any ideas: the domino didn't mean anything. I just thought up the domino as a way of getting acquainted … "

"Sorry, you've dripped some sardine oil on yourself," Nikolai Apollonovich interrupted him, while thinking to himself: "This is all a cunning game, to see what he can find out: have to be careful … " We forgot to mention that Nikolai Apollonovich had taken off the domino at the restaurant entrance.

"You must agree: it was a crazy idea that you were the domino … Hee-hee-hee: well, where would you get an idea like that from, eh? Listen. I said to myself: hey, Pavlusha, old chap, why that's just a sort of—sudden inspiration, like, and there's me standing by the fence answering a call of nature, as it were … The domino! … Nothing to it at all, just a pretext to make your acquaintance, my dear good fellow, because I've heard ever so much: about your intellectual capacities."

They moved away from the vodka counter, making their way between the tables. And again, like a dozen howling horns hurling their ear-splitting sounds into the fug, the machine bellowed out; swarms of little bells tinkled, smashing against ear-drums; and from a private room someone's shameless boasting drifted out.

"Waiter: a clean tablecloth … "

"And some vodka … "

"So that's it: we've finished with the domino. And now, my dear chap, about another little matter that links us together … "

"You mentioned a matter that links us together … What matter is that?"

They placed their elbows on the table. Nikolai Apollonovich was feeling intoxicated (from tiredness, no doubt); all the colours, all the sounds, all the smells struck with increasing ugliness his incandescent, white-hot brain.

"Yes-yes-yes: a most curious, fascinating little matter … Fine: I'll have kidneys in Madeira, and for you … kidneys too?"

"What matter is it?"

"Waiter, two portions of kidneys … You were asking about this fascinating matter? Well, it's like this—I must admit: those ties —the ties that link us —are sacred ties … "

"?"

"They are family ties."

"?"

"Ties of blood … "

At that moment the kidneys were served.

"Oh, don't imagine that those ties … —Salt, pepper, mustard!— are connected with the spilling of blood: why are you trembling, old chap? Goodness me, you've flared up so, blushing all over—like a young girl! Shall I pass you the mustard? Here's the pepper."

Just like Apollon Apollonovich, Nikolai Apollonovich over-peppered his soup; but he stopped with the pepper-pot hanging in mid-air.

"What did you say?"

"I said to you: here's the pepper … "

"About blood … "

"Ah? About the ties? By ties of blood I mean family ties."—The little table set off around the room (the vodka was having its effect); the little table began to expand without rhyme or reason; Pavel Iakovlevich meanwhile flew away together with the edge of the table, tied a dirty napkin round himself, fiddled around with the napkin and looked like a maggot on a corpse.

"All the same, excuse me, I can't have understood you at all: tell me, what do you understand by our family ties?"

"Nikolai Apollonovich, I am your brother … "

"What do you mean, my brother?"

Nikolai Apollonovich even stood up, but leant his face across the table towards the gent; with nostrils palpitating nervously his face now seemed a pinkish-white beneath a shock of hair that stood on end; his hair was of a misty colour.

"Illegitimate, stands to reason, for I am no more or less than the fruit of your father's unhappy love-affair … with the family dressmaker … "

Nikolai Apollonovich sat down; his dark-blue eyes, now darker still, the faint aroma of *White Rose* scent, his slender fingers torturing the tablecloth—all expressed the anguish of death: the Ableukhovs had always treasured the purity of their blood; he too treasured his blood;—how could that be, how could that be: so his papa had had a …

"So in his youth your papa had an interesting little love-affair … "

Nikolai Apollonovich suddenly thought that Morkovin was going to continue his sentence with the words: "which resulted in my appearance" (what nonsense, what a wild thought!).

"Which resulted in my appearance in the world."

Madness!

This had happened before.

"And on this occasion of our family meeting let's have another glass."

Viciously, tormentingly, in that wild machine, with a bellow and a clash of tambourines, terrible antiquity, like a scream hurtling upon us from the depths, grew ever louder, swelled and wailed out into the restaurant from golden trumpets.

"You mean to say that my father ... "

"Our shared father."

"If you like, our shared father," Nikolai Apollonovich flinched.

"A-a-a: that shoulder of yours? How you're flinching!" Pavel Iakovlevich interrupted him. "Do you know why you flinched?"

"Why?"

"Because for you, Nikolai Apollonovich, being related to a non-descript like me is, say what you will, an insult ... And then, you know, you've picked up courage."

"Picked up courage? Why should I be afraid?"

"Ha-ha-ha!" Pavel Iakovlevich was not listening to him. "you've picked up courage because you think that ... —Some more kidneys ... "

"No, thank you ... "

"My remarkable curiosity and our conversation by the fence have been explained ... And some sauce ... Do please forgive me for applying to you, my dear chap, a psychological method of torture, so to speak—by keeping you waiting, I mean, of course; I'm probing you, old fellow, this way and that; I'll come at you from this side, then from the other; I'll lie in ambush. And then jump out."

Nikolai Apollonovich narrowed his eyes, and from behind his long eyelashes his eyes shone blue with a wild, keen determination not to ask for mercy, at the same time as his fingers drummed on the table.

"And it's the same about our being related; that's a kind of probing too: to see how you take it ... And now I have to gladden you and sadden you at the same time ... No, you must forgive me—when I meet a new person I always act like this: I only need to tell you that we're brothers, but ... with different parents."

"?"

"It was nothing more than a joke about Apollon Apollonovich: there never was any love-affair with a dressmaker; there never was—hee-hee-hee—any love-affair at all ... An exceptionally moral man in our immoral age ... "

"Then in what sense are we brothers?"

"By conviction ... "

"How can you know my convictions?"

"You, Nikolai Apollonovich, are an utterly convinced terrorist." Everything in Nikolai Apollonovich merged together in unremitting anguish; everything merged into a single torment.

"I'm an out-and-out terrorist too: if you would kindly notice, it wasn't by chance I dropped some names that are not unfamiliar to you: Butishchenko, Shishiganov and Peppóvich ... Do you remember, I mentioned them just now? That was a subtle hint, suggesting you could take it however you liked ... Alexandr Ivanovich Dudkin, the Fugitive! ... Eh? Eh? ... Do you get my drift? Don't be embarrassed: you got my drift all right, because you are a well-read man, our theoretician, a clever old rogue: ooo-ooo, you old rascal, let me kiss you ... "

"Ha-ha-ha," Nikolai Apollonovich leant back on the flimsy chair, "ha-ha-ha-ha-ha ... "

"Hee-hee-hee," Pavel Iakovlevich joined in, "hee-hee-hee ... "

"Ha-ha-ha," Nikolai Apollponovich went on chortling.

"Hee-hee-hee," Morkovin giggled in accompaniment.

The colossus from the next table turned angrily towards them and looked at them intently.

"What'ya doing?"

Nikolai Apollonovich became angry.

"And his own knew him not."

"This is what I'll tell you," Nikolai Apollonovich said completely seriously, pretending he had overcome his fit of uncontrolled laughter (he had been forcing himself to laugh), "you are mistaken, because my attitude to terrorism is negative; and apart from everything else: tell me, on what basis did you come to that conclusion?"

"For heaven's sake, Nikolai Apollonovich! I know everything about you: about the package, about Alexandr Ivanovich Dudkin and about Sofia Petrovna ... "

"I know it all out of personal curiosity and moreover: in the line of official duty ... "

"Ah, you are in the service?"

"Yes: in security ... "

"In security?"

"Why do you grasp at your chest like that, my good chap, with an expression as though you had a most dangerous and secret document there ... A glass of vodka! ... "

I destroy irrevocably

For a moment they both sat stock still; from the other side of the table Pavel Iakovlevich Morkovin, agent of the security service, grew, extended, stretched out with a finger pointing upwards; and then the sharp point of this hook-shaped finger caught hold of Nikolai Apollonovich's button from across the table; then Nikolai Apollonovich with an entirely new guilty smile pulled from his side pocket a small bound volume which turned out to be a notebook.

"Ah, ah, ah! Be so kind as to give me that book … for examination … " Nikolai Apollonovich did not resist; he sat there with the same guilty smile; his torment had passed all bounds; the ecstasy of torture undergone and the afflatus of the sacrificial role had vanished; what was left was: humiliation, submission (the remnants of destroyed pride); before him one single path remained: the path of unfeeling apathy. Be that as it may: he handed the detective his little book for examination like a criminal caught red-handed and crucified by suffering, and like a slandered prude (shameless deceiver!).

Pavel Iakovlevich meanwhile, bending over the notebook, stuck his head over the edge of the table so that it seemed to be attached not to his neck but to his two hands; for a moment he turned into a straightforward monster: what Nikolai Apollonovich saw at that moment was a hideous head with blinking eyes, with hair like dog's fur standing on end, leering with ghastly laughter, as it peeped across the table in yellow folds of skin, running over the leaves of the notebook with its ten skipping fingers, for all the world like some immense insect: a ten-legged spider, its paws rustling across the paper.

But it was all play-acting …

Pavel Iakovlevich evidently wanted to frighten Ableukhov with this appearance of a search (what a delightful joke!); still leering with loud laughter, he tossed the notebook back across the table to Ableukhov.

"For goodness' sake, why such obedience … It's not as though I was planning to interrogate you … Don't be afraid, old chap: I'm in the security service on the party's behalf … And there's no reason for you to be so upset, Nikolai Apollonovich: honestly, no reason at all … "

"Are you making fun of me?"

"Not for a second! ... If I were really in the police you'd already be under arrest, because that gesture of yours, you know, was worthy of attention; first of all you grasped at your chest with a terrified expression on your face, as though you had some document there ... If you do meet a detective in future, don't repeat that gesture; that was what gave you away ... Agreed?"

"If you like ... "

"And then, if you don't mind my saying so, you made another blunder: you took out a perfectly innocent notebook at a time when nobody had asked you for it; you took it out in order to distract attention from something else; but you didn't achieve your purpose; you didn't distract attention, you attracted it; you made me think that you did still have a document of some sort in your pocket ... Oh, you are so careless ... Just look at this page of the notebook you gave me; you've accidentally revealed an amorous secret to me: here, have a good look at this ... "

The animal howls of the machine filled the air: the cry of an immense bull being butchered: tambourines were bursting, bursting, bursting.

"Listen!"

Nikolai Apollonovich uttered this 'listen' with genuine fury.

"What's all this torture for? If you're really who you say you are—waiter, here you are!—then all your behaviour, all this charade of yours—is unworthy."

They both stood up.

Nikolai Apollonovich stood there in the white billows of stench coming from the kitchen—pale, white, furious, his red mouth torn wide open with no trace of laughter, his misty-flaxen hair, fair as fair, formed a halo round his head; like a snarling beast at bay he turned contemptuously to Morkovin, slipping a fifty-copeck piece to the waiter.

The machine had already fallen silent; the neighbouring tables had long since been standing empty, and the hybrid race had dispersed through the Lines of the island; suddenly the white electric light went out everywhere; the rusty light of candles pierced the deathly emptiness here and there; the walls dissolved in darkness: only where a candle stood and the edge of the painted wall was visible, white foam tumbled hissing into the room. And from there, from afar, the Flying Dutchman was flying towards Petersburg on his shadowy sails (it must have been Nikolai Apollonovich's head reeling from the seven glasses he had drunk); the forty-five-year-old sailor rose from the table (wasn't he a Dutchman?); for a moment his eyes flashed with green sparks; but he vanished in the darkness.

Mr Morkovin, adjusting his frock coat, glanced at Nikolai Apollonovich with a kind of pensive tenderness (the latter's state of mind had evidently touched him too); he gave a melancholy sigh; and lowered his eyes; for a minute or so they did not utter a word.

Eventually Pavel Iakovlevich spoke up slowly and distinctly.

"That's enough: it's just as hard for me as it is for you ... "

"And what sense is there is hiding it, comrade? ... "

"I didn't come here for fun ... "

"We have to come to an agreement, don't we? ... "

"?"

"Well, yes, yes: agree about the day you will carry out your promise ... Really, Nikolai Apollonovich, you're an unusually strange man; did you really imagine for one minute that I was just dragging round the streets after you because I had nothing better to do, when I'd taken so much trouble to strike up a conversation with you ... "

And then, looking Ableukhov sternly in the eyes, he added with dignity: "The party, Nikolai Apollonovich, is expecting an immediate answer."

Nikolai Apollonovich went quietly down the stairs; the end of the staircase slipped away into the darkness; and at the bottom— by the door—*they* were standing; he could give no positive answer to the question who *they* were: a black outline and a murk that was green through and through, like dully burning phosphorus (it was a streetlamp outside shining in); and *they* were waiting for him.

And when he reached that door he sensed the sharp gaze of an observer on either side of him; and one of them was that selfsame giant who had been sipping kümmel at the nearby table: illuminated by the light of the streetlamp outside, he stood at the door like a bronze-headed colossus; a metallic face with a phosphorescent gleam fixed Ableukhov with a momentary stare as it entered the beam of light; and a green hand, many tons in weight, shook a finger at him.

"Who is that?"

"He who destroys us irrevocably … "

"A detective?"

"Never … "

The restaurant door slammed to.

Tall, many-eyed streetlamps, tormented by the wind, trembled with strange lights, expanding outwards into the long Petersburg night; black, black pedestrians drifted past out of the darkness; once again the bowler hat began to run along beside them on the wall.

"What if I refuse the commission?"

"I shall arrest you … "

"You? Arrest me?"

"Don't forget that I am a … "

"That you're a conspirator?"

"That I am an officer of the security department; as an officer of the security department I shall arrest you … "

The wind from the Neva whistled in the telegraph wires and sobbed in the archways; icy scraps of half-torn clouds could be seen; and it seemed that out of the most ragged cloud strips of bustling rain would tear off—to rattle, to hiss, to beat on the flagstones in flinty drops, spinning their icy bubbles on the foaming puddles.

"What will the party say?"

"The party will find me innocent: I shall be using my position in security to take revenge on you on the party's behalf … "

"And if I denounce you?"

"You just try … "

And out of the most ragged cloud strips of bustling rain tore off— to rattle, to hiss, to beat on the flagstones in flinty drops, spinning their icy bubbles on the foaming puddles.

"No, Nikolai Apollonovich, I beg you—joking aside: because I am very, very serious; and I have to say: your doubts, your indecision are killing me; you ought to have weighed up all the chances earlier … In the last resort, you could have refused (you had two months, thank God). You did not take the trouble to do that in time; there is only one path for you now; and the choice that lies before you is: arrest, suicide, or murder. You understand me now, I hope? ... Goodbye ... "

The bowler hat trotted off in the direction of the Seventeenth Line, the greatcoat—towards the bridge.

Petersburg, Petersburg!

Sediment of mist, you pursued me too with idle cerebral play; you are a cruel-hearted tormentor: but you are also a restless ghost: for years you used to attack me; I too ran along your terrible Prospects, till my momentum brought me flying to this glittering bridge ...

Great bridge, gleaming with electric light! Green waters, teeming with bacilli! I remember one fateful moment; I leaned over your grey parapet one September night; a moment more: and my body would have tumbled into the mists.

On the great cast-iron bridge Nikolai Apollonovich turned round; behind him he could see—nothing, nobody: there above the damp, damp parapet, above the greenish water teeming with bacilli, he was dolefully seized by nothing but the gusts of the cold Neva gale; here, at this very place, two-and-a-half months before, Nikolai Apollonovich had made his terrible promise; the same waxen face, with lips apart, protruded from the grey greatcoat above the damp parapet; he stood over the Neva, staring dully at the green—but no: gazing away to where the banks cowered down; and then he quickly strutted off, clumsily wrapped in the folds of his greatcoat.

A phosphorescent blur floated mistily and furiously across the sky; the expanse of the Neva was covered with a misty, phosphorescent glow; and this imparted a green gleam to the surfaces that were gliding soundlessly by, glinting here and there with a spark of gold. Now the huge buildings of the islands were rising up beyond the Neva, casting their fiery eyes into the mist. Higher still—indistinct outlines spread their ragged arms furiously; they rose up, swarm on swarm.

The Embankment was empty.

Occasionally the black shadow of a policeman passed by; the square was empty; on the right the several storeys of the Senate and the Synod rose up. A rock rose up too: Nikolai Apollonovich stared wide-eyed and with especial curiosity at the huge outline of the Horseman. As he and Pavel Iakovlevich had passed by here before, it had seemed to Ableukhov that the Horseman was not there (a shadow had been hiding it); now a fitful half-shadow hid the Horseman's face; and the metal of the face smiled ambiguously.

All at once the heavy clouds split open, and wisps of cloud wound in a green haze of molten bronze beneath the moon ... For a moment everything flared up: the waters, the roofs, the granite; the Horseman's face flared up, his bronze laurel wreath; a vast bulk of metal hung down from the shoulders of the bronze-headed colossus, that shone an unreflecting green; the moulded face, the wreath, green with time, and the arm, many tons in weight, stretching imperiously straight at Nikolai Apollonovich, all had a phosphorescent gleam; in the bronze eye-sockets bronze thoughts shone green; and it seemed: the hand would move (the heavy folds would ring against the elbow of the cape), the metallic hooves would fall with a loud crash on to the rock and across all Petersburg would sound a voice that shatters granite:

"Yes, yes, yes ... "

"It's me ... "

"I destroy irrevocably."

For a moment everything around was lit up for Nikolai Apollonovich; yes—now he understood what colossus it was that had sat there at the table in the drinking-den on Vasilevskii Island (had he too been visited by a vision?); as he walked towards that door it was this face that had risen up before him, lit by the streetlamp; and it was this green hand that had shaken its finger at him. For a moment everything became clear to Ableukhov: his fate was lit up: yes—he must; and yes—he was doomed.

But the clouds cut across the moon; fragments of witches' tresses flew across the sky.

With loud laughter Nikolai Apollonovich ran from the Bronze Horseman:

"Yes, yes, yes ... "

"I know, I know ... "

"I am destroyed irrevocably ... "

In the empty street a shaft of light flew by: it was a black carriage from the court carrying bright-red lanterns, like bloodshot eyes; the ghostly outline of a footman's tricorn hat and the outline of coat-flaps flew by with the lights from mist to mist.

Gryphons

The Prospects spread out—over there, over there: the Prospects spread out; a morose pedestrian did not quicken his step: the morose pedestrian gazed around in anguish: infinities of buildings! The morose pedestrian was Nikolai Apollonovich.

... There was something he had to do at once, without losing a minute—but what? Was it not he himself who had sown so thickly the seeds of theories about the madness of all compassion? Was it not he who had once before that taciturn gathering declared his views—always about the same thing: about the dull disgust he felt for the master, for the master's aged ears, for everything to do with overlords and Tatars, up to and including ... that bird-like protruding neck ... with the vein beneath the skin.

In the end he hailed a belated cab: four-storey buildings moved off and flew along past him.

The Admiralty thrust out the eight columns of its aspect: a glimpse of pink and it vanished; from the other side, across the river, between white stucco fringes the walls of an old building cast a bright carrot-coloured flash; a black-and-white sentry box was now behind and to the left; an old grenadier of the Pavlovskii regiment was striding to and fro in his grey greatcoat; his sharp, glinting bayonet hung from his shoulder.

Evenly, slowly, languidly the cab trotted past the grenadier; evenly, slowly, languidly Nikolai Apollonovich bounced past the grenadier as well. The bright morning, gleaming with sparks from the Neva, turned all its water into an abyss of burnished gold; the funnel of a hooting steamer hurtled into the abyss of burnished gold; he saw a gaunt figure on the pavement quicken its belated step, as it skipped across the stones—a gaunt figure, which ... which he recognised: it was Apollon Apollonovich. Nikolai Apollonovich wanted to hold the cab back, to give that figure time to put enough distance between ... but it was too late: the old, shaven head turned towards the cab, shook once and turned away. So as not to be recognised Nikolai Apollonovich turned his back to the belated pedestrian: buried his nose in his beaver collar; all that could be seen was a collar and a cap; the yellow mass of the house already rose up in the mist.

Apollon Apollonovich Ableukhov, who had seen the young girl to her home, was now hastening to the threshold of the yellow house; the Admiralty had just thrust at him the eight columns of its aspect; the black-and-white striped sentry-box was now behind and to his left; he was now walking along the Embankment, contemplating, out on the Neva, the abyss of burnished gold into which the funnel of the hooting steamer had just hurtled.

Then Apollon Apollonovich heard behind him the rumble of a cab; the old shaven head turned towards the cab; and when the cab came level with the senator, the senator saw: there, over the seat—an old-fashioned and misshapen young man was slumped, wrapped most unpleasantly in a greatcoat; and when this young man looked at the senator, keeping his nose tucked into his coat (only his eyes and his cap could be seen), the senator's old head shot back so rapidly towards the wall that his top hat struck against the stone fruit on a black protuberance of the house (Apollon Apollonovich adjusted his hat methodically), and Apollon Apollonovich stared for a moment into the water's depths, into the chasm of emerald and red.

It seemed to him then that the eyes of that unpleasant young man, as soon as they saw him, had instantly started to expand, expand, expand: they had instantly expanded unpleasantly and stopped still in a gaze full of horror. Apollon Apollonovich stopped still in horror in front of that horror: this gaze had been pursuing Apollon Apollonovich more and more often; it was the gaze of his subordinates as they looked at him, it was the gaze of the hybrid race as it passed by: and of the student, and of the shaggy Manchurian hat; yes, yes, yes: they had looked at him with that same gaze and had expanded with that same gleam; the cab that had overtaken him was now irritatingly marking time on the cobblestones; and the number on its badge could be glimpsed: nineteen hundred and five; and in utter terror Apollon Apollonovich gazed into the crimson, many-chimneyed distance; and Vasilevskii Island gazed tormentingly, insultingly, impertinently at the senator.

Nikolai Apollonovich jumped out of the cab, tangled clumsily in the flaps of his coat, old-fashioned and angry through and through, ran as fast as he could to the entrance of the yellow house, waddling like a duck from side to side and flapping the folds of his coat in the air against the background of the crimson dawn; Ableukhov stopped at the entrance: Ableukhov rang the bell; and as had happened multitudes of times before (just the same now) from somewhere in the distance the night-watchman Nikolaich's voice was projected towards him:

"Good health to you, Nikolai Apollonovich! ... Much obliged to you, sir ... It's very late ... " And as had happened multitudes of times before, so just the same now, a fifteen-copeck coin dropped into Nikolaich, the night-watchman's hand.

Nikolai Apollonovich tugged hard at the bell pull: let Semyonych come quickly to open the door, or else—that gaunt figure would appear out of the mist (why wasn't it in its carriage?); and on either side of the house's ponderous portico he saw the gaping jaws of a gryphon, pink from the dawn, holding in its claws the ring for a flagpole, for a red-white-and-blue flag, which would flutter with its tricolour banner over the Neva on specific days of the year; above the gryphons the Ableukhov coat of arms was hewn into the stone; this coat of arms depicted a knight with long plumes and rococo curls, impaled by a unicorn, a crazy thought passed through Nikolai Apollonovich Ableukhov's mind, like a fish that momentarily flits across the surface of the water: Apollon Apollonovich, who lived beyond the threshold of that embossed door, was himself the impaled knight; and after that thought another flitted by, quite nebulously, without rising to the surface (as the dark shape of a fish is glimpsed from afar): the ancient family crest was addressed to all the Ableukhovs; he too, Nikolai Apollonovich, was also one impaled—impaled by whom?

All this chaos of thoughts rushed through his mind in a tenth of a second: and over there already, over there, on the pavement—in the mist—he saw that gaunt figure hurrying towards the house: the gaunt figure was running towards the house at speed—that gaunt figure in which ... which from a distance had appeared to him like a retarded runt: with his yellow, yellow face, emaciated, haemorrhoidal, Apollon Apollonovich Ableukhov, his progenitor, looked like death in a top hat; Nikolai Apollonovich—such stray thoughts occur—imagined the figure of Apollon Apollonovich at the moment of fulfilling his conjugal obligations to his mother, Anna Petrovna: and Nikolai Apollonovich felt with renewed force a familiar nausea (it was at one such moment that he had been conceived).

He was overwhelmed with disgust: no, let what would be, be!

The figure, meanwhile, was approaching. Nikolai Apollonovich saw to his shame that his tide of fury, artificially enhanced, was ebbing and ebbing: a familiar embarrassment took hold of him, and ...

An unpleasant spectacle presented itself to Apollon Apollonovich's sight: Nikolai Apollonovich, old-fashioned and angry through and through, with a yellow, yellow face, with eyelids inflamed bright red, with lips apart—Nikolai Apollonovich tripped hastily down the steps of the porch and, waddling like a duck from side to side, ran guiltily to meet his parent, blinking and avoiding his father's eyes and with his scented hand extended from the fur of his coat:

"Good morning, Papa ... "

Silence.

"What an unexpected meeting, I've just come from the Tsukatovs ... "

Apollon Apollonovich Ableukhov had the thought that this apparently reticent young man was just a scoundrel; but Apollon Apollonovich Ableukhov was embarrassed by this thought, especially in his son's presence; and, in embarrassment Apollon Apollonovich Ableukhov muttered reticently:

"I see, I see: good morning, Kolenka ... Well now, fancy that—so we meet ... Ah? Yes, yes, yes ... "

And as had happened multitudes of times before, so just the same today, the voice of the night-watchman rang out in the mist:

"Good health to you, your Excellency!"

On the portico, on either side of the door, the gaping gryphons showed their beak-like jaws; the stone knight with his long plumes and rococo curls, his breast split open, was being impaled by the unicorn; the more blindingly and ethereally the rosy-fingered harbingers of day dispersed across the sky, the more distinctly the protrusions of the buildings took on weight; the more scarlet, the more purple were the jaws of the gaping gryphon.

The doors were thrown open; the smell of the familiar rooms embraced the Ableukhovs; into the opening of the door the thick-veined fingers of the valet were inserted: the grey Semyonych himself, half-asleep, his jacket donned in haste, with his seventy-year-old hand grasping his collar, narrowed his eyes as he admitted the masters from the unbearable brilliance of the Neva.

The Ableukhovs slipped sideways through the opening of the door.

As red as any flame

Both knew they had a conversation in store; this conversation had been maturing during many years of silence; handing to the servant his top hat, his overcoat and gloves, Apollon Apollonovich had a spot of trouble with his galoshes; poor, poor senator: how was he to know that Nikolai Apollonovich had received such a commission with regard to him? And in just the same way Nikolai Apollonovich could not have guessed that his parent was entirely aware of the whole story of the red domino. At that moment they both breathed the smell of the familiar apartment; the luxurious beaver, with a glint of silver, fell softly into the servant's veiny hand; the overcoat slipped off as though in a dream—and Nikolai Apollonovich finally stood before his parent's gaze in his domino. At the sight of this domino a line of verse, learnt long ago, went through Apollon Apollonovich's mind:

Colours of a fiery might
I'll cast upon my palm,
That he may stand in pools of light
As red as any flame.

With a hand no less veiny than Semyonych's (only better washed) he stroked his side-whiskers:

"Aha ... A red domino? ... Well I never! ... "

"I was in fancy dress ... "

"I see ... Kolenka ... I see ... "

Apollon Apollonovich stood in front of Kolenka with a kind of bitter irony, either muttering something or simply sucking his lips; the skin on his forehead was gathered together somehow shoddily, ironically—into wrinkles; it was somehow shoddily stretched taut on his scalp. An imminent explanation was in the air: it could be sensed that the fruit growing on the tree of their lives had ripened; and was about to fall: it fell and ... all at once:

> Apollon Apollonovich dropped a pencil (by the steps of the velvet stairs); Nikolai Apollonovich, obedient to time-honoured habit, rushed to pick it up; Apollon Apollonovich, in his turn, rushed to forestall his son's civility, but tripped, falling on all fours with his hands on the stairs; his bald head swept swiftly

down and forwards; to find itself unexpectedly beneath the fingers of his son's outstretched hand: Nikolai Apollonovich in an instant saw before him his father's yellow, veiny neck, resembling a crayfish tail (a vein pulsating at the side); Nikolai Apollonovich did not measure his clumsy movements, as he accidentally touched that neck; its warm pulsation frightened him, and he snatched his hand away, but—he snatched it away too late: at the touch of his cold hand (always sweating slightly) Apollon Apollonovich turned round and saw—that *selfsame* glance; the senator's head twitched in a momentary tic, his skin gathered shoddily together into wrinkles on his scalp and his ears twitched slightly. In his domino Nikolai Apollonovich seemed all on fire; and the senator, like a nimble Japanese schooled in the art of Ju-Jitsu, jerked to the side, straightening himself on his creaking knees—upwards, upwards, and to the side ...

All of this lasted the merest moment. Nikolai Apollonovich picked up the pencil without a word and handed it to the senator.

"Here you are, Papa!"

This trivial incident, bringing them into collision with one another, gave rise in both of them to an explosion of the most disparate wishes, thoughts and feelings; Apollon Apollonovich was thoroughly embarrassed by the disgraceful nature of what had happened: his fear in response to the deference in his son's meaningless courtesy (this man, red all over, was after all his son: flesh of his flesh: and it was shameful to be afraid of his own flesh, what had aroused his fear?); nevertheless this disgraceful event had taken place: he had squatted under his son and physically felt upon himself that *selfsame* gaze. Along with his embarrassment Apollon Apollonovich also felt annoyance: he resumed a dignified posture, bowed whimsically from the waist, and proudly compressed his lips into a ring as he took the proffered pencil in his hand.

"Thank you, Kolenka ... I'm very grateful to you ... Sleep well ... "

The father's gratitude immediately embarrassed the son; Nikolai Apollonovich felt a rush of blood to his cheeks; and when it occurred to him that he was turning pink, he was already crimson. Apollon Apollonovich stole a glance at his son; and, seeing that his son was turning crimson, he began to turn pink himself; in order to conceal this colouring he dashed with whimsical grace swiftly up the stairs, dashed off to his bedroom to sleep enveloped in the finest linen.

Nikolai Apollonovich was left alone on the steps of the velvet staircase, immersed in a deep and insistent thought: but his train of thought was interrupted by the servant's voice.

"Oh, my goodness! ... What a scatterbrain! ... It completely slipped my mind ... My dear master: why, you'll never guess what's happened! ... "

"What has happened?"

"Something that ... I hardly dare to say it ... "

On a step of the grey staircase, carpeted in velvet (trodden by the feet of ministers), Nikolai Apollonovich paused; on the very spot where his father had stumbled a pattern of purple stains fell through the window at his feet; this pattern of purple stains for some reason reminded him of blood (on the ancient weapons blood shone crimson too). A familiar, abhorrent nausea arose, though not on the previous (terrifying) scale, from his stomach: was it indigestion he was suffering from?

"What a thing to happen! It's like this: the mistress ... "

"Our mistress, Anna Petrovna, sir ... "

"She's come back!!"

From the nausea Nikolai Apollonovich at that moment started yawning: and the huge orifice of his mouth opened wide towards the dawn: he stood there, red as a torch.

The aged lips of the servant stretched out to the shock of fair, fine, luxuriant hair:

"She's come back, sir!"

"Who's come back?"

"Anna Petrovna, sir ... "

"Who's that?! ... "

"How d'you mean, who? ... Your mother ... What's the matter with you, my dear master, you might be a complete stranger: your mama ... "

"?"

"She's returned from Spain to Petersburg ... "

"She sent a note with a messenger: she's staying at a hotel … Because—you know, sir … Her position's a bit … "

"?"

"Just as soon as His Excellency, Apollon Apollonovich, had left, this messenger turned up: with a letter, sir … Well, I put the letter on the table, and gave the messenger twenty copecks … "

"And can you believe it, not another hour had passed, when—goodness gracious: she turned up herself! … She obviously knew for sure that there wasn't anybody at home … "

A pike glinted in front of him: a patch of slanting light shone such a strange crimson; the patch of slanting light shone a tormenting crimson: a pillar of crimson stretched from wall to window; in that pillar specks of dust danced, seeming scarlet. Nikolai Apollonovich thought that blood was dancing inside him just like that; Nikolai Apollonovich thought that man himself was nothing but a pillar of steaming blood.

"She rings the bell … And I go to open the door … And I see: an unknown lady, a respectable lady; only dressed quite simply; and all in black … And I says to her: 'What can I do for you ma'am?' And she says to me: 'Mitry Semyonych, don't you recognise me?'—And I kissed her hand: 'Why, Anna Petrovna, ma'am, dear mistress' … "

All it needs is for any old villain simply to stick a blade into a man, and the white, hairless skin splits open (just like carving a sucking-pig in aspic with horseradish), and the blood that thumps in your temples will flood out in a stinking puddle …

"And then Anna Petrovna—God give her good health—has a look: she looks at me, like … She has a good look at me and then bursts into tears: 'I wanted to see how you're getting on without me … ' She gets a little handkerchief out of her *réticule*, not the sort you see here, sir …

"As I'm sure you know, sir, I've been strictly ordered not to let her in ... Only I did let the mistress in ... And she ... "

The old man stared wide-eyed; he stood there with his mouth agape and thought, no doubt, that in this lacquered house the masters had long since lost their wits: instead of any surprise, sympathy or joy—Nikolai Apollonovich shot up the stairs, his bright-red satin billowing eccentrically in the air behind him like the tail of a lawless comet.

It was him, Nikolai Apollonovich ... Or was it not him? No, it was him—it was: he must have said to them then that he hated the repulsive old man; that the repulsive old man, the bearer of bejewelled insignia, was quite simply a thorough villain ... Or had he said all that to himself?

No—to them, to them! ...

Nikolai Apollonovich had shot off up the stairs, interrupting Semyonych, because he had vividly imagined: a hideous act by one scoundrel upon another; he suddenly imagined a scoundrel; a gleaming pair of scissors rasped in this scoundrel's fingers, when he rushed clumsily to sever the scrawny old man's carotid artery; the scrawny old man's forehead gathered in wrinkles; the scrawny old man had a warm, throbbing neck ... a bit like a crayfish; the scoundrel slashed with the scissors across the scrawny old man's artery, and sticky, stinking blood oozed over his fingers and the scissors, while the little old man—beardless, wrinkled, bald—wept unrestrainedly and stared straight into his eyes, Nikolai Apollonovich's, with an expression of supplication, sinking on to his haunches and trying to stop up with his finger the gash in his neck, from which with a just audible whistle red streams kept on—trickling, trickling, trickling ...

This image arose so vividly before him, as though it were something that had just happened (when the old man fell on to all fours, he could, after all, have seized the pike from the wall and lunged ...). This image arose so vividly before him that he was afraid.

That is why Nikolai Apollonovich took to flight through the rooms, past the lacquer and gleam, clattering with his heels and risking summoning the senator from his distant bedchamber.

A bad sign

If I were to put to their Highnesses, their Excellencies, to the ladies and gentlemen, and to the citizens the question: what kind of apartment is occupied by our imperial dignitaries, then the holders of these various titles would most probably reply directly in an affirmative sense, that the apartment of a dignitary is, in the first place, a space, by which we all understand an aggregate of rooms; these rooms consist of: a single room which may be called a hall or a ballroom, which—kindly take note—makes no difference; they consist further of a room for the reception of miscellaneous guests; and so on, and so on (the rest is trivialities).

Apollon Apollonovich Ableukhov was an actual privy councillor; Apollon Apollonovich was a person of the first class (which again is the same thing), and lastly: Apollon Appollonovich was a dignitary of the Empire; we have seen all that from the very first pages of our book. Therefore: as a dignitary, even as an official of the Empire, he could not do otherwise than reside in spaces possessing three dimensions; and he did reside in spaces: in cubic spaces, consisting, please note: of a ballroom (or hall) and so on, and so on, and so on, as we have had the opportunity cursorily to observe (the rest is trivialities); among these trivialities was his study, and other—just ordinary—rooms.

These just ordinary rooms were already lit by the sun; and the inlay of the tables was already glinting in the air, and the mirrors were gleaming merrily: and all the mirrors burst out laughing, because the first mirror, which looked into the hall from the drawing room, reflected the white countenance of Petrushka, as though covered in flour, while the fairground Petrushka himself, bright red as blood, came running from the hall (his footfalls pattered); at once the mirror threw the reflection across to another mirror; and the fairground Petrushka was reflected in all the mirrors: it was Nikolai Apollonovich, who had come rushing into the drawing room and stopped as though rooted to the spot, his eyes wandering in the cold mirrors, because of what he had seen: the first mirror, which looked into the hall from the drawing room, had shown Nikolai Apollonovich the reflection of a certain article: a deathly skeleton in a buttoned-up frock coat, possessed of a skull, to right and left of which protruded a naked ear and a small side-whisker; but between the side-whiskers and the ears there emerged, larger than was right, a pointed nose; and over the pointed nose two dark eye-sockets were raised reproachfully …

Nikolai Apollonovich realised that Apollon Apollonovich was waiting here for his son.

Instead of his son all that Apollon Apollonovich saw in the mirrors was a red fairground marionette; and catching sight of the fairground marionette, Apollon Apollonovich froze; the fairground marionette stopped in the middle of the hall in such strange perplexity …

Then Apollon Apollonovich to his own surprise shut the door into the hall; retreat was cut off. What he had begun, he needed as quickly as possible to finish. Apollon Apollonovich viewed a conversation about his son's strange behaviour as a burdensome act of surgery. Like a surgeon approaching the operation table, on which were laid out scalpels, saws and drills—Apollon Apollonovich, wiping his yellow fingers, went right up to Nicolas, stopped, and, seeking his evasive eyes, unintentionally took out his glasses case, twisted it about in his fingers, put it away again, cleared his throat in a restrained manner, and after a moment's silence, said:

"So that's how it is: a domino."

At the same time he thought that this to all appearances reticent young man, grinning from ear to ear and looking at him with that *selfsame* gaze, but not straight in the eye—this reticent young man and the brazen Petersburg domino that the Jewish press had been writing about were one and the same person; that he, Apollon Apollonovich, a person of the first class and a nobleman of ancient lineage—he had begotten him; at this same time Nikolai Apollonovich observed in some embarrassment:

"Yes, well … a lot of people were in masks … So I got myself a … costume, too … "

At the same time Nikolai Apollonovich was thinking that this slight, five-foot body of his father's, which couldn't be more than a couple of feet in circumference, was the centre and the periphery of a certain immortal centre: that was where, when all was said and done, the 'self' was located; and any plank of wood, if it toppled down at the wrong time, could crush that centre: crush it once and for all; perhaps it was under the influence of this intuited thought that Apollon Apollonovich ran so quickly to that distant table and drummed upon it with two fingers, while Nikolai Apollonovich, advancing, laughed guiltily:

"It was fun, you know … We danced, you know … "

But what was in his mind was: skin, bones and blood, without a single muscle; yes, but this cordon of skin, bones and blood was destined by the ordinance of fate to be blown to pieces; if that was avoided today, it would come rushing back tomorrow evening, and by tomorrow night it would …

Then Apollon Apollonovich, catching in the glistening mirror that *selfsame* glance from under lowered brows, turned on his heel and caught the tail-end of the sentence.

"And then, you know, we played *petits jeux*."

Apollon Apollonovich, staring straight at his son, made no reply; and that *selfsame* gaze from under lowered eyebrows fixed on the parquet blocks of the floor … Apollon Apollonovich recalled: why, this extraneous 'Petrushka' used to be a little body; he used to carry that little body in his arms with paternal tenderness; the fair-haired little boy would put a paper cap on and clamber on to his shoulders. Apollon Apollonovich would sing hoarsely, out of tune and out of time:

> *Silly laddie, simple chap,*
> *Little Nicky's dancing:*
> *On his head a dunce's cap,*
> *On a horse he's prancing.*

Afterwards he used to carry the child up to this very mirror; in the mirror the old man and the little one were reflected; he would point out the reflections to the boy, and say:

"Look, my boy, at those funny people … "

Sometimes Kolenka would cry and then shout out in the night. But now, now? Apollon Apollonovich saw not a little body, but a big one, an alien one … Was it alien, though?

Apollon Apollonovich began to circulate around the drawing room, forwards and back:

"You see, Kolenka … "

Apollon Apollonovich lowered himself into a deep armchair.

"I need, Kolenka, to … That is, it's not me, but—I hope—*we* need … need to talk things through: do you have sufficient time available just now? The question, and it's a disturbing one, is a matter of … " Apollon Apollonovich stumbled in the midst of his speech, and ran up to the mirror again (at that moment the clock chimed), and from the mirror death in a frock coat glanced at Nikolai Apollonovich, a reproachful gaze focused on him, fingers drummed; and with a shout of laughter the mirror cracked: like lightning a crooked needle flashed across it with a slight crackle; and came to rest there forever in a silver zigzag.

Apollon Apollonovich Ableukhov cast his gaze at the mirror, and the mirror split; superstitious people would have said:

"A bad sign, a bad sign … "

Done, it was finished: the conversation was upon them.

Nikolai Apollonovich was clearly trying with all the means at his disposal to delay the explanation for as long as possible; after tonight the explanation would be superfluous: everything would be explained without it. Nikolai Apollonovich regretted that he had not made his escape from the drawing room in good time (so many hours these death-throes had been dragging on: and under his heart something was swelling, swelling, and swelling); in his horror he was experiencing a strange voluptuousness: he could not tear himself away from his father.

"Yes, Papa: I must confess, I was expecting we'd discuss things."

"Ah … you were expecting it?"

"Yes, I was expecting it."

"Are you free?"

"Yes, I'm free."

He could not tear himself away from his father: in front of him … But here I have to make a brief digression.

O, worthy reader: we have revealed the outward appearance of the bearer of bejewelled insignia in exaggerated, overly harsh lines, but without any humour; we have revealed the outward appearance of the bearer of bejewelled insignia merely as it would appear to any extraneous observer—and not at all as it would undoubtedly be revealed to itself, and to us: we, after all, have looked at it very closely; we have delved into its inordinately perturbed soul and its furious maelstroms of consciousness; it would not come amiss to remind the reader of that outward appearance in the most general terms, because we know: as are the visible lineaments, so too is the essence. Here it is sufficient merely to observe that if that essence were to stand before us, if in front of us all these maelstroms of consciousness were to rush by, blowing apart the frontal bones, and if we were able coldly to dissect those blue sinewy swellings, then … But—silence. In short, in short: the extraneous gaze would see here, at this very place, the skeleton of an old gorilla in a tight frock coat …

"Yes, I'm free … "

"In that case, Kolenka, you go to your room: gather your thoughts together first. If you find something in yourself that it would be appropriate for us to discuss, come to my study."

"Very well, Papa … "

"And, by the way: take off that fairground frippery … Speaking frankly, I dislike it in the extreme … "

"?"

"Yes, in the extreme! I dislike it to the utmost degree!!"

Apollon Apollonovich dropped his hand; two yellow knuckles drummed distinctly on the cardtable.

"Actually," Nikolai Apollonovich became confused, "actually, I ought to … "

But the door slammed: Apollon Apollonovich circulated through into his study.

By the table

Nikolai Apollonovich just stayed standing by the table: his gaze flitted across the leaves of the bronze inlay, across the little boxes and the shelves that protruded from the walls. Yes, this was where he had played; he used to sit here for long periods—here on this armchair, where little garlands curled around on the pale-azure satin of the seat; and the copy of David's *The Distribution of the Eagle Standards* hung there just as before. The picture depicted the great emperor in a laurel wreath and porphyry, stretching out his hand to a gathering of marshals.

What would he say to his father? Would he once more torment himself by lying? Lying, when lying was already useless? Lying, when the situation he was now in precluded any lying? Lying … Nikolai

Apollonovich remembered the lies he used to tell in the distant years of his childhood.

Here was the piano, a yellow, fashionable one: it touched the parquet with the casters on its slender legs. How his mother used to sit down at it, Anna Petrovna, how the old sounds of Beethoven would set the walls trembling here: age-old antiquity, explosive and plaintive, would rise up in the child's heart with the same hankering as the paling moon that rises all red and bears aloft above the city its pastel-yellow melancholy …

Wasn't it time to go and explain—explain what?

At that moment the sun glanced in at the window, the bright sun cast from above its incisive beams: a golden Titan from antiquity with a thousand arms furiously veiled the void, illuminating the spires, the roofs, the torrents and the stones, as well as the godlike, sclerotic forehead pressed to the windowpane; the golden Titan with a thousand arms mutely mourned his solitude: "Come to me, come—to the ancient sun!"

But the sun seemed to Nikolai Apollonovich to be a huge tarantula with a thousand paws attacking the earth with demented passion …

And Nikolai Apollonovich unwittingly screwed up his eyes, because everything had burst into flame: the lampshade burst into flame; the glass of the lamp was spattered with amethysts; sparks glistened on the wing of a golden cupid (the cupid beneath the mirror's surface thrust its heavy flame into the golden roses of a wreath); the mirror's surface burst into flame—yes: the mirror had split.

Superstitious people would have said:

"A bad sign, a bad sign … "

Meanwhile, amidst everything golden and bright, behind Ableukhov's back a vague outline appeared; against the general silence, like a gleam of sunshine, a distinct muttering drifted by.

"What are… we … "

Nikolai Apollonovich raised his countenance …

"What about … the mistress?"

And he caught sight of Semyonych.

He had quite forgotten about his mother's return; yet she, his mother, had returned; and with her the old days had returned— with all the ceremony, the scenes, childhood with twelve governesses, every one of whom was an embodied nightmare.

"Well ... I don't know, really ... "

Semyonych sucked his lips anxiously in front of him.

"I'll tell the master, shall I?"

"Doesn't Papa know yet?"

"I didn't make so bold ... "

"Then go, tell him ... "

"I'll go then ... I'll tell him ... "

And Semyonych went into the corridor.

The old days were returning: no, the old days will not return; if the old days come back, they look different. And the old days looked at him—with horror!

Everything, everything, everything: all this glitter of sunlight, the walls, the body, the soul—everything was going to collapse; it was already collapsing, collapsing; and what would be was—bedlam, abyss, bomb.

Bomb—a swift expansion of gases ... The roundness of the gases' expansion aroused in him a forgotten absurdity, and against his will a sigh burst into the air from his lungs.

In childhood Kolenka had been liable to delirium; at night an elastic ball had sometimes started jumping up and down in front of him, made of rubber, perhaps, or else of the material of very strange worlds; this elastic ball, as it bounced on the floor, made a soft, lacquered sound: *pépp-peppép*; and again: *pépp-peppép*. Suddenly the ball would expand horribly, and take on all the appearance of a fat, rotund gentleman; this fat gentleman, turning into a tormenting sphere—expanded, and expanded, and expanded, threatening finally to overwhelm him and to burst.

And while it was swelling, turning into a tormenting sphere, about to burst, it jumped around and turned crimson, making a soft, lacquered sound as it bounced on the floor:

"*Pepp* ... "

"*Péppovich* ... "

"*Pepp* ... "

And it burst into pieces.

And Nikolenka, quite delirious, began to shout out vain, nonsensical things—all about the same thing: that he too was becoming spherical, that he too was a big round zero; everything in him was zeroing— zero-oing—zero-o-oing ...

But his governess, Karolina Karlovna, in her white nightgown, with diabolical curling-papers in her hair that took on the hue of the horror he had just experienced—Karolina Karlovna, the Baltic German, who had jumped up from her downy bed at the sound of his cry—looked at him angrily from the yellow circle of her candle, while the circle—expanded, and expanded, and expanded. Karolina Karlovna just repeated a multitude of times:

"Calm down, little Kolenka: it's just—growing pains … "

She didn't look, she shrank away; and it wasn't growing pains, he was expanding: expanding, swelling, bursting:—

Pepp Péppovich Pepp …

"What's this, am I delirious?"

Nikolai Apollonovich pressed his cold fingers to his brow: what would be was—bedlam, abyss, bomb.

And out of the window, far, far away beyond the window, where the river banks cowered down, where the cold buildings of the islands settled submissively, the spire of the Peter and Paul Cathedral, gleaming speechlessly, sharply, tormentingly, mercilessly prodded the lofty sky.

Semyonych's steps passed along the corridor. No delaying now: his father, Apollon Apollonovich, was waiting for him.

Packets of pencils

The senator's study was plain in the extreme; in the middle, of course, the desk towered up; and that is not the main thing; incomparably more important here is the following: bookcases stood along the walls; on the right were bookcases numbers one, three and five; on the left, numbers two, four and six; their densely filled shelves sagged under systematically arranged books; in the middle of the desk lay a textbook on *Planimetry*.

Before going to bed Apollon Apollonovich usually opened this book, in order to calm the sleep-resistant life in his head by contemplating the most beatific figures: parallelepipeds, parallelograms, cones, cubes and pyramids.

Apollon Apollonovich settled into the black armchair; the back of the chair, upholstered in leather, would have tempted anyone to lean back, and would have tempted anyone to lean back all the more on a wearisome, sleepless morning. Apollon Apollonovich was punctilious towards himself; even on a wearisome morning he sat bolt upright at his desk, waiting for his worthless son to come to him. While awaiting his son he opened a drawer; there, under the letter '*p*' he retrieved a diary entitled *Observations*; and into it, into the *Observations*, he began to write down his thoughts, the fruit of his experience. The pen started to scratch: *A statesman is marked by his humaneness ... A statesman ...*

An observation always began with a maxim; but at the point of the maxim he was interrupted; a frightened gasp reverberated behind his back; Apollon Apollonovich permitted himself to press hard (his pen snapped), and on turning round he espied Semyonych.

"Master, your Excellency, sir ... May I make so bold as to inform you (I forgot to tell you just now) ... "

"What's all this!"

"It's just that, ee-ee ... I really don't know how to say it ... "

"Ah! I see, I see ... "

Apollon Apollonovich's whole body stood out as though engraved, displaying to outward observation the most perfect combination of lines: grey, white and black; he looked like an etching.

"You see, sir: our mistress, sir—if I may be so bold as to inform you—Anna Petrovna, sir ... "

Apollon Apollonovich suddenly turned his immense ear angrily towards the butler ...

"What is all this—eh? ... Speak louder: I can't hear you."

The trembling Semyonych bent right down to the pale-green ear that was gazing at him with such anticipation:

"The mistress ... Anna Petrovna, sir ... She's come back ... "

"? ... "

"From Spain—to Petersburg ... "

"I see, I see: very well! ... "

"She sent a note with a messenger ... "

"She's staying at a hotel ... "

"Just after your Excellency was pleased to depart, sir, the messenger, sir, with the letter ... "

"Well, I put the letter on the table, and gave the messenger twenty copecks … "

"And not an hour had passed, when all of a sudden I heard someone ring the bell, like … "

Apollon Apollonovich, one hand upon the other, sat utterly impassive, immobile; it appeared he sat there unthinking: his gaze fell indifferently upon the spines of books; from the spine of one book there glinted in gold the impressive inscription: *Code of the Laws of Russia. Volume One.* Then: *Volume Two.* On the desk lay piles of papers, an inkwell glowed gold, pens and pencils were in evidence; on the desk stood a heavy paperweight in the form of a plump stand on which a silver peasant (a loyal subject) was raising an old-fashioned winebowl to the health of his betters. Apollon Apollonovich sat in front of the pens, the pencils, the piles of papers, his arms folded, motionless, without a quiver …

"So I opens the door, your Excellency, sir: a lady, sir, a stranger, but a respectable lady …

"And I says to her: 'What can I do for you?' … And the mistress says right out: 'Mitrii Semyonych … '

"So I kissed her hand; Anna Petrovna, I says, my dear mistress …

"She looks at me, like, and bursts into tears …

"And she says: 'I wanted to see how you're getting on without me … '"

Apollon Apollonovich made no reply, but opened another drawer and took out a dozen pencils (extremely cheap ones), picked up a couple of them in his fingers—and the stem of a pencil cracked in the senator's fingers. Apollon Apollonovich used sometimes to express his inner torment in this way: he broke packets of pencils, which were scrupulously kept for this eventuality in a drawer under the letter '*b*'.

"Very well … You may go … "

But, even as he snapped the packets of pencils, he still maintained with dignity his appearance of impassivity; and no one, no one at all, could have said that shortly before this moment this punctilious gentleman had been seeing a cook's daughter home through the slush, gasping for breath and almost in tears; no one, no one at all, could have said that this immense frontal protrusion had so recently harboured the wish to sweep away the unsubmissive crowds by girding the earth, as though with chains, in an iron Prospect.

But when Semyonych had left, Apollon Apollonovich threw the remnants of the pencils into the wastepaper basket and leant his head right back against the back of the black chair: his aged face became younger; quickly he began to straighten the tie at his neck; quickly he jumped up and started moving round hastily, circulating from one corner to the other: short in stature and quite nimble in a way, Apollon Apollonovich might have reminded anyone of his son: most of all he resembled a photograph of his son taken in 1904.

At that moment from a distant room, from the ordinary rooms, the sounds of one impact after another rang out; starting somewhere far off, the sounds came nearer; it was as though someone terrible, metallic, was walking there; and a blow rang out that could smash everything to pieces. Apollon Apollonovich stopped involuntarily and was about to rush to the door and lock the study, but … he became pensive, stayed where he was, because the blow that could smash everything turned out to be the sound of a slamming door (the noise came from the drawing room); someone was walking in unutterable anguish towards the door, coughing loudly and shuffling his slippers in an unnatural way: terrible antiquity, like a howl that comes upon us from the depths, suddenly took on strength in his memory in the sounds of long-forgotten singing, to the strains of which Apollon Apollonovich had once upon a time first fallen in love with Anna Petrovna:

"*Be soothed now, you feelings of passion* … "
"*And sleep now, you heart without hope* … "

Why, then, what was this?

The door opened: on the threshold stood Nikolai Apollonovich, in his uniform and even with his sword (that was how he had been dressed at the ball, only he had removed the domino), but in slippers and a multicoloured Tatar skullcap.

"Here I am, Papa ... "

The bald head turned towards his son; seeking the right words, he snapped his fingers:

"You see, Kolenka," instead of talking about the domino (what did the domino matter now?) Apollon Apollonovich began to talk about another circumstance: about the circumstance that had just caused him to take recourse to a tied packet of pencils.

"You see, Kolenka: I have not yet shared with you, old chap, a piece of news which you have no doubt already heard ... Your mother, Anna Petrovna, has come back ... "

Nikolai Apollonovich sighed with relief and thought: "So that's what it was," but pretended to be excited:

"Of course, of course: I do know ... "

And indeed: for the first time Nikolai Apollonovich pictured to himself precisely that his mother, Anna Petrovna, had come back; but having done that, he resumed his previous occupation: the contemplation of the crushed chest, neck, fingers, ears, chin of the old man who was now bustling about in front of him ... These hands, this neck (something of the crayfish!). The frightened, bewildered look and the purely girlish diffidence with which the old man ...

"Anna Petrovna, my dear boy, committed an act which ... which ... I find it difficult, as it were ... difficult, Kolenka, to qualify with sufficient composure ... "

Something rustled in the corner: trembling, trying to hide, squeaking—a mouse.

"In short, this act is, I hope, familiar to you; as you will have noticed—I have hitherto refrained from discussing this act in your presence, out of consideration for your natural feelings ... "

Natural feelings! Those feelings were at all events unnatural ...

"For your natural feelings ... "

"Yes, thank you, Papa: I do understand you ... "

"Of course," Apollon Apollonovich stuck two fingers into his waistcoat pocket and once again started bustling up and down along the diagonal (from one corner to the other). "Of course: your mother's return to Petersburg is a surprise to you."

(Apollon Apollonovich, rising on to tiptoes, fixed his gaze upon his son.)

"A complete ... "

"Surprise to all of us … "

"Who could have imagined that Mama would come back … "

"That's just what I say: who could have imagined," Apollon Apollonovich spread his arms in perplexity, raised his shoulders, made a bow to the floor, "that Anna Petrovna would come back … " And he set off again: "This complete surprise may result, as you have good grounds for supposing, in a change (Apollon Apollonovich raised a finger portentously, thundering across the whole room in his bass voice, as though he were delivering an important speech before a crowd of people) in our domestic status quo, or (he turned round) everything may remain as it has been."

"Yes, I suppose so … "

"In the first case—she is welcome."

Apollon Apollonovich made a bow to the door.

"In the second case," Apollon Apollonovich blinked in confusion, "you will see her, of course, but I … I … I … "

And Apollon Apollonovich raised his eyes to his son; his eyes were sad: the eyes of a trembling, hunted deer.

"I really don't know, Kolenka: but I think … However, it is so hard to explain this to you, taking into account the naturalness of the feeling that … "

Nikolai Apollonovich began to tremble from the gaze with which the senator turned towards him, and a strange thing happened: he felt an unexpected surge of—can you imagine what? Love? Yes, love for this aged despot who was destined to be blown to pieces.

Under the influence of this feeling he made an impulsive move towards his father: another moment, and he would have fallen to his knees before him, to confess and beg for mercy; but at the sight of his son's movement towards him the old man once again compressed his lips, ran away to one side and began to wave his arms in disdain:

"No, no, no! Please leave me alone … Yes, I know what you all want! … You have heard what I said, now take the trouble to leave me in peace."

Two fingers tapped imperiously on the desk; the hand was raised and pointed to the door:

"You, my good sir, are making a fool of me; you, my good sir, are no son of mine; you are the most frightful villain!"

Apollon Apollonovich did not say all this, he shouted it out; the words burst from him unexpectedly. Nikolai Apollonovich did not remember how he sprang out into the corridor with the same feeling of nausea and flow of grisly thoughts: those fingers, that neck and those two protruding ears would become—a slurry of blood.

Pepp Peppovich Pepp

Nikolai Apollonovich all but banged his forehead against the door of his room; then the electric switch clicked (why did it do so—the sun, the sun was staring in at the windows); knocking a chair over on the way, he ran up to his desk:

"Oh, oh, oh … Wherever is the key?"

"?"

"!"

"A! … "

"So here it is … "

"Fine … "

Just like Apollon Apollonovich, Nikolai Apollonovich talked to himself.

And—yes: he was in a hurry … He pulled at a reluctant drawer, but the drawer would not comply; out of the drawer he threw on to the desk tied bundles of letters; there was a large studio portrait under the bundles; his gaze slid across the portrait; and a pleasant-looking lady cast a return glance from there: her gaze was mocking—the studio portrait flew aside; under the portrait was a package; with feigned indifference he balanced it on the palm of his hand: there was a weight in it; he quickly put it down.

Nikolai Apollonovich quickly began to undo the knots in the towel, pulling at an embroidered end depicting a pheasant: short in stature—quite nimble—Nikolai Apollonovich now resembled the senator: most of all he resembled a photograph of the senator taken in 1860.

But why was he so flustered? Self-control, oh, for more self-control! No matter, his trembling fingers did not unravel the knot; there was nothing to unravel anyway: everything was clear as it was. All the same, he did undo the package; and his astonishment knew no bounds:

"A sweet-box … "

"Ah! … "

"A ribbon! … "

"Well I never … "

Just like Apollon Apollonovich, Nikolai Apollonovich talked to himself.

But when he broke the ribbon, his hope broke with it (he had been hoping for something), for inside it—in the sweet-box, beneath the pink ribbon—instead of delicious sweets from Balle's was a simple tin can; the lid of the tin can was so unpleasantly cold it burned his finger.

Then he noticed in the process a clockwork mechanism attached to the side: you had to turn a little metal key at the side to make a sharp black pointer indicate the appointed hour. Nikolai Apollonovich sensed a dull certainty arising in his mind which would prove his worthlessness and weakness: he sensed that he would never be able to turn that key, for there was no means of stopping the mechanism once it was activated. And in order to cut off immediately all further retreat, Nikolai Apollonovich at once grasped the metal key between his fingers; whether because his fingers shook, whether because Nikolai Apollonovich, in an attack of dizziness, tumbled into that very abyss that he had wished with all his soul to avoid—only, only: the key slowly turned to one hour, then it turned to two hours, and Nikolai Apollonovich … made an inadvertent *entrechat*: he leapt off to one side; completing his leap to one side he cast another sideways glance at the desk: just as before a tin can full of greasy sardines was still standing on the desk (he had once made himself sick by eating too many sardines and had since stopped eating them); a sardine-tin like any other: shiny, with rounded edges …

No—no—no!

Not just a sardine-tin, but a sardine-tin of terrible import!

The metal key had already turned two hours, and a particular kind of life, beyond the mind's comprehension, had already started seething in the sardine-tin; and although the sardine-tin was still the same, it wasn't the same; an hour hand and a minute hand were creeping along for sure; a fussy little hair-spring measuring seconds had set off on its circular gallop, right up to the moment—that moment was not far off now)—to the moment, the moment, when …

—the sardine-tin's terrible import would suddenly distend hideously; in a trice it would start to expand beyond measure; and then, and then: the sardine-tin would fly apart …

—streams of that terrible import would promptly hurtle out in circles, tearing the table to pieces with a tempestuous roar: something would burst in him with a crash, and his body—would be blown to pieces too; along with the wood-splinters, along with the gases spurting in all directions it would be spattered in a loathsome slurry of blood over the cold stones of the walls …

—in a hundredth of a second all that would come about: in a hundredth of a second the walls would collapse, and the terrible import, expanding, expanding, expanding, would be hanging in the air in a mess of splinters, blood and stone.

Ragged smoke-plumes would spread out swiftly across the leaden sky, dragging their tails over the Neva.

What had he done, whatever had he done?

The box was after all still standing on the desk; since he had turned the key what he had now to do was to seize the box immediately and put it in the appropriate place (for instance—in the white bedroom under the pillow); or else at once to crush it under his heel. But to hide it in the appropriate place, under his father's fluffed-up pillow, so that the old, bald head, wearied by all that had just happened, should fall with all its weight upon the bomb—no, no, no: of that he was not capable; that would be betrayal.

Crush it under his heel?

At that thought he felt something which positively made his ears twitch: he experienced such an immense attack of nausea (from the seven glasses he had drunk), as though he had swallowed the bomb like a pill; and now in the pit of his stomach something was distending: made of rubber, perhaps, or else of the material of very strange worlds …

He would never crush it, never.

It remained to throw it into the Neva, but there was still plenty of time for that: he needed only to turn the key another twenty times or so; and everything would be postponed for the time being; since he had turned the key, he must immediately prolong that time being;

but he delayed, and dropped into an armchair in utter impotence; nausea, a strange weakness, somnolence were taking a terrible toll; and his enfeebled thought, separating from his body, was painting for Nikolai Apollonovich quite senselessly a mass of shoddy, idle, powerless arabesques ... as it drifted off into drowsiness.

Nikolai Apollonovich was an enlightened man; it was not without meaning that Nikolai Apollonovich had devoted the best years of his life to philosophy; all prejudices had fallen from him long ago, and Nikolai Apollonovich was decidedly a stranger to magic practices and all manner of miracles; magic and miracles obscured (why was he thinking of extraneous things, he had to think about *that* ... Think about what? Nikolai Apollonovich struggled to escape from his somnolence; but he could not escape) ... obscured ... all manner of miracles ... the idea of the source of perfection; for a philosopher the source of perfection was Thought: God, so to speak, that is to say, the Perfect Rule ... The lawgivers of the great religions had expressed various rules in the form of images; Nikolai Apollonovich respected the lawgivers of the great religions, as it were, without, it goes without saying, believing in their divine essence.

Yes: why was he thinking about religion? Was there time to think ... Why, it was done: quickly ... What was done? ... Nikolai Apollonovich's last effort to escape from his somnolence was not crowned with success; he remembered nothing; everything seemed quiet ... to the point of banality, and his enfeebled thought, separating from his body, kept painting senselessly those shoddy, idle, powerless arabesques.

Nikolai Apollonovich particularly respected Buddha, considering that Buddhism outshone all other religions both in a psychological and a theoretical respect; in the psychological—by teaching the love even of animals; and in the theoretical: logic had been developed lovingly by the Tibetan lamas. Nikolai Apollonovich recalled that he had once, for instance, read the logic of Dharmakirti with a commentary by Dharmottara ...

That was the first thing.

In the second place: in the second place (this is our observation), Nikolai Apollonovich was an unconscious man (not Nikolai

Apollonovich number one, but Nikolai Apollonovich number two); from time to time, between the entrances to two houses a certain strange, very strange, exceedingly strange condition would come upon him (as it did upon Apollon Apollonovich); as though everything on the other side of the door was not what it was, but something else: what it was—Nikolai Apollonovich could not have said. Simply imagine that on the other side of the door—there is nothing, and that if you throw the door open, then the door will open upon an empty, cosmic infinity, into which ... you can only throw yourself head first, to fly, and fly, and fly—and only after flying there will you learn that that infinity is the sky and the stars—that same sky and those same stars which we see above us, and which, as we see them, we do not see. All that is left is to fly past strangely static, no longer twinkling little stars and crimson planetary spheres at absolute zero, in an atmosphere of two hundred and seventy-three degrees below zero. That was what Nikolai Apollonovich was experiencing at this moment.

A strange, very strange semi-somnolent condition.

The Day of Judgement

And in just such a condition he sat before the sardine-tin: he saw—and did not see; he heard—and did not hear; it was as though at that lifeless moment when this weary body had tumbled into the embrace of the armchair, this spirit had tumbled straight from the parquet of the floor into some lifeless sea, into a temperature of absolute zero; and he saw—and did not see: no, he did see. When his weary head bent down silently on to the desk (on to the sardine-tin), in through the open door to the corridor the bottomless infinity gazed at its own reflection, that strange thing that Nikolai Apollonovich had tried to cast off as he made the transition to the current business: to his distant astral journey, or sleep (which, we observe, is the same thing); but the open door went on gaping amongst all that was current, opening into it its own profundity, not current at all: cosmic infinity.

Nikolai Apollonovich had the impression that something standing outside the door in the infinity had looked at him, that some kind of head was poking through (the moment you looked at it, it vanished): the head of a *god* (Nikolai Apollonovich would have classified this head among the heads of wooden deities, such as can to this day be encountered among the tribes of the north-east, who have since time immemorial peopled Russia's tedious tundra). Maybe it was just such gods that in ancient times his Kirgiz-Kaisak ancestors had worshipped; these Kirgiz-Kaisak ancestors, according to tradition, had been in contact with Tibetan lamas; there was no shortage of them in the blood of the Ab-Lai-Ukhovs. Was that perhaps the reason why Nikolai Apollonovich felt such sympathy for Buddhism? His heredity was making itself felt; heredity was coursing into consciousness; in his sclerotic veins his heredity was beating in millions of yellow blood corpuscles. And now, as the open door revealed infinity to Ableukhov, he responded to this exceedingly strange circumstance with admirable composure (it had, after all, happened before): he lowered his head into his hands.

Another moment—and he would have calmly set off on his customary astral journey, uncoiling from his mortal coil a tenebrous, cosmic tail that pierced the walls into the infinite, but his dream broke off: ineffably, tormentingly, mutely someone was moving towards the door, swirling in winds of non-being: terrible antiquity, like the assailing cry of a rushing taxicab, suddenly gathered strength in the sounds of ancient singing.

Nikolai Apollonovich intuited this singing, rather than recognised it:

"*Be soothed now, you feelings of passion* … "

Only just before an automobile's roar had been heard:

"*And sleep now, you heart without hope* … "

"A-a-a," came a roar in the doorway: a gramophone's loudspeaker? The horn of a taxicab? No: in the doorway stood an ancient, ancient head.

Nikolai Apollonovich leapt up.

An ancient, ancient head: was it Confucius or Buddha? No, it was no doubt his ancestor Ab-Lai peeping in at the door.

A multicoloured iridescent silk gown rustled and swished; for some reason Nikolai Apollonovich remembered his own Bukhara dressing gown with its iridescent peacock feathers … A multicoloured iridescent silk gown, across whose smoky, smoky-sapphire background (and into that background) little dragons were crawling, sharp-beaked, golden, winged, miniature; the pyramidal cap with its five layers and its golden base looked like a mitre; an effulgent halo glowed and crackled above his head: a wondrous vision, familiar to us all! In the middle of that halo a wrinkled countenance spread open its lips with a *chronic* look; the worshipful Mongol entered the colourful room; and behind him wafted the winds of millennia.

In the first instant Nikolai Apollonovich thought that in the guise of his ancestor, Ab-Lai, Khronos had come to pay him a visit (that was what was hidden in him!); his gaze shifted anxiously: he looked to see the blade of the traditional scythe in the Stranger's hands; but there was no scythe in his hands: in his yellowish hand, scented like the first lily, there was only an oriental platter with a small pile of pink aromatic Chinese apples on it: apples of paradise.

Nikolai Apollonovich rejected paradise: paradise, or a garden (which, as he saw it, was the same thing) was incompatible in Nikolai Apollonovich's understanding with the ideal of the highest good (let us not forget that Nikolai Apollonovich was a Kantian; indeed, he was a follower of Cohen); in that sense he was a Nirvanic man.

By Nirvana he understood—Nothing.

And Nikolai Apollonovich recalled: he—the old Turanian—had been embodied a multitude of times; he was embodied now: in the flesh and blood of the Russian imperial nobility of ancient lineage, with the task of fulfilling an age-old, sacred purpose: to dislodge all foundations; in the degenerate Aryan blood the Ancient Dragon was to flare up and consume everything in its flame; the age-old East was scattering a hail of invisible bombs into our time. Nikolai Apollonovich—the old Turanian bomb—was now exploding with delight at the sight of his homeland; on Nikolai Apollonovich's face a forgotten, Mongol expression appeared; he seemed now to be a mandarin of the Middle Empire, clad in a frock coat for his passage to the West (he was here with a single, top secret mission).

"I see … "

"I see … "

"I see … "

"Very well, sir!"

How strange: he suddenly so resembled his father!

And so with breathless, soul-searing enthusiasm the ancient Turanian, clothed for the time being in the mortal coil of an Aryan, rushed up to a pile of old exercise books, in which the premises of the metaphysics he had developed were sketched out; he grasped the exercise books with a mixture of embarrassment and joy: all the exercise books in front of him amounted to a single immense undertaking—the business of his whole life (they could be compared to the sum of Apollon Apollonovich's business). The business of his life was however more than the business of *his* life: a single, immense Mongol business shone through in the notes under all points and all paragraphs: the great mission entrusted to him before his birth: the mission of destroyer.

This guest, the worshipful Turanian, stood motionless: the impenetrable, nocturnal darkness of his eyes spread all round; while his hands—his hands: were raised rhythmically, melodically, smoothly to limitless heights; his garments fluttered; the sound they made was reminiscent of the trembling of passing wings; the smoky background became clear, deepened, and became a fragment of the distant sky that gazed through the riven air of this little study: a chink of dark sapphire—how could it have appeared in this room crammed with bookcases? The little dragons embroidered on the iridescent gown flew off in that direction (the gown itself had become a chink); in the depths they glittered like stars ... And age-old antiquity itself stood there as sky and stars: and from there blew the indigo air, infused from stars.

Nikolai Apollonovich rushed up to the guest—Turanian to Turanian (subordinate to master) with a pile of exercise books in his hand:

"Paragraph one: Kant (proof that Kant, too, was a Turanian)".

"Paragraph two: the value, understood as nobody and nothing."

"Paragraph three: social relations built upon value."

"Paragraph four: the destruction of the Aryan world by the system of values."

"Conclusion: the age-old Mongol business."

But the Turanian replied.

"The exercise has not been understood: instead of Kant should be the Prospect."

"Instead of value—numbering: by houses, floors and rooms for all time."

"Instead of a new order: the circulation of the citizens of the Prospect—even and in straight lines."

"Not the destruction of Europe—its stagnation … "
"That is the Mongol business … "

It occurred to Nikolai Apollonovich that he was condemned: and the pile of exercise books in his hands disintegrated into a heap of ashes; the wrinkled countenance, familiar to the point of horror, bent right down to him: thereupon he glanced at its ear, and—he understood, understood everything: the old Turanian who had once upon a time instructed him in all the rules of wisdom was Apollon Apollonovich; he it was against whom, misunderstanding science, he had raised his hand.

This was the Day of Judgement.

"Whatever is this? Whoever is this?"
"Who is it? Your father … "
"Who is my father?"
"Saturn … "
"How is that possible?"
"Nothing is impossible! … "

The Day of Judgement was at hand.

Bygone dreams were here in reality; the cycles of the planets ran their course here in reality—in a wavelength of a billion years: there was no Earth, no Venus, no Mars, only three nebulous rings ran round the Sun; the fourth had only just exploded, and great Jupiter was about to become a world; only ancient Saturn raised from its fiery centre aeonian waves: nebulae swept by; and Nikolai Apollonovich was cast down into the immeasurable by Saturn, his parent, and nought but distances flowed by.

At the close of the fourth kingdom he was on earth: at that time the sword of Saturn hung as an unquenched thunderstorm; the continent of Atlantis had collapsed; Nikolai Apollonovich, Atlas, was a depraved monster (the ground beneath him did not hold—it sank beneath the waters); later he was in China: Apollon Apollonovich, the Emperor of China, commanded Nikolai Apollonovich to slaughter many thousands (which was done); and in those relatively recent times, when thousands of Tamberlaine's horsemen flooded over Russia, Nikolai Apollonovich came galloping from the steppes to that same Russia on his steed; later he became embodied in the blood of a Russian nobleman; and took up the same old business: just as he had slaughtered thousands then, so now he planned explosion: he planned to throw a bomb at his father; to throw a bomb at swift-flowing time itself. But his father was Saturn, the cycle of time turned upon itself, and closed; the empire of Saturn returned (from sweetness here the heart may burst).

The flow of time ceased to be; for thousands of millions of years matter had been ripening in the spirit; but he had craved to blow up time itself; and lo, everything was perishing.

"Father!"

"You planned to blow me up; and therefore everything is perishing."

"It was not you, but … "

"Too late: the birds, the beasts, people, history, the world—everything is collapsing: it is all falling back to Saturn … "

Everything was falling on to Saturn; the atmosphere outside the windows darkened, turned black; everything came into its ancient molten state, expanding beyond measure, all bodies ceased to be bodies; everything revolved the other way—revolved terribly.

"*Cela … tourne …* " Nikolai Apollonovich howled in utter terror, finally bereft of his body, but not noticing …

"No, *Ça … tourne …* "

Bereft of body, still he felt his body: some invisible centre that had previously been both his consciousness and his 'self', turned out to possess a semblance of the former, burnt to ashes: Nikolai Apollonovich's logical premises turned into bones; the syllogisms around these bones wrapped themselves into rigid sinews; the content of his logical activity developed flesh and skin; and so the 'self' of Nikolai Apollonovich again displayed its bodily form, although it was not a body; and in this *non-body* (in the exploded 'self') someone else's 'self' was revealed: this 'self' had rushed in from Saturn and to Saturn it returned.

He sat in front of his father (as he used to sit before)—without a body, but in a body (a strange business!): outside the windows of his study, in utter darkness, a loud mumbling could be heard: turn—turn—turn.

This was the calendar running backwards.

"What calendar are we in?"

But Saturn, Apollon Apollonovich, replied with loud laughter:

"None at all, Kolenka, none at all: time, old chap, is at zero … "

The terrible import of Nikolai Apollonovich's soul revolved restlessly (there, where the heart should be), like a whistling top: it swelled and expanded; and it seemed: the terrible import of his soul—a round zero—was turning into an agonising sphere; it seemed: there was the logic—the bones would be blown to pieces.

This was the Day of Judgement.

"Oh, oh, oh: what does 'I am' mean?"

"I am? Zero … "

"Well, and zero?"

"That, Kolenka, is a bomb … "

Nikolai Apollonovich understood that he was only a bomb; and he burst with a bang: from the place where a semblance of Nikolai Apollonovich had just arisen in the armchair and where there was now nothing to be seen but a tawdry broken shell (like an eggshell), a zigzag of lightning flashed, tumbling into the black, aeonian waves …

Then Nikolai Apollonovich awoke from his dream; with a shudder, he realised that his head was lying on the sardine-tin.

And he jumped up: a terrible dream … But what kind? He could not remember the dream; his childhood nightmares had returned: Pepp Peppovich Pepp, swelling up from a little ball into a colossus, had evidently fallen quiet there for the time being—in the sardine-tin; his age-old childhood delirium was returning, because

—Pepp Peppovich Pepp, this little ball of terrible import, was quite simply a bomb belonging to the party: it was ticking away there inaudibly with its hairspring and its hands; Pepp Peppovich Pepp would expand, expand, expand. And Pepp Peppovich Pepp would burst: everything would burst …

"What is it … am I delirious?"

Again things started revolving in his head with terrifying speed: what was he to do? There was a quarter of an hour left: turn the key again?

He turned the little key another twenty times; and twenty times something wheezed there, in the tin-can: the age-old delirium withdrew for a while, so that the morning might remain morning, the day might remain day, and the evening—evening: but when the night came to an end no movement of the key could postpone things further: something would happen that would make the walls collapse, and the purple-lighted skies split asunder, mixing with spattered blood into one leaden, primeval darkness.

CHAPTER SIX

In which the events of a drab grey day are recounted.

> *Where'er he turned, the Horse of Bronze*
> *Came galloping with thund'rous hooves.*
>
> A Pushkin

Retrieving the thread of his being

I T WAS A DULL PETERSBURG MORNING.
Let us return, though, to Alexandr Ivanovich; Alexandr Ivanovich
woke up; Alexandr Ivanovich slightly opened his reluctant eyes: the
night's occurrences ran off into the world of his unconscious; his
nerves were unhinged; the night had been for him an occurrence of
gargantuan proportions.

In the transitional state between wakefulness and sleep he was being
thrown somewhere: as though he were jumping from his fourth-floor
window; his sensations revealed to him a gaping breach in his world;
he flew into that breach, transported into a swarming world, of which
it was not enough to say you were assailed by substances akin to Furies:
the very fabric of the world there seemed to be a fabric of Furies.

It was only just before morning that Alexandr Ivanovich overcame
that world; and then he entered a state of bliss; his awakening swiftly
cast him down from there: there was something he felt sorry for, and
with that his whole body ached and throbbed.

The first instant after his awakening he noticed that he was wracked
by a violent shivering; he had been tossing and turning all night:
something had happened—for certain … Only what?

All night long a delirious flight through misty Prospects had gone on and on, or sometimes—up the steps of a mysterious staircase; most likely it was fever racing through his veins; his recollections tried to tell him something, but—his recollections slipped away; and he could not tie anything down with his memory.

It was all the fever.

Frightened in earnest (in his solitude Alexandr Ivanovich was afraid of falling ill), he thought that it would not be a bad idea to spend the day at home.

With this thought he began to drift into oblivion; and as he drifted, he thought:

"I could do with some quinine."

He fell asleep.

And waking up—he added:

"And some strong tea … "

And after more thought, he added further:

"With raspberry jam … "

He reflected that all these days he had been living in a state of lightness that was not permissible in his position; this lightness seemed to him all the more disgraceful because stupendous, weighty days were on the way.

He gave an involuntary sigh.

"And what I also need—is strict abstinence from vodka … Stop reading *Revelation* … Stop going down to see the caretaker … And all those conversations with that Styopka who's living at the caretaker's: no more chattering with Styopka … "

These thoughts about tea with raspberry jam, about vodka, about Styopka, about the *Revelation* of St John calmed him down at first, reducing the night's events to utter nonsense.

But after washing in the ice-cold water from the tap with the help of his wretched little lump of soap and its yellow slime, Alexandr Ivanovich felt another flood of nonsense.

He cast a glance round his twelve-rouble room (an attic space).

What a miserable abode!

The principal adornment of this miserable abode was the bed; the bed consisted of four cracked boards placed any old how on a wooden trestle; the splintered surface of that trestle was marked by some repulsive, dark-red, dried-up stains, no doubt from bedbugs, since for many months Alexandr Ivanovich had been doing stolid battle with those dark-red stains by means of Persian powder.

The trestle was covered with an emaciated mattress stuffed with bast; on top of the mattress on the single grimy sheet Alexandr Ivanovich's hand had solicitously thrown a knitted blanket, which could hardly be described as striped: meagre hints of one-time stripes of blue and red were covered with a patina of grey, arising most probably not from dirt, however, but from many years of thorough use; Alexandr Ivanovich kept hesitating to part with this gift from someone (maybe from his mother); perhaps he hesitated to part with it for lack of means (it had been with him to the Yakutsk province).

Apart from the bed … —yes: here I have to say: over the bed there hung a little icon, depicting the thousand nights of prayer by Seraphim of Sarov, on a rock amidst the pine-trees (and here I have to say—Alexandr Ivanovich wore a silver cross beneath his shirt).

Apart from the bed there could be seen a small, smoothly planed table, bereft of any decoration: precisely such tables do service as the humble support of washbasins—in cheap summer-cottages; tables of exactly this kind are sold everywhere at Sunday markets; in Alexandr Ivanovich's abode this table served at once as writing desk and bedside table; there was no washbasin at all: when performing his ablutions Alexandr Ivanovich employed the services of the tap, the sink and a sardine-tin holding a scrap of Kazan soap that floated in its own slime; there was also a hanger: with his trousers on it; the punctured toe of a well-worn shoe peeped out from under the bed (Alexandr Ivanovich had had a dream in which this punctured shoe was a living creature: a domestic pet, a dog or a cat, perhaps; it shuffled along of its own accord, crawling round the room and rustling in the corners; when Alexandr Ivanovich made to feed it with some masticated bread, this shuffling creature bit his finger with its punctured aperture, making him wake up).

There was also a brown suitcase which had long since changed its original form and which stored objects of the most terrible import.

All the accoutrements of the room (if I may use that expression) faded into the background against the colour of the wallpaper, distasteful and importunate, something between dark-yellow and dark-brown, and exposing huge patches of damp: in the evenings a woodlouse would crawl across this patch or that. The room's accoutrements were veiled by layers of tobacco-smoke. You would need to smoke incessantly for at least twelve hours on end to turn the colourless atmosphere into such a dark-grey, blue colour.

Alexandr Ivanovich Dudkin cast a glance round his abode, and again (as had happened before) he felt drawn out of his smoke-laden room—away: he was drawn out on to the street, into the grimy mist, in order to mesh, to merge, to fuse with the shoulders, the backs, the green-hued faces on the Petersburg Prospects and turn into one single, huge, grey—face and shoulder.

Swarms of green October mists clung to the window of his room; Alexandr Ivanovich Dudkin felt an irresistible desire to become infused with mist, to infuse his thoughts with it, in order to drown in it the nonsense rattling round his brain, to quench that nonsense in flashes of delirium that rose like balls of fire (the balls then burst), to quench it with the gymnastics of striding feet; he had to stride out—stride out again, stride all the time; from Prospect to Prospect, from street to street; stride out until his brain was fully numbed, and then to collapse on to a tavern table and scald himself with vodka. Only in this aimless wandering through streets and crooked alleys— beneath the streetlamps, fences, chimneys—could the thoughts that oppressed his soul be quenched.

As he put his coat on Alexandr Ivanovich felt himself shivering again; and he thought sadly:

"Oh, if only I could have some quinine now!"

But what chance was there of getting quinine …

And as he went down the stairs, he thought again with sadness:

"Oh, if only I had some strong tea with raspberry jam! … "

The staircase

The staircase!

Threatening, shadowy, damp—it echoed pitilessly his shuffling steps: threatening, shadowy, damp! That was last night. Alexandr Ivanovich Dudkin recalled now for the first time that he really had passed here yesterday: that had not been a dream: that had really happened. But what had happened?

What?

Yes: from all the doors—a baleful silence had spread out around him; it resounded limitlessly, making rustling sounds of some sort; and limitlessly, tirelessly, some unknown slobberer was swallowing his own spittle with leisurely distinctness (that was not a dream either); there were terrible, unidentified sounds, all woven from the muffled keening of the times; from above, through the narrow windows you could see—and he did see—how the darkness brushed by from time to time and swept up into misty outlines, how everything became illuminated when the pale, matt turquoise spread out soundlessly beneath his feet, to lie there lifeless, tremorless.

There, over there: it was the moon gazing down there.

But the swarms kept scurrying on: swarm upon swarm—shaggy, spectral, hazy, thunder-bearing—these swarms all hurled themselves upon the moon: the pale, matt turquoise was occluded; from everywhere the shadows swept about, and everything was clothed in shadow.

Here Alexandr Ivanovich recalled for the first time how he had come rushing up this staircase last night, straining the last of his expiring strength without the slightest hope (what hope?) of overcoming—overcoming what precisely? And all the while a black outline (had that really happened too?) ran for all it was worth—at his heels, after him.

Destroying him irrevocably.

The staircase!

On a grey weekday it is peaceful, ordinary; down below dull thuds ring out: it's cabbages being chopped—the occupant of flat number four has stocked up on cabbage for the winter; it all looks ordinary—banisters, doors, steps; over the banisters hangs a worn and ragged carpet, smelling of cats—from flat number four; a floor-polisher with a swollen cheek is beating it with a carpet-beater; and a fair-haired slattern sneezes into her apron from the dust as she squeezes out of the door; between the floor-polisher and the slattern words, of course, arise:

"Ugh!"

"Give us a hand, there's a good chap … "

"Stepanida Markovna … What a load you've brought now! … "

"All right, all right … "

"I mean to say, what a ... "

"Now it's 'a load', but when you've got a cup of tea in front of you ... "

"What a job it is—I was saying ... "

"You shouldn't go sloping off to them meetings: then you'd get your work done faster ... "

"Don't you knock the meetings: there'll come a time when you'll be glad of them yourself!"

"Come on, beat that feather-bed, a fine cavalier you are!"

Doors!

One there, another here, and that one ... The oil-cloth has come loose on that one; horsehair sticks out roughly from the holes; and on this door a card has been attached with a pin; the card has turned yellow; and on it is written: '*Zakatalkin*' ... Who Zakatalkin is, his Christian name and patronymic, what profession he pursues—I leave the curious to judge for themselves: '*Zakatalkin*'—and that's all there is to it.

From behind the door a violin bow laboriously saws out a familiar song. And a voice is heard:

"My fatherland dear ... "

I rather assume that Zakatalkin is employed as a violinist: playing in the orchestra of some restaurant or other.

That's all you can tell from observation of the doors ... One more thing: in the old days there used to be a water-butt standing by the door, with a sour smell to it: for filling from the water-carriers: but since running water has been introduced the water-carriers have become extinct in the cities.

The steps?

They are littered with cucumber skins, dirt from the street and eggshells ...

And, tearing free, he ran

Alexandr Ivanovich Dudkin cast his eyes over the staircase, the floor-polisher and the slattern, who was struggling through the door with another feather-bed; and—strange to say: the everyday simplicity of the staircase did not dispel what he had experienced here the previous night; even now, in broad daylight, amidst the steps, the eggshells, the floor-polisher and the cat, that was devouring a chicken's innards on the windowsill, the terror Alexandr Ivanovich had once experienced here returned to him: everything that had happened to him the night before—had really happened; and tonight what had really happened would come back again: he would come back home at night: the staircase would be shadowy and threatening; a black outline would once again chase at his heels; through the door where the card said '*Zakatalkin*' the slobberer would once again be swallowing his spittle (maybe swallowing his spittle, and maybe—blood) ...

And the familiar, impossible words would ring out again in perfect clarity ...

"Yes, yes, yes ... It's me ... I destroy irrevocably ... "

Where had he heard that before?

Away from here! Into the street! ...

He had to start striding out again, to stride, to stride away: until his strength was quite exhausted, until his brain was fully numbed, and then to collapse on to a tavern table, so that these hallucinations should appear no more; and then to start all over: pacing out Petersburg, losing himself in the damp reeds, in the floating mists of the sea-shore, casting everything aside in utter apathy, only to come to his senses among the drizzling lights of the Petersburg suburbs.

Alexandr Ivanovich Dudkin was on the point of strutting off down the staircase with its multitude of stone steps; but suddenly he stopped; he noticed that some strange type in a black Italian cape and a fantastically cocked hat of the same ilk was rushing up towards him, three steps at a time, with his head bowed low and twirling desperately in his hand a heavy cane.

His back was arched.

This strange type in the black Italian cape bumped into Alexandr Ivanovich in his haste; he all but thrust his head into his chest; and when he raised his head, Alexandr Ivanovich Dudkin caught sight, right in front of his nose, of the deathly pale and perspiration-covered forehead of—can you imagine!—Nikolai Apollonovich: the forehead with its swollen, throbbing vein; it was by this characteristic sign alone (by the quivering vein) that Alexandr Ivanovich recognised Ableukhov: not by his wildly squinting eyes, not by his strange outlandish garb.

"Good morning: I was on my way to see you."

Nikolai Apollonovich snapped these words out very fast; and—what was this? He snapped them out in a threatening whisper? Goodness, how out of breath he was. Without even offering his hand, he uttered hastily—and in a threatening whisper:

"I have to tell you, Alexandr Ivanovich, that I can't do it."

"?"

"You understand, of course, what exactly it is that I can't do: I can't, and I don't want to; in short—I won't."

"!"

"This is a refusal: an irrevocable refusal. You can pass that on. And I ask you to leave me in peace … "

As he said this, Nikolai Apollonovich's face reflected embarrassment, perhaps even alarm.

Nikolai Apollonovich turned round; and, twirling his heavy cane, Nikolai Apollonovich rushed back down the stairs, as though he was fleeing.

"But wait, wait a moment," Alexandr Ivanovich rushed after him and felt beneath his feet the rapid patter of the staircase steps.

"Nikolai Apollonovich?"

At the exit he caught Ableukhov by the sleeve, but the latter tore free. Nikolai Apollonovich turned to face Alexandr Ivanovich; with a slightly trembling hand Nikolai Apollonovich held the brim of his flamboyantly cocked hat; and, summoning his courage, he blurted out in a half-whisper:

"This is, so to speak … loathsome … Do you hear me?"

He set off across the yard.

Alexandr Ivanovich grasped the door for a moment; Alexandr Ivanovich felt the profoundest anxiety: an insult—and for no reason at all; he hesitated for a second, wondering what he ought to do; he twitched involuntarily; with that involuntary movement he revealed his extraordinarily delicate neck; then in two bounds he caught up with the fugitive.

He buried his fingers in the hem of the black cape as it flew away from him; the owner of the cape thereupon began trying desperately to tear himself free; for a moment they struggled among the piles of firewood and in the struggle something fell to the ground, ringing on the asphalt. With his cane raised and breathless with anger, Nikolai Apollonovich began to shout out loudly, fitfully, some outrageous and, above all, insulting nonsense of his own: insulting to Alexandr Ivanovich.

"And this you call an action, work for the party? Surrounding me with spies ... Dogging my steps at every point? ... Losing all conviction yourself ... Spending your time reading *Revelation* ... And at the same time snooping ... My good sir, you are a ... a ... a ... "

Finally, tearing free again, Nikolai Apollonovich ran: they flew along the street.

The street

The street!

How it had changed: how these sombre days had changed it!

Over there—those cast-iron railings round a little park; the crimson leaves of the maples used to beat in the wind and strike against the railings; but the crimson leaves have all been blown away; and only the branches—dry skeletons—stand there black and clamouring.

It used to be September: the sky was blue and clear; but now it's not like that: from early morning the sky has begun to fill with a flood of heavy pewter; it's not September now.

They flew along the street:

"But come on, Nikolai Apollonovich," Dudkin, upset and offended, kept at him, "you must agree that now we cannot possibly part without an explanation ... "

"We have nothing more to talk about," Nikolai Apollonovich uttered curtly from beneath his flamboyantly cocked hat.

"Explain yourself more coherently," Alexandr Ivanovich insisted in his turn.

A sense of insult and an anxious astonishment were expressed in his twitching features; the astonishment, we may say for our own part, was quite unfeigned, and so unfeigned that Nikolai Apollonovich, despite the distraction of his anger, could not fail to notice its genuineness.

331

He turned round and, without his previous fury but still with tearful anger, drummed out rapidly:

"No, no, no! ... What more can there be to explain? And don't you dare dispute it ... I am the one who has a right to call you to account ... I am the one who is suffering, not you, or your comrade ... "

"What? ... What is it?"

"To hand over the package ... "

"Well?"

"Without any warning, any explanation, any request ... " Alexandr Ivanovich turned a deep red.

"And then to disappear ... Through some kind of proxy to threaten me with the police ... "

At this undeserved accusation Alexandr Ivanovich made an impulsive movement towards Ableukhov:

"Stop: what police?"

"Yes, the police ... "

"What police are you talking about? ... What abomination is this? ... What are you hinting at? ... Which of us is out of his mind?"

But Nikolai Apollonovich, whose tearful anger had turned back into fury, hissed into his ear:

"I'd like to ... " his hoarse words rang out (his mouth, with teeth bared, seemed to be smiling: attacking Dudkin's ear, as though to bite it) ... "I'd like to ... right now—here in this very place: I'd like ... in broad daylight as a warning to all the people watching, Alexandr Ivanovich, my very good friend ... " (he became confused) ...

Over there, that way ...

—On summer evenings in July a little old woman used to suck her gums in the sunset from the carved window of that gleaming house (—"I'd like to ... " Alexandr Ivanovich caught the words in the distance); since August the window had been closed and the little old woman had vanished; in September a brocaded coffin had been carried out; a group of people walked behind the coffin: a gentleman in a worn overcoat and a cap with a cockade; and with him—seven tow-headed little urchins.

The coffin was nailed down.

("Yes, Alexandr Ivanovich, sir," reached Alexandr Ivanovich's ears from somewhere.)

Later uniform caps started traipsing in and out of the house and making a mess on the stairs; it was said that they'd been making bombs there behind the walls; Alexandr Ivanovich knew that that very bomb had first been brought to his attic—from that house.

And he gave an involuntary shudder.

How strange: rudely returned to reality (he was a strange man: he was thinking about that house at the same time as Nikolai Apollonovich was showering him with words ...)—well, like this: from the senator's son's incoherent outpourings about the police, his decisive and irrevocable refusal, Alexandr Ivanovich understood only:

"Listen," he said, "the little that I understand, that makes sense to me in what you say, is just this: it's all a question of the package ... "

"Of course it is: you yourself handed it to me for safe keeping."

"That's odd ... "

It was odd: their conversation was taking place beside that very house where the bomb had arisen: the bomb itself, having become a mental bomb, had described a perfect circle, so that this talk about the bomb had arisen at the place of the bomb's own origin.

"Talk more quietly, Nikolai Apollonovich: I don't understand your agitation, I must admit ... Here you go insulting me: what is it you find so reprehensible in that act of mine?"

"How can you ask?"

"Yes, what is base in the party asking you," he spoke these words in a whisper, "to look after the package for the time being? You had agreed yourself, hadn't you? And—that's all there is to it ... So if you find it awkward to keep the package at your house, it's no problem for me to drop in and pick it up ... "

"Oh, drop this pose of innocence, please: if it were a matter of nothing but the package ... "

"Shhh! Quiet: we might be overheard ... "

"Nothing but the package—then ... I would understand you ... That isn't the point: don't pretend to be so uninformed ... "

"What is the point, then?"

"The coercion."

"There was no coercion ... "

"The organised inquisition ... "

"I repeat, there was no coercion: you agreed willingly; as for an inquisition, I ... "

"Yes, back then—in the summer ... "

"What about the summer?"

"In principle I agreed, or, rather, I suggested, and ... I dare say ... I made a promise, assuming that there could be no question of compulsion, just as there is no compulsion in the party; but if you do employ compulsion here, then—you're just a bunch of dubious adventurers ... So what, then? ... I made a promise, but how could I imagine that the promise couldn't be withdrawn ... "

"Wait ... "

"Don't interrupt me: how was I to know that they would take the offer that way: twist it like that ... And suggest *that* to me ... "

"No, wait, I will interrupt you ... What promise is it you're talking about? Express yourself more precisely ... "

At this point Alexandr Ivanovich vaguely recalled something (how could he have forgotten it all!).

"Ah, so it's *that* promise you're talking about? ... "

He remembered that once in a grubby tavern *a certain person* had told him (the thought of this *person* caused him an unpleasant feeling)—that *person*, that is to say, Nikolai Stepanovich Lippanchenko—well, he had told him that Nikolai Apollonovich—ugh! ... You don't want to remember! ... And he quickly added:

"That's not what I'm talking about, that isn't the point at all."

"Of course it's the point. The whole essence is in the promise: in the promise understood in a base way and as irrevocable."

"Quiet, quiet, Nikolai Apollonovich, what do you find base in all this? Where is the baseness?"

"It's obvious, isn't it?"

"No, no, no: where? The party asked you to look after the package for the time being ... That's all ... "

"Do you really think that's all?"

"That's all ... "

"If it were simply a matter of the package, I would understand you: but I'm sorry ... " And he waved an arm in despair.

"There's no point in our discussing things: can't you see, our whole conversation is just marking time: going nowhere at all ... "

"And I notice ... All the same: you keep on about coercion, but I've remembered: even I heard rumours—back then, in the summer ... "

"Well?"

334

"About an act of violence that you proposed to us: so that intention had its origin not with us, but with you!"

Alexandr Ivanovich remembered (*that person* had told him everything then, plying him with liquor in a grubby tavern): through a third person Nikolai Apollonovich Ableukhov had offered then that he would do away with his father with his own hands; he remembered that the *person* had talked then with revolting calmness, adding, however, that the party had no choice: it would have to decline the offer; the extraordinary nature of the intention, the unnaturalness in the choice of victim and the shade of cynicism, bordering on obscenity—all that affected Alexandr Ivanovich's sensitive heart with an attack of out-and-out abhorrence (Alexandr Ivanovich was drunk at the time; and so the whole conversation with Lippanchenko seemed to him afterwards to be nothing but the play of his inebriated brain, and not sober reality): all that he remembered now:

"And I must admit ... "

"To demand of me," Ableukhov broke in, "that I ... with my own hands ... "

"Just so, just so ... "

"It's horrible!"

"Yes—horrible: and, as it were, Nikolai Apollonovich, I didn't believe it then ... If I had believed it, you would have fallen ... in the party's estimation ... "

"So you think it's horrible too?"

"I'm sorry: I do ... "

"There you are, then! You call it horrible yourself; yet you yourself have got involved in this horrible business, evidently?"

Something suddenly disturbed Dudkin: his sensitive neck twitched:

"Just a moment ... "

And, grasping with a trembling hand the buttons of the Italian cape, he fastened his eyes on a neutral spot:

"Don't start wandering off the point: here we are, accusing each other, and yet we both agree ... " he turned his eyes in surprise to meet Ableukhov's, "what to call this act ... It's base, isn't it?"

Nikolai Apollonovich shuddered:

"Well, of course, it's base! ... "

They were silent for a moment.

"You see, we both agree … "

Nikolai Apollonovich took a handkerchief from his pocket and stopped to wipe his face.

"That surprises me … "

"Me, too … "

They looked each other in the eye in consternation. Alexandr Ivanovich (he had now forgotten that he was shaking with fever) extended his hand again and touched with his finger the hem of the Italian cape:

"In order to unravel this knot completely, answer me this: in promising with your own hands (and so on) … —Did that promise not originate from you? … "

"No! It didn't!"

"And so in thought you have nothing to do with any such murder? I put the question like that because a thought sometimes expresses itself unwittingly through involuntary gestures, intonation, glances— even: a quivering of the lips … "

"No, no … that is … " Nikolai Apollonovich faltered, then realised that he had faltered out loud over a dubious train of thought; and, faltering out loud, he reddened; and—started explaining himself:

"I mean, I didn't love my father … And I may have let it be known more than once … But to suggest I might? … Never!"

"Very well, I believe you."

At that Nikolai Apollonovich, as ill luck would have it, reddened to his very ears; and, having reddened, he tried to do some more explaining, but Alexandr Ivanovich shook his head decisively, not wishing to touch upon a certain delicate nuance of an uncommunicated thought which had flashed through both their minds simultaneously.

"No, don't … I believe you … That's not it—I've something else in mind: this is what I want you to tell me … Tell me now perfectly frankly: do I have anything to do with it?"

Nikolai Apollonovich looked in surprise at his naïve interlocutor: he looked, he reddened, and with excessive vehemence, with a forced conviction that he needed now in order to conceal a certain thought—he cried out:

"I believe you do … You helped *him* … "

"Who do you mean?"

"The Incognito ... "

"?"

"The Incognito demanded ... "

"!"

"The performance of a horrible act."

"Where?"

"In his ghastly note ... "

"I don't know such a person ... "

"The Incognito," Nikolai Apollonovich went on insisting in perplexity, "your party comrade ... Why are you so surprised? What's surprised you like that?"

"I assure you: there is no Incognito in the party ... "

It was Nikolai Apollonovich's turn to be surprised:

"What? No Incognito in the party ... "

"Don't talk so loud ... No ... "

"I've been getting notes for three months ... "

"Who from?"

"From him ... "

They both fell silent.

They both breathed heavily and both fixed their eyes on the eyes of the other, raised in query; and in proportion as one lowered his eyes in perplexity, horrified, fearful, a shadow of faint hope flitted across the eyes of the other.

"Nikolai Apollonovich,"—a limitless disgust, overwhelming his fear, spread across Alexandr Ivanovich's pale cheeks in two patches of crimson—"Nikolai Apollonovich!"

"Well?" the other seized him by the arm.

But Alexandr Ivanovich was still unable to catch his breath; in the end he raised his eyes, and—lo and behold: something sad, that occurs in dreams—something beyond expression, but comprehensible to everyone without words, suddenly issued from his brow, from his numbed fingers.

"Come on, then—don't torture me!"

But Alexandr Ivanovich Dudkin, placing a finger to his lips, went on shaking his head in silence: something beyond expression, yet comprehensible in dreams, flowed from him invisibly—from his brow, from his numbed fingers.

At last he said with effort:

"I can assure you—my word of honour: I have nothing at all to do with this shady story … "

At first Nikolai Apollonovich did not believe him.

"What did you say? Repeat it, don't keep silent: try to understand my situation … "

"I—have nothing to do with it … "

"What does that mean, then?"

"I don't know … " and he added in a staccato: "no, no, no:—this is a lie, it's insanity, abracadabra, a mockery … "

"How do I know? … "

Nikolai Apollonovich looked at Alexandr Ivanovich with unseeing eyes; then into the distance of the street: how the street had changed!

"How do I know? … That doesn't make it any easier for me … I haven't slept all night."

The hood of a cab was rushing at pace into the distance of the street: how the street had changed—how these sombre days had changed it!

There was a rush of wind from the sea: the last leaves fluttered down; there would be no more leaves till May; how many people would be there no more in May? These fallen leaves were truly the last leaves. Alexandr Ivanovich knew it all by heart: there would be bloody days, full of horror; and then—everything would collapse; so swirl then, whirl around, you last, incomparable days!

So swirl then, whirl in the air, you last of the leaves! Another idle thought …

A helping hand

"So *he* was at the ball?"

"Yes, he was … "

"Talking to your papa … "

338

"Exactly: and he mentioned you … "

"And afterwards you met in the side street? … "

"And he took me off to a restaurant."

"And what did he call himself? … "

"Morkovin … "

"Abracadabra!"

When Alexandr Ivanovich Dudkin finally tore himself away from the contemplation of the swirling leaves and returned to reality, he realised that Nikolai Apollonovich, running ahead, was gabbling on nineteen to the dozen with a vivacity uncharacteristic of him; he was gesticulating; he was bending his profile forwards with his gaping mouth leering unpleasantly, resembling an ancient tragic mask, which quite failed to create a harmonious whole with the brisk restlessness of a lizard: in short, he looked like a jack-in-a-box with a petrified face.

Alexandr Ivanovich merely inserted the occasional comment:

"And then he talked about the security service?"

"Yes, he tried to frighten me with that … "

"Insisting that such intimidation was part of the party's plan and that the party approved of it? … "

"Well, yes, approved of it … " Nikolai Apollonovich confirmed with some irritation, and, reddening, made to inquire:

"You said yourself, I remember, at that time, that party prejudices … "

"What did I say?" Dudkin flared up sternly.

"I remember you said that the party prejudices of the lower echelons were not shared by the higher ones, whom you serve … "

"Rubbish!" and Dudkin twisted his whole body away: in his agitation he kept quickening his pace.

Nikolai Apollonovich in his turn grasped at his arms with a faint shadow of hope, answering his questions like a schoolboy and smiling unnaturally. In the end, seizing his moment again, he continued his outpourings about the events of the previous night: about the ball, the mask, his flight through the ballroom, sitting on the step of the little black house, the archway, the note; finally—about the wretched little tavern.

It was genuine delirium.

Abracadabra had mixed everything up; they had all long since lost their wits, unless that which *destroys irrevocably* existed in reality.

From the street a black porridge of humanity rolled towards them: swarms of bowler hats rose in their thousands like waves. From the street there rolled towards them: lacquered top hats; rising from the waves like the funnels of steamers; from the street ostrich feathers foamed in their faces; caps like pancakes grinned with their peaks; there were blue peaks, yellow ones, and red ones.

They were importuned on all sides by insistent noses.

Noses flowed past in their multitudes: an aquiline nose and a cockerel's; the nose of a duck or a chicken; and so on, and so on … one nose was twisted to the side; another nose was not twisted at all: shades of green, pale, white and red.

All of this rolled from the street towards them: senselessly, hastily, abundantly.

Nikolai Apollonovich, trying obsequiously to keep up with Dudkin, seemed wary of formulating in front of him his fundamental question, arising from the discovery that the author of the terrible note could not be the bearer of a party directive; this was now the substance of his principal thought: a thought of immense importance—on account of its practical consequences; this thought was now fixed in his head (their roles had changed: now it was Alexandr Ivanovich, not Nikolai Apollonovich, who was furiously jostling aside the bowler hats that surrounded them).

"So that means you presume—it means: a mistake has crept into all this?"

When he had made this timid approach to his thought, Nikolai Apollonovich felt as though hordes of ants were crawling over his body: but what if he was putting on an act—he thought—and—fear overcame him.

"You're talking about the note?" Alexandr Ivanovich glanced up; and he tore himself away from his gloomy contemplation of the flowing abundance of bowlers, heads and moustaches.

"Well, of course: mistake isn't the word … It's not a mistake, it's some revolting imposture that has got mixed up in all this; a perfectly consistent absurdity—with a conscious purpose: to make an arbitrary breach in the relations between a group of people who are closely bound to one another, to confuse them; and in the party's chaos to drown the party's action."

"So help me then … "

"An absolutely intolerable piece of mockery," Dudkin interrupted him, "has got mixed in—made up of gossip and hallucinations."

"I implore you, advise me what to do … "

"And there's treachery mixed up in it too: it reeks of something threatening, ominous … "

"I don't know … I'm confused … I … didn't sleep last night … "

"And it's all a hallucination."

Now Alexandr Ivanovich Dudkin stretched out his hand to Ableukhov in an impulse of sympathy; and here, incidentally, he noticed that Nikolai Apollonovich was considerably shorter than him (Nikolai Apollonovich was not distinguished by his stature).

"Gather all your composure … "

"Lord above! It's easy for you to say *composure*—I didn't sleep last night … I don't know what to do now … "

"Sit and wait … "

"Will you come to me?"

"I tell you   sit and wait: I undertake to help you."

He said this so confidently, with such conviction, almost inspiration, that Ableukhov immediately calmed down; but to tell the truth, in his impulse of sympathy for Ableukhov Alexandr Ivanovich had overestimated the help he could give … In truth: how could he help? He was on his own, cut off from community; conspiracy closed off for him access to the very body of the party; Alexandr Ivanovich had never been a member of the Committee, although he had boasted to Ableukhov about the headquarters; if he was able to help, then exclusively by means of Lippanchenko; he could tell Lippanchenko, affect the course of events through Lippanchenko. First of all he had to catch Lippanchenko. But as a preliminary he had to reassure as quickly as possible this man who was shaken to his very core.

And he reassured him:

"I'm sure I shall be able to unravel the knots of this ghastly trickery: today, straight away, I'll make the necessary inquiries, and … "

And—he broke off: the necessary inquiries could be answered

only by Lippanchenko; no one else … What if he were not in Petersburg?

"And? … "

"And I'll give you an answer tomorrow."

"Thank you, I'm very, very grateful," and Nikolai Apollonovich rushed to shake his hand; Alexandr Ivanovich couldn't help feeling embarrassed (everything depended on where *that person* was now to be found and what information he had at his disposal).

"Oh, please don't: your business concerns all of us personally … "

But Nikolai Apollonovich, who until this moment had been in a state of utter terror, was only able to respond to any word of support either apathetically or effusively.

And Nikolai Apollonovich responded effusively.

Meanwhile Alexandr Ivanovich drifted back into his own thought; he was struck by one little fact: Nikolai Apollonovich gave his word and swore that the terrible commission originated from the unknown Incognito; this person had written to Ableukhov several times; and it was quite clear: that unknown Incognito was, actually, an *agent provocateur*.

Moreover …

From Ableukhov's confused tirade one conclusion could nevertheless be drawn; his own special relations with the party were clearly in evidence, and from those special relations something nefarious emerged; Alexandr Ivanovich struggled to clarify for himself something else as well; and struggled in vain: his thought trickled away into the abundance flowing towards them—moustaches, beards, chins.

Nevskii Prospect

Beards, moustaches, chins: that abundance comprised the upper extremities of human torsos.

Shoulders flowed by, shoulders and shoulders; all together, the shoulders formed a pitch-black porridge; all the shoulders formed a slow-flowing porridge of extreme viscosity, and Alexandr Ivanovich's shoulder immediately became attached to that porridge; stuck to it, you might say; and Alexandr Ivanovich Dudkin followed that self-willed shoulder, in accordance with the law of the indivisible wholeness of bodies; thus he was disgorged on to Nevskii Prospect; and there he was compressed like a single grain into the porridge that flowed with blackness.

What is a grain? It is both a world and an object of consumption; as an object of consumption a grain—of caviar, say—does not represent in itself a satisfactory wholeness; that wholeness—is caviar: the aggregate of grains; the consumer is not aware of grains of caviar; but he is aware of caviar, that is, the porridge of grains of caviar, spread on a proffered sandwich. In just the same way the bodies of individuals who emerge on to the pavement are transformed on Nevskii Prospect into the organs of a communal body, into the grains of the caviar: the Nevskii pavements are a field of sandwiches. Exactly the same happened to the body of Dudkin as he emerged here; exactly the same happened to his persistent thought: it instantly became attached to an alien, incomprehensible thought—to the thought of a huge, many-legged creature that ran along the Nevskii.

They left the pavement; multitudinous legs were running there; and they stared speechlessly at the multitudinous legs of the dark porridge of people as it ran past: this porridge, incidentally, was not flowing, but creeping: creeping and shuffling—creeping and shuffling on a tide of legs; the porridge was composed of many thousands of tiny constituents; every tiny constituent was a torso: and the torsos ran on legs.

There were no people on Nevskii Prospect; what was there was a creeping, clamouring myriapod; a miscellany of voices—a miscellany of words—was pouring out into a single moisture-laden space; coherent sentences clashed against each other and broke; and words flew apart there senselessly and terribly like the shards of empty bottles, all broken in a single spot: all of them, mixed at random, were woven together again into a sentence that flew for all infinity, without beginning or end; this sentence seemed senseless and woven from fantasy: the unalleviated senselessness of the sentence thus composed hung like black soot over the Nevskii; the black smoke of fantastic tales enveloped all its space.

And the Neva, swelling now and then, roared at those fantastic tales and beat against the massive granite walls.

The creeping myriapod is terrible. Here, along the Nevskii, it has been running for centuries. But higher up, above the Nevskii—it's the seasons that do the running: springs, autumns, winters. There the sequence is changeable; but here—the sequence is unchanging in its springs, summers and winters; through springs, summers, winters the sequence is the same. And, as we know, a limit is set to periods of time; and—period follows upon period; after spring comes summer; autumn follows upon summer and passes over into winter; and in spring everything thaws. There is no such limit to the human myriapod; nothing takes its place; its segments may change, but it—is forever the same; somewhere over there, beyond the railway station, its head bends round; its tail protrudes into Morskaia; but along the Nevskii its segments, the legs that are its members, shuffle by—with no head, no tail, no consciousness, no thought; the myriapod creeps past as it has always crept; and as it has crept, so it will go on creeping.

Truly a scolopendra!

And a frightened metal steed has long been standing at the corner of the Anichkov Bridge; and a metal groom is hanging on to it: will the groom saddle the horse, or will the horse destroy the groom? This struggle has been going on for years, and—past them, hasten past!

Past them, hastening past: people on their own, couples, groups of four and couples upon couples—they blow their noses, cough, shuffle, gossiping and laughing, scattering into the moisture-laden space with their miscellany of voices a miscellany of words, detached from the sense that gave them birth: bowler hats, plumes, caps; caps, cockades and feathers; a tricorn, a top hat, a flat cap; an umbrella, a head-scarf, a feather.

Dionysus

But someone was talking to him!

Alexandr Ivanovich Dudkin dragged his thought out of the surging abundance again; the ambient absurdities had made a substantial mess of it; after immersion in the thought-collective it had become an absurdity itself; with great difficulty he focused it upon the words that were pattering into his ear: these were Nikolai Apollonovich's words; Nikolai Apollonovich had been assailing his ear with words for some time already; but a passing word, entering his ear like a piece of shrapnel, shattered the sense of the sentence; that was why Alexandr Ivanovich found it so hard to fathom what was being dinned into his eardrums; into those eardrums, vainly, lengthily and tiresomely, drumsticks were beating a tattoo: that was Nikolai Apollonovich, extricating himself from the porridge and prattling away at speed, ceaselessly.

"Do you understand," he kept repeating, "do you understand me, Alexandr Ivanovich … "

"Oh, yes, I understand."

And Alexandr Ivanovich tried to extract with his ear the sentences addressed to him: this was not all that easy, because a passing word would smash against his ear like a hail of stones:

"Yes, I do understand you … "

"There, in the tin-can," Nikolai Apollonovich kept insisting, "there was definitely life stirring: the clockwork mechanism was ticking away so strangely … "

At this Alexandr Ivanovich thought:

"What does he mean, tin-can, what tin-can is this? And what has any tin-can got to do with me?"

But as he listened more intently to what the senator's son kept repeating, he realised that he was talking about a bomb.

"No doubt life began to stir there when I activated it: it was just like that, lifeless … I turned the key; and it even started, yes, sobbing, I assure you, like a drunkard in his sleep when someone tries to wake him … "

"So you wound it up?"

"Yes, it started ticking … "

"The minute-hand?"

"It's on twenty-four hours."

"What did you do that for?"

"I had put the can on my desk and was looking at it, I kept looking at it: my fingers reached out to it of their own accord; and—just like that: they somehow turned the key by themselves … "

"What have you done?! Into the river with it, straight away!?!" Alexandr Ivanovich threw up his hands in unfeigned terror; his neck twitched.

"D'you understand, it pulled a face at me? … "

"The tin-can?"

"Altogether, an extraordinary variety of sensations took hold of me, changing constantly, while I was standing over it: an extraordinary variety ... The devil only knows what ... I've never experienced anything like it in my life, I have to admit ... I was overcome by revulsion—so much so, that the revulsion was tearing me apart ... All sorts of drivel came into my head and, I repeat—a terrible revulsion towards *it*, unbelievable, incomprehensible: towards the very form of the tin, towards the thought that maybe some time before it had had sardines floating in it (I can't bear the sight of them); my revulsion towards it grew, as though it were a huge, hard insect droning into my ears with its incomprehensible insect-prattle; do you understand—it had the gall to jangle away at me like that ... Eh? ... "

"Hm! ... "

"Revulsion, as though towards a huge insect with a shell that had a nauseating gleam like tin-plate; at one moment it seemed like an insect, and at another like untinned tableware ... Can you believe it— it tore me apart so, made me feel sick ... As though, well, as though I had ... swallowed it ... "

"Swallowed it? How horrible ... "

"Devil only knows what it was—swallowed it; do you understand what that means? It means I turned into a walking bomb on two legs with a ghastly ticking going on in my stomach."

"Not so loud, Nikolai Apollonovich—not so loud: people might hear us here!"

"They won't understand anything: it's quite impossible to understand ... What you have to do is keep it in your desk for a while and stand there and listen closely to the ticking ... In short, you'd have to go through all the same experiences yourself ... "

"You know," Alexandr Ivanovich now began to take an interest in his words, "I understand you: ticking ... You can perceive sound in different ways; if you listen closely to a sound, you'll find that it's all the same, yet not the same ... I once put the wind up a neurasthenic; during our conversation I started tapping on the table with my finger, meaningfully, you know, in time with the conversation; then he suddenly looked at me, went pale, fell silent, and asked: 'What's that you're doing?' And I said to him: 'Nothing,' and went on tapping on the table ... Can you believe it, he had a seizure: he was so offended that he stopped replying to my bow when we met in the street ... I understand that ... "

346

"No, no, no: it's impossible to understand … Something there—came up from below, came back to memory—some delirious sensations that were both familiar and unfamiliar … "

"Your childhood came back to you—didn't it?"

"It was as though a blindfold had been removed from all my sensations … Something was moving about above my head—you know? Hair standing on end: now I know what that means; only that's not it—it's not your hair, because you're standing there with the top of your head wide open. Hair standing on end—I came to understand that expression last night; and it's not your hair; my whole body was like hair standing on end: bristling with little hairs; my legs and arms and chest—all seemed to be made of some invisible animal hair that was being tickled with a straw; or like this, too: as though you had sat down in a cold bath full of Narzan mineral water and the carbon dioxide was bubbling all over your skin—tickling, pulsating, running up and down—faster and faster, so that if you keep quite still, then the throbbing, the pulses, the tickling turn into a powerful feeling, as though you are being torn to pieces, as though your limbs are being pulled apart in different directions: your heart is pulled out at the front, and at the back, like a stake out of a fence, your own spine is tugged out; you're dragged upwards by your hair; and dragged into the abyss by your legs … If you move—everything stands still, as though … "

"So in short, Nikolai Apollonovich, you were like Dionysus in his torment … But—joking aside: you're talking a completely different language now: I don't recognise you … It's not the language of Kant you're talking now … I've never heard this language from you before … "

"But I've already told you: a blindfold was removed—from all my sensations … Not the language of Kant—you're right about that … It couldn't be! … There—it's all different … "

"There, Nikolai Apollonovich, logic is passed through into the blood, there's a sensation of the brain in the blood—or deathly stagnation; but here you've been hit by a real shock in your life and the blood has rushed to your brain; that's why even in your words I can hear the throbbing of real blood … "

"I'm standing there, you know, right over it, and—can you believe it: it seems to me—now, what was I talking about?"

"You said it 'seemed' to you," Alexandr Ivanovich confirmed ...

"It seems to me—that I'm swelling up all over, I've been swollen up for a long time: maybe it's hundreds of years that I've been swelling; and there I am walking around, without noticing it—like some swollen freak ... That's really horrible."

"It's all your sensations ... "

"Tell me, I'm ... not ... "

Alexandr Ivanovich gave a sympathetic grin:

"On the contrary, you've shrunk: your cheeks are pinched, you've got rings under your eyes."

"I was standing there over it ... Only it wasn't me standing there—it wasn't me, it wasn't me, but ... a kind of, how shall I put it, giant with a huge idiotic head and a skull that hadn't grown together; and all the time—my body was pulsating; everywhere, all over my skin—pinpricks: shooting, piercing; and I could feel the jab clearly—at a distance of at least eight inches from my body—outside my body! ... Just imagine! ... Then another, a third: many, many jabs with a perfectly physical sensation—outside my body ... And those jabs, the throbbing, the pulsation—you have to understand this!—followed the contour of my own body—outside the confines of my body, outside my skin: my skin—was inside the sensations. What is that? Either I was turned inside out, with my skin on the inside, or my brain had jumped out?"

"You were simply beside yourself ... "

"It's all very well for you to say 'beside yourself'; 'beside yourself'—is something everyone says; that expression is simply an allegory, with no foundation in any physical sensations, but, at best, in the emotions. But what I felt was being *beside myself* in an entirely bodily sense, physiologically, if you like, and not emotionally at all ... It goes without saying that besides that I was also *beside myself* in your sense: that's to say I was shocked. But the main thing isn't that, it's that my sensory perceptions were spread around me, they suddenly expanded, were scattered into space: I was flying apart, like a bomb ... "

"Shhh! ... "

"Into pieces! ... "

"People might hear ... "

"Who was it standing there having these sensations—me, or not me? It was happening to me, in me, outside me ... Look what balderdash I'm talking ... "

"Do you remember, the other day, when I came to your house with the package, I asked you why am *I—I?* You didn't understand me at all then … "

"But now I understand everything: but this is—terrible, it's terrible … "

"It's not terrible, it's the genuine experience of Dionysus: not in words, not from books, of course … Dionysus dying … "

"It's just the devil only knows what!"

"Do calm down, Nikolai Apollonovich, you're awfully tired: and it's not surprising: going through so much in just one night … It's enough to knock out a much stronger man." Alexandr Ivanovich put his hand on his shoulder; the shoulder before him protruded at the level of his chest; and that shoulder was shaking; Alexandr Ivanovich now felt a pressing need to get rid of Nikolai Apollonovich, babbling away nervously in front of him, in order to reflect calmly and clearly on what had happened.

"I am calm, I'm perfectly calm; now, you know, I wouldn't even mind having a drink; I feel so much better, in such good spirits … I'm sure you can tell me for certain that the commission was a trick?"

Alexandr Ivanovich could not tell him that for certain; nevertheless Alexandr Ivanovich just blurted out, with an unusual fervour:

"I promise … "

Revelation

Finally he said goodbye.

Now he had to go striding away: striding and striding, striding again—till his brain was completely addled, to collapse on to a tavern table—think things through and drink vodka.

Alexandr Ivanovich remembered: the letter, the letter! He had been supposed to hand over the letter—on the instructions of *a certain person*: hand it over to Ableukhov.

How had he come to forget it all! He had taken the letter with him when he set off to see Ableukhov—with the package: but he had forgotten to hand the letter over; he had handed it over a little later—to Varvara Evgrafovna, who told him she was going to meet Ableukhov. That letter could turn out to have been the fatal letter.

No, surely not!

It wasn't that one; why, that one, the *fatal* one, had been handed to Ableukhov, by his own account, at a ball; and by some mask or other … A mask, a ball and—Varvara Evgrafovna.

No and no again!

Alexandr Ivanovich calmed down: that meant that *that other* letter could not be *this one*, which he had received from Lippanchenko and handed over to Solov'eva; so that he, Alexandr Ivanovich Dudkin, was not involved in this business; but most importantly: the terrible instruction could not have come from *that person*; that was the main trump in his hands: a trump which beat the madness and his crazy suspicions (these suspicions had passed through his head again when he had promised, had given a guarantee on behalf of the party—on behalf of Lippanchenko, because Lippanchenko was his organ of communication with the party); if it were not for this trump he held in his hands now, if, that is, the letter came from the party, from Lippanchenko, then the *person*, Lippanchenko, would be a suspicious *person*, and he, Alexandr Ivanovich Dudkin, would turn out to be mixed up with a suspicious character.

That way madness lies.

He had just worked all this out and was on the point of crossing the stream of carriages in order to jump on to a horse-tram running the other way (there were no electric trams yet, of course), when a voice called him:

"Alexandr Ivanovich, wait … One moment … "

Turning round he saw that Nikolai Apollonovich, whom he had left only a moment earlier, was running after him through the crowd, breathless—shaking all over and covered in sweat; with a feverish gleam in his eyes he was waving his cane over the heads of the astonished passers-by …

"Just a moment … "

Good Lord above!

"Wait: it's hard for me, Alexandr Ivanovich, to part from you … There's just one other thing I want to say to you … " and he took him by the arm and led him away to the nearest shop window.

"It was also revealed to me … This revelation, or whatever—there, over the tin can? … "

"Listen, Nikolai Apollonovich, I really must go; it's time to see about your business … "

"Yes, yes, yes: I'll be very quick ... just a second, a fraction of a second ... "

"Well, go on then: I'm listening ... "

Now Nikolai Apollonovich's outward appearance displayed nothing short of inspiration; in his joy he had evidently forgotten that not everything was yet unravelled for him, and—above all: *the tin was still ticking, tirelessly overcoming twenty-four hours.*

"It was like a revelation that I was growing; I was growing, you know, into infinity, overcoming space; I assure you that it was quite real: all other objects were growing with me; the room, and—the view over the Neva, and—the spire of the Peter and Paul Cathedral: everything was growing, expanding; and the growth was coming to an end (there was simply nowhere left, nothing to grow into); and in that which was coming to an end, in that end, that completion— it seemed to me there was another beginning: the beyond, or something ... It was something utterly absurd, highly unpleasant and preposterous—preposterous, that was the main thing; preposterous, perhaps, because I don't have any organ that can make sense of this meaning beyond meaning, so to speak; in the place of sense organs I just had a feeling of—'zero'; I had a sensation of something that wasn't zero and wasn't one, but—something less than one. All the absurdity may have come from the fact that this sensation was a sensation of 'zero minus something', maybe five, for example."

"Listen," Alexandr Ivanovich interrupted him, "you'd do better to tell me this: I suppose you received that letter through Varvara Evgrafovna Solov'eva? ... "

"The letter ... "

"Not that one, not the *note*: the letter that came via Varvara Evgrafovna ... "

"Oh, you mean those verses signed *'An ardent soul'*?"

"That I really don't know: in short, the one that came via Varvara Evgrafovna ... "

"I got it, I got it ... No I'm telling you that this 'zero minus something' ... What is it?"

Good Lord, on and on he goes! ...

"You ought to read the *Apocalypse* ... "

"I've heard you reproach me before for not knowing the *Apocalypse*; now I will read it, I really will; now that you have reassured me about … *all that,* I feel an interest awakening in me for your circle of reading; I'll settle down at home, you know, I'll sip bromide and read the *Apocalypse*; I have an immense interest in it: there's something left from last night: everything's the same—and yet different … Look at that shop window, for instance … There are reflections in it: there's a man in a bowler hat going by—look … he's gone … There are you and me, can you see? And it's all—somehow strange … "

"Somehow strange," Alexandr Ivanovich nodded in assent: Lord above, as far as the realm of the 'somehow strange' was concerned, he was quite an expert.

"Or again: objects … The devil knows what they are in fact: they're the same—and yet different … I realised that with the tin can: a tin can like any other; but no, no: it's not a tin can, but … "

"Shh"

"A tin can of terrible import!"

"You go and throw that tin can into the Neva straight away; and everything will right itself; everything will return to its proper place … "

"It won't return, it can't, that isn't going to happen … "

He gazed round miserably at the passing couples; he sighed miserably, because he knew: it wouldn't return, it couldn't, that wasn't going to happen—ever, ever!

Alexandr Ivanovich was surprised at the flood of loquacity spilling from Ableukhov's lips; in truth, he didn't know what to do with that loquacity: whether to calm it, to support it, or on the contrary—to break the conversation off (Ableukhov's company was weighing heavily upon him).

"It's just to you, Nikolai Apollonovich, that your sensations seem strange; it's just that up till now you've been poring over Kant in an unventilated room; you've been hit by a squall—and you've started noticing things in yourself: you've started listening to the squall; and you have heard yourself in it … Your state of mind has been variously described; it is the subject of observation, study … "

"Where, though, where?"

"In fiction, in poetry, in psychiatry, in studies of the occult."

Alexandr Ivanovich smiled unintentionally at such glaring ignorance (from his point of view) on the part of this scholar with such a highly developed intellect, and, after smiling, he continued earnestly:

"A psychiatrist … "

"?"

"Would call … "

"Yes-yes-yes … "

"All of this … "

"That everything's 'the same, but different'?"

"Well, the same but different—call it that if you like—for him the most usual term is: pseudohallucination … "

"?"

"That is to say a kind of symbolic sensation, a sensation that doesn't correspond to the stimulus."

"So what of it: to say that is tantamount to saying nothing at all! … "

"Yes, you're right … "

"No, that doesn't satisfy me … "

"Of course: a modernist would call that sensation— the sensation of the abyss, that is, for this symbolic sensation that is not normally experienced he would try to find a corresponding image."

"Well that's just an allegory."

"Don't confuse allegory with symbol: an allegory is a symbol that has become a standard cliché; for example, the ordinary understanding of your 'beside yourself': but a symbol is an appeal to what you experienced there—sitting over the tin can; an invitation to experience artificially something that was experienced like that … But a more suitable term would be another one: the pulsation of the elemental body. That is precisely how you experienced yourself; under the influence of the shock your elemental body was convulsed, quite literally, for a moment it became detached, unstuck from your physical body, and so you experienced everything that you experienced there: hackneyed verbal combinations like 'bottomless pit' or 'beside yourself' acquired depth, became for you a living truth, a symbol; the experience of the elemental body, according to the teachings of certain mystical schools, changes verbal meanings and allegories into real meanings, symbols; since the works of mystics are full of symbols like that, I really advise you now, after what you've experienced, to read those mystics … "

"I told you I would: and I will … "

"And as for what has happened to you I can just add one thing: this kind of sensation will be your first experience beyond the grave, as

Plato tells us, referring in evidence to the assertions of Bacchantes … There are schools of experience where sensations of that kind are consciously provoked—don't you believe me? There are: I can tell you this with confidence because my only friend, the one person I am close to, is there, in those schools; by working on your nightmare these schools of experience can turn it into a harmonious pattern, by studying the rhythms, the movements, the pulsations, and drawing all the sobriety of consciousness into the experience of expansion, for example … However, what are we standing here for: we've got lost in our chatter … It's essential you go home straight away, and … into the river with that tin can; and stay there, stay there: don't go anywhere— don't put a foot outside (you're probably being followed); so just sit there at home, read the *Apocalypse*, take bromide: you're terribly overwrought … However, better without bromide: bromide dulls the consciousness; anyone who abuses bromide becomes incapable of anything … Well, it's time I was off—to see to your business."

Alexandr Ivanovich shook Ableukhov's hand and suddenly slipped away from him into the black torrent of bowler hats, turned round from that torrent and from there cried out once more:

"And into the river with that tin!"

His shoulder became attached to other shoulders: he was swiftly borne away by the headless myriapod.

Nikolai Apollonovich shuddered: life was rasping away in the tin can; the clockwork mechanism was working even now; quickly back home, as quickly as possible; he would hire a cab immediately; and as soon as he got back home he would pop it into his side pocket; and—into the Neva with it!

Once again Nikolai Apollonovich began to feel that he was expanding; at the same time he felt that it was beginning to drizzle.

The caryatid

Over there, on the opposite side, the black of a crossroads could be seen; and there was a street there; the caryatid at an entrance loured there stonily.

The *Establishment* rose up there: the *Establishment* where Apollon Apollonovich Ableukhov held sway.

There is a limit to autumn; and to winter there is a limit too: periods of time themselves pass by in cycles. And over all these cycles the bearded caryatid at the entrance loured; its stone hoof was thrust dizzyingly into the wall: it seemed that it was all about to crumble and collapse piecemeal on to the street.

But—it is not collapsing.

What it sees above its head is as inconstant, as inexplicable, as incoherent as life itself: clouds float there; fleecy white clouds wind about amidst the inexplicable; or else—a shower sprinkles down; sprinkles down, just as it does now: as it did yesterday, and the day before.

But what it sees beneath its feet is as changeless as the caryatid itself: the flow of the human myriapod across the illuminated pavement is changeless; or, as now—in the dark and damp; the rustle of the passing feet is deathly; and the faces are eternally green; no, you cannot tell from them that the roar of great events is in the air.

Observing the procession of bowler hats you would never say that the roar of great events was in the air, for instance, in the little town of Ak-Tiuk, where a worker at the station, who had fallen out with a railway policeman, appropriated the policeman's banknote and introduced it into his stomach by way of his oral aperture, for which reason an emetic was also introduced into that same stomach—by the railway doctor; observing the procession of bowler hats, no one would ever say that in the theatre at Kutais the audience had cried out: "Citizens! ... " No one would have said that in Tiflis a local constable had discovered a bomb-factory, that the library in Odessa had closed or that in ten Russian universities a meeting of many thousands was taking place—on the same day, at the same time; nobody could have said that at precisely this time thousands of dedicated members of the Bund had come swarming to a gathering, that the men of Perm were showing what they were made of and that at this very moment, surrounded by Cossacks, the Revel iron-foundry had started unfurling its red banners.

Observing the procession of bowler hats, no one could have said that new life was gushing forth, that Potapenko was putting the finishing touches to a play by that title, or that a strike had already begun on the Moscow-Kazan railway; windows were being smashed, warehouses were being broken into, and work was stopping on the

Kursk, Vindavsk, Nizhnii Novgorod and Murom railway lines; and wagons in their hundreds of thousands, struck by paralysis, were coming to a halt in spaces far and near; communications were on the point of rigor mortis. Observing the procession of bowler hats, no one could have said that the roar of great events was in the air in Petersburg, that the typesetters in almost all the printworks, having elected delegates, had swarmed together; and that factories were on strike: the ship-building yards, the Alexandrov factory, and so on; or that the suburbs of Petersburg were alive with Manchurian hats; observing the procession of bowler hats, no one could have said that those processing were the same, but not the same; that they were not simply striding along, but concealing within them, as they strode, an alarm, a sense that their heads were idiotic heads whose skull had not grown together, but had been cracked open by a sabre, or simply smashed with a wooden stake; if you put your ear to the ground, you would hear someone's gentle whisper: the whisper of incessant revolver fire—from Arkhangelsk to Colchis and from Libava to Blagoveshchensk.

But the circulation was not disrupted: unvaried, sedate and deathly, the bowler hats still flowed by under the feet of the caryatid.

The grey caryatid bent down to look beneath its feet: at ever the same crowd; there is no limit to the contempt in the old stone of its eyes; no limit to the tedium; no limit to the despair.

And, oh, grant me strength!

The muscular arms on those elbows thrusting high above the stone head would straighten; and the chiselled skull would jerk up wildly; the mouth would fly open in an echoing roar, a long drawn-out and desperate roar; you would say: "That is the roar of a tempest" (that was how the thousands of city thugs in their black caps roared during pogroms): the street would be swathed in steam, as though from a locomotive's hooter; the cornice of a balcony, torn from the wall, would soar up over the street; and would fall asunder into sturdy, thunderously clattering stones (and it would not be long before those stones were used to smash the windows of *zemstvo* offices and provincial *zemstvo* assemblies); this ancient sculpture would collapse on to the street in a hail of stones, describing in the air a rushing, blinding arc; and in blood-stained fragments it would settle on the frightened bowler hats that passed here—deathly, unvaried, sedate ...

On this grey Petersburg day a heavy, sumptuous door was flung open: a grey, clean-shaven servant with gold braid on his lapels rushed from the entrance-hall to make signs to the coachman; horses hurtled to the entrance, pulling a lacquered carriage; the grey, clean-shaven servant lost his wits and stood to attention, as Apollon Apollonovich Ableukhov, round-shouldered, bent, unshaven, his face unhealthily swollen and his bottom lip drooping, touched the brim of his top hat (the colour of a raven's wing) with his gloves (the colour of a raven's wing).

Apollon Apollonovich Ableukhov cast a momentary glance, full of indifference, at the upright servant, at the carriage, at the coachman, at the great black bridge, at the indifferent expanse of the Neva, where the misty, many-chimneyed distance was so dimly outlined and where the indistinct Vasilevskii Island rose ashen with its hundreds of thousands of strikers.

The upright servant slammed the carriage door, on which an ancient aristocratic coat of arms was emblazoned: a unicorn, impaling a knight; the carriage sped off into the grimy mist—past the dully looming black cathedral of St Isaac, past the equestrian statue of Emperor Nikolai—on to the Nevskii, where a crowd was swarming, where with a faint whistling sound a flailing sheet of red calico, straining free of its wooden pole, made wave-crests as it rippled in the air, fluttering and tearing; the black contour of the carriage, the outline of the servant's tricorn hat and the tails of his greatcoat flapping in the air suddenly sliced into a black, unkempt mass, where Manchurian hats, uniform caps, workmen's caps, all swarming together, thundered out in raucous singing straight into the carriage windows.

The carriage came to a halt in the crowd.

Get off me, Tom

"*Mais j'espère* ... "

"You are hoping?"

"*Mais j'espère que oui,*" the speech of a foreigner tinkled through the door.

357

Alexandr Ivanovich's steps rang with intentional firmness on the planks of the terrace; Alexandr Ivanovich did not like to overhear others' conversations. The door leading into the rooms was half-open.

It was turning dark: turning blue.

They did not hear his steps. Alexandr Ivanovich Dudkin decided not to overhear anything; and so he stepped over the threshold.

There was a heavy scent in the room; a mixture of perfume with some pungent acid: medicine of some sort.

Zoia Zakharovna Fleisch was as welcoming as ever. She was endeavouring to get a visiting foreigner to take a seat; the foreigner was resisting.

It was turning dark: turning blue.

"Oh, I am so glad to see you ... Very, very glad to see you: wipe your feet, take your coat off ... "

But no reciprocal gladness ensued; Alexandr Ivanovich shook Zoia's hand.

"I do hope you have received a good impression of Russia ... Don't you think ... " she turned to the sunburnt foreigner. "What extraordinary élan?"

And the Frenchman tinkled dryly:

"*Mais j'espère ...* "

Wiping her plump fingers, Zoia Zakharovna Fleisch directed her gentle, slightly perplexed gaze at the Frenchman and at Alexandr Ivanovich in turn; she had prominent eyes: they protruded from their sockets. Zoia Zakharovna seemed about forty; Zoia Zakharovna was a brunette with a large head; her strong cheeks were enamelled; powder was flaking from her cheeks.

"He isn't back yet ... I suppose it's him you want?" she asked Alexandr Ivanovich apropos of nothing; in her cursory question a hidden anxiety was revealed: perhaps there was hostility concealed there; or maybe, even hatred; but the anxiety, hostility and hatred were courteously covered up: a smile and a look; just as all the revolting filth of unventilated sweet factories is hidden in the sticky sugary sweets as they are sold.

"Well, never mind, I'll wait for him."

Alexandr Ivanovich bowed to the Frenchman; he reached out for a pear (there was a bowl of Duchess pears standing on the table); Zoia

Zakharovna Fleisch immediately moved the bowl away from Alexandr Ivanovich: Alexandr Ivanovich had such a weakness for pears.

Pears were all very well, but they were not what made the real impression.

The real impression came from a voice: a voice that had struck up somewhere; it was an overstrained voice, impossibly strident and sweet; and at the same time: the voice had an outrageous accent. At the dawn of the twentieth century it is out of the question to sing like that; it's even somehow shameless; in Europe they don't sing like that. It occurred to Alexandr Ivanovich that the singer was a sensual, black-haired man; dark-haired, for certain; he had a sunken chest, collapsed between his shoulder-blades, and the eyes of an absolute cockroach; he might be consumptive; and he was probably a southerner: from Odessa or even a Bulgarian from Varna (that was probably the most likely); he went round in not entirely salubrious underwear; he had a bee in his bonnet, and hated the countryside. As he built up his ideas about the invisible performer of the song, Alexandr Ivanovich reached out again for a pear.

Meanwhile Zoia Zakharovna Fleisch did not for one moment let go of the Frenchman:

"Yes, yes, yes: we are experiencing events of historical significance ... Such vigour and youthfulness everywhere ... The historian of the future will write ... Don't you believe it? Go to the meetings ... You'll hear such fervent effusions of feeling, just look: everywhere—such enthusiasm."

But the Frenchman had no wish to sustain the conversation.

"Pardon, madame, monsieur viendra-t-il bientôt?"

In order not to be a witness of this distasteful conversation, which for some reason demeaned his national pride, Alexandr Ivanovich went right up to the window and almost tripped over a shaggy St Bernard, gnawing a bone on the floor.

The cottage looked out on to the sea: outside it was turning dark, turning blue.

The eye of a lighthouse revolved; the light flashed: 'one-two-three'—and was extinguished; out there the dark raincoat of a distant pedestrian flapped in the wind; even further away wave-crests curled; lights on the shore were scattered like luminous grains; the many-eyed shoreline bristled with reeds; in the distance a siren moaned.

What a wind!

"Here's an ashtray … "

The ashtray was set down under Alexandr Ivanovich's nose: but Alexandr Ivanovich was quick to take offence, and so he stubbed his cigarette end in the flower-vase: he stubbed it there as a sign of protest.

"Who is it singing there?"

Zoia Zakharovna made a gesture which clearly signified that Alexandr Ivanovich was behind the times: unpardonably behind the times.

"What? Don't you know? … No, of course, you don't know … Well, let me tell you: it's Shishnarfiev … that's what comes of living like a hermit … Shishnarfiev—he's really become one of us … "

"I've heard the name somewhere … "

"Shishnarfiev is incredibly artistic … "

Zoia Zakharovna uttered this sentence with a decisive mien—such a mien, as though he, Alexandr Ivanovich, had long since placed an unwarranted question mark over the artistic aptitude of the universally renowned and congenial possessor of that name. But Alexandr Ivanovich had no intention of disputing the talents of that gentleman.

He merely asked:

"An Armenian? Bulgarian? Georgian?"

"No, no … "

"A Croatian? Persian?"

"A Persian from Shemakha, who very nearly became a victim of the massacre in Isfahan … "

"One of the Young Persians?"

"Of course … Didn't you know? … Shame on you … "

A glance of pity, of condescension in his direction, and—Zoia Zakharovna Fleisch turned to the Frenchman. Alexandr Ivanovich naturally did not listen to their conversation: he listened to the hopelessly cracked tenor; the activist of the Young Persia movement was singing a passionate gypsy romance and casting gloom over his audience. Incidentally, Alexandr Ivanovich reflected in passing that the features of Zoia Fleisch's face were in all honesty taken from the faces of the most varied beauties: the nose—from one, the mouth—from another, the ears—from a third beauty.

Taken all together they were distinctly irritating. And Zoia Zakharovna seemed to be compiled from many beautiful women, without herself being beautiful in the least—truly! But her most essential feature was that she belonged to the category known as the dark-eyed Eastern beauty.

All the same Zoia Zakharovna's pretentious chatter pursued Alexandr Ivanovich and caught him up:

"Are you here about money?"

Silence.

"Money from abroad—will be necessary ... "

An impatient movement of the elbow.

"Your editor had better not come now that T T's organisation has been broken up ... "

But the Frenchman—said not a word.

"Because documents have been found."

If Alexandr Ivanovich had been able to think about the cause, the news that T T had been broken up might (this is our comment) have shaken him to the core; but he was listening to the Young Persia activist warbling his romance. The Frenchman, meanwhile, his patience exhausted by Zoia Zakharovna's insistent attentions, cut her short:

"*Je serai bien triste d'avoir manqué l'occasion de parler à monsieur.*"

"Never mind: talk to me ... "

"*Excusez, dans certains cas je préfère parler personellement ... *"

Outside the window a bush was thrashing about.

Through the branches of the bush the spume of the waves could be seen and a sailboat, crepuscular and blue, bobbing up and down; with its sharp-winged sails it cut a thin slice from the darkness; the blue-tinged night slowly established itself on the surface of the sail.

It seemed the sail was being altogether extinguished.

Just then a cab drew up to the little garden; the body of an overweight man, obviously short of breath, toppled unhurriedly out of the carriage; his ungainly hand, burdened by half-a-dozen parcels that dangled uneasily on strings, began slowly to fiddle with a leather purse; one of the parcels, held clumsily under his arm, fell into a puddle; tearing the paper as they fell, a pile of Antonov apples rolled in the mud.

The gentleman fussed about over the puddle, gathering up the apples; his overcoat fell open; he was breathing with obvious difficulty; as he closed the gate, he all but shed his purchases again.

The gentleman approached the cottage along the yellow garden path between two rows of bushes, bending in the wind; a familiar oppressive atmosphere spread all round; his sinister head, covered by a hat with ear-flaps, was drooping acutely on to his chest; his deep-set eyes on this occasion were not wandering at all (as they did before any intensive scrutiny); the deep-set eyes gazed wearily at the window.

Alexandr Ivanovich was able to glimpse in those eyes (can you imagine!) a certain special, personal joy, mixed with tiredness and sadness—a purely animal joy at the prospect of getting warmed through, having a sound sleep and a good supper after so many exertions. Like a bloodthirsty beast: returning to its lair, a bloodthirsty beast appears harmless and domesticated, displaying a mildness of which even it is capable; this beast then sniffs amicably at its mate; and licks its whimpering cubs.

Could this be *that person?*

Yes: this was the *person in question;* and on this occasion the *person* was not terrible; his mien was quite prosaic; but the *person* it was.

"Here he is!"

"*Enfin* ... "

"Lippanchenko! ... "

"Good evening ... "

The yellow St Bernard hurled itself across the room with a joyful roar and leapt up to place its shaggy paws right on the *person's* chest.

"Get off me, Tom! ... "

The *person* did not even have time to notice his uninvited guests, so busy was he desperately defending his shopping from the shaggy St Bernard; on his broad, flat, square face was imprinted a mixture of humour and helpless anger; even something childlike slipped through:

"He's licked me all over again."

And, turning helplessly away from Tom, the *person* shouted:

"Zoia Zakharovna, get him off me ... "

But the broad canine tongue disrespectfully licked the tip of the *person's* nose; the *person* cried out in a penetrating voice—cried out helplessly (yet at the same time, can you imagine, he was smiling) ...

"Tom-mie!"

But noticing that he had guests, and that the guests were waiting, letting out little impatient laughs at this domestic idyll, the *person* stopped laughing and blurted out with no semblance of politeness:

"Excuse me, excuse me! Straight away: just let me … "

And his drooping lip gave an offended twitch; on his lip was written:

"Even here there's no peace … "

The *person* hurried into the corner; he stamped around a bit there—in the corner: he was in no hurry to take off his galoshes, which were new and somewhat tight; for a long time he stood there in the corner, delaying removing his coat and digging around in his well-filled pocket (as though he had a twelve-shot revolver concealed there); finally his hand emerged from the pocket—with a child's doll, a tumbler.

He threw this doll on to the table.

"This is for Akulina's Manka … "

At this, it must be admitted, the visitors' mouths fell open.

Afterwards, wiping his numbed hands, he turned to the Frenchman with a kind of timid suspiciousness:

"Would you, please … This way … this way."

And to Dudkin he snapped:

"You'll have to wait … "

Frontal bones

"Zoia Zakharovna … "

"Yes?"

"Shifnarfiev—I understand: a Young Persia activist, a fiery artistic nature; but—where does the Frenchman come in?"

"Knowing too much makes you age too soon," said Zoia Zakharovna in an un-Russian way, and her abundant bosom began to heave under her tightly fastened bodice; a spray hissed in her hand.

A heavy aroma made itself felt in the room: a smell of perfume mixed with that of denture preparation (anyone who has sat in a dentist's surgery is certain to be familiar with this smell—not a pleasant smell).

Zoia Zakharovna moved closer to Alexandr Ivanovich.

363

"But you keep to yourself … like a hermit … "

Alexandr Ivanovich compressed his lips a little crookedly:

"Your better half saw to that long ago … "

"?"

"If it isn't me who's a hermit, it makes no difference: someone has to be the hermit … "

The direction of this conversation was evidently not to Zoia Zakharovna's liking, and the spray in her hand began its nervous hissing again; Alexandr Ivanovich gave a disagreeable smile, and— set things back on course.

"In any case: distraction doesn't suit me."

Zoia Zakharovna accepted this new train of thought; and hastened to make a witticism:

"That's why you're so distracted: you've scattered ash all over my tablecloth, haven't you?"

"I'm sorry … "

"Never mind: here's an ashtray … "

Alexandr Ivanovich reached out again for a pear; having performed this action, Alexandr Ivanovich said to himself in annoyance:

"What a skinflint … "

He had noticed that the bowl of Duchess pears (he had such a weakness for Duchess pears) was not there any more.

"What do you want? Here's the ashtray … "

"I know: I was reaching for a pear … "

Zoia Zakharovna did not offer him the pears.

The doors into the further room were not fully closed: he gazed avidly, insatiably, through the half-open door; he could see two seated silhouettes there. The Frenchman was talking nineteen to the dozen; and he seemed to be tinkling; the *person* was emitting dull rumbling sounds, and interrupting the Frenchman; during the conversation he kept impatiently grasping at various writing implements—first this one, then that; and was scratching the back of his head with his arm at a strange angle; evidently the *person* was alarmed in earnest by the Frenchman's message; Alexandr Ivanovich noted a gesture of pure self-defence.

"*Bu-bu-bu* … "

That was what it sounded like.

The St Bernard was leaning its slobbering muzzle on the *person's* checked knee; and the *person* was absent-mindedly stroking its coat. At this point Alexandr Ivanovich's observations were interrupted: interrupted by Zoia Zakharovna.

"Why have you stopped coming to see us?"

He gave an absent-minded glance at her grinning mouth: he glanced, and then commented:

"No reason in particular: you said yourself—I'm a hermit … "

The gold of her filling gleamed in reply:

"Don't try to wriggle out of it."

"I'm not … "

"You've simply taken offence at him … "

"What an idea … " Alexandr Ivanovich tried to object, but broke off his attempt at justification: it had turned out unconvincing.

"You've simply taken offence at him. Everyone does. *Lippanchenko's* mixed up in this too … That *Lippanchenko*! … Spoiling his reputation … You have to understand: *Lippanchenko* is a necessary, assumed role … Without *Lippanchenko* he would have been caught long ago … He's covering for all of us with this *Lippanchenko* … But everyone believes in *Lippanchenko* … "

Some creatures have an unfortunate quality: bad breath … Alexandr Ivanovich moved away.

"Everyone takes offence at him … But tell me," Zoia Zakharovna seized the spray, "where would you find another worker like him? … Eh? Where would you find one? … Who would be willing, you tell me, to forego all natural feelings like him and just be *Lippanchenko*— through and through … "

Alexandr Ivanovich thought that *that person* was rather too good at being *Lippanchenko*: but he chose not to object.

"I assure you … "

But she interrupted him:

"You ought to be ashamed of yourself, leaving him like that, hiding away like that, concealing yourself; Nicky suffers, you know; to break off all intimate links … "

Alexandr Ivanovich recalled with astonishment that it was *that person* who was called Nicky: how many months was it, honestly, since he had remembered that?

"Well, and what if he does sometimes drink too much, and gets rowdy; and—well, gets carried away … Why, the best people have drunk themselves silly and gone in for debauchery ... Because they wanted to. But Nicky does it just to distract attention—as *Lippanchenko*: it's for safety's sake, for publicity, under the eyes of the police, for the good of the cause that he's destroying himself."

Alexandr Ivanovich gave an involuntary grin, but caught an angry, distrustful gaze fixed upon him:

"What ... "

And he reacted quickly:

"No ... I didn't mean ... "

"That's the most terrible sacrifice, you know ... Believe me, he's in danger from lots of things; Nicky will bring himself to an early grave with these frequent, forced drinking bouts and all this debauchery, which is obligatory in his position ... "

Alexandr Ivanovich knew that Zoia Zakharovna suspected him of spending too much time with Lippanchenko in taverns, and teaching Lippanchenko ... lots of things ...

"All this may end badly, you know ... "

What a life: here—it might end badly; he, Alexandr Ivanovich, was slowly going out of his mind. Nikolai Apollonovich was crushed by difficult circumstances; something damaging had settled in their souls; it wasn't a matter of the police, or of arbitrary force, or of danger, but a rottenness in the soul; was it permissible to set out upon the great cause of the people without first being cleansed? He recalled: "With the fear of God and with faith go forward." But they had gone forward without any fear. And did they have faith? Going forward like that, they had gone beyond, they had transgressed a law of the soul: they had become transgressors, not in the ordinary sense, of course ... but in another.

All the same they had transgressed.

"Remember Helsingfors and our boat trip ... " there was unfeigned sadness in Zoia Zakharovna's voice. "And then: all those rumours ... "

"What rumours?"

His interest was awoken, he shuddered.

"The rumours about Nicky! ... Do you think he doesn't suspect, doesn't suffer from it, doesn't cry out at night," (Alexandr Ivanovich made a point of remembering that he *cries out at night*)—"the way they talk about him after so much. And—no gratitude, no awareness that the man has sacrificed everything ... He knows it all, he keeps quiet, suffers inwardly ... That's why he's so gloomy ... He doesn't know how to dissemble. He always has a nasty look," something almost like tears could be heard in Zoia Zakharovna's voice, "he has a nasty look … with that … unfortunate appearance. Believe me: he's just a child, a child … "

"A child?"

"Does that surprise you?"

"No," he hesitated, "only, you know, it's a bit strange to hear that, my impression of Nikolai Stepanovich somehow doesn't fit … "

"A real child! Look here: a doll—a tumbler," she pointed with her hand at the doll, her bracelet glittering … "You will go away in a moment: you'll tell him a load of home truths, and he—he! … "

"?"

"He'll sit the cook's little daughter on his knee and play dolls with her … Do you see? And they accuse him of double-dealing … Good Lord, he even plays at soldiers! … "

"Does he really!"

"Lead soldiers. he buys Persians, sends for boxes of them from Nuremberg … Only—that's a secret … That's what he's like! … But," her eyebrows made a sharp movement, "but with his child's quick temper he's capable of anything."

Alexandr Ivanovich became more and more convinced from her words that *that person* was compromised in earnest; that was something he hadn't known; he now took full note of all these hints about *something*, as his gaze drifted to where they were sitting …

The head with its narrow forehead was drooping sharply on to his chest; the deep-set, inquisitorial, drilling eyes were buried in their sockets, hopping about from object to object: the lip trembled slightly and sucked the air. There was a lot in that face: the face confronted Dudkin with insurmountable revulsion, as it formed itself into that same strange whole, carried away by his memory to his attic, where it would pace around there at night, rumble—drill, suck, hop about and squeeze from itself inexpressible meanings that had no existence anywhere.

Now he looked intently at those oppressive features which nature itself had built so heavily.

That frontal bone …

—That frontal bone protruded outwards in a single concentrated effort—to understand: come what may, at any price—to understand, or … to burst into smithereens. The frontal bone betrayed no intelligence, or frenzy, or treachery; simply effort—without thought, without feeling: to understand ... And the frontal bones were unable to understand; the forehead was pitiful: narrow, with diagonal furrows; it seemed to be weeping.

The little eyes, drilling inquisitorially ...

—The little eyes, drilling inquisitorially (if only the eyelids were raised!)—turned into nothing more than ... just ... little eyes.

And they were sad.

And the lip that sucked at the air was reminiscent—it was, truly!—of the lips of an unweaned eighteen-month-old child (only there was no nipple); if a real nipple were inserted into those lips, then it would not be surprising that the lips kept sucking; without a nipple, though, this gesture gave the face a very nasty tinge.

And on top of that: he played at soldiers!

So a careful analysis of this monstrous head revealed only one thing: the head was that of a premature baby; someone's feeble brain had been prematurely encased in layers of fat and bone; at the same time as the frontal bone protruded outwards to excess in the arcs above the eyebrows (have a look at a gorilla's skull), so beneath that bone a distasteful process was maybe taking place that is known in the vulgar parlance as softening of the brain.

This combination of inner feebleness with the obstinacy of a rhinoceros—could it be this combination that had created Alexandr Ivanovich's chimera, a chimera that grew with every night: on a patch of the dark-yellow wallpaper it grinned like a real Mongol.

Such were his thoughts; and in his ears the words droned on:

"A tumbler ... Cries out at night ... Sends for boxes from Nuremberg ... A real child ... "

And to this was added his own:

"Good at smashing heads together ... Something of the vampire ... Gives himself over to debauchery ... And—dragging us to our doom ... "

And again the words droned on:

"A child ... "

But they droned only in his ears: Zoia Zakharovna had already left the room.

A bad business ...

A funny thing!

Up till now in his attitude to Alexandr Ivanovich the behaviour of *a certain person* had been of an exclusively obliging nature, insistently so; for many months, on many occasions, in many ways *that person* had woven his pattern of flattery around Alexandr Ivanovich; he wanted to believe that flattery.

And he did believe it.

He felt revulsion towards the *person*; he felt a physiological aversion to him; more than that: all these recent days Alexandr Ivanovich had been avoiding the *person*, as he was experiencing a tormenting crisis of disillusionment with everything. But the *person* kept catching up with him everywhere; often he would mockingly throw out excessively frank challenges to him; the *person* received these challenges stoically—with cynical laughter, and if he had asked the *person* what that laughter meant, the *person* would have answered:

"That's addressed to you."

But he knew that the *person* was laughing at their common cause.

He kept telling the *person* that their party's programme was untenable, abstract, blind; and the *person*—agreed; he knew, though, that the *person* had taken part in the formulation of the programme; if he had asked whether there was not some provocation mixed up in the programme, the *person* would have replied:

"No, no: audacity ... "

In the end he had tried to impress him with his mystical creed, his assertion that Society, Revolution—were not categories of the reason, but divine Hypostases of the universe; the *person* had nothing against mysticism: he listened attentively; and— even tried to understand.

But was unable to understand.

Only—only: the *person* stood there before him; he accepted all his protests and all his extreme conclusions with submissive silence; he patted him on the shoulder and dragged him off to the tavern; there, at the table, they downed cognac; sometimes, to the accompaniment of the machine's tambourines the *person* would say to him:

"What of it? What am I: I'm nothing ... I'm nothing more than a submarine; you are our battleship, a large vessel needs a deep draught ... "

Nevertheless he had driven him up into the attic: and having done so, he hid him there; the battleship stood at the wharf without crew, without cannons; the only draughts Alexandr Ivanovich had seen these last few weeks were draughts of cognac in their trips from tavern to tavern; it could be said that in these weeks of protest the *person* had turned Alexandr Ivanovich into a drunkard.

He greeted him hospitably; from all their previous talks he had been left with one indubitable impression: if Alexandr Ivanovich had suddenly needed some serious help, the *person* would have been bound to provide it; all this was merely implied, of course; but Alexandr Ivanovich was afraid to ask for any help, any service, for himself.

It was only today that the occasion had arisen.

He had given Ableukhov his word that he would sort it out; and sort it out he would: with the help, of course, of the *person*. This fatal concatenation of circumstances had thrown Ableukhov quite simply into some kind of abracadabra; he would tell the *person* about the abracadabra, and the *person*, he was sure, would know how to sort it all out.

His appearance here was brought about solely by the fact that he had given Ableukhov his word; and now—what do you make of this?

The *person's* tone towards him had changed in an offensive way; he had noticed that on the *person's* first appearance at the cottage; the *person's* tone had become unrecognisable—unpleasant, offensive, strained (the kind of tone in which the heads of departments receive petitioners, or newspaper editors receive news reporters, gatherers of information about fires and thefts; and that is how the chairman of the governors speaks to an applicant for a teaching post in … Solvychegodsk, or Sarepta …).

So there now—what do you make of this? …

And so: after his conversation with the Frenchman (the Frenchman had now departed) the *person*, contrary to his usual manner with Alexandr Ivanovich, did not come out of his study, but went on sitting there—at his desk; and it made an insulting impression: as though he, Alexandr Ivanovich, wasn't there at all; as though he wasn't a close acquaintance, but—devil only knows what—an unknown petitioner, with all the time in the world at his disposal. Alexandr Ivanovich Dudkin was, after all, the Fugitive; his party alias

370

resounded throughout Russia and abroad; and, apart from that: he was by ancestry a hereditary aristocrat, while *that person, that person*—ahem; he regarded his own appearance at *that person's* dwelling as an honour bestowed upon the *person*.

It was growing dark, growing blue.

And in the spreading darkness, in the twilight of the study, the *person's* jacket made a patch of horrible yellow; his square head was bent right down to the desk (over his back only a tuft of dyed hair could be seen), displaying a broad, muscular back and a no doubt unwashed neck; his back seemed to protrude as it was displayed to the gaze; and the way it was displayed was all wrong: it wasn't decent, it was … somehow … derisive. From here it seemed to Alexandr Ivanovich that those hunched shoulders and that back in the twilight of the study were making a coarse mockery of him; and in his mind's eye he undressed them; what was displayed was fatty skin that could be cut as easily as the skin of a roast sucking-pig with horseradish; a cockroach crawled by (there was evidently an abundance of them here); it made him feel sick: he—spat.

Suddenly between the back and the nape of the neck a fatty fold in the neck squeezed itself into a faceless smile: as though a monster had settled in that armchair; the neck presented itself as a face; as though in the armchair a monster had settled with a noseless, eyeless dial for a face; and the fold of the neck appeared as a toothlessly gaping mouth.

There, in the twilight of the room, a deformed, splay-legged monster was leaning back unnaturally.

Ugh, hideous!

Alexandr Ivanovich made a brusque movement and presented his back to that back; he started plucking at his whiskers with an air of nonchalance; he wanted to demonstrate that he was offended, but managed only a show of indifference; he plucked away at his whiskers as if to say that he and that back had nothing to do with one another. He wanted to slam the door and leave; but he couldn't leave: the peace of Nikolai Apollonovich's life depended on this conversation; and that meant it was out of the question to slam the door and leave; and that meant that he was still dependent on *that person*.

We said that Alexandr Ivanovich presented his back to that back; but that back with its fold of the neck was still a magnetic back;

371

and he turned round to it: he could not help turning round …
Thereupon the *person*, in his turn, turned sharply on the chair: the
bowed, narrow-browed head stared straight at him like a wild boar
ready to sink its fang into any pursuer; he turned towards him and
turned away again. This action was performed with a gesture that
spoke eloquently of a single wish—to inflict an insult. But that was
not all the gesture expressed. The *person* must have noticed something
in the gaze fixed on his back, because the glance of those blinking
eyes caustically expressed:

"Aha, aha … So that's what you're up to, old chap? … "

Alexandr Ivanovich clenched his fist in his pocket. And turned
away again.

The clock ticked. Alexandr Ivanovich cleared his throat twice, so
that his impatience should impinge upon the *person's* hearing (he had
to stand up for himself and at the same time not offend the *person* too
much; were he to offend the *person*, Nikolai Apollonovich might well
suffer from that offence) … But Alexandr Ivanovich's throat-clearing
came out like the timid spasms of a first-former in front of the class
teacher. Whatever had happened to him? Where had that timidity
come from? He was not in the least afraid of *that person*: he was afraid
of the hallucination that appeared there on his wallpaper—not of
the *person*, though …

The *person* went on writing.

Alexandr Ivanovich cleared his throat again. And again. And this
time the *person* responded.

"Just wait, would you … "

What sort of tone was that? What coldness?

At last the *person* half-rose and turned round; the ponderous hand
described a gesture of invitation in the air:

"Please come in … "

Alexandr Ivanovich lost his composure; his anger, which had
exceeded all bounds, expressed itself in his forgetting, in his anxiety,
all ordinary words:

"I've … you see … come … "

"?"

"As you know, or rather … To hell with it! … " And suddenly he
just blurted out:

"I've come on business … "

But *that person*, leaning back in his chair with an annihilating expression (Dudkin was ready to strangle him mercilessly in that armchair), drummed on the desk with a chewed fingernail; and burst out in a hollow voice:

"I have to warn you … I don't have time today to listen to any long drawn out explanations. And therefore … "

How about that!

"Therefore I would ask you, my dear fellow, to express yourself as precisely and briefly as possible … "

And pressing his chin into his Adam's apple, the *person* stared out of the window; and the space outside, empty of light, tossed in rustling clusters of fallen leaves.

"Just tell me, since when have you adopted this … this tone," Alexandr Ivanovich snapped out not only with irony, but also some perplexity.

But again the *person* interrupted him: interrupted him in a most unpleasant manner:

"Well, then?"

And folded his arms on his chest.

"My business … " and he stopped short …

"Well, then? … "

"Is a matter of great importance … "

But the *person* interrupted him for a third time:

"We'll consider its degree of importance later."

And screwed up his little eyes.

Alexandr Ivanovich Dudkin, his composure incomprehensibly dissipated, reddened and felt that he could not squeeze out another sentence. Alexandr Ivanovich was silent.

The *person* was silent.

Falling leaves beat on the windows: red leaves, striking against the glass, drifted down, whispering; branches—dry skeletons—formed a tenebrous black network; it was windy outside: the black network started swaying, the black network began to hum. Incoherently, helplessly, stumbling over his expressions, Alexandr Ivanovich expounded the incident with Ableukhov. But as he got carried away with his story, overcoming the potholes in the construction of his speech, so the *person* became colder and sterner: more and more dispassionately his forehead jutted out and lost its frown; his puffy lips stopped sucking; and at that point in the story where the *agent provocateur* Morkovin made his appearance, the *person* raised his eyebrows meaningfully and twitched his nose: as though up till this point he had been trying to appeal to the narrator's conscience, as though from this point on the narrator had abandoned his conscience entirely, so that all the bounds of toleration, of which the *person* was capable, were now transgressed; and his patience—finally snapped:

"Ah? ... You see? ... And you were saying? ... "

Alexandr Ivanovich shuddered.

"What was I saying?"

"Never mind: carry on ... "

Alexandr Ivanovich cried out in utter despair:

"I've said it all! What more is there to add!"

And, pressing his chin into his Adam's apple, the *person* lowered his gaze, reddened, sighed, and stared reproachfully at Alexandr Ivanovich with eyes that no longer blinked (his gaze was sad); and—he whispered faintly:

"It's a bad business ... A very, very bad business ... You ought to be ashamed of yourself! ... "

In the adjoining room Zoia Zakharovna appeared with a lamp; the servant, Malania, was laying the table: glasses were being set out; Mr Shishnarfiev appeared in the dining room; his light tenor floated and flattered, but all its flattery was absorbed by ... the accent of Young Persia; Shishnarfiev himself was concealed from view by a flower-vase; Alexandr Ivanovich noted all this from a distance, and—as though in a dream.

Alexandr Ivanovich felt a trembling in his heart; and—horror; at the words "you ought to be ashamed" he felt a bright flush spread across his cheeks; an evident threat lurked ominously in his terrible interlocutor's words; Alexandr Ivanovich squirmed involuntarily on his chair, recalling some guilt which he had not incurred at all.

It was strange: he could not summon the courage to inquire what was meant by the threat concealed in the *person's* tone and what "ashamed" could mean, addressed to him. But still he swallowed that "ashamed".

"What message am I to give Ableukhov about that *provocateur's* note?"

Then those frontal bones came right up to his own forehead:

"What do you mean, *provocateur's*? There was no provocation in it at all ... I have to cool your ardour. The letter to Ableukhov was written by myself."

This tirade was delivered with a dignity that overrode not only anger, but reproach and offence as well; with a dignity that overrode itself and now stooped ... to a disparaging humility.

"What? The letter was written by you?"

"And it was delivered —through you: do you remember? ... Or have you forgotten?"

The word "forgotten" the *person* pronounced with an expression suggesting that Alexandr Ivanovich knew all this perfectly well himself, but was for some reason feigning ignorance; and in general the *person* gave him clearly to understand that he was now going to play a cat-and-mouse game with this sham of his ...

"If you recall: I handed that letter to you there—in the tavern ... "

"But I passed it on, I assure you, not to Ableukhov, but to Varvara Evgrafovna ... "

"Come on now, Alexandr Ivanovich, come on now, old man: we have no need for such subtleties between ourselves: the letter found its addressee ... The rest is just—sophistry ... "

"And you are the author of the letter?"

Alexandr Ivanovich's heart was fluttering so, and beating so, that it seemed on the point of leaping out; it lowed like a bull; and ran ahead.

But the *person* rapped on the table meaningfully with his finger, and, changing his appearance of nonchalance into one of granite firmness, he cried out:

"What do you find so surprising? ... That the letter to Ableukhov was written by me? ... "

"Of course ... "

"You must forgive me, but I would say that your astonishment is bordering on plain disingenuousness ... "

The black profile of Shishnarfiev emerged behind a flower-vase: Zoia Zakharovna began whispering something to the profile, and the profile nodded its head; and then it stared at Alexandr Ivanovich. But Alexandr Ivanovich saw nothing. He merely exclaimed, rushing at the *person*:

375

"Either I've lost my mind, or—you have! … "

The personage winked at him:

"Come on, then,"

But his appearance was saying:

"Now, now, old chap: I saw the way you looked at me just now … Do you think I'm going to let you get away with that? … "

Something happened: cheerfully, merrily almost, even with a kind of simple-minded relish, the *person* clicked his tongue, as though he was about to exclaim:

"Yes, old chap, it was baseness all right, but on your part—only on yours: not on mine … "

But all he said was:

"Well? … Well? … "

Then, making a show of suppressing with difficulty a sardonic guffaw, the *person* placed his heavy hand sternly, forcefully, condescendingly upon Alexandr Ivanovich's shoulder. He lapsed into thought for a moment and added:

"It's a bad business … A very, very bad business … "

And Alexandr Ivanovich was seized by that same strange, oppressive and familiar state: the state of perdition before a patch of dark-yellow wallpaper, on which something fateful—is about to appear. Alexandr Ivanovich became aware of an unknown guilt; as he looked a cloud seemed to come and hang over him, enveloping him from the direction where *that person* was sitting, and emanating from the *person*.

And the *person* stared at him with his narrow-browed head; kept sitting there, repeating:

"A bad business … "

A burdensome silence ensued.

"However, I will, of course, wait for the relevant evidence; you can't act without evidence … However: the charge—is a serious one; the charge, I'll tell you straight, is so serious, that … " here the *person* sighed.

"What evidence do you mean?"

"I don't want to judge you personally yet … In the party we act, as you know, on the basis of facts … But the facts, the facts … "

"What facts are you talking about?"

"Facts about you are being gathered … "

That was all he needed!

Rising from his chair, the *person* snipped off the tip of a Havana cigar and began to hum a song ambiguously; now he shut himself into an impenetrable show of good humour; strode off into the dining room, took Shishnarfiev amicably by the shoulder.

He called out in the direction of the kitchen, from where a delectable smell of roast was wafting.

"I could eat a horse … "

He looked round the table and commented:

"Could do with some fruit liqueur … "

Then he strode back through into the study.

"All the time you spend sitting in the caretaker's lodge … Your friendship with the house police, with the caretaker … Finally, your drinking with Voronkov the police clerk … "

And in reply to a questioning, bewildered glance—a glance full of horror Lippanchenko, that is to say, *that person*, continued his biting, cryptic whisper, putting his hand on Alexandr Ivanovich's shoulder.

"As though you didn't know yourself? Pulling surprised faces? Don't you know who Voronkov is?"

"Who Voronkov is? Voronkov?! … Goodness … what of it … what is this all about? … "

But the *person* roared with laughter, holding his sides:

"You don't know? … "

"I'm not saying that: I do know … "

"Delightful! … "

"Voronkov is a clerk from the police station: he visits the caretaker of the house, Matvei Morzhov … "

"You keep company with a detective, you go drinking with a detective, like I don't know who, like the lowest little nark … "

"Really! … "

"Not a word, not a word," the *person* waved an arm, seeing Alexandr Ivanovich's attempt, now that he was frightened in earnest, to say something.

"I repeat: the fact of your obvious involvement in provocation is not yet established, but … I warn you—I warn you in all friendship: Alexandr Ivanovich, my dear fellow, you've set something shady in train … "

"I have?"

377

"Step back: there's still time … "

For a moment Alexandr Ivanovich had the clear impression that the words "step back: there's still time" were a kind of condition set by the *person*: not to insist on clarification of the incident with Nikolai Apollonovich; and something else occurred to him as well—the *person* (he remembered) had himself earned quite some notoriety; something of the sort had happened here—it was clear: Zoia Zakharovna's hints just now—what else were they about!

But hardly had that thought occurred to Alexandr Ivanovich, and brought him a mite of encouragement, when the familiar, ominous expression—the expression of that hallucination—flashed across the fat man's face; and the frontal bones strained in a single determined effort—to break his will: cost what it may, at any price at all—to break it, or else … to burst into smithereens.

And the frontal bones broke it.

Alexandr Ivanovich, sleepy and depressed, began to droop, while the *person*, taking revenge for the moment of resistance to his will, was already back on the attack; his square head bent right down.

His little eyes—his little eyes were trying to say:

"Now then, old chap … So that's what you're up to?"

And his mouth frothed with spittle:

"Don't pretend to be such a simpleton … "

"I'm not pretending … "

"The whole of Petersburg knows about it … "

"Knows about what?"

"About the collapse of T T … ."

"What?!"

"Yes, yes … "

If it was the *person's* conscious intention to distract Alexandr Ivanovich's thoughts from the possibly impending revelation of the true motives for the *person's* behaviour, then it was a complete success, because the news of the collapse of T T struck the enfeebled Alexandr Ivanovich like a bolt from the blue.

"Oh, my Lord Jesus Christ! … "

"Jesus Christ!" the *person* mocked. "You knew of that before any of us … Until we get expert evidence let's assume it's as you say … Only don't go increasing the suspicions against you: and not a word about Ableukhov."

At that moment Alexandr Ivanovich must have had an extremely idiotic expression on his face, because the *person* went on guffawing and mocking him with his bared teeth and the black cavity of his wide-open mouth: it is with just such a grinning cavity that a flayed and blood-smeared carcass gazes at us from a butcher's shop.

"Don't pretend, my dear fellow, that Ableukhov's role was unknown to you; or that you didn't know the reasons that forced me to do away with Ableukhov by giving him those orders; or that you didn't know how that wretched cur played his part: mind you, he played it cleverly; and he'd reckoned correctly—he reckoned on all this sentimentality, all this sloppiness, like yours," the *person* softened: by admitting that Alexandr Ivanovich was also suffering from sloppiness he magnanimously lifted from him the accusation levelled against him the moment before; no doubt that was why at the word "sloppiness" something fell from Alexandr Ivanovich's soul; and he began trying ever so faintly to convince himself that regarding the *person* he had been wrong.

"Yes, he reckoned correctly: the son is so noble he hates his father, is planning to do his father in, and in the meantime swans around amongst us with his little reports and all that nonsense: collecting bits of paper, and when he's got a big enough collection of papers, then he'll go and present his collection to—his papa ... And all of you feel some unaccountable attraction towards this bastard ... "

"But, you know, Nikolai Stepanych, he was crying ... "

"And his tears surprised you ... You're a funny fellow: tears are the normal condition of the intelligent informer; when an intelligent informer has a good cry he thinks he's crying sincerely; and I dare say he even regrets being an informer; only those intelligentsia tears don't make things any easier for us ... And you, too, Alexandr Ivanovich— you're crying too ... I don't at all mean to say that you're guilty too." (That wasn't true: the *person* had only just been insisting on his guilt; and for a moment this falsehood horrified Alexandr Ivanovich; it flashed like lightning just below his consciousness: "There's a trade-off going on: I am supposed to believe this horrible calumny, or, rather, to accept it without believing it, and in exchange a calumny will be lifted from me ... " This flashed through just below the threshold of consciousness, because the terrible truth had been locked away on the other side of the threshold by the *person's* frontal bones, looming over his eyes, and by the

379

oppressive atmosphere of an approaching thunderstorm, and by the gleam of those little eyes with their "Now then, old chap ... " And he thought he was beginning to believe that calumny.)

"You, I'm sure, Alexandr Ivanovich, you're clean, but as for Ableukhov: here, in this box, I'm keeping a dossier: later I shall hand this dossier over for the party to judge." At this the *person* began stamping frantically round the study—from one corner to the other—and clumsily thumping his over-starched chest with the palm of his hand. In the tone of his voice unfeigned distress could be heard, despair—simply nobility of feeling (evidently the bargain had been successfully concluded).

"Later on I shall be understood, believe me: at present the situation compels me to tear out the infection by the roots, without delay ... Yes ... I'm acting like a dictator, just by my own will ... But—believe me—I'm sorry to do it: I was sorry to sign his death-warrant, but ... dozens of people are coming to grief ... because of your ... senator's son: dozens are perishing! ... Peppovich, and Pepp have already been arrested ... Remember how you once nearly came to grief yourself (it went through Alexandr Ivanovich's mind that he already had come to grief) ... If it hadn't been for me ... Remember the Iakutsk province! ... And here you are taking his side, feeling sorry for him ... You can weep all right, do weep! There's plenty to weep about: there are do-zens perishing!!! ... "

At this the *person* looked up quickly and left the study.

It had grown dark: all was blackness.

Darkness descended; and came to stand between all the objects in the room; the tables, cupboards, armchairs—all disappeared into profound darkness; in the darkness sat Alexandr Ivanovich—utterly alone; the darkness entered his soul; he—wept.

Alexandr Ivanovich recalled all the nuances of the *person's* speech and found all those nuances sincere; the *person* was surely not lying; and the suspicions, the hatred—all of that might be explained by Alexandr Ivanovich's own morbid condition: some chance nocturnal nightmare, in which *that person* played the main role, might be linked fortuitously with some ambiguous expression of the *person's*; and the food for mental illness on the basis of alcoholism was to hand;

the hallucination of the Mongol and the senseless whisper heard at night:—"*Enfranshish*"—completed the picture. What was the Mongol on the wall? Delirium. And an infamous word.

"Enfranshish, enfranshish … "—what was that?

An abracadabra, an association of sounds—nothing more.

True, he had held unkind feelings towards *that person* even before: but it was also true: he was obliged to the *person*—the *person* had helped him out; his disgust, his horror had no justification, except perhaps … in his delirium: *the patch on the wallpaper.*

Oh, he was ill, ill …

The darkness was attacking him; it fell upon him, surrounded him; table, armchair, cupboard—stood out with solemn ominousness; the darkness entered his soul—he wept: the moral character of Nikolai Apollonovich stood out now for the first time in its true light. How could he have failed to understand?

He remembered his first meeting with him (at the house of some common acquaintances Nikolai Apollonovich was reading a paper, in which all values were overthrown): the impression he made was not a pleasant one; then—later: Nikolai Apollonovich had, in all honesty, shown a particular curiosity about all manner of party secrets; with the absent-minded air of a clumsy degenerate he poked his nose into everything: why, that absent mindedness could be a pose. Alexandr Ivanovich thought: an *agent provocateur* of the finest type could of course very well have the external appearance of Ableukhov—that melancholy and pensive gaze (avoiding the other's eyes) and the frog-like expression of those elongated lips; gradually Alexandr Ivanovich came to the conviction: Nikolai Apollonovich had behaved very strangely in all this business; and dozens—were coming to grief …

As he convinced himself of Ableukhov's involvement in the affair of the collapse of T T, the threatening, oppressive feeling that had possessed him during his conversation with the *person* disappeared; something light, almost carefree entered his soul. For a long time Alexandr Ivanovich had felt an especial hatred for the senator: Apollon Apollonovich aroused in him a particular disgust, akin to the disgust we feel for a poisonous spider or a tarantula; for Nikolai Apollonovich, however, he now and then felt a liking; now, though, the senator's son united in him with the senator in a single access of disgust and a desire to eradicate that brood of tarantulas—to destroy them.

"What scum! ... Dozens perishing ... What scum ... "

Better even the woodlice, the patch of dark-yellow wallpaper, better even *that person*: in the *person* there was at least the majesty of hatred; you could still make common cause with the *person* in the desire—to destroy spiders:

"Oh, the scum! ... "

Two rooms away the table was already glinting hospitably; on the table delicacies were set out: sausage, salmon and cold veal cutlets; from the distance there carried the satisfied mumbling of the now exhausted *person* and the voice of Shishnarfiev; this latter was making his farewells; finally he left.

Soon the *person* burst into the room, came up to Alexandr Ivanovich and placed his heavy palm on his shoulders:

"That's it, then! It's better we don't fall out, Alexandr Ivanovich; if you quarrel with your own people, then ... what else can you expect? ... "

"Well, come and have something to eat ... Have supper with us ... Only let's not say a word about all this at supper ... It's a sorry business ... And there's no need for Zoia Zakharovna to know about it: she's tired, poor thing ... And I'm pretty tired too ... We're all pretty tired ... It's all from nerves ... You and I are nervous people ... Come on—supper, supper ... "

The table glinted hospitably.

Again the sad and sorrowful one

Alexandr Ivanovich rang a great number of times.

Alexandr Ivanovich rang at the gate of his sombre house; the caretaker did not open it for him; on the other side of the gate the only answer was the barking of a dog; in the distance a nocturnal cockerel raised its voice to midnight; and—fell silent. The Eighteenth Line ran away there: into the depths, into the emptiness.

Emptiness.

Alexandr Ivanovich experienced something actually akin to pleasure: his arrival in these wretched walls was postponed; all night long in these wretched walls whispers and crackles and squeals resounded.

Finally—and the main thing: he would have to surmount in the darkness twelve cold steps; turning, he would have to count the same number again.

Alexandr Ivanovich did that four times.

A total of ninety-six echoing stone steps; further: he would have to stand in front of the felt-covered door; in fear he would have to insert his half-rusted key into the keyhole. It was risky to strike a match in this pitch darkness; the light of the match might suddenly illuminate all manner of filth; like a mouse; or something else …

That was what Alexandr Ivanovich thought.

That was why he went on hesitating at the gate of his sombre house.

And—would you believe it …

—someone tall and sad, whom Alexandr Ivanovich had seen many a time by the Neva, appeared again in the depths of the Eighteenth Line. This time he trod quietly into the pool of light round a streetlamp; but it seemed as though this bright golden light were streaming sadly from his brow, from his fingers, numb with cold …

—that was how this unknown friend made his appearance this time too.

Alexandr Ivanovich remembered that once an old woman passing by in a straw bonnet with purple ribbons had called out to this dear inhabitant of the Eighteenth Line.

On that occasion she had called him Misha.

Alexandr Ivanovich shuddered each time that the tall and sad one turned upon him, as he passed, his inexpressible, all-seeing gaze; and always his sunken cheeks bore the same white hue. After these meetings by the Neva Alexandr Ivanovich could see without seeing and hear without hearing.

"If only he would stop! … "

"Oh, if only! … "

"And, oh, if he would hear me out! … "

But the tall and sad one, without looking or stopping, had already passed by.

The sound of his retreating footfalls was still distinct: this sound's distinctness came from the fact that this pedestrian's feet were not, like those of others, clad in galoshes. Alexandr Ivanovich turned round, wanting to say something to him quietly; he wanted quietly to call an unknown Misha …

But the spot where Misha had vanished without trace—that spot stood empty now in a quivering pool of light; and there was nothing there, but wind and slush.

And from there the fiery yellow tongue of a streetlamp flickered.

All the same he rang again. The Petersburg cockerel once again gave answer; the damp wind from the sea whistled in the chinks; the wind groaned in the archway and across the road it struck with violence the iron inn-sign '*Cheap meals*'; and the iron clattered in the darkness.

Matvei Morzhov

At last the gate creaked.

The bearded caretaker, Matvei Morzhov, an old friend of Alexandr Ivanovich's, admitted him across the threshold of the house: his retreat was now cut off; and the gate closed.

"Bit late, aren't you?"

"So many things to see to … "

"Been looking for a job?"

"A job, yes … "

"Naturally: there's no jobs going now … Only if one came free at the police station … "

"They wouldn't have me at the station, Matvei … "

"Naturally: what would you be wanting at the station … "

"You see?"

"There's no jobs going now … "

The bearded caretaker, Matvei Morzhov, sometimes sent his plump wife with her perpetual earache up to Alexandr Ivanovich with a piece of pie, or an invitation to drop in; and so they would have a drink in the caretaker's lodge on high days and holidays: as an illegal it was important for Alexandr Ivanovich to maintain the closest possible friendship with the house police.

And besides.

That provided a good opportunity for him to come down from his cold attic (as we have seen, Alexandr Ivanovich hated his attic, and yet he sometimes sat there for weeks on end when emerging from it seemed dangerous).

Sometimes Voronkov the police clerk and Bessmertnyi the cobbler joined their company. And lately Styopka had taken to sitting in the caretaker's lodge all the time: Styopka was out of work.

Once in the yard, Alexandr Ivanovich heard distinctly the same song coming over and over again from the lodge:

There's those as don't like scribblers—
I'd have one straight away;
'Cos educated people
Can find nice things to say …

"Got guests again?"

Matvei Morzhov scratched the back of his head in ferocious pensiveness:

"We're having a bit of fun … "

Alexandr Ivanovich smiled:

"The police clerk, I bet? … "

"Who else? … Himself … "

Alexandr Ivanovich suddenly remembered that the name of Voronkov the clerk had for some reason been insistently mentioned— there, by *that person*; why did the *person* know Voronkov the clerk, and about Voronkov the clerk, and about the time they spent sitting there? It had surprised him then, but he had forgotten to ask.

Mama, won't you buy me
Some grey poplin for a dress:
Vasia Alexeev won't
Walk out with me, unless …

Morzhov the caretaker, seeing some hesitation on Alexandr Ivanovich's part, sniffed loudly and gloomily blurted out:

"Well … Come on in … Into the lodge … "

And Alexandr Ivanovich would have gone in: it was warm in the lodge, there were people there, and drink; in the attic it was cold and lonely. But—no, no: Voronkov the clerk was there; and *that person* had said ambiguous things about Voronkov; and—devil only knows! But the main thing was that going into the caretaker's lodge would be definite cowardice: he would be running away from his own walls.

Alexandr Ivanovich replied with a sigh:

"No, Matvei: it's time to sleep … "

"Naturally: you know best! … "

How they were singing there:

> *Mama, won't you buy me*
> *Some blue poplin for a dress:*
> *Sonny-boy Vasiliev won't*
> *Walk out with me, unless …*

"You could come and have some vodka, though?"

And with something like desperation, something simply like anger, he shouted:

"No, no, no!"

And set off at a run towards the silvery piles of firewood.

Matvei Morzhov, as he moved off, threw open for a moment the door of the lodge: white steam, a sheaf of light, a roar of voices and the smell of warmed-up mud, carried in from the street on monstrous boots, surged out momentarily; and—crash: the door slammed to behind Matvei Morzhov.

His retreat was cut off a second time.

Again the moon was lighting the precise, square yard and the silvery piles of aspen logs, which Alexandr Ivanovich slipped quickly past on his way to the black entrance to his staircase. Behind his back words were carried from the caretaker's lodge; it was probably Bessmertnyi the cobbler singing:

> *The railway tracks in the distance,*
> *Embankments! And signals and points!*
> *The train, washed away in the mudslide,*
> *Crashed down from the sleepers and joints.*
> *A picture of carriages shattered,*
> *A picture of folk in distress …*

He couldn't hear any more.

Alexandr Ivanovich stopped: just so, just so—it was starting; he hadn't even had time to shut himself into his dark-yellow cube, and already it was starting, it was under way—the inescapable nightly torment. And this time it had begun right by the black outer door.

It was the same as ever: *they* were keeping watch on Alexandr Ivanovich … It had started like this: once, when he was returning home, he had seen a stranger coming down the stairs, who had said to him:

"You are linked with Him … "

Who the man coming down the stairs really was, who was this He (with a capital letter), Who created a link with Himself, Alexandr Ivanovich made no attempt to discover, but rushed impetuously up the stairs away from the stranger. The stranger had not followed him

And a second thing had happened to Dudkin: he met a man in the street with a cap pulled down over his eyes and with a face so terrible (inexpressibly terrible) that an unknown lady passing by seized Alexandr Ivanovich by the sleeve in her horror:

"Did you see that? It's—terrible, simply terrible … It's quite unheard of! … Oh, what can it be? … "

But the man went on by.

And one evening on the second-floor landing Alexandr Ivanovich had been grabbed by hands that pushed him towards the banisters, obviously trying to push him over—down there. Alexandr Ivanovich fought free and struck a match, and … there was no one on the staircase: no sound of footsteps going either up or down. It was empty.

And latterly, to cap it all, Alexandr Ivanovich had been hearing an inhuman cry at night … from the staircase: what a cry! … One cry, and nothing more.

But the other occupants had not heard this cry.

Just once he had heard this cry in the street—there, by the Bronze Horseman: it had been exactly the same cry. But that had been an automobile with its headlights glaring. Just once the out-of-work Styopka, who kept him company in the nights, had heard the cry. But to all Alexandr Ivanovich's pestering he just gloomily replied:

"It's *them* after you … "

As to who *they* were Styopka wouldn't say a thing. And not another word about it. Only Styopka started steering clear of Alexandr Ivanovich, didn't drop in so often; and as for spending the night there—no fear … And Styopka didn't say a word about it to the caretaker, or to Voronkov the clerk, or to the cobbler. And Alexandr Ivanovich didn't say a word either …

But what did it feel like to be forcibly driven into all this, and not share it with anyone!

"It's *them* after you … "

Who were *they*, and why were *they* after him? …

And now again.

Alexandr Ivanovich involuntarily cast his eyes upwards: to the little window in the attic on the fourth floor; there was a light in the window: he could see an angular shadow moving restlessly about in the window. In a second—he anxiously felt in his pocket for the key to his room: he had the key all right. Who could be there in his locked room? …

Perhaps it was a police search? Oh, if only it were just a police search: stumbling upon a police search would make him the happiest man in the world; let them arrest him and stick him away, even … into the Peter and Paul Fortress. Those who stick you away in the Peter and Paul Fortress are at any rate people—not *them*, anyway.

"It's *them* after you … "

Alexandr Ivanovich took a deep breath and promised himself in advance that he would not be excessively horrified, because the kinds of events that might happen to him now—were nothing but idle cerebral play.

Alexandr Ivanovich went in through the black entrance.

A lifeless beam of light fell through the window

Just so, just so: they were standing there; they had been standing there just the same the last time he had come home late. And they were waiting for him. There was no telling precisely who they were:

two outlines. A lifeless beam of light fell through the window from the second floor; it settled in a dull-white gleam on the grey stairs.

And in that utter darkness the dull-white patches lay there so terribly peacefully—unwavering.

The banisters of the staircase lay within this dull-white patch; and *they* were standing by the banisters: two outlines; they let Alexandr Ivanovich pass, standing to right and left of him; they had let him pass in just the same way then; they said nothing, did not move, did not bat an eyelid; all he could feel was someone's evil, narrowed, unblinking eye strained upon him in the darkness.

Should he not go up to them and whisper in their ears the talisman that had surfaced in his memory from his dream?

"Enfranshish, enfranshish! ... "

What would it be like to move under their fixed gaze into that dull-white patch: to be illuminated by the moon, sensing on either side the sharp gaze of an observer; and further—to sense these observers of the black staircase behind his back, capable of anything at any second; what would it be like to resist quickening his pace and nonchalantly clear his throat?

For Alexandr Ivanovich had only to rush at full tilt up the steps of the staircase for the observers to come rushing after him.

At that moment the dull-white patches became grey patches and then began in unison to dissolve; and they dissolved completely in the utter darkness (evidently a black cloud had covered the moon).

Alexandr Ivanovich stepped calmly into the place which had just been white, so that he did not see the eyes, and concluded from this that his eyes had not been seen either (poor fellow, he cherished the vain idea that he might slip up to his attic unseen). Alexandr Ivanovich did not quicken his pace, and he even—started plucking at his moustache; and ...

Alexandr Ivanovich could not keep it up.

He shot like an arrow up to the first-floor landing (so tactless!). And once arrived there, he permitted himself something that finally destroyed his reputation in the eyes of the outline standing there.

Leaning over the banisters, he cast a distressed, terrified glance downwards, after throwing down as a preliminary a lighted match:

the iron rods of the banisters flared up; and amidst this yellow glimmer Alexandr Ivanovich made out distinctly the silhouettes.

What was his astonishment!

One silhouette turned out to be no more or less than the Tartar, Makhmudka, who lived in the basement; in the yellow tremor of the match, as it fell past him and burnt itself out, Makhmudka leant over to a gent of ordinary appearance; the gent of ordinary appearance was wearing a bowler hat, but had the hook-nosed face of an oriental person; this hook-nosed, oriental person was trying to ask Makhmudka something, and Makhmudka was shaking his head in denial.

After that the match burnt out: it was impossible to distinguish anything.

But the burning match had given Alexandr Ivanovich's presence away to the hook-nosed oriental person: feet shuffled swiftly upwards; and then a lively voice rang out right at Alexandr Ivanovich's ear, but ... —can you imagine, a voice without an accent.

"Excuse me, are you Andrei Andreich Gorelskii?"

"No, I am Alexandr Ivanovich Dudkin ... "

"Yes, according to your false passport ... "

Alexandr Ivanovich shuddered: he was indeed living under a false passport, but his name was: Aleksei Alekseevich Pogorelskii, not Andrei Andreich Gorelskii.

Alexandr Ivanovich shuddered, but ... decided that concealment would serve no purpose:

"I am, what can I do for you? ... "

"Please forgive me: I am calling on you for the first time and at such an unsuitable hour ... "

"Never mind ... "

"This black staircase: your apartment was locked ... And there's somebody there ... I preferred to wait for you at the entrance ... And then this black staircase ... "

"Who's waiting for me there? ... "

"I don't know: an uneducated voice answered when I called ... "

Styopka! ... Thank goodness: it's Styopka who's there ...

"So what can I do for you? ... "

"Forgive me, I have heard so much about you: we have some friends in common ... Nikolai Stepanych Lippanchenko, where I am treated like a son … I have long wished to make your acquaintance … I heard that you were a night-bird … So I took the liberty … I actually live in Helsingfors and come here occasionally, although my homeland is—the south … "

Alexandr Ivanovich quickly calculated that his guest was lying; and moreover in the most flagrant manner, for the same story had been repeated once before (where and when—he could not now bring to mind: perhaps it had occurred in an immediately forgotten dream; and now—it had surfaced).

No, no, no: it was altogether a dirty business; but he mustn't let on that he knew; and Alexandr Ivanovich responded into the utter darkness.

"With whom do I have the honour of speaking?"

"Shishnarfne, subject of Persia … We have already met … "

"Shishnarfiev? … "

"No, Shishnarfne: the e-v ending has just been stuck on—for Russianness, if you like … We were together today—there, at Lippanchenko's; I sat there for two hours, waiting for you to finish your business discussion, and couldn't wait any longer … Zoia Zakharovna didn't warn me in time that you were with her. I have been seeking a meeting with you for a long time … *I've been after you for a long time* … "

This last sentence, just like Shishnarfiev's transformation into Shishnarfne, again reminded Dudkin dreamily of something or other: it was distasteful, depressing, wearisome.

"Have we met before?"

"Yes … do you remember? … In Helsingfors … "

Alexandr Ivanovich vaguely remembered something; to his own surprise he lit another match and held this one right up to Shishnarfiev's—sorry: Shishnarfne's—nose: the walls lit up for a moment with a yellow reflection, the rods of the banisters glinted; and out of the darkness right in front of his face the face of the Persian subject suddenly took shape; Alexandr Ivanovich now remembered clearly that he had seen that face in a certain café in Helsingfors; then, too, that face had for some reason not taken its suspicious eyes off Alexandr Ivanovich.

"Do you remember?"

Alexandr Ivanovich called something else to mind: and it was this: it was in Helsingfors that all the symptoms of the illness threatening him had started; and it was in Helsingfors that all that idle cerebral play had started too, in response, it seemed, to someone's suggestion.

He recalled that at that time he had had occasion to develop the most paradoxical theory about the necessity of destroying culture, because the era of historically outlived humanism was at an end, and all cultural history stood before us now like an eroded ruin: a period of healthy bestialism was beginning, emerging from the depths of the ordinary people (hooliganism, the riotous behaviour of the apaches), from aristocratic high society (the uprising of the arts against established forms, love of primitive culture, the exotic), and from the bourgeoisie itself (oriental ladies' fashions, the cake-walk—a negro dance; and—so on); at that time Alexandr Ivanovich advocated the burning of libraries, universities, and museums; he advocated the summoning of the Mongols (later he became afraid of the Mongols). All contemporary phenomena were divided by him into two categories: symptoms of outlived culture and healthy barbarism, which was compelled for the time being to conceal itself under a mask of refinement (the appearance of Ibsen and Nietzsche), and under that mask to infect the hearts of men with the chaos that was already secretly calling in their souls.

Alexandr Ivanovich called on people to remove their masks and live openly with chaos.

He remembered preaching this at that time, in the Helsingfors café; and when someone asked him what would be his attitude to Satanism, he had replied:

"Christianity has outlived its time: in Satanism there is a vulgar worship of the fetish, that is to say a healthy barbarism … "

And at that time—he recalled—at a table to one side sat Shishnarfne and did not take his eyes off them.

The advocacy of barbarism had ended in a surprising way (in Helsingfors, at that very time): it had ended in an absolute nightmare; Alexandr Ivanovich had a vision (in a dream, perhaps, or at the moment of falling asleep) of being rushed through something indescribable, which might most easily be called interplanetary space (but wasn't that): he was being rushed there in order to perform a certain act, an ordinary act *there*, but all the same from our point of view a revolting one; undoubtedly this had taken place in a dream (between ourselves—what is a dream?), but in an ugly dream, which had induced him to abandon his advocacy; in all of this the most unpleasant thing of all was that Alexandr Ivanovich did not remember whether he had performed the act or not; afterwards Alexandr Ivanovich noted this dream as the beginning of his illness, but all the same: he did not like remembering it.

And it was then that in secret from everyone he took to reading *Revelation*.

And now, here on the staircase, the reminder of Helsingfors had a terrible effect. Helsingfors appeared before him. He thought involuntarily:

"That is why all these recent weeks I've been hearing without any meaning at all: Hel-sing-fors, Hel-sing-fors ... "

And Shishnarfne went on:

"Do you remember?"

The matter had taken a revolting turn: he ought to take to flight at once—up the stone staircase; he ought to take advantage of the darkness, otherwise the phosphorescent light would cast its dull-white patches through the window. But Alexandr Ivanovich hesitated in utter horror; for some reason this ordinary visitor's surname particularly struck him:

"Shishnarfne, Shishnarfne ... I do know it from somewhere ... "

And Shishnarfne went on:

"Well then, will you allow me to come to your room? ... I have to admit, waiting for you has made me tired ... I hope you will forgive me my nocturnal visit ... "

And in an access of involuntary fear Alexandr Ivanovich cried out:

"You are welcome ... "

And thought to himself:

"Styopka will help me out ... "

Alexandr Ivanovich ran up the stairs. Shishnarfne ran after him; the endless string of steps seemed not to be leading them to the fourth floor: there seemed to be no end of the staircase in sight; and there was no running away: Shishnarfne was running at his shoulders, while in front a stream of light poured from his room.

Alexandr Ivanovich thought:

"How could Styopka have got into my room? I've got the key myself."

But when he felt in his pocket he realised that he did not have the key: instead of the door-key he had the key to his old suitcase.

Petersburg

Alexandr Ivanovich came flying into his wretched room at his wits' end to see Stepan settled on the dirty trestle bed over the last burning remnants of a candle-end; his unkempt head was bent low over an open book with Church Slavonic letters.

Stepan was reading a breviary.

Alexandr Ivanovich remembered Stepan's promise: to bring the breviary with him (he was interested in a certain prayer in it—the prayer of Vasilii the Great: an admonitory prayer to demons). And he seized hold of Styopka.

"It's you, Stepan: I'm so glad!"

"I've brought you the brev—," but glancing at the visitor coming through the door, Styopka just added, "the thing you were asking for ... "

"Thank you ... "

"I got lost in reading while I was waiting for you ... (another glance in the direction of the visitor) ... It's time I was off ... "

Alexandr Ivanovich put out a hand to hold Styopka:

"Don't go, stay and sit with us ... This gentleman is Mr Shishnarfiev ... "

But from the door a metallic voice rapped out gutturally:

"Not Shishnarfiev ... Shishnarfne ... "

Whatever need was there for him to insist on the absence of the letters '–ev'? He became more visible at the door; he took off his bowler hat; he kept his coat on and cast a questioning glance round the room:

"Not much of a place you have here ... It's damp ... And cold ... "

The candle was burning its last: its wrapping paper flared up, and all of a sudden the walls began to dance in watery-red flames.

"No, master, let me go: it's time I was off," Styopka fussed about, squinting at Alexandr Ivanovich with a hostile gaze and not looking at the visitor at all, " ... let me go—I'll come another time."

He took the breviary away with him.

Under Stepan's fixed gaze Alexandr Ivanovich lowered his eyes: that fixed gaze, it seemed to him, was a gaze of condemnation. And how was he to behave—with Stepan? There was something he wanted to say—to Stepan; he had offended Stepan; Stepan would not forgive him; and it seemed Stepan was now thinking:

"No, master, if *that sort* have started coming to see you, then there's nothing to be done; and the breviary's no use to you ... Not everybody lets *that sort* in, and those that does, well—they're birds of a feather ... "

So that meant, then, if Stepan considers that the visitor's a suspicious type ... Then, how would he manage on his own, without Stepan:

"Stepan, stay."

But Stepan waved him away not without a hint of disgust: as though he was afraid that *this* might rub off on him:

"It's you he's come to see, not me ... "

But in his soul there echoed:

"It's you they're after ... "

The door slammed behind Stepan. Alexandr Ivanovich was on the point of shouting after him to leave the breviary, but ... felt ashamed. He might go and say the word 'Breviary', so compromising for a freethinker: but Alexandr Ivanovich had promised himself in advance that he would not be excessively horrified, because the things that might happen to him after Stepan was gone—were a hallucination of hearing and a hallucination of sight. The flames, the blood-red flashes, finishing their dancing, died on the walls; the paper had burnt away: the candle-flame was dying; everything—was a deathly green ...

With a gesture of his hand he invited his visitor to take a seat by the table on the trestle bed with its ragged blanket; he stayed standing in the doorway, in order should the need arise to be out on the stairs and able to lock the visitor in, while he himself went clattering down all ninety-six steps.

His visitor, leaning on the windowsill, was lighting a cigarette and prattling away; his black outline stood out against the luminescent background of green spaces outside the window (the moon was running by there in the clouds) …

"I see that I've come at a bad time … that I seem to be disturbing you … "

"Not at all, I'm very glad," Alexandr Ivanovich Dudkin tried unconvincingly to reassure his guest, much in need of reassurance himself and cautiously checking with his hand behind his back whether the door was closed or not.

"But … I so meant to call on you, was looking for you everywhere, that when by chance we failed to meet at Zoia Zakharovna Fleisch's, I asked her to give me your address; and I came straight from her, from Zoia Zakharovna, to you: to wait for you … Especially since I'm leaving at first light tomorrow."

"You're leaving?" Alexandr Ivanovich checked, because he had the impression that his visitor's words were duplicated: his outer ear perceived the words "I'm leaving at first light"; but some other ear perceived quite clearly other words:

"I leave in the daytime, but I arrive with the dusk … "

But he did not insist, and went on hearing the words beating at his ears as they sounded, not as they resounded.

"Yes, I'm leaving for Finland, Sweden … That's where I live; however, I originally come from Shemakha; but I live in Finland: the climate of Petersburg, I must admit, is harmful to me too … "

That "me too" echoed in his consciousness, redoubled. The climate of Petersburg is harmful to everyone; there was no need at all to emphasise "me too".

"Yes," Alexandr Ivanovich responded mechanically, "Petersburg stands on a swamp … "

The black outline on the background of the green spaces outside the window (the moon was running by there in the clouds) suddenly broke loose and romped away in a flood of utter drivel.

"Yes, yes, yes … For the Russian Empire Petersburg is the most typical point … Take a geographical map … But concerning the fact that our capital city, so well adorned with monuments, belongs also to the world beyond the grave … "

"Oh-ho!" thought Alexandr Ivanovich: "I'd better keep my ear to the wind now, so as to be able to escape in good time … "

But what he said by way of objection was:

"You say our capital city … But it isn't yours: *your* capital city isn't Petersburg, it's Teheran … For you, as an oriental person, the climatic conditions of *our* capital … "

"I'm a cosmopolitan: I've been in Paris, you know, and in London … Yes—what was I talking about: about the fact that *our* capital city," the black outline continued, "belongs to the world beyond the grave—it somehow isn't done to talk about that when composing maps, guidebooks, catalogues; even the venerable Baedeker himself maintains an eloquent silence on that score; and the humble provincial, who has not been informed of this in good time, will come a cropper as soon as he arrives at the Nikolaevskii or the Warsaw railway station; he takes due account of the overt administration of Petersburg; but he does not have a shadow passport."

"What do you mean?"

"Just that, it's very simple: when I set off for the land of the Papuans, I know that in the land of the Papuans there will be a Papuan waiting for me: Karl Baedeker has warned me in advance about this sad phenomenon of nature; but what would happen to me, tell me, if on the way to Kirsanov I were to meet a tribe of the black-skinned Papuan hordes—something which will soon happen in France, by the way, since France is arming the black hordes on the quiet and bringing them into Europe—you'll see: anyway, that's all grist to your mill—your theory of bestialisation and the destruction of culture: do you remember? … In that café in Helsingfors I listened to you with sympathy."

Alexandr Ivanovich was beginning to feel more and more uncomfortable: he was wracked with fever; it was especially ghastly to have to listen to this reference to a theory he had abandoned; after the terrible Helsingfors dream he had become clearly aware of the link between that theory and Satanism; he had cast all that aside, as an illness; and now that he was ill again the black outline was bringing it all back to him with a vengeance, revoltingly.

There against the window, in the moonlit cubby-hole, the black outline was becoming ever finer, lighter, more ethereal; it seemed to be a sheet of dark, black paper, stuck firmly on the window frame; its resonant voice, existing outside of it itself, echoed of its own accord in the middle of the square room; but most astonishing of all was the circumstance that the voice centre itself was moving in space in the most noticeable way—from the window—in the direction of Alexandr Ivanovich; it was an autonomous, invisible centre from which ear-splitting sounds were gathering strength:

"So, what was I talking about? Yes … About the Papuan: the Papuan, so to speak, is an earth-born creature; the biology of the Papuan, even if it is a little primitive—is not alien even to you, Alexandr Ivanovich. You'll come to terms with the Papuan sooner or later; well, even if it takes a strong drink, such as you have been indulging in lately and which created such a propitious atmosphere for our meeting; moreover: even in Papua there exist some legal institutions, approved, quite possibly, by the Papuan parliament … "

It occurred to Alexandr Ivanovich that his visitor's behaviour was not at all seemly, because the sound of the visitor's voice had quite indecently separated itself from the visitor; and the visitor himself, transfixed motionless on the windowsill—unless his eyes deceived him—had manifestly turned into a layer of soot on the moonlit glass, while his voice, becoming more and more resonant and assuming a tinge of a gramophone's stridency, rang out right beside his ear.

"The shadow—is not even a Papuan; the biology of the shadow has not yet been studied; and that is why you will never come to terms with a shadow: you won't understand its demands; in Petersburg it makes its way into you through the bacilli of all manner of illnesses, which you swallow along with water from the tap … "

"And with vodka," Alexandr Ivanovich responded and found himself thinking: "What am I doing? Have I taken the bait of delirium? I responded, I countered in kind?" And thereupon he decided to distance himself once and for all from the drivel; if he did not dissolve the drivel at once with his consciousness, then his consciousness itself would be dissolved into drivel.

"No: the only thing you introduce into your consciousness with vodka is me … It's not with vodka, but with water that you swallow bacilli, and I am not a bacillus; so there you are: not being in possession of the necessary passport, you become subject to all kinds of consequences: from the very first days of your stay in Petersburg your stomach ceases to digest; you are in danger of contracting cholera … And then cases arise which cannot be helped by any petitions or complaints to the Petersburg police; your stomach isn't digesting?

… What about Dr Inozemtsev's drops?! … You're tormented by longing, hallucinations, melancholy—all effects of cholera—go to the Farce … Get a little distraction … Tell me, Alexandr Ivanovich, as a friend—you do suffer from hallucinations, don't you?"

"Now he's just making fun of me," thought Alexandr Ivanovich.

"You suffer from hallucinations—and it is a psychiatrist, not a policeman, who will give you an opinion about them … In short, your complaints addressed to the visible world will produce no effect, like all complaints: after all we do not live, it has to be admitted, in the visible world … The tragedy of our situation is that, like it or not, we are in the invisible world; in short, complaints in the visible world produce no effect; so that means you are left with no option but respectfully to submit your petition to the world of shadows."

"Is there such a thing?" Alexandr Ivanovich cried out provocatively, making ready to slip out of his cubby-hole and shut the visitor in, who was becoming ever more subtle: into this room had come a portly young man possessing three dimensions; leaning against the window he had turned into nothing but an outline (and moreover—of two dimensions); then: he had become a thin layer of black soot, rather like that which emerges from an oil-lamp if it has been badly trimmed; and now this black soot on the window, forming a human outline, grey all over, was decomposing into ash, glinting in the moonlight; and now the ash was blowing away: the outline was covered all over with patches of green—apertures into the spaces of the moon; in short: the outline was not there. It was obvious—what was happening here was the dissolution of matter itself; this matter had been transformed entirely, without residue, into a sonic substance, clattering deafeningly—only where? It seemed to Alexandr Ivanovich that it was clattering inside himself.

"You, Mr Shishnarfne," Alexandr Ivanovich was saying, addressing himself to empty space (for Shishnarfne was no longer there), "are perhaps the bearer of a passport from the transcendental world?"

"That's original," Alexandr Ivanovich jabbered, in answer to himself—or rather a jabbering came out of Alexandr Ivanovich … "Petersburg doesn't have three dimensions, it has four; the fourth is subject to uncertainty and is not marked on maps at all, unless by a point, for a point is the place of contact between the plane of this existence and the spherical surface of the immense astral cosmos; so any point in the spaces of Petersburg is capable in the twinkling of an eye of throwing up a resident of this dimension, from which no wall can save you; so a moment before I was there—among the points situated on the windowsill, and now I have appeared … "

"Where?" Alexandr Ivanovich wanted to exclaim, but he could not exclaim, because it was his throat that exclaimed:

"I have appeared … out of the point of your larynx … "

Alexandr Ivanovich gazed all round distractedly, while his throat went on automatically, regardless, hurling out deafening sounds:

"It's a passport you need … However, you're registered with us there: you just have to complete the ultimate pact in order to receive your passport; this passport is inscribed in you; you must just sign it inside yourself, with some extravagant deed, such as … Well, anyway, the deed will occur to you: perform it yourself; that kind of signature is acknowledged as the best in our parts … "

If at that moment my deranged hero had been able to glance at himself from outside, he would have been horrified: in the green-tinged, moonlit room he would have seen himself, holding his hands to his stomach and straining for all he was worth to bellow into the absolute emptiness in front of him; his head was thrown right back, and the huge aperture of his bellowing mouth would have seemed to him a black abyss of non-being; but Alexandr Ivanovich could not leap out of himself: and he did not see himself; the voice that resounded so thunderously from him seemed to him an alien automaton.

"When was I registered with you there," flashed through his brain (the drivel had overcome his consciousness).

"Then: after the act," his mouth split wide, deafeningly; and having done so, closed.

Then all of a sudden a veil was torn open before Alexandr Ivanovich: he remembered everything distinctly … That dream in Helsingfors, when he was being propelled through some kind of … well … spaces, linked to our spaces at the mathematical point of contact, so that while remaining attached to space, he was all the same truly able to be carried away into other spaces—so, then: when he was being propelled through other spaces …

He had performed it.

And by that act he had attached himself to *them*; Lippanchenko was merely an image which hinted at it; he had performed it; and with this the power had entered him; dashing from one organ to another and seeking the soul in his body, this power had taken hold little by little of the whole of him (he had become a drunkard, his sensuality had got out of control and so on).

And all the while this was happening to him he had thought that *they* were after him; but *they*—were inside him.

And while he was thinking this, roars were bursting out of him like the roaring of automobile horns:

"Our spaces are not yours; everything there flows the other way … And a simple Ivanov there is a Japanese, for the name, read backwards, is a Japanese one: Vonavi."

"So you too have to be read the other way round," flashed through his brain.

And he realised: "Shishnarfne, Shish-nar-fne … " It was a familiar word that he had pronounced on performing the *act*; only this dreamily familiar word had to be turned inside out.

And in a surge of involuntary fear he strained to cry out:
"Enfranshish."

From deep inside himself, beginning at his heart, but through the agency of his own laryngal apparatus, the answer came:

"You called me … Well—here I am … "

Enfranshish itself had now come for his soul.

With an ape-like leap Alexandr Ivanovich sprang out of his own room: the key clicked; silly man—he needed to spring out of his body, not his room; maybe the room actually was his body, and he was nothing but a shadow? That was how it must be, because from beyond the locked door came the ominous thunder of a voice that a moment before had been roaring out of his throat:

"Yes, yes, yes … It's me … I destroy irrevocably … "

Suddenly the moon lit up the steps of the staircase: in the utter darkness greyish patches stood out, just starting to be outlined, then grey patches, dull-white, pale, and ultimately patches burning with phosphorescence.

The loft

Through someone's carelessness the loft was not locked; and Dudkin rushed into it.

He slammed the door behind him.

It's strange in the loft at night: there's a layer of earth on the floor; you walk smoothly on this soft surface; all of a sudden: a thick beam pops up under your feet and knocks you down on all fours. Transverse strips of moonlight stretch brightly across: and you walk through them.

Suddenly …

—A transverse beam treats you to a violent blow on the nose; you risk being left forever with a broken nose.

Motionless white patches—underwear, towels and sheets … A draught skips through—and the white patches stretch out soundlessly: underwear, towels and sheets.

It is all empty.

Alexandr Ivanovich had found his way to the loft straight away; and, once there, he was astonished to find that the loft was not locked; no doubt the laundry-girl, lost in thoughts of her fiancé, had left the door open behind her. When Alexandr Ivanovich slipped through this door he—calmed down, kept hidden: breathed a sigh of relief; there were no footsteps running after him, no gramophone bellowing its abracadabra; not even an echoing door.

All that could be heard through the broken panes of the window was a song in the distance:

Mama, won't you buy me
Some blue poplin for a dress …

The hollow banging of the door was resolved into the beating of his heart; and the shadow that assailed him from below—simply into the shadow of the moon; all the rest was hallucinations; he needed treatment—that was all.

Alexandr Ivanovich strained to listen. And—what could he hear? You know very well yourself, of course, what he could hear: the absolutely distinct sound of a cracking beam: and—dense silence: that is to say—a net woven of nothing but rustles; there, in the first place—in the corner there was a hissing and hushing at work; secondly—a pressure in the atmosphere from inaudible footsteps; and—some slobberer swallowing his spittle.

In short—nothing but everyday, domestic noises: and no reason to be afraid of them.

At this Alexandr Ivanovich regained his self-control; and he could have gone back: in his room—he knew this now for certain—there was nobody and nothing (his attack of illness had passed). But still he didn't want to leave the loft: he moved cautiously between the underwear, towels and sheets to the window with its sheath of autumnal cobwebs and stuck his head through the remnants of glass: what he saw now wafted over him a breath of tranquillity and pacific melancholy.

Beneath his feet he could see—distinctly, in blinding simplicity: the precise square of the yard, which from here looked like a plaything, the silvery piles of aspen logs, from where he had so recently looked up at his windows with unfeigned terror; but the main thing was that in the porter's lodge they were still making merry; from the porter's lodge a hoarse song rang out; the pulley-block on the door gave a crash; and two small figures emerged; one of them hollered out:

> *Lord, I see the error of my ways:*
> *Falsehood did deceive my vision,*
> *Falsehood did bedim my eyes ...*
> *I took pity on my own white body,*
> *I took pity on my coloured raiment,*
> *On my honeyed victuals*
> *And my heady wine—*
> *I was afraid, I Pontius, of the arch-priest,*
> *I went in fear, I Pilate, of the Pharisees.*
> *I washed my hands—and washed my conscience!*
> *And sent an innocent to crucifixion.*

It was Voronkov the police clerk and Bessmertnyi, the cobbler from the basement, singing away. Alexandr Ivanovich thought for a moment: "Shall I go down and join them?" And he would have gone down ... If it weren't for—the staircase.

The staircase terrified him.

The sky had cleared. A turquoise rooftop, as though itself an island, now situated somewhere down below him, to the side—a turquoise rooftop was whimsically sketched with silver scales, and in their turn those silver scales merged with the living tremor of the river's waters.

The Neva was seething.

And a despairing cry came from the hooter of a belated steamer, of which all that could be seen was the receding eye of a red lantern. Further away, beyond the Neva, the Embankment stretched out; above the boxes of yellow, grey, and red-brown houses, above the columns of the grey and red-brown palaces, Rococo and Baroque, rose the dark walls of an immense temple, raised by human hands, prodding the moon's realm with its golden dome—rising from the walls with its grey-black, lofty cylindrical stone form, surrounded by a colonnade: St Isaac's …

And, barely visible, the golden Admiralty shot into the sky with its spire.

A voice was singing:

Lord, have mercy!
Jesu, forgive me!
I will return my title to the emperor—and mourn my soul,
I will sell my mansion—and endow the poor,
I will set free my wife—and go in quest of God …
Lord, have mercy!
Jesu, forgive me!

At this midnight hour—there, in the square, surely the old grenadier was already breathing heavily in his sleep, leaning on his bayonet; and his shaggy hat was resting against the bayonet; and the grenadier's shadow lay motionless on the interwoven pattern of the railings.

The whole square was empty.

At this midnight hour metal hooves dropped with a ringing sound on to their rock; a steed snorted with its nostrils into the incandescent mist; the bronze outline of the Horseman now separated itself from the horse's crupper, while a ringing spur scratched impatiently against the horse's side, to make the horse spring down from the rock.

And the horse sprang down from the rock.

Across the cobbles surged a cumbersome, clangorous clatter—over the bridge: towards the islands. The Bronze Horseman flew by into the mist; in his eyes was a greenish depth; the muscles of his metal arms—straightened, became taut; and the bronze head soared; the horse's hooves, in headlong, blinding arcs, barely touched the cobblestones; the horse's mouth gaped open in a deafening whinny like the whistle of a locomotive; dense steam from its nostrils drenched the street in scalding light; horses meeting it scuttled aside with a snort, in horror; and passers-by in horror closed their eyes.

Line after Line flew past: a section of the left bank flew past—in wharves, steamer funnels and a dirty heap of sacks stuffed with hemp; bits of waste land flew past, barges, fences, tarpaulins and a multitude of houses. And from the edge of the sea, from the city limits, the side of a building gleamed out of the mist: the side of a restless drinking-den.

The oldest Dutchman, dressed in black leather, twisted his way out from the mildewed threshold—into the freezing pandemonium (the moon had vanished into a cloud); a lantern trembled in his fingers beneath the blue-tinged face in its black leather hood: evidently the Dutchman's sensitive ear had picked out from here the horse's cumbersome clatter and its locomotive whinny, for the Dutchman had left the company of seamen like himself, who clinked their glasses from one dawn to the next.

Evidently he knew that the crazy, drunken feast would carry on here until the dullest dawn of all; evidently he knew that when the clocks struck long after midnight the mighty Guest would come flying to the clink of glasses: to down a glass of fiery kümmel; to shake many a calloused hand that from the captain's bridge would turn the steamer's heavy wheel at the very forts of Kronstadt; and the iron muzzle of a cannon would hurl its roar in the wake of a stern that ploughed the foam but did not answer to the signal.

But there was no catching that vessel: it would slip into a white cloud that had settled on the sea; it would merge with it, and move away with it—into the bright blue that heralds dawn.

All this the oldest Dutchman knew, dressed in black leather and stretched out into the mist from the mildewed steps: now he could discern the outline of the hurtling Horseman … The clatter of hooves could be heard; and—nostrils snorting as they blazed and pierced the mist with a pillar of incandescent light.

Alexandr Ivanovich moved away from the window, reassured, calmed, frozen (he had been in a draught through the remnants of the windowpanes); patches of white fluttered towards him—underwear, towels and sheets; a breeze blew up ...

And the patches began to move.

Timidly he opened the loft door; he had decided to go back to his cubby-hole.

Why this had happened ...

Illuminated, covered in phosphorescent patches, he now sat on his dirty bed, resting from the bouts of fear; here—was where his visitor had been; and here—a dirty woodlouse had been crawling: there was no visitor. These bouts of fear! There had been three, four and five of them in a night; after a hallucination came a period of lucidity.

He was now in such lucidity, like the moon shining into the distance—before receding clouds; and his consciousness was shining like the moon, lighting up his soul as the labyrinths of the Prospects are lit by the moon. His consciousness cast its light far in front and far behind—cosmic times and cosmic spaces.

In those spaces there was not a single soul: neither man nor shadow.

And—the spaces were empty.

Amidst his four reciprocally perpendicular walls he seemed to himself a captured prisoner in those spaces, unless a captured prisoner has a greater sense of freedom than all others, unless this cramped interval of walls is equal in extent to the whole world's expanse.

The whole world's expanse is deserted! His deserted room! ... The world's expanse is the last attainment of wealth ... The world's monotonous expanse! ... His room had always been marked by monotony ... The dwelling of a beggar would seem too luxurious before the beggarly surroundings of the world's expanse. If he had really withdrawn from the world, then the luxurious magnificence of the world would seem beggarly before these dark-yellow walls ...

As he rested from his attacks of delirium, Alexandr Ivanovich lost himself in dreams about how high he had raised himself above the sensual morass of the world.

A voice objected mockingly:

"Vodka?"

"Smoking?"

"Carnal longings?"

Was he really raised so far above the world's morass?

He dropped his head; that was where his illnesses and his fears came from, where his persecutions came from—from insomnia, cigarettes, abuse of alcohol.

He felt a very strong twinge in his bad molar; he clasped his hand to his cheek.

He saw his bout of acute insanity in a new light; he became aware now of the truth of his acute insanity; his insanity itself, in essence, stood before him now as an account rendered by his deranged sense organs to his conscious 'self'; and the Persian subject Shishnarfne symbolised an anagram; it was not he, in essence, who chased, pursued, hunted, but it was the overburdened organs of his body that chased and attacked his 'self'; and by running away from them, the 'self' became the 'non-self', because the 'self' returns to itself through the organs of the senses, not by running away from them; alcohol, smoking, insomnia were gnawing away at his feeble physical make-up; our physical make-up is tightly bound to spaces; and when it began to collapse, all the spaces cracked apart; and now bacilli had crawled into the gaps in his sensations, and ghosts had started fluttering in the spaces that enclose the body … So then: who was Shishnarfne? His obverse—an abracadabra dream, Enfranshish; and that dream undoubtedly came from vodka. Drunkenness, Enfranshish, Shishnarfne— were just stages of alcohol.

"Stop drinking. Stop smoking: and your sensory organs will work again!"

He—shuddered.

Today he had performed an act of betrayal. How could he have failed to understand that it was a betrayal? Why, without doubt it was: he had surrendered Nikolai Apollonovich to Lippanchenko out of fear: he remembered that ugly trade-off so distinctly. Without believing, he had believed, and there lay the betrayal. Lippanchenko was even more of a traitor; that Lippanchenko was betraying them Alexandr Ivanovich knew; but he hid his knowledge from himself (Lippanchenko had an unaccountable power over his soul); and that was where the root of his illness lay: in that terrible knowledge that Lippanchenko was a traitor; alcohol, smoking, dissoluteness—were merely consequences; so his hallucinations must be simply the final links in the chain with which Lippanchenko had knowingly bound him. Why? Because Lippanchenko knew that he knew; it was only by virtue of that knowledge that Lippanchenko kept so close to him.

Lippanchenko had enslaved his will; this enslavement of his will came about because his terrible suspicion would have given everything away; because he kept trying to dispel the terrible suspicion; he sought to chase the terrible suspicion away through intensified contact with Lippanchenko; and, suspecting his suspicion, Lippanchenko did not let him out of his sight; and so they bound themselves to each other; he poured mysticism into Lippanchenko; and the latter poured alcohol into him.

Alexandr Ivanovich now remembered distinctly the scene in Lippanchenko's study; that shameless cynic, that scoundrel, had pulled a fast one that time too; he remembered Lippanchenko's horrible, fatty neck with its horrible folds of fat; as though that neck was laughing brazenly there, until Lippanchenko turned round and caught how he was gazing at it; and, catching his gaze, Lippanchenko had understood everything.

That was why he had set about frightening him off: he took him by surprise with his attack and mixed up all the cards; he insulted him mortally with his suspicion and then offered him the only way out: to pretend that he believed in Ableukhov's treachery.

And he, the Fugitive, had believed it.

Alexandr Ivanovich leapt up; and in impotent fury he shook his fists; the deed was done; it was completed.

That was what his nightmare had been about.

Alexandr Ivanovich now translated the inexpressible nightmare with absolute precision into the language of his senses; the staircase, the little room, the attic were Alexandr Ivanovich's disgustingly neglected body; the frantic inhabitant of these miserable spaces, whom *they* attacked, who tried to escape from *them*, was the conscious 'self', laboriously lugging the discarded organs; Enfranshish was a foreign body that had entered his spirit's abode, his body—with the vodka; developing as a bacillus, Enfranshish ran from one organ to another; this was how he caused all the feelings of persecution, only to strike later at his brain and cause there a serious inflammation.

He remembered his first meeting with Lippanchenko: the impression was not a pleasant one; Nikolai Stepanovich, to tell the truth, displayed an especial curiosity towards the human weaknesses of those who came into contact with him; a high-class *provocateur* could, of course, perfectly well be the possessor of such an ungainly appearance and such a pair of senselessly blinking eyes.

He, no doubt, had looked a complete simpleton.

"The scum ... Oh, what scum!"

And the more he dwelt on Lippanchenko, on the contemplation of the parts of his body, his mannerisms, affectations, the more there rose before him not a man, but—a tarantula.

And then something steely entered his soul:

"Yes, I know what I shall do."

A brilliant thought occurred to him: everything would end so simply; why hadn't that come to mind earlier; his mission was drawn distinctly.

Alexandr Ivanovich burst out laughing:

"That scum thought he'd pull the wool over my eyes."

And again he felt a very strong twinge in his molar: Alexandr Ivanovich, snatched away from his dreaming, grasped his cheek; the room—the world's expanse—once again seemed a poverty-stricken room; his consciousness dimmed (like the moonlight in the clouds); fever made him shiver with anxiety and fears, and the minutes took their course sluggishly; one cigarette was smoked after another—down to the cardboard, down to the tip ...

When all of a sudden ...

The guest

Alexandr Ivanovich Dudkin heard a strange, booming sound; the strange sound boomed out down below; and then it was repeated (it began to boom repeatedly) on the stairs: blow after blow resounded between intervals of silence. It was as though someone was dropping from a height on to the stone a heavy metallic object, many tons in weight; and the blows of the metal, shivering the stone, rang out ever higher, rang out ever nearer. Alexandr Ivanovich realised that an intruder of some sort was knocking the staircase to pieces down below. He listened carefully, to see whether one of the doors on the staircase would open and allay the awfulness of this nocturnal vagabond. Hardly a vagabond, though …

Blow after blow thundered out; step after step was smashed; and stones spattered down from the blows of these ponderous footfalls: someone metallic and terrible was stubbornly mounting the stairs, from landing to landing, towards the dark-yellow attic; many thousands of tons now fell with a shattering roar from one step down on to the next: the steps collapsed; and—here it was: with a shattering roar the landing outside the door fell through.

The door itself split and snapped off: a violent crash, and—it flew off its hinges; melancholy swathes of lustreless green vapour poured in; there the expanses of the moon began—from the shattered door, from the landing, so that the attic room itself opened on to the inexplicable, while in the middle of the threshold, from the riven walls admitting spaces of a vitriolic hue—bowing his wreathed and green-hued head, extending his heavy, green-hued arm, stood an immense body, burning with phosphorus.

It was—the Bronze Guest.

The lustreless metallic cape hung down heavily—from the shoulders with their mottled gleam and the scaly armour; the moulded lip was molten and trembling ambiguously, because now Evgenii's fate was being repeated; and so the previous century repeated itself—now, at this very moment, when beyond the threshold of that wretched entrance the walls of the old building collapsed in expanses of vitriol; and in exactly the same way Alexandr Ivanovich's past gaped open; he cried out:

"I have remembered … I was expecting you … "

The bronze-browed giant chased through periods of time right up to the present moment, closing the well-forged circle; quarter centuries passed by; and Nikolai mounted the throne; and the Alexanders—mounted the throne; but Alexandr Ivanych, a shadow, tirelessly overcame the same circle, all the periods of time, traversing days, and years, and minutes, traversing the damp Petersburg Prospects, traversing—in dream, in wakefulness, traversing … drearily; and along behind him, along behind them all—thundered the metallic blows that shattered lives: metallic blows thundered—in waste lands and in villages; they thundered in towns; they thundered through gateways, across landings and up the steps of midnight staircases.

It was the thunder of periods of time; I have heard that thunder. Have you heard it?

Apollon Apollonovich Ableukhov is one such blow of the thundering stone; Petersburg is a blow of the thundering stone; the caryatid at the entrance, about to crash down—is another such blow of the stone; the chase is ineluctable; and the blows are ineluctable; no hiding in the attic; the attic is of Lippanchenko's making; and the attic is a trap; break out of it, break out—with blows … that strike Lippanchenko!

Then everything will turn around; under the blows of the metal that shatters stone Lippanchenko will fly apart, the attic will collapse and Petersburg will be destroyed; the caryatid will be destroyed under the blows of that metal; and from the blow to Lippanchenko the bare head of Ableukhov will split in twain.

Everything was now illuminated, everything, now that after ten decades the Bronze Guest himself appeared and said to him in hollow tones:

"Greetings, my son!"

Only three paces: three crashes of the sundered beams beneath the feet of the colossal visitor; the bronze-cast emperor crashed down upon a chair with his metallic bottom; his elbow with its green gleam dropped the weight of all its bronze from the folds of his cape on to the cheap little table, with bell-like, plangent sounds; with absent-minded leisureliness the emperor lifted his bronze laurels from his head; and the wreath of bronze laurels broke off from his brow with a crackle.

411

And with a jingle and a jangle, the hand of massive weight took from the folds of his camisole a red-hot pipe, and indicating the pipe with his eyes, he winked at it:

"Petro Primo Catharina Secunda … "

He inserted it into his mighty lips and wisps of green smoke from the unsoldered copper twined about beneath the moon.

Alexandr Ivanovich, Evgenii, now for the first time fathomed that for a century he had been running in vain, that the blows were thundering behind him with no anger—through villages, through towns, through gateways and up staircases; he had forever been forgiven, and everything past together with all that was to come—was only a spectral transition through ordeals until the Archangel's trump.

And—he fell at the Guest's feet:

"Teacher!"

In the Guest's bronze cavities gleamed a bronze melancholy; the hand that shatters stones, becoming incandescent, dropped amicably on to his shoulder and broke his collar-bone.

"Never mind: die, suffer … "

The Metallic Guest, glowing beneath the moon with thousand-degree heat, now sat before him, scorching, crimson-red; now, fired right through, he turned a blinding white and released on to Alexandr Ivanovich, as he bent before him, a searing torrent; in utter delirium Alexandr Ivanovich trembled in the hundred-ton embrace: the Bronze Horseman was infused into his veins.

Scissors

"Master: you asleep?"

Alexandr Ivanovich had long been dimly aware through his heavy oblivion that someone was shaking him.

"Hey, master? … "

At last he opened his eyes and emerged into the sullen day:

"Come on, master!"

A head bent down.

"What is it?"

Alexandr Ivanovich only now realised that he was stretched out on the trestle.

412

"The police?"

A corner of the warm pillow stuck out in front of his eye.

"There's no police here … "

A dark-red patch on the pillow crawled away—brrr: and—it flashed through his consciousness:

"That's a bedbug … "

He tried to raise himself on to his elbow, but dropped back to sleep.

"Heavens above, do wake up … "

He raised himself on to his elbow:

"Is that you, Styopka?"

He caught sight of a rushing jet of steam; the steam was from his kettle: on his table he saw his kettle and cup.

"Oh, that's wonderful, a cup of tea."

"What's wonderful about it: you're burning, master … "

Alexandr Ivanovich noticed with astonishment that he was not undressed, he hadn't even taken his overcoat off.

"How do you come to be here?"

"I dropped in to see you: there's strikes everywhere—in lots of factories; they've sent police reinforcements … I dropped in to see you, with the Breviary, I mean."

"But as far as I remember, I've got the Breviary."

"What do you mean, master: you must have imagined it … "

"Didn't we see each other yesterday … "

"We haven't seen each other for a day or two."

"And I thought: it seemed to me … "

What had he thought?

"I dropped in this morning; and I saw—you were lying there groaning; tossing and turning—in a fever from top to toe."

"I'm in perfectly good health, Styopka."

"That's not what I call health! … I've boiled the kettle for you; brought some bread; a nice warm roll; have something to drink— you'll feel better. No good just lying there … "

In the night it was boiling metal that had flowed through his veins (that he remembered).

"Yes—yes: in the night, old chap, I had a mighty fever … "

"I don't wonder … "

"A hundred-degree fever … "

413

"You'll get stewed in alcohol."

"Stewed in my own juice, eh? Ha-ha … "

"What of it? They say that one alcoholic fellow had little puffs of smoke coming out of his mouth … And he got stewed … "

Alexandr Ivanovich grinned an unpleasant grin.

"You've already started seeing demons … "

"There were some demons, that's true … That's why I asked for the Breviary: to exorcise them."

"You'll finish up seeing the Green Serpent … "

Alexandr Ivanovich gave another crooked grin:

"But the whole of Russia, my friend … "

"Well?"

"Is the offspring of the Green Serpent … "

But he was actually thinking:

"What did I say that for! … "

"It's not like that at all: Russia's a Christian country … "

"Rubbish … "

"It's you who's talking rubbish: you'll drink yourself—to, to … that one … "

Alexandr Ivanovich jumped up in terror.

"Which one?"

"You'll drink yourself—to the white … woman … "

That he was on the point of delirium tremens there was no doubt.

"Oh! I tell you what: you might pop down to the chemist's … Buy me some quinine … "

"All right, if you like … "

"Only remember: not the sulphate; the sulphate is just kids' stuff … "

"It isn't quinine, master, that … "

"Off with you! … "

Stepan rushed out of the door, and Alexandr Ivanovich—after him:

"And Styopushka, while you're at it, some raspberry jam: I'd like some raspberry jam with my tea."

But he was actually thinking:

"Raspberries are a splendid sudorific," and with vigorous, almost flowing gestures he ran over to the tap; but hardly had he washed, when everything inside him flared up again, confusing reality and delirium.

So. While he had been talking to Styopka he had felt all the time that something was lying in wait for him outside the door: something forever familiar. There, outside the door? And he slipped out there; but outside the door the landing revealed itself; and the banisters on the stairs dangled over the abyss; Alexandr Ivanovich stood there above the abyss, leaning against the banisters, clicking his tongue, which was completely dry and felt as though made of wood, and shivering from cold. He had a sensation of taste, a sensation of bronze: both in his mouth and on the tip of his tongue.

"*It* must be lying in wait for me in the yard … "

But in the yard there was nobody, nothing.

In vain he ran all round the side streets and the alleyways (between the piles of firewood); the asphalt glistened silvery; the aspen logs glistened silvery; no one, nothing.

"Wherever is *it*?"

Styopka ran by with his purchases; but he ducked behind the logs to hide from Styopka, because it dawned on him:

"*It*—is in a metallic place … "

What kind of a place might that be, why was *it* a metallic *it*? To all such questions Alexandr Ivanovich's whirling consciousness gave only very vague replies. He strained in vain to recall: there was nothing resembling memory left of the consciousness that dwelt within him; one single recollection was left: some other consciousness had really been there; that other consciousness had been unfolding harmonious images before him; it was in that world, not in the least like ours, that *it* resided.

It would appear again.

On waking, any other consciousness turned into a mathematical point, not a real one; and *it*, therefore, must be compressed in daytime into a small part of a mathematical point; but a point has no parts; so—it followed—*it* did not exist.

What was left was the memory of the absence of memory and of the task that had to be performed, which would brook no delay; what was left was the memory—of what?

Of the metallic place …

Something dawned on him: and with light, springy steps he ran to the intersection of two streets; on the intersection of these two streets (he knew) an iridescent gleam flickered from a shop window … Only where was the shop? And where—the intersection?

There were objects shining there.

"Are there metals there?"

What an extraordinary predilection!

Why had such a predilection revealed itself in Alexandr Ivanovich? Indeed: on the corner of the crossroads there were metals gleaming; it was a cheap little shop with all manner of items like knives, forks, scissors.

He went into the shop.

Out of a dirty office an ugly sleepy face dragged itself to the gleaming steel of the counter (presumably the proprietor of these drills, blades and saws); a narrow-browed head fell at a steep angle on to the chest; reddish-brown eyes were concealed in their sockets behind a pair of spectacles:

"I'd like, I'd like … "

And not knowing what to take, Alexandr Ivanovich caught his arm on the tooth of a saw; it glittered and squealed: "vizz-vizz-vizz". The proprietor scrutinised this chance customer from under lowered brows; it was not surprising that he looked at him suspiciously: Alexandr Ivanovich had slipped out of his attic unprepared; he had slipped out just as he had lain on the bed, in his overcoat: the coat, though, was crumpled and soiled; but the main thing was: he hadn't put his hat on; his shaggy, uncombed head and his immoderately gleaming eyes would have given anyone a fright.

That was why the proprietor scrutinised him suspiciously, frowning, raising his oppressive features, which were heavily built by nature itself; this face stared at Dudkin with insurmountable distaste.

But, overcoming itself, the face boomed out plaintively:

"D'you want a saw?"

And the eyes, drilling into him querulously, were saying ferociously:

"Oh, oh, oh! … A real DT case: that's a fine business … "

It only seemed so.

"No, you know, a saw—it would be awkward, a saw … What I want, you know, is a sharp Finnish knife."

But the person snapped gruffly:

"Sorry: haven't got any Finnish knives."

But the drilling eyes seemed to be saying decisively:

"Give you a knife, and you'll get up to all sorts … "

If the eyelids had been raised these querulously drilling little eyes

416

would just have turned into ordinary eyes; still a certain resemblance struck Alexandr Ivanovich; just imagine—a resemblance to Lippanchenko. Just then the figure for some reason turned its back; and cast such a glance at the customer as would have felled an ox.

"Well, never mind: some scissors … "

And actually he was thinking: why this ferocity, this resemblance to Lippanchenko? But then he consoled himself: what resemblance was there, after all!

Lippanchenko was clean-shaven, while this podgy fellow had a curly beard.

But at the thought of *a certain person* Alexandr Ivanovich remembered everything—everything! He remembered with absolute clarity why he had had the idea of coming to a shop selling objects of this kind. What he was planning to do was in essence simple: like striking a match—nothing to it.

He even began to shiver over the scissors:

"Don't wrap them —no, no … I only live nearby … I can manage like that: I'll get them home like that … "

So saying, he stuffed the miniature scissors, with which a dandy would no doubt trim his nails of a morning, into his pocket—and rushed away.

Surprised, frightened, suspicious, the square, narrow-browed head stared after him (from behind the gleaming counter) with its protruding frontal bone; this frontal bone protruded outwards in a single concentrated effort—to understand what had happened: to understand, come what may, to understand, at any price; to understand, or … to burst into smithereens.

And the frontal bone was unable to understand, the forehead was pitiful: narrow, with diagonal furrows; it seemed to be weeping.

CHAPTER SEVEN

Or: the events of a drab grey day continue.

> *I'm tired, my friend, I'm tired: for peace my heart now aches.*
> *Days hasten after days …*
>
> A Pushkin

The immeasurable

WE LEFT NIKOLAI APOLLONOVICH at the moment when Alexandr Ivanovich, astonished by the torrent of loquacity that had suddenly burst from Ableukhov's lips, shook his hand and slipped smartly off into the black surge of bowler hats, while Nikolai Apollonovich felt that he was once again expanding.

We left Nikolai Apollonovich at the moment when his troublesome concatenation of circumstances had unexpectedly reached a benign resolution.

Up till this moment he had been beset by towering crags of delirious visions and monstrous delusions; ominous Everests of events had towered over him and toppled—in twenty-four hours: waiting in the Summer Garden with the anxious cawing of the jackdaws; wrapping himself in red silk; the ball—that is to say: striped Harlequins with bells, jesters in flame-red leggings, a hunch-backed yellow Pierrot and a pale clown with deathly mien that scared young ladies—all flying in fear through the rooms in one great harlequinade; a pale-blue mask, that curtseyed as it danced, delivering with a curtsey a little note; and—his shameful flight from the ballroom out to the archway that was all but a latrine, where the moth-eaten gent had waylaid him; and in the end—Pepp Peppovich Pepp, otherwise known as: a sardine-tin of terrible import, which … was still … ticking.

A sardine-tin of terrible import, capable of transforming everything around it into one great slurry of blood.

We left Nikolai Apollonovich by a shop window; but we abandoned him; quick drops began to drip between the senator's son and ourselves; a net of drizzling rain came upon us; and in this net all the usual weighty objects, protrusions and niches, caryatids, entrances, the cornices of brick-built balconies—all lost distinctness of outline, gradually blurring and barely discernible.

Umbrellas were raised.

Nikolai Apollonovich stood by the shop window, thinking there was no name for that crushing atrocity: for that atrocity that had lasted a day and a night, twenty-four hours, or—eighty thousand six hundred seconds, that chattered away in his pocket: eighty thousand moments, meaning that number of points in time; but barely did the moment arrive and provide a foothold—a second, a moment, a point—than, spreading swiftly in circles, it gradually turned into a swelling, cosmic sphere; and this sphere burst; your heel slipped off into the void: and the wanderer in time tumbled no one knew where or into what, cast down, perhaps, into cosmic space, until ... a new moment; and so the circular day and night, the eighty thousand seconds, chattering away in your pocket, stretched away, each second bursting: and your heel slipped away into the immeasurable.

No, there was no name for that crushing atrocity!

It was better not to think. But—thinking was going on somewhere; maybe in his swelling heart some thoughts were hammering away which had never arisen in his brain but had all the same arisen in his heart; his heart was thinking; his brain was feeling.

Of its own accord an extremely clever plan, worked out in detail, was arising; a relatively safe plan, too, but ... a base one: yes ... base!

Who was it who had thought it out? Was it possible that Nikolai Apollonovich could have hit upon this plan?

Here's what it was all about:—all these recent hours barbed fragments of thoughts had been flickering before his eyes, tinged with lurid, flame-red flashes and star-like sparks, like the merry tinsel on a Christmas-tree: they kept falling incessantly into one spot that was lit by consciousness—from one darkness into another; now the figure of a jester might be pulling faces there, now a lemon-yellow

Petrushka might go galloping by—from one darkness to another—across that spot that was lit by consciousness; and consciousness illuminated dispassionately all the swarming images; and when they melted into one another, consciousness sketched upon them an astounding, inhuman meaning; then Nikolai Apollonovich all but spat in disgust:

"A matter of conviction?"

"There was no matter of conviction at all … "

"There's just a base fear and a base animal feeling: saving your own skin … "

"Yes, yes, yes … "

"I'm an out-and-out scoundrel … "

But we have seen already that his venerable papa was gradually reaching exactly the same conviction.

Could it be that all this (what, we shall see anon) took its course consciously in his will, in his swiftly beating heart and in his inflamed brain?

No, no, no!

But all the same there were certain swarms of thoughts there, thinking themselves; it was not he who thought the thoughts, but … the thoughts thought themselves … Who was the author of the thoughts? All morning he had been unable to answer that question, but … —thinking happened, images took shape, ideas arose; something jumped about in his hammering heart and drilled in his brain; it arose over the sardine-tin—precisely there: it had probably crawled across out of the sardine-tin when he had awoken from a dream he had now forgotten and seen that his head was resting on the sardine-tin—it had crawled across from the sardine-tin; and that was when he had hidden the sardine-tin—he didn't remember where, but … it seemed … in his desk; and that was when he had made good his escape from that accursed house, while everyone else was asleep; and he had wandered around the streets, drifting from one coffee-house to another.

It was not his head thinking, it was … the sardine-tin.

But out on the streets all this went on arising, taking shape, forming images, drawing lines; if it was his head thinking, then his head—it too!—had also turned into a sardine-tin of terrible import, which … went on … ticking, or else it was not he who was in charge of his thoughts, but the thundering Prospect (on the Prospect all personal thoughts turn into an impersonal porridge); but if it was indeed the porridge thinking, he was doing nothing to prevent the porridge from pouring in through his ears.

And that was why the thoughts were thinking themselves.

Something grey and soft was wriggling unhealthily beneath the bones of his skull: soft and, above all—grey, like the Prospect, like the flagstones of the pavement, like the flannel of fog pressing ceaselessly from the sea-shore.

Finally—the fully thought out plan, ready in all respects (about which we shall tell anon) had appeared in the field of consciousness—at the most inopportune moment, when Nikolai Apollonovich, who Lord alone knows why had popped into the university vestibule (where the church is), was leaning nonchalantly against one of the four massive columns, in conversation with a lecturer who had dropped in, and who was bending over towards him, spattering him with spittle, and losing no time in hurriedly communicating to him the contents of a German article, where … —yes: in his soul something suddenly burst (the way a doll inflated with hydrogen bursts into flabby little pieces of celluloid, such as balloons are made of): shuddering, recoiling, breaking free—he set off at a run, with no idea where, because— precisely: at that time it was revealed to him:—

—the author of the plan—was he himself …

He was an out-and-out scoundrel! …

And when he realised that he rushed to the Eighteenth Line of Vasilevskii Island; a bedraggled cabby took him there; and from the cab an intermittent, indignant whisper could be heard, directed at the driver's back,:

"Well? … What do you say to that? … A fraud … a deceiver … a murderer … Simply—saving his own skin … "

He was evidently expressing his indignation out loud, because the cabby turned round to him in irritation.

"What's that?"

"No … Never mind … "

And the cabby thought to himself:

"Got a weird one here, that's for sure … "

Like Apollon Apollonovich, Nikolai Apollonovich talked to himself. And the winds took up his words:

"Parricide! … "

"Fraud! … "

At his wits' end, Nikolai Apollonovich jumped out of the cab; crossing the asphalt yard and passing the piles of aspen logs, he rushed into the black staircase, to go hurtling up the steps and—for whatever reason; probably just out of curiosity: to look straight in the eye the culprit of this occurrence, who had brought the package, since the 'refusal' that he had thought up was, of course—a pretext: it was perfectly possible not to throw this 'refusal' in their faces (and thereby to save time).

And it was then that he ran into Alexandr Ivanovich: the rest we have seen.

There is no name for this crushing atrocity!

Yes —but his heart, heated up by all that had happened to him, began slowly to melt: the lump of cardiac ice—became after all a heart; up till now it had been beating senselessly; now it was beating with meaning; and feelings were beating in him too; all unheralded, those feelings quivered; and now those palpitations—shook his entire soul and turned it upside down.

That monster of a house was just now towering over the street with its clusters of brick balconies; by simply running across the street, he could have touched its stone side; but when the light rain started falling, its stone side began to float in the mist.

Just as everything else was floating now.

The light rain started falling—and this monster of assembled stones had already come apart; and now it was raising up—out of the rain to meet the rain—the lace of its fragile contours and barely discernible lines—simply rococo: the rococo vanishes into nothing.

A wet gleam brightened on the shop-fronts, on the windows, on the chimneys: the first rivulet shot out of a drainpipe; from another drainpipe a steady flow of drops began to drip; the pale pavements were sprinkled with tiny spots: their deathly dryness gradually turned a greyish brown; the wheel of a rushing cab sent up a spattering of mud.

And off it went, off it went …

In the hazy, wafting wetness, hidden by the umbrellas of passers-by, Nikolai Apollonovich disappeared: the Prospects floated in the mists; it seemed that these monsters of buildings had been squeezed out of one space into some other space; from there their interwoven patterns—of caryatids, spires, walls—flickered vaguely. His head was in a whirl; he leant against a shop window; something in him burst, flew apart; and—a fragment of childhood arose.

He saw—his head resting on the unsteady lap of his old governess, Nockert; the old woman is reading under the lamp:

Wer reitet so spät durch Nacht und Wind?
Es ist der Vater mit seinem Kind …

Suddenly stormy squalls rampage outside the window; darkness rages there, and noise: what's happening out there must be the chase after the little boy; the governess' shadow flickers on the wall.

And again …

—Apollon Apollonovich—small, grey-haired, ageing—is teaching little Kolia a French *contredanse*; he steps out smoothly, and, counting the steps, beats time by clapping: he trips out to the right and to the left; he trips out to the front and to the back; instead of music he barks out—in a loud, rapid voice:

O, who rides by night through the woodland so wild?
It is the fond father embracing his child …

Then he raises his hairless brows to Kolenka:

"What is the first, hm-hm, figure of the quadrille, my dear?"

All the rest was *woodland wild*, because they were caught by the chase: and the son was torn away from the father:

But, clasp'd to his bosom, the infant was dead.

All of his life that had passed since that moment turned out to be only a play of the mist. The fragment of childhood closed.

A wet gleam brightened on the shop-fronts, on the windows, on the chimneys; the rivulet wove its way out of a drainpipe; the greyish-brown moisture on the pavement glistened; a wheel spattered mud. In the hazy, wafting wetness, hidden by the umbrellas of passers-by, Nikolai Apollonovich disappeared; it seemed that these monsters of buildings had been squeezed out of one space into another; from there their patterns of interwoven lines—of caryatids, spires, walls—flickered vaguely.

Cranes

Nikolai Apollonovich felt drawn to his homeland, the nursery, because he realised: he was a little child.

He needed to shake off everything, forget everything, he needed to learn—everything—all over again, as you learn in childhood; his old, forgotten homeland—now he could hear it. And: over everything there suddenly rang out the voice of his orphaned, but nonetheless beloved childhood, a voice that had not sounded for a long time; but which sounded now.

That voice's sound?

It is inaudible, as the cry of the cranes is inaudible over the city; in the roar of the city people do not hear the cranes as they fly so high; but there they are, flying, flying past over the city—the cranes! … Somewhere, on the Nevskii Prospect, say, in the tremor of hurtling cabs and the clamour of newspaper vendors, where only the throaty voice of an automobile is raised above everything—amidst these metallic voices, in an early evening hour, in spring, on the pavement, a dweller of the fields, who has come to the city by chance, will stand still, rooted to the spot; he will stop—and, tilting his shaggy, bearded head to one side, will stop you too.

"Shhh! … "

"What is it?"

And he, the dweller of the fields, who has come to the city by chance, will shake his bearded, shaggy head at your astonishment and give you a sly grin:

"Can't you hear it?"

"?"

"Just listen … "

"What? What is it? … "

And he will sigh:

"Up there … the cranes … are calling."

And you will listen too.

At first you will hear nothing; but then, from somewhere in the spaces high above, you will catch a familiar, forgotten sound—a strange sound …

The cry of the cranes.

You both raise your heads. Then a third raises his head, a fifth, a tenth.

At first the ethereal spaces blind you all; nothing but air … Yet— no: the air is not all … for amidst all that blue there is something that stands out clearly—something familiar: the cranes … flying … north!

A whole circle of onlookers gathers around; all have their heads raised, and the pavement—gets blocked; a policeman pushes through; and—no: he can't contain his curiosity; he stops, throws back his head; he—gazes.

And there's a rumble:

"The cranes! … "

"They're coming back … "

"How lovely … "

Over Petersburg's accursed roofs, over its wood-block pavements, above the crowd—that image of early spring, familiar voice!

And the voice of childhood is like that!

Sometimes it is inaudible; but it is there; the cry of the cranes over the Petersburg rooftops—just wait, it will ring out! The voice of childhood is like that.

It was something of that sort that Nikolai Apollonovich now heard.

It was as though someone sad, whom Nikolai Apollonovich had never once seen, had drawn around his soul a penetrating circle of redemption and had stepped into his soul; the bright light of his eyes began to penetrate his soul. Nikolai Apollonovich shuddered; something that had been compressed in his soul gave way; now it moved with ease away into the boundless; yes, the boundless was there, and unflinchingly it said:

"You all drive me away! ... "

"What, what, what?" Nikolai Apollonovich too tried to make that voice out; and the boundless said unflinchingly:

"I keep watch over you all ... "

Such were its words.

Nikolai Apollonovich cast his eyes all round in astonishment, as though he expected to see before him the owner of that voice that sang unflinchingly; but what he saw was something else; to be precise: he saw a floating porridge of bowler hats, moustaches, chins; as he went further—just the misty Prospect; and people's eyes were floating in it, as everything was now floating.

The misty Prospect seemed familiar and dear to him; oh my, oh my—how sad the misty Prospect seemed; and the flow of bowler hats and faces? All these passing faces—passed by deep in thought, in unutterable sadness.

But the voice's owner was not there.

Only who was that over there? Over on the other side? Beside that monster of a building? And—under that cluster of balconies?

Yes, there was someone standing there.

Just like himself, Nikolai Apollonovich; like him, beside a shop window, just standing there—beneath an open umbrella ... Looks all right: maybe just looking at something ... seems so; can't make his face out. So what's so special about him? Here on this side is Nikolai Apollonovich, just standing there, minding his own business ... And the other one—he's all right too: just like Nikolai Apollonovich, like all the passers-by—just happens to be walking this way; and he is sad and dear, too (as they are all now dear); he glances over with an independent air: as if to say, I'm all right, there are no flies on me! ... No beard, either, clean-shaven ... The outline of his coat is a bit like—what, though? Isn't he nodding? ...

Just wearing some cap or other.

Where can it have been?

Ought to go up to him, maybe, to the dear owner of that cap? It's a public Prospect, after all: it really is! There's plenty of room for everyone on this public Prospect ... Just like that—go up to him:

have a look at the things there … under the glass in the shop window. Anyone has the right …

Just stand beside him in an independent way, and when the chance arises cast an eye over him, make it look an absent-minded glance, but really it'll be close scrutiny!

Make certain what's going on here.

No, no, no! … Touch his fingers that are surely numb with cold, and weep with silly happiness! …

Fall down upon the pavement!

"I am sick, and deaf, and heavy-laden … comfort me, teacher, protect me … "

And hear in reply:

"Rise … "

"And walk … "

"Sin no more … "

No, of course there would be no answer.

Of course—the sad one would make no answer, because there cannot be any answers yet; the answer will come later—in an hour, in a year, in five, or maybe even longer—in a hundred, in a thousand years; but the answer—will come! But now the tall, sad one, who had never been seen in dreams, but who turned out to be nothing but a stranger—not a straightforward stranger, though, but, as it were, an enigmatic one—the tall, sad one would simply glance at him and put his finger to his lips. Without looking, without stopping, he would walk off in the slush …

And in the slush would disappear …

But the day will come.

All this will change in the twinkling of an eye. And all these passing strangers—those who have walked by one another (somewhere in an alleyway) at a moment of mortal danger, those who have spoken of that unutterable moment with unutterable glances and have then walked off into the boundless—all, all of them, shall meet!

And no one shall take from them the joy of that meeting.

I'm just walking here ... not getting in anyone's way ...

"What am I doing," thought Nikolai Apollonovich, "this is no time to be daydreaming ... "

There was no time to lose ... Time was passing, and the sardine-tin was still ticking away; straight to his desk; wrap it all carefully in paper, put it in his pocket, and into the Neva with it ...

And he began to look away from that monster of a building where the stranger was standing under the cluster of brick-built balconies with his umbrella open, because that notorious porridge of bodies on their many legs had started to flow again—that porridge of human bodies that ran here spring, summer, winter: unchanging bodies.

And he couldn't keep it up, but had another look.

The stranger had not moved from the spot; evidently he was waiting, just as Nikolai Apollonovich was: waiting for the rain to stop; suddenly he moved off, suddenly merged with the flow of people—those groups of two and four; he was hidden by a tricorn hat with its brilliant shine; his umbrella stuck out helplessly.

"Ought to turn my back and walk away! To hell with him, that stranger—really, what a thing!"

But he had barely had that thought when (as he noticed) the inquisitive cap began to emerge once more from behind the shining tricorn and the hurrying shoulders; risking being run over by a cab he ran across the road; he was holding out his umbrella, in danger of being snatched by the wind, in a ridiculous way.

Well, how could he turn his back then? How could he walk away?

"What is he up to," Nikolai Apollonovich thought and to his own surprise noted as a shock:

"So that's what he looks like?"

At close quarters the stranger definitely lost; he made a better impression at a distance; he looked more mysterious; sadder; his movements—more unhurried.

"Hey! ... Gracious me: doesn't he look idiotic. What a cap! Is that how you wear a cap? Running along on legs like a crane's; his coat flapping, his umbrella torn; and one galosh doesn't fit ... "

"Phew!" any self-respecting citizen would have uttered incoherently and gone on his way, pursing his lips in indignation and with an independent air: a self-respecting citizen would have sensed some-thing—something rather like this:

"So what! ... I'm just walking here ... not getting in anyone's way ... I might give way if the occasion arises. But don't expect me to ... Not on your life: I'll walk where I want to ... "

Nikolai Apollonovich, it has to be admitted, did not feel like a self-respecting citizen (where would respect come from!); but the stranger probably did feel like one, despite his coat, his umbrella and the galosh that was slipping off his foot.

As though he was saying:

"May I make myself plain: I just happen to be passing by, but I'm a self-respecting passer-by ... And I won't let anyone get in my way ... I won't give way to anybody ... "

Nikolai Apollonovich felt hostility at this; and, on the point of standing aside, he changed his tactics: he did not stand aside; and so they all but bumped noses; Nikolai Apollonovich—in astonishment; the stranger—without the slightest surprise; what was surprising was that his big hand (with goose-pimples), numb with cold, was raised to his cap; and a hoarse, wooden, clipped voice rasped out with determination:

"Ni-ko-lai A-pol-lo-no-vich!! ... "

It was only then that Nikolai Apollonovich noticed that this nondescript who had advanced upon him so abruptly (might be a tradesman of some sort) had a bandage round his throat; most likely he had a boil on his throat, and a boil, as is well known, restricting your freedom of movement, appears most inconveniently on your Adam's apple, on your back (between your shoulder-blades)—and may appear ... in an unmentionable place! ...

But any more detailed reflection on the properties of nefarious boils was interrupted:

"You don't appear to recognise me?"

(Oh dear, oh dear!) ...

"To whom do I have the honour," Nikolai Apollonovich made to begin, pursing his lips in indignation, but, looking more attentively at the stranger, he suddenly recoiled, pulled off his hat and cried out with a distorted face:

"No ... is it you? ... What a contingency! ... "

He probably meant to exclaim: "what a coincidence" ...

Naturally: it was difficult to recognise Sergei Sergeevich in this chance passer-by with the appearance of a beggar, because, in the first place, Likhutin had garbed himself in a civilian suit which sat on him like a saddle on a cow; and secondly: Sergei Sergeich Likhutin was—oh, dear, oh dear!—clean-shaven: that was what really did it! Instead of a curly blonde beard there was a senseless, spotty emptiness protruding there; and—where had his moustache gone? This hair-free place (between his lips and nose) transformed a familiar face into an unfamiliar one—into just a disagreeable emptiness.

The absence of Likhutin's proper beard and Likhutin's proper moustache gave the Second Lieutenant the extraordinary appearance of an idiot:

"No ... Either my eyes are deceiving me, or ... it seems, Sergei Sergeevich, that ... you ... "

"Perfectly correct: I'm in civilian dress ... "

"That wasn't what I meant, Sergei Sergeich ... It's not that ... That's not what surprised me ... What is surprising is .. "

"What is surprising?"

"You are somehow completely transformed, Sergei Sergeich ... You must, please, forgive me ... "

"That's of no consequence ... "

"No, of course, of course ... I was just ... I meant to say that you have shaved ... "

"Oh, what does that matter," Likhutin took offence, "what does it matter: 'shaved': why shouldn't I? Well, so I've shaved ... I haven't slept all night ... Why shouldn't I shave? ... "

In the Second Lieutenant's voice Nikolai Apollonovich was struck by a kind of anger, an overwhelming fraughtness, which sat so uneasily with his shaven mien.

"Well, so I shaved ... "

"Of course, of course ... "

"That's all there is to it!" Likhutin pressed on. "I'm leaving the service ... "

"How do you mean, leaving it? ... Why are you leaving it? ... "

"For private reasons that are entirely my own business ... These details, Nikolai Apollonovich, have nothing to do with you ... Our private business has nothing to do with you."

Second Lieutenant Likhutin thereupon began to move closer.

431

"However, there are matters which … "

Nikolai Apollonovich, jostling other pedestrians with his back, began very obviously to retreat:

"There are matters, Sergei Sergeich?"

"Matters which, my good sir … "

Nikolai Apollonovich caught an obviously ominous note in the Second Lieutenant's hoarse voice; and it seemed to him that the other was distinctly attempting to take hold of his arms for some reason.

"Have you caught a cold?" he abruptly changed the topic of conversation and stepped off the pavement; in explanation of his comment he touched his own neck, implying the bandage on Likhutin's neck, some kind of cold in the throat—a quinsy, maybe, or perhaps—influenza.

But Sergei Sergeevich turned red, stepped swiftly off the pavement to continue his assault with a view to … a view to … a view to … Some of the passers-by stopped and looked:

"Ni-ko-lai A-pol-lo-no-vich! … "

"?"

"Really, I didn't come running after you in order to talk about some neck, for God's sake … "

A third man stopped, a fifth, a tenth, probably imagining that a petty thief had been apprehended.

"This has all got nothing to do with the matter … "

Ableukhov's attention became more acute; to himself he whispered:

"Is that the case? … So what does have something to do with it?" And, avoiding Likhutin, he stepped back on to the damp pavement.

"What is this all about?"

Where was his memory?

The business to be settled with the lieutenant was no laughing matter. Why—the domino, of course! For God's sake, the domino! Nikolai Apollonovich had thoroughly forgotten about the *domino*; it was only now that he remembered:

"There is a matter, there is … "

No doubt Sofia Petrovna Likhutina had let the cat out of the bag about the incident in the unlit entrance; and about the incident at the Winter Canal.

And it was about this matter that Likhutin was now assailing him.

"This is all I needed ... Oh, damn it: what a bad time for this to happen! ... What a bad time! ... "

And suddenly everything took on a frown.

The swarms of bowlers darkened; the top hats gleamed vengefully; from all sides the noses of men-in-the-street began to spring out: noses flowed by in their multitudes: aquiline noses, cockerels' noses, the noses of chickens, greenish, blue-grey ones; and—a nose with a wart: senseless, hurrying, huge.

Nikolai Apollonovich, avoiding Likhutin's gaze, took this all in and buried his eyes in the shop window.

Meanwhile Sergei Sergeevich Likhutin, taking hold of Ableukhov's hand and either shaking it or simply squeezing it, gathering around himself a crowd of inquisitive gawpers—relentlessly, tirelessly snapped out in his wooden falsetto: just like drumsticks!

"I ... I ... I ... have the honour of informing you, that since early morning I ... I ... I ... "

"?"

"Have been on your heels ... And I have been ... I have been everywhere—at your house, among other places ... I was taken into your room ... I sat there ... I left you a note ... "

"Oh, how annoy ... "

"All the same," the Second Lieutenant interrupted him (the rattle of drumsticks), "since I had business with you: an urgent business conversation ... "

"Here we go, now it's starting," darted through Ableukhov's brain, and he was reflected in the big shop window among the gloves, umbrellas, and things of that kind.

In the meantime a chill pandemonium began to whistle down the Nevskii, to attack with tiny, fine and steady drops, to clatter and splutter on umbrellas, on backs severely bowed, to soak the hair, to soak the frozen, veiny hands of tradesmen, students, workers; in the meantime a chill pandemonium began to whistle down the Nevskii, drenching the shop-signs with a venomous, mocking, metallic gleam, to twist the billions of wet dust specks into funnels, set vortices whirling, drive them on and on along the streets and smash them on the stones; and then to drive the bat's wing of clouds out of Petersburg across the wastes; and already a chill pandemonium began to whistle across the wastes; it roamed the spaces—of Samara, Tambov and Saratov—with its reckless, robber's whistle, it roamed the gullies, the sandstone cliffs, the thistles and the wormwood, tearing thatch from roofs, tearing down tall pointed hayricks and spreading its sticky grime all over the threshing-floor; it makes the heavy, grain-laden sheaf germinate in the barn; it clogs with rubbish the well of clear water; it makes the woodlice multiply; and through many a sodden village typhus will rampage.

The wing of clouds was torn apart; the rain came to an end: the wetness was exhausted …

The conversation continued

In the meantime the conversation continued.

"I have something to discuss with you … I mean to say—something to sort out, which will brook no delay; I've been asking after you everywhere, to see how we might meet: incidentally, I went to ask about you to … what's her name? … our common acquaintance, Varvara Evgrafovna … "

"Solovyova?"

"Precisely … I had an extremely painful exchange with Varvara Evgrafovna—concerning you … Do you understand? … So much the worse … Now what was I talking about … Yes—this Solovyova, Varvara Evgrafovna (I locked her in, by the way) gave me a certain address: of a friend of yours … Dudkin? … Well, never mind … I went to that address, of course, but before I got as far as Mr— Dudkin's, was it?—I met you in the courtyard … You were running away from there … Yes … And moreover—not alone, but with an individual I do not know … No, don't bother: *nomina sunt odiosa* … he looked unwell … I couldn't bring myself to interrupt your conversation with Mr … I'm sorry—you can keep that gentleman's name to yourself … "

"Sergei Sergeevich, I … "

"Wait a moment! … I couldn't bring myself to interrupt your conversation, of course, although … to tell the truth, it had taken me so much effort to catch you … Anyway: I started following you; keeping a certain distance, it goes without saying, so as not to be an inadvertent witness to your conversation: I do not like, Nikolai

Apollonovich, sticking my nose into … But we can talk about that later … "

At that Likhutin fell into thought, and turned round for some reason, gazing into the distance of the Nevskii.

"I followed you … Right to this spot … All the time the two of you were talking about something … I—was walking along behind you, and, I must admit, getting annoyed … Listen," he broke off his narration, which resembled a page of type that had been scattered and re-assembled, and was now being read at random, "can you hear that?"

"No … "

"Shhh! … Listen … "

"What is it?"

"It's like a note—an 'uuu' sound … There … there … there's a humming sound … "

Nikolai Apollonovich turned his head; it was strange—how quickly the cabs had started flying past—and all in the same direction; the movement of the pedestrians became faster (constantly jostling them); some of them were turning to look back; and bumping into those coming the other way; everything was completely off balance; he looked about him without listening to Likhutin.

"Then you were left on your own and leant against the shop window; and it started raining … So I leant against a shop window too, on the other side … All the time, Nikolai Apollonovich, you were staring straight at me, but you pretended you hadn't noticed me at all … "

"I didn't recognise you … "

"But I bowed to you … "

"I was right," Nikolai Apollonovich's annoyance increased, "he's pursuing me … He's planning to … "

What was he planning?

Two-and-a-half months before Nikolai Apollonovich had received a note from Sergei Sergeich, in which Sergei Sergeich Likhutin had requested him in the most pressing tone not to disturb the peace-of-mind of the wife he so dearly loved—this was after the episode of the bridge; certain expressions in the note were underlined three times; they had an air of something very serious about them—there was a kind of nasty verbal draught, no direct hints, but—still … In his letter of reply Nikolai Apollonovich had promised …

435

He had made the promise, but—had broken it.

What was this?

Passers-by came to a halt, blocking the pavement; the wide, wide Prospect was empty of cabs; there was no bustling rattle of their wheels to be heard, no clatter of horses' hooves: the cabs had all rushed by, to form—there in the distance—a black, unmoving mass, and to form—here—a bare emptiness of wooden blocks, on to which the tumult of the elements was once more hurling in cascades its swarms of crashing raindrops.

"Just look at that?"

"Oh, how strange, how strange?"

It was as though in an instant huge granite boulders had been revealed, over which the white foam of waterfalls had been tumbling for millennia; but from afar, from the depth of the Prospect, out of utter pristine emptiness, between the two black rows of people crowding on the pavement, where ran an ever-growing roar of a thousand voices (like the roar of a swarm of hornets)—from there a stylish cab came hurtling; half-standing on it, bending nearly double, was a beardless, scruffy gentleman without a hat, clutching in his hand a tall, heavy, pole: and straining free of that wooden pole with a faint whistling sound a flailing sheet of red calico made wave-crests as it rippled in the air, fluttering and tearing—out into that huge, cold emptiness; it was strange to see the red flag flying along the empty Prospect; and when the cab rushed by, all the bowlers, tricorns, top hats, cap-bands, feathers, uniform caps and shaggy Manchurian hats—began to buzz, to shuffle, to jostle each other with their elbows and suddenly surged from the pavement into the middle of the Prospect; out of the ragged clouds the sun's pale disk spilled for a moment its straw-coloured gleam—on to houses, on to reflecting windowpanes, on to bowler hats and cap-bands. The pandemonium rushed by. The rain stopped.

The crowd swept both Ableukhov and Likhutin off the pavement; separated by a pair of elbows, they ran where everyone else was running; taking advantage of the crush, Nikolai Apollonovich planned to escape this inopportune heart-to-heart and to throw himself into the first cab standing there in the distance and, without losing valuable time, to speed off in the direction of his home: the bomb, after all ... there in his desk ... was ticking! Until it was in the river there could be no peace.

People running by bumped him with their elbows; black figures came tumbling out of shops, yards, barbers' shops, perpendicular Prospects; and into shops, yards, side-roads black figures ran hurriedly back; they keened, they howled, they stamped: in short—there was panic; from far away, as though above the heads, blood seemed to surge; seething red crests kept unfurling from the blackening soot, like flashing fires or antlers.

Oh, what a bad time for this!

Out from behind a little cluster of shoulders, and at the same level as himself, that odious cap and two staring eyes fixed anxiously upon him: Second Lieutenant Likhutin was not losing sight of him even in all this tumult, but was straining to the utmost to make his way through to Ableukhov, who was straining to escape him through the crowd: Ableukhov was on the point of gasping with relief, when:

"Don't lose me ... Nikolai Apollonovich; anyway, I shan't get left behind."

"I was right," Nikolai Apollonovich now conclusively convinced himself, "he is pursuing me: he's never going to let me go ... "

And they made their way through to a cab.

Behind them, from the further reaches of the Prospect, banners licked out above the heads and the roar of voices, like fluid tongues and fluid gleams of light; and suddenly all the banners, all the flames, stopped stock still: the sound of singing echoed out distinctly.

Nikolai Apollonovich succeeded at last in forcing his way through to a cab; but hardly had he raised his foot to climb in and make the driver force his way further through the crowd, when he felt the Second Lieutenant's hand stretching over someone else's shoulder and seizing hold of him; at that he stopped as though rooted to the spot, and, feigning indifference, said with a forced smile:

"It's a demonstration! ... "

"Doesn't matter: I have something to discuss with you."

"I ... don't you see ... I ... am entirely in agreement with you ... We do have things to talk about ... "

Suddenly from somewhere in the distance came scattered bursts of gunfire; and from the distance, torn to shreds, all the gleams of light that had risen over the heads of the crowd up into the soot began to sway this way and that over the heads of the crowd; the red whirlpools of banners were thrown into confusion and quickly fell apart into solitary protruding crests.

"In that case, Sergei Sergeevich, let's talk in a coffee-house … Why shouldn't we … in a coffee-house … "

"In a coffee-house! … " Likhutin took umbrage. "I am not in the habit of conducting discussions in such places … "

"Sergei Sergeevich? Where then? … "

"Well I'm wondering too … Since you've taken a cab, let's get in together and go to my flat … "

These words were spoken in an obviously disingenuous tone: Nikolai Apollonovich bit his lip till it bled:

"In his flat, in his flat … How can we—in his flat? That means shutting myself in with the Second Lieutenant eyeball to eyeball, and accounting for all the unseemly tricks I've played on Sofia Petrovna; maybe even in Sofia Petrovna's presence rendering account to this outraged husband for not keeping my word … It's obvious that this is a trap … "

"But, Sergei Sergeevich, I believe that for a number of reasons which you very well understand, it would be awkward for me in your flat … "

"Oh, come, come!"

To Nikolai Apollonovich's credit—he stopped contradicting; he submissively said: "I'm ready." And he bore himself calmly; his lower jaw trembled a little—that was all.

"As an enlightened man, Sergei Sergeevich, a humane man, you will understand me … In short, in short … and concerning Sofia Petrovna."

He suddenly broke off in confusion.

They got into the cab. And—in good time: where the banners had just been swaying and from where the rasping crackle had come in scattered bursts, there was not a single banner left; but such a crowd surged in from there, pressing against those running in front, that the cabs standing there in clusters shot off to the distant end of the Nevskii—in the opposite direction, where the traffic had already been restored, and where grey constables were running along the street and the police were prancing by on horseback.

They set off.

Nikolai Apollonovich saw that here the human myriapod was flowing as though nothing had happened; as it had flowed for centuries; it was up there, on high, that time ran by; to it too there was a limit set; but there was no such limit to the human myriapod; it will go on creeping as it creeps today; and it creeps now as it has always crept: in ones and twos and fours; couples upon couples: bowler hats, feathers, caps; caps, caps, feathers; a tricorn, a top hat, a cap; a scarf, an umbrella, a feather.

And then it was all gone: they turned off the Prospect; in the sky above the stone buildings ragged clouds hurtled towards them with a strip of slanting rain; Nikolai Apollonovich sat hunched up, burdened by the weight that had abruptly fallen on him; the ragged cloud crept nearer; and when the blue-grey strip enveloped them—bustling raindrops started beating, clattering, lisping, as they set their cold bubbles swirling on the gurgling puddles; Nikolai Apollonovich sat in the cab hunched over, with his Italian cape pulled up to cover his face; for a moment he forgot where he was going; he was left with just a vague feeling that he was going there against his will.

Once again a troublesome concatenation of circumstances had befallen him.

A troublesome concatenation of circumstances—is that the right thing to call the pyramid of events that had accumulated in these past twenty-four hours, like one massif on another? A pyramid of massifs fragmenting the soul, and precisely—a pyramid! ...

There is something in the pyramid that exceeds all human conceptions; the pyramid is the delirium of geometry, that is to say, delirium that cannot be measured; the pyramid is a satellite of the planet, created by man; it is yellow, like the moon, and dead, like the moon.

The pyramid is delirium measured in numbers.

There is a horror in numbers—the horror of thirty signs placed next to each other, where the sign is, of course, zero; thirty zeros together with a unit is horror; strike out the unit, and the thirty zeros will vanish.

There will be—zero.

There is no horror in a unit either; a unit in itself—is nothing; precisely—one! ... But a unit plus thirty zeros turns into the monstrosity of a quintillion: the quintillion—oh, oh, oh!—dangles on a thin black stick; the unit of a quintillion repeats itself more than a billion billion times, repeated more than a billion times.

It drags its way through the immeasurable.

And in just the same way man drags himself through ethereal spaces from times immemorial into times immemorial.

Yes—

It was as a human unit, that is to say as this skinny stick, that Nikolai Apollonovich had hitherto lived in space, fulfilling his course from times immemorial—

> —Nikolai Apollonovich in the costume of Adam was a stick; ashamed of how skinny he was, he had never been to the baths with anyone else—

—into times immemorial!

And now the monstrosity of the quintillion had fallen on to the shoulders of this stick, that is: more than a billion billion, repeated more than a billion times; the unprepossessing *something* had taken into itself a huge *nothing*; and this immense *nothing* had been swelling in its prepossessing aspect since times immemorial—

> —just as the stomach swells from the development of the gases from which all the Ableukhovs suffered—

—into times immemorial!

The unprepossessing *something* had taken into itself the huge *nothing*; *something* from that empty, null immensity was expanding to the point of horror like tumescent Everests; he though, Nikolai Apollonovich, was exploding like a bomb.

Aha? Bomb? Sardine-tin?

In the twinkling of an eye everything passed through his mind that had been passing through it since the morning: his plan flew through his head.

What plan?

The plan

Yes, yes, yes! …

To secrete the sardine-tin under his father's pillow; or—no: to place it in the appropriate spot under his mattress. And—his expectations would not be deceived: precision was guaranteed by the clockwork mechanism.

While he would be saying to him:

"Good night, Papa!"

And would hear the reply:

"Good night to you, Kolenka! ... "

A peck on the lips, and off to his own room.

Get undressed impatiently—essential to get undressed! Slip the lock on the door and pull the blankets over his head.

Play the ostrich.

But in the warm, fluffy bed to start trembling, breathing unevenly—from the throbbing of his heart; to listen intently, in anguish and fear: for a bang ... for a crash—through the mass of stone walls; to wait for that bang and that crash that would shatter the silence, would shatter the bed, the table and the wall; and would shatter, maybe ... —would shatter, maybe ...

To listen intently, in anguish and fear ... And to hear the familiar shuffle of slippers on the way to ... the room comparable with no other.

To abandon his light French novel for—for the cotton wool, to stop up his ears with it: bury his head in the pillow. To realise once and for all. now nothing could help! Throwing off the blanket, to poke out his sweat-covered head—and in the abyss of terror to dig yet another abyss.

To wait and wait.

Now there is a mere half-hour or so left; here is the green-tinged brightening of dawn; the room is turning blue, then grey; the candle flame dwindles; and—just fifteen minutes; the candle goes out; eternities flow by sluggishly, not minutes, but precisely—eternities; then the strike of a match: five more minutes have passed ... Reassure himself that it all wouldn't happen very soon, only after ten sluggish rotations of time, and be astoundingly wrong, because—

—an unrepeated, irresistible sound, never heard before, would still ...

—crash out!! ...

And then:—

hastily sticking bare legs in his underpants (no, why underpants: better to go as he was, without underpants)—or even in nothing but his night-shirt, with his face distorted, completely white—

—yes, yes, yes!—

—to jump out of the warm bed and patter off with bare

feet to a space full of mystery: the blackness of the corridor; to hurry and hurry—like an arrow: towards the unrepeated sound, to bump into servants and inhale into his chest a special smell: a mixture of smoke, fumes, gas and … something else, more horrible than fumes, and gas, and smoke.

However, there probably wouldn't be any smell.

Go running into a very cold room full of smoke; loudly coughing, choking, rush back out again and quickly poke his way once more through a black aperture in the wall, that had appeared since the sound (a haphazardly lighted candelabra would be bobbing about in his hand).

There: on the other side of that aperture …

—in place of the demolished bedroom, a rust-red flame would light up … It would light up something of no importance at all: clouds of churning smoke on all sides.

And something else would be lit up too … —no! … Throw a curtain over that picture—of smoke, of smoke! … Nothing else: just smoke and smoke!

And yet …

Slip under that curtain if only for a moment, and—oh, oh! Half the wall completely red: the redness dripping; the walls must be wet, then; must be sticky, so sticky … All that would be the first impression of the room: and no doubt the last. In between, between those two impressions, what would impress itself would be: the plaster-work, fragments of shattered parquet blocks and torn scraps of charred carpets; the scraps still smouldering. No, best not go that way, but … the shin-bone?

Why should it alone have survived, and not the other parts?

That would all be instantaneous; and other instantaneous things would go on behind his back: an idiotic hubbub of voices, an irregular clatter of feet at the far end of the corridor, the despairing wail of—can you believe it!—the kitchen-maid; and—the crackle of the telephone (obviously they were phoning the police) …

Drop the candelabra … Squatting down by the aperture, shiver from the October wind rushing in through the aperture (all the window panes had flown apart at the sound); and—shiver, pluck at his night-shirt, until one of the servants took pity on him—

—perhaps the valet, that same one upon whom it would very soon be the simplest of matters to shift the blame (a shadow would fall on him in any case)—

—until one of the servants took pity on him and dragged him forcibly into the next room and started forcing cold water into his mouth …

But to see, as he got up from the floor:—

beneath his own feet that same dark-red stickiness that had splashed in here after the thunderous sound; it had splashed in from the aperture along with a scrap of torn-off skin … (from what part of the body?). To raise his eyes—and above his head see something sticking to the wall …

Brrr! … And suddenly to lose consciousness.

To keep up the play-acting right to the end.

At most a day later to pronounce the acathistus in front of the firmly closed coffin (for there is nothing to bury), leaning over the candle in his uniform with its close-fitting waist.

No more than two days later, freshly shaven, his marble, godlike countenance buried in the fur of his cape, to process out on to the street, to the hearse, with the air of an innocent angel; and to clutch his cap in his white kidskin fingers as he mournfully followed to the cemetery in the company of all that high-ranking retinue … a heap of flowers (the coffin). This heap of flowers would be borne down the staircase in their trembling hands by golden-breasted, white trousered old men wearing swords and ribbons.

And eight little bald old men would carry the heap of flowers.

And—yes, yes!

Give evidence to the inquiry, but of such a kind that … on somebody or other (not intentionally, of course) … but, all the same, a shadow would be cast; a shadow had to be cast—on somebody or other; if not—the shadow would fall on him … How should it be otherwise?

A shadow would be cast.

443

Silly laddie, simple chap,
Little Nicky's dancing:
On his head a dunce's cap,
On a horse he's prancing.

And it became clear to him: it was that moment itself when Nikolai Apollonovich had heroically condemned himself to be the executioner—*in the name of an idea* (as he thought), it was that moment, and nothing else, that had been the creator of that plan, and not the grey Prospect, where he had been rushing around all morning; action in the name of an idea had been combined, however upset he may have been, with a diabolical, coolly composed pretence, and, maybe, with slander: slander of the most innocent people (the valet was most convenient: his nephew kept dragging along to visit him, after all, a pupil at a trade school, who didn't seem to belong to any party, but … all the same …).

He had definitely been banking on his own composure. To parricide was added falsehood, was added cowardice; but, the main thing was—baseness.

Noble, elegant and pale,
Locks of hair, like flax;
Rich in thought and poor in feeling,
N A A—who's that?

He was a scoundrel …

Everything that had occurred in these two days was fact, where a fact was a monster; a pile of facts, that is to say, a flock of monsters; there had been no facts before these last two days; and no monsters had pursued him. Nikolai Apollonovich had slept, read, eaten; he had even lusted: after Sofia Petrovna; in short: everything had flowed within its banks.

But, and—what a but! …

His eating was not like other people's eating, and his loving was not like other people's loving; his experience of lust was not like others': his dreams were heavy and dull; his food seemed tasteless, and lust itself since the episode of the bridge had taken on a tincture of absurdity—of mockery with the help of the domino; and then again: he hated his father. There was something stretching out behind him, casting a particular light on all the functions of his organism (why did he keep shuddering, why did his arms dangle like flippers? And his smile had turned into a frog's); this *something* was not the fact, but the fact remained; the fact was in the *something*.

What did the *something* consist of?

Of his promise to the party? He had not retracted his promise; and although he did not think, nevertheless ... others were probably thinking (we know what Lippanchenko was thinking); and here he was, eating in a strange way, sleeping in a strange way, lusting, hating in a strange way too ... And his squat figure in the street seemed strange as well; with the tails of his cape flapping in the wind, and hunched ...

Of his promise to the party, then, that had arisen by the bridge—just there, just there: in the gusts of the Neva gale, when behind him he saw a bowler hat, a cane, a moustache (the inhabitants of Petersburg are distinguished by—ahem—qualities! ...)

And then again, standing by the bridge was itself only a consequence of that which had driven him on to the bridge; and what had driven him was lust; the most passionate feelings were experienced by him *in the wrong way*, he became aroused *in the wrong way*, not in a good way, coldly.

So it was all a matter of coldness.

Coldness had entered him in childhood already, when people called him not Kolenka, but—his father's sprog! He became ashamed. Later the meaning of the word 'sprog' was fully revealed to him (through observation of shameful antics in the lives of domestic animals), and, he remembered—Kolenka cried: he transferred his shame at his own generation on to his shame's culprit: his father.

He used to stand for hours in front of the mirror watching his ears grow: and grow they did.

And it was then that Kolenka understood that everything there was living in the world was—a 'sprog', that there weren't any people, because they were all—'offspring'; even Apollon Apollonovich himself turned out to be an 'offspring'; that is to say an unpleasant amalgam of blood, skin and flesh—unpleasant because skin—sweats, and flesh—spoils in the warmth; while blood gives out a smell that is not the smell of May-tide violets.

And so his warmth of feeling came to be identified with boundless ice, with the Antarctic, perhaps; while he—a Pirie, Nansen, Amundsen—went round and round there in the ice; or else his warmth turned into a bloody slurry (man, as is well known, is just slurry sewn into a skin).

So there could be no soul.

He hated his own flesh; and lusted after another's. And so from earliest childhood he harboured in himself the larvae of monsters: and when they reached maturity, then in twenty-four hours they all came crawling out and massed around him—as facts of terrible import. Nikolai Apollonovich was eaten alive; he was ingested by monsters.

In short, he turned into those monsters himself.

"Frog!"

"Freak!"

"Red clown!"

That's how it was: they joked about his blood and called him 'sprog'; and the 'clown'—joked about his own blood; the 'clown' was not a mask, Nikolai Apollonovich was the mask …

His blood was prematurely decomposed.

It was prematurely decomposed; that was evidently why he aroused disgust; that was why his figure in the street appeared so strange.

This ancient, fragile vessel was destined to explode: and it was exploding.

The Establishment

The Establishment …

Someone established it; since that time it has existed; prior to that time—there were simply times of yore. So the 'Archive' tells us.

The Establishment.

Someone established it, before it was darkness, and someone moved over the darkness; there was darkness and there was light—circular number one, under the circulars of the past five years has stood the signature: "Apollon Ableukhov"; in the year 1905 Apollon Apollonovich Ableukhov was the soul of circulars.

The light shineth in darkness. The darkness comprehended it not.

446

The Establishment ...

And—the torso of a goat-footed caryatid. Since such time as a carriage drawn by a pair of lathery black horses came hurtling up to the entrance-porch, since such time as a court footman in a loose-flowing cape with a tricorn askew on his head first threw open the lacquered, emblazoned orifice, and the door, with a click, cast aside a coat of arms (a unicorn, striking a knight) embellished with crowns; since such time as a statue with a face of parchment, rising from the coach's funereal cushions, set foot upon the granite of the entrance-porch; since such time as a suede-gloved hand touched the rim of a top hat as it returned other people's bows:—since such time a yet more mighty power had subdued the Establishment which cast its own mighty power all across Russia.

Paragraphs long buried in dust were resurrected.

I am struck by the very lineaments of the paragraph-sign: two conjoined hooks fall on to the paper—and piles of paper are destroyed; the paragraph-sign is a devourer of paper, that is, a paper phylloxera, the paragraph-sign sinks its teeth, like a tick, into the arbitrariness of the dark abyss—and truly: there is something mystical in it: it is the thirteenth sign of the zodiac.

Over an immense part of Russia a frock coat without a head was being multiplied by the paragraph-sign, and the paragraph-sign, inflated by the senator's head—rose up above the starch of the collar; through unheated halls lined with white columns and down staircases swathed in red cloth this headless circulation became established, and Apollon Apollonovich was in charge of it.

Apollon Apollonovich was the most popular official in Russia with the exception of ... Konshin (whose invariable autograph you carry on all your banknotes).

And so:—

The Establishment—is. And in it is Apollon Apollonovich: or rather 'used to be', because he has died ...

> —Recently I visited his grave: over a heavy block of black marble rises an eight-pointed black marble cross; under the cross is a distinct high relief on which is hewn an immense head that drills right into you from under lowered brows with the void of its pupils; a demonic, Mephistophelean mouth! Underneath—an

447

> unassuming signature: '*Apollon Apollonovich Ableukhov—senator*'... date of birth, date of death ... An obscure grave! ...

—Apollon Apollonovich—is: he is in the office of the Director: he is to be found there every day, with the exception of his haemorrhoidal days.

Besides that there are in the Establishment offices for ... reflection.

And there are rooms pure and simple; and most of all—halls; in every hall, desks. Scribes at the desks; a couple of them per desk; in front of each: a pen and ink and a respectable pile of paper; the scribe scratches across the paper, turns the sheets over, rustles a sheet and rasps with his pen (like blowing a raspberry); like the autumn wind, wind of misfortune, that the gales bring through forests and gullies; like the rustle of sand—in the wastes, in the saline expanses—of Orenburg or Samara or Saratov;—

> —the same rustle hung over the grave: the melancholy rustle of birches; their catkins were falling, their fresh leaves were falling on to the eight-pointed, black marble cross, and—peace to his dust!—

In a word: the Establishment is.

It is not the fair Proserpina, borne off to the realm of Pluto through the land where Cocytus foams with white spray: it is the senator, abducted by Charon and carried away every day on tousled, lathery, black-maned steeds to Tartarus; over the gates of gloomy Tartarus hangs Pluto's caryatid. The waves of Phlegethon splash: papers.

In his office as Director Apollon Apollonovich Ableukhov sits every day with the veins in his temples tensed, one leg over the other, and his veiny hand tucked into the lapel of his frock coat; the logs in the fireplace crackle, while the old man of sixty-eight breathes the bacilli of the paragraph, that is to say, of the conjoining of hooks; and his breath girds the vast expanse of Russia: every day a tenth part of our country is shrouded by bats' wings of cloud. Apollon Apollonovich Ableukhov, struck by a happy thought, with one leg over the other, and his hand in the lapel of his frock coat, then puffs up his cheeks like a bubble; then he makes as if to blow out (such is his habit); a chill then blows through the unheated halls; eddies and vortices of miscellaneous papers swirl up; the gale begins in Petersburg, and somewhere in the provinces a hurricane begins to rage.

Apollon Apollonovich sits in his office ... and blows.

And the scribes' backs bend; and the leaves rustle: and so the winds rush through the tops of the austere pine-trees ... Then he draws his cheeks in; and everything—rustles: an arid paper flock, like fatal falling leaves, rushes with gathering pace from Petersburg ... to the Sea of Okhotsk.

This chill pandemonium will spread—through fields, through forests and through villages, to hum, to harry and to laugh out loud, to maul with hail and rain and ice the paws and hands—of birds and beasts and the travelling wayfarer, to topple on to him the striped beams of turnpikes—to leap out from a ditch on to the highway in the form of a striped milepost, to flaunt a grinning number, and to reveal the homelessness and the journey's endlessness and to stretch out the murky nets of hovering delusions.

The north, the north we know and love! ...

Apollon Apollonovich Ableukhov is an urban man and a thoroughly cultivated gentleman: he sits there in his office while his shadow, piercing the stone of the wall ... hurls itself on travellers out in the fields: with its reckless robber's whistle it roams the expanses—of Samara, Tambov, Saratov—it roams the gullies and the yellow sandstone cliffs, the thistles and the wormwood or the wild thornbushes, it lays bare the bald tracts of sand, it tears the tall pointed hayricks, and tickles into life a suspicious flame in the drying-barn; the red cockerel in the village—is born of it; it clogs with rubbish the well of clear water; when it falls as noxious dew on fresh-sown crops—the crops wither from it; and the cattle—waste away ...

It digs and multiplies ravines.

Jokers would be right to say: he's not Apollon Apollonovich, but ... Aquilon Apollonovich.

The multiplication of the amount of paper that passes each day before each scribe, then to be discharged from the Establishment's doors, the multiplication of that paper by the number of scribes in pursuit of it creates a product, a proliferation, that is, of paper, that needs not wheelbarrows to transport it, but wagons.

Under every paper is the signature: "Apollon Ableukhov".

All that paper rushes along the branch lines from the railhead: from St Petersburg; all the way—to the provincial capital; scattering his flock to the appropriate centres, Apollon Apollonovich creates in those centres new seats of paper proliferation.

As a rule the paper with the said signature circulates as far as the provincial administration; all the state councillors receive the paper: the Chichibabins, the Sverchkovs, the Shestkovs, the Teterkos, the Ivanchi-Ivanchevskiis; from the provincial capital the Ivanchi-Ivanchevskiis correspondingly distribute the papers to the towns of Mukhoedinsk, Likhov, Gladov, Morovetrinsk and Pupinsk (all of them regional capitals); and then Kozlorodov, an assessor, receives the paper.

The entire picture changes.

Kozlorodov, the assessor, having received the paper, ought to have settled into a britzka, a cabriolet, or simply a rickety cab, to go rollicking over the ruts—through the fields and the forests, past hamlets and hovels—and to have got gradually stuck in the clays or the mud-coloured sands, exposing himself to assaults from striped upright mileposts and striped turnpike beams (in the wastes Apollon Apollonovich waylays travellers); but instead of this Kozlorodov simply sticks Ivanchi-Ivancheskii's demand into his side-pocket.

And nips off to his club.

Apollon Apollonovich is on his own: as it is he spreads a thousand versts; he can't manage it all by himself; nor can the Ivanchi-Ivanchevskiis. There are thousands of Kozlorodovs; and behind them stands the man-in-the-street, whom Ableukhhov fears.

Therefore Apollon Apollonovich demolishes only the boundary markers on his horizon: and the Ivanchevskiis, the Teterkos and the Sverchkovs lose their posts.

Kozlorodov is permanent.

Since he lives beyond the limits of accessibility—beyond the ravines, the ruts, the forests—he goes on playing whist in Pupinsk.

He still has time for another game of whist.

His games are over

Apollon Apollonovich is on his own.

He can't keep up. And the arrow of his circular does not pierce the provinces: it breaks. Only here and there an Ivanchevskii falls, pierced by the arrow; and the Kozlorodovs mount a raid on Sverchkov. Apollon Apollonovich will set up a cannonade of paper from Palmyra, from St Petersburg—but (lately) he will miss.

The men-in-the-street have long since christened these bombs and arrows soap-bubbles.

An archer—it was in vain he sent Apollo's barbed lightning; history has changed; no one believes in ancient myths; Apollon Apollonovich Ableukhov is not at all the god Apollo: he is Apollon Apollonovich, a Petersburg official. And his shooting at the Ivanchevskiis was in vain.

All these recent days the paper circulation had been falling off; the wind was in the opposite direction: paper smelling of fresh printer's ink began to undermine the Establishment—with petitions, lawsuits, illegal threats and complaints; and so on and so forth: treachery of that kind.

And what a disgusting attitude towards the authorities was circulating among the men-in-the-street? A tone of agitation had appeared.

And—what did this mean?

It meant a lot: the impenetrable, inaccessible Kozlorodov, the assessor, somewhere out there, got too big for his boots; and set off from the provinces on the track of the Ivanchi-Ivanchevskiis: at one point in space a crowd demolished a wooden palisade to make pickets, and ... Kozlorodov wasn't there; at another point the windows of an Official Institution were found to be broken, and Kozlorodov—wasn't there either.

From Apollon Apollonovich came plans, advice and orders: the orders spattered out like gunshot; Apollon Apollonovich had been sitting in his office with a swollen vein in his temple all the last days of this week, dictating one order after another; and order after order winged its way like a demented thunderbolt into the darkness of the provinces; but the darkness was approaching; previously it had merely threatened from the horizon; now it was flooding the distant districts and surged into Pupinsk in order to threaten from there, from Pupinsk, the provincial centre from where Ivanchevskii, overwhelmed by darkness, had disappeared into darkness.

At that time in Petersburg itself, on the Nevskii, the darkness of the provinces made its appearance in the form of the dark Manchurian hat; gathering in swarms, this hat marched in serried ranks along the Prospects; on the Prospects it made sport with a red calico rag (that's the sort of day it was): and on that day the ring of many-chimneyed factories stopped emitting smoke.

Apollon Apollonovich turned the vast wheel of this mechanism, like Sisyphus; for five years he had been rolling this wheel uninterruptedly up the steep slope of history; his powerful muscles were bursting; but from under the muscles of power more and more often protruded the quite inessential skeleton, that is to say—Apollon Apollonovich Ableukhov protruded, who lived on the English Embankment.

For he truly felt he was a weathered skeleton, from which Russia had fallen away.

To tell the truth: even before this fateful night Apollon Apollonovich had seemed to many a dignitary observing him to be somewhat threadbare, consumed by a secret illness, transfixed (it was only in this last night that he had swollen); every day he hurled himself, groaning, into the carriage the colour of a raven's wing, dressed in his overcoat the colour of a raven's wing and top hat the colour of a raven's wing; and two raven-maned steeds bore this pale Pluto away.

They bore him on the waves of Phlegethon to Tartarus: here, in the waves, he floundered.

In the end—through dozens of catastrophes (such as the removal of the Ivanchesvskiis and events in Pupinsk) the Phlegethonic waves of paper struck the wheel of the immense machine that the senator turned; the Establishment revealed a crack—the Establishment, of which there are so few in Russia.

And that is when there occurred a similar scandal, comparable with no other, as people said afterwards—from the frail body of the bearer of bejewelled insignia in a mere twenty-four hours his genius evaporated; many even feared that he had lost his mind. In twenty-four hours—no, in no more than twelve (from midnight to midday)—Apollon Apollonovich Ableukhov flew headlong down the steps of his political career.

He fell in the opinion of many.

It was said afterwards that the cause was the scandal that had occurred with his son: yes, it was a statesman of national importance who had arrived at the Tsukatovs' party; but when it was revealed that it was his son who had run away from that party, all the senator's failings were revealed as well, starting from his manner of thought and ending with his—paltry stature; and when the still-damp newspapers appeared in the early morning and the urchins selling them ran through the streets shouting "Secret of the Red Domino", then there was no further doubt at all.

Apollon Apollonovich Ableukhov was conclusively struck off the list of candidates for a responsible post of exceptional importance.

The newspaper paragraph is infamous—but here it is:

It has been established by officers of the criminal investigation department that the rumours about the appearance on the streets of Petersburg of an unidentified domino, which have created such concern in recent days, are based on indisputable fact; the perpetrator's traces have been found: suspicion has fallen upon the son of a highly placed dignitary who occupies an administrative post; the police have taken all necessary steps.

From that day began the decline of senator Ableukhov.

Apollon Apollonovich Ableukhov was born in the year 1837 (the year of Pushkin's death); his childhood passed in the Nizhnii Novgorod province, in an old manorial estate; in 1858 he completed the course at the Institute of Law; in 1870 he was appointed Professor at the University of St Petersburg in the Faculty of J ... ; in 1885 he became deputy director and in 1890 director of N N Department; in the following year he was appointed by Imperial Edict to the Governing Senate; in 1900 he became Head of the Establishment.

Such is his *curriculum vitae.*

Charcoal tablets

Here already are the greenish glimmerings of morning, and Semyonych has not closed his eyes all night! All the time he was wheezing away in his little room, tossing and turning, fussing about; spasms of yawning came over him, of scratching and—Lord, forgive us our trespasses!—of sneezing; and all the while—ruminations of this ilk:

"Anna Petrovna, the dear lady, is back from Spain—she came to visit … "

And to himself Semyonych said of this:

"Yes … So I opens the door, like … And I sees this lady, a stranger … No one I recognise and dressed in foreign clothes … And she says to me … "

"Aaaa … "

"Says to me … "

"Lord, forgive us our trespasses."

And he was overcome by yawning.

Now the Tetiurin hooter has its say (at the Tetiurin factory); and the little steamers give a whistle; the electric lights on the bridge: puff—and they're out … Throwing off his blanket, Semyonych sat up: his big toe scratched on the mat.

And he started mumbling.

"I told him: your Excellency, sir—it's like this, I says … And he, sort of—yes … "

"No notice at all … "

"And the young master: the pipsqueak … And—Lord, forgive us our trespasses!—he's still wet behind the ears—a milksop."

"They're not real gentlemen, just Hamlets … "

Semyonych mumbled away to himself; and—back under the pillow with his head; the hours passed slowly; pink clouds, ripening with the sun's gleam, sailed high above the river, ripening likewise with the gleam of the sun … While Semyonych, warmed by his blanket—went on mumbling and moping:

"They're not gentlemen, they're … phoneys … "

Then there was a crash and a clatter from the door to the corridor: was it thieves, maybe? … Avgiev the merchant had been robbed, Agniev the merchant had been robbed.

And they'd come to murder Khakhu from Moldavia.

Throwing off his blanket, he stuck out his head, covered in perspiration; hastily inserting his legs into his underpants, he sprang out of his well-warmed bed with an anxious and offended look and his jaws munching, and shuffled with bare feet into a space fraught with mystery: the murky corridor.

And what should he see?

A door-latch clicked in … the lavatory: his Excellency Apollon Apollonovich, the master, with a lighted candle in his hand, was pleased to pass from there—to his bedroom.

The dark-blue expanse of the corridor was turning grey, and the other rooms too were lightening; the crystal chandeliers were glinting: half-past-seven; the bulldog was scratching itself and catching its collar with its paw, and trying to reach its back with its tiger-striped muzzle and bared teeth.

"O, Lord, oh, Lord!"

"Avgiev the merchant has been robbed! … Agniev the merchant has been robbed! … And Khakhu the inspector has been murdered! … "

Rays of light flashed wildly across the crystal-clear, resonant blue sky.

Discarding his pyjama trousers, Apollon Apollonovich became clumsily entangled in tassels, as he donned his mousy padded dressing gown, half worn through; from its bright raspberry-red lapels he revealed his unshaven chin (which had, however, been quite smooth the day before), peppered all over with completely white, dense, prickly stubble, like hoarfrost that had settled in the night, and which set off even more the dark recesses of his eyes and of his sunken cheeks, which—we will add on our own account—had grown much larger in the night.

He sat there on his bed with his mouth open and his hairy chest uncovered, drawing lengthily in and fitfully breathing out the air that would not pass into his lungs; every minute he felt his pulse and glanced at his watch.

Evidently he was suffering from an unremitting fit of hiccups.

And without a thought for the series of most disturbing telegrams that were hastening towards him from everywhere, nor for the fact that the responsible post was slipping away from him forever, nor—even!—for Anna Petrovna—he was probably thinking the thoughts that might come to one in front of an open box of charcoal-coloured lozenges.

That is to say—he thought that the hiccups, the spasms, the missed beats and the constricted breathing (the longing to drink the air), that were causing, as always, a throbbing and slight pins and needles in the palms of his hands, were happening not on account of his heart, but —from the accumulation of gases.

He tried all this time not to think about the ache in his left arm and the shooting pains in his left shoulder.

"Don't you know? It's all the stomach!"

That was how Sapozhkov the chamberlain had once tried to explain it to him; Sapozhkov was an old man of eighty who had recently died of cardiac angina.

"Gases, you know, expand the stomach: the diaphragm is compressed … And that's where the spasms come from and the hiccups … It's from the development of gases … "

Once not long ago, when Apollon Apollonovich was analysing a report in the Senate, he had turned blue, begun to splutter, and been taken out; to insistent admonitions that he should see a doctor he explained to all and sundry:

"It's just gases, you know … That's where the spasms come from."

By absorbing those gases, the dry black lozenges sometimes helped him—not always, though.

"Yes, it's gases," and he made his way to … to … : it was—half-past eight.

That was the noise Semyonych heard.

Shortly after that the door to the corridor banged and clattered and another one creaked in the distance; removing his striped travelling rug from his chilled knees, Apollon Apollonovich moved off once more, went up to the closed bedroom door, opened that door and stuck out his perspiring face, only to meet, right by the door, another equally perspiring face:

"Is that you?"

"It's me, sir … "

"What do you want?"

"I was just walking about here … "

"Aa: yes, yes … Why so early … "

"Have to keep an eye on everything … "

"What's that, tell me? … "

"? … "

"A noise of some sort ... "

"What, sir?"

"Something slammed ... "

"Oh, you mean that?"

Then Semyonych grasped the edge of his immensely loose underwear and shook his head disapprovingly:

"It's nothing, sir ... "

The point was that ten minutes earlier Semyonych had noticed with astonishment that a fair-haired head had emerged from the young master's door: it had looked to left and right, and—disappeared.

And then—the young master had skipped like a grasshopper up to the old master's door.

He had stood there for a bit, breathed deeply, shaken his head, turned round, without noticing Semyonych, who was pressed into the shadowy corner of the corridor; he had stood there, breathed deeply some more, and then—put his face to the keyhole with its shaft of light: and—how he had stuck to it, unable to detach himself from the door! His curiosity wasn't proper curiosity for the master's son, something wasn't nice about it—it wasn't right.

As though he was some kind of snooper. And then— it was somehow indecent.

It would be a different matter if he'd been spying on some stranger or other who might be hiding there—but he was spying on his own flesh and blood, his own papa; he might have been keeping watch on his health; but all the same: he sensed that it wasn't a matter of filial anxiety, but something else: pure idleness. But then there was only one possible conclusion: he was a wastrel!

He wasn't just some lackey or other—he was a general's son, educated in the French manner. At that Semyonych started humming and hawing.

And how the young master jumped!

" My frock coat," he said angrily, "get it cleaned for me quickly ... "

And made off from his father's door to his own: just a wastrel, that's what he was!

"Very well, sir," Semyonych sucked his lips disapprovingly, thinking to himself:

"His mother's come, and first thing in the morning he's—'clean my frock coat … ',

"It isn't nice, it's improper!"

"They're just some kind of Hamlets … Oh, good Lord … Peeping through the keyhole!"

Thoughts like this swarmed round in the old man's head as he grabbed the top of his ill-fitting trousers and shook his head disapprovingly, muttering ambiguously under his voice:

"Eh? … What was it? … There was a bang: that's for sure … "

"What went bang?"

"Nothing, sir: nothing to worry about … "

"? … "

"Nikolai Apollonovich … "

"Yes?"

"Slammed the door when he was going out: he went out ever so early … "

Apollon Apollonovich looked at Semyonych, made as if to ask a question, and stayed silent, but … sucked his lips like an old man: as he recalled his recent, highly unsuccessful attempt to have things out with his son (it was the morning after the evening at the Tsukatovs'), bags of loose skin dangled as though aggrieved from the corners of his lips. This unpleasant sensation evidently stuck in Apollon Apollonovich's throat: he tried to drive it away.

And he glanced at Semyonych timidly, beseechingly:

"The old man did at least see Anna Petrovna … Say what you will—he did talk to her … "

The thought flashed through his mind insistently.

"No doubt Anna Petrovna's changed … Grown thinner, weaker: and I dare say she's gone grey: I expect she's got more wrinkles … Ought to find a way of asking, carefully, in a roundabout way … "

"And—no, no! … "

Suddenly the face of this sixty-eight-year-old gentleman dissolved into unnatural wrinkles, his mouth split open to his ears, and his nose disappeared in folds of flesh.

And the man of sixty turned into a thousand-year-old; straining to the point of stridency, this grey-haired ruin started trying to wring from himself by force a pun:

"Ah ... me-me-me ... Semyonych ... Are you ... me-me-me ... barefoot?"

Insulted, Semyonych flinched.

"Beg pardon, your Excell ... "

"That's not ... me-me-me ... what I meant," Apollon Apollonovich struggled to formulate his pun.

But he did not succeed in formulating it, and stood there staring into space; then he perched on a chair for a moment, and blurted out something monstrous:

"Er ... tell me ... "

"?"

"Have you got —yellow heels?"

Semyonych took offence:

"It's not me, sir, who has yellow heels: it's them, sir, those pigtailed Chinamen ... "

"Hee-hee-hee ... Then pink ones, maybe?"

"Human ones, sir ... "

"No—yellow ones, yellow ones!"

And Apollon Apollonovich, a thousand-year-old, squat, trembling figure, stamped his foot insistently.

"Well, suppose my heels were like that, sir? ... It's my corns, your Excellency—that's what does it ... The minute you put a shoe on it drills into you, it burns ... "

And he thought to himself:

"Oh, what's heels got to do with it? ... It isn't a question of heels, is it? ... I bet the old toadstool hasn't closed his eyes all night ... And herself right on the doorstep here, in a waiting state ... And the son—is playing the Hamlet ... And he goes on about heels! ... Yellow heels—if you please ... He's the one with yellow heels ... There's a public figure for you! ... "

And he took offence even more.

But Apollon Apollonovich, as always (when the mood came over him), showed nothing short of obduracy in his puns, his nonsense, his jokes: sometimes, in an effort to keep his spirits up, the senator would become (and he was, after all, a real privy councillor, a professor and bearer of bejewelled insignia)—restless, fidgety, importunate, insufferable, and would resemble, at times like that, flies that crawl into your mouth, your nostrils, your ears—on a sultry day before a thunderstorm, when a livid cloud climbs languorously above the lime-trees; flies like that are squashed in their tens—on arms, on whiskers—on a sultry day before a thunderstorm.

"But a young lady's got—hee-hee-hee … A young lady … "

"What's a young lady got?"

"She has … "

What a fidget!

"What's she got?"

"A pink heel … "

"I don't know … "

"Well, you have a look … "

"You are a card, master … "

"It's from her stockings, when her foot starts sweating."

And without finishing his sentence, Apollon Apollonovich Ableukhov—real privy councillor, professor, head of the Establishment—shuffled away in his slippers to his bedroom; and—click: locked himself in.

There, on the other side of the door—he slumped into a chair, he calmed down, softened.

And he began to gaze around helplessly: oh, how small he had become! Oh, how stooped he had become! And his shoulders seemed unequal (as though one shoulder was broken). Now and then he pressed his hand to his side, which ached and throbbed.

Yes! …

Alarming reports from the provinces … And, you know—his son, his son! … A fine thing—disgraced his father … A terrible situation, you know …

That silly old woman, Anna Petrovna, had been robbed: a good-for-nothing troubadour with a moustache like a cockroach … So she'd come back …

Never mind! … We'll find a way! …

An uprising, the downfall of Russia … And already … they're preparing: they've already made one attempt … some undergraduate chappie comes bursting into a respectable, aristocratic house with his eyes and his moustache ...

And then—the gases, the gases! ...

Then he took one of the lozenges ...

A spring that is overloaded with weights ceases to be resilient; there is a limit to resilience; for the human will there is a limit too; even an iron will can melt; in old age the human brain goes mushy. Today the frost might strike—and a firm block of snow will sprinkle glittering sparks in all directions; and out of frosty snowflakes it will mould a gleaming human bust.

But when the thaw comes rushing by— that block will turn a dirty brown and start to dribble: it will turn soggy, slimy: and—will shrink.

In childhood Apollon Apollonovich Ableukhov had already frozen: he had frozen and grown firm; under the frosty night of the capital his gleaming bust seemed sterner, stronger, more terrible— that glittering, sparkling bust that rose higher and higher above the northern night until that tainted breeze that struck his friend down, and which in recent times had blown a hurricane.

Apollon Apollonovich Ableukhov's rise had continued until the hurricane; and—after ...

For long now, proud and solitary, Apollon Apollonovich Ableukhov had been standing in the hurricane's fusillade—glittering, ice-bedecked and firm; but there is a limit to everything: even platinum will melt.

In a single night Apollon Apollonovich Ableukhov had grown hunched; in a single night he had collapsed and his large head had come to droop; and he, resilient as a spring, had been brought low; how used things to be? Not long ago on his unwrinkled profile, that stared in challenge up towards the skies to meet the trials to come, red bursts of flame had fluttered, enough ... to set ... all Russia ... on fire! ...

But just one night had passed.

And on the fiery background of the Russian Empire in flames instead of a firm statesman in a golden uniform there was just— an old man with haemorrhoids, standing there with his hairy chest uncovered, breathing intermittently—unshaven, uncombed, perspiring—in a tasselled dressing gown—he, for sure, could no longer steer (through ruts and pits and potholes) the course of our rickety wheel of state! ...

Fortune had betrayed him.

It goes without saying—it was not events in his personal life, not that out-and-out scoundrel, his son, and not fear of succumbing to a bomb, like a simple soldier on the field of battle, not the arrival of some Anna Petrovna or other, a person of no consequence who could not make a success of any calling—not Anna Petrovna's arrival (in her darned black coat and with her little *réticule*), and certainly not that red rag—that had turned the bearer of gleaming bejewelled insignia into nothing but a block of melting snow.

No—it was time ...

Have you ever seen old men, still grand, but sinking into childhood, who for half-a-century have gallantly withstood all manner of blows—white-haired old men (more often bald, in fact), leaders clad in the iron of battle?

I've seen them.

In meetings, conferences, congresses they would clamber up in snow-white starch and gleaming shoulder-padded tailcoats to the lectern; bent old men with drooping jaws, no teeth and dentures—

—I've seen them—

—went on by force of habit tugging heart-strings, maintaining their composure on the dais.

I have seen them at home, too.

With feeble-minded fussiness they would drop anaemic, silly whispered witticisms in my ear; surrounded by their acolytes, they would shuffle into their studies and boast with dribbling lips about their shelf-full of collected works, all morocco bound, which once upon a time I also used to read, to which they treated me, and themselves too.

It makes me sad!

At ten exactly the door-bell rang: it was not Semyonych who opened it; someone passed through there—into Nikolai Apollonovich's room; he sat a while, and left a note there.

I know what I'm doing

At ten exactly Apollon Apollonovich took his coffee in the dining room.

As we know, he would run into the dining room—icy, stern, shaven, spreading a smell of eau de cologne and measuring his coffee by his chronometer; and today, scratching the floor with his shoes, he shuffled in for his coffee in his dressing gown: not scented, not shaved.

From nine-thirty until ten in the morning he had been sitting behind locked doors.

He did not glance at his correspondence, contrary to custom he made no reply to his servants' greetings; and when the bulldog's slobbering snout rested on his knees, his mouth that was rhythmically mumbling—

And my beloved Delvig calls me,
The comrade of my merry youth,
The comrade of my youth downhearted—

—his rhythmically mumbling mouth just choked on his coffee:

"I say: take the dog away, would you … "

Plucking at his roll and crumbling it, he stared with leaden eyes at the black coffee grounds.

At half-past-eleven Apollon Apollonovich, as though he had remembered something, started fidgeting and fussing; his eyes began to dart about like a grey mouse; he jumped up—and with tiny steps, trembling, he made off to the study, revealing under the open flap of his dressing gown his half-unbuttoned underpants.

Shortly afterwards a servant glanced into the study, to remind his master that the horses were ready; he glanced in—and stopped at the threshold as though rooted to the spot.

With astonishment he observed that Apollon Apollonovich was

trundling the heavy office stepladder from shelf to shelf along the velvety carpet-runners that were laid everywhere—gasping, groaning, stumbling, sweating—clambering up the ladder and, when he reached the top, endangering his own life by checking the dust on the volumes with his finger; when he caught sight of the servant Apollon Apollonovich sucked his lips disdainfully, and made no answer to the mention of departure.

Banging a volume against the shelf, he demanded dusters.

Two servants brought him dusters; these dusters had to be conveyed to him on the end of a raised broom (he allowed no one up to him, and himself refused to come down); two servants took a stearin candle each; two servants stood on either side of the stepladder with arms extended upwards, petrified.

"Raise the candle a bit … No, not like that … And not that way … Oh, higher: still higher … "

By this time ragged clouds had come clustering out from behind the buildings across the river, their sullen, matted clumps came towering up; the wind beat on the windowpanes; twilight reigned in the greenish, frowning room; the wind howled; higher and higher two stearin candles stretched on either side of the stepladder as it soared up to the ceiling; and there, in a cloud of dust, under the very ceiling, was a flurry of mouse-coloured flaps and a flutter of raspberry tassels.

"Your Ex'lency!"

"Is that a job for you? … "

"If you would be so good, sir … "

"Heavens above … Have you ever seen anything of the sort … "

Apollon Apollonovich Ableukhov, actual privy councillor, could not even hear them at all in his cloud of dust: he didn't care! Forgetting everything on earth, he wiped away at the spines, furiously banging the volumes against the steps of the stepladder; and—in the end had a fit of sneezing:

"Dust, dust, dust … "

"Well I never … Well I never! … "

"I'll just have a … with the duster: that's the way, that's the way … "

"Very good! … "

And he hurled himself on the dust with a grubby duster in his hand.

There was an anxious rattle from the telephone: the Establishment was ringing; but from the yellow house the telephone's anxious rattle was answered by:

"His Excellency? ... Yes ... He's just taking his coffee ... We'll tell him ... Yes ... The horses are ready ... "

And the telephone rattled a second time; and the telephone's second rattle was answered by:

"Yes ... yes ... He's still sitting at the table ... We have already told him ... We'll tell him ... The horses are ready ... "

And the telephone's third, now indignant rattle, was answered by:

"Not at all, sir!"

"He's sorting out his books ... "

"The horses?"

"They're ready ... "

After standing there a while, the horses were dispatched to the stable; the coachman spat: he didn't dare to swear ...

"I'll give it a wipe!"

"Oh dear, oh dear! ... Did you see that?"

"Atishoo ... "

And trembling yellow hands, laden with books, banged at the shelf.

Bells jangled in the entrance-hall: they jangled intermittently; the silence between two bouts of bells spoke eloquently; the silence flew through the space of the lacquered rooms as a reminder—a reminder of something forgotten, something dear; and—it came unbidden into the study; something old, old—was standing there; and climbing the stepladder.

An ear protruded from the dust, a head turned:

"Can you hear? ... Listen ... "

It might be any number of people.

It might turn out to be: Nikolai Apollonovich, that frightful good-for-nothing, wastrel, liar; or it could be: German Germanovich, bringing papers; or maybe—Kotoshi-Kotoshinskii; or possibly, Count Nolden: it could, indeed, turn out to be—me-me-me—Anna Petrovna ...

Another jangle.

"Can't you hear it?"

"Your Excellency, of course we can hear it: someone there will open the door for certain … "

Only now did the servants respond to the jangling; they went on giving light, as though transfixed.

Only Semyonych, wandering along the corridor (he kept on mumbling and moping), enumerating out of boredom the compass points in the chest of drawers for the master's toilet articles: "Northeast: black ties and white ties … Collars, cuffs—east … watches—north"—only Semyonych, wandering along the corridor (he kept on mumbling and moping), only he—became alert and apprehensive, and strained to hear the jangling sound; he trotted into the study.

Just as a faithful cavalry horse responds to the sound of the horn:

"If I may make so bold: someone's ringing … "

The servants took no notice.

Each of them stretched out his candle—up to the ceiling; from right at the top of the stepladder, under the very ceiling, a bare head emerged in clouds of dust; a cracked and agitated voice responded:

"Yes! I heard it too."

Apollon Apollonovich, tearing himself away from a thick bound volume—was the only one to respond:

"Yes, yes, yes … "

"Don't you know … "

"Someone's ringing … the bell … "

Something inexpressible was there, but something they both understood, evidently they had both sensed it, because they both shuddered: "hurry up—get a move on—be quick about it! … "

"It's the mistress … "

"It's Anna Petrovna!"

Hurry, get a move on, be quick: it jangled again!

Then the servants put down their candles and trotted out into the dark corridor (Semyonych trotted out first). Right under the ceiling in the greenish light of the Petersburg morning Apollon Apollonovich Ableukhov—a mousy-grey lump—cast his eyes about him nervously; breathing heavily, he started climbing down as best he could, grunting, leaning his hairy chest, his shoulder and his stubbly chin against the steps of the stepladder; down he came—and off he pattered with little steps in the direction of the staircase with a grubby duster in his hand and the flaps of his dressing gown wide open and sticking out in the air at a fantastic angle. Now he stumbled, stopped, began breathing heavily and with his finger felt his pulse.

And already a gentleman with downy side-whiskers, in a tightly buttoned uniform drawn in at the waist, with blindingly white cuffs and the cross of St Anne on his breast, was coming up the stairs, with Semyonych deferentially leading the way; on a tray that wobbled slightly in the old man's hand lay a glossy visiting card with an aristocratic crown.

Apollon Apollonovich, his dressing gown flap wide open, peeped anxiously from behind the statue of Niobe at the dignified and downy old man.

Truly, he looked like a mouse.

You will wander like a madman

Petersburg is a dream.

If you have been to Petersburg in your dreams you are bound to know a certain ponderous entrance: there are oak doors there with plate-glass windows; people passing by see those windows; but they never pass beyond them.

A heavy bronze mace gleams soundlessly from behind those panes.

There is a sloping, octogenarian shoulder there: it appears year in year out in the dreams of those chance passers-by for whom everything is a dream and who are a dream themselves; a dark tricorn hat also slips on to the sloping shoulder of this old man of eighty; the octogenarian doorman gleams just as brightly with his silver braid, resembling a funeral parlour official in the execution of his duties.

So it is always.

The heavy bronze mace rests peacefully upon the doorman's octogenarian shoulder; and for years, adorned with tricorn, the doorman drowses over *The Stock Exchange Gazette*. Then the doorman rises and throws open the door. Whether you pass that oaken door in the afternoon, the morning, or the evening—you will see, in the

467

afternoon, the morning or the evening, the bronze mace too; you will see the braid; and you will see—the dark tricorn hat.

You will stop still in astonishment before that selfsame vision. You saw the same exactly on your previous visit. Five years have passed: restless events have rumbled by; China has awoken; and Port Arthur has fallen; our Amur provinces have been inundated by men with yellow faces; and the tales of Chingiz Khan's iron horsemen have come to life again.

But the vision from years of old is unchanging, permanent: an octogenarian shoulder, a tricorn hat, braid, beard.

One moment—if the white beard moves behind the glass, if the great mace starts to rock, if the silver braid begins to glitter blindingly like the toxic trickle from the drainpipes that threatens those living in the basement with cholera and typhus—if all that should happen and the years of old should change, then you will wander like a madman round the Petersburg Prospects.

The toxic trickle from the drainpipe will drench you in the dank October cold.

If the heavy mace there, beyond the plate-glass entrance, had given a peremptory flash, then surely cholera and typhus would not be flying round: China would not be in turmoil; Port Arthur would not have fallen; our Amur provinces would not be inundated by men with slanting eyes; the horsemen of Chingiz Khan would not have risen up from their centuries-old graves.

But listen, listen hard: a clatter … A clatter from the steppes beyond the Urals. The clatter is approaching.

It is the iron horsemen.

Over the entrance of the grey-black, many-columned building, unmoved for years, the same old caryatid still hangs: a stone colossus with a clotted beard.

For years he has hung there with his thousand-year-old sad smile, with the dark vacuity of eyes that penetrate the day: he hangs in anguish; for a hundred years the cornice of the balcony's protrusion has weighed upon the bearded creature's skull and on the elbows of those stone arms. His loins are shrouded in vine leaves hewn from stone and clusters of stone grapes. His black-hoofed, goat-like feet are firmly set in the wall.

Bearded old creature of stone!

For many years he has smiled above the noise of the street, for many years has risen up above the summers, winters, springs—with the rounded, florid decorations of his ornamental moulding. Summer, autumn, winter: and again—summer and autumn; he remains the same; in summer he is porous; in winter, iced all over, he would scatter particles of ice; in spring those particles and icicles would drip with thawing drops. But he—remains the same: the years pass him by.

Time itself is only waist-high to the caryatid.

Since a time without time, as though above time's continuity, he has bent over the straight arrow of the Prospect. A raven settles on his beard: it caws monotonously at the Prospect; this slippery, wet Prospect is shot with a metallic gleam; in these wet slabs of stone, lit so miserably by the October day, are reflected: the greenish swarm of clouds, the greenish faces of the passers-by, the silvery trickles that pour out from the rumbling drainpipes.

This bearded stone creature, raised high above the turmoil of events, has for days and weeks and years supported the entrance to the Establishment.

What a day!

Since early morning raindrops had been beating, rattling, hissing; from the sea grey fog pressed in like a layer of felt; scribes passed in pairs; the doorman in his tricorn hat admitted them; they hung their hats and wet clothes on hangers, ran up the red-carpeted steps, ran through the marble vestibule, raising their eyes to the portrait of the minister; and traversed unheated halls—to their own cold desks. But the scribes did no writing: there was nothing to write; no papers were brought from the Director's office; there was no one in the office; just logs crackling in the fireplace.

The bald head was not tensing the veins in its temples over the severe oak desk; it was not looking from under lowered brows at the cornflowers of coal-gas dancing in frisky swarms in the hearth: in that solitary room flames of coal-gas nevertheless were dancing idly in the hearth above the incandescent piles of crackling flames; red cockscombs were bursting up, together and apart, flying off at speed up the chimney, to merge above the rooftops with the fumes, the toxic soot, and to hang above the roofs in an unchanging, suffocating, corrosive gloom. There was no one in the office.

This day Apollon Apollonovich had not come striding through into the Director's office.

They were tired of waiting; a perplexed whisper flitted from desk to desk; rumours fluttered round; delusions dallied; the telephone receiver rattled in the office of the deputy director:

"Has he left yet? ... That's impossible? ... Tell him that his presence is imperative ... it's impossible ... "

And the telephone rattled a second time:

"Have you told him? ... Still sitting at table? ... Tell him there's no time to lose ... "

The deputy director stood with his jaw trembling; he spread his hands in perplexity; an hour or an hour-and-a-half later he descended the velvet steps in his immensely tall top hat. The entrance doors flew open ... He sprang into his carriage.

Twenty minutes later, as he climbed the stairs in the yellow house, he was astonished to see Apollon Apollonovich, his immediate superior, peeping anxiously out at him from behind a statue of Niobe, and pulling around himself the flaps of a graceless mousy dressing gown.

"Apollon Apollonovich," the white-haired knight of the order of St Anna cried out, catching sight of the senator's stubbly chin behind the statue, and began hastily to adjust the large medal round his neck beneath his tie.

"Apollon Appollonovich, so this is how you are, this is where you are? And I have been, we've been trying to—we've been ringing you, telephoning. You—were expected ... "

"I'm ... me-me-me," the bent old man sucked his lips, "sorting my library ... Do forgive, old chap," he added grumpily, "my informal dress."

And he pointed at his ragged dressing gown.

"What's this, are you ill? Oh, oh—you do seem a bit puffy ... Oh, isn't that a spot of dropsy?" the visitor deferentially touched the dust-covered finger.

Apollon Apollonovich dropped his dirty duster on to the parquet.

"You haven't chosen a good time to fall ill ... I have brought you news ... May I congratulate you: there is a general strike—in Morovetrinsk ... "

"Why do you say that? ... I'm ... me-me-me ... I'm quite well," and the old man's face collapsed into wrinkles of displeasure (he received the news of the strike with indifference: evidently nothing could surprise him any more), "and look here: there's a lot of dust, you know ... "

"Dust?"

"So I'm—dusting."

The deputy director with his downy whiskers now leant deferentially forward in front of this hunched wreck and kept trying to set about the exposition of the extremely important paper which he had spread out before him in the drawing room on a little mother-of-pearl table.

But Apollon Apollonovich interrupted him again:

"Dust, you know, contains the micro-organisms of disease ... So I'm—dusting ... "

Suddenly this grey-haired wreck, that had only just sat down in an Empire armchair, jumped up hurriedly, leaning one hand on the arm; one finger of the other hand prodded hurriedly at the paper.

"What's this?"

"That's just what I was reporting to you ... "

"No, sir, if you will ... " Apollon Apollonovich bent down captiously to examine the paper: he seemed younger, whiter, and became—a pale pink colour (turning red was already beyond him).

"Wait! ... Have they all gone mad? ... Does this need my signature? Under a signature like that?!"

"Apollon Apollonovich ... "

"I won't sign it."

"But it's a revolt!"

"Dismiss Ivanchevskii ... "

"Ivanchesvkii's already been dismissed: have you forgotten?"

"Well, I won't sign it ... "

With his face rejuvenated and the flap of his dressing gown indecently open, Apollon Apollonovich shuffled back and forth around the drawing room, clutching his hands behind his back, his bald head bent low: coming up close to his astonished visitor, he spattered him with spittle:

"How could they imagine? Firm administrative power is one thing, but the breach of direct legal procedures—is quite another."

"Apollon Apollonovich," the knight of St Anna urged, "you are a firm man, you are a Russian ... We hoped ... No, of course you will sign it ... "

But Apollon Apollonovich began to twist a fortuitously available pencil between two skeletal fingers; he stopped, and gave the paper a penetrating glance: the pencil snapped with a crack; then he nervously made to tie the tassels of his dressing gown, his jaw trembling in anger.

"I am a man of the school of Plehve, my good fellow ... I know what I am doing ... It isn't for eggs to teach chickens ... "

"Me-me-me ... I will not put my signature to it."

Silence.

"Me-emme ... Me-emme ... "

And he blew his cheeks out in a bubble ...

The gentleman with the downy sideburns descended the stairs in consternation; it was clear to him: senator Ableukhov's career, built up over so many years, had disintegrated into dust. After the departure of the deputy director of the Establishment Apollon Apollonovich continued to march up and down among the Empire armchairs in high dudgeon. Soon he went away; soon he returned again: he was carrying under his arms a weighty folder with papers which he set down on the mother-of-pearl table, leaning his shoulder and his still aching side against the folder; placing this pile of papers in front of him, Apollon Apollonovich rang and ordered that a fire should be lit in front of him immediately.

From all the *nota bene*'s, question marks, paragraph-signs and underlinings, from this *last* piece of work, a lifeless head rose over the fire in the hearth; his lips mumbled of their own accord:

"Doesn't matter ... It's all right ... "

The incandescent mass—bright red, golden—began to seethe and snort, giving off scorching crackles and flashes; the logs collapsed into charcoal.

The bald head rose above the hearth with a sardonic, grinning mouth and narrowed eyes, picturing that furious, inveterate careerist flying off through the slush after offering him, Ableukhov, nothing less than a base compromise with his unblemished conscience.

"I, my good sirs, am a man of the school of Plehve ... And I know what I'm doing ... That's how it is, gentlemen ... "

472

A sharply pointed pencil was already dancing in his fingers; the sharply pointed pencil fell on to the paper in flocks of question marks; this was his last task; in an hour this task would be completed; in an hour the telephone would rattle in the Establishment: with an inconceivable piece of news.

The carriage flew up to the caryatid at the entrance, but the caryatid—did not move: the bearded old stone creature that supported the entrance to the Establishment.

The year 1812 had freed him from his scaffolding. 1825 had seen the tumult of December days; their tumult passed; recently the tumult of January days had been seen: the year was 1905.

Bearded stone creature!

Everything had happened at his feet and everything at his feet had ceased to be. What he has seen he will tell no one.

He remembers a coachman reining in his thoroughbred pair and the steam rising in clouds from the horses' heavy rumps; a general in a tricorn hat, in a loose-flowing, ermine-trimmed greatcoat, jumped gracefully from the carriage and, accompanied by cries of "hurrah", ran through the open door.

Later, still accompanied by cries of "hurrah", the general trod the floor of the protruding balcony in white buckskin boots. The bearded creature, holding up the cornice of that protruding balcony, will keep his name a secret; the bearded stone creature knows the name to this day.

But he will not tell.

Nor will he tell anyone, ever, about the tears of the prostitute who took shelter beneath him last night on the steps of the entrance.

And he will tell no one about the recent visits of the minister: he was wearing a top hat; and in his eyes—was a green profundity; the grey-haired minister, as he climbed out of the light sleigh, stroked his sleek moustache with a grey Swedish glove.

Then he rushed hastily through the open door, to sink into thought beside the windows.

The pale blur of a face, pressed to the windowpane, could be made out—from far away; the chance passer-by would not have discerned in that flattened blur, as he gazed at it, would not have discerned in it the commanding personage who from here directs the fate of Russia.

The bearded creature knows him; and—remembers; but he will not tell—anyone, ever! …

> *'Tis time, my friend, 'tis time; for peace my heart now aches …*
> *Days hasten after days, and each, departing, takes*
> *Away with it a part of being; you and I*
> *Had thought to live together; lo, we die.*

That was how the lonely, grey-haired minister, now at rest, used to speak to his lonely friend.

> *He is no more—and Russia he has left,*
> *Upraised by him …*

And—peace to his dust …

But the doorman with the mace, drowsing over the *Stock Exchange Gazette*, knew that weary face well: Viacheslav Konstantinovich, the Lord be thanked, is still remembered in the Establishment, but Emperor Nikolai Pavlovich of blessed memory is no longer remembered in the Establishment: the white halls remember him, the columns, the banisters.

And the bearded stone creature remembers.

Since a time without time, as though above time's continuity, is it the straight arrow of the Prospect that he has bent over, or the bitter, alien, salt tear—of man?

> *Earth knows no happiness, but peace it knows and leisure …*
> *I've long been dreaming of an unencumbered pleasure:*
> *I've long, exhausted slave, prepared my flight*
> *To some far sanctuary of work and chaste delight.*

A bald head rises up—a mouth, Mephistophelean, drained of colour, responds with a senile smile to flashes of light; the face turns crimson from those flashes; the eyes, after all, are flecked with flame; yet they are eyes of stone: blue eyes—and in green orbits! A cold, astonished gaze; and—empty, empty. Times, suns, worlds—all consumed in delusion. All of life—is nothing but delusion. So is it worth it? No, it is not:

"I, my good sirs, am a man of the school of Plehve ... I, gentlemen, am ... I'm—me-me-me ... "

And the bald head drops back.

In the Establishment a whisper was flitting from desk to desk; suddenly the door opened: an official with a completely white face rushed up to the telephone.

"Apollon Appollonovich ... is going into retirement ... "

Everyone jumped up; Legonin, the departmental head, burst into tears; and all the following occurred: an idiotic hubbub of voices, an irregular tramp of feet, an assuaging voice from the deputy director's office; and—the rattle of the telephone (to the ninth department); the deputy director stood with trembling jaw; the telephone receiver in his hand jumped up and down: Apollon Apollonovich Ableukhov, actually, was no longer head of the Establishment.

A quarter-of-an-hour later, his close-fitting uniform buttoned to the top, the grey-haired deputy director with the cross of St Anne on his chest was already giving orders; twenty minutes later he was parading his face, freshly shaven and growing younger from exhilaration, through all the rooms.

That was how an event of indescribable significance came about.

A reptile

The seething waters of the canal surged towards the spot where the wind from the bare expanses of the Field of Mars roared into a grove of groaning branches: what a terrible place!

This terrible place was crowned by a magnificent palace; with its upward thrusting tower it resembled a fantastic castle: reddish-pink, of ponderous stone blocks; within those walls lived a crowned head; that was not now; that crowned head is no longer among us.

Remember his soul in Thy kingdom, O, Lord!

The reddish-pink palace stood out with its upward thrusting turret from the humming hordes of knotty branches, utterly devoid of leaves; the branches thrust into the sky in muffled gusts and as they swayed caught fleeting wisps of mist; a crow shot upwards with a caw; it flew aloft, swayed among the wisps of mist, and dropped again.

475

A carriage was crossing that place.

Two little red buildings, forming something like a ceremonial exit on the square in front of the palace, came rushing towards it; to the left of the square a cluster of trees emitted an ominous hum; and the leaning tops of the trunks seemed about to collapse; a lofty spire protruded from the wisps of mist.

An equestrian statue appeared from the misty square as an indistinct black outline; passing visitors to Petersburg pay this statue no attention; I always stand before it for a long time: it is a magnificent statue! It is only a shame that the last time I passed it some mean-spirited joker was painting its pedestal gold.

This statue was raised to his noble great-grandfather by an autocrat and great-grandson; the autocrat lived in this castle; and it was here that his joyless days came to an end—in the pink stone castle; he did not pine here long; he was not able to pine here; his soul was torn apart between a tyrant's vanity and noble impulses; and from that sundered soul the youthful spirit departed.

A snub-nosed face with fair curls probably appeared many times in the embrasure of the window; there's a window—was it from that one? And the snub-nosed face with curls surveyed in anguish the expanses beyond the windowpanes; and its eyes drowned in the fading pink of the sky; or maybe: those eyes stared at the play of silver and the shimmer of the moon's reflections in the thick foliage of the grove; at the entrance stood a sentinel of the Pavlovskii regiment in a wide-brimmed three-cornered hat, presenting arms as a general with golden breast and the ribbon of St Andrew came out and made his way to a golden carriage with water-colour decoration; a flame-red coachman towered up on the raised box; on the footboard of the carriage stood thick-lipped negroes.

Emperor Pavel Petrovich, casting a single glance at all this, returned to his sentimental conversation with a lady-in-waiting in muslin and gauze, and the lady-in-waiting smiled; two sly dimples imprinted themselves on her cheeks, and—a black beauty-spot.

On that fateful night the silver of the moon cascaded through those same windowpanes, falling on to the heavy furniture of the imperial bedchamber; it fell on to the bed, gilding the artful cupid with his flashing sparks; and on the pale pillow a profile was outlined, as though sketched in Indian ink; somewhere clocks chimed; from somewhere steps were heard ... Not three moments passed—and the bed was crumpled: where the pale profile had been was just the shadow in the hollow from the head; the sheets were warm; the sleeper was not there; a little bunch of fair-haired officers with drawn swords bent their heads towards the empty bed; they broke into a locked door at one side; a woman's voice was wailing; suddenly the hand of a pink-lipped officer raised the heavy window blind; under the draped muslin at the window, in the silver shimmer—a gaunt, black shadow trembled.

And the moon went on spilling its weightless silver as it fell on the heavy furniture of the imperial bedroom; it fell on the bed, gilding the cupid that glittered from the bed-head; it fell upon the profile, deathly pale, as though outlined in ink ... Somewhere clocks chimed; in the distance footsteps echoed everywhere.

Nikolai Apollonovich surveyed this dismal place vacantly, not even noticing that the shaven face of the Second Lieutenant who was escorting him turned now and then in the direction of his, if one may be allowed the expression, neighbour; the gaze which Second Lieutenant Likhutin cast over the victim under escort seemed full of curiosity; he kept twisting round restlessly throughout the journey; and throughout the journey he kept knocking into his side. Gradually Nikolai Apollonovich came to realise that Sergei Sergeevich could not bear to touch him ... even with his side; and so he kept jostling him, bestowing on his companion a constant battering of bumps.

At just this time the wind tore off Ableukhov's broad-brimmed Italian hat, and the latter, with a spontaneous movement, caught it on Sergei Sergeevich's knee; for a moment he came into contact with his numb fingers, but a shudder went through Sergei Sergeich's fingers as they sprang away to the side with an evident shock of disgust; his angular elbow began to quiver. Second Lieutenant Likhutin was experiencing, no doubt, not so much contact with the skin of a friend, indeed, one might say, of a bosom friend from childhood, as ... with that of a reptile that ... should be crushed ... on the spot ...

Ableukhov took note of that movement; in his turn he started looking round in fear at this childhood friend, with whom he used to

be on Christian name terms; this Serezhka, that is, Sergei Sergeevich Likhutin, had grown younger since their previous conversation, truly, by a good eight years, and thus turned back from Sergei Sergeich into Serezhka; but now that Serezhka no longer listened with rapt attention to the flights of Ableukhov's thoughts, as he had in times of yore, sitting in the elder-bush in his grandfather's park—all those eight years ago; eight years had passed; and those eight years had altered everything: the elder-bush was long since broken, while he …
—now glanced with rapt attention at Sergei Sergeich.

Their unequal relationship was reversed; and everything, everything, began to move in the reverse direction; his idiotic appearance, his unbecoming overcoat, the jolts of his angular elbow and other nervous gestures, which Nikolai Apollonovich read as gestures of contempt—all this gave rise to sad reflections on the vicissitudes of human relations; this terrible place likewise gave rise to sad reflections: the reddish-pink palace, the garden with its wild howling and its crows that shoot into the sky, the two little red buildings and the equestrian statue; however, the garden, the castle and the statue had now been left behind.

And Ableukhov shrank.

"You're leaving the service, Sergei Sergeevich?"

"What?"

"The service … "

"As you see … "

And Sergei Sergeevich gave him such a look as though till now he had not known Ableukhov; he looked him up and down, from head to toe.

"I would advise you, Sergei Sergeevich, to turn your collar up: you have a cold in the throat, and in weather like this it only takes a moment, it's really terribly easy to … "

"What?"

"To catch a quinsy."

"And on your account," Likhutin blurted out gruffly; his anxious spluttering was heard.

"?"

"I'm not talking about throats … I'm leaving the service *on your account*, that's to say, not exactly on your account, but precisely: because of you."

"That's a hint," Nikolai Apollonovich all but exclaimed and caught his glance again: you never look at friends like that, but you might look like that at, say, some outlandish creature from distant climes, whose proper place is in the *Kunstkammer*, (not in a carriage, and certainly not on the Prospect …).

It is with a look like that that passers-by might lift their gaze to elephants, that are sometimes led through the city in the evening— from the railway station to the circus; they lift their gaze, take a step backwards, and—don't believe their eyes; at home they'll tell about it:

"Can you believe it, we met an elephant in the street!"

But everyone will laugh at them.

It was just such curiosity that Likhutin's gaze expressed; there was no sense of outrage in it; there was, maybe, disgust (as at the proximity of a boa-constrictor); crawling reptiles do not give rise to anger—you simply crush them, with whatever is to hand: there and then …

Nikolai Apollonovich considered the words the Second Lieutenant had muttered through clenched teeth about leaving the service— exclusively because of him; yes—Sergei Sergeich would lose the chance of staying in the service of the state after what was about to happen there between the two of them; the flat was evidently going to be empty (and the *reptile* would be crushed there) … Something was going to happen that … Then Nikolai Apollonovich lost the remnants of his courage; he started wriggling on the spot and—and: all ten cold, trembling fingers seized the Second Lieutenant's sleeve.

"Ah? … What's this? … Why are you doing that?"

A house flashed by, a small blancmange-coloured house, with grey stucco moulding from top to bottom: rococo convolutions (maybe it once did service as a refuge for that same lady-in-waiting with the black beauty-spot and two sly dimples on her lily-white cheeks).

"Sergei Sergeich … I, Sergei Sergeich … I must confess to you … Oh, how deeply I regret … It is extremely, extremely regrettable: my behaviour … I, Sergei Sergeich, have behaved … Sergei Sergeich … disgracefully, deplorably … But I do, Sergei Sergeich, have an excuse: yes, I do have an excuse. As an enlightened man, humane, as a good person, not just anybody, Sergei Sergeich—you will be able to understand it all … I haven't slept all night, I mean, what I meant to say was, I'm suffering from insomnia … The doctors consider me," he was reduced to simple lying, "that is, consider my condition—very,

479

very dangerous ... Mental exhaustion with pseudo-hallucinations, Sergei Sergeevich (for some reason he remembered Dudkin's words) ... What do you say?"

But Sergei Sergeevich said nothing: he looked at him with no sense of outrage; and there was disgust in his gaze (as in the proximity of a boa-constrictor); reptiles don't give rise to anger: you crush them ... there and then ...

"Pseudo-hallucinations ... " Ableukhov insisted imploringly, terrified, small, clumsy, with an ingratiating gaze into the other's eyes (the other's eyes did not respond); he wanted to explain himself at once; here—in the cab: to explain himself here—not in the flat; as it was that fateful entrance was already near; if he and the officer could not come to terms before they reached the entrance, then—that was it: everything would be over! Finished! A murder would take place, or a physical insult, or simply an ugly fight would occur:

"I ... I ... I ... "

"Get out: we've arrived ... "

Nikolai Apollonovich glanced in front of him with leaden, unblinking eyes—he glanced at the scraps of mist, from which drops kept splashing, making circles of metallic bubbles in the gurgling puddles.

Jumping down on to the pavement, Second Lieutenant Likhutin tossed some money to the driver and stood in front of the cab, waiting for the senator's son; the latter seemed to be in no hurry.

"Just a moment, Sergei Sergeevich: I had a cane with me ... Oh, wherever is it? Surely I can't have dropped my cane?"

He really was looking for his cane; but the cane had disappeared without trace; Nikolai Apollonovich, completely white, anxiously turned imploring eyes in all directions.

"Well? What is it?"

"My cane."

Ableukhov's head sank deep into his shoulders, while his shoulders shook; his mouth was open and twisted; Nikolai Apollonovich glanced in front of him with leaden, unblinking eyes at the bluish scraps of mist; and—did not move.

Then Sergei Sergeich Likhutin began to breathe angrily, impatiently; seizing Ableukhov by the sleeve he courteously, but firmly began carefully to pull him out of the cab, arousing as he did so the obvious curiosity of the caretaker—he began to unload him like an over-laden bundle.

But Nikolai Apollonovich, thus unloaded, seized Likhutin's hand firmly with his fingernails: in the darkness that hand might, after all—as they made their way through that door—assume an improper posture in relation to his, Nikolai Apollonovich's, cheek; there was no room to jump aside in that darkness; and it would be over: the act would be performed; and the Ableukhov clan would be disgraced for ever (no one had ever struck them).

And already Second Lieutenant Likhutin (he was crazy!) seized the collar of his Italian cape with his free hand; and Nikolai Apollonovich turned as white as a sheet.

"I'll come, I'll come, Sergei Sergeich … "

He instinctively lodged his heel against the edge of the entrance step; he immediately thought better of it, though, afraid of making himself look ridiculous.

The entrance door slammed behind them.

Pitch darkness

Pitch darkness embraced them in the unlit hallway (that is what it is like the first moment after death); immediately the Second Lieutenant's puffing was heard in the darkness, accompanied by a fine volley of exclamations.

"I … was standing here: just here—standing here … Just standing, minding my own … "

"What's this you're doing, Nikolai Apollonovich? … What's this, sir? … "

"In a total attack of nerves, surrendering to morbid associations of ideas … "

"Associations? … Why are you standing still? … Associations, did you say? … "

"The doctor said so … Hey, why are you pulling me? Don't pull me: I'm quite capable of walking by myself … "

"Then why are you holding on to my hand? … Don't grab hold of me, please," the words came from further up the stairs …

"It never occurred to me … "

"You are grabbing hold … "

"But I keep telling you … " was heard still further up …

"The doctor said, the doctor said: a very rare … mental indisposition, all that business of the domino and suchlike … A mental indisposition … " came a squawk from somewhere up above.

But from somewhere higher still a well-fed stentorian voice exclaimed unexpectedly:

"Good day to you!"

This was right beside the Likhutins' door.

"Who is there?"

Sergei Sergeevich Likhutin raised his voice in displeasure out of the utter darkness.

"Who is this?" Nikolai Apollonovich raised his voice too with immense relief; at the same time he was aware: the hand that had hold of him let go and dropped away; and a match was struck—with relief.

The unfamiliar, well-fed voice went on perorating:

"Here I am standing there … Ringing and ringing—no one opens the door. And what do you know: familiar voices."

When the match caught light, puffy white fingers came into view holding a bunch of the most magnificent chrysanthemums; and after them, in the darkness, there came into view the stately figure of Vergefden—what was he doing here at this time of day?

"What's this? Sergei Sergeich?"

"You've shaved off your beard? … "

"How's this! … In civilian dress … "

And then, pretending that he had only just noticed Ableukhov (we can say on our own account that he had noticed Ableukhov at once), he struck another match and with eyebrows raised high started peeping out at him from behind the chrysanthemums swaying in his hand.

"Nikolai Apollonovich here too? … How is your health, Nikolai Apollonovich? … After yesterday evening I must admit I thought … You weren't very well, were you? … You disappeared rather noisily from the ball? … Since yesterday evening … "

Another match struck; two mocking eyes stared out from the flowers: Vergefden knew very well that Nikolai Apollonovich was not admitted to the Likhhutins' house; seeing him so obviously being dragged to the door, Vergefden, out of considerations of decorum, began to bustle about:

"Am I disturbing you? ... The thing is, I was only coming for a moment ... I don't really have time ... We're up to the neck in work ... Your papa, Apollon Apollonovich, is expecting me ... All signs suggest there's going to be a strike ... Up to the neck ... "

They had no time to reply, because the door opened abruptly; an over-starched linen butterfly appeared in the doorway—a butterfly perched upon a mob-cap.

"Mavrushka, is this a bad time?"

"Come in, sir, the mistress is at home ... "

"No, no, Mavrusha ... It's better if you hand these flowers to your mistress ... It's a debt," he smiled to Sergei Sergeich, shrugging his shoulders as one man shrugs and smiles to another after a day spent together in the company of ladies ...

"Yes, my debt to Sofia Petrovna—for the number of *whiffies* I've told ... "

And he smiled again: and—stopped short:

"Well, good bye then, old chap. Adieu, Nikolai Apollonovich: you do look exhausted, jittery ... "

His steps pattered down the stairs; and from there, from the bottom landing, his words reached them:

"You can't spend all your time with books ... "

Nikolai Apollonovich was on the point of shouting down:

"I'm coming too, German Germanovich ... It's time I was off home, too ... Are we going the same way?"

But the steps descended, and—bang: the door slammed to.

Then Nikolai Apollonovich again felt alone; and he felt—caught; yes—and this time finally; caught in front of Mavrusha. Horror was written on his face, and on Mavrusha's face were written perplexity and fright, while on the face of the Second Lieutenant an unconcealed satanic delight was written quite distinctly; drenched in perspiration, he pulled his handkerchief out of his pocket with one free hand—while with the other free hand pressing the resisting figure of the student against the wall, squeezing, dragging, pulling, pushing him.

The resisting figure of the student, in its turn, showed itself as supple as an eel; this figure, in its turn, struggling free, pushed away from the door—to get away; the more it was pushed in, the more it pushed back and squeezed away; just as when we tread on an anthill with our foot, we leap away instinctively as we see thousands of tiny red ants rushing fretfully around on the heap our foot has squashed; and then a horrid rustle emerges from that heap; could it be that the once so beguiling house had turned for Nikolai Apollonovich into a squashed anthill? Whatever might the astonished Mavrusha be thinking?

In the end Nikolai Apollonovich was pushed inside.

"Please come in, you're welcome … "

He was pushed inside; but in the vestibule, maintaining the last vestiges of dignity, scrutinising the familiar oak-finish coat-stand and on the box beneath the mirror scrutinising likewise the broken handle, he observed:

"I haven't … actually … come for long … "

And he very nearly handed his cape to Mavrusha (oh—the smell and heat from the steam heating); and—the pink kimono! … A patch of its satin flitted from the vestibule into the next room: a piece of Sofia Petrovna herself; or, more precisely of Sofia Petrovna's dress …

There was no time to think.

The cape was not handed over, because Sergei Sergeich Likhutin intercepted Mavrusha's hands and hissed abruptly:

"Into the kitchen … "

And without observing the most elementary niceties of the welcoming host Sergei Sergeich shoved the broad-brimmed hat and the flapping cape straight into the room with the Fujiyamas. It does not need to be added that beneath the hat with its broad brim and the folds of the flapping cape the owner of the cape, Nikolai Apollonovich, came flapping into that room too.

As he flew into the dining room Nikolai Apollonovich for a moment caught sight of a kimono, fleeing through the door; and—the door slammed to behind a scrap of kimono.

Nikolai Apollonovich traversed the room with the Fujiyamas without noticing any significant change, without noticing the traces of plaster on the bright, striped carpet; it had been trodden in—*since the occurrence*; afterwards the carpets had been cleaned; but traces of plaster still remained. Nikolai Apollonovich noticed nothing: neither the traces of plaster, nor the mess of the fallen ceiling. Turning the fearful leer of his mouth to the executioner who was pulling him, he suddenly noticed …

—A door there opened slightly—through the door of Sofia Petrovna's room, open a crack, a head emerged: all Nikolai Apollonovich could see was—two eyes: the eyes turned upon him in horror from a torrent of black hair.

But no sooner did he turn round to the eyes, than the eyes turned away from him; and an exclamation rang out:

"Oh dear, oh dear!"

Sofia Petrovna saw: in front of the alcove the sweat-soaked Second Lieutenant was dragging himself across the carpets and the parquet with his winged victim (Nikolai Apollonovich in his cape appeared to have wings), sweat-soaked too—with his victim, under the wings of whose cape green trousers protruded most indecently, treacherously revealing their straps.

"Trrr"—his heels dragged across the carpet; and the carpet was covered in wrinkles.

It was just then that Nikolai Apollonovich turned his head and, seeing Sofia Petrovna, shouted to her tearfully:

"Leave us, Sofia Petrovna: this is a matter between men," and at that moment the cape flew from him and fell floridly upon the couch like some fantastic creature with two wings.

"Trrr"—his heels dragged across the carpet.

After such a thorough shaking, Nikolai Apollonovich for a moment hung in space, his legs dangling, and … —the broad-brimmed hat was parted from his head with a gentle thud. He himself, with dangling legs and describing an arc, crashed through the unlocked door of the firmly closed study; the Second Lieutenant was like a sling, and Nikolai Apollonovich was like a stone: he crashed like a stone against the door; the door flew open: he vanished into the unknown.

Man-in-the-street

Finally Apollon Apollonovich stood up.

He began to look around anxiously; he tore himself away from the piles of parallel files: *nota bene's*, paragraphs-signs, question marks, exclamation marks; his hand, poised with a pencil, trembled and shook—over the yellowing sheets, the mother-of-pearl side-table; his frontal bones strained in a single concentrated effort: to understand, come what may, at any price.

And—he understood.

The lacquered carriage with its coat of arms would never again come flying up to the old stone caryatid; there, behind the windows, no one would start up to meet him: not the octogenarian shoulder, not the tricorn hat, not the braid and the bronze-headed mace; Port Arthur would not take shape again from the ruins; but—China would rise in turmoil; hark—listen carefully: it's like a distant rumbling; those are the horsemen of Chingiz-Khan.

Apollon Apollonovich listened carefully: a distant rumble; no, that wasn't a rumble: that was Semyonych walking through, crossing the frigid magnificence of the gleaming rooms; now he enters, glancing round, and passes through; he sees—the mirror has cracked: a silver arrow glints in zigzags across it; and—is set there forever.

Semyonych passes through.

Apollon Apollonovich did not like his spacious apartment with its unvarying view of the river: clouds rushed by in a greenish swarm; they thickened at times into a yellowish smoke that bent low towards the sea-shore; the dark watery depths beat firmly at the granite with their steely scales; a motionless spire swept off into the greenish swarm … from the Petersburg Side. Apollon Apollonovich began to look around anxiously: those walls! He would be confined here for a long time—with that view of the river. This was his domestic hearth; his professional activity was over.

So what?

The walls were snow, not walls! True, they were a little cold … So what? Family life; that is to say: Nikolai Apollonovich—the most frightful, so to speak—and—Anna Petrovna, who in her declining years had turned into … Lord alone knows what!

Me-emme …

Apollon Apollonovich clasped his head firmly in his fingers, as his gaze drifted off into the crackling hearth, exhaling warmth: idle cerebral play!

It, too, drifted away—drifted off beyond the bounds of consciousness: there it went on swirling up into the swarms of chaotic clouds; and Nikolai Apollonovich came to mind—quite short of stature with a penetrating blue gaze and a cluster (one must be fair) of the most varied intellectual interests, hopelessly confused.

And a young girl came to mind (that was—thirty years ago); a host of suitors; among them a still relatively young man, Apollon Apollonovich Ableukhov, already a state councillor and—a desperate admirer.

And—the first night: the horror in the eyes of his consort, when she was left alone with him—the expression of disgust, contempt, disguised by a submissive smile; that night Apollon Apollonovich Ableukhov, already a state councillor, performed a hideous act, sanctioned by custom: he raped a girl; this rape went on for years; and on one such night Nikolai Apollonovich was conceived— between two smiles of different kinds: between smiles of lust and of submission; was it surprising that Nikolai Apollonovich became thereafter a combination of revulsion, fear and lust? They should have embarked forthwith upon the joint upbringing of the horror they had begotten: the humanising of that monster.

Instead they just inflated it ...

And once they had inflated the horror to the limit, they ran away from it in different directions; Apollon Apollonovich—to direct the fate of Russia; and Anna Petrovna—to gratify her sexual proclivities with Mantalini (an Italian singer); Nikolai Apollonovich- into philosophy; and from there- -into gatherings of undergraduates from non-existent institutions (all those moustaches!). Their domestic hearth had now become a desolate abomination.

And now he must return to that abominable desolation; instead of Anna Petrovna he would encounter nothing but a locked door, leading to her apartments (unless Anna Petrovna conceived a desire to return to this abominable desolation); he had the key to these apartments (he had been into this part of the cold house no more than twice: to sit there; each time there he had caught a cold).

Instead of his son he would see there an elusive, blinking eye- huge, cold and empty: of cornflower blue; or maybe—shifty; or maybe—frightened out of its wits; horror would be hiding there—that same horror that had flared up in the bride the night that Apollon Apollonovich Ableukhov, state councillor, for the first time ...

And so on, and so on ...

After he left government service these formal rooms would probably be closed up too; so what would be left would be the corridor and the adjacent rooms for him and for his son; his life itself would be limited by the corridor: he would shuffle along there in his slippers; newspaper reading would be left, the performance of organic functions, the room comparable with no other, his last memoirs and the door leading to his son's room.

Yes, yes, yes!

Looking through the keyhole; and—springing away on hearing a suspicious rustle; or—no: drilling a hole with an awl in the appropriate place; and—his expectations would not be disappointed: his son's life on the other side of the wall would open up before him with just the same precision as is revealed to the gaze when a clockwork mechanism is dismantled. Instead of the interests of the state he would be met by a new set of interests—from this observation point.

This would all come about:

"Good morning, Papa!"

"Good morning to you, Kolenka!"

And—they would go to their separate rooms.

And—then, and—then: he would lock the door and settle down to the drill hole, to see and hear and now and then to tremble, to shudder fitfully—from the revelation of a burning secret; to languish, cower, eavesdrop: on the heart-to-heart confessions of Nikolai Apollonovich and that stranger, the one with the moustache; at night, throwing off his blanket, he would stick his sweat-soaked head out; and, reflecting on what he had overheard, he would fight for breath amidst the thumping of his heart that tore his heart to pieces, he would suck lozenges and run ... to the room comparable with no other: shuffling along the corridor in his slippers until ... a new morning.

"Good morning!"

"Yes, indeed, Kolenka ... "

That was the life of a man-in-the-street!

An irresistible urge drove him into his son's room; the door creaked timidly: the sitting room revealed itself; he stopped on the threshold; he was small and old; his fingers shook as he fiddled with the pale-red tassels of his dressing gown, surveying the muddle: the cage with green budgerigars in it, the Arabian stool with incrustations of ivory and bronze; and he saw—absurdity: from the stool in all directions spread the seething scarlet folds of the flamboyantly discarded domino, like leaping flames and flowing antlers—right up to the head of the spotted leopard, spread-eagled on the floor with snarling jaws; Apollon Apollonovich stood there a while, sucking his lips, scratched his chin that seemed sprinkled with hoar-frost and spat in disgust (he knew the story of that domino); it lay there, headless and preposterous, in satin folds and empty sleeves; on a rusty Sudanese arrow the little mask was hanging.

Apollon Apollonovich felt that it was stuffy: instead of air the atmosphere was full of lead; as though terrible, intolerable thoughts had been pondered here ... A nasty room! ... And—a suffocating atmosphere!

Here was—a mouth with a tormented smile, here were—eyes of cornflower blue, here—a shock of lambent hair; clad in an extremely tight-waisted uniform and clutching in his hand a white kid glove, Nikolai Apollonovich, clean-shaven (possibly perfumed), complete with sword, gazed longsufferingly from a frame: Apollon Apollonovich gave the portrait, painted the previous spring, an attentive glance, and—passed through into the next room.

The unlocked desk seized Apollon Apollonovich's attention: one of the drawers was open; Apollon Apollonovich was taken with an instinctive curiosity (to examine its contents); he rushed with swift steps across to the desk and grasped—a huge portrait that had been forgotten on the desk; in deep distraction he began to twirl it around (his absent-mindedness distracted his thoughts from the content of the drawer); the portrait depicted a lady—a brunette ...

His absent-mindedness arose from the contemplation of a certain lofty matter, because this matter had developed into a train of thought along which the senator had embarked; this train of thought had nothing to do with his son's room, nor with his own sojourn in his son's room, into which Apollon Apollonovich had most likely penetrated quite mechanically (an irresistible urge is a mechanical act); he then lowered his eyes mechanically and saw that his hand was no longer twirling a portrait, but some heavy object, while his thoughts were surveying the type of government official who is known in the vulgar parlance as a careerist, with a representative of which he had recently had the misfortune to have discussions: in the days of the deceased minister they had been on the same side as him, but now they were planning to ...

Planning to do what?

The heavy object resembled a sardine-tin in shape; it had been pulled out mechanically by the senator's hand; Apollon Apollonovich had grasped mechanically the studio portrait, and had surfaced from his cogitation—with a round-edged object: something inside it made a jangling sound; least of all did the senator at this point remember the abyss (we often drink coffee with cream over the abyss), but he examined the round-edged object with the minutest attention, bending his head over it and listening to the ticking of a clock: a clockwork mechanism in a heavy sardine-tin ...

He took a dislike to the object ...

He took the object with him for a more detailed examination— across the corridor into the drawing room—bending his head over it and looking like a grey, mousy bundle; all this time he went on thinking about that same type of government official; people of that type protected themselves from responsibility with vacuous phrases such as 'as is well known', when nothing is yet known at all, or: 'science teaches us', when science does not teach (his thoughts were always pouring poison on to the opposing party) ...

Apollon Apollonovich rushed with the object to the end of the drawing room where an incrusted side-table rose up on lion's legs; a long-legged bronze rose primly from the table; he set the heavy object down on a Chinese lacquered tray, bending his bald head, over which the lampshade spread its pale-violet, delicately decorated glass.

But the glass had grown dark with time; and the delicate decoration had grown dark with time too.

He failed to explain himself properly

Sent flying into Likhutin's study, Nikolai Apollonovich crashed heels first on to the floor at full speed; the shock was transmitted to his skull; his knee-joints trembled; he dropped involuntarily to his knees, ramming into the unpleasantly slippery parquet with the dark-green cloth of his trousers; he hurt himself.

He fell and …

—immediately sprang up again, breathing heavily and limping, hurled himself in fear towards the heavy oak armchair, presenting a clumsy and pretty ridiculous figure with his trembling jaw, his obviously trembling fingers and a single instinctive urge—to get there in time: to seize hold of the armchair in time, so that in the event of attack from behind he could quickly run round the armchair, flying this way and that to evade his merciless opponent, who would himself be flying this way and that, his movements resembling the convulsions of someone suffering from hydrophobia; to seize hold of the armchair in time! …

Or else, using the armchair as a weapon, to knock his opponent over, and while he was struggling beneath the heavy oak legs, rush as quickly as possible over to the window (better to crash down on to the street from a first-floor window, smashing the glass, than to stay face to face with … with …)

Breathing heavily and limping, he rushed over to the oak armchair.

But hardly had he reached the armchair when the Second Lieutenant's hot breath scorched his neck; turning round, he just had time to make out a wan, twisted mouth and a five-fingered hand, about to drop on to his shoulder: a face, purple with rage, the face of an avenger, with swollen veins, stared at him with an unflinching eye; in that hideous face no one would have recognised the gentle face of the Second Lieutenant, serenely uttering one *whiffy* after another. The five-fingered hand was more like a huge paw, and would for certain have dropped on to Ableukhov's shoulder and broken his shoulder; but he managed in time to jump over the armchair.

The five-fingered paw dropped on to the armchair.

And the armchair broke; the armchair crashed on to the floor; above their ears resounded—an unrepeatable, inhuman sound, never heard before:

"Because a human soul is doomed to perish here!"

And an angular body flew after the receding figure; from an oral orifice bubbling with spittle thin, squeaky notes burst out, gurgled, broke in a splintered mass of wheezing—voiceless notes, and somehow red …

"Because I ... got involved ... you understand? In all this business ... This business ... You understand? ... This business is a ... Nothing to do with me ... I mean, no: it is to do with me ... But do you understand? ... "

And the crazed Second Lieutenant, having caught up with his victim, raised over that figure, who was bent double, anticipating a box on the ears, two trembling palms (the figure went on trying to hide his sweating head under his arched back), nervously clenched them into fists, leaning with his whole body over the bundle of muscles that was wriggling under his hands; the *bundle* twisted and turned with its teeth bared in fear, imitating all the rhythms of those hands and protecting his right cheek with his open palm:

"I understand, I understand ... Sergei Sergeevich, calm down," the bundle squeaked, "take it easy, I beg you, take it easy: my dear fellow, I beg you ... "

This bundle of body (Nikolai Apollonovich was retreating, unnaturally contorted)—this bundle of body was tiptoeing on two crooked legs; and not towards the window—away from the window (the Second Lieutenant was obstructing the way to the window); at the same time this bundle saw through the window—(strange as it may be, this was still Nikolai Apollonovich)—the protruding funnel of a steamer; and beyond the canal—the wet roof of a house; above that roof was a huge, cold emptiness ...

He retreated into the corner and—can you imagine: the leaden five-fingered hands dropped on to his shoulders (one hand scorched his neck with a forty-degree heat as it slid across it); so that he collapsed—in the corner on to all fours, bathed in cold sweat, like ice.

He was on the point of screwing up his eyes and blocking his ears, so as not to see the half-crazed crimson face and not to hear the cries of the hoarse, high-pitched voice:

"Aaa ... A matter ... where any respectable person, where ... a-a-a ... any respectable person ... What did I say? Yes—respectable ... must get involved, regardless of propriety, or social position ... "

It was strange, listening to this incoherent succession of words that had meaning in themselves, but were accompanied by facial features and gestures that were meaningless; Nikolai Apollonovich wondered:

"Maybe I should shout out, call for help?"

No, what use was it to shout; and who would hear a call there; no—it was too late; just shut your eyes and ears; in a moment it would all be over; crash: a fist struck the wall above Ableukhov's head.

For a moment he opened his eyes.

In front of him he saw: the two legs were placed so wide apart (he was on all fours, remember); a single dizzying thought—and: without considering consequences, his teeth bared in fear, as though he was laughing, his flaxen hair flailing, Nikolai Apollonovich swiftly crawled between those widely spaced legs; he leapt up and rushed unthinking straight for the door (the leaden edge of the roof swept by in the window), but ... the five-fingered paws that scorched with their touch seized him humiliatingly by the tail of his coat; they gave a tug: the expensive material ripped.

The piece of torn-off tail flew off to one side:

"Wait ... Wait ... I'm ... I'm ... I'm not ,,, going to kill you ... Stop ... You're in no danger of violence ... "

And Nikolai Apollonovich was roughly thrust away; he banged his back into the corner; he stood there in the corner, breathing heavily, almost weeping from the overpowering ugliness of what had happened; and it seemed that his hair was not hair, but some lambent luminosity on the crimson background of the smoke-stained study wallpaper; and his usually dark-cornflower eyes now seemed black from his immense, cold terror, because he realised: it was not Likhutin raging over him, not the officer he had insulted, not even an enemy in a paroxysm of vengeful wrath, it was ... a violent lunatic, with whom no talk was possible; this violent lunatic, possessed of immense muscular strength, was not attacking him just now; but he surely would.

And this violent lunatic, turning his back (that would have been the time to do him in), tiptoed up to the door; and the door clicked: on the other side of the door some sounds were heard—maybe weeping, maybe the shuffle of shoes. And all fell silent. Retreat was cut off: only the window was left.

In this locked room they silently gasped for breath: parricide and madman.

The room with the fallen ceiling-plaster was empty; in front of the slammed door lay a soft, wide-brimmed hat, while from the sofa dangled the flap of a fantastic cape; but when the dull thud of the armchair was heard in the study, then at the opposite side, from Sofia Petrovna's room, a door shot open with a creak; and from there Sofia Petrovna Likhutina came tripping through in her shoes and with a torrent of black hair tumbling down her back; a diaphanous silk scarf, like liquid brightness, dragged along behind her; on Sofia Petrovna's diminutive forehead a frown was clearly marked.

She crept up to the keyhole of the door; she squatted down by the door; she looked and saw: just two pairs of passing feet and two … trouser straps; the feet pattered away into the corner; now the feet were nowhere to be seen, but from the corner, with a gurgle, soft wheezing sounds emerged as though from a bubbling throat: an unrepeatable, inhuman, high-pitched whisper. And the feet pattered by again; right beside Sofia Petrovna's eyes, on the other side of the door, the metallic sound rang out of the door-lock clicking to.

Sofia Petrovna burst into tears, sprang away from the door and saw—an apron and a cap: it was Mavrusha just behind her burying her face in her clean, snow-white apron; Mavrusha was crying too:

"Whatever is it, ma'am? … Ma'am, dear? … "

"I don't know … I don't know anything … Whatever is it? … What are they doing there, Mavrusha?"

Half-past-two in the afternoon.

In its solitary study a bald head that rested on a roughened palm is raised above the sombre oaken desk; it gazes under lowered brows at the fireplace where cornflowers of escaping gas swirl in a mischievous swarm above the incandescent pile of crackling coals, and where red cockscombs burst out, scatter and explode—acrid, light, flying swiftly up the chimney, to merge above the rooftops with the fumes, the toxic soot, and hang there in perpetuity as a suffocating, caustic gloom.

The bald head is raised—a wan, Mephistophelean mouth smiles a senile smile at the spurting flames; the face is purpled by the spurts; the eyes are kindled too; and yet—they're eyes of stone: blue—set in green sockets! A huge, cold emptiness has glanced out of them;

it clings to them, peers out of them, without detaching itself from delusion; this world spreads out in front of it as a delusion.

Cold, astonished eyes; and—empty, empty: with their delusions they have set times, suns, and worlds on fire; history has run its course from distant times right to this very moment, when—

> —the bald head that rested on a roughened palm is raised above the desk and gazes under lowered brows with a huge, cold emptiness—at the fireplace where cornflowers of escaping gas swirl in a mischievous swarm above the incandescent pile of crackling coals. The circle is closed.

What was that?

Apollon Apollonovich tried to remember where he was and what had happened between two moments of thought; between two movements of his fingers as they twirled a pencil; the sharply pointed pencil—here it was, dancing in his fingers.

"Never mind ... Doesn't matter ... "

And the sharpened pencil drops on to the paper in a swarm of question marks.

Mumbling Lord alone knows what, the lunatic went on attacking; mumbling Lord alone knows what, he went on stamping his feet: he went on striding to and fro along a diagonal line across the stuffy study. Nikolai Apollonovich, standing spread-eagled against the wall, over in the shadowy corner, went on watching the movements of the poor lunatic, who was still capable of turning into a wild beast.

Every time his arm shot upwards in an abrupt gesture, he shuddered; and the lunatic—stopped tramping up and down, stood still, diverged from the fatal diagonal: two paces from Nikolai Apollonovich his ominous, gaunt hand began to shake again. Then Nikolai Apollonovich sprang away: the hand made contact with the corner—it hammered on the wall in the corner.

But the demented Second Lieutenant (pitiable, rather than pugnacious) was pursuing him no longer; he was sitting with his back turned and his elbows pressed to his knees, which made his back bend and his head disappear into his shoulders; he sighed deeply; he was deep in thought.

He blurted out:

"Oh, Lord!"

And groaned again:

"Save me and have mercy!"

Nikolai Apollonovich carefully took advantage of this lull in his delirium.

He raised himself surreptitiously and, trying to make no noise, he straightened up; the Second Lieutenant's head did not turn, as it had been turning lately with a danger—honestly!—of untwisting from his neck; the paroxysm of madness was clearly spent; and now was on the wane; then Nikolai Apollonovich, limping, hobbled soundlessly to the desk, trying not to let his shoe squeak, or to let the floorboard squeak—he hobbled along, presenting a pretty ridiculous figure in his elegant uniform ... with its coat-tail torn off, in new rubber galoshes and his scarf still round his neck.

He made his way to the desk: he stopped beside it, listening to the beating of his heart and the quiet mumbled prayers of the sick man as he quietened down: in an inaudible movement his hand reached for the paperweight; but disaster struck: on top of the paperweight lay a pile of writing-paper.

If only he could avoid catching the paper with his sleeve!

But as bad luck would have it he did catch the pile of paper; a treacherous rustle was heard and the pile of paper scattered all over the desk; this rustling of paper awoke the Second Lieutenant from his reverie; his paroxysm, having erupted once and receded, now erupted again with new force; his head turned and caught sight of Nikolai Apollonovich with hand outstretched, clutching the paperweight; Nikolai Apollonovich's heart fell: he sprang away from the desk, the paperweight stayed in his hand—as a precaution.

In two bounds Sergei Sergeich Likhutin flew up to him, dropped a hand on his shoulder and started squeezing his shoulder: in short— he was up to his old tricks again:

"I have to ask your forgiveness ... I am sorry: I lost my temper ... "

"Please calm down ... "

"This is all terribly unusual ... Only, please, be so kind: don't be afraid ... Why are you shaking like that? ... It seems I make you feel afraid? I ... I ... I ... tore off your coat-tail: that was ... an accident, because you, Nikolai Apollonovich, revealed an intention of avoiding an explanation … But, you must understand, there is no way you can leave me without an explanation … "

"Why, I'm not trying to avoid it," Nikolai Apollonovich pleaded, still clutching the paperweight in his hand, "I began to tell you about the domino myself on the way in: I'm trying to clear it up with you myself; it's you, Sergei Sergeich, who is dragging it out: you're not giving me the chance to explain."

"Mm … yes, yes … "

"Don't you see, that domino is explained by nervous exhaustion; and it certainly isn't a breach of my promise: it wasn't of my own free will that I stood there in the entrance, but … "

"Well, I'm sorry about the coat-tail," Likhutin interrupted him again, by which he merely proved that he really was *non compos mentis* (however, he did for the time being leave Ableukhov's shoulder alone) … "We'll get the coat-tail sewn on again; if you like—I'll do it myself. I've got needle and thread … "

"That's all I needed," flashed through Ableukhkov's head: he scrutinised the Second Lieutenant with surprise, concluding from the visible evidence that the paroxysm had nevertheless passed.

"But that's not the point: it's not about needles and thread … "

"Really, Sergei Sergeevich, it's … It's—trivial … "

"Yes, yes: trivial … "

"Trivial in relation to the main topic of our discussion: in relation to all that standing in the entrance … "

"But it's not about standing in the entrance!" the Second Lieutenant waved his hand in irritation, starting once again to stride in the same direction: along the diagonal of that stuffy study.

"Well, about Sofia Petrovna … " Nikolai Apollonovich ventured from the corner, now noticeably more courageous.

"It's not … not … about Sofia Petrovna … " the Second Lieutenant shouted at him: "you haven't understood me at all!! … "

"Then what is it about?"

"That's all—trivial! … That's to say, it's not trivial, but it is trivial in relation to the topic of our conversation … "

"What is the topic?"

"The topic, don't you see," the Second Lieutenant stopped in front of him and brought his bloodshot eyes right up to Ableukhov's eyes, that were dilated with fear ... "The essential thing, you see, is simply that you—are locked in ... "

"But ... Why am I locked in?" and the paperweight was once more firmly clutched in his fist ...

"What have I locked you in for? Why did I, so to speak, drag you here more or less by force? ... Ha-ha: that has absolutely nothing to do with the domino, or with Sofia Petrovna ... "

"He's definitely out of his mind: he's forgotten all the reasons, his brain is only responding to morbid associations: and he is planning to ... " flashed through Nikolai Apollonovich's head, but Sergei Sergeevich, as though guessing his thought, hastened to reassure him, which could well have seemed more like a joke and some wicked mockery:

"I repeat, you are in no danger here ... It's just the coat-tail ... "

"He's making fun of me," Nikolai Apollonovich thought and a mad idea shot through his brain in its turn: to bring the paperweight down on the Second Lieutenant's head; and after knocking him out, to tie his hands, and through this act of violence save his own life, which he needed if only because ... the bomb ... in his desk ... was ticking away!! ...

"You see: you aren't going away from here ... But I ... I shall leave here with a letter I shall dictate—with your signature ... I shall go to your house, into your room, where I was this morning already, but didn't notice anything ... I shall turn everything there upside down; and in the event that all my searches turn out fruitless, I shall warn your papa ... because," he wiped his brow, "it's not your papa who has the power; you're the one with the power: yes, yes, yes, my good sir—you alone, Nikolai Apollonovich!"

He prodded him in the chest with one rough finger and stood there with an upward soaring eyebrow (only one).

"Listen, Nikolai Apollonovich, this shall not happen—it shall never happen!"

And on his crimson, clean-shaven face was a play of:

"?"

"!"

"!?!"

Totally out of his mind!

But strange to say, Nikolai Apollonovich listened intently to this utter nonsense; something in him winced: in truth—was this nonsense?

It was more like hints, incoherently expressed; but hints—at what? Surely not hints at … at … at? …

Yes, yes, yes …

"Sergei Sergeevich, what is all this about?"

And his heart fell: Nikolai Apollonovich felt that it was not a body that his skin enveloped, but … a pile of cobblestones; in place of his brain—was a cobblestone; and there was a cobblestone—in his stomach.

"What's it about? … Why, I'm talking about the bomb … " and Sergei Sergeevich took two steps back, astonished in the extreme.

The paperweight fell from Ableukhov's unclasped fist; a moment before it had seemed to Nikolai Apollonovich that it was not a body that his skin enveloped, but … a pile of cobblestones; but now his horror crossed another line; he felt that something had thrust itself sharply into the enormity of the quintillion (between the zeros and the unit); the unit remained.

And the quintillion became—zero.

The enormity suddenly burst into flames: the cobblestones that filled his body turned into gases, and in the blinking of an eye spurted out from every aperture in the pores of his skin, wove once more a spiral of events, but wove them in reverse order; they wove his very body into a receding spiral; and so the sensation of his body itself—became a zero sensation; the features of his face assumed clear outline, took on extraordinary meaning, revealing in the young man the face of a venerable sixty-year-old: they assumed clear outline, took on meaning, became as though etched; the face—white, pale-white—became a countenance lit from within, flooding all with scalding light; on the other hand: the Second Lieutenant's face turned a bright carrot colour; it became even sillier with its shaven cheeks, and his stunted jacket became more stunted still …

"Sergei Sergeevich, I am surprised at you … How could you believe, that I, that I … could you attribute to me consent to such a ghastly act of baseness … And yet I am not a scoundrel … I, Sergei Sergeevich, am not yet—I believe—a thorough villain … "

Nikolai Apollonovich was evidently unable to continue; and—he turned away; and having done so, turned back again …

From the shadowy corner emerged a proud, bowed figure, seemingly re-composed, and consisting, as the Second Lieutenant perceived it, of liquid luminosity—with a mouth smiling in martyrdom, with eyes of cornflower blue; the shock of shining flaxen hair formed a transparent circle, like a nimbus, over the lofty, gleaming brow; he stood with outspread hands, palms upwards, indignant, offended, beautiful, somehow raised on high against the bloody background of the wallpaper: the room had red wallpaper.

He stood there—his scarf hanging loosely round his neck and with only one coat-tail: the other had—alas—been torn off ...

So he stood: from the huge abysses of his eyes a cold, immense emptiness and darkness gazed unremittingly at the Second Lieutenant; it clung to him, it chilled him; Second Lieutenant Likhutin somehow felt that for all his physical strength, for all his good sense (he thought he had good sense) and, moreover, for all his nobility—he was nothing but a fleeting delusion; so that Ableukhov had only to approach the Second Lieutenant with that gleaming appearance for the Second Lieutenant, Sergei Sergeevich, to start manifestly retreating from him.

"But I believe you, I believe you," he waved his arms in perplexity.

"You see," he became conclusively embarrassed, "I didn't have the slightest doubt ... I'm really ashamed ... I'm very worried ... My wife told me ... She had that note foisted on her ... So she read it—she opened it by mistake, of course," he lied for some reason, blushed, and lowered his eyes ...

"Since the note to me had been opened," the senator's son seized upon his remark with pleasurable malice, "then," ... he shrugged his shoulders, "then Sofia Petrovna, of course, had every right (this smacked of irony) to tell you, as her husband, about its content," Nikolai Apollonovich muttered arrogantly through clenched teeth; and—continued to advance.

"I ... I ... lost control," Likhutin offered in his defence: his gaze fell on the unfortunate coat-tail, and he fastened on to that.

"That coat-tail, don't you worry: I'll sew it on myself ... "

But Nikolai Apollonovich, with the faintest of smiles on his lips— handsome, his face lit from within—went on reproachfully waving his hands in the air:

"You knew not what you did."

His dark-cornflower, deep blue eyes and his shock of shining hair expressed a vague, unutterable sadness:

"Go: denounce me, don't believe me! ... "

And he turned away ...

His broad shoulders began to shake fitfully ... Nikolai Apollonovich was weeping uncontrollably; at the same time: freed from his crude, animal fear, Nikolai Apollonovich became entirely fearless; more than that: at that moment he even wished to suffer; that, at all events, was how he felt at that moment: he felt he was a hero, offered up for torment, suffering publicly, debased; his body, in his sensations, was a body in torment; his senses were torn apart, as his whole 'self' was torn apart; from the rupture of his 'self'—he expected—a blinding ray of light would flash and a familiar voice would pronounce to him, as always—would pronounce within himself: and for himself:

"You have suffered for my sake: I am standing over you."

But there was no voice. There was no ray of light either. There was—darkness. That feeling arose, no doubt, because he only now realised: ever since his meeting on the Nevskii up to this last minute he had been undergoing undeserved insults; he had been brought here by force, pulled and dragged into the study: by force; and here in the study he had had his coat-tail torn off; why, he had been suffering incessantly for twenty-four hours anyway: so why on top of that did he have to experience fear of physical assault? Why was there no voice of reconciliation: "You have suffered for my sake?" Because he had not suffered for anyone's sake: he had suffered for himself ... He was supping, as it were, the brew he had himself concocted out of ugly incidents. That was why there was no voice. And why there was no ray of light either. In the place of his previous 'self' there was darkness. He could not bear that: his broad shoulders began to shake fitfully.

He turned away: he was weeping.

"Honestly," a voice behind his back was heard, conciliatory, humble, "I was mistaken, I did not understand ... "

Yet there was still a touch of irritation in that voice: of shame and ... irritation: and Sergei Sergeevich stood there, biting his lip painfully; was it perhaps that Likhutin regretted, now that he was calm, that he had been mistaken, that he could not crush his enemy: either with this great fist of his, or with nobility; just so a maddened bull, driven

501

wild by a red rag, hurls itself at its antagonist and—strikes against the iron bars of its cage: and stands there bellowing, not knowing what to do. On the Second Lieutenant's face was written the struggle of distasteful memories (the domino, of course) with the noblest of sentiments; his antagonist, meanwhile, still weeping, and his back still turned to him, was saying in an unpleasant way:

"Taking advantage of your physical superiority, you dragged me … in the presence of a lady, like a … like a … "

The noblest of impulses won the day; Sergei Sergeevich Likhutin crossed the study with his hand extended; but Nikolai Apollonovich, turning round (a teardrop trembled on his eyelash), abruptly uttered in a voice half-strangled by the fury that had seized him and by—alas!—a pride that had arrived too late:

"Like a … like a … pipsqueak … "

If he had proffered his hand now—Sergei Sergeich would have deemed himself the happiest of men: utter self-composure would have played across his face; but his access of nobility, just like his access of fury, was at once sealed inside his soul; his noble impulse fell into a dark void.

"You wanted to make certain, Sergei Sergeevich? … That I was not—a parricide? … No, Sergei Sergeevich, no: you should have thought of that sooner … But you … like a pipsqueak. And—you tore my coat-tail off … "

"The coat-tail can be sewn on again!"

And before Ableukhov had recollected himself, Sergei Sergeevich rushed to the door:

"Mavrusha! … Some black thread! … And a needle … "

But the door, as it opened, very nearly struck Sofia Petrovna, who had been eavesdropping just behind it; caught in the act, she sprang away, but—too late: caught in the act, red as a peony, she was trapped: and at them—both of them—she cast an indignant, annihilating glance.

The coat-tail was lying between the three of them.

"Ah? … Sonechka … "

"Sofia Petrovna! … "

"Have I disturbed you? … "

"Goodness me … Nikolai Apollonovich here … You know … has torn his coat-tail off … He needs it … "

"No, don't trouble yourself, Sergei Sergeich; Sofia Petrovna—if you would be so kind … "

"He needs it sewn on."

But Nikolai Apollonovich, his mouth contorted from his absurd situation, wiping his perfidious eyelashes with his sleeve and still limping on one leg, appeared in the room with the Fujiyamas … in his battered frock coat with one coat-tail dangling; as he picked up his Italian cape, he raised his head and, noticing the mess the ceiling was in, turned his contorted mouth to Sofia Petrovna for decorum's sake.

"Tell me, Sofia Petrovna, something's been changed here: on the ceiling there's some sort of … Something not quite right: have you had painters in?"

But Sergei Sergeevich interrupted:

"It was me, Nikolai Apollonovich: I was … mending the ceiling … "

But he thought to himself:

"Ha! How do you like that: last night— I failed to hang myself properly; and now—I failed to explain myself properly … "

Nikolai Apollonovich limped across the room on his way out; his fantastic cape, slipping off his shoulder, dragged along behind him like a black train.

From the *nota bene's*, question marks, paragraph-signs, underlinings, from this *final* task the bald head is raised; and—drops again. The burning mass—scarlet, golden—exhaling warmth, seethed and snorted, emitting fervid crackles and flashes; the logs collapsed into charcoal—and the bald head was raised over the hearth with a sardonic smile on its lips and its eyes narrowed; suddenly the lips parted in fear.

What was that?

Seething red flares—thrusting flames, flowing antlers—splayed out in all directions: branching out, licking out from everywhere— tree-like, golden, diaphanous; they came leaping out of the hearth's red muzzle; jumping up at the walls: the fireplace started moving, expanding, turning into a stone dungeon where the liquid luminosity, the flames, the dark cornflower-coloured escaping gases and crests all froze (stopped suddenly, ceased moving): in the now transparent light—a figure re-composed itself, raised upwards into the disappearing vault and stretched out in a stooping posture; red, five-fingered hands stretch out—singeing with flames whatever they might touch.

What was that?

Here was—a mouth smiling in martyrdom, here—eyes of cornflower blue, here—a shock of shining hair: clad in the fury of flames, with wide-spread arms nailed in the air by sparks, with hands palms upwards in the air—palms that were pierced—

> —Nikolai Apollonovich, splayed out in the form of a cross, was suffering there in the light's luminosity and pointing with his eyes at the red sores on his hands; and from the gaping heavens a broad-winged archangel was pouring on him cooling dew— into the incandescent furnace ...

—"He knows not what he does ... "

Suddenly ... —a dizzying crash, a hissing, a snorting: the bright luminosity starts to pulsate and shatters to pieces, sweeping away the tormented image in vortices of sparks.

A quarter-of-an-hour later he ordered the horses to be harnessed; forty minutes later he made his way through to his carriage (we saw this in the previous chapter); an hour later the carriage was standing in the middle of an idle crowd; and—was it merely idle? ...

Something had happened there.

A half-inch of space, the side of his carriage, separated Apollon Apollonovich from the mutinous crowd; the horses snorted, and in the windows of the carriage Apollon Apollonovich saw nothing but heads: bowler hats, caps, and, above all, Manchurian hats; he saw a pair of indignant eyes staring at him; he saw the ragged mouth of a ragamuffin: a singing mouth (people were singing). The ragamuffin, catching sight of Apollon Apollonovich, shouted out rudely:

"Get out, can't you see: there's no way through."

To the ragamuffin's voice were added the voices of other ragamuffins.

Then Apollon Apollonovich Ableukhov, in order to avoid unpleasantness, was compelled by the coercion of the crowd to open slightly his carriage door; the ragamuffins saw the old man climbing out with trembling lips, holding on to the brim of his top hat with his glove: Apollon Apollonovich saw in front of him howling mouths and a tall pole: straining free of that wooden pole with a faint whistling sound, a flailing sheet of red calico made wave-crests as it rippled in the air, fluttering and tearing, splashing into the void:

"Hey, you, off with your hat!"

Apollon Apollonovich removed his top hat and began hastily to squeeze his way over to the pavement, abandoning carriage and coachman; soon he was stepping carefully along in a direction opposite to that of the swarming mass; little black figures were streaming out of shops, yards, side streets, taverns; Apollon Apollonovich was running out of strength: and—he ran out into the empty side streets, from where … cossacks … were galloping …

The cossack detachment rushed by; the area was emptied; the backs of cossacks could be seen rushing towards the sheet of calico; and the back of an old man in a tall top hat could be seen, running for all he was worth.

A little game of patience

A samovar was boiling on the table; from the dresser a completely new, completely clean samovar cast a metallic gleam; the samovar that was boiling on the table, however, was unpolished, dirty; the completely new samovar was used when there were guests; in the absence of guests this lopsided monstrosity was set on the table: it snorted and hissed loudly; and now and then a red spark shot out from the holes in it. Someone's uncouth hand had rolled some balls of white bread; and they were squashed on the stained and crumpled tablecloth; a slovenly damp stain showed under a half-finished glass of sour tea (sour from the lemon in it); and a plate stood there with the remains of a cold cutlet and cold mashed potato.

And where was the luxuriant hair? A paltry plait protruded instead.

Zoia Zakharovna Fleisch probably wore a wig (when there were guests, of course); and—by the way: she probably used immodest quantities of make-up, because last time we saw her as a brunette with luxuriant hair, and with enamel skin, excessively smooth; but now before us was simply an old woman with a sweaty nose and a rat's tail of a plait; she was wearing a blouse: and, again, a dirty one (she probably slept in it).

Lippanchenko was sitting half turned away from the tea table, presenting to both Zoia Zakharovna and the dirty samovar his square, hunched back. In front of Lippanchenko lay a half completed game of patience, leading one to assume that after supper Lippanchenko had taken up his customary pastime, which had so beneficial an effect upon his nerves, but—had been disturbed: he had reluctantly torn himself away from the cards; a lengthy conversation had taken place, during which, of course, the glass of tea, the patience and all the rest—had been forgotten.

And it was after that conversation that Lippanchenko had turned his back: to the conversation.

He was sitting without his starched collar, without his jacket, and with his belt, which evidently restricted his stomach, loosened, as a result of which a little tongue of shirt, uncomfortably starched, protruded perfidiously between his waistcoat and his sagging trousers (of a dark yellow colour—the same as before).

We have caught Lippanchenko just at the moment when he was contemplating pensively the black spot of a cockroach crawling with a rustling sound from the direction of the clock; there were cockroaches in the cottage: huge, black ones; and in profusion—in such unbearable profusion that, regardless of the lamplight—there was a rustling in the corner, and from a crack in the sideboard a whisker occasionally protruded.

Lippanchenko was distracted from the contemplation of the crawling cockroach by the plaintive lamentations of his life's companion.

Zoia Zakharovna pushed the tea tray away from her with such a noise that Lippanchenko jumped.

"Well? ... Whatever is this? ... And what's the reason for it?"

"What's what?"

"Surely a faithful woman, a woman of forty, who's given her life to you—a woman like me ... "

And she rested her elbows on the table: one elbow was torn, and through the tear her old, faded skin could be seen and what was probably a flea-bite she had scratched.

"What's that you're mumbling, old lady: talk more clearly ... "

"Doesn't a woman like me have the right to ask? … An old woman," and she covered her face with her hands: just her nose stuck out and two dark eyes bristled.

Lippanchenko turned round in his chair.

Evidently her words had touched him; for a moment some semblance of an attack of conscience appeared on his face; he blinked both eyes in a cross between limp timidity and childish caprice; evidently he wanted to say something; and evidently he was afraid to say it; something of the sort he now slowly cogitated—maybe wondering how his companion's soul would react to such a terrible confession; Lippanchenko's head dropped; he snuffled and looked at her from under lowered brows.

But the call to truthfulness collapsed; and truthfulness itself tumbled into the dim depths of his soul. He took up his patience again:

"Hm: yes, yes … The five on to the six … Where's the queen? … Here's the queen … And … the jack is blocked … "

Suddenly he cast a searching, suspicious glance at Zoia Zakharovna, and his short fingers with golden hairs moved a pile of cards: over from one pile of cards—to another pile of cards.

"Well—that turned out a fine game … " he went on angrily laying out rows of cards.

Zoia Zakharovna carefully carried a cup she had wiped quite clean over to the dresser, treading heavily in her slippers.

"Well? … What is there to be cross about?"

Now, still treading heavily, she started walking round the room, making a shuffling sound (a cockroach's whisker vanished into the crack in the sideboard).

"I'm not cross, old girl," and again he cast a searching glance at her: folding her arms over her stomach and sticking out her estimable stomach, unconstrained by any corset, her sagging chin wobbling as she walked; she came quietly up to him and gently touched him on the shoulder:

"You'd do better to ask why I'm asking you … Because everyone's asking … They shrug their shoulders … So I think,"—she leant against his chair with her stomach and her breasts—"it's better for me to know everything … "

But Lippanchenko, biting his lip, went on laying out the cards with a restless efficiency.

He, Lippanchenko, had not forgotten that tomorrow was for him

507

a day of quite exceptional importance; if tomorrow he did not succeed in proving her innocence to them, did not succeed in shaking off the ominous weight that had come down on him from certain documents, then—it was checkmate for him. And, remembering all this, he simply sniffed:

"Hm: yes, yes … There's a space here … Nothing for it: into the space with the king … "

And—he could not keep it up:

"You say they're asking? … "

"Did you think they weren't?"

"And they come when I'm away? … "

"They come, they come: and shrug their shoulders … "

Lippanchenko threw the cards aside:

"It won't work: the twos are all blocked … "

It was clear that he was worried.

At that moment something tinkled plaintively in Lippanchenko's bedroom, as though someone were opening the window. They both turned their heads towards Lippanchenko's bedroom; they both kept cautiously silent: who might that be?

No doubt Tom, the St Bernard.

"You must understand, you funny woman, that your questions"—Lippanchenko stood up, groaning—perhaps to check the reason for the strange noise or perhaps to wriggle out of answering.

"Are a breach of party … " he took a sip of the thoroughly sour tea, "discipline … "

Stretching, he went through the open door—into the depths, the darkness …

"What's party discipline got to do with me, Kolenka," Zoia Zakharovna objected, resting her face on her hand and lowering her head, still standing over the now empty chair … "Just think what you're saying … "

But she fell silent, because the chair was empty; Lippanchenko trotted off towards the bedroom; and she absent-mindedly flicked through the cards.

Lippanchenko's steps came closer.

"There have been no secrets between us … " She said this to herself.

She immediately turned her head towards the door—towards

the darkness, the depths—and started talking anxiously to the approaching footsteps:

"You didn't warn me that basically we've got nothing to talk about (Lippanchenko appeared in the doorway), that you have secrets now, while I … "

"No, it's all right: there's nobody in the bedroom," he interrupted her …

"They keep pestering me: the way they look, the hints, the questions … There have even been … "

His mouth split open in a yawn of boredom; and, unfastening his waistcoat, he mumbled under his breath in displeasure:

"What's the point of these scenes?"

"There have been threats against you … "

A pause.

"So I'm obviously going to ask … Why are you shouting so? What have I done, Kolenka? … Don't I love you? … Can't you see I'm afraid?"

And she wound her arms round his plump neck. And—sobbed:

"I'm an old woman, a faithful woman … "

And he saw on his own face her nose; it was a hawk's nose; or more precisely—a hawk-like nose; it would have been a hawk's, if it hadn't been for its fleshiness: it was full of pores; the pores shone with sweat; two compact areas in the form of juxtaposed cheeks were criss-crossed with imprecise folds of skin (when there was neither cream nor powder on them)—of skin that was not exactly flabby, but was unpleasant, stale; two wrinkles ran sharply from her nose down to her lips, pulling her lips downwards; and her eyes were staring into his little eyes; it was as though those eyes were hatching out and pressing insistently—like two eager, black buttons; and the eyes did not shine.

They merely pressed.

"Well, stop it … Stop it … That's enough … Zoia Zakharovna … Let me go … I'm short of breath: you'll throttle me … "

And he grasped her hands with his fingers and took them off his neck; and he sank into his chair; and breathed heavily:

"You know what a sentimental and nervous person I am … Here I am again … "

They fell silent.

And in the profound, oppressive silence that comes after a long, joyless conversation, when everything has been said, all anxieties over words have been exhausted and there is nothing left but dull submissiveness—in that profound silence she washed the glass, the dish and two teaspoons.

He, though, sat half turned away from the tea table, presenting to Zoia Zakharovna and the dirty samovar his square back.

"You said—threats?"

How she shuddered.

How she shot out: from behind the samovar; her lips were drawn back again: her anxious eyes all but jumped out of their sockets; they ran anxiously across the tablecloth, clambered up the plump chest and broke into those blinking eyes; and—what had time done?

No, what had it done?

Those light-brown eyes, those eyes that used to shine with humour and a sly merriment at the age of twenty-five, had grown dull, had sunk and been veiled in an ominous shroud; they were misted by the fumes of all the most noxious atmospheres: dark-yellow, dark-saffron ones; true, twenty-five years is no mean span of time, but all the same—to fade, to shrink like that! And under the eyes those twenty-five years had drawn out stupid-looking bags of fat; twenty-five years—is no mean span of time; but ... —why that popping Adam's apple under the round chin? The pink hue of the face had yellowed, gone greasy, faded—and it aroused horror with its corpse-like pallor; hair had grown over the forehead; and the ears had grown; there are, surely, such things as decent old men? And he wasn't an old man ...

Time, what have you done?

The fair-haired, pink-cheeked twenty-five-year old Parisian student—the student Lipenskii—swelling to the point of delirium, had been turning doggedly into a forty-five-year-old, indecent, arachnid paunch: into Lippanchenko.

Inexpressible meanings

A bush was writhing ... On the sandy shore pools of salty water puckered here and there.

White-crested bands kept surging in from the gulf; the moon lit them up, band after band simmered up in the distance and roared; then it broke, rushing right up to the shore in ruffled foam; a band rushing in from the gulf laid itself across the flat shore—submissively, transparently; it licked the sands: it trimmed them—honed them; like a fine glass blade, it swept across the sands; here and there a glassy band trickled all the way to a salty pool; and poured a salt solution into it.

And already it was running back. A new band of roaring foam was casting it aside.

A bush was writhing ...

Over here, and over there—were bushes in their hundreds; the black and desiccated arms of bushes stretched out some distance from the sea; these leafless arms rose into space with demented gestures; a small black figure without hat or galoshes was running fearfully between them; in the summer soft sweet murmurs wafted from them; those murmurs had dried up long ago, and only groans and creaking rose from this place now; mists sprang up from here; moisture sprang up from here; and still the rough stumps stretched—out of the mist and moisture; in front of the little figure a knotty arm stuck up askew out of the mist and moisture, festooned with twigs, like fur.

Now the figure bent over to a hollow tree—into a swathe of black moisture; and there it fell to thinking bitterly; there it dropped its unsubmissive head into its hands:

"My soul," rose from its heart: "my soul—you have gone away from me ... Answer my call, my soul: poor as I am ... "

From its heart rose:

"I fall before you with my shattered life ... Remember me: poor as I am ... "

Pierced by a glittering point, the night was coming to pass in brightness; a barely visible point trembled on the very skyline of the sea; evidently a trading schooner was approaching Petersburg; a light fledged out from the puncture in the night, and filled with brightness like a ripening ear of corn, whiskered in rays.

And now it was transformed into a broad, crimson eye, revealing behind it the dark body of the vessel, and above it—a forest of rigging.

And above the little languishing black figure ramified wooden arms flew out beneath the moon to meet the flying spectre; the bush's head, its knotty head stretched out into space, rocking like a spider's web a network of black branches; and—swayed in the sky; the lightweight moon became entangled in that network, trembled, gleamed more blindingly still: and seemed to shed a tear: the airy intervals between the branches filled with a phosphorescent gleam, revealing things beyond expression, and out of them a figure was composed;—that was where it took shape—that was where it began: an immense body, burning with phosphorus, in a cape of vitriolic hue, that hovered away into the mist-laden smoke; an imperious hand, pointing to the future, stretched out towards the light that winked from the cottage garden, where the taut branches of the bushes struck against the fence.

The figure stopped and reached out in supplication to the phosphorescent intervals between the branches, that formed a body:

"But come now, come now; you can't just do it like that—on mere suspicion, without an explanation … "

The hand pointed imperiously at the lighted window that gleamed through the scraping black branches.

The little black figure cried out and ran off into space; behind it rushed a ramified black outline, forming on the sandy shore that same strange whole that was able to squeeze out of itself monstrous, inexpressible meanings that had never existed anywhere; the little black figure struck its chest against the fence of a certain garden, climbed over the fence and now slid soundlessly, catching its feet on the dew-soaked grass, towards that grey cottage, where it had been so recently, where now—everything was different.

It crept cautiously to the terrace and placed a hand on its chest; without a sound, in two leaps, it was at the door; the door was not curtained; the figure then pressed against the window; there, inside, light was dispersed.

They were sitting there …

     —On the table stood a samovar; under the samovar stood a plate with the remains of a cold cutlet; and a woman's nose peeped out with an unpleasant, awkward, slightly repressed appearance; the nose peeped out timidly; and—timidly withdrew: it was a hawk-like nose; against the wall there wobbled the shadow of a woman's head with a short plait; this sorry head dangled from an arched neck. Lippanchenko sat with one elbow on the table; the other arm lay loosely on the back of an armchair; the palm of his coarse hand was bent back, unclenched; its breadth was striking; the shortness of the five seemingly truncated fingers was striking too, with their hangnails and the yellow coloration of the nails ...

—In two bounds the little figure flew back from the door; and—was once again in the bushes; it was seized by an access of indescribable pity; from the hollow trunk, beneath two branches—an excrescence, like a huge browless head, rushed towards the little figure; the winds began to groan in the rotten funnel of the bush.

And the figure whispered angrily beneath the bush:

"You can't just do it so simply ... How can that be ... Why, nothing's been proved yet ... "

Swansong

Turning right round from Zoia Zakharovna and her sighing, Lippanchenko reached out with his hand—just imagine!—to a violin hanging on the wall:

"A man has all kinds of unpleasantness when he's away ... He comes home for a rest, and straight away—that's what he gets ... "

He took a block of rosin: with a ferocity that passed all measure— he threw himself upon the rosin; he took the block of rosin between his fingers with relish; with a shamefaced mien that bore no relation to his position in the party, nor to the conversation that had just taken place, he began to rub his violin bow on the rosin; then he took hold of the violin:

"He's met, you might say—with tears ... "

He pressed the fiddle to his stomach and bent over it, holding its broad end hard against his knees; he pushed the narrow end into his chin; with one hand he started tightening the strings with relish, while with the other he extracted sounds:

"Twang!"

His head was bent forward and tilted to the side as he did this; with a questioning expression, half humorous, half pathetic (there was something child-like in it), he glanced at Zoia Zakharovna and smacked his lips; as though he was asking:

"Did you hear that?"

She sat down on a chair: with a questioning face, half tenderness, half anger, she looked at Lippanchenko and Lippanchenko's finger; the finger was testing the strings; and the strings twanged.

"That's better!"

And he smiled; she smiled too; they nodded to one another; he—with a youthful vigour; she—with a shade of embarrassment, that betrayed a muted pride and her old adulation of him (of Lippanchenko?)—and she cried out:

"Oh, what an … "

"Twang- twang … "

"Incorrigible infant!"

And at these words, despite the fact that Lippanchenko looked for all the world like a rhinoceros, he twisted his violin round with a swift and skilful movement of his left hand; its broad end was inserted at lightning speed into the angle between his immense shoulder and his head that rested on it; the narrow end found its place between his scuttling fingers:

"Here we go, then."

The arm with the bow flew up: and—hung in the air: motionless, with the gentlest lowering of the bow it made contact with the string; the bow shot off across the strings; and behind the bow—came the whole arm; behind the arm came the head; behind the head—the corpulent body: everything tilted to the side.

The little finger was bent like a hook: it—did not touch the bow.

The armchair cracked under Lippanchenko, who seemed to be tensed in a single concentrated effort: to emit a tender sound; his slightly hoarse but still pleasant bass voice suddenly filled the room, drowning out both the snoring of the St Bernard and the rustling of the cockroach.

"No, do not te-e-empt me," sang Lippanchenko.

"Without rea-ea-ea … " the strings joined in tenderly, with a quiet sigh.

"-son," sang Lippanchenko, bending over to one side; he seemed to be tensed in a single concentrated, irresistible effort: to emit a tender sound.

In the days of their youth they had sung for hours on end this old romance, which nowadays no one sings any more.

"Shhh!"
   "Listen?"
   "The window? ... "
   "I must go and look."

Looming vaporous shapes, shot through with green, were sailing by despondently; the moon came out from behind a cloud; and everything that had stood there looming—was opened up and fell apart; the skeletons of bushes were outlined black in open space; their shadows tumbled on to the ground in shaggy clumps; the phosphorescent air was laid bare in the gaps between the branches; all the spots of air combined together—here it is, here it is: a body, burning with phosphorus; with its hand it pointed imperiously to the window; the little figure sprang up to the window; it was not locked, and as it opened it gave a faint tinkling sound; the figure sprang away.

Shadows moved around inside the windows; someone passed with a candle—in the curtained windows; this window too, unlocked, was lit up; the curtain was pulled aside; a corpulent figure stood there a moment and looked out—into the phosphorescent world; it seemed to be a chin looking out, because only a chin protruded; the eyes could not be seen; instead of eyes just two dark sockets loured; two eyebrow arches, lacking eyebrows, glistened unnaturally beneath the moon. The curtain was pulled to again; someone, huge and corpulent, went back across the curtained windows; soon all was peaceful. The warbling of the fiddle and the voices were once more issuing from the cottage.

The bush was writhing. Its excrescence, like a huge browless head, moved out into the moonlight in one concentrated effort: to understand—come what may, at any price; to understand—or to burst into smithereens; this aged, browless growth protruded from the hollow trunk, all covered in moss and lesions; it stretched out into the wind; it begged for mercy—come what may, at any price. The little figure separated itself once more from the hollow trunk; and

515

crept up to the window; retreat was cut off; it had only one option left: to complete what had been begun. Now it was hiding … in Lippanchenko's bedroom it waited impatiently for Lippanchenko— to come.

Even villains, when all is said and done, experience a need to sing their swansong.

"To him who o-o-once has kno-o-own disappointment, all the sedu-u-uctions of past days are alien … I believe no mo-o-ore in your assu-u-urances …

"No more do I believe in lo-o-ove … "

Did he know what he was singing? Or what he was playing? Why he was sad? Why did he feel his throat constricted—so that it hurt? … Was it the sounds? Lippanchenko did not understand this, just as he failed to understand the tender sounds he was producing … No, his frontal bone could not understand: his brow was small, with diagonal furrows: it seemed to be weeping.

And so on an October night Lippanchenko sang his swansong.

A perspective

So here he was!

He'd had a sing, he'd played his fiddle; putting the violin down on the table, he wiped his sweaty head with a handkerchief; his indecent, arachnid, forty-five-year-old paunch wobbled slowly; finally, picking up a candle, he set off to his bedroom; on the threshold he turned round once more in indecision, gave a sigh and sank into thought; the whole figure of Lippanchenko expressed a vague and inexplicable sadness.

And—Lippanchenko vanished in the darkness.

When the flame of the candle suddenly cut its way into the completely dark room (the blinds were down), the darkness was shattered; and the pitch darkness split up into crimson-yellow gleams; on the periphery of the fierily dancing centre there noiselessly revolved in a circular movement scraps of darkness in the form of shadows cast by all the objects; and following behind the dark door-jambs and the shadows of the objects, a huge, fat shadow-man, emerging from under Lippanchenko's heels, began to dance around with fretful movements.

Between the wall, the table and the chair this shapeless, soundless figure leapt from here to there, was fractured on the door-jambs and torn to shreds in agony, as though he was undergoing all the torments of purgatory.

So the soul is seized, when it has cast aside the body as ballast no longer needed, seized by all the hurricanes of its emotions: the hurricanes rampage through emotional space. Our body is a little vessel; it sails across the ocean of emotions from one spiritual continent—to another.

And so ...

—Imagine an endlessly long rope; and imagine that your body is entwined at the waist by this rope; and then—the rope is swung around: at a crazy, indescribable speed; flung out in expanding, ever increasing circles, describing spirals in space, you will fly off into the outer atmosphere head downwards, advancing with your back; and then, a satellite of earth, you will fly away from earth into ethereal infinity, overcoming in an instant unfathomed spaces, and becoming those spaces yourself.

It is by such a hurricane that you will instantly be seized, when your soul casts off your body as ballast no longer needed.

And let us also imagine that every point of the body experiences a mad urge to expand beyond measure, to expand to the point of horror (for example, to occupy a space equal in diameter to the orbit of Saturn); and let us imagine too that we are consciously aware not only of a single point, but of all points, and that all of them have swollen—and are rarefied, incandescent—and are passing through the stages of the expansion of bodies: from a solid to a gaseous state, and that the planets and the suns are circulating freely in the gaps between the molecules of the body; and imagine further that all centripetal sensation is completely lost; and in the urge to expand beyond measure physically we have been torn to pieces, and only our consciousness remains in one piece: consciousness of our dismembered sensations.

What would we feel then?

We would feel that our flying, burning, gaping organs, no longer linked together, were separated from each other by billions of versts; but our consciousness binds that monstrous atrocity—in a simultaneous aimlessness; and while in our spine, rarefied to the point of emptiness, we feel the seethe of Saturn's masses, into our brain the stars of all the galaxies drill their way ferociously; and in the centre of our seething heart we feel the senseless, painful thrusts—of a heart so huge that the sun's candescent torrents, as they fly in all directions from the sun, would still not reach the surface of that heart, if the sun were inserted into that igneous, senselessly beating centre.

If we were able physically to imagine all that, then before us would arise a picture of the first stages in the soul's life after it has cast off the body: these sensations would be all the stronger in proportion to the violence with which our bodily composition collapsed before us …

Cockroaches

Lippanchenko stopped in the middle of the darkening room with a candle in his hand; the shadowy door-jambs stopped with him; the huge fat shadow-man, Lippanchenko's soul, hung by his head from the ceiling; Lippanchenko felt no interest in the shadows of the objects, nor in his own; he was more interested in the rustling sound—familiar and not mysterious at all.

He felt a nauseous disgust for cockroaches; and now—he saw—there were dozens of the creatures; they scuttled off with a rustle to their dark corners, as soon as the light of the candle caught them. And—Lippanchenko fumed:

"Damn them … "

And he trotted into the corner for the floor-brush, which consisted of a very long stick with a mop on the end:

"Haven't you had enough?! … "

He put the candle on the floor; with the mop in his hand he clambered on to a chair; now his heavy, panting body protruded over the chair; his blood vessels were bursting with the effort, his muscles strained; and his hair was dishevelled; he chased the retreating hordes with the prickly end of the mop; one, two, three! And—there was a crunch beneath the mop: on the ceiling, on the wall; even—in the corner of the bookcase.

"Eight … Ten … Eleven," his ominous whisper hissed; and with each crunch, stains fell on to the floor.

Every evening before settling to sleep he squashed cockroaches. When he had squashed a goodly crop, he made his way to bed.

Finally, stumbling into his little bedroom, he locked the door; and after that: he had a look under the bed (for some time now this strange custom had become an inalienable attribute of his undressing), and set the guttering candle down in front of him.

And then he undressed.

Now he sat on the bed, naked and hairy, with his legs apart; two effeminate convexities were clearly visible on his hirsute chest.

Lippanchenko slept naked.

At an angle from the candle, between the wall with the window and the wardrobe, in a dark shadowy niche an elaborate outline appeared: of the trousers that hung there; and it formed into the likeness of a person watching from there; more than once Lippanchenko had hung his trousers somewhere else; but the result was always the same: the likeness of a person watching.

He saw that same likeness now

But when he blew out the candle the likeness quivered and stood out more distinctly; Lippanchenko reached out his arm towards the window curtain; the curtain was torn aside: the calico rustled as it flew back; the room shone with the greenish gleam of bronze; from over there, from the pale pewter of the clouds a flaming disk thundered across the room: and ...

—On the background of the wall, completely green, like copper sulphate—there!—a little figure stood, in a shabby overcoat, with an impassive face, as white as chalk: it seemed—a clown; smiling with chalk-white lips. Lippanchenko pattered across towards the door with his bare feet, but with his stomach and breasts he crashed hard against the door (he had forgotten that the door was locked); then he was pulled abruptly back; a scalding stream slashed down his naked back from shoulder blades to bottom; falling on to the bed, he realised that his back had been cut open: just the way you cut the white hairless skin of a cold sucking-pig in horseradish; and no sooner had he realised what had happened to his back, when he felt the same scalding stream—beneath his navel.

And from there something gave a mocking hiss; somewhere a thought occurred, that it was gases, because his stomach was split open; with his head drooping over his throbbing stomach that stared insensibly into space, he sagged down sleepily, groping at the viscous fluids—on his stomach and the sheet.

That was the last conscious impression of ordinary reality; now his consciousness expanded; its monstrous periphery sucked within itself the planets; and experienced them as—organs of the body, split from one another; the sun floated in the dilations of his heart; his spinal column was scorched by contact with the mass of Saturn; a volcano opened in his stomach.

All this time the body sat senselessly with its head drooping on to its breast and its eyes staring at its riven stomach; all at once it collapsed—stomach first into the sheet; the arm dangled over the blood-stained rug, moonlight playing on its reddish hairs; the head with its drooping jaw lolled over in the direction of the door and stared at the door with an unblinking pupil; the eyebrow arches with no eyebrows gleamed; the imprint of five blood-stained fingers showed through the sheet; and a fleshy heel stuck out.

The bush was writhing; from the gulf white-crested bands came surging in; they rushed up to the shore in ruffled foam; they licked the sands; like fine glass blades, they swept across the sands; they trickled to a salty pool and poured a salt solution into it; and then ran back. Between the branches of the bush a sailing ship could be seen bobbing up and down—turquoise, spectral; with its sharp-winged sails it sliced a thin swathe of space; a wisp of mist clung to the sail's surface.

When they came in in the morning Lippanchenko was no longer there; there was a pool of blood; and there was a corpse; and there was the figure of a man—with a grinning white face, out of his mind; it had a small moustache; it was twisted upwards; it was very strange: this man had seated himself astride the dead body; he was clutching a pair of scissors in his hand; this hand was stretched out; across his face—over his nose, along his lips—the black patch of a cockroach crawled away.

He had clearly lost his wits.

CHAPTER EIGHT

The last chapter.

> *My mind's eye scours the past as it goes by ...*
> *Was it so long ago that, rich in deeds,*
> *It seethed and thundered, like the very sea?*
> *And now it lies untroubled and unspeaking:*
> *Few are the faces that my memory has preserved,*
> *Few are the words that now still reach my ears ...*
> A Pushkin

But first ...

ANNA PETROVNA!
We had forgotten about her: but Anna Petrovna had returned; and now she was waiting ... but first:

—those twenty-four hours!—

those twenty-four hours in our narration expanded and scattered throughout psychic spaces: as a hideous dream; and they closed off the vista all round; and the author's vision became embroiled in psychic space; it was occluded.

And with it Anna Petrovna was lost to view.

Like sombre, leaden clouds, leaden cerebral games dragged by in this closed vista, in a circle that we have drawn—with no way out, no way out, ad nauseam—

—in those twenty-four hours! ...

And through these baneful events in their sombre flow the news of Anna Petrovna fluttered like the glow of a soft light—from somewhere. We lost ourselves in sad thoughts then—but only for a moment; and—forgot; but we ought to have remembered ... that Anna Petrovna—had returned.

Those twenty-four hours!

A day and a night, that is: a relative concept, a concept—consisting of a multitude of moments, where a moment—

—is either the minimal segment of time, or—something quite other, something psychical, determined by the fullness of psychic events—not by a number; if determined by a number, it is precise, it is—two tenths of a second; and in that case it is unchanging; if determined by the fullness of psychic events it is—an hour, or—zero: experience burgeons in a moment, or—is absent in a moment—

—where a moment in our narration was like a full cup of events.

But Anna Petrovna's arrival is a fact; indeed, a huge one; true, it contains no terrible import, as certain other facts we have noted do; and that is why we, the author, forgot about Anna Petrovna; and, as tends to happen, in our wake, the heroes of the novel forgot as well.

All the same …

—Anna Petrovna had returned; she did not witness the events we have described; she had no knowledge or suspicion—of those events; only one occurrence was of concern to her: her own return; and it should have been of concern to the characters I have described; these characters ought immediately to have reacted to that occurrence; to have showered her with notes and letters, expressions of joy or anger; but no notes, no messengers to her were forthcoming: to this immense occurrence no attention was paid—either by Nikolai Apollonovich, or by Apollon Apollonovich.

And—Anna Petrovna was sad.

She did not go out of doors; the deluxe hotel enclosed her in her tiny room; and Anna Petrovna sat for hours on the single chair; Anna Petrovna sat for hours, staring at the speckles on the wallpaper; the speckles danced before her eyes; she transferred her gaze to the window; but the window looked out upon a wall in shades of olive-green that stared back brazenly; instead of sky there was yellow smoke; just in one window, at an angle, could piles of dirty plates, a tub, and rolled-up sleeves be seen through the reflections in the panes …

Not a letter, not a visit: from husband or son.

Now and then she rang; a frisky damsel in a cap like a butterfly would appear.

And Anna Petrovna—for the umpteenth time!—was pleased to request:

"To my room, please, *thé complet*."

A waiter in a black frock coat would appear, with a starched collar and a tie gleaming with freshness—with a tray of immense proportions, poised precisely on his palm and shoulder; he cast contemptuous glances at the tiny room, at its occupant's ineptly mended dress, the motley Spanish rags lying on the double bed, the battered suitcase; with no show of courtesy, but no noise either, he swung the tray of immense proportions from his shoulder; without the slightest sound the *thé complet* dropped on to the table. And without the slightest sound the waiter left.

Nobody, nothing: the same speckles on the wallpaper; the same laughter and commotion in the next room, the conversation of two chambermaids in the corridor; a piano—from somewhere below (in the room of a visiting pianist preparing for her concert); and she turned her eyes—for the umpteenth time—to the window, but the window looked out upon a wall in shades of olive-green that stared back brazenly; instead of sky there was smoke, just in one window, at an angle, through the reflections in the panes—

—(all of a sudden there was a knock at the door; in bewilderment Anna Petrovna splashed tea all over the spotless napkins on the tray)—

—just in one window, at an angle, could piles of dirty plates, a tub and rolled-up sleeves be seen.

A chambermaid came flying in and handed her a visiting card; Anna Petrovna flushed all over; she stood up noisily from the table; her first gesture was that gesture she had acquired in youth: a quick movement of the hand to adjust her hair.

"Where is he?"

"Waiting in the corridor, ma'am."

Flushing, passing her hand across her hair towards her chin (a gesture she had acquired but recently, occasioned, no doubt, by shortness of breath), Anna Petrovna said:

"Please ask him in."

She breathed deeply and blushed.

Laughter and commotion were heard from the next room, the conversation of two chambermaids in the corridor and the piano from somewhere below; footsteps were heard, running— so fast, so fast—up to the door; the door opened; Apollon Apollonovich Ableukhov strained in vain, without crossing the threshold, to make out something in the twilight of the tiny room; and the first thing he saw was the wall in shades of olive-green, staring in through the window; and—smoke instead of sky; just in one window, at an angle, could piles of dirty plates be seen through the reflections in the panes, a tub, rolled-up sleeves and hands, washing something.

The first thing that struck him was the mean appointments of the cheap and tiny room (the shadows fell in such a way that Anna Petrovna was somehow obscured); a room like this—in a deluxe hotel! How could that be? There's nothing to be surprised at; there are tiny rooms like that in all deluxe hotels—in all deluxe capital cities: there will be one, or two at most, in each hotel; but they are advertised in all the catalogues. You read, for instance: "*Savoy Premier ordre. Chambres depuis 3 fr.*" That means: the lowest price for a tolerable room is not less than 15 francs; but for the sake of appearances somewhere in the entresol you are bound to find an untenanted nook or cranny, dirty and unkempt—in all deluxe hotels of deluxe capital cities; and it is to it that the catalogue's advertisement "*depuis trois francs*" refers; this room is kept under wraps; it's impossible to stay in it (instead of it you will finish up in a room costing fifteen francs); in "*depuis trois francs*" there is neither light nor air; even the servants would disdain it, to say nothing of you, a gentleman; there are no fittings there, nor anything else; woe betide you if you stay in it: you will earn the contempt of the multifarious crowd of chambermaids, waiters and bell-boys.

And you will move to a second-class hotel, where for seven or eight francs you will rest in cleanliness and comfort and respect.

"*Premier ordre—depuis 3 francs*"—Lord preserve you!

There were—a bed, a table and a chair; scattered in disorder on the bed were a *réticule*, some straps, a black lace fan, a small Venetian cut-glass vase, wound round with—of all things—a long stocking (of the purest silk), a travelling rug, some more straps and a bundle of loud, lemon-yellow Spanish rags; all of this, Apollon Apollonovich concluded, must be the accoutrements of travel and souvenirs from Granada or Toledo, most probably once valuable but now bereft of all their looks, and all their shine—

—the three thousand roubles in silver which had been sent so recently to Granada evidently could not have been received—

—so that a lady of her station in life must feel deeply embarrassed at carrying round with her such old tatters; and—his heart missed a beat.

Then he noticed the table, gleaming with a pair of spotless napkins and a *"thé complet"*: the property of the hotel, perfunctorily delivered here. A silhouette emerged from the shadows: his heart missed another beat, because on the chair—

—and no, not on the chair!—

—standing up from the chair he saw—was it the same?—Anna Petrovna, flaccid, plump, and—her hair streaked with grey; the first thing he realized was the regrettable fact: in her two-and-a-half years in Spain (and—where else, where else?)—her double chin had come to stand out more clearly from her collar, and her rounded stomach had come to stand out more clearly below her corset; only the two azure-filled eyes of her once beautiful and even quite recently attractive face shone as before; in their depths the most complicated feelings were now in play: timidity, anger, sympathy, pride, humiliation from the wretched furnishings of the room, a secret bitterness and ... fear.

Apollon Apollonovich could not bear that look: he lowered his eyes and crumpled his hat in his hands. Yes, the years spent in the company of the Italian singer had changed her; where had her respectability gone, her innate sense of her own dignity, her love of cleanliness and order; Apollon Apollonovich allowed his eyes to roam about the room: scattered in disorder were—a *réticule*, some straps, a black lace fan, a stocking and a bundle of lemon-yellow rags, presumably Spanish.

In front of Anna Petrovna … —was it really him? Two-and-a-half years had changed him too; it was two-and-a-half years ago that she had seen in front of her for the last time that precisely etched face of grey stone, as it looked coldly at her across the mother-of-pearl table (during their last argument); every feature had engraved itself distinctly on her memory with its ossifying frost; but now the face showed—the complete absence of features.

(Let us add on our own account: those features had been there very recently; and at the beginning of our narrative we described them …). Two-and-a-half years ago, it is true, Apollon Apollonovich was already an old man, but … there was something ageless about him; and he looked a doughty man; but now—where was the statesman? Where was the iron will, the stony gaze, from which flowed only whirlwinds— cold, sterile, cerebral (not feelings)—where was that stony gaze? No, everything had retreated before his old age; the old man outweighed everything else: his place in society and his will; his terrible gauntness was striking; his stoop was striking; the trembling of his lower jaw was striking, and the trembling of his fingers; and above all—the colour of his overcoat: never in her days had he ordered clothes of that colour.

So they stood in front of one another: Apollon Apollonovich—not crossing the threshold; and Anna Petrovna—beside the table: with a trembling and half spilt cup of strong tea in her hands (she had splashed tea on to the tablecloth).

At last Apollon Apollonovich raised his head towards her; he chewed his lips and said with a stutter:

"Anna Petrovna!"

Now he was able to inspect her in full clarity (his eyes had grown accustomed to the half-light); he saw: all her features were lit up beautifully for one moment; and then again her features were overtaken by wrinkles, flab, pockets of fat: and they imposed on the clear beauty of her childlike features the coarseness of age; but for one moment all her features were lit up beautifully—at the moment when with a sharp movement she pushed away from her the tea that had been brought; and she made as if to rush towards him; but still: she did not move from the spot; and from the table merely blurted out to the old man standing there chewing his lips:

"Apollon Apollonovich!"

Apollon Apollonovich rushed across to her (he had been rushing towards people like that for two-and-a-half years, to proffer two fingers, snatch them away and administer a cold shower); he ran to her right across the whole room—in his overcoat, his hat in his hand; her face leaned over to the bald pate; the surface of that huge skull, bare as a knee, and the two protruding ears reminded her of something, and when the cold lips made contact with her hand, wet from the spilt tea, the complicated expression of her features was replaced by an unconcealed feeling of satisfaction: just imagine—something childlike flared up in her eyes, flickered there and vanished.

And when he straightened up, the figure before her stood out even with excessive clarity, in loose-hanging trousers and overcoat (of an unheard-of colour), a mass of new wrinkles, and an unfamiliar gaze that somehow split his face in two; these two bulging eyes did not seem to her, as before, like two transparent stones; what stood out in them now was an unknown power and firmness.

But the eyes were lowered. Apollon Apollonovich, his eyes flitting about, was struggling for words:

"I want ... "—he thought for a moment and went on:—"I would like ... "

"?"

"I have come, Anna Petrovna, to pay my respects ... "

"And to welcome you here ... "

And Anna Petrovna caught his embarrassed, perplexed glance, a gentle, sympathetic glance—of a dark cornflower blue, like a breath of warm spring air.

From the next room came the sounds of laughter and commotion; outside the door—the conversation of the same two chambermaids; and from somewhere below—the piano; scattered in disorder round the room were: straps, a *réticule*, a black lace fan, a Venetian cut-glass vase and a bundle of loud lemon-yellow rags, that turned out to be a blouse; the speckles on the wallpaper stared at you; the window stared at you as it revealed the brazen gaze of a wall in shades of olive-green; instead of sky there was smoke, and in the smoke was—Petersburg: streets and Prospects; pavements and roofs; drizzle settling on a tin windowsill; cold trickles tumbling from tin drainpipes.

"But here ... "

"Wouldn't you like some tea? ... "

"There's a strike starting ... "

527

Nodding over a pile of objects ...

The door burst open.

Nikolai Apollonovich found himself in the entrance-hall from which he had run in such haste in the early morning; on the walls an ornamental arrangement of ancient weaponry gleamed; here swords were rusting; there—sloped halberds: Nikolai Apollonovich seemed beside himself; with an abrupt gesture of his hand he tore off his broad-brimmed Italian hat; his shock of flaxen hair softened this cold, almost severe appearance with its imprint of obstinacy (it was hard to find hair of that shade in a grown-up man; this shade is often found in peasant children—particularly in Belorussia); the lines of his completely white face, like the face on an icon, stood out cold, dry, precise, when for a moment he paused in thought and stared across to where beneath a verdigris encrusted shield there shone a Lithuanian helmet with its spike and the cruciform hilt of a knight's sword glittered.

Suddenly he flushed; and in his wet, crumpled cape he limped swiftly up the steps of the carpeted staircase; why was it he flushed now and then, glowing scarlet as he never had before? And—he coughed; and—he was out of breath; he was wracked with fever: indeed you cannot stand out in the rain unpunished; strangest of all was that on the knee of the leg on which he limped the cloth was torn away; and—a shred of it trailed free; the frock coat of his student's uniform was hoisted up under his cape, giving both back and front a hunched appearance; between the coat flap that was whole and the one that was torn a dancing half-belt stuck out; truly, truly: Nikolai Apollonovich looked lame, hunchbacked, and—with a tail, when he flew for all he was worth up the soft shallow staircase, his shock of flaxen hair billowing out—past the walls against which a blunderbuss and a pike were leant.

Outside the door with the cut-glass doorknob he slipped; and as he ran past the gleaming lacquered rooms, it seemed that only the illusion of rooms was building up around him; and then disintegrating without trace, raising its misty planes beyond the borders of consciousness; and when he slammed the door into the corridor behind him and his heels went tapping along the echoing corridor, then it seemed to him that it was the veins in his temples that were hammering: the quick pulsation of those veins marked distinctly on his forehead the signs of premature sclerosis.

Beside himself he rushed into his multicoloured room: the green budgerigars squawked desperately and flapped their wings in their cage; this cry interrupted his rush; for a moment he stared ahead of him; and saw: a brightly coloured leopard, thrown down on the floor with gaping jaws: and—he rummaged in his pockets (he was trying to find the key to his desk).

"Ah?"

"Devil take it … "

"Lost it?"

"Forgot it!?"

"Well, I'll be damned."

And he started rushing helplessly around the room, looking for the treacherous key he had forgotten, riffling through completely inappropriate articles of furnishing, seizing a three legged golden ashtray in the form of a perforated sphere with an aperture, surmounted by a half-moon, and muttering to himself: just like Apollon Apollonovich, Nikolai Apollonovich had a habit of talking to himself.

In horror he rushed into the next room—to the desk: on the way he caught his foot against an Arabian stool with ivory incrustation; it crashed to the floor; he was astonished to find that the desk was not locked; a tell-tale drawer protruded; it was half-opened; his heart sank: how could he have been so careless as to forget to lock it? He tugged at the drawer … And …

No: no, it couldn't be!

Various objects lay in disorder in the drawer; on the desk a studio portrait lay sideways where it had been thrown: but … the sardine-tin was not there; the lines of his crimson face with its eyes now huge and black, ringed in blue, stood out ferociously, furiously, fearfully above the open drawer: they were black from the dilation of the pupils; and so he stood between the green-upholstered armchair and the bust of: Kant, obviously.

He went over to the other table. He opened a drawer; objects lay in that drawer in perfect order: bundles of letters, papers; he pulled them all out on to the desk; but … —the sardine-tin was not there …

Then his legs gave way; and, just as he was, in his Italian cape, in his galoshes—he collapsed on to his knees, dropping his feverish head into his cold, wet hands, dampened by the rain; for a moment—he stayed transfixed like that: his shock of flaxen hair formed a strange, motionless, yellowish, deathly patch in the twilight of the room amongst the green-upholstered armchairs.

And—up he leapt! And—to the wardrobe! And the wardrobe burst open; things went tumbling higgledy-piggledy on to the floor; but—the sardine-tin was not there either; he started rushing round the room like a whirlwind, resembling a frisky monkey both in the swiftness of his movements (like those of his Excellency his father), and in his unprepossessing stature. And indeed: fate had played a trick on him; from room—to room; from the bed (where he rummaged under the pillows, the blanket, the mattress)—to the fireplace: here he soiled his hands with ashes; from the fireplace—to the rows of bookshelves (and the light silk that concealed the spines slipped along on little bronze wheels); here he pushed a hand between the volumes; and many volumes tumbled to the floor with a rustle and a crash.

But the sardine-tin was nowhere to be found.

Soon his face, smeared all over with ashes and dust, was nodding without rhyme or reason over a pile of objects, thrown in a senseless heap, through which he was riffling with long, spidery fingers extending from trembling hands; those hands emerged from the outspread Italian cape to wriggle across the floor; in this bent posture, trembling and sweating all over, with the veins of his neck swollen, he would truly have reminded anyone of a pot-bellied spider, devourer of flies; like the spectacle an observer sees when he tears apart the delicate web: a huge, anxious insect, slithering down a silver thread that hangs in space from ceiling to floor, starts running clumsily across the room on its furry legs.

In just this posture—over the heap of objects—Nikolai Apollonovich was caught unawares by Semyonych, who came rushing in.

"Nikolai Apollonovich! ... Young master! ... "

Nikolai Apollonovich, still in a squatting position, turned round; catching sight of Semyonych, with a swift movement of the cape he covered the heap of jumbled objects—sheets of paper and gaping books—resembling a broody hen on her eggs: his shock of flaxen hair formed a strange, motionless, yellowish, deathly patch in the twilight of the room.

"What is it? ... "

"May I be so bold as to inform you ... "

"Not now: you can see ... I'm busy ... "

With his mouth stretched open to his ears, he looked for all the world like the head of the multicoloured leopard leering on the floor:

"I'm sorting out my books, you see."

But Semyonych was not to be deterred:

"Please come, sir: there ... they're asking for you ... "

"?"

"A family joy: the mistress, your mother, Anna Petrovna, sir, she's been so gracious as to come and visit us."

Nikolai Apollonovich raised himself mechanically; the cape fell from him; on the ash-stained contours of his face, like the face on an icon—through ashes and dust—a blush flared up like lightning; Nikolai Apollonovich presented an absurd and comical figure in the frock coat of his student's uniform that spread out to create two humps, with its single coat-flap—and loose-hanging half-belt, when he started coughing; hoarsely, through his cough, he cried out:

"Mama? Anna Petrovna?"

"She's there with Apollon Apollonovich, sir; in the drawing room ... Only a moment ago she ... "

"They're calling for me?"

"Apollon Apollonovich is asking you to come, sir."

"Straight away, then ... I'll come straight away ... I'll just ... "

In this room, Nikolai Apollonovich had so recently grown into an autonomous, self-existent centre—into a series of logical premises flowing out from that centre, which determined everything: the soul, thought, and this armchair right here: here he had so recently comprised the sole centre of the universe; but ten days had passed; and his self-consciousness had got shamefully mired in this jumbled heap of objects: just as a fly, running at liberty round the edge of a plate on its six legs, suddenly becomes inescapably stuck by both leg and wing in a sticky mass of honey.

"Shhh! Semyonych, Semyonych—listen," Nikolai Apollonovich skipped nimbly out of the door in pursuit of Semyonych, jumped over the overturned stool and grasped the old man's sleeve (and how his fingers clung!)

"You haven't seen somewhere here—the point is … " he became confused, stooping down to the ground and pulling the old man away from the door to the corridor, "I forgot … You haven't seen a sort of thing like? … Here, in this room … A thing like: a toy … "

"A toy, sir?"

"A children's toy … a sardine-tin … "

"A sardine-tin?"

"Yes, a toy (in the form of a sardine-tin)—it's quite heavy, with a wind-up mechanism: the clockwork is still ticking … I put it here: a toy … "

Semyonych turned round slowly, freed his sleeve from the clinging fingers, stared for a moment at the wall (there was a shield hanging on the wall—a negro one: made from the carapace of a fallen rhinoceros), he paused for thought and quite disrespectfully blurted out:

"No!"

Not even "No, sir": simply—"No" …

"It's just, I thought … "

How do you like that: a happy ending, family joy; the master, the *minister*, all smiles: for such an occasion … And here we have: a sardine-tin … quite heavy … with a wind-up mechanism … a toy: and he's got a coat-tail torn off! …

"So may I announce you?"

"Straight away, I'll be there straight away … "

And the door closed: Nikolai Apollonovich stood there without realising where he was—beside the overturned dark-brown stool, in front of the hookah; in front of him on the wall hung a shield, a negro shield made from the thick skin of a fallen rhinoceros and with a rusty Sudanese arrow hanging beside it.

Without realising what he was doing, he hurried to change his tell-tale frock coat for a completely new one; as a preliminary he washed his hands and face clean of ash; as he washed and dressed, he muttered to himself:

"What can have happened, what can have happened … Where ever did I actually put it … "

Nikolai Apollonovich was not yet aware of the full extent of the horror that had befallen him as a result of the chance disappearance of the sardine-tin; it was as well that for the time being it did not occur to him: *in his absence someone had been in his room and, discovering the sardine-tin of terrible import, had as a precaution removed the said sardine-tin from him.*

The servants were astonished

And exactly the same houses still rose up there, and the same grey streams of people passed by, and the same yellow-green mist hung there; faces ran past deep in concentration; the pavements shuffled and whispered—under the horde of giant houses; towards them flew—Prospect upon Prospect; and the spherical surface of the planet seemed to be entwined, as though by the rings of a snake, by the grey-black cubes of houses; and the network of parallel Prospects, intersected by another network of Prospects, spread into the abysses of the universe with its surfaces of squares and cubes: one square per man-in-the-street.

But Apollon Apollonovich was not looking at his favourite figure: the square; he was not surrendering himself to the unthinking contemplation of stone parallelepipeds or cubes; bouncing on the soft cushioned seat of a rented carriage, he was glancing with agitation at Anna Petrovna, whom he was himself taking—to the lacquered house; what they said to one another over tea there in the hotel room remained forever an impenetrable secret to everyone; it was after that conversation that they decided: Anna Petrovna would move on the morrow to the Embankment; while today Apollon Apollonovich was taking Anna Petrovna—to meet their son.

And Anna Petrovna was ill at ease.

In the carriage they did not talk; Anna Petrovna gazed out of the carriage windows: for two-and-a-half years she had not seen these grey Prospects: there, outside the window, the numbering of the houses could be seen; and circulation was taking place; from over there—on clear days, far, far away, a golden spire, clouds, the crimson rays of sunset, would glitter brilliantly; from over there, on misty days—was nobody and nothing.

Apollon Apollonovich leaned with unconcealed pleasure against the carriage walls, separated from the mire of the street in this enclosed cube; here he was segregated from the flowing crowds of people, from the red magazine-covers on sale at a nearby crossroads, getting miserably drenched; and his eyes flitted about; only occasionally Anna Petrovna caught: his perplexed, uncomprehending, and—can you imagine—quite simply gentle gaze: blue as blue, infantile, vacant even (was he regressing into childhood?).

"I've heard, Apollon Apollonovich: you're in line to become a minister?"

But Apollon Apollonovich interrupted:

"Where is it you've come from just now, Anna Petrovna?"

"Why, I've come from Granada … "

"I see, I see, I see … " and, blowing his nose—he added … "Well, you know how things are: some trouble at work … "

And—what was this? On his hand he felt a warm hand: his hand was being stroked … Hm-hm-hm: Apollon Apollonovich was perplexed; he became embarrassed, even a little afraid; he even found it unpleasant … Hm-hm: no one had treated him like that for fifteen years … She just went and stroked his hand … That was something he hadn't expected from a person … hm-hm … (For two-and-a-half years Apollon Apollonovich had regarded this person as … a lady … of easy … virtue …).

"I'm going to retire … "

Was it possible that the cerebral play that had divided them for so many years and had been so ominously intensified these last two-and-a-half—had finally erupted from this obstinate brain? And that outside that brain it had condensed into clouds above them? And that at last it had exploded all around in unprecedented storms? But as it exploded outside the brain, it became exhausted inside it; gradually the brain became cleansed; sometimes—through the slanting strips of rain—you see in the clouds a chink of azure running along beside them; so what if the downpour lashes you; so what if dark clumps of cloud burst with a crash in crimson lightning! The chink of azure is approaching; soon the sun will break out blindingly; you are already expecting the end of the storm; and suddenly—a flash, a crash: lightning has struck a pine-tree.

The greenish daylight pressed in through the carriage windows;

streams of people coursed past like undulating breakers; and those human breakers—were like thunder.

It was just here that he had seen the man of uncertain status; it was here that that man's eyes had gleamed and recognised him, about ten days ago (yes, only ten days: in ten days everything had changed; Russia herself was different!) ...

The flight and the thunder of carriages hurtling past! The melodious cries of automobiles' roulades! And—detachments of police! ...

Over there, where nothing but pale-grey putrefaction hung, there emerged first as a pale outline and then in full clarity: the grimy, grey-black St Isaac's ... And disappeared back into the mist. And an expanse opened out: depths, greenish murk, into which the black bridge ran, where the mist obscured the many-chimneyed distance, and from where advanced a wave of scudding clouds.

Really and truly: the servants were astonished!

This is how sleepy Grisha, the boy who was on duty in the entrance-hall, told about it afterwards:

"There was me, sitting counting on my fingers: how many days from the Protection—all the way to the Nativity of the Virgin ... It comes out at ... And from the Nativity of the Virgin—right up to the Winter Nikola ... "

"Come on, tell us what happened: Nativity of the Virgin, Nativity of the Virgin!"

"What d'you think I am doing? The Nativity of the Virgin is our village festival—'cause our church is named after Her ... So anyway—it'll be: and I keeps on counting ... Then I hears someone arriving; so I'm straight to the door. Opened the door wide, like, and—oh, my goodness! It was the master himself, in a hired carriage (and a pretty lousy one, too!); and there was, like, a middle-aged lady with him in a cheap waterproof."

"It's not a waterproof, you twerp: no one wears waterproofs nowadays."

"Don't put him off: he's off his rocker as it is."

"Well anyway—in a coat. The master's all fussing around: jumps down from the cab—from the carriage, I mean—gives his arm to the lady—all smiles: like a real cavalier; helping her in every way."

"Well I never ... "

"What a to-do ... "

"I should think so; they haven't seen each other for two years," voices rang out all round.

"That's just it: the mistress gets out of the carriage; only I could see—the mistress was a bit put out with all that business: she was smiling—but not like she really meant it; just to keep her spirits up: started holding her chin; and I can tell you, she wasn't well dressed; holes in her gloves; hadn't been darned, I could see, her gloves: maybe she hadn't anyone to darn them; perhaps they don't darn gloves in Spain ... "

"Get on with it, that's enough! ... "

"I am getting on with it: anyway, the master, our master, Apollon Apollonovich, dropped all his airs and graces; standing there by the carriage he was, over a puddle, in the rain; and what rain—oh my goodness! The master was wriggling about, like he was running on the spot, dancing up and down on his toes; and when the mistress put all her weight on his arm as she was getting off the footboard—she's no fairy, like—the master got pressed right down; the master's very short; how's he going to hold a big heavy woman like that, I wondered! He's hasn't the strength ... "

"Don't prattle on so; get on with it."

"I'm not prattling; I am getting on with it; what's the point, anyway ... Mitrii Semyonych here will tell you: he met them in the entrance-hall ... What is there to tell? The master just said to the mistress: welcome, he said, Anna Petrovna ... And that was when I recognised her."

"And?"

"She's aged ... I didn't recognise her at first; and then I did recognise her, because I remembered, like: she used to give me sweets."

That was how the servants talked about it afterwards.

But really!

An unexpected, unanticipated fact: it was two-and-a-half years since Anna Petrovna had left her husband for an Italian singer; and now two-and-a-half years later, abandoned by the Italian singer, she had come hastening back by express train, from the beautiful palaces of Granada across the range of the Pyrenees, through the Alps, through the mountains of the Tyrol; but what was most astonishing of all was that the senator could not bring himself to breathe a word about Anna Petrovna not only for the past two years and more, but even a mere two-and-a-half days ago (even the day before he had bridled at it!); for two-and-a-half years Apollon Apollonovich had consciously avoided the very thought of Anna Petrovna (and all the same he did think of her); the very sound combination "Anna Petrovna" had struck his ear-drums just as a paper pellet, flicked from under a desk, strikes the forehead of a teacher; except that the schoolteacher will then hammer on the desk with his fist in anger; whereas Apollon Apollonovich would merely compress his lips in disdain at this combination of sounds. So why was it that at the news of her return the usual compression of the lips burst out into an angry and agitated trembling of the jaws (the night before—during his conversation with Nikolenka): why had he not slept that night? Why, in the course of a single day, had that anger dissipated and been replaced by an ache of longing that turned into alarm? Why could he not bear the anticipation, but went to the hotel himself? He talked her round—himself: he brought her home—himself. What was it that had happened there in the hotel room; Anna Petrovna had also forgotten her earnest promise: she had made that promise to herself—here, the day before: here in the lacquered house (when she visited it and found no one at home).

She made a promise: but—she did return.

Anna Petrovna and Apollon Apollonovich were excited and confused by their heart-to-heart talk; and so on entering the lacquered house they exchanged no lavish effusions of emotion; Anna Petrovna looked sideways at her husband: Apollon Appollonovich began to blow his nose ... beneath the rusty halberd; after emitting a stentorian noise, he began to snort into his sideburns. Anna Petrovna graciously responded to the servants' deferential bows, displaying the reserve that we have just observed in her; only Semyonych she embraced and seemed about to cry; but, casting a fearful, confused glance at Apollon Apollonovich, she overcame herself: her fingers moved towards her *réticule*, but did not pull out her handkerchief.

Standing above her on the steps, Apollon Apollonovich cast stern and imperious glances at the servants; they were the kind of glances he would cast in moments of perplexity: at ordinary times Apollon Apollonovich was impeccably polite and formal with the servants— offensively so (apart from his jokes). As long as the servants were standing there, he maintained a tone of indifference: nothing had happened—until now the mistress had been living abroad, for the sake of her health; that was all: and now—the mistress had returned … What of it? Everything was fine! …

However, there was one servant here (all the rest had changed except Semyonych and the boy Grishka); that one remembered what he remembered: he remembered the manner in which the lady of the house had executed her departure abroad—without any warning to the servants: with a little travelling bag in her hands (and that—for two-and-a-half years!); and the day before her departure she had locked herself away from the master; for two days before she left that *fellow with the moustache* had been sitting with her all the time: that visitor with the dark eyes—what was his name? Mindalini (they called him Mantalini), who used to sing un-Russian songs in their house: "Tra-la-la … Tra-la-la … " And didn't give any tips.

And that same servant, remembering such things, kissed her Excellency's hand with particular respect, feeling a sense of guilt that the details of the elopement—of the departure, that is—had not been erased in his head; for he was afraid in earnest that his days in the lacquered house were numbered—in view of the return to the lacquered house of their Excellencies.

Here they were—in the grand hall; the parquet floor in front of them gleamed with its little squares like a mirror: in these two-and-a-half years this room had rarely been heated; the expanses of this enfilade of rooms evoked an involuntary sadness; Apollon Apollonovich spent most of his time sitting in his study with the door locked; he always had the feeling that someone familiar and sad would come running to him from here; and now he thought that he was no longer alone; he would not be striding across the squares of the parquet floor on his own, but … with Anna Petrovna.

It was not often that Apollon Apollonovich strode across the squares of the parquet floor with Nikolenka.

Bending his arm double, Apollon Apollonovich led his guest across the grand hall: it was a good thing he had offered her his right arm; his left arm—was wracked with aches and shooting pains from the rapid, restless thrusting of his heart; but Anna Petrovna stopped him, led him over to the wall and, pointing at the pale mural, smiled at him:

"Ah, they're still the same! ... Do you remember that fresco, Apollon Apollonovich?"

And—she tilted her head slightly, she blushed slightly; his cornflower-blue gaze settled upon two eyes that were filled with azure; and—that gaze, that gaze: something dear, that has been before, that existed long ago, that all people have forgotten, but which forgot no one and stands *at the door*—something like that suddenly came to stand between their gazes; it was not within them; and it did not arise—within them; but it stood—*between them*: as though a breath of spring had wafted in. The reader will have to forgive me: I shall express the essence of that gaze with the most banal of words: *love*.

"Do you remember?"

"Of course I do ... "

"Where?"

"In Venice ... "

"Thirty years have passed! ... "

He was seized by the memory of a misty lagoon, an aria sobbing in the distance: thirty years ago. Recollections of Venice seized her, too, and split in two: thirty years ago, and—two-and-a-half years ago; she blushed at the untimely memory, which she chased away; and something else flooded in: Kolenka. In the past two hours she had forgotten about Kolenka; her conversation with the senator had squeezed out everything else for the time being; but two hours previously it was only Kolenka that she had thought about with tenderness; with tenderness and resentment, because from Kolenka she had had no greeting or response.

"Kolenka ... "

They went through into the drawing room; masses of porcelain trinkets struck the eye on all sides; delicate incrustations—mother-of-pearl and bronze—glittered on boxes and shelves, protruding from the wall.

"Kolenka is all right, Anna Petrovna … he's fine … he's doing very well,"—and he retreated—sideways, somehow.

"Is he at home?"

Apollon Apollonovich, who had just lowered himself into an Empire chair, with a pattern of entwined garlands on the pale-blue satin of the seat, pulled himself up reluctantly as he pressed the bell-push:

"Why didn't he come to see me?"

"He's, Anna Petrovna … mme-emme … been, in his own turn, very-very," the senator faltered strangely, and then took out his handkerchief: he blew his nose at great length with stentorian noises; snorting into his sideburns, he then at great length stuffed his handkerchief back into his pocket:

"In short, it made him very happy."

A silence ensued. His bald head swayed under a cold, long-legged bronze; the lampshade did not gleam with its delicate decoration of a violet hue: the nineteenth century had lost the secret of that colour: the glass had darkened with age; the delicate decoration had darkened with age too.

Semyonych appeared in response to the bell:

"Is Nikolai Apollonovich at home?"

"Indeed he is, sir … "

"Mmm … listen: tell him that Anna Petrovna—is here; and—requests him to come … "

"Perhaps we could go to him," Anna Petrovna became flustered and with an alacrity that belied her years stood up from her chair; but Apollon Apollonovich, turning sharply to Semyonych, interrupted her:

"Me-emme … Semyonych: I say … "

"Very well, sir! … "

"The wife of a Phoenician—tell me—who is she?"

"A suppose—a lady Phoenician … "

"No—a Phoenix! … "

"Hee-hee-hee, sir … "

"I'm displeased with Kolenka, Anna Petrovna … "

"What are you saying?"

"For a long time now Kolenka has been—don't be distressed—behaving: actually—please don't be distressed—rather strangely … "

"?"

The golden pier glasses between the windows swallowed the drawing room on all sides with their greenish mirror surfaces.

"Kolenka has become rather secretive … ahem, ahem," in a fit of coughing, Apollon Apollonovich drummed on the side-table with his fingers, recalled something—of his own, frowned, and began rubbing the bridge of his nose with his hand; however, he quickly regained his composure: and with excessive cheerfulness he almost shouted:

"Anyway—no: it doesn't matter … It's quite trivial."

The mother-of-pearl side-table gleamed on all sides amidst the pier glasses.

Utter absurdity

Struggling with an acute pain at the back of his knee (he really had injured himself), Nikolai Apollonovich limped slightly as he ran through the echoing space of the corridor.

A meeting with his mother! …

He was overwhelmed by a maelstrom of thoughts and implications; or not even a maelstrom of thoughts and implications: simply a maelstrom of absurdity; just as the particles of a comet, as in their flight they penetrate a planet at incredible speed, will produce no change at all in the planet's composition; as they penetrate hearts, they will produce no change at all in the rhythm of the heartbeats; but if the speed of the comet is reduced: the hearts will burst: the planet itself will burst; and all will turn to gas; if we held back even for a moment the swirling maelstrom of absurdity in Ableukhov's head, then that absurdity would discharge itself in furiously erupting thoughts.

And—here are those thoughts.

In the first place, the thought of the horror of his situation; the terrible situation was building up now (as a result of the sardine-tin's disappearance); the sardine-tin, that is to say, the bomb, had disappeared; it was clear that it had disappeared; that must mean: someone had taken the bomb; but who, who? One of the servants; that would mean: the bomb had found its way to the police; and he would be arrested; but that was not the main thing, the main thing was: if Apollon Apollonovich had taken the bomb himself; and carried it off just at the moment when all accounts with the bomb were settled; and—he knew: he knew everything.

Everything—what was that? After all there hadn't really been anything; an assassination plan? There was no assassination plan; Nikolai Apollonovich emphatically denied any such plan: it was a hideous calumny—that plan.

There remained the fact of the discovered bomb.

Since his father was now calling for him, since his mother—no, he couldn't know: and he hadn't taken the bomb from his room. And the servants ... The servants would have discovered everything long ago. But nobody—said anything. No, they didn't know about the bomb. But—where was it, where was it? Had he definitely put it in the desk drawer, hadn't he stuffed it away somewhere under the carpet, mechanically, by chance?

Such things did happen to him.

It would turn up by itself in a week ... But no: it would announce its presence somewhere this very day—by the most ear-splitting crash (the Ableukhovs positively could not bear crashes).

Somewhere, maybe—under the carpet, under a pillow, on a shelf—it would announce its presence: it would roar out and burst; the bomb had to be found; and now he had no time to look for it: Anna Petrovna had arrived.

In the second place: he had been insulted; in the third place: that moth-eaten Pavel Iakovlevich—he felt he had just seen him somewhere on the way back from the flat on the Moika; and Pepp Peppovich Pepp—in the fourth place: Pepp was a terrible expansion of the body, a tautening of the veins, a ferment in the head ...

Oh, everything was in havoc: maelstroms of thoughts swirled round at an inhuman speed, roaring in his ears, so that there were no thoughts: there was utter absurdity.

And so with this absurd ferment in his head Nikolai Apollonovich ran along the echoing corridor without straightening his hastily donned frock coat and presenting to the gaze some kind of puff-chested cripple, limping on his right leg and with his knee joint aching excruciatingly.

Mama

He opened the drawing room door.

The first thing he saw was … was … But what can be said: he saw his mother's face as she sat in the chair with both arms outstretched: her face had aged, and her arms were trembling in the tracery of the golden streetlamps that had just been lit—outside the windows.

And he heard a voice:

"Kolenka: my dear, my darling!"

Able to contain himself no longer, he rushed towards her:

"Is it you, my little boy … "

No, he could contain himself no longer: dropping to his knees before her, he wound firm arms around her waist; he pressed his face to her knees, and burst into convulsive sobs—sobbing for no obvious reason: his broad shoulders rose and fell uncontrollably, shamelessly, unrestrainedly (let us remember: Nikolai Apollonovich had experienced no tenderness these last three years).

"Mama, mama … "

She also wept.

Apollon Apollonovich stood there in the semi-darkness of a niche; and fingered a little porcelain doll—a Chinese figurine: the Chinaman shook his head; Apollon Apollonovich then emerged from the semi-darkness of the niche; and quietly cleared his throat; he moved with small steps up to the weeping pair; and suddenly boomed out above the chair:

"Calm down, my dears!"

He had, of course, no reason to expect such feelings from his cold, secretive son—on whose face for the last two-and-a-half years he had seen nothing but grimaces; a mouth, split open to the ears, and lowered eyes; then, turning round, Apollon Apollonovich ran anxiously from the room—to fetch something.

"Mama … Mama … "

The fear, the humiliations of these past days, the disappearance of the sardine-tin, finally the feeling of utter insignificance, all of this, swirling round, developed into momentary thoughts; and drowned in the moisture of meeting:

"My darling, my little boy."

The icy touch of fingers on his hand brought him back to his senses.

"Here you are, Kolenka: have a sip of water."

And when he raised his tear-stained face from his kneeling position, he saw something childlike in the eyes of the old man of sixty-eight: Apollon Apollonovich, short of stature, was standing there in his jacket with a glass of water; his fingers were twitching; rather than actually patting him, he was attempting to pat Nikolai Apollonovich—on the back, the shoulders, the cheeks; all of a sudden he stroked his flaxen hair. Anna Petrovna was laughing; quite inappropriately she made to straighten her collar; she kept turning her eyes, drunk with happiness, from Nikolenka—to Apollon Apollonovich; and back: from him to Nikolenka.

Nikolai Apollonovich slowly got up from his knees:

"I'm sorry, mama: I'm all right … "

"It's, it's—so unexpected … "

"Just a moment … It's nothing … Thank you, papa … "

And took a gulp of water.

"There."

Apollon Apollonovich set the glass down on the mother-of-pearl table; and suddenly—laughed out loud at something in an old man's way, as little boys will laugh at the tricks of some merry grown-up, nudging each other with their elbows; two familiar faces from long ago!

"I see … "

"I see … "

"I see … "

Apollon Apollonovich stood there by the pier glass, which was surmounted by the wing of a golden-cheeked Cupid: beneath the Cupid laurels and rosebuds pierced the heavy flames of torches.

But like lightning it shot through his memory: the sardine-tin! …

How could it be? What was happening? And his spasm of feeling was stilled again.

"Just a moment … I'll come back … "

544

"What's the matter, my dear?"

"It's nothing … Leave him, Anna Petrovna … I advise you, Kolenka, to be by yourself for a bit … five minutes … Yes, you know … And then—come back … "

And simulating slightly the feeling he had just experienced, Nikolai Apollonovich stumbled, and lowered his face into his fingers with a touch of the theatrical: his shock of flaxen hair created a strange, deathly patch in the semi-darkness of the room.

He went out unsteadily.

The father looked in astonishment at the happy mother.

"To tell the truth, I hardly recognised him … Those, those … Those, as it were, feelings," Apollon Apollonovich ran across from the mirror to the windowsill … "Those, those … bursts,"—and he patted his sideburns.

"Show," he clasped his hands behind his back (under his jacket) and rotated one hand behind his back (which made his jacket wiggle); and it seemed that Apollon Apollonovich was running round the drawing room wagging his tail:

"Show a naturalness of feeling in him, and, so to speak," at this point he shrugged his shoulders, "good natural qualities … "

"I never expected … "

A snuffbox lying on the table seized the distinguished statesman's attention; and, wishing to endow its position on the table with a more symmetrical appearance in relation to the tray that lay there, Apollon Apollonovich went swiftly up to the table and took hold of … a visiting card from the tray, which he for some reason started twisting around in his fingers; his absent-mindedness arose from the fact that at this moment he was visited by a profound thought, which ramified into the receding labyrinth of extraneous discoveries. But Anna Petrovna, sitting in her armchair with a look of blissful perplexity, commented with conviction:

"I have always said … "

"Yes, you know … "

Apollon Apollonovich stood up on tiptoe with his jacket-tail raised; and—ran over from the table to the mirror:

"You know … "

Apollon Apollonovich ran from the mirror to the corner:

"Kolenka surprised me: and I must confess—this behaviour of his has reassured me," he furrowed his brow, "in respect of … in respect of," he withdrew his hand from behind his back (the edge of his jacket dropped down), and drummed with his fingers on the table:

"Mmm-yes! … "

He interrupted himself abruptly:

"Never mind."

And sank into thought: he looked at Anna Petrovna; he met her gaze; they smiled to one another.

And a roulade pealed out

Nikolai Apollonovich went into his room; he stared at the overturned Arabian stool: he followed with his eyes the incrustation of ivory and mother-of-pearl. He went slowly over to the window: there the river ran; and a boat rocked; and a wave splashed; from the drawing room, from far in the distance, pealing roulades suddenly filled the silence; she used to play like that before: and to those same sounds he used to fall asleep over his books.

Nikolai Apollonovich stood still over the heap of objects, reflecting tormentedly:

"Wherever can it … How did such a thing … Wherever did I actually? … "

And—he could not remember.

Shadows, shadows and shadows; out of the shadows the chairs showed green; a bust stood out from the shadows: of Kant, of course.

Then he noticed on the table a sheet of paper, folded in four: visitors who do not find the master of the house at home, tend to leave sheets of paper folded in four on the table; he took hold of the paper mechanically; mechanically he saw the handwriting—familiar handwriting, Likhutin's. Why yes—of course: he had quite forgotten that Likhutin had been there that morning, in his absence: he had riffled around and rummaged (he had told him about this himself during their distasteful encounter) …

Yes, yes, yes: he had searched the room.

A sigh of relief escaped from Nikolai Apollonovich's chest. Everything was explained in an instant: Likhutin! Well—of course, of course; he had definitely been rooting around here; he had searched and he had found; and having found it, he had carried it off; he had noticed the unlocked desk; and he had looked into it; the sardine-tin had struck him both by its weight and its appearance, and by the clockwork mechanism; and the Second Lieutenant had carried the sardine-tin away. There was no doubt.

He sank down with relief into an armchair; at that moment the pealing roulades filled the silence again; that's how it used to be before: roulades would come pealing from there; nine years ago; and ten years ago: Anna Petrovna used to play Chopin (not Schumann). And now it seemed to him that there hadn't been any events, since everything could be explained so simply: Second Lieutenant Likhutin had taken the sardine-tin (who else, unless you allowed that ... but why should you!); Aleksandr Ivanovich would see to everything else (at this very time, we remind the reader, Aleksandr Ivanovich Dudkin was indeed having things out in the cottage with the late Lippanchenko); yes, there had been no events.

There outside the window Petersburg was prowling with its cerebral play and its plaintive expanses; the cold, wet wind came thrusting in assault; the huge nests of diamonds were shrouded in mist—beneath the bridge. Nobody—nothing.

And the river ran; and the wave splashed; and the boat rocked; and a roulade pealed out.

On the other side of the Neva's waters great masses rose up—the outlines of islands and buildings; and cast their amber eyes into the mists; and it seemed they were weeping. A row of lanterns on the Embankment dropped fiery tears into the river: and the river's surface was scorched with seething flashes.

The watermelon is a vegetable

After two-and-a-half years there were three of them at dinner.

The cuckoo-clock on the wall cuckooed; a servant brought in the hot soup tureen; Anna Petrovna gleamed with contentment; Apollon

547

Apollonovich … —apropos: looking at the frail old man in the morning, you would not have recognised this ageless patriarch, who had suddenly regained his strength and his bearing, and had taken his place at the table and grasped his napkin with an elastic gesture; they had already started the soup when the side door opened: Nikolai Apollonovich, slightly powdered, shaven, washed, came hobbling in from there to join his family in his buttoned student frock coat with its immensely high collar (reminiscent of the collars of a past time, that of Alexander).

"What's the matter, *mon cher*," Anna Petrovna raised her pince-nez to her nose with affectation, "I see you're limping?"

"Ah? … " Apollon Apollonovich cast a glance at Kolenka and grasped the pepper-pot. "You really are … "

With a youthful gesture he began to over-pepper his soup.

"It's trivial, maman: I tripped over … and now my knee hurts … "

"Don't you want some embrocation on it?"

"Yes, really, Kolenka," Apollon Apollonovich, raising a spoonful of soup to his lips, looked at him from under lowered eyebrows, "with injuries like that, in the hamstring, you can't afford to take risks; injuries like that can take a nasty course … "

And he swallowed his spoonful of soup.

Nikolai Apollonovich, smiling charmingly, set about over-peppering his soup in his turn.

"Maternal feeling is an astonishing thing," and Anna Petrovna put her spoon down on her plate and opened wide her big, childlike eyes, lowering her head (in such a way that her second chin sprang out from her collar), "it's astonishing: he's quite grown up and here am I, worrying about him just as I used to … "

Somehow it seemed natural to forget that for two-and-a-half years it was not Kolenka she had been worrying about: Kolenka was obscured from her by another person, with dark skin and a long moustache, and eyes like a pair of prunes; perfectly natural—and she forgot how, for two years and more, there in Spain, she had fastened this other man's tie every day: a silk one, violet in colour; and for two-and-a-half years she had given him his morning laxative—Hunyadi Janos.

"Yes, maternal feeling: do you remember—when you had *dysenterie* … " (she pronounced the word in the French way).

"Of course, I remember it well … You're thinking of those pieces of bread?"

"Exactly … "

"I think even now, dear boy, you still suffer the after-effects of dysentery,"—Apollon Apollonovich rumbled from his plate, stressing the first syllable emphatically.

And he swallowed his spoonful of soup.

"It's bad for him … to eat berries … even now, sir," Semyonych's contented voice rang out from the door; his head peeped round: he was keeping watch from there—he was not serving at table.

"Berries, berries!" Apollon Apollonovich thundered in his deep bass and suddenly turned round fully to face Semyonych: or rather, to face the key-hole.

"Berries," and he chewed his lips.

Then the servant who was serving at table (not Semyonych) smiled in anticipation, with a look on his face as though to tell everyone:

"That's how it's going to be now!"

But the master shouted out.

"Now you tell me, Semyonych: a watermelon—is that a berry?"

Anna Petrovna turned only her eyes to Kolenka: she concealed her smile indulgently and cunningly; she looked across at the senator, who was as though transfixed in the direction of the door, and seemed totally absorbed in the anticipation of an answer to his absurd question; with her eyes she was saying:

"So he's still the same?"

Nikolai Apollonovich reached in embarrassment for his knife, then his fork, until a voice, quite unfazed by the question, sailed in from the door, precisely and dispassionately:

"A watermelon, your Excellency, is by no means a berry—it is a vegetable."

Apollon Apollonovich quickly turned round with his whole body, and suddenly let loose with his—oh, dear, oh, dear!—impromptu:

So for you, Semyonych,
The question was a doddle,
You have guessed the answer right,
With your bald old noddle.

Anna Petrovna and Kolenka kept their eyes down on their plates: in short—it was just like old times!

After the scene in the drawing room Apollon Apollonovich made it clear to them in all his bearing: everything had now returned to normal; he dined with a healthy appetite, he joked and listened attentively to stories about the beauties of Spain: a strange, sad feeling arose in the heart; as though (it occurred to Kolenka) there had been no time; as though all this had happened yesterday: he, Nikolai Apollonovich, was five years old; he was listening intently to his mother's conversations with his governess (the one that Apollon Apollonovich dismissed); and Anna Petrovna—was exclaiming in excitement:

"Zizi and I; and right behind us again—two tails; we went to the exhibition; and the tails came right to the exhibition after us … "

"Really, what an impertinence!"

Kolenka imagined a huge room, a crowd, the rustle of dresses and so on (he had been taken to an exhibition once): and in the distance, hanging in space, huge, black-brown *tails* floating up out of the crowd. And—the boy was afraid: in his childhood Nikolai Apollonovich could not understand at all that Countess Zizi called her high-society admirers *tails*.

But this ridiculous recollection about tails hanging in the air aroused in him a muted anxiety; he ought to go to the Likhutins': to make sure that—really …

"Really,"—what?

The ticking of the clockwork mechanism kept sounding in his ears: tick-tock, tick-tock; the hairspring was scampering round in a circle; not scampering round here, of course—in these gleaming rooms (somewhere under the carpet, for instance, where any one of them might accidentally tread …), but—in some black cesspool, out in a field, in the river: just going "tick-tock"; the hairspring scampering round—until the fateful hour …

What nonsense!

All this came from the senator's awful joke, of truly spectacular tastelessness; that was where it had all started: the recollection about black-brown tails, floating along in the air, and—the recollection about the bomb.

"What is it, Kolenka, you seem very preoccupied: and you're not eating your *crème*? … "

"Oh, yes, yes … "

After dinner he strolled along this unlit hall; the hall was slightly illuminated; by the moon, and by the tracery of the streetlamp; here he strolled across the squares of the parquet floor: Apollon Apollonovich; and with him—was Nikolai Apollonovich; they crossed—from the shadows into the tracery of the lamp-light; they crossed: from that bright tracery—into the shadow. With an unwonted, trusting gentleness, his head bent low, Apollon Apollonovich talked: half to his son, half to himself:

"You know: it's a difficult position—being a statesman."

They turned round.

"I told them all: no, facilitating the import of American reaping-machines—isn't such a trivial thing; there's more real humaneness in that than in long-winded speeches ... Civil law teaches us ... "

They walked back across the squares of the parquet floor; they crossed; from the shadow—into the moonlight glinting on the window-frames.

"All the same, we need humane principles; humanism is a great thing, developed at the price of great suffering by such minds as Giordano Bruno, as ... "

And for a long time yet they strolled about here.

Apollon Apollonovich spoke in a cracked voice; sometimes, with two fingers, he took hold of his son by the button of his frock coat: he stretched his lips right up to his ear.

"They're just windbags, Kolenka: humaneness, humaneness! ... There's more humaneness in reaping-machines: reaping-machines are something we need! ... "

Then he put his free hand round his son's waist, drawing him over to the window—into a corner; he muttered and shook his head; they weren't taking account of him, he wasn't needed any more:

"You know—they passed me over!"

Nikolai Apollonovich dared not believe his senses; yes, how naturally all this had happened—without explanations, without storms, without confessions: this whispering in the corner, this affection from his father.

Why all these years had he ...

—"So that's it, Kolenka, my dear boy: let's be more open with each other ... "

"What's that? I can't hear ... "

The demented whistle of a steamer rushed stridently past the windows; the bright, flame-red lantern on its prow was borne away obliquely into the mist; ruby-red rings expanded. And so, with confidential gentleness, his head bent low, Apollon Apollonovich talked: half to his son, half to himself. They crossed: from the shadow—into the tracery of the lamplight; they crossed: from that bright tracery—into the shadow.

Apollon Apollonovich—small, bald and old—lit by flashes from the dying coals, started laying out a game of patience on the mother-of-pearl side-table; he hadn't played patience for two-and-a-half years; that was how he was imprinted on Anna Petrovna's memory; but this was, why—two-and-a-half years ago: before that fateful conversation; the little bald figure had sat at the same table playing the same game of patience.

"There's a ten … "

"No, my dear, it's covered … In the spring, I tell you what: why don't we go, Anna Petrovna, to Prolyotnoe." (Prolyotnoe was the Ableukhovs' hereditary estate: Apollon Apollonovich hadn't been to Prolyotnoe for a good twenty years.)

There, beyond the ice, beyond the snows, beyond the jagged outline of the forest, he had all but frozen to death once by a stupid chance— fifty years ago; at that hour of his solitary freezing someone's frigid fingers had seemed to caress his heart; an icy hand had beckoned to him; behind him—the centuries ran off into immeasurable expanses; in front—the icy hand revealed: immeasurable expanses; immeasurable expanses flew towards him. Hand of ice!

And—look: it was melting.

Only now for the first time, as he took his leave of the service, did Apollon Apollonovich remember: the forlorn expanses of the provinces, the smoke of villages; and—a jackdaw; and he wanted to see: the smoke of villages; and—a jackdaw.

"Shall we, then? Let's go to Prolyotnoe: there are so many flowers there."

And Anna Petrovna, allowing herself to get carried away again, talked excitedly about the beauties of the Alhambra palaces; but in her rush of enthusiasm she forgot, it has to be admitted, that she was adopting the wrong tone, that instead of "I" she kept saying "we"; that is: Mindalini and I (it seemed like—Mantalini).

"We arrived in the morning in a sweet little coach, drawn by donkeys; we had such great big pompons on our harness, Kolechka; and do you know, Apollon Apollonovich, we got quite used to ... "

Apollon Apollonovich went on listening as he turned over the cards; then—he gave it up: he didn't finish the game of patience; he bent double, hunched himself up in the armchair, lit by the bright purple of the coals; several times he took hold of the arms of the Empire chair, on the point of jumping up; but he evidently realised in time that it would be tactless to interrupt this verbal torrent in the middle of an unfinished sentence; and he slipped back into the chair with a slight yawn.

In the end he observed plaintively:

"I must admit, I really am—tired ... "

And he moved from the armchair into the rocking-chair.

Nikolai Apollonovich offered to see his mother back to her hotel; as he left the drawing room, he turned to look at his father; from the rocking-chair—he saw (or so it seemed to him)—a melancholy gaze directed at him; sitting in the rocking-chair, Apollon Apollonovich rocked the rocking-chair slightly with a nod of his head and a movement of his foot; that was his last conscious perception; indeed, he never saw his father again; in the country, at sea, and—in the mountains, in cities—in the gleaming halls of important European museums—it was this gaze that he remembered; and it seemed: Apollon Apollonovich was consciously bidding him goodbye—with a nod of his head and a movement of his foot: that aged face, the quiet creaking of the rocking-chair; and—that gaze, that gaze!

Clockwork

Nikolai Apollonovich took his mother to her hotel; then—he turned off to the Moika; in the windows of the apartment was darkness: the Likhutins were not at home; nothing for it: he turned back home.

He hobbled into his bedroom; he stood a while in utter darkness:

shadows, shadows and shadows; the lamplight's tracery cut across the ceiling; out of habit he lit a candle; he took off his watch; he looked at it absent-mindedly: three o'clock.

Everything surged up again.

He realised—his fears had not been overcome; the assurance that had kept him going all evening had vanished somewhere; and everything—became unstable; he wanted to take some bromide; there wasn't any; he wanted to read *Revelation*; it wasn't there; at that moment a distinct, disturbing sound reached his ears: tick-tock, tick-tock—resounded quietly; surely—not the sardine-tin?

And this thought gained strength.

But that was not what tormented him, he was tormented by something else: an old, delirious feeling; forgotten in a day; arisen in a night:

"Pepp Peppovich ... Pepp ... "

It was him, swelling up into something monstrous, penetrating from the fourth dimension into the yellow house; and tearing round the rooms; clinging to his soul with unseen surfaces; and his soul became a surface: the surface of an immense and swiftly swelling bubble, inflated to the size of Saturn's orbit ... oh-oh-oh: Nikolai Apollonovich became distinctly cold; gales blew across his brow; then everything burst: and became simple.

And—the clockwork was ticking.

Nikolai Apollonovich reached out for the exasperating sound: he tried to find its location; he crept quietly up to the table, his shoes creaking; the ticking became more distinct; but at the table—it disappeared.

"Tick-tock"—sounded quietly from the shadowy corner; and he crept back: from the table—into the corner; shadows, shadows and shadows; the silence of the grave ...

Nikolai Apollonovich was panting, rushing around with a candle in his outstretched hand amidst the dancing shadows; all the time trying to catch the fleeting sound (this is how children chase after yellow butterflies with a net).

Now he set off in the right direction; the strange sound revealed itself; the ticking resounded clearly: another moment—and he would catch it (this time the butterfly wouldn't escape).

Where, where, where?

And when he started looking for the source of the sound, he immediately found it: in his own stomach; truly: a huge weight had distended his stomach.

Nikolai Apollonovich saw that he was standing by the bedside table; and at the level of his stomach, on the surface of the table—the watch he had taken off … was ticking; he looked at it absentmindedly: four o'clock.

Things fell back into place (Second Lieutenant Likhutin had taken the wretched bomb); the delirious feeling disappeared; the weight in his stomach disappeared; quickly he threw off his suit; with relish he unfastened his starched collar, his starched shirt; he pulled off his underpants: on his leg, at the knee, an inflamed bruise stood out; and his knee was swollen; now his legs disappeared under the snow white sheet, but—he fell to thinking, leaning on his hand; the white features of his icon-like face were clearly set off against the white of the sheet.

And—the candle went out.

The watch was ticking; utter darkness surrounded him; in the darkness the ticking fluttered off again, like a butterfly taking off from a flower: now—it was here; and now—over there; and his thoughts—were ticking; in various places on his inflamed body—thoughts were beating like pulses: in his neck, in his throat, in his arms, in his head; even in his solar plexus.

These pulses started chasing round his body, trying to catch each other.

Then, letting go of his body, they were outside it, forming around him on all sides a throbbing and conscious contour; half-a-metre away; and—more; then he realised quite distinctly that it was not he who did the thinking, that is to say: it was not his brain thinking, but this clearly drawn, throbbing, conscious contour outside his brain; within this contour all the pulses, or projections of the pulses, turned instantly into self-fabricated thoughts; in his eyeball, in its turn, a tempestuous life was going on; ordinary dots, visible in the light and projected into space—now flared up like sparks; leapt from their sockets out into space; danced all round, forming tiresome tinsel-strings, forming a swarming cocoon—of lights; half-a-metre away; and—more; this now was the pulsation: now it flared up.

These were swarms of thoughts that thought themselves.

The gossamer fabric of these thoughts—he realised—was by no means thinking what the owner of the fabric would have liked to think, not at all that which he was trying to think with the aid of his brain, and which—escaped from his brain (to tell the truth—the convolutions of his brain were merely preening themselves; there were no thoughts in them); only the pulses were thinking, scattering precious stones—like sparks, or stars; across this golden swarm there ran a little ball of light, reverberating with the assertion:

"It's still ticking, still ticking ... "

Another ran across ...

What was being thought was the affirmation of the statement that his brain denied, with which it battled obstinately: the sardine-tin—is here, the sardine-tin—is here; a little second-hand is running round it; the second-hand is tired of running: it will run as far as the fatal point (that point is now near) ... Fluttering pulses of light scattered wildly, as the sparks of a bonfire scatter if you give the fire a great thump with a log—they scattered: and beneath them a blue and insubstantial something was laid bare, from which a sparkling kernel instantaneously pierced the sweat-soaked head of a man who had lain down there; with its prickly, trembling lights it resembled a giant spider, intruding from another world, and—reflected in the brain:

—and unbearable crashes will resound, which you might not even have time to hear, because before they strike your ear-drum, your ear-drum will be shattered (and that's not all)—

—what was blue and insubstantial disappeared; and with it—the sparkling kernel beneath the rushing tinsel-string of light; but with mindless movements Nikolai Apollonovich shot out of bed: a torrent of thoughts not thought by him now suddenly turned into pulses; these pulses clung to him and throbbed: in his temple, his throat, his neck, his arms, but ... not outside those organs.

He padded off barefoot; and finished up in the wrong place: not the door, but—the corner.

It was growing light.

Quickly he threw on his underpants and padded through into the darkening corridor: why, why? Oh, he was simply afraid ... He was simply seized by an animal feeling for his own invaluable life; he had no desire to return from the corridor; he did not have the courage to glance into his own rooms; he now had neither strength nor time to look for the bomb a second time; everything got mixed up in his head, and he could no longer remember exactly either the minute or the hour when the time expired: any moment might prove to be the fatal one. All he could do was wait here trembling in the corridor until daybreak.

And, retreating into the corner, he crouched down there.

The moments passed slowly within him; the minutes seemed like hours; many hundreds of hours flowed by; the corridor turned dark blue; the corridor turned grey; day was breaking.

Nikolai Apollonovich became more and more convinced that the thoughts thinking themselves were nonsense; these thoughts were now located in his brain; and his brain could handle them; and when he came to the conclusion that the time had long since expired, the version in which the Second Lieutenant had taken the sardine-tin somehow of its own accord diffused all round the vapours of most blissful images, and Nikolai Apollonovich, sitting crouched in the corridor—whether from a sense of safety, whether from fatigue— only, only: he dropped asleep.

He was woken by something sticky touching his forehead; opening his eyes, he saw—the bulldog's slobbery muzzle: in front of him the bulldog was snuffling and wagging its tail; he pushed the dog away nonchalantly with his hand, trying to resume where he had left off: to continue something he was doing; to finish spinning some reeling images, so as to make a discovery. And— -suddenly he realised: why was he on the floor?

Why was he in the corridor?

Half-asleep he stumbled off to his own room: as he approached his bed, he was still finishing spinning his sleepy reeling images …

—There was a crash: he understood everything.

—In the long winter evenings afterwards Nikolai Apollonovich returned many times to that heavy crash; it was a special crash, not comparable with any other; deafening and—not reverberating in the least; deafening and—dull: with a bass, metallic, oppressive shade to it; then everything fell still.

Soon voices were heard, the irregular patter of bare feet and the hushed whining of the bulldog; the telephone rang: in the end he opened his door; a blast of cold air struck him in the chest; and lemon-yellow smoke filled the room; in the blast of the wind and the smoke he tripped quite inopportunely over a chip of wood; and he sensed, rather than understood, that it was a piece of a shattered door.

Here was a pile of cold bricks, here were shadows running round: out of the smoke; scorched tatters of carpet—how did they get here? Here one of the shadows, emerging from a veil of smoke, growled at him coarsely.

"Hey, what'yer doing there: something terrible's happened, can't you see!"

And another voice rang out; the words were heard:

"I'd hang them all, the bastards!"

"It's me," he tried to say.

He was interrupted.

"A bomb … "

"Oh!"

"That's what it was … blew up … "

"?"

"In Apollon Apollonovich's study … "

"?"

"Thank God, he's safe and sound … "

Let us remind the reader: Apollon Apollonovich had absent-mindedly taken the sardine-tin from his son's room into his own study; and had quite forgotten about it; he was, of course, in ignorance of the sardine-tin's import.

Nikolai Apollonovich ran to the place where until recently there had been a door; and where—there was no door: there was a huge chasm, from which smoke came in clouds; if anyone had looked out into the street, they would have seen: a crowd gathering; a policeman was pushing it back from the pavement; and gawpers watched with upturned heads as from the black chasms of the windows and the splitting cracks ominous lemon-yellow clouds burst out.

Without knowing why, Nikolai Apollonovich ran back from the chasm; and without knowing where he was going, arrived …

—on the snow-white bed (right there on the pillow) sat Apollon Apollonovich with his bare legs pressed to his hairy chest; he had only his nightshirt on; with his arms round his knees, without any restraint, he was—not sobbing, but roaring; in the general clatter he had been forgotten; none of the servants was with him, not even ... Semyonych; there was no one to comfort him; and here he was, utterly alone ... straining fit to burst, till his voice went hoarse ...

> —Nikolai Apollonovich rushed towards this helpless body, as a nurse might rush into the middle of the roadway to grasp a three-year-old mite who had fallen down there, who had been put in her charge, but whom she had forgotten in the rush of traffic; but this feeble little body—this mite—at the sight of his son rushing towards him –leapt up from the pillow—and how he waved his arms: with indescribable horror and a far from childish vigour.

And—how he fled from that room, leaping out into the corridor!

With a cry of "stop him" Nikolai Apollonovich set off after it: after that demented figure (though which of them was demented?); they both tore away to the far end of the corridor past the smoke and the tatters and the gesticulations of clattering people (they were putting something out); there was something uncanny about those fleeting figures, bellowing strangely at the far end of the corridor; a nightshirt flapped in flight; a patter of faintly glimpsed heels; Nikolai Apollonovich set off in pursuit with an abrupt leap, limping on his right leg; he grabbed with his hand at his plummeting underpants; and with the other hand he endeavoured to grasp hold of the flailing tails of his father's nightshirt.

As he ran he shouted:

"Wait ... "

"Where are you going?"

"Do stop."

When he reached the door leading into the room comparable with no other, Apollon Apollonovich, with unimaginable cunning, seized hold of the door; and as quick as a flash he was inside: he made good his escape to that incomparable room.

Nikolai Apollonovich momentarily recoiled from the door; in

one moment—the turn of the head, the sweaty brow, the lips, the sideburns, the eye that gleamed like molten stone—were etched upon his memory; the door slammed to; everything vanished; the door latch clicked; he had made good his escape to that incomparable room.

Nikolai Apollonovich hammered desperately at the door; and begged—straining fit to burst, till his voice went hoarse:

"Open it … "

"Let me in … "

And—

"Ahh … ahh … ahh … "

He fell down in front of the door.

He lowered his arms on to his knees; he dropped his head into his hands; and then he lost consciousness; servants came clamouring up to him. They dragged him away into his room.

Here we put a full-stop.

We will not describe how the fire was extinguished, how the senator, suffering from a severe heart-attack, explained things to the police: after that explanation a group of doctors were called in for a consultation: the doctors found that he had dilation of the aorta. And nevertheless: throughout those days of strikes, in chancelleries, offices, and ministers' apartments he kept appearing—haggard, lean; his powerful bass voice thundered out persuasively—in chancelleries, offices, and ministers' apartments—with a hollow, oppressive tinge. Let us simply say: he succeeded in proving something. Someone somewhere was arrested; and then—released for lack of evidence; various connections were brought to bear; and the matter was hushed up. No one else was touched. All those days his son lay in bouts of nervous fever, without regaining consciousness at all; and when he did come round, he saw that only his mother was with him; there was no one else in the lacquered house. Apollon Apollonovich decamped to the country and spent all that winter cloistered in the snows, having taken indefinite leave; and from that leave he passed into retirement. For his son he prepared in advance: a foreign passport and some money. Ableukhova, Anna Petrovna, accompanied Nikolenka. She returned only in the summer: Nikolai Apollonovich did not return to Russia until his father's death.

EPILOGUE

T HE FEBRUARY SUN IS SETTING. Ragged cacti are scattered here and there. Soon, very soon sails will come flying in to the shore from the gulf; here they come: with pointed wings, rocking; a little dome disappears into the cacti.

Nikolai Apollonovich, in a pale-blue Arab shirt and a bright-red fez, is squatting motionless, a long, long tassel dangles from his fez; his silhouette is distinctly moulded on the flat roof; below him are the village square and the sounds of a tam-tam: they strike the ear with a hollow, oppressive tinge.

Everywhere are the white cubes of the village houses; a vociferous Berber drives his donkey along with his cries; a bundle of branches on the donkey's back shines silver; the Berber is an olive colour.

Nikolai Apollonovich does not listen to the sounds of the tam-tam; and he does not see the Berber; what he sees is that which stands before him: Apollon Apollonovich—small, bald and old—sitting in his rocking-chair, rocks the rocking-chair with a nod of his head and a movement of his foot; that movement is lodged in memory …

The pink of almond blossom is visible in the distance; that jagged ridge—is purple and amber; that is the ridge of Zaghouan, and the promontory is the cape of Carthage. Nikolai Apollonovich is renting a little house from an Arab in a village on the shore near Tunis.

The branches of the firs bend under the weight of their glistening caps of snow: green and ragged; in front is a wooden building with five columns; snowdrifts spread over the balustrade of the terrace like hills; on them lies a pink gleam from the February sunset.

A hunched figure appears—in warm felt boots and mittens, leaning on a stick; his fur collar is raised; his fur hat is pressed down over his ears; he is making his way along the cleared path; he is supported by another figure carrying a warm travelling-rug.

In the country spectacles have appeared on Apollon Apollonovich's face; they are steamed up in this frost, and neither the jagged forest in the distance, nor the smoke of the villages, nor—the jackdaw are visible through them: what can be seen are—shadows and shadows; between them are the glint of the moon on the door-jambs and the squares of the parquet floor; Nikolai Apollonovich—gentle, attentive, responsive—with his head bent low, crosses: from the shadow—into the tracery of the streetlamp's light; crosses: from the brightness of that tracery—into the shadow.

In the evening the old man sits at his desk among round frames; in the frames are portraits: of an officer in buckskin, and an old lady in a satin bonnet; the officer in buckskin is his father; the old lady in the bonnet is his late mother, née Svargina. The old man is scribbling his memoirs, so that they shall appear in the year of his death.

They have appeared.

The wittiest of memoirs: the whole of Russia knows them.

The sun's flame is ferocious: it fills the eyes with purple; if you turn round—it strikes furiously at the nape of your neck; it makes the desert look greenish and deathly; however, life itself is deathly; it would be good to stay here forever—by the deserted shore.

Nikolai Apollonovich sits down on a mound of sand in his thick pith helmet with its veil waving in the wind; in front of him is an immense, mouldering head—on the point of collapsing into a heap of millennial sandstone;—Nikolai Apollonovich sits for hours before the Sphinx.

Nikolai Apollonovich has been here for two years; he is working in the Bulaq museum. The *Book of the Dead* and the records of Manetho have been wrongly interpreted; for the inquisitive eye there is a broad expanse here; Nikolai Apollonovich is lost to view in Egypt; and in this twentieth century he discerns—Egypt, the whole of culture—is like this mouldering head: everything is dead; there is nothing left.

It is good that he is thus occupied: sometimes, when he tears himself away from his diagrams, he starts to imagine that not everything is dead; that there still are some sounds; these sounds rumble away in Cairo: a very special rumble; it reminds him of that same old sound: deafening and—dull: with a metallic, bass, oppressive tinge; and Nikolai Apollonovich is drawn to the mummies; it was that 'occurrence' that brought him to the mummies. Kant? Kant is forgotten.

Evening falls: and in the dimness after dusk the colossi of Gizeh stretch out formless and ominous; everything in them is dilated; and they make everything dilate; dark-brown lights appear in the dust that hangs in the air; the atmosphere is close.

Nikolai Apollonovich leans thoughtfully against the side of the lifeless pyramid.

In an armchair, in the full warmth of the sun, the old man sat motionless; with his huge cornflower-blue eyes he kept glancing at the old lady; his legs were wrapped in a travelling-rug (evidently he had lost the feeling in them); on his knees a bunch of white lilac had been placed; the old man kept straining towards the old lady, leaning out of the chair with his whole body:

"He's finished it, you say? ... Maybe he'll come?"

"Yes, he's putting his papers in order ... "

Nikolai Apollonovich had at last brought his monograph to an end.

"What is it called?"

And—the old man smiled all over:

"The monograph is called ... me-emme ... *On the letter of Daufsekhrut.*" Apollon Apollonovich was in the habit of forgetting absolutely everything: he forgot the names of the most ordinary things; but that word Daufsekhrut —he remembered clearly; Kolenka was writing about 'Daufsekhrut'. If you throw your head back, the gold of the greening leaves is there: raging furiously: blue sky and fleecy clouds; a wagtail was running along the path.

"He's in Nazareth, you say?"

Oh, what a mass of bluebells! The bluebells gaped wide with their purple mouths; just there, among the bluebells, stood a wheelchair; Apollon Apollonovich, all wrinkles, his stubble unshaven, silvering his cheeks, sat in it—under a canvas sunshade.

In 1913 Nikolai Apollonovich went on striding for days on end through the fields, the meadows, the forests, watching with a sullen indolence the work in the fields; he wore a cap during his walks; he wore a light camel-coloured coat; his boots creaked; a full, golden beard had changed him astoundingly; and his shock of hair was marked by one distinct, completely silver strand; this strand had appeared suddenly; his eyes had begun to hurt in Egypt; he had started wearing dark-blue glasses. His voice had coarsened, and his face had become tanned; the quickness of his movements had been lost; he lived alone; he invited no one to visit him; and he visited no one; he was seen in church; it is said that most recently he had been reading the philosopher Skovoroda.

His parents had died.

TRANSLATOR'S AFTERWORD

Few of the world's great cities have given rise to national myths as powerful as the myth of Petersburg. Founded in the early eighteenth century by Peter the Great as the new imperial capital, with the express purpose of re-directing Russian history and creating a new identity for the nation, it became from the early nineteenth century the dominant symbol of Russian historical experience. In one aspect it proclaims the triumph of human endeavour over elemental forces; but more consistently it is perceived as a city built against nature, lost in the mists and marshes where no human habitation previously existed or ought to exist, a spectral city whose inhabitants lose touch with their own roots and become unreal themselves. In the nineteenth century this tradition is most forcefully expressed in the work of Pushkin, Gogol and Dostoevskii, and echoes of them can be detected on every page of Bely's novel. Indeed, it is hardly an exaggeration to claim that the central hero of Petersburg *is none of the shadowy human figures that populate its pages, but the equestrian statue of Peter, who descends from his pedestal as he did in Pushkin's* The Bronze Horseman *to compel the obedience of his reluctant vassals. Many a conversation between the characters recalls the dialogues of Dostoevskii with their psychological tension and threat. And the depiction of the city streets, the scampering pedestrians defined by the hats they wear or the shape of their noses, could only come from Gogol's* Petersburg Tales.

Petersburg *shows us the city at a time of crisis. Russia is reeling from defeat in the war with Japan, and the revolution of 1905 is beginning to seethe. Subversive nondescripts crowd the city streets, through which the main upholder of order and stability, Senator Apollon Apollonovich Ableukhov, must make his way to his government office in his black cube of a carriage. The novel's material is almost all derived from real circumstances and events which can be traced in the historical record of the time, but that does not make it a* historical novel in any customary sense. Time does not move in straight lines here, it turns back to devour its own tail, and it is only in myth that anything can truly be explained. When he published his first novel, The Silver Dove, in 1909, Bely stated in a preface that it was to be the first novel of a trilogy entitled East or West. If that first novel was a study of the Eastern aspect of Russian culture, the darkness and religious ferment of the countryside, then it was natural for its sequel to focus upon the most Western of Russian cities. But what we find is that this utterly rational, Western city is no less chaotic than its rural counterpart.

In the course of composition the links with Bely's first novel became more and more tenuous, although there are glimpses of it in the character of Styopka and the tales he tells. Bely was never fully satisfied with Petersburg, and published a much shortened redaction of it in Berlin in 1922; however, it was shortened almost exclusively by a process of excision, leaving a text which, though critics have appreciated its increased pace, is not in the last resort entirely coherent. He also dramatised it for production at the Moscow Arts Theatre. The dramatic text went through innumerable modifications before it saw the stage, and then it survived only one performance in 1925. This translation is of the longer original version, written between 1911 and 1913 and first published in the Moscow journal Sirin in 1913-14.

Petersburg is the work for which Bely is best known, though he was the author of seven novels in all, much poetry, extensive works of philosophy and literary theory, and a vast output of memoirs. Born into a Moscow academic family in 1880 (his real name was Boris Nikolaevich Bugaev), his career spanned an equal period on either side of the 1917 revolutions. Most of his life was spent in or very near to Moscow, though he lived in Switzerland for two years in 1914-16, and in Berlin for two years in the early 1920s. One of the acknowledged leaders of the Russian Symbolist movement in the first decade of the century, in demand as a contributor to all the cultural debates of that time, he fell out of favour after the revolution and lived his last years in relative seclusion and considerable penury. He died in January 1934.

There is a strong autobiographical substratum to Petersburg. There are considerable similarities between Nikolai Apollonovich's relations with his parents and the known biographical facts of the Bugaev family—not that Bely's mother really fled the family home, nor that Bely ever sought to kill his father. His triangular relationship with the Likhutins bears a clear resemblance to Bely's relations with his friend and fellow poet Alexandr Blok and his wife, Liubov Dmitrievna, with whom Bely at one time nearly eloped. But the interest of these *personal elements lies in the way they are threaded into the broader canvas and become typical images of the psychological and philosophical malaise that Bely diagnoses in the culture of his time. The conflicting aspects of the city itself, its rational geometry and its haunting nebulousness, are reflected both in the political conflict between reactionary status quo and revolutionary turmoil, and in the unresolved tensions between logic and emotion in the characters themselves. Neither aspect can hope to win; it is only in a faintly mooted apocalypse that redemption may be found.*

Petersburg *is the culmination of the pre-revolutionary tradition of the city's depiction, absorbing and re-interpreting a century of literary history. Very soon after Bely wrote this novel, the city was renamed Petrograd out of wartime chauvinism, to become Leningrad a decade later, by which time the capital had been moved back to Moscow. Nevertheless, the Petersburg tradition did not disappear, even if for much of the twentieth century it took refuge in the more private realm of poetry. In post-Soviet Russia the city's historical name has been restored and its cultural reverberations have come to resound afresh.*

JOHN ELSWORTH

ACKNOWLEDGEMENTS

I am immensely grateful to Roger Keys for reading the entire manuscript of this translation and making many very valuable suggestions for its improvement.

I am also deeply indebted to my wife, Katya Young, for her unstinting help in identifying nuances of meaning in the Russian text, as well as for her constant encouragement and support.

I dedicate this translation to the memory of Dmitrii Evgenevich Maksimov (1904-87), teacher and friend, who loved and understood this novel, in gratitude for many conversations about it and much else.

All remaining inadequacies are my responsibility alone.